The Dancing Barber

AC MICHAEL

THE DANCING BARBER
by
AC Michael
Copyright © AC Michael 2015
Cover Copyright © Antonio Gresko 2015

First published by White Stag 2015
Second edition published by White Stag 2016
(White Stag is an Imprint of Ravenswood Publishing)

Names, characters and incidents depicted in this book are products of the author's imagination, or are used fictitiously. Any resemblance to actual events, locales, organizations, or persons, living or dead, is entirely coincidental and beyond the intent of the author or the publisher.

All rights reserved. No part of this book may be reproduced or transmitted in any form or by any means whatsoever, including photocopying, recording or by any information storage and retrieval system, without written permission from the publisher and/or author.

Ravenswood Publishing
Raeford, NC 28376
www.ravenswoodpublishing.com

Printed in the U.S.A.

ISBN-13: 978-1517473648
ISBN-10: 1517473640

Contents

Prelude
The Feast of Our Lady
1

Act 1
Good Friday
12

Act 2
Easter Saturday
63

Act 3
Easter Sunday
104

Act 4
Easter Monday
269

Act 5
The Sunday of St Thomas
415

Act 6
A Normal Day
448

Encore
A few days later…
628

Dedication

To my Mother, Father and Grandparents.

The Dancing Barber

Prelude

---- ✂ ----

Autumn 1933
The Feast of Our Lady

> ' "If you can?" said Jesus.
> "Everything is possible for him who believes." '
>
> *Mark 9:23*

The Village of Chaplinka, Khersonska Oblast, South-eastern Ukraine

'Here,' said Tato, 'dinner is served.' He held out an old saucepan lid, piled high with cubes of boiled shoe leather, its weight almost too much for his weakened arms to bear. 'But,' he advised, 'only swallow when *properly* chewed.'

His youngest daughter selected the largest, most succulent piece and put it in her mouth, being careful not to burn her lips. As she chewed, she tried to imagine it to be a nice piece of pork: crisp on the outside and juicy on the inside, like they used to have every Sunday. But not even her imagination was that good.

AC Michael

The wooden farmstead was only a few yards from the patrolled perimeter fence of the Collective Farm, behind which the unwilling army of conscripted Ukrainian workers was bringing in the grain harvest. Wheat, barley and corn were piled into enormous silos; the deliciously sweet smells wafting over to the one remaining farmstead in Chaplinka, tempting the small family to join the other villagers and work for the Soviets.

Mama had just finished dicing up another piece of shoe leather, employing her husband's well-used cobbler's knife. She tipped the little cubes into the pan of boiling water and stepped back to avoid being splashed. So as not to attract unwanted attention, she cooked well away from the house, on an open fire in the corner of their barren field, the rising steam camouflaged behind the branches of a dead cherry tree.

'Perhaps,' she said with a sigh, 'it wouldn't be so bad if we worked on Collective Farm? At least then, we get something proper to eat?'

Tato spat to the ground, 'I will <u>never</u> work for the Soviet occupiers!' He glared at his wife with animal eyes, 'and I <u>never</u> want to hear you speak like that again! Is that understood?'

Mama would have cried, if she thought it would have made a difference. But her mouth could only water as she watched the workers behind the barbed-wire fence eating their ration of watery soup and mouldy bread that would be their only meal today. They ate quickly, but not quickly enough. Once the work bell rang, whether they'd finished or not, the guards snatched the tin plates and viciously kicked anyone who crouched to pick up what they could from the dusty ground.

She turned back to her husband, 'but surely even *that* is better than chewing old shoe leather?'

'You think working twenty hours a day for the Soviets and only getting a mouthful of soup and a bit of old crust as payment is better than being free? Don't be so stupid!'

Mama picked up her youngest daughter, a veritable bag of bones with the swollen abdomen characteristic of woeful malnutrition. 'Just look at her!' she said, 'your own daughter is dying and you just sit there chewing bits of your old shoes! None of us have eaten properly for six months!'

'We are <u>all</u> dying!' he cried, 'but we will never work for the

The Dancing Barber

Soviets! Just like the Cossacks in the olden days, we will stand up for our country!' He swallowed with difficulty, 'and if that means we all starve to death, then so be it!' He looked through the barbed-wire fence and said, 'those cowards are dying too, but it's better to die free than to die a prisoner.'

His wife slapped him hard across his bony, unshaven face. She cried, 'you stubborn old – !' before bursting into tears. She was convinced that if only they'd cooperated straight away instead of upsetting the Soviets, then perhaps they'd have been better off.

Her youngest daughter started to cry and threw up the leather she'd swallowed. But all her mother could do was clean up the mess: surely watery soup and mouldy bread was better than eating such deplorable things? At least then – even though they'd be worked like dogs – their lives would be extended, if only by a few weeks. But then she glanced at the smoke from the latest pyre beyond the horizon, the appalling stench of burning flesh drifting on the breeze; she thought that maybe her husband was right.

Holding the carved wooden crucifix that had hung around his neck for many years, Tato said, 'have faith my dear. Have faith.' But even his faith was being tested to the limit.

Bang! Bang! Bang! The pistol shots ricocheted across the Steppes, and the emaciated bodies of three workers on the Collective Farm fell to the dusty ground with a thud. Then two guards hauled them up, one by one, as if they were old sacks, and slung them onto a heap of many others, who'd also been caught with grain in their pockets. They were the lucky ones; others caught stealing from the State had already been marched half way to the Siberian Gulags, where they would be worked to death building roads or mining gold, assuming they survived the journey through the tundra often wearing little more than rags.

Tato let go of his crucifix and it dangled in its usual position against the cross-shaped patch of un-tanned skin on his hollow chest. He said a small prayer for the men who would never have a proper funeral.

'Tato! Tato!' shouted his eldest twin daughters as they bounded across the field, their bare feet kicking up clouds of dust. 'Look what we have just caught!'

The old fellow didn't know where these two got all their

energy. He turned around and, with a shaky wave of his hand, beckoned them closer. As they approached, the muscles around his mouth ached from smiling for the first time in weeks. 'You have done very well,' he said, admiring their wonderful bounty.

In each hand, dangling by their long, bald tails were the fattest rats he'd ever seen. He kissed his crucifix with gratitude before hugging the huntresses, thanking God that the twins hadn't been caught trespassing. The rats were the only animals thriving; the Soviet silos were full of them.

Upon hearing the news, his youngest daughter scampered over to help her mother skin and gut the precious carcasses. She used to be squeamish of such things, but as with all desperate times, the need for food brought the hunter-gatherer instincts to the fore.

That turned out to be one of the best meals the little family had eaten in six months: spit-roasted rat, accompanied by nettle soup with a garnish of grated tree bark. It made a welcome change from the usual grass and earthworms; and after all this time, the prawn-like treat that was the occasional woodlouse had completely lost its sheen. 'Remember, *Kapusta* everyone, *Kapusta*,' said Tato, fastening his lips with an imaginary button, 'no-one must ever know…'

His three daughters mimed his actions and smiled.

'Do not forget salad,' said Mama, unveiling a selection of peppery basil, woodsy sage and earthy oregano. 'I found a few tussocks growing by river… It will be last of year, so enjoy it.'

'Thank you,' said Tato, 'herbs, they really are food of poor… and they complement our roast dinner so well.'

Their happy peasant existence was now a depressingly distant memory. Their animals had long ago been confiscated, their crops seized and their small stream, previously teeming with trout, diverted. It saddened everyone to watch the fertile black loam – the *Chornozem* Ukraine is famous for – that was the family's field being gradually swallowed up by the fescue and feather grasses of the surrounding Steppes. But even if they still had their plough, there was no point in ploughing it, because the family didn't have any seeds to plant. Not even one.

As the year went on, even the most simple-minded peasants realised that Stalin's strategy was to starve them into working on the Collective Farm; the troublemakers would die one way or the other and the land would be cleansed of the people who call themselves "Ukrainians" forever.

Even the Orthodox Church had been converted into a Soviet cinema, its precious Byzantine icons smashed and its white-painted wooden exterior desecrated with Soviet propaganda. The Priest's skeleton lay unburied by the side of the road, as a reminder that all resistance was futile.

Tato licked the last morsels from his bony fingers and declared, 'that was delicious!' He smacked his lips together and then poured a little sorrel tea into an old earthenware cup without a handle. Cradling the cup in his hands, he allowed himself to feel slightly content. He sipped the bitter liquid, feeling it trickle warmingly down his throat and into his blessedly full stomach.

He watched with pride as his daughters nibbled the last strands of meat from the rat's legs, and then used the smaller bones as toothpicks to remove the gristle lodged between their craggy teeth. They each burped with satisfaction and relished the feeling of having stomachs filled with the closest thing to proper food they'd had in a long time. Even the bits of gristle had been eaten, and the juicy marrow sucked out of the bones as if they were drinking straws. These scraps used to go to the dog, but they didn't have a dog any more: when it died, Mama treated it in the same way as the rats.

Always the last to start a meal and the first to finish, Mama crossed herself in the Ukrainian Orthodox fashion: with her left hand at her chest, and holding together the thumb, first and second fingers of her right hand, moving from her forehead to chest, then from right to left shoulders. She said, 'in the name of the Father, the Son and the Holy Spirit. Amen.'

She collected the tin plates and the forks that were made from long nails welded together... the sooner the evidence was cleared away, the better. The chilly evening was fast approaching, so she went indoors to stoke the fire. She was thankful the thatched roof had been patched with sheets of rusty corrugated iron, because although today had been warm, she knew snow and bitter cold were just around the corner. So the furry rat skins would make a welcome pair of gloves or maybe even a nice warm hat.

With the chimney blocked, the earthy little house soon filled with the calming fragrance of pine-smoke, reminding Mama of the good times on the farmstead she shared with her own parents before the Soviets took them from her. Her parents taught her well, and every square inch of land had been used to the full. The fields once yielded some of the best crops in the village, and her little kitchen garden provided the family with a supply of cabbages, carrots, potatoes, onions, garlic, lettuce and radish; and in the summer, the crop of juicy tomatoes was a joy to behold and a delight to eat. She understood the land, knew all its little quirks, and treated the soil as if it were a member of the family. But the Soviets didn't understand or care about any of this; they treated the land in the same way as they treated the peasants, working it brutally until it could do no more.

Like a deer hearing a twig snap in the woods, Mama stopped and listened. She'd noticed the distant thunder of hooves and the rumble of cartwheels slowly getting louder. There wasn't any time to waste. Even though she'd been extra careful, it seemed the smoke from the spit-roasted rats had attracted unwanted attention.

'Quickly,' she shouted to her husband and daughters, 'clear all this stuff away!'

The dust kicked up by the horses was like a fast approaching storm cloud. 'Brace yourselves everyone,' Tato said with trepidation as he peered through the unglazed window, and saw the usual platoon of soldiers, riding in a V-shaped formation. 'It looks like Captain Stanislaw again.'

Mama swore under her breath; she threw his clay pipe and what was left of his tobacco at her husband. 'Quick, light your pipe! If he smells we've had a cooked meal, we are all as good as dead!'

Captain Stanislaw needed a big, strong horse, because anything less would crumble beneath his immense weight. But even this formidable steed wasn't strong enough, and it emitted an audible gasp of relief when the Soviet officer descended. The Captain's heels crashed into the parched earth as if they were a pair of anvils; he clicked his clammy fingers for his Privates to follow. He straightened his great-coat, positioned his bearskin hat squarely on his perspiring head and thrust his whip under his left armpit. 'Hurry up!' he barked at his Privates, who like obedient dogs, immediately took up positions by their master's side.

Mama waited behind the creaky wooden door for the Captain's usual knock. But this time, the door was kicked open and the Captain barged in, pushing the weakened woman to the floor. With his hands behind his back, he strutted to the centre of the room and clicked his heels. He said, 'good evening filthy peasants.'

From his flea-ridden bed, Tato replied, 'and same to you.' The pain of the whip striking his face was worth it, just to aggravate the Soviet swine. Tato smiled even though blood trickled down his cheek.

The Captain unscrewed his bearskin hat and checked the furry ear-flaps were properly secured before handing it to one of his Privates, as if it were his favourite pet cat. The man's pale bald head was covered with beads of sweat that ran down his deeply tanned cheeks and under his wide collar, where it slowly soaked through his vest, shirt and tunic and was beginning to be visible through the hefty material of his great-coat. His boots probably contained half a gallon each and made a squelching sound as he strutted about.

He surveyed the peasants with repulsion and truly hoped they wouldn't last much longer. The greyish-yellow skin draped over their bones, the bulging, immobile eyes, and the necks that seemed to have shrunk into their shoulders made him feel queasy. The sooner the "Ukrainian Problem" was solved, the better.

But for now, he had to stick to protocol.

'That is an interesting smell,' the Captain said, sniffing the air by twitching the fungal growth that was his nose. 'It smells as though you've had a roasted meal? But surely that cannot be?' He looked at his Privates who shook their heads disapprovingly, 'because you kindly donated all of your animals and crops to the State some time ago. And as you stupidly chose not to join in the fun at the Collective Farm, you therefore have not been allocated a food ration. So,' he said, looking around the austere room, 'I can only assume that the food has been stolen!' The pale northern hemisphere of his bald head turned as red as his cheeks, and the veins on the side of his neck bulged like drainpipes, pressing against the collar of his great-coat; the restricted blood flow gradually transforming his head into a monster aubergine.

Nobody moved, secretly hoping the Captain's head would explode. Not even Tato dared speak, preferring to puff on the pipe, whose smoke hadn't fooled the wily old Captain.

'That is,' the Captain said calmly, 'unless you *have* decided to join the Collective Farm and,' he consulted the official documents he kept in a leather case, 'my records are wrong, which is *highly* unlikely.'

Tato held his breath when the Captain came and stared at him; but there was no escaping the man's putrid halitosis… it was worse than over-boiled cabbage. He braced himself for another lash of the whip when he said, 'even someone as stupid as you should have realised by now that neither I nor any member of my family would ever work for Soviets!'

'So you *admit* you have eaten stolen food!' the Captain said smugly, 'and therefore it is *you* who is the stupid one!'

Tato looked at his wife, and said nonchalantly, 'tell him what we ate for dinner.'

When Captain Stanislaw had listened to what Mama had said, both he and his Privates laughed as if they'd just watched a Laurel and Hardy film. 'Roasted rat!' the Captain said, 'a fitting meal for such filthy peasants!'

But the grin soon became a sneer; the Captain clicked his fingers for his Privates to set to work tearing the small house apart, looking for any evidence of stolen grain.

'Leave that alone!' Mama protested, but she could only watch as one of the Privates pulled her beloved embroidered icon of the Madonna and Child from above the fireplace.

'Silence,' said the Private, striking her across the face.

'Do you not know what day it is?' she said defiantly. But she could only watch as the soldier tore the icon from its simple frame and cast it to the floor, treading on it with both boots.

The soldiers continued their search, tapping the roof beams and examining the walls and beneath the floor for any evidence of secret grain stores.

The Dancing Barber

The family were unconcerned; there wasn't a speck of flour in the whole house. They knew it wasn't worth taking the risk, not after what happened to their neighbours when the Soviets discovered their hollowed-out roof beams, crammed with grain.

'As you are aware,' Tato said, standing up a vase of bright orange marigolds that had been knocked over by the soldiers, 'eating rats is <u>not</u> offence. Unless Soviet Union has confiscated all vermin too?'

Captain Stanislaw had nothing to say. He gave an *"I'll get you next time"* shrug of the shoulders, clicked his heels and headed for the splintered door. Although marigolds were not the most fragrant of blooms, his nose became twitchy and inflamed at the very sight of them... He paused; right on cue one of the Privates announced, 'Comrade Captain, come and look what *I* have found!'

A slash of a smile emerged across Captain Stanislaw's face as he examined the little pouch. He unfastened the string and poured the contents into the palm of his clammy hand. Rolling a pinch of the coarse grains between his thumb and forefinger, sniffing at the stale aroma and crunching a grain between his stained teeth was all the proof he needed to show. He turned to Tato and said proudly, 'I have here some stolen grain that was found concealed in your house. Do you have anything to say?'

It didn't matter what anyone could say. The Captain had won – by cheating – but had won nevertheless. It looked as though the Siberian Gulag beckoned.

'Captain Stanislaw,' announced the surliest Private, a man with bow legs and an enormous chin. '*I* have found something even better!'

When the Captain saw the stash of propaganda leaflets, it was as though all his Christmases had come at once. He'd never seen so much anti-Soviet filth in one place before...

'It seems I am to be promoted,' the Captain said smugly, 'because not only have I finally cleansed Chaplinka of every single filthy "Ukrainian" peasant, but it seems I have also captured an associate of the hated Voloshin!'

He clicked his fingers and his Privates hauled Tato to his feet. He dusted off the drab epaulette on his shoulder and said, 'maybe they will make me a General for this?'

The surly private with the enormous chin couldn't help saying, 'and maybe they will make me a Sergeant?' He knew instantly that he had spoken out of turn, so held up a hand of apology.

Captain Stanislaw ignored the comment and put the bag of wheat grain back in his pocket. He looked at the propaganda leaflets his Private had found beneath a straw-filled mattress and allowed the slash of a smile to bisect his entire face. He laughed so much that his flabby cheeks rippled concentrically around his mouth.

Mama could do nothing but watch her husband being dragged to a waiting barred carriage, his heels gouging tramlines in the dirt that ended abruptly when he was thrown into the cage.

Tato's protests fell on deaf ears: 'I know <u>nothing</u> about propaganda. You know I don't! You planted it there just like you planted bag of grain! Captain Stanislaw – you will go to Hell for this!'

The Captain laughed, tugging the cage's padlock, ensuring it was definitely locked. 'You may or may not know about Voloshin's plans; that is yet to be determined.' He shrugged his shoulders. 'For some reason, filthy peasant, I respect your resilience,' he tapped the blood-stained bars with his whip, 'but you know that I couldn't let you defy me indefinitely: I <u>do</u> have a reputation to uphold... So because I respect you, you will travel via train to Siberia, instead of being forcibly marched like all the other Enemies of the State. There – should you survive my colleagues in the *Chamber* – you will help build Comrade Stalin's finest road.' He laughed evilly, 'and when you die, your bones will <u>become</u> part of Comrade Stalin's finest road for all eternity!'

From the depths of his throat, Tato somehow mustered a mouthful of green mucous and spat in the Captain's face. He shouted, 'even Hell is too good a place for likes of you!' He moved further into the cage to avoid the Captain's backlash, which disappointingly never came.

The Captain cleared the slime from his eyes, wiping his fingers down his clammy great-coat. He snapped, 'take this pig away,' and watched the horses drag the barred carriage to the railway station. He smiled... even travelling by train, sitting in a windowless carriage without a coat, this peasant would probably die well before he reached Siberia.

The Dancing Barber

Captain Stanislaw looked hatefully at the anti-Soviet propaganda leaflets in his hands and turned to stare at Mama. He stepped towards her, almost tripping over the embroidered icon of the Madonna and Child that partially covered a rusty sickle the Privates had cast to the floor during their search. He gently put the end of his whip beneath her chin and lifted her head with it. Looking the petrified woman straight in the eye, he said, 'as there isn't a printing press in your grubby little house, I want to know where you got these from... otherwise the Collective Farm will be the least of your worries.'

All Mama could do was burst into tears; she looked at the icon beneath the Captain's feet and prayed for help. She knew the Soviets would inevitably tear her family apart, but she didn't think it would be so soon. And she couldn't believe they would stoop so low as to plant such propaganda in her house. Being caught with only one leaflet such as this meant you'd be found guilty of Anti-Soviet Agitation, an offence punishable in a most severe way. But the Captain held a stack of leaflets; she shuddered to imagine what would happen to her and her daughters. One thing she knew... she'd never see her beloved husband again...

One of her twins and her youngest daughter also cried.

But the other twin stared at the propaganda in the Captain's hands and muttered, 'what have I done? What have I done?'

Act 1

Spring 1963
Good Friday

> 'If any one of you is without sin, let him be the first to throw a stone...'
>
> John 8:7

The Dancing Barber

Chapter 1

---✂---

The City of Bradford, West Yorkshire, Northern England

If there were any passers-by, they would have thought the body, lying face down in the gutter was just another tramp. Perhaps he was the latest unfortunate soul to have been kicked out of his home by Bradford's most heinous landlord. Judging by his frayed suit and long, unkempt moustache, he may have been sleeping rough for some time. And the worn leather soles of his boots looked as if they'd circumnavigated the globe, twice.

But on closer inspection, the suit looked anything but "off the peg": its dark grey weave was finely pinstriped, the jacket with blue silk, and the trousers with yellow silk. And the boots were made of bright red leather, worn cowboy-fashion beneath his trouser legs.

The rain intensified, darkening his clothes as they slowly became saturated, his face now half submerged in a puddle between the cobblestones with the kelp of his moustache floating on the surface. The man held a leash made of intertwined blue and yellow leather cords, at the end of which a most miserable creature sat patiently. The damp fur of his Russian Blue pedigree cat made the animal look half its normal size; it would have sought shelter had it not been loyal to its owner, or tethered to him by the leash. Droplets of rain the size of marbles bounced off the cat's head as it pawed at its owner's bulbous nose, almost getting its claws entangled in the sodden tendrils of his dark moustache. But the man still did not stir.

For the third hour, the chimes of the man's pocket watch went unnoticed. The cat shook with disgruntlement, as if it were a dog emerging from the river, flicking water droplets everywhere. It sniffed at its damp fur with dismay, before turning its back on its owner.

Moments later the man screwed up his face and tried to bury it deeper into the gutter. He groaned and uttered, 'thanks a bunch

Mister Pushkin,' as he observed the flagellating tail before his eyes, the verdant stream emanating from beneath, accurately aimed up his left nostril. 'A-hem, I am not a skirting board,' he said, wiping his face with his wet sleeve before levering the cat's silky tail back down so as to shut off the faucet.

After enduring hypothermic conditions for so long, the man felt as though he was suffering from *Riga Mortis*, unable to move most of his body. He groaned and cursed, then rolled onto his back, straight into a puddle as deep as a half-filled bath. A brace of rats that had been lapping at the water's edge darted over his body and into the darkness, inducing the man to scream with fright, taking the cat completely by surprise.

When his heart stopped pounding, the man performed a laboured sit up and struggled to get onto his haunches, taking the time to catch his breath before attempting any more movements. Eventually he gathered the strength to stand, his short body struggling to remain upright; he tried to look around but was still unable to move his head more than an inch in any direction. And he was sure Mister Pushkin was laughing at him splashing around in the ankle-deep puddles, trying to wring out as much water as he could from his heavy, saggy suit. At least the rain had eased off...

The Russian Blue head-butted the man's shin so hard that he almost fell over again. 'Mrryaw!' it said, shaking its fur with disgruntlement and then gently tugging on the leash in the direction of shelter.

'In a minute Mister Pushkin,' the man said impatiently, transferring the leash to his left hand and using his right to verify the flat oblong plastic box was still nestled safely in his inside pocket. Even though the case was cracked, the contents were undamaged... for the moment. He then grasped the green ribbon that hung from his waistcoat pocket and fished out the bulky gold watch. Relieved that the water hadn't damaged the movement, he checked the time through the half-hunter case. He swore under his breath and muttered, 'three hours late,' as he rubbed the lump on his shaking head. He rotated the watch's winding crown the usual seven times and placed it back in his pocket.

'Look at the state of me,' he muttered, 'I should change my suit... but I don't have time...' He shook his head again, sniffed the damp cloth of his sleeve and flinched away. He had at least half a dozen tailored suits hanging in his wardrobe, but only ever wore one of them, saving the rest for 'special occasions' that never seemed to happen.

The sound of muffled groaning echoing almost indiscernibly down the damp alley really put a spring in his step. So much of a spring that he almost slipped on the soaking wet cobblestones and knocked himself out again. 'Come on then,' he said to the Russian Blue, 'let's get into the dry.' And the pair headed off down the alleyway in the direction of the Club, where a nice cup of tea would wash away the taste of water from the puddle and from the cat.

The man was thankful to get out of the cold, dank, rat-infested alleyway and into the relative warmth of the sodium streetlights that lined the steep incline of Great Horton Road. Alleyways were always filled with too many rats, and he'd seen quite enough of them to last a lifetime.

As the rain intensified, he saw an enormous lightning fork almost touch the top of Lister Mill's soaring chimney, momentarily illuminating the landscape that was corrugated with terraced houses. 'One, two, three,' he counted until he heard the first rumbles of thunder that built into an almost deafening crescendo. The Russian Blue didn't need any encouragement to speed up and almost dragged its owner along the greasy sandstone pavement, the leather soles of the man's boots gliding across the flagstones.

The pair skipped onto the road to overtake a troika of headscarved old women that marched and gossiped in step. As if he were a stranger walking into a saloon in the Wild West, the gossip immediately ceased when he passed by. But he knew he'd become the new topic of conversation the second he was out of earshot. He smirked, skipping back onto the pavement... The Gossipmonger and her Gaggle didn't bother him anymore.

It was a little-known fact that flat-cap wearing, middle-aged Ukrainian men were capable of gossiping with just as much enthusiasm as headscarf wearing, middle-aged Ukrainian women. During their lunch breaks they would frequent the benches of Manningham Park to debate their latest gripes, which were currently their hatred of the Soviet Union and their detestation of their odious landlord. But every evening, the ones who managed to escape their nagging wives would congregate in the Ukrainian – or "Uki"– Club bar.

'Would you like another?' one fellow said while scratching the scalp beneath his flat-cap.

'Can you afford it?' came the reply.

'I can if we both have halves,' said the first fellow, rummaging in the depths of his pocket to extract sufficient change from amongst the fluff. He sighed, 'then I suppose we'll have to go back home.'

'Well let's drink slowly,' said the other fellow with a frown. 'My wife's in an awful mood and I need to give my ears a rest.'

On the next table, another couple of men loosened their woven ties and stretched luxuriantly as they deliberated whether to have beer or bitter. Their strong hands, hardened through decades of farming in Ukraine were now moisturised every day by the oil they used to keep the looms running smoothly at Lister Mill. Tonight, the furrows on their brows were almost as deep as the ones they ploughed on their farmsteads before 1933.

'What does that durak think he's playing at?' said the first fellow, examining his screwed-up letter of eviction. 'He can't just chuck everyone out on the street and sell our houses from beneath us… We paid enough for them? My wife's expecting another child any day now, but that durak doesn't give a toss!'

'And what do you expect?' said the other fellow as he ordered two pints of beer by giving his usual hand signal to the inebriated barman. 'You knew Ivan was a piece of work when you agreed to rent a house from him.'

The first fellow begrudgingly agreed, 'but I didn't think he'd kick us out after only three months!'

The other fellow smirked, 'we've always referred to him as The Ginger Rasputin… But others have begun calling him The Count, because he bleeds them dry… And he never has the guts to tell you to your face... he always sends his bad news in a letter!'

'The Count?' said the first fellow. 'That's one letter too many in my opinion…'

'He's obviously in trouble,' the other fellow said, shrugging his shoulders. 'Why else would he be in such a rush to sell <u>all</u> his

The Dancing Barber

houses?'

'I couldn't give a toss about how much trouble he's in! I paid that durak six months' rent in advance, and when I asked him for a refund, he told me to... you know...'

'I wish *he'd*... you know... and leave us alone! Try not to let it worry you... pieces of work like Ivan always get what's coming to them. Drink up,' he said, handing a pint of frothy beer to his friend, 'it'll make you feel better.'

In amongst all the flat-caps, a solitary headscarf glittered like iron pyrites in a bucket of grit. And it was this headscarf's presence that made the flat-caps tone down their conversations from their usual lurid heights.

Halyna had been sat at the corner table for the best part of three hours and couldn't cross her legs any tighter; she couldn't even look at the dregs in the bottom of her eighth teacup without thinking longingly about the loo. But she certainly was not waiting for her husband, because he was at the Ballet Studio, engrossed in a last-minute dress rehearsal until at least midnight. She looked at the time on her mechanical Sekonda wristwatch, its ticking almost keeping pace with her pounding heartbeat. She thought about starting to panic.

The rain had come on heavy once more and Halyna watched as the last remnants of bird droppings finally eroded from the windowpane. This reinforced her belief that – given enough time – windows kept themselves clean, thus saving money on window cleaners.

She checked the time again; noticing the watch's case had gone green with her sweat after the silver plating had worn off. She thought *come on Klem? Where are you? You've never been <u>this</u> late before; I knew something would go wrong.*

Through the torrential rain she watched half a dozen sodden figures dash to and fro, failing to stay dry beneath inadequate umbrellas. But none of them was Klem.

She stood up and adjusted the apron that had moved out of place after hours of fidgeting. But pulling the cord tighter pressurised her bladder so much that she feared flooding the bar; wisely, she scampered to the loo before embarking on what she'd decided was to be a rescue mission...

'Looks like her boyfriend has stood her up, doesn't it?' said one of the flat-caps. 'The husband may be an artist, but the boyfriend is an *artist*!'

Another flat-cap positioned his pint glass in the centre of the square beer mat. He said, 'I don't think the boyfriend's an *artist* any more... he's been tea-total for decades... even the thought of booze turns his stomach.' He laughed, 'the boyfriend might be five years younger than the husband, but they're both old gits compared to Halyna...' He sipped his pint, giving himself a frothy white moustache, 'anyway... I'm glad he's stood her up.'

'I'm surprised Taras lets his wife get away with it,' said a third flat-cap. 'Because if she were my wife, I'd sort her out good!' he said with a nod of the head.

'Oh would you now?' shouted a severe-looking headscarved woman from across the bar. 'I'm interested in finding out how you would "sort me out good"?'

The flat-cap gulped, then uttered the semblance of an apology, but was soon escorted out, guided by his wife's firm grip of his ear lobe.

The remaining flat-caps erupted into laughter, but quickly simmered down when they spied another Gaggle of headscarved women entering the bar... and any one of them could be next!

A greatly relieved Halyna emerged from the lavatory to find the bar completely desolate. The only evidence of human activity being the accumulation of uncollected glasses on every table, the heady smell of mothballs hanging in the air and the darts still quivering in the well-perforated image of Josef Stalin on the dartboard. She looked out of the window while buttoning her coat and noticed the multitude of wives – *that explained the mothballs* – steering their alcoholic husbands home as if they were a bunch of naughty schoolboys.

She waved goodbye to the inebriated barman who couldn't care less, and carefully squelched across the carpet that was forever saturated with every alcoholic drink imaginable towards the exit.

'Mrryaw!'

She instinctively looked to the floor upon hearing the recognisable greeting, coupled with the gentle tinkle of cat urine against the skirting board. She said, 'hello Mister Pushkin,' noticing he was detached from his leash, 'and where's your owner?'

As the sharp smell of mothballs dissipated, Halyna detected the delicate floral aroma that meant only one thing…

'Will you join me for some of my special Darjeeling?' the silky voice she knew so well sang across the empty bar.

'Klem! Thank Goodness you're all right!' she said, rushing over to greet the man who emerged like an apparition from behind his steaming teapot. She wanted to hug him, but didn't wish to give the wrong impression, especially as the inebriated barman with the Robert Mitchum eyes had sat up so as to get a better view. Instead she said, 'thank you for bringing your special tea, because,' she cocked her head towards the eavesdropper, 'I'm fed up of drinking *his* puddle water.'

Klem raised an eyebrow; he knew more than most what puddle water tasted like.

The barman was suitably offended and stomped off in a huff. He'd probably go finish the bottle of samahon he'd been emptying all night.

'Here you are,' Klem said, decanting the steaming tea into a fresh cup and passing it to his dear friend. 'This is an extra special blend… smell it…' he said, taking in a deep lungful, 'can you detect that subtle hint of muscatel grapes? Ahhh, this truly is the *Champagne* of Teas!'

'Mmm,' Halyna said, 'it tastes very goodski.' Although it was much nicer than her usual PG Tips, it still tasted like tea to her. Yes, it smelled floral, but she wouldn't recognise a muscatel grape if one fell from the sky and bounced off her head!

Klem allowed the tea to linger on his pallet and used the time to examine his dear friend's appearance. For a woman once admired for her Margaret Lockwood good looks (even down to the naturally occurring "beauty spot" on her cheek), tonight he thought Halyna resembled a sack of spuds. He looked at her reddened cheeks and her ever so slightly swollen nose (undoubtedly the result of too much samahon), and the prematurely grey strands of hair peeking out from beneath her colourful headscarf. And why did she always have to wear that damned apron? By the look of its plentiful beetroot stains, it was probably borsch for dinner. He wondered what made a woman age so quickly in such a short space of time.

He listened as she said, 'Taras won't be happy if I'm not in the kitchen when he comes up from the studio. He wants all the *Pasky* baked tonight!'

That answered his question... Taras expected far too much from his wife: how could one woman be a full-time housewife and a full-time factory worker? It wasn't any wonder she'd turned into a Margaret Rutherford years before her time.

After her initial elation at seeing her friend, Halyna was rather shocked by his appearance. Usually so immaculately dressed – even though his suit had seen better days – tonight he looked like he'd had a bath fully clothed! She noticed that Klem's attempt at a Cossack-style moustache was stuck to the dried blood on his face, so she reached over to gently release it. Watching as he winced at the pain, she asked, 'I take it things didn't go as you'd planned?' She also noticed her friend's gaping jacket pocket: this was the first time she'd seen him without his trusty Thermos flask.

'On the contrary... my plan went *precisely* as expected,' he said confidently, whilst unsuccessfully attempting to twist his floppy moustache back into place. He picked up his cup, holding it to his nose so as to wallow in the delightful aroma. 'Our friend decided to go back on his word, and became rather violent.'

'Pardonski?' Halyna said, her tinnitus giving her trouble again. She cupped her ears in her hands and leaned forward.

Moving the teacup away from his mouth, Klem repeated: 'I said that things became rather violent!'

'Violent! I *knew* there'd be trouble,' Halyna slammed her cup onto its saucer. 'I knew it was too much for you to cope with on your own!' She narrowed her eyes, 'but you said your plan went *precisely* as expected... does that mean you *expected* him to turn violent?'

'Relax,' Klem said, placing his reassuring hand on hers, 'I'm all right, and the outcome was quite satisfactory.' He felt her warm hand beneath his, with its hardy skin and tough nails, and on her third finger, the gold wedding ring formed from one of Taras' melted-down ballet medals. He took his hand away, realising it had lingered that little bit too long. He coughed and straightened the green ribbon on the collar of his embroidered shirt and said, 'I must admit I'm famished: I don't suppose you've brought any food?'

Halyna delved into the bottomless pit that was her handbag, and rummaged in amongst the bottles of medicine, tissues, newspapers, bottles of samahon and spare underwear, until she found the emergency pork pie that she never left the house without.

'Here,' she said, unwrapping the tin foil and displaying the stale-smelling pie before him, 'enjoy!' She watched Klem put down his teacup and rub his hands together gleefully. He then reached out to grab the pie as if he were a hungry schoolboy.

Just before he picked it up, Halyna snatched it away and said, 'oh, I am so sorry! Of course, meat is not allowed today.'

'Isn't it?' Klem asked, frowning. 'Why not?'

'It's Good Friday! *You* of all people should know that!'

Klem crossed himself in the Ukrainian Orthodox fashion and said, 'today, I will be allowed to make an exception.' He snatched the pie and carefully surveyed it, deducing it was likely a couple of days old and probably not too poisonous. 'Thank you kindly,' he said before devouring the pie with much enjoyment: Halyna's pastry was rather tough, but the ball of pork nestled within was sufficiently seasoned to disguise its age. After over a decade of practice, she was finally getting the hang of English cooking… even though it did no favours for the waistline… He still felt guilty for enjoying his food, but not because it was forbidden to eat meat on Good Friday…

He watched the stair rods of rain lashing down against the window, the relentless booms of thunder and the pitch-forks of lightening striking the very fabric of the sky. He stopped eating and said, 'this weather is God's punishment for what I've just done.'

Halyna wrinkled her nose, 'why do you say that?' She knew it couldn't be punishment for eating the pie; she looked seriously at him, 'what <u>have</u> you done?'

'You know I'm not a violent man, don't you?' he said, crossing himself in the Ukrainian Orthodox fashion, 'but I never imagined that durak pulling a gun on me!'

Halyna almost dropped her cup.

Klem continued, 'he decided that the cassette tape would cost <u>twice</u> as much as we'd agreed and said he'd shoot all my fingers off, one by one, if I didn't pay up!'

Halyna thought *this was getting serious*. She couldn't believe Ivan would stoop to such barbaric Mafiosi threats just to get some more money; surely he had enough already...? 'Hang on a minute,' Halyna said, 'but you told me that you weren't going to pay him anything in the first place... I thought you were going to do a bit of blackmail of your own?'

'A-ha, this is true,' he said, sipping his tea, trying not to allow his moustache to droop into it. 'But that's not the point. It was typical of that durak to be greedy and threaten me with violence instead of blackmailing me like a gentleman.'

'Come on! Ivan may be a lot of things, but a gentleman isn't one of them!'

'You can say that again...' Klem mused.

Halyna was about to until she realised it was a figure of speech.

'When I refused to pay him a single penny, regardless of what he threatened to do to me, he had some sort of infantile tantrum: stomping his feet and thumping his fists!' Klem almost knocked over his teacup as he made a demonstration. 'Then without warning, he smashed me across the face with the butt of his gun! Well, that knocked me straight to the floor and he shoved his filthy paws in my pockets and stole my wallet and watch before saying that the price was now <u>three</u> times as much, otherwise he'd send the cassette to the BBC! He then nonchalantly walked off, swinging around my beautiful watch as if it were a worthless bunch of keys!'

Halyna knew that contrary to Klem's opinion, the evening's events had undoubtedly not gone to plan. Maybe he had a Plan B all along, or maybe there never really was a plan...

'So,' Klem continued, 'for the first time in three decades I saw red and threw my Thermos flask at him with all my strength!' He demonstrated his version of a bowler's over arm throw, and then opened his eyes widely, 'never in a million years did I think I'd actually hit him! I got him right on the back of the head!' He punched his fist into the palm of his hand, 'whack! And that was that! Ivan crumbled to the ground in a heap of raincoat and corduroys. Well... this was too much of an opportunity to ignore!'

The Dancing Barber

Halyna closed her eyes.

Klem shrugged deviously, 'besides I couldn't leave him in a heap on the ground, could I?' He popped the last morsel of pork pie into his mouth, 'the rain was getting heavier...'

Halyna blew on her perspiring palms, cooling them down. 'Please tell me you've not done anything silly?'

'Don't worry yourself Halyna. The silliest thing I did tonight was trip up in the alleyway on the way to meet you and knock myself out: you know how clumsy I can be when I'm excited!'

Halyna folded her arms and said, 'mmm.'

'There really is no need to worry. Ivan's nicely sheltered out of the rain! Drink up your tea and we'll go and see him!'

Halyna rolled her eyes to the ceiling. Her instincts told her that she wouldn't like what she was going to see...

Chapter 2

There is no worse a sound than a cane thwacking down against the flesh. But as all professional torturers know, the cries of anguish that follow the first strokes soon diminish as the victim's body is numbed to the pain.

The longer the cane the better, as the end whips through the air much quicker, delivering a far more effective blow. And the four-foot cane is the ballet teacher's cane of choice. But Mr Taras' preference is for a <u>five</u>-footer, because he isn't a mere ballet teacher. He is a Ballet <u>Master</u>, who naturally requires a superior cane, especially when keeping his most insubordinate pupils in line.

The youngest dancers were always scared of Mr Taras, but tonight they were petrified. His cane seemed to strike Oksana's buttocks in time with the bolts of lightning that illuminated the night sky, glimpsed only through the tiny barred window high up on the wall. To the youngsters, it was as if Mr Taras had so much anger that he could control the weather.

'If you dare answer me back again,' Mr Taras said, 'I'll cane you until your skin is cut to ribbons! And then I'll cane you some more! You understand?' He shouted so loudly that his face went tomato-red and he almost spat out the cigarette that was perpetually glued to his lip.

Oksana wept, 'I am very sorry Mr Taras. I will never answer you back again!' She struggled to get up from her prostrate position across the well-worn 'caning chair'. Her buttocks throbbed in time with the metronome on top of the piano and she knew that after this, her status as Queen Bully was lost forever.

'And let that be a lesson to you all!' Mr Taras shouted at the rest of his class, 'I will <u>not</u> tolerate bad manners from any of my pupils! Understand?' He then flexed the cane so much that it almost became a hula-hoop, and shouted at Oksana, 'get to your place at once!' Swoosh! Mr Taras released the cane under her and she shot across the floor. He shouted, 'move quicker, you fat pig!'

Not even Oksana dared to rile her Ballet Master any more.

The Dancing Barber

Normally she would have pulled a face, blown a raspberry or given him the two-fingered salute when he wasn't looking. But there were too many mirrors in the studio... with her recent luck, someone was bound to tell on her. And her buttocks couldn't bear another caning.

From across the studio, Sofia grinned at her foe, thinking *oh how the mighty had fallen.* And to her surprise, Oksana didn't bat so much as an eyelid. Sofia tried to be a good Christian, so didn't truly hate anyone. But Oksana tried just as hard to be the one and only exception. If Sofia had the inclination, she could quite easily have turned the tables on Oksana, the only girl at school who could never call her "Saddlebags"... The obese heifer looked ridiculous with her milk bottle glasses, uneven teeth and her woolly mammoth face; she had an unnatural habit of constantly scratching down below and would always eat whatever she managed to extract from in her ears or up her nose.

Sofia agreed that *it didn't matter how big or ugly they were, people in glass houses should never dare throw stones.* But that didn't stop Oksana launching the stones of insult at every opportunity...

Earlier that day, at school, the tell-tale pong of cheese and onion crisps was the early warning signal that Oksana was in the vicinity. The heifer enjoyed nothing more than mocking Sofia in the playground, and to begin with, she said, 'I like your zippy boots!'

'Why thank you,' Sofia played along, rotating each foot in turn, admiring every angle of her leatherette boots with the rusty zips running down the sides.

'Did you get them from a second hand shop? Or did you steal them from a tramp?' Oksana asked, seeking approval from her followers, who raucously laughed whether they thought it funny or not.

Sofia looked at her feet and said, 'but what's wrong with my zippy boots? They're very comfortable?' She thought: *as it happens, my father had purchased them from a second hand shop, but they look brand new. The heifer's probably just jealous because she couldn't get a pair to fit her elephant feet!*

Dissatisfied with not getting a reaction and determined not to disappoint her entourage, Oksana decided to vent her criticism at Sofia's tatty satchel and threadbare coat. Again, Sofia said, 'I like my tatty satchel and threadbare coat: they're very comfortable.'

Oksana then lost her temper and clenched her fists. Sofia half expected her to begin beating her chest like Queen Kong! Instead, she snatched the tatty satchel and tore open the catches.

'Well what have we here?' Oksana scoffed, scattering Sofia's school books across the playground, upon discovering the shabby plastic "Minnie Mouse" lunchbox. 'A sandwich... for me... why *thank* you!' And she promptly thrust Sofia's lunch into the black hole of her mouth... After a brief gnawing, she shouted, 'that's disgusting!' and spat the half-chewed salami sandwich onto the ground. She declared: 'it's like eating cat turds!' And she continued spitting on the ground, throwing the remnants of the sandwich over her shoulder.

Sofia thought: *if anyone knew what cat turds tasted like, it would be you Oksana!* She did well to remain calm. But when Oksana spat all over her zippy boots, she decided enough was enough...

Oksana's entourage gasped as they watched their leader emit a piercing scream. They immediately disbanded, leaving Oksana to look down at the blood oozing from the wide gash in her shin, forming a dark red ribbon as it soaked into her white sock.

'My Mama made me that sandwich,' Sofia said calmly, examining the sharp toe of her zippy boot. 'And don't you know that it's a sin to waste food?'

'You're gonna pay for this,' Oksana hissed, 'you horrible little...' She cried out again, this time much louder as Sofia used her zippy boot to give the heifer a matching pair of blood-stained socks.

Sofia grabbed her nemesis by the second chin and said, 'you dare take the mickey out of me again and I'll do much worse!' She pushed the fat bully over and watched as her ample behind cushioned her fall.

The upturned tortoise took so long to get back up that she was late for class, thus incurring the first of many canings she'd accrued that day.

'Right! From the top!' Mr Taras shouted so as to be heard over

The Dancing Barber

the din of traffic rumbling along Great Horton Road. Although the subterranean studio was down a side street, the speeding juggernauts still managed to shake the cement from the walls. He looked at Sofia and said, 'that means you too! Stop daydreaming and concentrate!'

Sofia shook the happy thoughts from her mind and did as she was told. She knew Mr Taras would never cane her, but it was wise not to annoy him, just in case.

With every dancer in attendance, the studio was jam packed and so hot that Sofia wished the only opening window wasn't actually a coal hatch, high up the wall. The recently mopped wooden floor smelled of damp, as did many of the dancers. She tried to refocus her attention to the task in hand, but flinched when she thought she saw a rodent scuttling along the skirting board. But it was only the fluff that collected in the corners, where the Ballet Master's overworked wife's mop could not reach.

Sofia stood in first position – her feet heel-to-heel, lined up with the floorboards, her arms slightly bent and raised level with her stomach – waiting for the music to commence. She watched the peacock of a Ballet Master strutting around in front of the enormous arched mirror, and imagined how awful it would be if his reflection jumped out and inflicted twice as much belligerence to the already tense dress rehearsal... As it was Good Friday, everyone should have been at church... But Mr Taras' dress rehearsal was much more important, regardless of what the Priest could say. For the first time ever, Sofia would have preferred to have gone to church; anything was better than this... But she wouldn't think that way on Sunday morning, not after attending the gruelling All-Night Easter Service...

'And one, two, three, four...' Mr Taras shouted, marking time by whipping his smoking table with the cane, scattering cigarette butts to the floor... But the piano was silent... he looked around and noticed Mrs Wiggins had gone home; the little pile of snotty tissues beside the metronome was the only evidence she'd actually been there. Despite her ability to play wondrously without requiring sheet music, he cursed the wretched woman for sticking to her contracted hours. Moodily, he cranked up his record player with one hand and selected his favourite Tchaikovsky LP with the other, letting the brown paper sleeve flutter to the floor...

But less than a minute into Act One, Mr Taras tore the needle from the record and shouted, 'STOP!'

Every dancer gulped; who'd gone wrong this time? All eyes turned to Oksana, but for once it wasn't only her fault.

'Té-ori!' Mr Taras shouted to everyone, 'why do none of you remember your Té-ori? You dance like you know nothing and yet you should, because you have all been taught the Té-ori!'

One of the smaller dancers, who was on the verge of bursting into tears, looked up to Sofia. With a slight shrug of the shoulders, she mouthed, 'Té-ori?'

Sofia bent down to the little girl's ear and whispered, 'he means *theory*.'

'Why then, doesn't he *say* theory?'

'Silence!' shouted Mr Taras, dabbing his perspiring brow with an ironed handkerchief. He thwacked the cane against his smoking table harder than ever, splinters of wood exploding into the air. 'I cannot keep going through the basics! When I say do the Batman, then *do* the Batman! How hard can it be?'

Oksana managed to resist laughing out loud as she imagined how silly Mr Taras would look if he were dressed as the Caped Crusader... Actually, the costume would suit him rather well...

Another one of the smaller dancers looked up to Sofia. She mouthed, 'Batman?'

Sofia bent down to the little girl's ear and whispered, 'he means *Battements*, you know, swinging the leg...'

'Oh, I see,' said the little girl, 'oh that's easy...'

'Silence!' shouted Mr Taras, wondering how much more ineptitude he could tolerate. 'Right!' he clapped his hands harshly, 'from the top!'

Mr Taras' dual roles of choreographer and principle dancer necessitated – much to the class' sheer delight – each of the four acts to be rehearsed twice. Once with Mr Taras in the role of Prince Siegfried, and once as he watched from the side-lines while Natalka, his beautiful Odette, and Oksana, his anything but beautiful Odile took it in turns to dance with an imaginary Prince. It wasn't his fault there were no boys in his class. And he certainly didn't want to turn his beloved *Swan Lake* into a Pantomime by getting one of the girls to play a boy! Although as he watched Oksana destroy his meticulous choreography with each stomp of her elephant feet, he thought a Pantomime it might well become...

Only five minutes into Act One, Mr Taras shouted, 'no, no, <u>no</u>! Stop! How many times do I have to tell you? Pirouette first, *then* plié! And for goodness sake, dance <u>lightly</u> on your feet: you are <u>not</u> a herd of stomping elephants! And <u>listen,</u> you <u>must</u> have an ear for the music: you cannot dance without listening... Get it right! We start again!'

It had already gone nine, and every dancer was exhausted and more desperate than ever not to put a single foot wrong. Any mistake – no matter how small – meant starting again, and everyone was sick of hearing the words 'from the top!'

'Give me strength!' shouted Mr Taras, 'why can none of you do the Enter-Shat?'

Every dancer in the studio looked at each other and shrugged.

The smallest dancer plucked up the courage to put up her hand.

'Yes?' Mr Taras snapped, 'what do you want?'

'Excuse me sir, but *I* have read *all* my theory and not *once* did I come across a dance step called the Enter-Shat... What is it, please sir?'

'What is it? *What is it?* It's <u>Enter-Shat</u>! That's what it is!' Mr Taras threw his cane to the floor and breathed deeply. After standing in fifth position, he fluttered up in the air as elegantly as a mayfly at dawn, alternating his stretched feet, then landing back in the original fifth position. He repeated the step another twice... 'Enter-Shat! Understand?'

The smallest dancer said, '*Entrechat,* is what I think you are trying to say, sir.'

A groan of understanding reverberated around the studio. Their Ballet Master's pronunciation was getting worse every day... No wonder they didn't know what he was on about half the time...

'Listen, smart aleck,' Mr Taras said, glaring down at the little girl and leaning on his flexing cane as if he were Charlie Chaplin. 'Enter-Shat is what I just said... I cannot help it if you cannot hear me... Besides it is the way in which the movements are performed that is important, and not what they are called!' He repositioned the needle of the record player and hollered: 'right! From the top!'

The little girl made a mental note to pencil in Mr Taras' names for the steps of Classical Ballet in her copy of Vaganova's seminal tome that she'd read from cover to cover, twice.

Sofia had only read this book once – mainly looking at the pictures – but as the dress rehearsal continued, she wished she'd spent more time both studying and practicing... then she might, one day, dance as superbly as Natalka...

Sofia watched Natalka prance across the floor, moving her lithe body from pointe to pointe with economy and elegance, displaying her disgustingly svelte thighs for all to see. Mr Taras scooped her up in his arms and lifted her above his head as if she weighed nothing. Natalka could probably perform a pirouette on the palm of his hand; she was a perfect dancer and if she weren't Sofia's best friend, she'd hate her for it.

In the back yard, Klem looked down through the cellar window at the parody of Degas' painting of *The Ballet Class*. As in the painting, he reflected that the dancers looked exhausted, but unlike the painting, they listened to every instruction their Ballet Master gave them: they dare not do otherwise. Klem watched Taras swagger around the studio with his cane thrust beneath his arm, as if he were a General inspecting his troops and surmised that in his mind, he probably was. But this was a General wearing white tights and a billowing, unbuttoned shirt who critically examined his troops with his twenty-twenty vision, looking for even the slightest mistake... any excuse to shout and whip.

Klem watched the strained faces of the ballerinas, concentrating so intently that they'd carry on dancing even if the walls collapsed around them. He used to think dancers danced for pleasure, for the sheer enjoyment of the art form, but he doubted any of Taras' students ever experienced the slightest whiff of enjoyment...

And what on earth did Taras stuff down his tights? If the ballerinas weren't so frightened of him, they'd probably be giggling at the excessiveness of his protuberance, wondering how many rolled-up socks he'd shoved down this time...

Halyna coughed, 'sorry to interrupt, but can you explain *why* you've brought me back home?' She tugged at the crumpled sleeve of Klem's pinstripe jacket, 'and move away from the window: you *don't* want to distract him when he's in the middle of a dress rehearsal. I can tell his mood is not goodski.'

But Klem was engrossed; he watched Taras tear off yet another length of carpet tape to temporarily fix the latest rupture in a fat girl's costume, making her look like an obese mummy from a Hammer film…

'Klem,' Halyna said impatiently, 'I thought you were going to take me to Ivan?'

'And I have,' Klem said, moving away from the window.

Halyna thumped him hard on the upper arm, 'are you insane? You can't bring him here? If Taras finds out, he'll kick you out. Then where will you go?'

'He won't kick me out,' Klem said with a wink, 'I know you wouldn't let him.'

Chapter 3

The Village of Chaplinka, Khersonska Oblast, South-eastern Ukraine

'It very hot today, you cannot the blame him,' Lenka said to her sister. She turned to face the refreshing breeze blowing in from the distant Black Sea and wiggled her arms as if impersonating an enormous mutant chicken, the curly hair in her armpits drying off for the first time that day...

'But even Tarzan, he covered up the dangler. And Tarzan, he was the young man,' Zena replied. 'Viktor, he is ninety-two years old and wrinkled like the prune. Who want see that?'

The twins observed the faraway figure of their uncle wading through the field of waist-high wheat and watched him giggle as the crops tickled him.

'Look,' Lenka pointed at a squadron of crows flying low across the Steppes, 'see how they fly away instead of eating the wheat!'

Zena mused, 'if I were the crow, I would fly away if field had the scarecrow like Viktor in it!' She put two of her soiled fingers to her lips and whistled piercingly to attract her uncle's attention.

'What you want?' Viktor shouted from across the field, his naked walnut skin glistening in the sun like an antique grandfather clock with a stoop.

'We bring you the lunch!' Zena shouted, holding up an enormous rye loaf, stuffed with fiery radish and garlic-infused salami.

Ten minutes later, Viktor had devoured the sandwich, washing it down with a jug of strong black tea, fresh from the samovar. He rubbed his full stomach with glee and declared, 'that was delicious. Thank you.' He raised his body from the parched earth and stretched his lissom arms to the Heavens. Using his hands, he dusted-off his bare buttocks before wiping the crumbs and spilled tea from around his mouth. He said, 'time to get back to work. You help me, yes?'

Zena looked puzzled. 'No,' she said, 'have you forgotten?'

The Dancing Barber

'Forgotten what? It not your birthday, is it?'

'We go on the trip today, Lenka and I,' Zena said, 'I cannot believe you forget!'

Viktor pulled out his pocket watch and read off the time through the grimy glass. 'In that case, you'd better get going. Train goes soon.' He scratched his chin, 'where is it you are going?'

Lenka looked at the pocket watch with curiosity.

Zena shook her head... it was better not to ask.

'Of course!' Viktor said, clicking his grimy fingers, 'you going to see your sister and your beautiful niece!' He slapped himself on the forehead, leaving a dirty hand print, 'how could I forget such a thing?' He thought for a moment, 'how many suitcases are you taking?'

'Ten each,' Zena said, displaying her grubby fingers and thumbs.

'And you have list?'

'Of course,' Zena said, 'that is the most important thing...'

'Passports? You have passports?'

Lenka showed them to him and said, 'do not worry Uncle, we have everything.'

He held out his lithe arms and said, 'in that case, come here and give your uncle a hug and a kiss!'

Zena cringed as he pulled her towards his grimy and rough body. Both she and her sister had put on their least-filthy clothes for the journey and they didn't want them getting covered in *Chornozem*. But it was too late.

'You say hello from me, yes?' Viktor said, running his finger along the contours of the scar where the top of his ear used to be. 'And be sure to bring back *everything* on list!'

'Of course,' Zena said, 'leave it to me.'

'Good, good,' Viktor said, 'I know I can trust you...' He turned to Lenka, 'my dear, you had better saddle up horse, while I speak with your sister alone.'

Lenka waddled off to fix the special double saddle to the soon-to-be disgruntled horse.

'Now listen to me Zena,' Viktor said, 'you make sure you do not let that man bully you! You know what you want, so you have got to get it! It is about time everything was put right.'

'But I am the scared,' Zena said.

Viktor laughed, 'how can the wild boar wrestling champion of Chaplinka be afraid of that pile of stinking himno? *I* have faith in you, so have faith in yourself!' He puckered his lips and kissed her on her bristly cheek, 'now run along, your sister is waiting.'

As the setting sun rendered the Steppes with a warmingly orange tint, Viktor sipped his bitter black tea and listened to the radio with his scraggy dog on his lap in what Zena and Lenka called their "nightly exchange of the fleas". He looked forward to enjoying three whole weeks of blissful peace, quiet and solitude.

It was to be the first Ukrainian Orthodox Easter he'd be parted from his favourite nieces since returning to Chaplinka many years ago, so he'd probably miss them, eventually. Although the next living soul was over two miles away in Askanya Nova, he certainly wouldn't feel lonely; he looked over to the row of gravestones by the tranquil river and sighed...

Viktor placed his bare feet on an upturned crate that used to contain vodka, and turned up the volume on his crackly transistor radio. The Soviet military marching music thankfully fell silent and the newsreader barked out the headlines in harsh Russian. 'Same old rubbish,' Viktor said to the dog, 'how many weeks have they been saying that Voloshin is still alive? Such boring news! When are we going to hear what's going on in rest of world?'

The dog signalled its agreement by pungently breaking wind.

With the sun now resting on the horizon like a giant satsuma, the radio abruptly crackled to silence. Viktor gave it a smack, cursing the 'cheap Soviet rubbish.'

But after a moment, a beautiful sound Viktor hadn't heard for over three decades fluttered from the tiny speaker: a Ukrainian ladies' choir exploded into singing the banned national anthem, *"Ukraine Is Not Dead Yet!"*

Viktor immediately stood to attention; the dog dropping to the floor like a collection of ragged mop heads. He was about to salute, but didn't think his dog would appreciate the gesture. He never thought he'd live long enough to hear Ukrainian words spoken on the radio ever again, let alone sung in this forbidden national anthem.

He'd submitted long ago to the fact that even though he was brought up a Ukrainian, and raised his nieces in the same way,

The Dancing Barber

there actually was no such country, officially. Whether they liked it or not, they were subjects of the Soviet Union. But with the hopeful lyrics of the national anthem filling the tiny homestead, those feelings of belonging and pride in being a Ukrainian set his heart alight.

After the anthem ended, a man's voice spoke, in proper Ukrainian: 'Welcome to *Radio Kateryna*, Ukraine's newest Radio Station! And before we play some more Ukrainian songs, we have some of the breaking news: We have the pleasure to confirm that Voloshin really is alive and will be speaking on this very station in the coming days! Repeat Voloshin is still alive, so…'

The station went dead. Viktor thought the Soviets were slipping, it had never taken them so long to jam an illegally used frequency before, especially one declaring itself to be a Ukrainian radio station! He clicked off the radio and grinned with pleasure that Ukraine had found her voice once more…

And if the person claiming to be Voloshin really was Voloshin, he had no doubt Ukraine had a future after all… This was the only man who had the courage to prove to the world that 1933's Great Famine, in which six million innocent Ukrainians perished was without question Genocide ordered by Stalin to eradicate his "Ukrainian Problem".

Viktor remembered those notorious Collective Farms all too well: at that time, a Ukrainian was doomed whether he worked on them or not. He took comfort in the fact that Stalin would spend all eternity in the burning pits of Hell, together with his platoons of barbaric soldiers…

Viktor and his nieces thanked God every day that they'd somehow survived: they were living proof that Stalin's evil plan failed. They regarded the Soviets as the real problem: why couldn't they leave Ukraine alone? Viktor felt a tear run down his wrinkled cheek; he looked over to the river and remembered what became of the rest of his family…

Just beyond the horizon, the thunderous diesel train set off on its north-westerly trajectory towards Kyiv. Viktor blobbed some rather acidic samahon into his tea and toasted his nieces a safe journey… They were lucky. They were off to the free world, while he remained in the sprawling Soviet Gulag some people call Ukraine.

Chapter 4

The City of Bradford, West Yorkshire, Northern England

'Have you been at the wine again?' Halyna said, trying her best not to panic, 'because this is the <u>dumbskiest</u> idea you've had in a *long* time.'

'Certainly <u>not</u>,' Klem said moodily, wondering whether "dumbskiest" was actually a word. 'You know that I no longer am an expert of fine wine, but am a *connoisseur* of the finest <u>teas</u> in the world.'

Halyna raised her eyebrows and looked at him doubtfully over the plastic rims of her spectacles.

'Besides, this idea is not "dumbski". It is actually a very good one.' He straightened the green ribbon at the collar of his embroidered shirt, 'because nobody would ever think to look here!'

'*No*,' Halyna said, 'nobody would *ever* think to look here… Give me strength…'

Ignoring her sarcasm, Klem creaked open the flimsy wooden door of the outside lavvy and checked it was safe to enter. With Mister Pushkin waiting patiently outside, he flicked the light switch, opened the door wider and genially allowed Halyna to go in first…

The damp, musty stench peculiar to all lavvies, coupled with the pong of stale urine evaporating from the floor – Taras' aim was never that good – forced Halyna to press her hankie to her nose; such acrid stenches always irritated the back of her throat. The atmosphere in the lavvy was so clammy that the toilet paper had to be wrung out before it could be used, and the dampness had obviously permeated the electrics, for the grubby light bulb, festooned with cobwebs, took an age to flicker on. And when it did, Halyna had the shock of her life.

'Have you gone out of your mind?' Halyna shouted.

The Dancing Barber

'What's up with you?' said Klem, folding his arms moodily. 'This is <u>Ivan</u>, remember! If this shocks you, then I'd better not say what I *actually* wanted to do to him…'

'No, you'd better not! Now get him down at once!'

'Now it's <u>you</u> with the "dumbski" ideas! I haven't done this for fun, but – *even though it was rather fun* – it is all part of my plan. Relax,' he said, hopeful that Halyna would remain calm, 'all will be explained in the fullness of time…' He whispered, 'actually, a friend of mine from British Intelligence taught me this technique during the war… It works a treat…' He looked down at Ivan's pathetic face and smiled proudly.

'Hello my friend,' Klem said to the prisoner with much enjoyment, 'has the blood flowed to your head?'

Ivan made very unfriendly noises through the gag over his mouth, many of a four-letter variety.

'Now, now,' Klem said, 'you should watch your language…' He gestured over to Halyna, 'there is a lady present.'

Halyna was speechless. All she could do was stare at Ivan who was suspended from the ceiling by his feet, his entire carcass bound with what looked like two entire rolls of carpet tape, giving him the appearance of a wriggling six-foot long chrysalis. The crown of his recently-balded head rested neatly in the stained toilet bowl, as if it were an enormous egg in an oversized eggcup.

With dismay, she turned to Klem and said, 'did you do this all by yourself?'

'Of course,' he said proudly, 'people have always underestimated Klem; they say he's weak and feeble, but look at what he can do when he's riled.'

Halyna had no idea Ivan had upset her friend so much. Klem had been a pacifist for three whole decades; even during the Second World War, he only ever concerned himself with propaganda, occasionally passing information to the British and believing violence was never the answer. He must have been at the wine again.

'And do you know what I like doing best of all?' Klem said with a mischievous twinkle in his eye.

Halyna cringed, 'go on then,' and hoped it wouldn't be too nasty.

When Klem pulled the chain, Ivan's head received yet another deluge of brownish toilet water, making him wriggle and squirm and groan. The captive's displeasure worsened when Klem threatened to follow Mister Pushkin's example, contemplating whether to aim down his left or his right nostril.

Halyna allowed herself a guilty smile. She should have been appalled at this display of cruelty. But it was Ivan after all.

Klem delighted in flushing the toilet once more and then bent down to look his nemesis directly in the eye. Ivan's enormous beard was thoroughly drenched and clung to his face like a soaking wet ginger cat, whilst his angry, bloodshot eyes bulged like Halloween gobstoppers. Calmly, Klem said, 'I hate you. And with the exception of your club-handed hag of a mother, everybody else also hates you. I know we have some personal history and I can see that evicting me probably made you feel better…' He then adopted an angrier tone, 'but you went <u>too far</u> with blackmailing me over that cassette tape. I cannot believe you'd stoop so low as to fabricate such a disgraceful thing! But it doesn't matter now, because everyone will soon know what you tried to do and who could blame them if they decide your blackmail is tantamount to <u>treason</u>!'

Although Ivan knew more than most about the way traitors were dealt with, there was no remorse in his eyes, no fear and certainly no apology.

Klem let the idea dwell in Ivan's mind for a while. He continued, 'and your interference with Katya could ruin what my colleagues and I have been working towards for so long. Why would you want to do such a thing? Why would you betray your own country just to satisfy your own greed?' He yanked the damp gag from Ivan's mouth, and shouted, 'well, <u>answer me</u>!'

Even after being washed out by all those flushes, Ivan's coffee breath was so obnoxious that Klem couldn't help flinching away. And all Ivan could do was frown, but from Klem's angle it looked as though he was mocking him. Every vein on Ivan's balded scalp was protruding as though he had subcutaneous ivy trying to break through the skin… it was like something from a horror film.

Klem shouted, 'I said <u>answer me</u>! Or do you want another flushing?' He grabbed hold of the chain and pulled it just enough for the water in the cistern to gurgle.

Finally, the captive spoke: 'Why don't you go and drink some more t-t-tea you, you t-t-tea drinking t-t-twit! I n-n-never did l-l-like you! And I'm gonna tell my m-m-mother on you! My m-m-mother was right; all b-b-bad men have m-m-moustaches: H-H-Hitler, S-S-Stalin and y-y-you!'

Klem could only laugh at Ivan's infantile retort, 'the same could be said about beards: Lenin may not have had a ginger tom clinging to his face...' He shrugged his shoulders; such childishness could only come from a sixty-five-year-old man who still gets tucked in at night by this mother.

'That's it, l-laugh at me,' Ivan said, 'I'm not s-scared of a little t-t-twit like you. I dare you to do your w-worst!'

'Little twit?' Klem said, turning to look at an appalled Halyna, 'but I am five foot three.' He looked back at Ivan, 'so you dare me to do my worst, hmm? Then so be it.'

Before Halyna could stop him, Klem had retrieved the confiscated Soviet pistol from his jacket pocket and inserted its silenced muzzle into Ivan's left nostril.

She pleaded, 'Klem, this is not goodski, please <u>think</u> before you do something stupid!'

'Halyna, please leave it to me,' Klem almost snapped, 'I have *everything* under control.' He turned back to Ivan,

'When I refused to pay your extortionate ransom, you pulled this gun on me and threatened to shoot all my fingers off, even though you only had six bullets. Then after your little tantrum you knocked me to the floor and stole my wallet and watch.' Klem sneered, 'so really, you're just a common thief, and quite frankly a thug too.'

Ivan said, rather nasally, 'I'm n-n-not fr-fr-frightened of you! You're a c-c-coward. You'll never p-p-pull the t-t-trigger.'

Halyna looked away in horror. What was Klem thinking? Today was Good Friday, the day when Christ died on the cross, a day for contemplation, for meditation and for strengthening the faith. Klem, of all people, should not have forgotten it.

The muffled 'pft' sound was realistic, but that was all that happened...

Slowly, Halyna opened her eyes, dreading what she was about to see...

Klem unscrewed the muzzle from Ivan's nostril and examined it. 'It must have been a blank?' he said with apparent disappointment. He looked down at the prisoner and noticed he'd fainted, his body wobbling limply...

'That's odd,' Klem said to Halyna, 'Ivan must have known they were blanks, so why would he faint?' He shrugged his shoulders and pulled the damp gag back over Ivan's mouth, handing the gun to Halyna, 'here... take a look...'

Halyna's heart was beating faster than a sewing machine's needle; she'd never been so relieved in her whole life. Did Klem – a man she thought of as a brother – really want to shoot Ivan up the nose? Her body shuddered... If he'd killed him, it would have been murder... this wasn't the Soviet Union – it wasn't allowed – so the consequences would have been dire. Klem may have been many things, but stupid wasn't one of them. Maybe all this blackmailing business with the cassette tape had pushed him over the edge? But she knew it was impossible to guess what Klem was really thinking...

'Come on Halyna, let's leave him here for the night,' Klem said, pushing Halyna out of the lavvy. 'Tomorrow morning, I'll come back for a farewell chat before my friend comes to collect him. It may be the last time any of us see him...' He rubbed his hands together gleefully, 'right then Pushkin,' he said to the waiting cat, 'let's get into the warm... I might have some nice sir-a-loin for you...'

'Friend?' Halyna said. She hadn't a clue what Klem meant and didn't have chance to ask before he'd taken back the pistol, locked up the lavvy, scampered across the yard and up the stone steps into the kitchen, his leather soles skidding on the moss. 'What friend?' she said, but there wasn't any time to worry about that now... She looked through the cellar window and saw the dress rehearsal coming to an end. '*Pasky*!' she cried, dashing into the kitchen to squeeze five hours' baking into one...

The Dancing Barber

Chapter 5

From Chaplinka to Kyiv, Ukraine

'I no like this train,' Zena said to her sister, gnashing her craggy teeth and shaking her sweating head.

'You think I do?' Lenka replied, shuffling from one flabby buttock to the other, yet still unable to get comfortable on the juddering bench. 'These wooden seats, they create much distress for the haemorrhoids...'

Zena snapped, 'I do not talk about the seats! I talk about this train!' She gazed at her surroundings, finding it hard to believe how thick-headed her sister could be... 'Do you not recognise the type?'

The penny, as usual, took an age to drop. And when it did, the colour immediately drained from Lenka's face.

Zena said, 'it still has the bars on the windows, and look,' she pointed to the door, 'the locks, they are on the <u>outside</u>.'

Peering between the rusty bars, Lenka watched the Steppes at dusk trundle by... in the warm evening light, they looked more beautiful than ever. She said, 'so this view, it must have been the last our Tato saw of his beloved Ukraine...' She sniffled, then blew her nose on her embroidered headscarf, as if she were a bugler playing *The Last Post*.

Zena put a comforting hand on her sister's sturdy shoulder, 'it is all in the past. There is no point getting the upset about it.' She tried to smile, 'we have the much to look forward to...' She spoke the words, but didn't believed them. To her, the past was still in the present and if the propaganda were to be believed, no Ukrainian would be happy until every Soviet injustice was admitted and Ukraine regained her independence. So deep down, she knew she would never be happy...

Despite hundreds of mass graves being unearthed, the Soviets continued to deny all knowledge, laughing in the faces of the people they'd persecuted and butchered... The few people who survived the Gulags and were brave enough to speak out always "disappeared" without trace... But the number of people who had the courage to challenge the Soviets was growing every day: they couldn't make them all disappear, although they'd probably try...

The spasmodic journey to Kyiv Central Station couldn't have gone quickly enough... the twins were so desperate to escape the "Death Train" that they jumped out before it had even stopped. They landed comfortably on their multitude of suitcases, crushing them flat, and wasted no time heading for the Aerodrome.

Lenka's inept map reading skills didn't delay them too much and they reached the correct runway with half an hour to spare. All they had to do now was find the correct aeroplane...

'Hey you two!' a commanding voice roared at them. 'This is State-owned property, so get lost!'

The sisters turned to face the officious man marching towards them, his clipboard in hand and automatic pistol on belt.

Zena said, 'are you the talking to us?'

The man gaped up at the looming edifice of the twins, appalled by their cavernous nostrils that looked as if they supported their own ecosystem, and their downy chins, teeming with life. He was either very brave or very stupid when he held his nose and said, 'tramps are not allowed in Aerodrome! Go now or I <u>will</u> shoot you!'

'Tramps?' the twins said in unison, looking each other over from head to toe. 'But we are the prettiest girls in Chaplinka: <u>everyone</u> says so...' Nobody would dare to say otherwise.

The officious man reached for his automatic pistol. He said, 'I think all the people of Chaplinka – wherever that is – need to urgently make an appointment with the optician! They must all have cataracts...'

'We have the dog,' Zena said, 'but no cat...? Now listen: we are here to catch the aeroplane to the Bradford Aerodrome. Look,' she showed the man their tickets that were already soiled after spending time in her pocket, 'it flies to the sky very soon!'

Lenka added, 'and we not appreciate being called the tramps, either.'

The officious man examined the tickets and declared they were fakes. He said, 'such peasant women,' he almost spat out the words, 'could never afford to fly on an aeroplane.'

The Dancing Barber

Before the twins had opportunity to rearrange the officious man's face, a burly pilot, wearing a peaked cap and striped sleeves, escorted them to his aeroplane… 'Take no notice of him,' said the pilot, 'he's only jealous, because he's never flown!'

The sisters laughed. But then realised that, actually, neither had they…!

Chapter 6

The City of Bradford, West Yorkshire, Northern England

At the end of Act Four, every dancer collapsed to the floor in a pool of sweat and tears; midnight was a distant memory, as was the ability to stay awake. Although his dancers were dead from exhaustion, Mr Taras was happy. In fact, he was ecstatic. 'That was wonderful!' he sang, flouncing energetically to the front of the studio. 'We have finally banished the elephants! Now all we have to do,' he said, stubbing out his fortieth cigarette of the evening, 'is do it even better at The Alhambra on Sunday!' He stood with his hands on his hips, emulating Yul Brynner's interpretation of the fictional Cossack, Taras Bulba, his head cocked back and his eyes questing the studio, 'can anyone tell me why?'

Every dancer said wearily, but in unison, 'because the ballet critics will be there and if *Swan Lake* gets good reviews, then we will all be famous and rich!' By now, they knew it word for word...

'Good, good,' Mr Taras said, lighting his forty-first cigarette, using a Dunhill lighter with the flame of a Bunsen-Burner. 'Everyone have a good night's sleep and I'll see you all back here in the morning for the *final* dress rehearsal. Nine a.m. sharp!'

The groan of displeasure made the fabric of the building shake. But Mr Taras didn't notice. He was happier than he'd been in a long time, thanks in no small part to Natalka's sublime performance; even Oksana seemed to dance better than he'd expected... that last caning was obviously worthwhile.

'Oh, before you go,' Mr Taras said, clapping his hands, insisting the slouching dancers stopped and turned to face him. 'I have spoken to all of your parents and they agree that every one of you needs help with their Ballet! Therefore, as stated in the Té-Ori, I shall also be teaching Ukrainian National Dancing during your rest days: lessons start in the summer!' He enveloped the dancers with his gaze, 'good news, isn't it?' And when no one responded,

The Dancing Barber

he said, 'that is all... you can all go home now!'

If the dancers groaned any more, they'd cause the building to collapse... Having to do Ballet was bad enough, never mind the added ordeal of Uki Dancing... Even the little ones thought it typical of "the old man" to commandeer what little free time they had left... But at a shilling a week, it was cheaper tuition than anywhere else... And Mr Taras was an excellent teacher... Almost everyone thought so... But every dancer knew the real reason their parents sent them to his studio: with their children occupied, it meant they could spend more time boozing at the Uki Club... It never occurred to them how much their daughters suffered at the hands of the tyrannical Mr Taras and his stinging cane...

The air in the studio was suffocating... so hot and stale that the dancers felt as though they were breathing mustard gas. They dragged their feet to the changing area, their ballet shoes streaking though all the sweat that had been spilled over the past seven long hours. And the bags under their eyes could have contained a week's shopping: were fame and riches worth all this effort and all those bunions? And tomorrow was the first Saturday since Christmas when the Ukrainian School was closed: so the first chance of a lie-in for months had been scuppered... *thank you very much Mr Taras!* It was an impossibly long time to wait until the summer holidays... and even then, their free time would be spent on Uki Dancing, instead of having fun... some of them couldn't remember what fun actually felt like...

Mr Taras sat down, put his feet onto the smoking table and leaned back contentedly in his chair. After more than seven hours of non-stop rehearsals he took the time to unwind, letting the calming smoke of his cigarette hiss through his teeth, rising through the air as if from the mouth of a resting dragon.

Who'd have thought it'd take over thirty years, but I'm finally going to make it! He imagined his name in lights above every grand theatre in the country... *Better late than never! I'll show that Gossipmonger how talented I am! The club-handed old witch!*

Natalka walked gingerly over to her teacher. 'Excuse me,' she said, her voice shaking with nerves, 'I have something to show you...'

Mr Taras turned and said joyfully, 'ah my Odette, you were

simply fabulous. It has been a long time since I saw anyone who could mime as well as you; you have such an ear for the music, it is wonderfully sublime! I'm going to make you into a big star, an *enormous* star!'

Natalka sobbed as she crumpled onto a bench, clutching her ankle with both hands.

Mr Taras' heart sank to the pit of his stomach and then crashed straight through the floor. 'Oh no,' he twisted his barely-smoked cigarette into the ashtray, 'what on earth has happened?'

Natalka winced as Mr Taras picked up her leg and examined it on his knee. Her ankle was so swollen that the white laces of her ballet shoe cut into the flesh making it look like a stringed up joint of beef. She spoke shakily through the tears, 'you didn't notice sir,' she always addressed him as sir, even though he disliked it, 'but I fell when I came out of the last pirouette at the end of Act Three, but I carried on, because,' she sobbed even more, 'I didn't want to let you down.'

Mr Taras' eyes darted all over the place as if following a wasp buzzing around his head. He saw Sofia watching from a distance and shouted, 'go and get some ice! And be quick!'

When he wasn't looking, Sofia clicked her heels and saluted before heading upstairs to the kitchen.

He turned back to his injured protégé, unable to disguise his disappointment. 'You wouldn't have let me down, Natalka, had you stopped dancing after you fell. But now you have made your injury much worse and it will take so much longer to heal. I didn't think you were stupid enough to dance an entire Act with a sprained ankle?'

Natalka was inconsolable, her usually immaculate face covered in snot and tears and she only got worse when Mr Taras pulled off her shoe, allowing her foot to swell to three times its normal size... now she really could stomp around like an elephant. She was to be Mr Taras' star performer: her face was next to his on the enormous banner advertising *Swan Lake* above The Alhambra and on promotional leaflets, sent far and wide; but now it looked as if everything was ruined. She thought she did the right thing by dancing through the pain... obviously not... nothing ever pleased Mr Taras...

Sofia ambled into the studio holding a plastic tub, gripping the

The Dancing Barber

rim with her fingernails, because it was painfully cold to the touch. She said, 'sorry Tato, I couldn't find any ice. But I have brought some of Mama's vanilla ice-cream instead. Is that okay?'

'I suppose it'll have to be,' he snapped before giving his daughter a cursory 'thank you'.

Sofia despaired as she watched her father gouge out a handful of sweet-smelling ice-cream and smear it all over Natalka's ankle. Surely it would have been better to hold the plastic tub against the swelling? But her father never had much in the way of common sense.

Although Natalka flinched when the frozen dessert made contact with her sensitive skin, she soon emitted a seemingly endless 'ahhh...' as it quenched the fire of her injury.

At least Oksana wasn't watching: she never could resist the taste of vanilla ice-cream, so would have been lapping it up from the floor like an obese bespectacled cat.

'I don't think anything's broken,' said Mr Taras, roughly prodding Natalka's ankle with his strong thumbs.

'If it isn't,' said Natalka, 'then it bleeding will be soon... *Please* be gentle...'

Sofia tried to look concerned, but inside she was grinning from ear to ear: Natalka's misfortune could be her big chance to finally get a leading role in *Swan Lake*. She was just as good as Natalka in the official ballet exams and knew all the Té-Ori. But her father didn't agree; on the few occasions he bothered to speak to her, he'd say, 'Sofia, you are too short and your thighs are too big to <u>ever</u> be a *prima* ballerina. And as for those feet...'

She was sure her father would have preferred Natalka as his daughter. He told everyone that Natalka moved like a gazelle, with exquisite poise and delicacy; the girl chose every step carefully and her flowing, lithe movements were a joy to behold. He said that Natalka was destined for the Royal Ballet, while his own daughter would only ever amount to a ballet teacher in a backstreet school. *Like father, like daughter*.

Sofia's shoulders slumped... there was more chance of Oksana winning a beauty contest than there was of her father asking her to be Natalka's replacement... even though she knew all her positions off by heart and could probably dance them backwards. How could he hate his own daughter so much? Whatever she did was never good enough. She was top of the class at school, scored highly in her ballet exams and even ironed his shirts in his preferred finicky way, yet still he didn't acknowledge her...

When she came home from school that afternoon, she proudly placed her glowing end of term report in the centre of her Tato's tiny desk, hoping that for once, he would take an interest in what it contained. But when she went back only five minutes later, he'd dumped a heap of choreography notebooks directly on top of it... She knew he wouldn't read it; he never did.

And she couldn't understand why he'd overlooked her for the role of Odile? That was the worst snub of all, picking that horrible Oksana over her: the girl couldn't even see her toes, let alone touch them! The whole premise of *Swan Lake* was that Odette and Odile looked identical, so the ballet was doomed from the start!

Sofia watched her father fumbling with the mess of melting ice-cream and wondered whether the old man had finally lost the plot? If his precious ballet were to be the calamity she expected, he would only have himself to blame...

Never mind a beauty contest, it looked as though Oksana was leading an eating contest. The heifer enjoyed nothing more than gorging on crisps – cheese and onion as usual – like a horse from a nosebag, simultaneously pulling the underwear from between her bruised buttocks, where it crept several dozen times each day.

She'd been waiting so long for her father to come and pick her up that she'd got through five whole packets that currently littered the floor by her chunky feet. His lateness wasn't unusual, for he was often entangled in his various business dealings, frequently forgetting all about her. And when he did turn up in his tiny red Volvo sports car, she hated everyone laughing when she tried to squeeze into the passenger seat. And hated them even more when they waited to witness the impromptu fireworks display caused by the exhaust pipe scraping along the tarmac as the car pulled away.

For a Queen Bully, a lot of people laughed at her: if not in her face, then certainly behind her back. If only she hadn't let that little curly-haired troll kick her in the shins with those charity shop boots, then maybe she wouldn't have become a complete laughingstock. She was so traumatised by her sudden fall in status that she didn't want her sixth packet of crisps, even though it rustled temptingly in her pocket…

She blamed her father for inflicting Mr Taras' awful ballet classes on her. For such a supposedly tough businessman, her father was a weakling in front of his own mother and would do anything she said; maybe it was her overpowering stench of mothballs that gassed him into submission? Or maybe it was the threat of being beaten with her clubbed hand? And it was only because *she* failed as a ballerina thirty years ago, that she insisted on forcing her own granddaughter to endure the pompous "Ballet Master's" ridicule and canings, just so as to relive what might have been. Oksana hated the ballet. The only things she hated more were her father and grandmother.

All these thoughts made her feel so depressed that she decided to risk walking home and hoped The Ripper would do her in; at least then, she'd be saved from her horrible life…

Chapter 7

The skies above Europe

After a brief period of sweaty palms and clammy armpits, the twins managed to relax, and tried to enjoy the experience of 'flying like the birds'. Lenka ensured she had been to the toilet whilst the aeroplane was over Russia... Pulling the flush, she said, 'I hope it lands on Khrushchev himself!'

She then spent most of the time with her blackhead-covered greasy nose pressed tightly against the small window. She enjoyed the bird's eye view of Poland's verdant forests, but was disgusted by Germany's belching industrial cities, cloaked in pollution, and was calmed by the green-grey expanse that was the North Sea. She couldn't believe she was flying above flocks of seagulls and pigeons... she wished she could be a bird, probably an enormous albatross.

Once the aeroplane passed over the famous white cliffs, a thick blanket of damp, low cloud disappointingly obscured "the green and the pleasant land" she so looked forward to seeing. And the weather certainly matched Zena's mood...

While Lenka went to annoy the pilot by sitting on his control panel and momentarily turning off both engines, Zena was so deep in thought that she wouldn't have noticed if the plane spiralled out of control and plummeted to earth.

After being locked out of the cockpit, Lenka insisted the Steward gave her two mugs of milky tea, a heap of gone-off tuna sandwiches and a reasonably recent, albeit well-read, newspaper. She didn't think it strange that the Steward wore filthy overalls, or that the newspaper was cut into square sheets...

Squeezing her enormous bulk down the narrow aisle between the empty seats, she re-joined her sister, miraculously without spilling the milky tea.

Zena feigned a smile; 'I cannot believe it is the thirty years since we last saw our young sister... I wonder if she has changed much.' She slurped her milky tea and selected a gone-off tuna

The Dancing Barber

sandwich made with the whitest bread she'd ever seen. 'And her life, it is so different to ours. She is the very rich woman.'

'I suppose that is what happens when you marry the rich man,' Lenka said, admiring the photograph her young sister had sent of the beautiful Manor House with its long, sweeping drive, classical façade and neatly trimmed ivy. Over the years they'd received dozens of letters from Bradford with boastful news of success and wealth; so the twins were eager to experience some of it for themselves. 'I cannot wait to walk through the leafy gardens and maybe climb the trees. And then go into the haunted room where the ghost appears in the night: I would like to meet her... It will be the first ghost I have ever seen...'

'It is probably just the cleaning woman,' said Zena. 'The house, it has some very nice wooden beds made by someone called,' she examined her young sister's letter so closely that the paper almost touched her eyeball, "the Tom-ass Chip-in-dale"; so ghost or no ghost, we shall sleep like the dead.'

Lenka hoped not; she preferred to sleep like the living. She said, 'our sister, she also has many of the oil paintings; they are the expensive, yes?'

'All oil paintings are the expensive. And according to the letter of our sister, they were painted by someone called Reynolds, whoever she is... So you must not touch them... We cannot afford to pay for the damage.' She mumbled, 'we cannot afford to pay for anything...'

Lenka looked dreamily at the photograph of the Manor House's ornate dining room. She said, 'if we lived there, I would paint the walls the bright blue; and all that dark wood, I would paint the bright yellow. You agree, yes?'

Zena shook her head, 'this is not our house; our sister, she will not like it if we do the redecorating.' She looked Lenka in the eye, 'you are to promise not to touch nothing, yes?'

Lenka ignored her. She said, 'how many servants do you suppose they have?'

'<u>One</u> would be more than we have! Our sister, she is the lucky woman!' Zena poured a generous glug of samahon into her milky tea... anything to improve the flavour... 'Do you think our sister, she will the recognise us?'

Lenka admired the advertisement for *Swan Lake* her young

sister had included in her last letter. 'Even if she doesn't,' she said, smearing her tuna fishy fingers all over the glossy photograph, 'we will the recognise our niece…' She smiled, 'is she not the prettiest girl? So graceful, with such skinny thighs… The perfect ballerina…'

'I suppose so,' Zena said, putting the milky tea to one side and drinking her harsh samahon directly from the bottle. 'Our niece, she must have some of the same genes as we do… the good looks, they run in the family…' She too admired the advertisement, 'and her teacher, he is the very handsome: I think he looks like the Charlton Heston. You can tell he come from the good Ukrainian family; apparently he trained as the Ballet Master in St Petersburg.'

Even though Lenka knew the ballet school in St Petersburg was one of the best, it was nevertheless a Soviet city and the thought of it set her bowels on edge once more. She said, looking sideways at Zena, 'at least our young sister, she made the good choice when marrying the husband…'

Zena rolled her eyes, refusing to gratify the comment with an answer.

Darkness descended, and the sisters soon ran out of things to talk about, so Lenka amused herself by reading the cartoons in the newspaper before dozing off to a grunty sleep, whilst Zena, once again, lost herself in her thoughts. She sat twirling the tarnished wedding ring she wore on a frayed cord around her neck. The ring was such a narrow diameter that it couldn't even fit onto her little finger, let alone the third finger of her right hand that it used to occupy. She sighed and stared absentmindedly at the back of the empty seat in front of her. 'Ah,' she said with the wave of a hand, 'to Hell with it!' She decided to sweep away her sad and negative thoughts, refusing to waste any more time dwelling on the past.

She dropped the ring back into the clammy crevasse between her bosoms and used the corner of her headscarf to wipe the solitary tear from her eye. From now on, with Uncle Viktor's advice ringing in her ears, she felt confident and determined…

Chapter 8

The City of Bradford, West Yorkshire, Northern England

'I'm tired,' Taras said, confidently sweeping his hand across the array of tumbler switches on the wall. The studio was plunged into near darkness, leaving only the glossy floorboards illuminated by the flashing neon sign of a nearby curry shop shining in through the tiny window. At least darkness disguised the puddles of sweat and piles of cigarette ash sprinkled across the floor. He sighed, because he knew it would get a great deal filthier: Halyna may have been on strike, but there was no way he would lower himself to cleaning his own floor… the very thought of it appalled him. He still hadn't a clue why she was on strike… it was terribly inconvenient. He dismissed the thought with a yawn and said, 'I think I must be working too hard.'

The dress rehearsal may have overrun by two entire hours, longer than ever before, but he still refused to apologise for it, no matter how vocally the flat-caps complained. As the headscarves were all tucked up in bed with their hair in rollers, their flat-capped husbands had been ordered out to fetch their daughters, despite preferring to sleep off all the booze they'd consumed earlier in the evening. So Taras told it to them straight: 'don't you *dare* complain to me that we finished late. If your daughters danced as I told them to dance in the first place then we'd have finished *hours* ago! Understand? You want your daughters to come home on time, you tell them to listen to their Ballet Master!' Not even the roughest flat-cap could argue with that.

Natalka was by far Taras' biggest worry, but as her father worked at the Infirmary, he knew his star dancer would get the best possible treatment. He didn't know what he'd do if she wasn't able to perform, and he didn't have anyone remotely in mind who was worthy of replacing her. But he was confident that things would seem better in the morning… they always did after a long night's sleep…

'Come on Sofia,' he said, slipping on his fifty-shilling blue blazer with the ballet school logo embroidered on the breast pocket. He didn't have the patience to wait for his daughter to finish mopping up the mess he'd made with all that melted ice-cream... especially in near darkness. 'It's time we were all in bed. I don't know about you, but I'm exhausted... But I would be, because I've been working too hard!'

Sofia threw the mop into the bucket. *The old man only ever worked in the evenings, so how could he be tired? When he eventually crawled out of bed (around midday), everyone knew he spent the rest of the day sleeping in his barber's shop, waiting for customers that never came. And who could blame them: her Tato could give a customer any hairstyle he wanted, so long as it was a "short back and sides" or a "crew cut". And who wanted a crew cut in 1963?* She watched him admiring his appearance in the mirror: *Why does he need to put on his fifty-shilling blazer just to go up to the kitchen?*

Out of the corner of his eye, Taras saw a dark figure lurking at the small window, high up on the wall. 'Not again,' he said, dashing over to stop the absent-minded coal man from tipping another delivery into his studio. 'How many more times do I have to tell you? We do not need any coal!'

'Don't you?' asked the coal man, scratching the mat of hair beneath his flat-cap, 'why not?'

Taras tried to remain calm, 'because we've been on gas for two years!'

'Gas? Oh... Terribly sorry,' said the coal man, 'I keep forgetting... I've been tipping coal down this hatch for ten years... But don't worry, it won't happen again...' He made a scribbled note on a piece of grubby paper and stuffed it into a pocket filled with other crumpled pieces of grubby paper. He then wheeled his barrow out into the alley, leaving the unbolted gate flapping in the wind.

Taras reached up and made sure the window was firmly bolted; 'that idiot won't be ruining my floor again!'

Sofia smiled; she knew the coal man would be back the same time tomorrow night...

Father and daughter carefully stepped between the dented

aluminium pans of chilled soup Halyna stored on the stone stairs leading from the subterranean cellar-cum-studio, some of which displayed the hallmarks of Mister Pushkin on their sides. They then went through into the warm kitchen and were immediately bathed in the mouth-watering aromas of baking…

'Hello Taras,' Halyna said, watching her husband walk straight past her.

'Oh hello,' Taras grunted, 'I'm off to bed.'

Halyna gritted her teeth and thought about reaching for the rolling pin. He could have said 'thank you, my kind and wonderful wife for staying up so late to bake hundreds of *Pasky*.' But he hadn't said anything remotely like it in years. *And he wonders why I'm on strike…!*

'Are you okay Mama,' Sofia asked, knowing that she wasn't.

'Yes, thank you,' Halyna said, doing her best to smile, 'the hard work's all done.' She looked at Klem who was quietly sipping his cup of tea by the fire; she knew precisely what he was thinking. Their eyes met across the steamy room and she discretely shook her head to make sure he did not interfere. Klem was a good man, and his help with kneading the half-ton of *Paska* dough was most welcome. Taras would never dream of rolling up his sleeves.

It wasn't just her husband's ungrateful attitude that annoyed her; that cat also had a lot to answer for. It was her custom to leave the dough to prove in an earthenware bowl, covered with a tea towel on a chair in front of the blazing fire. She cursed Mister Pushkin who'd decided to jump onto it, thinking it was a nice warm cushion, thus squashing it flat. It took her far too long to pick all the fur out of it, whilst the cat sat grinning at her from its basket, meticulously washing its whiskers with a moistened paw. She was sure it did it on purpose; that sort of cat always did.

Sofia admired the platoons of perfectly baked *Pasky* cooling on the blackened wire racks on the table by the window, knowing her mother had been slaving over them for hours. She said, 'the *Pasky* look wonderful Mama,' even though she thought some of them looked like burned toadstools. 'Would you like my help with anything?' She knew they had to be decorated, but were probably still too hot for the icing sugar and Smarties.

'That's not necessary Sofia,' Halyna said gratefully, 'I've just put the last batch in the oven.' She blessed the oven with the sign of the cross, so that the last batch – destined to be taken to church the following night – had the best chance of not burning to a crisp like all the others. 'You *can* take the rubbish out,' she added, glancing across the yard to the locked lavvy door, 'but be careful not to dirty your costume.'

Sofia rolled her eyes to the ceiling and said, 'yes Mama,' thinking: *why do I always get the glamorous jobs?*

The bin bag smelled like it was filled entirely with Mister Pushkin's litter, so Sofia held it at arm's length and deposited it into the dented dustbin in the corner of the yard, being careful not to clatter the lid. It was one o'clock in the morning and she did not want to disturb the neighbours, even though they rarely repaid the favour, frequently turning up roaring drunk in the small hours, singing songs that would make the Priest faint. At least it had finally stopped raining…

She yawned and turned to look up at the house. Her father's bedroom light had gone out, so he'd be fast asleep the instant his head hit the pillow; and the attic light had just flickered on, so the tea-drinking lodger had gone to his own bed. And she could see that her mother was still in the kitchen, crouched by the oven, frequently opening the door to check the *Pasky* hadn't incinerated. So the coast was clear… Sofia crept over to the coal-shed beside the lavvy and quietly opened the stiff and creaky door. She lit a candle with a damp match and peered into the dinginess of what used to be her father's musty old pigeon loft: it was the loft that was musty and old, not the pigeons. The homing pigeons he'd bought from a man at the Club really were homers; the moment he released them, they flew all the way back to where they came from – Leicester.

'Hello Brenda, hello Audrey,' she said in an infantile way, illuminating the little cage with the flickering flame, 'would you like some more drinkipoos?'

Naturally the hamsters didn't reply, but Sofia imagined they did while she carefully replenished their water and food supplies. She thought: *Don't hamsters make such a peculiar noise? They sound like they've been gagged and are crying out for help.* But the odd noises didn't last long and the furry little rodents were soon competing for the largest dish, with Brenda crawling over Audrey to get to it first. Considering they were sisters, the hamsters were always fighting: Brenda was forever jumping on Audrey's back... it was about time they learned to get along.

She bid them goodnight and covered up their cage with the old towel. She thought: *one day gone, only another sixteen to go: then the damned things can go back to the safety of the school classroom!* She couldn't believe her teacher entrusted her with the class hamsters over the holidays again, especially after what happened last time. And she truly hoped they weren't ailing. One was so unbelievably fat and the other looked far too thin. But she never did have any luck with hamsters. She backed out of the coal-shed and blew out the candle.

Mister Pushkin looked terribly disappointed to get to the coal-shed just as Sofia bolted the door. He emitted a lengthy Meow and pawed at the door, demanding for it to be re-opened. She knew cats could smell rodents from hundreds of yards away, so gave the Russian Blue a carefully placed kick of deterrence beneath his tail. The blue furry flash shot directly into the house and straight up the stairs.

From her father's opened bedroom window she heard him shout something that sounded remarkably like 'Cooking Fat!' Sofia smiled... she knew Mister Pushkin had jumped straight onto the old man's face, again.

She must have been attending to the hamsters for longer than she thought, because now the house was completely in darkness... *thank you Mama for leaving the kitchen light on...* It seemed as though she was the only person awake in the whole world: even the bustling Great Horton Road was quieter than silence. She yawned so widely that her jaw almost dislocated; if she stayed up any longer, she'd be so over-tired that it would be impossible for her to get to sleep. And she would need all the sleep she could get, because she'd be back in the studio at nine a.m. sharp; not even her Tato would sleep in for the final dress rehearsal before such an important performance. She resolved to have a quick wash and go straight to bed...

Sofia tiptoed passed her father's bedroom, where the old man was snoring loudly and breaking wind contentedly; and probably still wearing his shoes beneath the duvet.

And across the landing, a surprisingly hefty amount of snoring was coming from her mother's bedroom. With all the *Pasky* left to cool until morning, it looked as though her Mama had decided to finish writing her monthly letter, by candlelight, before going to bed. Unsurprisingly she'd succumbed to tiredness and slumped across the little table, pen still in hand, deeply and soundly asleep, the gusts of her breath causing the candle flame to flicker.

Sofia had always been a nosy child and seeing her name cursively written on the thick, embossed paper only aroused her curiosity further. She quietly tiptoed closer, avoiding the creaky floorboard, and gently lifted her mother's arm, gradually wiggling the paper out from beneath. Her arm was so heavy that she almost dropped it. And when her mother began coughing, Sofia was sure she was about to wake up. Thankfully, she didn't need to rack her brain for a suitable excuse for trespassing into her bedroom, for the snoring soon resumed, louder than ever.

Her Mama wouldn't dream of using translucent Air Mail paper when writing to her mother in Ukraine. The paper she used was hand-made and so thick that it'd probably soak up a pint of water; it even smelled expensive. Sofia wished her handwriting were as neat as her mother's: the beautiful curls of her copperplate script were a joy to behold, enhanced by her use of an italic nib. If anyone were lucky enough to receive such a letter, they'd think it was from an aristocrat or even a member of the Royal family. And that was precisely the effect her mother wanted to achieve, a trick she'd picked up from Natalka's ostentatiously showy parents, who had a tendency to embellish the truth so much that it was only a hair's breadth away from becoming a fib.

Sofia skipped straight to the paragraph that concerned her. She read:

> *Our darling Sofia is becoming a truly wonderful dancer and is a real credit to Taras' expert teaching. And sometime soon, I am sure she will become a prima ballerina, but…*

The 'but' was obvious: her father had told her often enough that her thighs were too big, she was too short and her feet were too deformed to ever become a prima ballerina. But at least when her

The Dancing Barber

Mama got round to finishing the letter, she wouldn't put it quite so bluntly.

Oh well, Sofia thought, *at least Mama is hopeful that I might have the chance of success <u>one day</u>.* She carefully put the letter in its place and tiptoed back out of the room. *If only Natalka could remain injured beyond Sunday then I could, at last, have the chance to prove myself, if not to the old man, then certainly to everyone else... big thighs or no big thighs.* She knew it was wrong to wish misfortune on her best friend, but she couldn't help it.

Halyna awoke with a jolt, as she often did when her snoring got too loud. She could have sworn there had been someone in her room so she picked up her candle, stood up and peered out into the corridor. When she discovered there was no-one there, she shook her head: she must have been dreaming. Every time she had these feelings, there was never anyone there. She shook her head again and resolved to finish the letter before she went to bed.

She re-read what she'd already written and picked up the pen to continue. The gold nib of Klem's heavy Pelikan fountain pen scratched the thick paper, but left no ink. She thought: *why did he lend me his pen when he knew it would run out?* After the ordeal of refilling it from the ink bottle, Halyna continued where she left off; for the first time deciding to categorically ignore what Taras had told her to write. In fact she'd screwed up his scrawled notes and thrown them in the bin.

Enough was enough, she thought, *it's time to tell my mother the truth!* She didn't want her embellishments to catch her out, as Natalka's parents were soon to be: how she imagined they regretted lying to those twin sisters for all those years. Halyna wondered how they planned to explain to them why they actually only lived in a back-to-back terrace house?

But that was their problem; Halyna's only worry would be Taras' reaction when he found out what she'd done. Nothing would aggravate his temper so much as when his pride was hurt.

So like a monastic scribe, Halyna completed her calligraphy and examined it with care; she knew that checking for spelling mistakes was a waste of time, but she was a perfectionist. Besides, if the Soviets decided to intercept the letter, they would see that there was at least one literate Ukrainian left on the planet.

She hadn't received a reply from her Mama in weeks, and hoped everything was alright. But delays weren't unusual: for the Soviets, censorship was a national pastime. She made sure the ink was dry before folding and inserting the letter into an envelope made of the same thick paper, with the return address elegantly embossed on the flap. She licked the gummed edge, thinking it tasted like strawberry ice-cream and sealed down the flap resolving to post this important letter on the way to work in the morning. She'd have to be at her cleaning job by six and then run to the factory for the morning shift, so she was thankful that she didn't need much sleep.

And it was just as well, because the discordant chimes of the cheap plastic pendulum clock that echoed up the stairs from the kitchen told her it had just gone two o'clock.

Unlike many of the other housewives in the area, she was never afraid of a hard day's work. Her body had been hardened to it from a very young age: the Soviet Collective Farms were horrendous, the Nazi munitions factories were worse, but at least then, she had youth on her side. But after almost a decade of being a non-stop factory worker, charwoman and housewife, her body was screaming for a rest...

Halyna stretched and yawned before taking off her apron to get ready for bed. She threw the apron onto the chair and was intrigued by a metallic tinkling sound coming from the pocket. She picked it back up and rummaged in amongst the used tissues to retrieve the little bullets she'd removed from Klem's pistol. She knew they were only blanks, but with Klem being in such a funny mood, it wasn't worth the risk letting him keep them. So she'd carefully slid them out of the pistol's magazine when he wasn't looking, before handing the pistol back to him. The pistol was much lighter now, but she knew he'd never notice.

She hadn't held a bullet in years, so it would have felt strangely nostalgic had it not been for the smell of brass they left on her fingers; it was one of those things that reawakened memories she'd tried so hard to forget. These bullets were so much smaller than the rifle grenades she was forced to manufacture in the Nazi labour camp twenty years ago, yet would have been just as deadly if they were "live".

Halyna lined all four of the miniature rockets on her table. *Four? But the pistol's magazine held six bullets. Klem used one, so there should be <u>five</u> remaining!* She rummaged inside her apron pocket again, but apart from bits of old fluff, it was empty. She slapped her forehead with the palm of her hand and cursed: she'd forgotten to remove the bullet in the chamber and felt extremely cross with herself. There was nothing she could do about it now. And anyway, not even Klem could create much mischief with a solitary blank bullet…

AC Michael

Act 2

✂--------

Easter Saturday

> 'If anyone thinks he is something when he is nothing, he deceives himself.'
>
> *Galatians 6:3*

The Dancing Barber

Chapter 9

'How should I know?' Klem said, staring into the empty lavvy. For the first time, he realised how disgustingly mouldy it was in the cold light of day. 'Not even Houdini could break free from all that carpet tape!'

Halyna examined the situation as if she were Margaret Rutherford's Miss Marple, wearing a beetroot-stained apron. After a bit of umm-ing and arr-ing she said, 'but the door was locked from the <u>outside</u>, wasn't it? And the lock wasn't forced... so someone *must* have let him out. But who?'

'<u>I did</u>.' An authoritarian voice projected from the studio door. Taras stood there like Ben Hur, his hands at his hips and his chest thrust out, his white costume gleaming in the early morning sunshine. He directly said to Klem, 'how dare you use my lavvy to string up your enemies!'

'Taras,' Halyna said, 'it really isn't how you think.'

'Actually,' Klem interrupted, 'it probably is. The man deserved it and I had a plan! How *could* you release that durak?'

'How dare you speak to me in such a way?' Taras shouted, 'just because I let you lodge in <u>my</u> attic does <u>not</u> entitle you to use my lavvy to torture the local villain! Understand?'

'You don't know what you've done? Do you?' Klem said, brushing back his thinning hair with both hands. He started to panic, his eyes darting around. He unfastened the green ribbon at the collar of his embroidered shirt, and said, 'I've got to hide!'

'Klem,' Halyna said, 'don't worry, you'll be safe here.'

But in less than a minute, Klem bolted up the stairs and barricaded himself in the attic. He could barely hold his hands still as he frantically dialled *the* number on the ancient Bakelite telephone and waited for *him* to answer.

Sofia and Natalka's heads peeked around the studio door.

'What's going on Tato?' Sofia asked, wondering why her mother and father were having such a blaring argument in the back yard. The din was already attracting the attention of many passers-by, even a double-decker lingered a little longer at the bus stop to enable the passengers to enjoy the free show.

'It's none of your business,' Taras barked, almost spitting the cigarette from his mouth. 'Go and practice your plié. Now!'

The girls couldn't move quickly enough… But only as far as behind the door. Though out of sight, they still heard every word…

'Listen Taras,' Halyna said, 'Klem had to do what he did, because…'

'I should have known you'd take his side,' Taras interrupted, 'you think I don't know about you two skulking around behind my back… My friends at the Club keep me very well informed of your secret little liaisons.'

'Oh shut up!' Halyna said. And for the first time, she caught her husband's hand before it struck her face. She was determined and very strong.

Taras was so shocked that he had to listen.

'Ivan was going to betray Klem and Katya,' Halyna said calmly, 'you know what Klem's involved with! And it certainly is not me! So cut him some slack.' She'd only come home to prepare Sofia's breakfast; otherwise she'd have gone straight to Lister Mill from her cleaning job. The day hadn't properly begun and she was already feeling tired, so the last thing she wanted was an argument with her moaning husband… She stopped herself from screaming, and said, 'I could do without all this aggravation!'

Taras had never before seen Halyna act in such a way. There was no doubt in his mind she was telling the truth, in spite of what his friends at the Club had told him… they'd always been prone to exaggeration, especially after they'd had a few. And he'd forgotten just how strong his wife was… even though she'd let go of his hand, her white finger marks remained for some time. 'In that case,' Taras stated, 'you should know that Ivan said he was going to the Police. He said he'd keep you and me out of it, but there was no way Klem would go unpunished. Understand?'

'Police?' Halyna said, 'but the man's a criminal. He wouldn't dare go to the Police… They've got a file on him an inch thick!'

Taras shrugged, 'I'm simply telling you what he said…'

'Of course!' Halyna interrupted, 'this is not goodski! He must have meant the Secret Police, the <u>Soviet</u> Secret Police! It makes perfect sense.'

'The Vlads?' Taras said, taking the cigarette from his mouth, 'but why would Ivan go to the Vlads?'

Groaning, Halyna rolled her eyes to the sky. 'Don't you know anything? Come on... You know that Ivan was blackmailing Klem for a lot of money... Yesterday, he threatened to shoot him if he didn't pay. Naturally, Klem didn't pay, and we all know what Klem did to him... so Ivan's doing the worst thing he possibly could in spiteful retaliation! The treacherous pile of – ! And he calls himself a Ukrainian!'

Taras cursed under his breath, 'why didn't you tell me what was going on?' He only just stopped himself from putting the lit end of the cigarette to his mouth. 'If I'd have known...'

'You're always too busy, so there was no point bothering to tell you. Besides, you never listen...'

Taras realised she had a point. 'But I would have listened if I'd have known things had gotten so serious, understand?'

'No you wouldn't!' Halyna snapped, 'you'd have probably jumped for joy if Klem had been shot! At least then, you'd get your precious attic back, your "private penthouse"! And you call him a friend!'

Taras shook his head, 'stop talking such rubbish, woman! I may be fed up of him living in my attic, but I would never want to jeopardise any of his or Katya's work! Nobody wants them to succeed more than me!'

'But you know the rumours about Ivan, just as well as I do, and yet you still released him! I can't understand it...?'

'Bullocks!' Taras shouted – he still hadn't got the hang of swearing in English – 'the lavvy upstairs was blocked again, so I dashed outside to use this one. I'd just unzipped when I heard a noise coming from the toilet bowl. And when the light finally flickered on, I was shocked to see this enormous mummified thing dangling from the ceiling. As I didn't know what it was, I unhooked it at once; it was so heavy that I dropped it to the floor. It was only when I pulled off the stinking gag and saw that bald headed, ginger bearded face looking up at me that I wished I'd tried to unblock the indoor lavvy and risked being inundated with... you know what.'

Halyna shook her head. 'You should have put the gag back on

him, hung him up again and gone to find Klem…'

'But I didn't know it was Klem's doing! I didn't think he had it in him! Ivan has so many enemies that it could be down to at least a couple of dozen people!'

'Yes, but *they* wouldn't have strung him up in *our* lavvy, would they?' Halyna tapped the side of her head, 'why didn't you think?'

'Now just a minute,' Taras protested.

'No, you've said enough,' Halyna raised a hand and walked away.

But Taras was determined to speak. He said, 'I suppose you have forgotten who provided me with a mortgage for this house? Hmmm? Ivan could easily have demanded full repayment, especially after the incident with his hair! And then where would we be? Hmmm? We'd be turfed out onto the street just like everyone else! No barber's shop! No studio! We'd only have your factory job to rely on!'

Halyna raised her eyebrows… even after all these years, he still didn't know about her cleaning job.

Taras continued, 'at least this way, *I* remain on good terms with Ivan and he will only vent his anger at Klem. I know it's Unchristian to be so selfish, but can you understand that I really didn't have any choice?'

Halyna's expression thawed. In Taras' situation, she'd have probably done the same thing. She cursed the day The Ginger Rasputin entered their lives…

'We best keep an eye out,' Taras said, 'the Vlads won't waste much time in coming to "arrest" Klem. That's assuming they believe whatever Ivan's told them… But if they do believe him, we have to decide whether we should take the risk to protect him or not? Understand?'

'Yes, I understand. But I doubt we have anything to worry about: as far as the "Vlads" are concerned, Ivan is *The Boy Who Cried Wolf*. In any case, once Sunday's over, "arresting" Klem would do the Soviets more harmski than goodski.' Halyna crossed her fingers, 'we just have to keep him safe for less than forty-eight hours… Then Katya will ensure *his* words are heard loud and clear.'

Taras said, 'hmmm, perhaps you're right…'

'There's no perhaps about it, I *know* I'm right… Now, unless you want me to get the sack,' she said, picking up her handbag, 'I suggest you let me get to the factory.'

'Who's Katya?' Natalka asked, straining to eavesdrop through the door.

Sofia shrugged her shoulders and said, 'maybe it's Klem's sister?' She giggled, 'or maybe it's his...? Quick...' She nudged her friend back in front of the broad mirror where they re-joined the rest of the group and commenced their pirouettes just in time.

'Right,' Taras commanded the instant he entered the studio, his presence making every muscle of every dancer twitch with anxiety. 'I know it's only half past nine, but that's enough dancing for today.' He clapped his hands harshly, 'get changed quickly and then go!'

Every dancer gasped; and one little girl almost fainted.

He didn't even notice they were practicing pirouettes instead of plié, which took the girls completely by surprise. Whatever had happened out in the yard had seriously rattled him, which was unusual, because nothing ever rattled him... with the exception of dancers who didn't do what they were told.

He looked at Natalka's heavily bandaged ankle and said gravely, 'I shall see what it's like tomorrow and then a decision will be made.' He prayed that, as it was only a sprain, it should heal relatively quickly. But if it didn't, he perspired at the implications of cancelling *Swan Lake* all together...

Sofia was fed up of waiting on tenterhooks. She said, '<u>Tato</u>, what will you decide if Natalka's ankle *isn't* better tomorrow? Who will you choose as a replacement?'

'You will find out <u>tomorrow</u>, understand?' he snapped, disliking his daughter's tone. 'In the meantime,' he said to the group, 'you go and relax: tomorrow will be a long day. But I expect you <u>all</u> to do some extra practice this afternoon! No sneaking off to the park, understand?' He flicked off the studio lights, even though most of the dancers hadn't begun to get changed. 'I'm going to open the shop; as it's Easter, I'm hopeful for at least one customer today.'

With the old man out of the way, Sofia flicked the lights back on. The rest of the group were grateful for being able to see what they were doing, and also for witnessing Oksana struggling to put on a skirt that wasn't hers. It was obviously ten sizes too small and resembled a wide suspender belt on one of the girl's gargantuan legs.

Natalka could see Sofia was still reeling with the way Mr Taras had spoken to her. 'You'll be all right Sofia,' she said, 'you know my dance better than I do! He's bound to ask you to take my place... He's only annoyed because – even though I said I bleeding hated the idea – he's had my picture put on all the advertisements and wants to give the audience who they expect to see.'

'Maybe,' Sofia said, 'but somehow I think I'll still be dancing the part of "Cygnet Number Eight".'

'Whatever will be, will be,' Natalka said, wincing as she put even more strapping on her tender ankle. 'Things will be stressful enough for me tomorrow without also having to worry about the performance.' She whispered in Sofia's ear, 'to tell you the truth, I'm not that bothered if I <u>can't</u> dance!'

Sofia looked at her sideways.

'What?' Natalka said, 'haven't you heard?'

It couldn't have been good news, Sofia thought, watching her friend's expression turn more sombre by the second. She shook her head, 'heard what?'

'Well,' Natalka sighed, 'it seems that, in her wisdom, my mother has asked her twin sisters to come and stay with us over Easter.'

'Would these be the twin sisters your father calls the ugliest trolls in Ukraine?'

'<u>No</u>, he never called them that! He said they were the ugliest trolls in the <u>world</u>!'

Sofia smiled, 'they can't be that bad? Can they?'

Natalka nodded, 'but what makes it worse is they're expecting to find us all living in the lap of luxury. You see, my mother has been telling them for years that we live in Harewood House and have half a dozen servants. Oh, and that's not the half of it...'

Sofia's jaw dropped, 'a doctor! But I thought your father was a hospital porter?'

'He <u>is</u> a hospital porter,' Natalka's arms flopped by her side, 'but he's so vain that he makes my mother write all these things. It's bleeding silly if you ask me... I can't understand why he's such a snob; why can't he be happy with what he's got?'

'You're quite right,' said Sofia, 'as Klem says: *"The brother in humble circumstances ought to take pride in his high position."* James 1:9... So what are your parents going to do when they turn up?'

Natalka shrugged, 'they *should* tell the truth, but I can't imagine them doing that.'

It seemed to Sofia that Natalka's mother must have taken leave of her senses. Even the ugliest trolls in the world would realise Harewood House was not a back-to-back!

But Natalka was convinced her mother would concoct a way of temporarily commandeering Harewood House for the duration of the trolls' visit. She'd probably pose as Head Housekeeper and tell the servants she was inspecting the house on behalf of the Lord and the Lady. And she'd dress her husband in a white coat and give him a stethoscope to hang around his neck.

There was a cat in hell's chance of such an illusion being maintained... She imagined the atmosphere in her house would become rather awkward if the truth ever came out. Which it inevitably would...

As the nuns at school had taught her: Such vanity was a terrible sin.

For Sofia, all the intrigue with Natalka's aunties was a welcome distraction from worrying about her parents' argument. Normally her Tato would shout and her Mama would obey unquestionably. But this time, her Mama shouted loudest of all and her Tato listened. She reckoned it was something to do with this mysterious Katya...

Chapter 10

Taras watched the clock's minute hand go full circle, and realised today would turn out to be yet another customer free zone. He loosened his polyester tie and unfastened the top button of his nylon shirt: there was no point looking smart if there was no one to see it…

After all the money he'd spent renovating the shop – installing a shiny linoleum floor, glittering wallpaper and genuine PVC chairs – he didn't think he'd see the days of profitability again. He was a good barber, who specialised in the short back and sides, and he was cheap too. But he blamed those Beatles for encouraging men to grow their hair long. Long hair belonged to women and was cut with scissors by a hairdresser. But he was a traditional gentleman's barber, so preferred using his electric clippers… unless there was a power-cut, in which case he'd use his manual ones that pulled out more hair than they cut…

Who was he kidding? Changing fashions were not the real source of his woes; balding his last customer probably didn't help… especially as his last customer was Ivan…

He glanced at the burgeoning rack of mismatched clothes in the corner of the shop. Some of the second or third hand clothes were so threadbare that he struggled to give them away! Prior to going on strike, Halyna did the best she could to renovate them, sewing on a patch here and a button there, but even he had to agree that not even a tramp would be seen wearing any of these rags.

And selling cigarettes was another disaster; it didn't help that the "Benton and Wedges" packets he'd bought from a man at the Club had been banned for containing, amongst other things, cyanide and arsenic… thankfully he hadn't sold many…

He had to face facts: he was a <u>terrible</u> businessman. He'd known it for years, but had finally admitted it.

The only thing he'd ever been good at was ballet: dancing ballet, teaching ballet and choreographing ballet. So *Swan Lake* was "make or break", but he hadn't a clue whether it could go ahead without Natalka – no one was remotely good enough to take

The Dancing Barber

her place – and the critics could spot an amateur a mile off. He put his head in his hands and sighed. And he really didn't need Klem making any more trouble; now was not the time to lose focus...

He was about to go to the kitchen and attempt to make some tea, when a man walked through the door. Taras didn't bother to say hello. He knew this anonymous looking man hadn't come for a haircut, so without looking up from the newspaper he was pretending to read, he said, 'Klem's up in the attic. Go straight up.'

The man nodded from beneath his wide-brimmed black hat and made his way upstairs.

Taras listened as the footsteps on the spiral staircase grew fainter. He leaned over his desk and peered between the photographs of elaborate hairstyles displayed in the front window. He cursed: *Why does that man always bring his mutt with him every time he visits?* He observed the surly Alsatian occupying the front step like a ferocious draught-excluder: there would certainly be no more customers while it remained...

Klem immediately un-barricaded and opened the door upon hearing the secret sequence of knocks and invited the anonymous looking man into the attic. This man was medium height, medium build and looked so non-descript that he wouldn't be noticed even if he was the only other person in the room. Klem took the man's hat and black leather coat, flinching away from the strong smell of boot polish. Hanging them on a tubular steel hat-stand, that could have been designed by Le Corbusier, he asked, 'would you care for some tea?'

The man smiled and said, 'please,' before wasting no time getting down to business. 'I understand from your rather garbled message that things didn't go quite to plan yesterday?'

Klem remained silent, preferring to take his time to unlock the particularly fine eighteenth century tea caddy containing the PG Tips he always gave to this anonymous looking man.

'You shouldn't worry,' said the man, turning up the corner of his mouth, 'things rarely go to plan where Ivan's concerned...' He rubbed his hands together, 'but at least you have him captive. Is he still in the lavvy? Because I've got to see it: it'll really make my day!' He smiled eagerly, displaying his brown teeth.

'Sorry,' Klem said, shakily, 'my landlord inadvertently let him go. By the time I found out, Ivan was long gone.'

The anonymous looking man no longer smiled. He hitched up his trouser legs and sat in Taras' Eames chair, settling into the comfortable, if creaky PVC upholstery. 'Pity,' he said, strumming his fingers on the arm-rest, 'I would have liked to have given him a couple of flushes...' He sighed, 'I suppose it doesn't really matter, because you can tell me where he lives, can't you?'

'Of course,' Klem said confidently as he unclipped the fountain pen from his inside pocket, noticing it still smelled of Halyna's divine perfume. 'He'll either be at home or at his office.' Klem narrowed his eyes, 'but beware of his mother... she can be extremely vicious!'

The man laughed, 'you mean the woman they call The Gossipmonger? Don't worry; I can handle that hideous old bat. Besides, she gives you fair warning when she's about to pounce: you can smell that stench of mothballs from two miles away!'

Klem smiled and said, 'rather you than me!' as he finished meticulously etching the paper with the addresses. He screwed the golden cap back onto his pen and clipped it in his pocket. Passing the paper over his cluttered desk, he said, 'but our agreement still stands, yes?'

'Naturally. Unlike some, I am a man of my word.' The anonymous looking man scrutinised the addresses. Satisfied, he folded the paper perfectly squarely and carefully put it in his pocket. He then took a sip of his refreshing tea, before delving back into the depths of his pocket. He presented Klem with a small cubic box, covered in deep blue leather. 'Here you are,' he said, delicately placing it in a space between the clutter on Klem's desk, 'as agreed.'

Klem's eyes were wide open; gently, he picked up the expensive looking box with the distinctive wavy edges. Despite its age, the box smelled of the finest leather and was decadently soft to the touch. He grinned, 'A-ha, I've always wanted one of these...'

'And now you've got one... Savour your payment for a while. Enjoy it before you sell it. It's not every day one gets the chance to own a jewel of *such* quality... And it complements that pocket

The Dancing Barber

watch of yours rather well...'

Klem pressed the discrete turquoise button and slowly opened the hinged lid. Nestled within the velvet and silk interior, the object was smaller, but much more beautiful than he'd ever imagined. The hundreds of stones all twinkled at him as if he was holding a piece of the night sky in the palm of his hand. One-handedly, he hooked on his half-moon spectacles and moved over to the window, gently rotating the orb, examining the wonderfully faceted sapphires and exceptionally rare yellow diamonds.

'Although this isn't one of the official Imperial Easter Eggs,' Klem said with great authority, 'I still believe it to be one of the most beautiful man-made objects in the world. Just look at those stones: each one a perfect princess cut, claw set using eighteen carat yellow gold... Exquisite... That Mister Fabergé was a truly talented gentleman.'

The anonymous looking man smiled. 'I'm glad you approve; it wasn't easy getting it out of the Kremlin. But I doubt the idiots even know its missing! And it makes you one of the world's richest Cossacks.'

Klem shook with excitement, 'It certainly does! And the fact you liberated it from that pig Stalin's personal collection makes it all the more wonderful!' Klem laughed, 'so that butcher will be directly funding Katya! Isn't it a delicious thought?' He gently closed the lid, waited for the click of the catch and then set the box down on his desk.

'Alas,' he said, 'it is only an object: a very beautiful and valuable object, but an object nevertheless. And when it is sold, imagine what Katya can do with the money...' He rubbed his hands together so vigorously that they almost caught fire. 'Funding political election campaigns can be an expensive business...'

The anonymous looking man couldn't care less about politics; his business would be unaffected whatever happened. 'Cigar?' he asked, holding out something that looked like a cinnamon stick protruding from a well-used leather case.

'You know I don't,' Klem said, 'and I'd prefer you didn't either.'

The man pulled the face of a trout and pushed the cinnamon stick back into its case. 'Always health conscious and constantly having other people's interests at heart: that's what I like about you. Me, I only ever think of myself…'

'And as the Head of the Uki Mafia, I'm sure you wouldn't have it any other way…'

'Please Klem, I'd prefer it if you didn't use the "M" word; it has so many negative connotations. And you know I run a legitimate ship now.'

Klem looked at the man from above his half-moon spectacles.

The man smiled, '*virtually* legitimate… Anyway, I think that concludes our business. Many thanks for the delicious tea; you really do spoil me by giving me tea from such an expensive box. It must cost a fortune…'

'Not as much as you'd think,' said Klem.

Looking around the attic, the anonymous looking man said, 'what does Taras think about you inflicting all your heavy Victorian furniture on his "modernist penthouse"?'

'I haven't asked him,' said Klem, 'but Halyna says he doesn't mind… Much…'

Smiling, the anonymous looking man stood up and reached for his hat and coat. 'It won't take me long to find Ivan… he won't bother you anymore. And if he doesn't pay back every penny he stole from me, he won't bother anyone anymore!'

'Yes, well,' Klem said uneasily, 'please keep me out of *that* side of things.'

'At least now, he won't be dredging up your past history every time he needs some more money…'

Klem nodded, 'that will be something to look forward to… Although I doubt people would believe what he had to say. But such a revelation, especially for a man of my stature, could do a lot of damage.'

The anonymous looking man placed his wide-brimmed black hat squarely on his head. He said, 'I assume you've destroyed the man's cassette tape?'

Klem clicked his fingers, 'that is something I've yet to do…' He ambled to his desk, glanced at the anonymous looking man and deliberately coughed.

'Pardon me,' said the anonymous looking man, turning to look the other way.

Klem sat behind the broad mahogany roll-top desk and gently depressed a button that only slightly protruded beneath the writing surface. Simultaneously, a small, yet ornately carved panel behind the ink-wells slid open smoothly, revealing the cassette tape nestled in one of the desk's many secret compartments, some of which were so secret that not even Klem knew where they were. He checked the man wasn't peeking before extracting the cassette tape and closing the panel. 'How are you supposed to destroy one of these things?' he asked, peering at the object with confusion.

'Oh, that's easy,' said the anonymous looking man, extracting an almost empty packet of Swan Vesta matches from his pocket. 'Prise open the case and hand the tape to me...'

Klem did as he was told. He watched an anonymous looking finger pull every last inch of tape from the reel. An anonymous looking hand then scrunched it up to form an irregularly wound ball of dark brown ribbon.

'Pathetic job, really,' said the anonymous looking man, pointing to where Ivan had spliced the tape so it would say what he wanted it to say. 'Such a sloppy effort, considering he planned to send it to the BBC: they would have spotted such feeble tampering straight away!' He snapped the tape from its fixings and threw the empty cassette into Klem's bin.

Realising what the plan was, Klem dashed to the table out on the balcony and brought in Taras' molded-plastic Lalique ashtray. Moments later, the tape went up in flames, releasing a toxic-smelling cloud of blue-black smoke the instant the lit match made contact with it. The two men smiled and nodded affirmatively at a job well done. Mister Pushkin sneezed... the cat was obviously allergic to burning cassette tape...

'Oh, I almost forgot,' the man said, shaking Klem's hand, 'just in case Ivan really has told the Vlads of your whereabouts, I'll be leaving you my best bodyguard... He's trained to attack and defend in the usual ways... all you have to do is click your fingers... I tried to rename him Mykola, but,' he shrugged his shoulders, 'he prefers the name engraved on his medal. Goodbye for now. It's been a pleasure doing business with you!'

And before Klem could protest, the anonymous looking man was gone.

Slumped over his tiny desk, completely engrossed with refining the details of his *next* ballet, Taras didn't notice the anonymous looking man leaving the shop... and neither did he care. Even before *Swan Lake* achieved the critical acclaim he insisted it deserved, he busily filled yet another exercise book with an array of arrows, lines and notes using his multi-coloured felt-tip pens. He could have been an ancient Egyptian scribe writing in hieroglyphics for the sense they made to anyone not *au fait* with his choreographer's shorthand...

He'd already decided what to do about the Natalka problem: why didn't he think of it sooner? But he always did like to mull things over properly before making an important decision. He also knew that – providing Oksana did precisely as she was told (which would be a miracle) – the critics would give his adaptation of *Swan Lake* a perfect review... He'd already written down precisely what he wanted them to say. And they wouldn't dare question it.

So *The Nutcracker* was provisionally booked for The Alhambra at Christmas, regardless of the exorbitant fee, which Halyna had yet to learn about. For Taras, cost was irrelevant: fame and status were his treasures, as well as sharing his love for the ballet.

His concentration was suddenly interrupted and he annoyingly made a mistake on the page. Small, scuttling shadows dashed in front of his window, crouching down so as not to be seen. But they *were* seen and Taras was quick to give them a piece of his mind.

He swung open the door just as a mischievous finger was about to press the electric doorbell. He shouted: 'get away from here, you little, err...' he noticed the Priest strolling on the other side of the road, 'you little rascals! If you ring my bell once more, I'll wring your necks! Understand?'

After the initial shock of being caught, the local children with the dirty necks laughed and ran away, imitating him by saying, "understand" repeatedly, before they prepared to choose the next volunteer.

Taras sniffed the air and immediately knew what he'd done. Although the Alsatian had gone, it had left rather a lot with which to remember it by. Cursing, he hopped off to find something to scrape his shoe on.

The Dancing Barber

The mischievous children returned three more times and managed to escape without having their necks wringed, much to Taras' annoyance and disappointment. And that turned out to be the most excitement he had all morning. Not a single customer had darkened his door since the incident with the shampoo that had inadvertently balded Ivan. He still had no idea how the bottles of Head & Shoulders and Imaac got mixed up: he didn't even sell Imaac!

It didn't matter how much Taras professed his innocence, Ivan still blamed him for making it look as though his head had been put on upside down. He suggested Ivan shaved off his beard, but it didn't go down well...

In a rare gesture of goodwill, he even gave Ivan's useless daughter a part in *Swan Lake*, but it was too late... The Gossipmonger had already dripped her poison and his reputation as a barber was shot to pieces. He knew the gossip would be forgotten eventually, so had to get used to writing big zeroes in his cashbook for a few more days... or weeks...

The lack of customers should have induced Taras to embark on some much-needed housekeeping. He wasn't accustomed to such menial tasks, but since Halyna declared she was on strike, he didn't have any choice. He gazed lethargically over to the brush, propped up against the wall, gathering dust, and recollected his wife's harsh words:

'Listen to me Taras! That lino has been the bane of my life for years; no amount of cleaning and polishing is ever good enough for you! So seeing as you're the expert,' she said, thrusting the broom handle into his palm, *'you can do it yourself from now on, because I'm on strike!'*

As a result, the floor was dirtier than ever, with a large compost heap of multi-coloured hair clippings in the corner that had begun to ferment. On a windy day, the shop would be engulfed by a hirsute hurricane the moment the door opened, blasting his face with an attrition of sharp little needles.

Taras sighed and looked up at his yellowing ceiling: it had only been painted the purest white last month, but it never took long for his tobacco fumes to stain it the colour of ancient papyrus. It was a pity Halyna was on strike, for he'd have made her scrub it down with a soapy sponge the instant she came home from the factory...

it would have only taken her a couple of hours…

Watching the smoke rise from his nostrils, he wondered how long it would be before she'd have to cross the picket line. He was glad she'd briefly dismantled it for Easter; he wouldn't know where to start if he had to bake the *Pasky* himself… Going on strike was very selfish of her: she knew he was a busy man and as Head of the Household, he <u>demanded</u> respect.

Fortunately, he had a plan… He'd been deliberately blowing smoke at her pink flowering geranium that occupied a shelf by the window; the thing looked increasingly pitiful, especially as he'd been "watering" it with samahon. He was confident Halyna's strike would soon end once she noticed one of her precious houseplants was ailing! He didn't like being so sly, but sometimes it was necessary.

Even busy men needed to have a break now and then, so he turned on his stainless steel radio that occupied half his tiny desk, lit another cigarette and put his feet up to relax. Deep down, he knew he didn't deserve to relax, because he'd made no money, but he relaxed nevertheless.

So he twiddled the tuning knob, easily finding Radio Kateryna's new frequency and hummed along to some of the Ukrainian folk songs he hadn't heard for decades. The news bulletin at the top of the hour was concerned with the latest developments in the Cuban Missile Crisis: those Soviets really knew how to upset people… But after watching Kennedy and Khrushchev battle it out on the telly a few days ago, he was confident the tension would soon subside…

The jolly folk songs recommenced, so he popped a Mint Imperial into his mouth and hummed along to the Ukrainian version of "I've got a hole in my bucket…"

All of a sudden he heard a loud explosion, and instinctively looked at the radio expecting to see sparks flying and smoke spewing from the speaker. The thing was ancient; it wasn't even new when the man he bought it from, bought it originally. But to his surprise, the radio was fine. After a momentary silence, an angry Soviet newsreader's voice rumbled on air:

'We have received many reports that the so-called "Peaceful Partisan" whose real name is Voloshin has been located in England. Rest assured, my fellow Soviets, this leader of' the

newsreader spat loudly, *'the hated Ukrainian Partisans will be arrested in the next few days. And anyone caught protecting him will also be arrested.'*

Taras scoffed, 'arrested? That's a Soviet euphemism if ever there was one.'

'The President insists,' the newsreader continued, *'that everything this Voloshin said and will say is completely and utterly untrue. In fact it is a <u>lie</u> and should not be believed. You will hear this Voloshin say that the minor food shortage in southern parts of the Soviet Union in 1933 was deliberate. But the President insists that this is a <u>complete fabrication</u>! Ask yourselves why Soviets would want to deprive their loyal citizens of food?'*

Taras had heard quite enough and gruffly turned off the radio. He noted the newsreader's carefully chosen words – "deprive their <u>loyal</u> citizens of food" – and aggressively stubbed out his cigarette in the last remaining space in the ashtray.

He lost himself in his thoughts... The seven million Ukrainians who died in 1933 were innocent, peaceful peasants; and there wasn't one of Taras' friends who hadn't been affected by The Great Famine, in fact many of them – Klem included – lost their entire families. He crunched what was left of his Mint Imperial.

But as the political heat was gradually being turned up in Ukraine, nobody would be surprised that Voloshin fled to England; he might have been in England for years...

And Taras knew the Vlads would soon be sniffing around, demanding to "speak" to Klem, especially if they believed Ivan's poisonous words. And if his involvement with Katya led the Soviets to Voloshin – as implausible as it may seem – then all those involved would share the same fate, a fate that would make the Gulag seem like a holiday in Butlins.

Taras struck the small desk decisively with both his hands: he didn't want to depress his mind with thoughts of the Soviets any more.

He stood up, stretched to the ceiling and yawned. When the bright sun poured into his eyes, he decided he'd done quite enough work for one day. The advice of an Italian he once knew rang guiltily in his ears: *'if you feel like doing some hard work, relax, the feeling will soon pass.'*

So he took off his barber's smock and hung it on its hanger.

Striding over to the glazed door, he locked and bolted it securely, ensuring the "Closed" sign was displayed, as if it really mattered.

With Halyna refusing to cook for him, he had to make his own lunch or else go hungry. And he was fed up of going hungry. Unable to cook anything remotely edible, even if he had the inclination, he decided to pick up a small burnt *Paska* that would probably taste of charcoal and a boiled egg with a cracked shell, and head off to Manningham Park.

He decided a top-up to his spring suntan was necessary, because he knew it would impress the critics tomorrow evening. Besides, Taras believed sitting indoors on a warm, sunny day was sacrilegious. And he knew he wouldn't get caught skiving, because all the women would be at the factory and all his dancers would be at home, practicing their steps diligently…

Chapter 11

The skies above Europe

Even though she could barely see through the half-inch of nose grease smeared across the window pane, Lenka daren't look as the aeroplane plunged through the carpet of clouds and began its long descent. She pulled her headscarf over her eyes, peeking only once, just in time to watch the ground accelerating towards her far too quickly. She yanked across the little curtain and turned to look at her sister, 'I am scared out of the wits...'

But Zena wasn't listening; she was too busy rolling that old ring between her thumb and forefinger.

Lenka wafted her jumper, ventilating the accumulated perspiration. She said, 'why have you not thrown it away? The ring, it is not even made of the gold and all it gives you is the bad memories!'

Zena dropped the tarnished little ring in amongst her clammy cleavage, where it had resided for twelve long years, staining the skin the deepest green. 'Uncle Viktor, he told me not to tell you,' she said with a sigh, 'the reason I keep the ring is... I still do not have the divorce.'

'You are *still* the married to that fart of the pig? Even after *everything* that happened?'

Zena nodded. 'But hopefully not the much longer... Viktor, he has arranged the papers of divorce for me.' With a determined look, she said, 'so before we visit our sister, I will find the fart of the pig and make him the sign them.' From beneath her waistband, she pulled out the official papers and showed them to Lenka.

'Good,' Lenka said, pretending to read the documents. The paper was thick as tree bark, yet smooth as nylon; they looked official enough with the seals and signatures she expected of such things. 'And what about the daughter; are you going to tell <u>her</u> the truth?'

Zena shuffled around and looked at her sister squarely. She said, 'you know about the daughter?'

'Of course! I am not the thicko people take me to be! I have known for the many years that the girl is the daughter of you!'

'The Heavens above,' Zena exclaimed, 'but how? It was meant to be the secret...'

'I am the good eavesdropper,' Lenka said proudly, with a confident nod of the head. 'I even know that he is not the real father. So the daughter, she should not be the living with him!'

'He does not know he is not... Yet...' Zena smiled, 'but that is the easy to prove...' She shook her head, scattering dandruff across her shoulders, 'it seems I cannot hide the secrets from you.'

'And that is the way it should be!' Lenka said with even more pride. 'Does the fart of the pig know you are coming?'

Zena shook her head, 'if he did, he would flee the country!' She took the divorce papers from Lenka and put them safely, with the birth certificate and all the letters she'd received from her young sister, back beneath her clammy waistband. 'It best we make the surprise visit, and then,' she hoisted the tarnished ring from the ravine between her bosoms, 'I can stick this where the sun, it does not the shine!'

'The Steward,' Zena said, clicking her fingers when an overall-wearing member of the crew strode purposefully down the aisle. 'What is the meaning of this sign?' She pointed to the notice that stated:

ARRIVAL TIME AT MUNICH AIRPORT
30 MINS
REMEMBER TO TURN CLOCKS BACK BY ONE HOUR

'Isn't that obvious,' said the man in overalls, 'can't you read?'

Lenka was already on her feet, poised to clout him, but Zena restrained her just in time. She said, 'but that says the "Mun-Itch"... we are supposed to be going to the *Bradford* aerodrome?'

'And you will be,' said the man in overalls, 'if you bothered to check tickets, you'd have seen this was scheduled stop-over to refuel and reload. We land at Bradford tomorrow.'

'Tomorrow?' Zena said, 'but this will completely ruin the schedule.'

Lenka nodded, even though she hadn't a clue what "the

schedule" was. And for the first time, she began wondering why they seemed to be the only passengers on this aeroplane...

The bright red landing lights flashed on the wall above the twins' heads and the aeroplane suddenly became a hive of activity. Members of the crew emerged from every nook and cranny and purposefully commenced their allocated tasks.

The man in overalls marched over to the twins and said, 'here. You'd better put these on.' He handed them a couple of XXL sized grimy brown smocks, 'they'll keep your clothes clean...' It was only then that he realised the smocks were significantly cleaner than the twins' own clothes.

'I beg the pardon?' Zena said, thinking it to be a joke.

'Hasn't the pilot told you?' the man said with puzzlement. 'You'll be helping us unload all this...' he drew back the curtain behind the twins' seats to reveal several hundred wooden crates. 'Your Uncle, he only pays half cost of flight – and some of that was in grain – so the agreement was that you work to make up rest of cost and also to pay for,' he looked at the piles of empty plates and cups littering the twins' vicinity, 'all you ate and drank during flight, yes?'

'That cannot be? Our sister in Bradford, she sent us many of the dollars that we collected for many years.' Zena protested, 'surely that was enough?'

The man shook his head and made excuses about the rising cost of fuel before immediately setting the sisters to work. From his time as a farmer, he'd successfully coaxed many a stubborn beast into work... But these two were by far the most obstinate brutes he'd ever had the misfortune to encounter.

But once they'd calmed down and accepted their unforeseen task, the cargo hold was emptied in half the time, with the sisters carrying twice or even three times the weight of his regular crew. He'd offer them full-time jobs if it weren't for their attitude or the smell.

Chapter 12

The City of Bradford, West Yorkshire, Northern England

Taras couldn't stop cursing... So much for going to Manningham Park to escape his troubles... He felt like going back home when he saw Ivan reclined by the boating lake, as if he were a ginger-bearded Roman emperor, basting himself with suntan oil and crisping up nicely in the scorching sun. And judging by his smug expression, it didn't look as though Klem's attempt to drown him in the toilet had any lasting effect. Pity.

Taras observed that although Manningham Park was very busy, not one sunbather was in Ivan's vicinity. And who could blame them? Even if people were unaware of the man's villainy, they wouldn't dare approach such an odd-looking character. It must have been the first time Taras had seen him without his old mackintosh and high-waisted corduroy trousers. In fact, apart from a pair of baggy shorts, held up by red trouser braces, Ivan wore little else. And didn't he look ridiculous: not only did his head look as though he'd put it on upside-down, with that enormous ginger beard dangling from his cue-ball scalp, but his scrawny pigeon chest and watermelon belly had that distinct lobster colouration of someone completely unaccustomed to sitting in the sun.

Nevertheless, the villain looked content enough, drinking instant coffee from his flask, eating his fish-paste sandwiches and occasionally dipping his hand into a wicker picnic basket to extract a pickled gherkin. If only the ground would open up and swallow him, he would go to where he belonged: a place where Klem said he would weep and gnash his teeth for all eternity... How dare he look so pleased with himself...? But Taras surmised that signing Klem's death warrant was all in a day's work for an evil specimen like Ivan.

Taras muttered the worst expletive and went in search of somewhere more private, in which to sunbathe. Tonight was the

The Dancing Barber

All-Night Easter Church Service, and – if last year's was anything to go by – it would be a long one, probably ending at half four at the earliest, so if he had any hope of remaining conscious, he'd need all the rest he could get.

He wasted no time claiming a spot on an embankment that tilted perfectly to the south-west... he could stay there all afternoon, shuffling only occasionally in order to track the sun. Lying on his towel, wearing nothing more than a pair of the skimpiest shorts, he imagined himself to be on a secluded beach on the French Riviera... and looking up at the fresh spring leaves against the clear blue sky, it wasn't too difficult a task. And after smearing half a pot of Nivea Crème all over his body, he'd surely develop a suntan to rival Cary Grant...

It finally dawned on him that arranging his flagship *Swan Lake* performance for the day after the All-Nighter might not have been one of his better ideas... But it was the only available slot, especially at such an affordable price. He took a bite from his *Paska* and felt his cheeks instantaneously draw into his teeth as it soaked up all the moisture in his mouth. This was the driest one ever: it needed heaps of butter and jam... if only he'd brought some. Feeling the charcoal he'd swallowed lodge itself firmly in his throat, he hurried to buy a bottle of lemonade...

'Oh bleeding hell,' Natalka said, 'quick, look the other way!'
'Why?' Sofia replied, 'what's the matter?'
'Your father!' Natalka cried, 'he's coming this way!'
Sofia smirked, 'so much for opening up the shop...'
The girls were supposed to be putting in some extra practice, but it would have been such a waste of a sunny day to be stuck indoors. They hadn't had a sunny Saturday without the chore of going to Ukrainian School since last August, so this was a day to make the most of!

'Phew,' Natalka said, emerging from behind the park bench once Mr Taras turned the corner, 'that was a close one.' She smiled, 'it looked as though he were choking on that rock-bun he were trying to eat.'

Sofia said nothing; she knew the "rock-bun" was actually her Mama's *Paska*.

The friends quickly resumed their sunbathing positions: shoes and socks off, sleeves rolled up and the hems of their skirts lifted more than were permitted. Natalka tied back her long dark hair with a rubber band, while Sofia tamed her unruly perm with a plastic headband that clawed into her scalp. They took an occasional lick of their refreshing ice-creams, before angling their faces to capture the most sunlight possible…

They soon dozed off to the drowsy murmur of bees coming from the surrounding flowerbeds, only occasionally waking to swat away the bluebottles and hoverflies whose sole reason for existing was to annoy as many people as possible. The suntan was purely for their own enjoyment, because they'd be daubed with so much white make-up for tomorrow's ballet that the audience would think they were watching a pair of dancing ghouls.

But the biggest ghoul of all had just cleared out the ice-cream van and carried five cones in her chubby hands to join her father by the boating lake. As usual, none of the ice-creams were for him: Oksana was more than capable of polishing off the lot unassisted.

'Wouldn't it be humorous,' Sofia said, 'if my Tato was to see Oksana gorging on ice-cream instead of practicing like she was supposed to?' She smiled, 'do you suppose he'd cane her in public? Shall I go and tell him?'

'Don't be a thicko,' Natalka said, pushing back her brown fringe, ensuring her pale forehead received the maximum sunlight, 'we're skiving just as much as she is!'

'Oh yeah,' Sofia said, thinking she must have had too much sun. 'Pity, because it would have been funny…' She watched the heifer stand in front of the man with the upside-down head and braces, deliberating which ice-cream she was to scoff first.

The warm sunshine had a relaxing effect on Sofia and Natalka, and they soon closed their eyes and nodded off. Getting a tan was an effortless business, enhanced by the use of liberal quantities of Nivea Crème that had the same effect on their skin as lard had on frying chips.

The tranquillity was abruptly shattered when, by the boating lake, Ivan exploded into his most infantile tantrum yet, clenching his fists and stomping his feet. 'Get out of the way you great fat lump! You're like a total eclipse!' He leaned forward and shoved Oksana to one side before resuming his preferred sunbathing

The Dancing Barber

position now his pink flesh was out of the dark shadows.

Oksana mouthed a suitable obscenity and contemplated throwing all the ice-creams at her vile father. But that would be such a waste... the full-fat vanilla dairy ice-creams were smothered with plenty of raspberry and chocolate sauce... her favourites... especially from the Hilton's van.

Many of the dainty ladies sat on a nearby lawn wouldn't have looked out of place in an Edwardian costume drama. They obviously sympathised with Oksana's plight and wafted frilly fans in front of their faces to disguise their expressions. Before they were married, many of them had first-hand experience of Ivan's feigned charm, dubious wealth and explosive temper, not to mention his halitosis and his clammy, crawling hands. They all had lucky escapes and looked gratefully across the picnic rugs at their husbands for saving them from the clutches of The Ginger Rasputin.

With the excitement over, Sofia turned to speak to Natalka, but discovered the bench was empty. She spun her head around, as if she were an owl, but couldn't see her anywhere. She shouted, 'Natalka!'

'I'm over here,' Natalka said, from the lawn beside the bench, 'best keep the ankle supple...'

Sofia watched Natalka fold her lissom body in half, then reach out and grab her ankles. She then laid down and raised both legs, rotating each ankle in turn, first anticlockwise, then clockwise. Sofia was ashamed of herself, but she could only feel disappointed that her friend was recovering: whether Natalka wanted to or not, if she were fit to dance, her Tato would make her dance. The mischievous little voice inside her head made her say, 'you know, you're going to have a dreadful tan line when you take that bandage off?'

'Mmm, I suppose you're right,' said Natalka. 'In that case I shall take it off and let the healing rays of the sun get at my ankle... It might even do it some good.' She looked seriously at Sofia, 'but please remind me to put it back on before standing up.'

'Of course,' Sofia said, knowing she wouldn't. That mischievous little voice rarely spoke, but when it did, she never could resist doing what it told her. She dreamt of the applause *her* Odette would receive tomorrow night, and the look of pride on her

Tato's face. It wouldn't be a fair victory, but she could live with it.

Whilst contemplating the morality of her actions, Sofia listened to the groan of lawnmowers echoing across Manningham Park; she preferred the drowsy clang of the old machines that reminded her of her infancy, but that sound was lost forever... At least the scent of cut grass hadn't changed... She looked at the lawn beside her best friend's feet... the bandage was calling to her, desperate to be hidden...

'Bleeding hell!' Natalka said, sitting bolt upright, 'look at what Oksana's doing...'

But Sofia was too busy watching the beautiful daffodils swaying in the fragrant breeze, the tulip spears emerging from the ground before her eyes, listening to the calls of blue tits and blackbirds (why were female blackbirds not called 'brownbirds'?) and generally enjoying life too much to concern herself with the antics of that stupid heifer. She had never before seen a dragonfly; and now there were two directly in front of her, a pair of iridescent miniature helicopters whirring away at the water's edge, the lake itself shimmering in the heat as if it were a mirage. She wished she could stay there forever.

'Sofia!' Natalka nudged her on the arm, 'look, I think she's using bleeding sun block!'

Sofia was about to say 'so what' when she realised that the sun block was being carefully applied to the top of Ivan's head!

'We'd better tell him,' Natalka, always the do-gooder, was getting up.

'Don't you dare,' Sofia ordered, 'that man is a cruel bully and – I don't know how – but he's been trying to get Klem into trouble. So I couldn't care less what Oksana has done to him! Besides, it's the first artistic thing that heifer's ever done; it'll be nice to see how it turns out...'

'But,' Natalka said.

'No buts...' Sofia was most insistent. She crunched away at the remaining piece of wafer cone, pleased that it had been filled with ice-cream to the very tip. And she decided it wasn't true what they sang at school: Hilton's ice-cream didn't taste like whipped cream...

The Dancing Barber

'Oh no, don't look now,' said Natalka, 'here comes your Casanova... *Bless*, he's brought his bed sheet with him.'

Sofia groaned, *more like Carsey-Nova*. Although she'd seen him out of the corner of her eye, she continued to deliberately look the other way.

'Hi-ya, So-fear,' said the boy, wiping his snotty nose on the back of his hand. He held out a fine selection of dandelions he'd tied together into a bunch using what looked like a frayed shoelace. 'I picked these, special, just for you.' He pulled his threadbare shorts up to his waist, tightening the knot in the rope that failed to hold them up.

Slowly, Sofia turned around. Looking down her nose at him, she said, 'are you talking to me?'

'I should say so,' said the boy, displaying a grin of unbrushed teeth and scraping his unwashed hair to one side.

Sofia said, 'I would prefer it if you didn't.' She turned away again, lifting her nose higher than ever.

'But I've had a wash, special like, you know, to come and see you.' The boy wiped his nose on the back of his hand again and sniffled to prevent the descent of a long candle of green snot from one of his nostrils. 'But look at how clean I am...'

'Having a wash,' Sofia said, barely able to look at the boy, 'is more than simply wiping your face with an oily rag.' She looked down her nose at the boy's bed sheet, grimy after being dragged around the streets of Bradford. She said, 'aren't you a little old to still have a comfort blanket?'

The boy looked at the blanket as though she'd just insulted a member of his family, shielding it from her harsh words.

A boy with a basin cut, playing football close by, wolf-whistled at Sofia, shouting, 'hey Saddlebags, I think he fancies you...!'

'Shut yer cake 'ole,' shouted the boy, 'or I'll shut it for ye! And don't call 'er Saddlebags; it ain't polite!'

Sofia lowered her nose, slightly, and considered thanking the boy... But Natalka interrupted, 'sling your hook... And take your weeds with you!'

'But these ain't weeds,' he said, admiring the blooms, 'these are pretty yellow flowers, is what they are...' His eyes glazed over, 'just like So-Fear...'

'Sling your hook,' Natalka barked, threatening to hit him with her shoe…

'Has he gone?' Sofia asked, still facing the other way.

'Yes,' said Natalka. 'The bleeding cheek of someone like him to dare to come and speak to you! Common isn't the word!'

'I don't know why he keeps on pestering me? He smells worse than our outside lavvy and I've seen cleaner and better dressed tramps asleep on this very bench!'

'And your Tato hates him too: he's the one that calls him "Tar-Arse"!'

'I didn't know that was *him*…' *Maybe the boy isn't all bad…*

'And your Tato calls him a horrible little Urchin… He's right.' Natalka watched the Urchin throw his bunch of weeds into a waste bin, kicking his heels into the gravel path as he went to re-join his friends to play another rowdy game of football.

Sofia turned and glanced fleetingly at the boy. At least he was polite; it wasn't his fault his parents were a pair of layabouts…

'You hear that?' Sofia asked, referring to Lister Mill's "clocking off" buzzer echoing across Manningham Park.

Natalka said, 'bleeding hell, our mothers will have just finished work… We'll have to go!'

'I know,' Sofia said, making sure her friend's bandage was well hidden. 'But we don't have to go straight away, do we? Let's enjoy these last few rays of sunshine…'

The Dancing Barber

Chapter 13

For the third time, Halyna asked, 'so how *did* you meet this Gunter?'

Again, Klem ignored her, preferring to absentmindedly rub a tea towel around the circumference of a dry plate.

'Here,' Halyna said, thrusting a wet plate into his hands, 'there are plenty more on the draining board...' She watched as Klem clanged the wet plate into the cupboard and continued to dry the dry one. 'Give me strength... what is the matter with you?'

'Why would there be anything the matter?' Klem said, taking the wet plate from the cupboard and plopping it into the sink.

Halyna said, 'don't do that! What is *wrong* with you?'

'Wrong with me?' said Klem, 'nothing at all. It's you who's acting strange... What are you doing washing up when you're supposed to be on strike? And you cooked dinner... very nice it was too!'

'It's a one-off...' Halyna said, rasping out a little more Mild Green Fairy Liquid into the tiny sink, then balancing the bottle upside-down so as not to waste a drop. 'Taras knows it'll be his duty from tomorrow...' She noticed Klem still hadn't answered her question, so demanded for the fourth and final time, 'this Gunter? Where did you meet him, hmmm?'

'Shhh,' said Klem, 'don't say his name so loudly.'

Halyna shook her head and whispered, 'terribly sorry... how did you meet *him*?'

Klem shrugged his shoulders. Picking up a cup, he neatly wiped every speck of water from its surface. 'Oh, it was during the thirties,' he said vaguely, 'when I still lived in the village...' He counted Gunter as one of his closest friends, so always chose to ignore the man's shadier side: it wasn't any of his business after all. As Gunter insisted on anonymity, Klem never spoke about him to anyone, not even to Halyna.

'And how do you suppose he'll sort out your Ivan problem?' Halyna asked, scrubbing out the Pyrex dish with the coarsest of Brillo pads, flakes of burnt fish and cremated potato flicking all over the place.

Klem shrugged his shoulders again, 'I've left that up to him. Anyhow,' he said with a broad smile, 'at least I'm not destitute anymore!'

Halyna stopped scrubbing and wiped the suds from her hands with a towel – one of Sofia's old nappies – hanging on a hook beside the sink. She looked at him, holding out a dry palm.

Klem turned and said, 'ah, you'll be wanting some money for my share of the Easter meal...' He fumbled through his pockets, 'now, where did I put it?'

Halyna had seen this same act many times and the best he'd ever extracted from his pockets was an old mint covered in fluff.

'Aha,' Klem said jovially, 'here it is. Now I hope you've got some change.' He extracted a chunky box covered in blue leather and unveiled its contents with a 'Ta-Da!'

'Is it genuine?' Halyna asked, raising both eyebrows.

Klem said, 'of course it is genuine. This happens to be one of Mister Fabergé's most renowned unofficial jewels. Mind you, it may be a little difficult to sell at the moment...' He raised an index finger, 'but when it does, I'll be able to retire!' He clicked the box shut and inserted it back into his pocket. 'But don't worry,' he said with a wink, 'I'll see you right.'

Halyna raised her eyebrows even more. To her it looked like a Christmas tree bauble. 'Where did you get it from?' She whispered, 'from *him* I suppose?'

'Indeed, it was payment for a little favour I did; a favour that's in *all* our interests...'

If the egg was real, Klem could afford to buy the whole street; but when people like Gunter were concerned, that was a big *if*. 'Mmm,' she said, 'I see...'

She resumed the washing up, but was unable to settle into her usual rhythm. She narrowed her eyes and honed in on the source of a terrible noise in the back yard. She said, 'and I suppose he came from the same place too?'

'He?' Klem asked.

She pulled open the net curtain and said, 'yes, him. Remind me, how many more days do we have the pleasure of your bodyguard's company?'

'Oh him, don't you worry about him! He'll come in useful if

The Dancing Barber

the Vlads pay me a visit, but assuming, touch wood,' he tapped his head with his fingertips, 'they don't, Gunter said he'd collect him at the end of next week. But I must admit I've grown rather fond of him. Haven't you?'

'What's to grow fond of? He's a terrible beast! He just stands there by the back door scaring everyone away!'

'Shhh! He might hear!' Klem said with a finger at his lips. 'Well, I think he's rather cute. Just look at that hairy face and those deep blue eyes. And he has such a bushy tail!'

'Mmm,' Halyna said, 'it's what drops out from beneath that bushy tail that worries me. That stuff's already made a terrible mess of Taras' suede shoes! I can still smell it even though I've disinfected them thoroughly... And you can't just leave him tied up in the back yard all the time: you're supposed to walk him twice a day and make sure he drops his load as far away from home as possible.' Halyna looked at the Russian Blue, trembling with fear in the corner, 'and poor old Mister Pushkin can't stand him either. That beast is upsetting <u>everyone</u>!'

'Listen, if the Vlads come a-calling, you'll be grateful of good old...'

'That's enough,' Halyna interrupted just in time, 'you will <u>not</u> utter his name in this house!'

The cheap Chinese pendulum clock on the mantelpiece chimed ten o'clock. 'Is that the time?' cried Halyna, almost dropping the last plate as she rushed to put it away in the cupboard. 'We're due at church in half an hour and it will not be goodski if we are late!'

She scuttled to the foot of the stairs and shouted, 'Taras! Sofia! You'd better be getting ready for church, because we're leaving in <u>two</u> minutes!' She adopted the demeanour of a decapitated chicken, running around the kitchen, putting on her church clothes whilst simultaneously putting together the Easter basket; she was never usually this disorganised.

A sunburned Sofia ambled wearily downstairs wearing her zippy boots and tatty old coat... it was way past her bedtime and she couldn't be bothered dressing up. The boots were fine, but Halyna insisted her daughter wore her smart navy blue coat and demurely embroidered headscarf that made mother and daughter look identical, much to Sofia's displeasure.

'Where is the horseradish?' Halyna said after looking in every cupboard twice, 'we can't go to church without it!' Then to her horror, she realised she'd forgotten to finish the embroidered towel she'd created especially for this year's Easter basket: the Orthodox crucifix was complete, as was the wording, "Christ Has Risen", but the wavy border of yellow and blue thread was unfinished. She didn't have time to do anything about it now, so she tied off the thread and ensured the incomplete section was tucked away out of sight beneath the containers of butter and cheese. 'Sofia!' she shouted, 'have you found the horseradish yet?'

'Yes Mama,' Sofia said proudly, dashing in from the pantry holding in her white-gloved hand a whisky tumbler, full to the brim with horseradish mixed with grated beetroot. 'Here it is!' She slotted it into place in the basket already containing a *Paska* (that Sofia knew by its appearance would taste of cremated brioche), dozens of decorated *Pysanky*, cream cheese, numerous exceptionally pungent garlic-infused sausages and salamis, butter, lard, salt and what looked like bits of cold chicken wrapped in tin foil.

'Oh Sofia!' Halyna cried, observing her daughter's stained glove that gave the impression she was a doctor who'd just performed a surgical procedure. 'They're your best pair! Quickly, go and change them at once, we're leaving in half a minute!' She looked around the kitchen and shouted, 'Taras! Are you ready?' But the sound of creaking bedsprings from the ceiling suggested otherwise: knowing he'd spent the entire afternoon in the park, she marched directly upstairs, brandishing her heaviest rolling pin…

Klem rolled his eyes to the ceiling and sighed… He of all people should have been looking forward to the All-Night Easter Service, but as the years went by, he simply didn't have the stamina any more. He reached into the cupboard under the sink and extracted a fresh green bar of Fairy soap, before running up to the attic, climbing two stairs at a time: it'd take Halyna at least five minutes to coax Taras into getting ready, especially if the rolling pin was used to its full effect… plenty of time for Klem to give his face a scrub and change into his 'Sunday Best'…

He flicked on the tumbler switch and strode over to the small ceramic basin in the corner of the attic, filling it with lukewarm water… it seemed Halyna had used all the hot water for the washing up, but he didn't mind. Two storeys down, he heard the

The Dancing Barber

front door slam and the taxi speed away. He muttered, 'thanks for waiting! I'll make my own way there, I suppose?'

So instead of only scrubbing his face, he gave his entire body a thorough clean with plenty of soap and water, using one of Halyna's softest flannels. The soap was as hard as a pebble, so just like Army soap, it would easily last him a year.

His body soon gleamed with cleanliness, the dirt greying the basin water so that he couldn't see the plughole. But the water was still soapy, and it would have been wasteful to let it drain away... so he gave his shirts and underwear a good scrub, hanging them up in front of the fire... they should be dry by morning. He considered giving Mister Pushkin its weekly bath, but had second thoughts when the cat unsheathed its claws when he approached...

Klem's pocket watch chimed eleven times, but he wasn't bothered: the All-Night Service never started on time, especially with ten times more people than normal going to the pre-service confession...

He carefully shaved his face with the Bic razor he'd been using for months and slipped on a clean shirt with a zig-zagged embroidered collar, cuffs and bib. He then donned one of his better suits, with the trademark blue and yellow pinstripes, and examined his appearance in the mirror.

Deciding his scuffed boots weren't appropriate for church, he fitted his feet into a special pair made of red patent leather: they pinched a lot, but at least they were smart.

And as a finishing touch, he applied a smidgen of Fairy soap to his horseshoe of a moustache, pulling and twisting it until it resembled two black skewers poking from his nostrils.

Hiding the Fabergé Egg in amongst the clutter on the mantelpiece, he called for Mister Pushkin and made his way downstairs. Barely out of the room, he clicked his fingers and scampered back: how could he have forgotten his notebook and pen? There was no way he would survive the All-Night Service without them... His watch chimed a quarter past: being an hour late for church was acceptable, but any more would be decidedly rude...

The air was thick with the intermingled smells of garlic, boiled eggs and horseradish that oozed from the multitude of fully laden Easter baskets occupying every space in the former Methodist Church in the suburban village of Eccleshill. The baskets were on the pews, beneath the pews, on the windowsills, on the stairs, balanced on the balcony and even squeezed between people's feet.

The swollen congregation, resplendently clad in their Sunday bests, had unsuccessfully tried to mask their personal aromas of mothballs and stale tobacco by dowsing themselves with so much scent that the air was almost painful to breathe. But for Taras' dancers, standing dead on their feet by their mothers' sides, the air was sweeter than honey when compared to the mustard gas of his studio, post-dress rehearsal…

The choir on the balcony wailed, whilst the Orthodox Priest – wearing his whitest cassock, trimmed with gold – sang his prayers in the form of a rhythmic lullaby, swinging his incense-filled *Cadyllo* with all the skill of a professional hypnotist. And the thousand or so candles, whose flames danced in the dingy gloom burned away whatever oxygen remained, whilst adding to the hypnotic effect…

So if it weren't for the enormous oak door creaking open and bringing in some much-needed cool and fresh night air, there wouldn't have been a single person remaining upright in the entire church.

Klem crept his way in; somehow managing to stand on every creaky floorboard and eventually took his place beside Taras. Out of the corner of his eye, he noticed the bronzed Taras had applied some orange-tinted stage make-up to his swollen forehead: Halyna's rolling pin was a formidable weapon. And Taras' suit was terribly creased: with Halyna still on strike, he was too stubborn or lazy to iron it himself.

On a normal day, Klem tied a piece of thick green ribbon to his watch's bow and fixed it discretely to the lining of his waistcoat pocket. But on special occasions, he'd wear his watch on the end of an extremely heavy gold chain, which tinkled loudly each time he moved as if he were the ghost of Jacob Marley. Constantly shuffling on the spot in the quest to adopt the least uncomfortable position, tonight the watch chain tinkled as though an entire platoon of Jacob Marleys was attending church.

The Dancing Barber

'Sorry I'm late,' he whispered in Taras' ear, the skewer of his moustache almost perforating Taras' jugular, 'but Mister Pushkin decided to go for a walk on the roof again, and it took me ages to coax him down.'

'Shhh,' said Taras, knowing Klem had already attracted too much attention. He dabbed his neck with a crumpled handkerchief, checking Klem's moustache hadn't drawn blood.

'He couldn't settle at home because of that dog,' Klem whispered, 'so I've brought him with me.'

Taras thought for a moment, 'brought who: the cat or the dog?'

Klem remained silently apologetic...

Taras' damp ankle answered his question most succinctly. He looked down and said, 'you can't bring that Cooking Fat into church!'

'Sorry Taras... In that case...' Klem said, bending to the floor, fumbling around for a moment. 'There, that's better...' When he stood up, the cat had disappeared.

Taras looked down again, 'for Heaven's sake... don't tell Halyna you've put it in her basket. Otherwise she'll have your eggs for *Pysanky* next year!'

Halyna and Sofia, standing on the women's side of the church, had seen precisely where Mister Pushkin had been put. *That* look from Halyna ensured Klem extracted the cat from the basket before it had eaten all the salami, but only after it'd given the iced *Paska* a plentiful decoration of blue fur, which would add an interesting, if unpleasant texture to the sweet topping.

With the excitement over, Taras' mind soon began to wander; for the first time ever, he'd missed the *Wrestling* on the telly earlier that evening. He knew it was terribly Unchristian, but he'd much rather watch two men grappling with each other than be bored to death standing in church. The sooner he could buy a video recorder, the better... this wonderful gadget had been demonstrated recently at the BBC's Alexandra Palace... He made a rough calculation of how many tickets he'd have to sell to be able to afford one... He hoped Mick McManus won; he wasn't a fan of Jackie Pallo. And *Miss World* would be televised soon... *that* would be worth recording. But even after having the most restful of days, standing in church in the middle of the night was as sleep-inducing as watching an episode of *Armchair Theatre*...

After only a short while, Klem put his hand into his waistcoat pocket and pressed a small button on the side of his pocket watch, a Vacheron Constantin, a gift from a dear friend. He counted as it discretely vibrated twelve times. He thought: *how can it only be midnight? I feel like I've been here for days!* Listening to the lullaby of harmonic prayers meant people were falling asleep all around him: even the usually resilient Taras had wedged himself into a corner and remained upright, despite being fast asleep; the fact he'd painted eyeballs onto his closed eyelids didn't fool anyone... He'd soon be joining him if he couldn't find something, anything, to occupy his mind. He looked around the church in search of inspiration, but he only saw the same icons adorning the same walls. Inside these four walls was the only place the old men ever peeled off their flat-caps... Klem was always amused to discover who'd gone bald and who was obviously nurturing a comb-over... but even this didn't excite him for very long.

He then examined the ornate *iconostasis* separating the sanctuary from the rest of the church. He remembered the day Mrs Wiggins' husband installed this enormous screen – towering from floor to ceiling – and the ensuing arguments with the other volunteers when it came to deciding which icon was to be positioned where: the only thing Ukrainians could ever agree on was to disagree on everything. Every icon – representations of Jesus, Mary, angels and saints – was Ukrainian in origin and painted reverently on oak panels. One particular icon – that of the Virgin and Child – had always been Klem's favourite: it was enhanced by a golden *riza*, only leaving the face and the hands visible. He adored this icon, not just because of what it represented, but also because of where it came from: he'd risked his life to rescue it from the church in Chaplinka just before the Soviets closed it down in 1933. He was the Curate at the time and managed to save not only the icon, but also many ancient and sacred religious texts; he was lucky not to have shared the same fate as the unfortunate Priest.

He'd only been beyond this particular *iconostasis* once before, entering the sanctuary – the Holy of Holies – via one of the three doors where only ordained Priests may tread. Ordinary people – especially women and those expelled from the Orthodox Church –

were never allowed. As one of the doors opened, allowing the Priest to go and refill his *Cadyllo* – obviously the existing fog of incense wasn't pungent or thick enough – another of Klem's favourite icons was revealed, depicting Saint Michael slaying a demonic beast by cutting its throat with his sword of fire. Klem smiled, how apt… this demonic beast bore such a striking resemblance to Ivan!

He'd finally settled into a comfortable-ish position by bending one knee and keeping the other leg straight, alternating the pose at regular intervals so as to give himself something to do. He, along with everyone else would be expected to stand or kneel for the full five or six hours, only permitted to sit when the Priest counted the evening's collection, which never took very long. He watched with envy as the elderly snuffer – the only man, other than the Priest, permitted to move during the Service – ambled to one of the many candelabra and began systematically extinguishing the shortest candles with military precision: the moment any candle was less than an inch in height, it was snuffed. It must have been his way of keeping alert; and Klem wished he also had such a task. But once the snuffer returned to his seat, the only thing that moved was the Priest's *Cadyllo*, swinging to and fro, to and fro, to and fro…

An hour later, the subtle sound of scratching cut through the serenity of the most reverent part of the Service.

'I think it's disgraceful how he sits there writing,' The Gossipmonger said, not bothering to whisper.

'Quite right,' said her deep-voiced deputy. 'A complete disgrace!'

The entire Gaggle, stared, tutted and shook their heads.

Klem knew they were talking about him, but didn't care. He had to do something to stay awake, so took out his notebook and pen and began writing down some lines of poetry that had entered his head. His publisher had been nagging him to complete his latest compendium, but after the events of recent days, he'd unsurprisingly fallen behind. The ideas clustered like clouds above his head: at first they were wisps of cirrus, but soon became cumulonimbus and fell like an intense thunderstorm into his head, running down his neck, along his arm and onto the page. His scribbling became faster and louder as he populated page after page with carefully selected words.

'That's done it,' Taras said, giving Klem a nudge.

The nudge was forceful enough for Klem's italic nib to jab through the paper of his notebook. Seeing his concentration had been shattered, he looked up with disgruntlement and noticed that not only was The Gossipmonger and her Gaggle staring at him, but so was everyone else. Klem smiled, screwing the golden cap back onto his pen. Even the choir craned their necks over the balcony to gawk and the Priest had fallen silent for the first time in over two hours, strumming his fingers on the cover of his ceremonial Holy Bible.

The Priest only recommenced the order of service once Klem's notebook and pen had been firmly consigned back to his pocket.

Taras exhaled a long breath, 'well done Klem. Now the Priest's lost his place. He said all this half an hour ago! Now it'll be *five* o'clock before we're released!' He then gestured to the small side table, 'and go fetch your Cooking Fat before anyone sees it lapping at the communion wine!'

When the heavy oak door was flung open again, a strong gust of cold wind blew through the church and – much to the elderly snuffer's dismay – extinguished all the wrong candles. The door then slammed shut and loud widely-placed goon-like steps echoed around the building. As the tall man waded in, the congregation parted to make way for his broad shoulders and thrusting elbows. The Gossipmonger looked on with pride.

A flat-cap muttered, 'here comes The Count...'

'You mean The Ginger Rasputin...' said another flat-cap.

'More like The Devil,' mumbled the snuffer as he painstakingly relit every candle taller than one inch. He hated anyone else snuffing out the candles: it was *his* job.

Without asking permission, Ivan inserted his extra-wide expensive-looking wicker basket between several others, thus occupying the prime location. Its contents were traditional, but with the exception of the home-baked *Paska*, everything else appeared to have been bought from Fortnum's... Not even Busby's was good enough for The Ginger Rasputin...

Taras looked around and noticed Ivan still wore his corduroys and ancient mackintosh: typical of the man not to dress appropriately. At least he'd taken off his hat... He smiled and said to Klem from the corner of his mouth, 'some people just can't take the sun, can they?'

Klem smirked, 'he does right getting all the sun while he can... There won't be any where he's going. Plenty of heat,' he said, 'but no sun.'

The bright red snooker ball of a head – whose skin was already peeling away in big curly ribbons – went to stand beside his mother and was the only man on the women's side of the church. He didn't even have the courtesy to cross himself and kiss the Holy Bible before taking his place... Everyone hated Ivan and even the slightly tipsy Mister Pushkin growled when it mistook Ivan's facial fungus to be a ginger tomcat.

Klem took pleasure in watching his adversary squirm: no matter how Ivan stood, his rough clothing irritated his raw sunburn. And even through the dense smell of garlic sausage, Klem could detect the stench of cremated flesh.

When Ivan stared at him through slatted eyes, Klem immediately looked across to the anonymous looking man... The subtle wink from beneath the rim of the familiar black hat put his mind momentarily at ease. But that got him thinking, if the anonymous looking man could merge so well into the congregation, then who else could? There were so many unfamiliar faces tonight, which – although typical of Eastertime – made him think that any one of them could be a Soviet Secret Policeman. These people were professionals and would easily blend in... The only thing they had in common was they all seemed to be called Vladimir...

Klem tried his best to shake away the paranoia by amusing himself by watching a headscarved old woman cough and splutter so much that she almost lost her dentures. She'd put on her best overcoat... unfortunately, the Mint Imperial she'd found in her pocket wasn't a mint, but – as you'd might expect – a mothball!

Boredom soon returned; Klem let out the longest of sighs. He resisted the temptation to take out his notebook and pen, letting so many lines of poetry fade away, never to be remembered. He sighed again... With the outdoor masonry being re-pointed, there wasn't even the Easter Parade around the church to look forward to: it was always fun and it certainly entertained the locals, even though it was only the winos who were awake at this time in the morning. He depressed the button on his pocket watch again, but disappointingly, only a quarter of an hour had passed. So he slowly let his mind switch off, letting the choir ease him to sleep.

Klem was just entering the land of dreams when, all of a sudden, the choir's singing became more discordant... He drowsily looked up to the balcony and saw the headscarved choir peering down at the only man on the women's side of the church. One headscarf leaned over so far that she nearly plummeted over the edge, whilst another attempted to make a rudimentary pair of binoculars out of two pairs of spectacles; anything to have a closer view...

After years' of indifference, had Ivan's presence on the women's side of the church started to bother them...? Or – as Ivan had removed his hat – had they seen something else...?

Act 3

Easter Sunday

> 'Let us not become weary in doing good, for at the proper time we will reap a harvest if we do not give up.'
>
> Galatians 6:9

Chapter 14

With a mischievous twinkle in his eye, the Priest took his time to close the trellis gate and draw the altar curtains in the centre of the iconostasis with the same enjoyment that ensured his most long-winded sermons always coincided with the sunniest of summer days…

The moment the two halves of the embroidered curtain finally met, the congregation stampeded out so quickly that it was a miracle the Easter baskets weren't trampled. Due to Klem's interruption, and all the fuss surrounding The Ginger Rasputin, everyone had to wait half an hour longer for the interval… The race was now on for coffee, tobacco and even a snifter or two of samahon before proceedings inevitably recommenced…

Sofia and Natalka were in the deepest of sleeps on a rear pew; unable to wake them, Taras had no choice but to haul the girls onto his broad shoulders and carry them to the church hall… Halyna was right; maybe they were too young for such an ordeal.

Halyna had been first out the door… the ordeal obviously too much for her too… She and Klem were already in the church hall, half way through their first cup of tea…

Oksana however was wide-awake, fuelled by cheese and onion crisps and a pathological hatred of her club-handed grandmother for forcing her to attend the All-Nighter. And every time she saw Mr Taras, she was reminded of his swooshing cane and her throbbing buttocks. She stared at him coldly, hoping to be able to turn the horrible man to stone; then she could strike him with a sledgehammer and watch him shatter into a million pieces.

'Stop dawdling!' shouted The Gossipmonger, yanking her granddaughter from her seat, prodding her towards the exit with her clubbed hand. 'Hurry up! At this rate, by the time we get there, it'll be time to come back!'

Oksana scowled more than ever; if she could, she'd also turn the old hag to stone, and then drop her from the top of Blackpool Tower. Even though she wasn't particularly keen on religion, she knew her Grandmother's insistence on chewing tobacco throughout the Service was deeply disrespectful... but nowhere near as disrespectful as when she decided to use a collection plate as a spittoon. And as for her father, he spent most of his time chomping on pickled gherkins; she hoped he got indigestion... She smiled... At least her artistic endeavours were beginning to show: the symbol on top of his head glowed wonderfully by candlelight...

By two-thirty am, the entire congregation was sat in their family groups, slurping coffee and crunching biscuits in the church hall; bleary eyes were sluggishly reawakening...

For once, it seemed The Gossipmonger's Gaggle had a rival... a second clique of headscarves was feasting on the latest piece of succulent gossip, tearing strips off their victim as if they were vultures on a rotting carcass...

'Didn't I say he was a bad-un?' one headscarf said.

'And we all believe you,' said a second headscarf. 'Has the brute no shame?'

'Maybe it was a trick of the light?' said a third headscarf, 'those flickering candles can make you imagine the strangest things...'

Much tut-tutting and muttering ensued.

Halyna smiled when the gossip reached her table. Handing Taras one of her famously soggy tomato sandwiches, she said cheerfully, 'I hope he's not going to blame you for it...'

'If he dares...' Taras said, deciding how best to eat the sandwich without tomato juice dripping down his tie, 'then I'll punch him in the mouth!'

'Good for you,' Klem said, slurping his Earl Grey, washing down the last morsels of his sandwich, grateful it'd finally gone. 'I must admit, whoever was responsible for this artistic masterstroke should win a prize!'

Taras smiled, 'at least it'll make it easier for your friend,' he cocked his head over to the man hiding beneath a black hat in the corner, 'to keep tabs on him.' He laughed, 'I'm sure Ivan's head can be seen from space! Here,' he said, holding out a box of Halyna's soggy doorstops, 'have another sandwich.'

After reluctantly selecting another sandwich, Klem smiled at Halyna and prepared to take a small bite. His jaws were barely able to reach around the two inches of crust; but he knew she sought approval from him, more than from anyone else. But that was the bite that broke the camel's back... he clutched his groaning stomach: he knew yesterday's pork pie was poisonous. He looked up to the ceiling apologetically, knowing it was punishment for eating meat on Good Friday...

Leaving the adults to their boring gossip, Sofia and Natalka sneaked off to share a bar of Cadbury's Dairy Milk and some Fry's Turkish Delight. Neither of them had the energy to speak, as their minds were firmly in the land of dreams, but they were just about capable of allowing chocolate to melt on their tongues. Sofia liked chocolate too much... Cadbury's Dairy Milk and Chocolate Digestives were undoubtedly responsible for the enormity of her thighs. And although she was fed up of looking as though she wore jodhpurs, she was unable to curtail her addiction... Natalka gorged on just as much chocolate as she did, yet still remained disgustingly thin: it was *so* unfair.

Sofia had resolved to give up chocolate for Lent... she only managed three days, which although pathetic, was two days better than her Tato's attempt to give up cigarettes...

Sofia reached into her special church handbag – which was white, to match her gloves – and pulled out another bar; she was about to tear it open, but changed her mind... This bar was one of her Mama's: it was just as delicious as normal chocolate, but its effects were far from normal. After inadvertently eating one last year, Sofia was unable to stray more than ten yards from the nearest loo for two whole days; and Mrs Wiggins' husband had to use his biggest plunger to unblock the lavvy in the yard... But it wasn't long before it became blocked again... and again... and again... It was an episode of her life she never wanted to relive. Strangely, it would take three of these bars to have the same effect on her frequently constipated Mama.

The girls looked over to the table where the adults were still gossiping; how could they have so much energy at such an ungodly hour? Sofia then noticed her Mama's surreptitious swig from a small glass bottle hidden up her sleeve. She had several such bottles in her bottomless pit of a handbag; and all this time, Sofia thought they contained water...

Natalka said, 'why do Ukrainians drink so much?'

The Dancing Barber

Sofia shrugged, 'I can't understand it... it doesn't even taste very nice... When my Tato accidentally dropped some cigarette ash into a glass of the stuff, the whole lot instantaneously went up in flames... it was like a chemistry experiment... so drinking the stuff can't do them any good...'

'No... Especially at the rate they drink it...'

Very soon, Sofia's chin dropped to her chest and she began drifting off to sleep, content that although she had big thighs, at least the rest of her was normal... She thought herself lucky not to be the size of Oksana.

But Natalka couldn't sleep. She said, 'did you see Coronation Street last week?'

Sofia levered open her eyes, 'what? Err, no... Mama used to watch it. But she doesn't any more... She told Mrs Wiggins that she may as well look out of the window and see the same twitching net curtains, housewives with curlers in their hair and promiscuous milkmen.'

'Promiscuous milkmen?' said Natalka, 'what are they?'

'Not sure, but one always sneaks through the back door of number sixty-six when the husband goes to work...'

As usual, Klem kept an eye on the time, his half-hunter propped up on the table in front of him. He said, 'only fifteen minutes before the altar curtains reopen, so we'll have just enough time for another cup.' He knew that tea never failed to settle his churning stomach... especially after those soggy tomato sandwiches.

With Taras preferring a cup of deplorable instant coffee, Klem decanted his Earl Grey into his and Halyna's cups, from the usual height of seven inches, taking the time to aerate the delicious beverage, despite the air in the church hall being musty from disuse. He compared tonight's All-Nighter with the ones he remembered at his church in Chaplinka: the order of service was essentially the same, although back then, the congregations were smaller and the baskets contained hardly any expensive garlic sausage... There wasn't the need to show off; people in Chaplinka gathered to celebrate the Resurrection and to share their love of God. And the same was true tonight, although the cynical voice inside his head thought that tonight's Service was also highly lucrative for the Priest... Candles cost money, confession cost money and there were *two* collection plates that wouldn't move until a *silver* coin was placed on them both. No wonder the Priest lived like a Lord... To Klem, this was woefully wrong: focussing too much on material wealth was not acceptable; did the Priest really need to ride around in a Jaguar? Klem had never been a fan of this new Priest... it was a pity his predecessor had to retire... but at the youthful age of 103, he probably deserved a rest... Klem sighed, and hoped that at least some of tonight's collection would go to help the needy: there'd soon be plenty of them now Ivan had served eviction notices on half of Bradford...

And all that swinging of the *Cadyllo* and wailing of the choir was getting too much for Klem to take. And why did the Priest have to sing everything: it would be a pleasure to hear him read from the Holy Bible in his normal voice for a change... He cursed himself: why was he in such a critical mood all of a sudden; maybe he was overtired? He couldn't help feeling guilty – a Priest should relish a long, drawn out ceremonial Service – but the older he became, the more he felt that people should make their peace with God individually, as an intrinsic part of their lives. But the Church would never agree: how else would they make their money? He shook the negativity from his mind and recited a silent prayer of apology, repeating it three times.

After precisely forty-nine seconds, he smelled the tea, moving his nose back and forth through the rising steam, beckoning Halyna to do the same. He declared, 'ah, this is a good plucking! Smell the light fragrance, and that distinctive bergamot flavour!'

But Halyna could only smell tea. She was sure bergamot meant lemon, or was it orange?

Klem took a big sip of the tea, allowing it to bathe his entire mouth, his tongue wallowing in the delicious liquid. Once it had cooled to body temperature, he swallowed and said, 'yes, a damned good plucking!' Noticing Taras' perplexed expression, he raised an index finger and clarified, 'it means the pluckers have only plucked the *best* leaves.'

'Oh,' Taras said, thankful he hadn't misheard. 'I'll stick to my Maxwell House... *a good stirring*,' he chuckled to himself, swirling the dregs around the base of his cup.

'Very droll,' Klem said, taking another luxuriant mouthful and enacting his elaborate tasting routine once more. Then without

The Dancing Barber

warning, he jerked forward and sprayed out his precious beverage, completely saturating a soggy tomato sandwich he'd hidden beneath a napkin. He spun his head around to see what clumsy buffoon had walked into him...

Ivan stood behind him with a beaming grin, the hairs of his ginger beard splayed out in all their glory. He said, 'hello my dear, <u>dear</u> friend! How are you doing?' He genially tipped his fedora and gave a sly wink to Halyna, who immediately looked away with revulsion.

Klem flinched away from the man's appalling instant coffee and pickled gherkin halitosis. He said, 'you're no friend of mine. And I do <u>not</u> appreciate being slapped on the back!'

'D-D-Don't be like that,' Ivan said with false friendliness. He took a sip from a plastic mug of black sweet coffee, somehow finding his mouth in amongst all that ginger beard. 'Why can't we let b-bygones be b-bygones? Hmm? How about it?' He looked at his mother – who stood menacingly by his side – to ensure what he'd said met with her approval. It did.

Klem allowed Mister Pushkin to answer eloquently on his behalf.

'D-D-Delightful cat,' Ivan pretended to laugh, wiggling his wet ankle. A life-long ailurophobe, he somehow resisted kicking the horrible animal across the hall and straight through a windowpane.

Klem decided he wanted to say something suitably scathing. He looked at his foe's appearance: the sunburnt, blistering and peeling skin, the freshly hair-sprayed and combed ginger beard and the fedora disguising his decorated bonce... there were so many things to choose from...

He rather hoped Taras would be on hand to punch Ivan in the mouth as he'd promised, especially after that devious wink he'd given Halyna. Unfortunately he'd fallen fast asleep with his mug of coffee nestled warmingly in his lap. *Typical.*

So Klem picked up Taras' slim leatherette case from the table and worked out how to get into it. He held it open in front of Ivan and said: 'could I offer you one?'

Slightly surprised, Ivan said 'that's very c-c-civilised of you.' He took a cigarette and said, 'thank you,' sniffing at the working class tobacco before fitting the white stick into the mouth that was buried somewhere in amongst that hair-sprayed ginger beard.

Klem genially smiled as he took Taras' Dunhill cigarette lighter and held it at arm's length.

Ivan craned his neck to get closer to the light; surprised that Klem was willing to forgive so readily.

In an instant, a foot-high flame engulfed the ginger beard and incinerated it entirely. Ivan screamed like an insane woman, desperately searching for water with which to put out the flames.

'Here you go,' said a flat-capped man at an adjacent table, holding out a glass, 'use this.'

Ivan snatched the glass and threw its contents all over the flames.

The flat-capped man almost split his sides as he watched the flames intensify. 'That'll teach you for evicting me without notice!'

The other flat-caps around the table laughed, clapped and cheered, toasting his success. Even the headscarves nodded their approval, but only when The Gossipmonger wasn't looking...

Ivan ran straight for the toilet to plunge his face into a sink of cold water... Pity it was locked for refurbishment.

Every headscarf and flat-cap in the hall laughed more than they'd laughed in ages. In fact they made so much noise that Taras awoke with a jolt, wondering why his crotch was soaking wet. For a horrible moment, he thought he'd wet himself and was much relieved when he noticed the empty cup.

And he was awake just in time to stop The Gossipmonger from pulverising Klem's head with her handbag. 'Leave him alone you poisonous old hag!' Taras shouted, disarming the woman of her weapon, which judging by its pungency, must have been entirely filled with mothballs.

But The Gossipmonger quickly snatched back her handbag and clouted Taras over the head with her clubbed hand. She looked down at his trousers and shouted: 'I'd rather be a poisonous old hag than an incontinent old man!'

'It's coffee!' Taras said, though few believed him.

'You are a disgraceful man, Mr Taras,' The Gossipmonger said, 'not only do you beat and criticise my talented daughter, err, granddaughter at your rehearsals, but now you defend this idiot,' she jabbed at Klem with her clubbed hand, 'for setting fire to my darling son's beard! You should be ashamed of yourself!'

The Dancing Barber

'Oh shut your face,' Taras said, wafting away the smell of singed beard hanging in the air. 'A trained pig could dance better than your precious Oksana! Just because you failed at the ballet, does not mean you can relive your life through her. The girl is worse than useless and so fat that it's a wonder she hasn't crashed through the studio floor and ended up in the fiery pits of Hell!'

'How dare you criticise her weight,' The Gossipmonger snapped, wagging her clubbed hand as if it were a truncheon. 'Wouldn't you rather be well fed than starving to death? Or would you prefer she wasted away like so many of us did in The Great Famine?'

Taras said, 'being "well fed" is one thing, but Oksana is just plain spoilt and greedy. She has so much fat that she could probably survive years without eating!'

Halyna kept quiet; it was her opinion that if Oksana were put on a diet, The Gossipmonger would save a fortune on her shopping bill...

And Taras knew precisely why the wretched Gossipmonger hated him. Although he never regretted rejecting the woman's advances in St Petersburg, he reflected that he could have gone about it less discourteously; although in his experience, rudeness was the only way to get through to a woman who refused to take "NO" for an answer.

'And as for your darling son!' Klem sneered, brushing his thinning hair back into position, 'you don't know the first thing about him, do you?' He straightened the ribbon at his collar and pulled the embroidered cuffs precisely half an inch from his jacket sleeves, 'if you did, you wouldn't be so quick to defend him!'

'What are you talking about,' The Gossipmonger demanded.

Klem noticed the man in the shadows shaking his head discretely. So he took a deep breath and slotted his half-hunter into his pocket. 'This is the *holiest* day of the year and I do not wish to spoil it by speaking of the Devil.' Standing up, he looked at Halyna and Taras, 'come on, the Service recommences in three minutes.'

Whilst everyone vacated the hall, The Gossipmonger shouted, 'tell me what you mean Klem! Tell me!'

But her words only echoed back at her.

Chapter 15

Manchester Airport, Lancashire, Northern England

Zena folded her arms, puffed out her cheeks and declared: 'I <u>not</u> the happy!'

'You <u>never</u> the happy,' Lenka said, 'what is up this time?'

'What do you think?' Zena looked at her sister as if she were the most stupid thing on the planet.

Lenka shrugged her shoulders, 'there are so many of the things to choose from…'

'It is <u>Easter Sunday</u>, yes? And we should be at the church!' Zena cradled her bosoms in her arms as if rocking an obese baby to sleep, 'but are we at the church?'

Lenka shrugged her shoulders again. Secretly, she was glad not to be at "the church".

'<u>No</u>, we are here!' Zena allowed her arms to flop at her sides, 'and it is all the fault of Viktor! Not only is he the miser, giving us the cheap tickets and making us the cargo unloaders, but also he never told us the aeroplane would stop in the Germany. We are already one day late for the visit! And for the icing on the *Paska*, now we are in the Manchester Aerodrome and not the Bradford Aerodrome! We have missed the All-Night Easter Service, and that makes me the very upset! What else can go the wrong?'

Lenka shrugged her shoulders. There were plenty of things to go "the wrong"…

'And how are we to get to the Bradford? Hmm?'

Lenka thought for a moment before daring to submit an answer. She said, 'if we walk slowly by side of the road, maybe a car, it will stop and take us to the Bradford?' She waited for her sister's criticism and when none was forthcoming she continued, 'we could stick out the thumbs and be the hitchhikers!' She shielded her ears from the inevitable telling-off… 'Is the good idea, yes?'

Zena was truly flabbergasted and struggled to utter a single word. Her sister was always full of bad ideas, and often many of them were also very stupid, such as the time she suggested drying last year's grain harvest by lighting a fire beneath it, ignorant of the fact that it and the wooden barn could easily have gone up in flames.

Lenka pressed her hands tightly against her ears; she knew she should have kept her mouth shut.

Eventually Zena said, 'quite frankly, that is the *good* idea! Come on, let us walk this way…'

Pleased her idea was approved, Lenka offered to carry one of Zena's hefty suitcases so her sister could stick out her thumb and beckon a lift for them both…

Chapter 16

The City of Bradford, West Yorkshire, Northern England

'Which durak said the All-Nighter couldn't possibly be any longer than last years?' Taras sighed, steering the cup of strong instant coffee in the general direction of his mouth, whilst listening to the cheap plastic pendulum clock in the kitchen chime for the twelfth time.

Halyna groaned deeply, 'when are you going to stop moaning about it? It's all over so let's enjoy our blessed breakfast in peace.'

'We will when Sofia comes down,' Taras said, shuffling pompously in his seat at the head of the table. 'How long does it take her to get ready?'

'Sofia!' shouted Halyna, her loud voice rattling the multitude of picture frames against the kitchen walls and bombarding straight through Taras' and Klem's sleepy heads. Her tinnitus frequently forced her to shout over the ringing bells and whistling sounds in her ears... even though it was only she who could hear them...

After the pain in his ears subsided, Taras smiled and said, 'even the Priest knew he'd been going on too long... because of *you know who* and his scratchy pen.' He looked directly at Klem, 'he was in such a rush that he swung his incense-filled *Cadyllo* as if he were in a hammer-throwing contest! I thought it was going to fly off the end of the chain and knock someone out!'

Halyna didn't usually like people criticising the Priest, but this morning, she had to make an exception. She said, 'and at least the church was kept nice and warmski by the roaring flames of his burning cassock!' She held her nose, 'and didn't the nylon fumes stink.'

Taras said, 'how long *did* it take him to realise?'

'Ages,' said Klem, almost choking on his tea, 'and when the altar boy dowsed the flames with Holy Water, I thought the Priest was going to lose his temper! You know how he hates wasting Holy Water...'

The Dancing Barber

'Mmm,' said Taras, 'I wouldn't want to be in the altar boy's shoes: imagine telling everyone it was only tap water, and it was always only tap water!'

Halyna added, 'and the excuse the Priest gave that he'd blessed the cold water tap by the sink was *so* flimsy! I didn't think it was possible to do such a thing?'

'It isn't,' said Klem, 'and it's something I'm sure the Bishop will be speaking to him about in due course…'

Taras looked puzzled. He said, 'I'd forgotten about the Bishop… Curious, him turning up like that… and why do you suppose he didn't allow the Priest to perform Ivan's confession? That was very out of the ordinary…'

'Ah, but Ivan isn't an ordinary sinner, is he?' Halyna mused, discretely dipping her finger into the cream cheese, licking off the delicious velvety, chivey loveliness. 'Perhaps someone like Ivan is beyond a normal Priest's ability?'

Klem said, 'not even an Archbishop could deal with the wickedness of Ivan's sins…'

Halyna smiled, 'the Priest was nervous enough with the Bishop turning up unannounced and uninvited; I think he'd have a nervous breakdown if an Archbishop attended! And that would not be goodski!'

'Yes, that Bishop certainly kept the Priest on his toes,' Klem said, helping himself to a little of the fiery horseradish. 'Apparently this Bishop was in the Kyiv Seminary around the same time as me,' he scratched the side of his head, 'but I don't remember him?'

'He remembers you,' Taras said, 'and somehow, he's managed to get hold of a ticket for *Swan Lake,* just so he can hear your recital in the interval…'

Klem should have been honoured; but he didn't hold senior clergymen in particularly high regard… It was a Bishop who'd defrocked him all those years ago…

Sofia finally came downstairs displaying the glummest of expressions. She walked straight over to where Klem sat and placed one of her sheepskin slippers between the knife and fork on the table in front of him…

Delicately, Klem put his special moustache cup onto its saucer and looked inquisitively at the slipper. He then looked at Sofia and said, 'thank you for the Easter gift, but I don't think it will fit. Neither, do I think it will suit me...'

Taras and Halyna hoped there was going to be a good explanation for their daughter's behaviour. It was completely out of character for her to behave so oddly... but she had just been through the ordeal of the All-Nighter...

'Please look inside, Mr Klem,' Sofia said calmly, staring at the slipper's contents.

Klem peered into the well-worn fluffy slipper and immediately screwed up his face at the pungent little pile nestled within. He gave a terribly disappointed look to Mister Pushkin, who was innocently cleaning its face beneath the table. 'Are you responsible?' he asked the cat, which took absolutely no notice, 'I thought so...'

He shook his head, then looked back at Sofia, 'don't worry, I'll buy you a new pair.'

'And you can also give my sock a wash, please,' Sofia added, dropping the stained garment into the laundry basket by the sink. 'I didn't think it necessary to look inside my slipper before putting it on...'

Today and tomorrow were Holy Days, so Sofia knew the sock would lay there looking sorry for itself until at least Tuesday... Housework was not allowed, regardless of whether her Mama was on strike... But with *Swan Lake* looming this evening, for some reason dancing was allowed... and that was something Sofia would never understand...

With Sofia's soiled slipper consigned to the dustbin, Halyna dashed to the cutlery drawer and extracted the knife she used to cut up anything and everything. Since she liberated it from the US Army Camp in 1945, it had decapitated hundreds of chickens, gutted thousands of fish and was always sharpened by rubbing it on the capstones of the sandstone wall outside, rendering the blade with a curved, sickle-like shape. But today, Halyna would use the knife to ceremonially dissect the *Paska* that had been blessed – with a generous splash of tap, err... Holy Water – earlier that morning. For Ukrainians, this task was more important than carving the turkey on the twenty-fifth of December...

The Dancing Barber

The *Paska* stood to attention in the centre of the table as if it were an enormous toadstool, flanked by two-dozen decorated hard-boiled eggs known as *Pysanky*. Although Halyna tried her best to ease out the *Paska* without disturbing the display, as per usual, every *Pysanka* was dislodged and rolled rapidly towards the edge of the table. Sofia tried her best to rescue as many as she could, especially the ones she'd spent hours painstakingly decorating with melted candle-wax and brightly coloured dyes. Unfortunately a *Pysanka* that – judging by the half a candle's worth of wax still covering the shell – her Tato had probably decorated, rolled straight off the table and landed squarely on Mister Pushkin's head. The cat narrowed its eyes and sneezed before drifting off to a concussed sleep.

Halyna shrugged her shoulders apologetically, laying the *Paska* onto the wooden chopping board that perpetually reeked of garlic and onions. Using her sickle-like knife, she hacked off the top that had been beautifully decorated with icing sugar, Smarties and what was left of the church candle that still protruded from the top, its melted wax merging seamlessly with the hardened icing sugar, which would undoubtedly break someone's teeth or give them indigestion. With the decorated top – that would be the pudding – placed back in amongst the reassembled *Pysanky*, Halyna set to work sawing the cylindrical trunk of the *Paska* into round slices an inch thick... so everyone would be able to enjoy at least five slices each.

After prayers, the special candle was ignited and everyone gorged on the blessed breakfast of salami and buttered *Paska*, horseradish and cheese, smoked fat and salt. The *Pysanky* that decorated the table would be eaten later... but as beautiful as they were, none were a patch on Klem's Fabergé, which he admired as he ate.

Klem smiled broadly and rubbed his hands together with glee. With his stomach-ache gone, he was free to enjoy the blessed breakfast. He said, 'this is just what I need after the All-Nighter!' He smeared a disc of *Paska* with a generous amount of blessed butter, followed by an even more generous amount of blessed cream cheese (of the Philadelphia variety), on top of which he placed several slices of garlic sausage followed by a little more cream cheese and a tablespoonful of beetroot-infused horseradish.

He admired his creation with pride, while Halyna looked at him with horror, obviously wondering how he was going to eat this vastness of blessed fayre without spilling it all down his front. He smiled at her before buttering another disc of *Paska* and placing it butter-side down on top of his creation, thus making himself a gigantic sandwich. With his moustache chopsticks still soaped-up and clear of his mouth, he picked up the sandwich with both hands, squeezed it together to make it a little thinner and then bit off a sizeable chunk, thoroughly enjoying the peculiar intermingling of flavours as he chewed it around.

Halyna thought it was a pity that Klem wore his smartest embroidered shirt… it would be impossible for her to clean off the numerous beetroot stains subsequent to half the sandwich's contents falling down his front. She shook her head and delicately popped a morsel of *Paska* smeared thinly with horseradish into her mouth. She said, 'and who taught you to eat in such a way?'

With a full mouth, Klem said, 'tradition: it's how my family always ate our *Paska* when I was little…'

Halyna shrugged, 'I don't care how you eat it, just so long as you enjoy it!' Her gaze enveloped the entire table, 'Goodski Health to you All! Christ Has Risen!'

Everyone replied in unison, 'Praise Him!' before tucking in with gusto.

'And remember,' Halyna said, 'we must eat <u>everything</u> up! I don't want a crumb left!'

Sofia looked at the fully-laden table… why did her Mama always have to say that…? Such a feat was impossible… there was enough food to sustain an entire army for a whole month!

'Anyone for tea?' Klem asked, surreptitiously dropping a piece of salami to the carpet, where Mister Pushkin expectantly sat; he didn't want the cat missing out…

But everyone preferred the stimulating effects of coffee, even though it was only instant.

'Suit yourselves,' Klem said, decanting his special Lapsang Souchon, 'all the more for me.' But even his sensitive nose struggled to detect the tea's delicate pinewood smoke flavour through the whiff of boiled eggs, pong of garlic and stench instant coffee.

Although there were four diners, Halyna had set five places.

The Dancing Barber

This had been puzzling Klem for some time, so he asked, 'who are we expecting?'

Halyna shook her head... he should have known better than to have asked such a stupid question. '<u>No one</u>,' she said, 'it's tradition to set an extra place for those who are no longer with us.' She cast her eyes to the ceiling and crossed herself in the Orthodox fashion. Taras and Sofia did the same.

'Oh,' Klem said. He never liked showing his ignorance, especially when it was something he should have known.

With neither Taras' nor Klem's families having survived The Great Famine, it was impractical for Halyna to set that many extra plates of food. So one was enough, and after the meal, it would be the cook's reward for all her hard work...

'What's the matter, Sofia?' Klem asked, seeing that she wasn't her usual self. 'Are you still upset about what Pushkin did to your slipper?'

Sofia shook her head and continued to play with her food.

Taras slammed his fork down on the plate, 'well, what's up with you then?'

Sofia recoiled at her Tato's explosive questioning, 'Natalka said she's going to be busy all holidays with her Aunties; so I won't have anyone to hang around with...'

Taras shook his head; 'and what makes you think you'll have time for "hanging around"? You'll be at The Alhambra every day! Remember, dancers who try their best on stage do not have time for "hanging around"!'

Klem asked, 'Aunties? Are they Natalka's Mama's or Tato's sisters?'

'Her Mama's,' said Sofia, 'they're twins; apparently her Tato calls them the "ugliest trolls in the world"!'

'That's a bit harsh,' said Halyna.

'But he's right,' said Taras, 'although the last time I saw them, such a nickname would have been an insult to ugly trolls!'

Halyna said, 'I'm sure they're not that bad...'

'You haven't seen them,' said Taras, grimacing, 'gorillas in dresses would look more attractive!'

Sofia said, 'Natalka has never met them... so it sounds like she'll be in for a shock.' She smiled, 'apparently, there was some sort of delay with their flight?'

'Quarantine,' said Taras.

Halyna scowled at him.

Klem said, 'at least that means they'll be around for one day less: I bet Natalka's Tato's happy…'

But Halyna knew Natalka's Tato would be far from happy: he was probably *relishing* the prospect of telling them that the Manor House they lived in was actually a back-to-back down a terraced side street, and he was actually a hospital porter, not a hospital doctor! She said, 'any way, I think that's quite enough gossip; let's get back to our meal!' She turned on Radio Kateryna and they all listened to traditional Ukrainian Easter music as they ate.

With an over-filled mouth, Taras asked, 'Klem, are you prepared for tonight's recital?'

'Of course,' Klem said rather snobbishly, 'pity I'm only the *interval* entertainment.'

Taras shrugged his shoulders, 'it's the best that could be done. But the interval is half an hour. And,' Taras said positively, 'the Bishop is coming especially to hear you recite.'

'Well, that makes *all* the difference,' Klem said. 'And are all your dancers prepared for the biggest performance of their lives?'

'Most of them, so it should go smoothly,' Taras said, not believing it for a moment.

'Time for *stukaty*!' Halyna declared boisterously, steering the conversation back to the festivities. She held out her strongest *Pysanka*, 'who wants to go first?'

Sofia didn't need asking twice and bashed her *Pysanka* as hard as she could against her mother's.

Halyna shouted, 'champion!' when her daughter's egg cracked.

Sofia sulked. Her *Pysanka* took hours to create and only seconds to crack, peel and devour. She excused herself to her room, cradling the fragments of shell in her palm, hoping – with the aid of some PVA glue – to eventually reassemble this miniature Humpty Dumpty.

Halyna put down her wooden egg, looked at Taras and Klem and said, 'now it's your turn!'

Begrudgingly, the men picked up their *Pysanky* – Klem deciding against using his Fabergé – and bashed them together.

Klem smiled because he was the 'champion!' He sprinkled plenty of salt on his freshly peeled egg, devouring it in two bites.

The Dancing Barber

But Taras frowned. His raw egg had splattered all over his only remaining clean shirt...

Halyna contained her smile. *That'll teach him for forgetting our wedding anniversary!*

Watching the needle on the bathroom scales swing further than ever before, Sofia said, 'how could I have put on *half a stone* in just one day? The food I ate didn't even weigh half a stone!' She threw the fragments of her prized *Pysanka* down the toilet and pulled the chain: *how many calories does an egg contain? And what about all that cheese and salami?*

She hoisted up her skirt and flicked at her wobbly thighs with her fingers, watching the ripples dissipate beneath the beige stockings.

I am just too heavy; but it is impossible to lose weight in this house. I tried last year, choosing Corn Flakes for breakfast instead of the compulsory bar of Cadbury's Dairy Milk, and a salad sandwich for lunch instead of the usual leftover sausages and their congealed fat. But all Mama could do was make fun of me, tauntingly saying: "Sofia is doing the slimming! Silly Sofia! Nobody would have thought of doing such a thing in The Great Famine! Now, eat your bread and dripping: it's good for you! Here, have some more salt!" When will she realise that it can be just as bad for your health to eat too much... look at the state of Oksana...

Dismissing the thought from her mind, she wobbled into her bedroom and creaked open her wardrobe door. She sighed at the poster of Cliff Richard she had pinned on the inside of the door and blew him a kiss, pretending to catch the one he blew back at her, holding it lovingly to her heart. She then reached to the end of the chromium-plated rail and pulled out the garment she could only dream about wearing. It was a cheap mini-skirt she'd bought from a stall on John Street Market, and fitting into it was one of her personal goals.

After what she'd just eaten, squeezing those thighs into that constricting nylon tube was probably not the best idea, and neither was examining her reflection in the mirror: she looked completely out of proportion, a subject of a Picasso painting. She looked back at Cliff and was sure she saw him laughing at her.

She slammed the wardrobe door, tore off the mini-skirt and threw it into the bin. What was the point of having it, if she could never fit into it; besides, she knew her Tato would never let her out of the house wearing "such a thing". The only thought that cheered her was imagining what Oksana would look like in a mini-skirt... the sound of ripping nylon would probably be heard for miles!

The Dancing Barber

Chapter 17

The Village of Chaplinka, Khersonska Oblast, South-eastern Ukraine

Viktor blasphemed, cursed and swore as he juggled the hot cylinders of charcoal onto the cooling rack that was actually a radiator grille from an old Land Rover. He decided it was a reasonable first attempt at baking *Pasky*, but not up to his nieces' standard... But what did he expect? He was a man...

'Ah,' he said, 'they will have to do...' plunging his burned hands into a trough of cold water, shoving the disgruntled horse to one side. Being attired in his usual way, he was grateful not to have burned any other parts of his body... especially in the light of all that cursing on such a holy day.

After dressing in his favourite embroidered shirt and his only pair of trousers, he ambled behind the rambling rose bushes by the river, carrying two of his *Pasky* and a couple of *Pysanky* he'd simply decorated with beetroot.

'Good morning my dears,' he said with affection, 'and a very Happy Easter. I think today will be a *beautiful* warm day.' He looked up, 'there's not a cloud in the sky.'

He lit two candles and knelt down onto a small cushion he'd brought with him so as to preserve his trousers' cleanliness. He twisted the candles into the black soil beside the two wooden crosses and lost himself in prayer for half an hour...

Further along the riverbank, the church in Chaplinka – that thirty years ago had been converted into a cinema by the Soviets – was still boarded up, and the adjacent small churchyard had been invaded by the most colourful and fragrant wild flowers that slowly reclaimed the land back to nature.

Churches were expensive to maintain – especially with a small congregation – and Priests were even more expensive. Viktor deduced that if the church had been closed for thirty years then it would never reopen.

Unfortunately, the nearest church was in Askanya Nova, where he and his nieces would ordinarily trek every Sunday morning, picking their way along the miles of trails and gravely roads that juddered through his entire body, slowly grinding away his joints.

But this year was to be different: he was on his own, so decided to conduct a short Easter Service by the graves of his wife and brother. He was no longer sad about losing them; his faith was strong and he knew they accompanied him in spirit wherever he went and whatever he did. And he knew that – eventually – he'd be reunited with them for all eternity.

He was relieved at not having to endure another All-Nighter... he was getting far too old for them. Instead, he burned a small piece of incense and read from the precious prayer book he hid from the Soviets, taking comfort in the Resurrection of Our Lord.

He imagined Zena and Lenka would probably still be in bed after attending Bradford's legendary All-Nighter, and would undoubtedly awaken to a delicious blessed breakfast in the lavish guest suite of their young sister's Manor House...

Greater Manchester Police Headquarters, Lancashire, Northern England

'A likely story,' the Constable said, slamming his blunt pencil onto the desk. 'No self-respecting women would dare walk along *that* road in the middle of the night. Unless...' he pulled the starched collar from his neck, 'they were looking for *business*, so to speak.'

Zena had no idea why she and her sister had been arrested. 'Business?' she said, 'we not looking for the business, we looking for the Bradford!'

'Yes,' Lenka said, raising herself from the plastic chair and releasing a thunderous pocket of trapped wind that made the interview room smell worse than a farmyard, 'we do the hitchhiking... We going to visit the young sister and the niece: they live in the Bradford.' She turned to her sister, 'what does he mean when he speaks of the business? I no understand?'

The Dancing Barber

'Me neither,' Zena said, looking at the Constable, 'the explanation please.'

The Constable rolled his eyes to the ceiling and was about to explain, when his Sergeant walked in. 'Morning Sarge,' he said, looking up at his superior's wise, weather-beaten face.

'There's no need to detain these "ladies" any longer, I've checked their papers and they're tourists,' said the Sergeant, munching on a sugared almond. He then whispered in the Constable's ear, 'I can't believe you arrested them for *that*!'

'Sorry Sarge, I best get back on the beat.'

The Sergeant shook his head, 'and <u>think</u> before you arrest next time!'

Placing his paper bag of sugared almonds on the desk, the Sergeant handed back the grimy passports and crumpled, soiled papers to the twins. He said, 'apologies for any inconvenience caused. But can I suggest you think carefully about which streets you walk along in future...'

The twins were relieved when the handcuffs were removed, yet still had no idea why they had been arrested. They mulled it over, rubbing their stout wrists in the effort to regain some circulation in their hands. The handcuffs were flimsy compared to the Soviet ones... had they the inclination, they could have broken them effortlessly... But they were in a foreign country, so thought it best to cooperate with the authorities... at least for now.

The Sergeant said, 'the Bradford train leaves the station in half an hour and should arrive by midday.' He edged away when he noticed fleas leaping from the women's hair and landing on the desk in front of him, 'so if you walk briskly you should get there in plenty of time...' After spraying the room with air freshener, he led the two smelly women to the nearest exit...

Pondering where he'd put his sugared almonds, the Sergeant watched the two women trundle down the street, as if they were a pair of heavy wardrobes shuffling across the floor. Feeling something bite his leg, he headed back indoors for the flea powder...

He muttered, 'I've had to deal with some smelly and flea-ridden tramps in my time, but all of them combined wouldn't come close to those two! And why would they need twenty empty suitcases between them?'

Chapter 18

The City of Bradford, West Yorkshire, Northern England

Out in the yard, Sofia said, 'bleeding hell!' upon discovering the coal-shed door ajar. She never used to swear until Natalka started: and if Natalka swore, it must have been all right... just so long as her Tato didn't hear. She glared at Mister Pushkin, who sat innocently on the doorstep, licking his lips. Expecting the worst, she slowly crept, with her knees to her chest, into the dark, constricted space.

'Oh <u>No</u>! Not again!' she cried, seeing the upturned cage, completely devoid of hamsters, the little wire door wide open and sawdust spilled everywhere. Mister Pushkin followed her in, undoubtedly to admire his handiwork, cleaning his whiskers with great satisfaction.

Sofia started to panic... *How do I tell my teacher that the cat's eaten the school pets, <u>again</u>?* All her teachers were the strictest nuns imaginable: they could wield a cane just as savagely as her Tato, especially the dreaded Mother Superior.

While she rummaged in amongst the sawdust in the bottom of the cage, Mister Pushkin came and sat beside her. He had the nerve to purr.

Sofia said '<u>Hiss</u>!' in a serpentine way and watched the cat scuttle back into the house, its sharp claws scratching against the eroding concrete of the back yard.

Moments later Taras shouted something that sounded remarkably like 'Cooking Fat!' from his bedroom. She couldn't believe the lazy *so n so* had gone back to bed to sleep off some of his heavy breakfast, only to be savaged by the cat again...

Sofia angrily hit the cage; some of the sawdust that was piled into the corner shifted, the lighter particles fluttering into the air. She peered closer in the dim light... she was sure the sawdust was moving... And then she saw a chubby little paw emerge, followed by a very chubby hamster, slowly unwrapping itself from its

The Dancing Barber

sawdust blanket.

'At least there's <u>one</u> left!' she said with great relief, the tension in her head melting away. She looked at the size of the rodent and knew it was too fat to fit through the tiny door. 'It's very nice to see you Audrey,' she said in the infantile way she spoke to all hamsters. She reached in and stroked the rodent's coarse fur, grateful that Mister Pushkin wasn't greedy enough to have eaten them both.

'Sofia!' her Tato called from the kitchen door. 'Come <u>here</u> please!'

Sofia cursed the cat for waking him up, especially when he shouted the words she dreaded to hear: 'Haircut time!'

She gulped and thought: *I've just got my hair how I like it! So I'm not going to let the old man hack it all off and make me look like a brunette Shirley Temple again; or, if he puts the wrong comb on those clippers, Yul Brynner... I wonder... How long can I hide in the coal-shed?*

But there was no need to hide. Her Mama shouted, 'oh no you don't, Taras! You are <u>not</u> ruining your daughter's hair before the performance. There will be many photographs taken and I do not want her looking as if she was suffering from alopecia!'

Through the chicken-wire window, Sofia watched her Mama shove her Tato back indoors, confiscating the electric clippers that buzzed menacingly in his hand. Her Mama then swung on her headscarf, tied it under her chin and said, 'if you're hungry, there's plenty in the pantry. Cook something yourself for a change: it will do you goodski!' And before her Tato could protest, her Mama said, 'I'm off to meet Mrs Wiggins!' She poked him in the chest with her index finger, 'and you leave Sofia's hair alone!'

Sofia thought: *Good on you Mama, you show the old man who's boss!*

Before locking up the coal-shed, Sofia rummaged systematically through the sawdust, just in case Brenda was hiding. Sadly, she wasn't there, but Audrey was definitely not alone: a couple of tiny pink things were attached to her teats, and the hamster was still heaving...

Chapter 19

Taras lit a cigarette, sat back and imagined he was on the balcony of a hilltop villa in the south of France. He tilted his head towards the hot sun and looked through the mesh of his eyelashes. The fringe of clouds on the horizon may well have been the foot-hills of the Alps, while the terraced houses cloaking the landscape might have been the gently rolling waves of the Mediterranean, and the smoking factory chimneys could have been steam ships coming into harbour. He smiled… thirty-three years after leaving Ballet School, his imagination was still the only thing keeping him sane…

Three floors above the hustle and bustle of Great Horton Road was Taras' haven of tranquillity. He'd often come up to what he called his "Penthouse" to escape the madness of the world. And the south-facing, sheltered balcony was definitely <u>his</u> domain; but this wasn't a conventional balcony; being recessed into the tiled roof, thus occupying some of the attic space, it was completely camouflaged when viewed from street level. He liked nothing more than to watch the sun rise over Lister Mill and then follow the sunlight slowly creeping across the terraced landscape cascading away from him. This wasn't a place to work, so the white walls and minimalist, yet comfortable furniture ensured Taras could clear his mind for a little while, before the inevitable descent downstairs to a world of endless worries and chaos…

Halyna had threatened for some time to convert his haven into a student bed-sit so as to earn some extra money. In the light of her new-found aggression, he knew she'd probably get her way in the end, so resolved to enjoy the space while he could. As he never found it constructive to sit and worry about a forthcoming performance, he decided to turn his thoughts to matters he'd neglected in recent years. And having finally realised Halyna's moodiness (and the mischief with his raw egg) was down to him forgetting their wedding anniversary last week, he decided to mull over how he could best make it up to her.

He'd have at least five hours to himself before she returned

The Dancing Barber

from town, so he lit another cigarette and deliberated what he could buy her. She'd bought him some socks; so maybe he could buy her some stockings? On second thoughts, maybe not: he still remembered what she did with the stockings he'd bought her for their last anniversary…

But in the background, the incessant sound of typing persistently intruded on Taras' thoughts. 'Klem!' Taras shouted, 'give it a rest will you!'

'Shhh!' Klem said, 'please do not interrupt me!' And he continued to hammer the heavy keys fluidly for a further ten minutes, slurping his aromatic Peppermint tea and munching through half a packet of his favourite Digestive biscuits without dropping a single crumb.

Taras was annoyed. But not sufficiently annoyed to go back downstairs; the hot sun was too nice to miss and he was tanning wonderfully, especially with the aid of liberal amounts of Nivea Crème, spread over his smooth face and toned torso. Besides, those pesky kids would only wind him up if he went into his shop.

And he knew the interloping typist would soon be leaving the attic, taking all his ghastly furniture and clutter with him. He never did like Klem hanging gloomy pictures on his pristine walls, and his Victorian bookcase was so heavy that it made the floor bend in the middle… never mind his four-poster bed and three-ton desk… Taras was sure he could grin and bear it for a little while longer: but if Klem hadn't gone after a fortnight, something would *have* to be said.

At the precise moment when his pocket watch emitted its orchestral alarm, Klem pulled the final sheet of foolscap from the runners and added it to the ream he'd spent months writing. He numbered the pages carefully, blowing on each number to ensure the ink was dry, and proofread every single word, slowly and meticulously, even though there were never any mistakes.

Then, as a matter of routine, he used an enormous brass key to unlock the deep drawer beneath his desk, sliding it fully open. He lifted out the heavy books and files it contained, and carefully unclipped the false bottom, to reveal a space just large enough to accommodate his battered old typewriter.

'Still doing the two typewriter trick, eh?' Taras asked, coming inside, after the sky had inevitably clouded over. He slipped on his crumpled shirt, not bothering to fasten it until he'd cooled down.

'It is the safest way,' Klem said, placing a pristine Royal typewriter onto his desk, feeding through a fresh sheet of paper. 'The idiot Soviets would never imagine I had two... They'll see this one, and realise the type doesn't match the documents...' He allowed himself a chuckle, 'assuming they ever intercept any. They'll soon realise they can't pin anything on me!' He smugly straightened the silky ribbon at his collar.

'It's not like you to be over-confident,' said Taras. 'You know what they say: "pride comes before a fall..."'

Klem shook his head, 'I'm not being over-confident... Katya and I have done our best to second-guess the Soviets... I'm simply saying that I doubt they'll have the intellect to track me down until it's too late...'

Noticing the glint of something peeking out from beneath Klem's monstrosity of a four-poser bed, Taras said, 'have you still got that old Soviet Army helmet?'

'Of course,' said Klem, 'it's very useful if I'm caught short in the night...'

'I see,' said Taras, 'just make sure you don't spill any...'

Klem smiled, 'I won't.'

Taras flopped into his replica Eames chair, upholstered in black PVC instead of leather, propping his bare feet onto the matching footstool. His shirt remained unfastened, displaying his toned abdomen, while he wafted his perspiring brow with a folded newspaper.

Klem inspected his old friend, thinking how much of a slob he was in private. It was a far cry from when he first met him; back then, he even slept in his tailored suit. And he didn't need any stick-on moustaches for his ballets, because he had a wonderful moustache all of his own. One wouldn't expect anything less from the spoiled son of a Kyiv banker... But that was a lifetime ago...

Taras may have been impressed by the ingenuity and confidence Klem showed in his work, but he couldn't help thinking that – because he'd been running rings around the Soviets for so long – the time for them to catch him out was long overdue... Especially if – in the grand scheme of things – what he was doing wasn't worth the effort... He said, 'don't take this the wrong way... but surely the Cuban Missile Crisis will overshadow everything you've been doing? And even if you *do* make the headlines, the Soviets are only going to continue to deny The Great Famine ever happened.' He sighed, 'do you really still think all this is actually going to make a difference?'

'Of course it will make a difference! I remember a time when you wouldn't dare be so pessimistic...' Reaching for his pocket-sized Bible, he said, 'it is <u>imperative</u> that we try; an eternity under Soviet rule does *not* bare thinking about...'

Thumbing to James, 1:12, he continued, 'as it is written, *"Blessed is the man who perseveres under trial, because when he has stood the test, he will receive the crown of life that God has promised to those who love him."*'

He closed the Bible and rested it on his knee, 'once the West knows the truth about The Great Famine, they'll certainly be on our side! It is the all-important first step to Ukrainian independence! And the problems in Cuba mean that Moscow is already in America's bad books... Katya and I have done the hard work; so tomorrow, we can sit back and relax! Look,' he fanned all the typewritten sheets of foolscap across his desk, 'I have prepared articles for every newspaper I'm connected with... They will all be printed tomorrow to coincide with Voloshin's interview. I hope he'll even make the television news.' Klem smiled, 'the Soviets are going to go ballistic!'

'So I suppose you're Voloshin's "ghost writer"?' Taras asked.

'Indeed. He's not the most eloquent of writers... so Katya agreed that I was to be his "voice". And with a subject as fundamental as The Great Famine, it was imperative the message was compelling.'

'Just like the old days then?' said Taras, glad he wasn't involved.

'Indeed. But this time, Voloshin plans to avoid the cyanide-tipped umbrella!' Klem handed a wad of foolscap to his friend, the bottom sheet still hot, fresh from the typewriter. 'Here, have a read...'

The testimony of the survivors was harrowing: many people's experiences were much worse than Taras had endured and seeing it in black and white emphasised the extent of the suffering. But the shameless statements Klem had collated from some of the perpetrators of The Great Famine were the hardest of all to read.

Taras couldn't understand how these evil men could boast of their brutal treatment of innocent Ukrainians. These people were animals, who neither sought nor deserved forgiveness. He wondered how Klem obtained these statements? The Soviet thugs wouldn't volunteer such information if they knew it would be used against them... Klem must have posed as a Soviet and befriended these butchers... The man certainly kept his courage well hidden.

Watching Taras admire the few black and white copies of photographs paper-clipped to the foolscap sheets, Klem said, 'I think they'll add real resonance to the text... don't you agree?'

But Taras was obviously engrossed.

Of all the evidence Klem collated at the height of the famine, these images of emaciated bodies and heaps of rotting grain were the most dangerous of all to obtain... One of his trusty Leica cameras still bore the thirty year old dents caused by torrents of Soviet bullets.

'Good Heavens,' Taras said, noticing a familiar name. He asked, 'I hope Halyna hasn't read these?'

Klem shook his head, 'they are confidential. Besides, until tomorrow, the less anyone knows about them, the better.' As time ticked by, he became increasingly surprised that he hadn't had a visit. The Vlads were leaving it rather late. Or maybe they'd decided Ivan was as disingenuous as the Boy Who Cried Wolf.

'Oh, I almost forgot,' Klem said, retrieving a recently recorded cassette tape from a secret drawer in his desk. 'This is Voloshin's recording for Radio Kateryna: the one Ivan hasn't fiddled with.' He slid the documents and the cassette into a waterproof envelope, carefully sealed it with the stickiest carpet tape and tied the package with string. His task complete, he exhaled and said, 'can I offer you a drink?'

Taras hoped it would be a real drink, but as usual, he had to settle for a cup of Darjeeling.

When Klem skipped over to the kitchenette to faff with the tea things, Taras swivelled his creaky Eames chair three-hundred-and-sixty degrees, and took the time to survey the state of his beautiful Penthouse. The broad attic that stretched the full width of the house had only been decorated with Pure Brilliant White emulsion last month, yet every time he looked, he noticed Klem had hung up even more of his framed artefacts, gloomy paintings and depressing newspaper clippings, perforating the immaculately plastered walls with yet more nails. He supposed he shouldn't really complain, considering he'd lined Halyna's kitchen with hundreds of framed photographs of his ballet exploits from over the years... but it was *his* house. Klem was just a lodger, and a *temporary* one at that.

Taras had no idea why Klem insisted on displaying all these yellowing newspaper front pages? They must have constantly reminded him of the horrific time in Ukraine thirty years ago, and some of them were so faded that it was almost impossible to read the text... which was just as well. But it wasn't all doom and gloom... The lodger had also hung some particularly beautiful icons, mainly of the Madonna and Child, but also others depicting Biblical scenes he'd displayed on the wall behind his small altar, the centrepiece of which was a brass crucifix and a brass candelabrum that flanked an ancient Holy Bible that looked as though it were bound in leather. And Taras' bespoke copper fireplace – that Klem often referred to as a stove from a POW camp – once had a mantelpiece made from a dimpled sheet of hand-beaten copper... But it could no longer be seen beneath all of Klem's ornaments and knickknacks...

'I know what you're going to say,' said Klem, polishing a teaspoon, 'but...'

Taras interrupted, 'so why say it?'

Klem smiled, 'you know I don't ask for much...'

'Forget it,' snapped Taras, 'and I do not wish to discuss it further.'

Klem said, 'but...'

'No buts,' interrupted Taras, 'and let that be an end to it.'

'Okay,' said Klem, 'but I'm only going to keep asking...'

Taras sighed, 'and I'm only going to keep saying NO!'

Just as the hob kettle began its piercing whistle, three floors down, the electric doorbell emitted the usual sound of a swarm of trapped bees.

Taras immediately stood up and bolted straight down the stairs to his shop. He shouted up at an aghast Klem, 'if it's those damned kids again...'

Klem was so taken aback by Taras' actions that he'd picked up the steel kettle with his bare hand. 'Wait!' he shouted, but Taras was already in the shop with his cane at the ready. Klem thrust his sore palm under a stream of cold water and thanked the Lord the skin hadn't blistered. He wrapped a wet cloth around his hand and dashed downstairs, hoping to prevent Taras from making too much of a scene.

Taras hid the cane behind his back when he noticed the pesky kids were nowhere in sight. He looked blankly at the motorcycle despatch rider stood on his doorstep, who wore enormous leather gauntlets and Biggles goggles. And his motorcycle had, rather annoyingly, left tyre marks on the pavement in front of his shop, the smell of burning rubber still hanging in the air.

'Aye Up, sir,' said the rider, 'is Mr Smith available?'

'Go away!' Taras said, 'there is no Mr Smith here!'

Klem barged past, completely out of breath. He said, 'excuse me Taras, but I am Mister Smith.' He smiled at the despatch rider, 'hello George, sorry to keep you waiting.'

Taras thought, *Mr Smith?*

'T's quite all right, sir,' said the despatch rider, holding out his opened leather satchel for Klem's package. 'You hurt your hand, sir?' he asked, noticing Klem's make-do bandage.

'It's nothing,' said Klem, giving him two crisp one pound notes. 'And here's an extra couple of quid for your trouble.'

'Ta very much, sir, you are very kind, sir.'

Within ten seconds, the motorcycle had sped down the road and was out of sight.

Taras looked at Klem and said, 'Mister Smith?'

'It's probably unnecessary,' Klem shrugged, 'but it makes it that little bit more exciting, don't you think?'

Taras led the way back indoors. 'I suppose so,' he said, 'let's go make that tea… I'm parched and the taste of Darjeeling seems to be growing on me.'

'I'm glad,' Klem said with a relaxed smile, 'it's so much healthier than the horrible instant coffee you usually drink...'

The deafening sound of breaking glass and twisting metal echoed up Great Horton Road. Klem immediately ran out of the house and around the corner in time to be greeted by the smell of spilled petrol and to watch a lone motorcycle wheel bounce across the cobbles like tumbleweed…

The Dancing Barber

Chapter 20

From Manchester to Bradford

The Manchester to Bradford Express' ticket inspector cantered down the oak-panelled corridor with his clipper in hand. He whistled a merry tune, and swung the ragged leather window-openers as he went by with all the joy of a schoolboy scraping a stick against the railings. The midday sun shining through the windows made the dust hanging in the air dance and swirl as he went along, parting as his arms cut through it only to reform behind him, settling to the floor, awaiting the next person to come by.

He trotted through the double doors and stepped across into the final carriage, tap dancing down the corridor as if he were Fred Astaire. Weekend travellers were so much friendlier than the weekday misery-guts he normally had to deal with: he always enjoyed chatting with them whilst clipping their tickets, often having a good laugh and exchanging a joke or two. But after cantering through five of the most over-crowded carriages he'd ever seen, the last carriage on the train was eerily quiet, and there was a most disgusting pong hanging in the air. He scratched his head: the train was filled to capacity, and yet not a soul chose to sit in this particular carriage. And the further down the corridor he went, the stronger the fetid stench became: it was worse than Esholt Sewage Works on a summer's day.

As the odour in the air reached its peak, he heard deep voices emanating from the final compartment and the sound of incessant hawking and spitting emitted by the occupants. He gingerly peeked through the window and witnessed a most deplorable sight. Judging by the type of underwear they wore, these people were probably women, although the vast carpet of black hair covering their backs suggested otherwise; and he had to avert his eyes when they started washing each other's faces using copious amounts of their own spit. He put his clipper in his pocket: he didn't care whether these two had tickets or not... there was no way he was going to enter *that* compartment. He galloped back up the corridor to instruct the janitor to fumigate the entire carriage, the instant the train arrived at Bradford Exchange Station...

The twins soon finished their rudimentary ablutions, which comprised of a simple spit and polish of their faces and a quick rub of their grimy skins using a moistened cloth, thus carpeting the wooden floor with flakes of dead skin and tussocks of malted hair. On hearing over the tannoy of the train's imminent arrival at Bradford, they inserted their re-clothed bodies back into their great-coats and waddled over, with suitcases in hand, to what they thought was the exit door.

Lenka said, 'I did not know that the train travel in England was free of the charge?'

Zena shrugged her shoulders, 'I am the glad it is, for we do not have any of the money to pay for the tickets!' She tapped the side of her head, 'but if we have to pay on the platform, we can pretend to be the stupid and hopefully they will let us pass.'

'Yes,' said Lenka, 'I am good at pretending to be the stupid.'

'Mmm,' said Zena. *You have put in plenty of the practice.*

The sisters were surprised when the train smoothly eased to a halt. They'd braced themselves for the jerk they were accustomed to, having only ever travelled on Soviet trains, which often flung off several passengers before they'd even stopped.

After several tense minutes they realised there wouldn't be a jerk after all and agreed it was safe to disembark. So they lobbed down their suitcases, hoisted up their many layers of skirts and – having decided to exit the train from the wrong side – lowered their bodies onto the railway tracks. They narrowly avoided being hit by a locomotive coming the other way, the driver of which hung his head out of the cab and shouted several words the sisters didn't think were complimentary. So they shouted back plenty of their own, before traversing the tracks aimlessly, striding from rail to rail.

Once they'd finally clambered up onto the platform – Zena had stood on Lenka's back before reaching down to haul her sister and suitcases up – they found themselves standing in the noisiest and smokiest environment they'd ever experienced. Uncle Viktor had fought the Nazis twenty years ago and had often recounted the horrendous din of the battlefield with bombs being dropped overhead, exploding shells and relentless gunfire; and to the sisters, this station sounded pretty close to his description.

The waiting trains had bellowed out so much smog that the sisters could barely see the ends of their bulbous noses, let alone a sign marked "EXIT". So they groped their surroundings in search of a way out. And when the air – all too briefly – cleared, they counted at least eight steam trains, puffing away on the various platforms, bellowing out the blackest of smoke that settled on their great-coats, darkening the already grubby material.

And when an inter-city express stormed through the station, the noise became intolerably loud, especially when it emitted a piercing whistle: the sisters put their hands over their ears, unable to hear themselves break wind, let alone think. The noise from the steam trains briefly abated, only to be replaced by undecipherable announcements blasting from conical speakers high above their heads. The sisters had only their sense of touch to rely upon, so, like a pair of elephants leading each other out of the fog, trunk holding tail, they meandered around, often coming dangerously close to the platform's edge...

The hot, smoky, oily air trapped beneath the station's sprawling glass roof was the first smell neither of them could tolerate: and over the years, they'd smelled many appalling things, most of which were of their own creation. Very soon, their throats were dry, their eyes were watering and their noses bunging up. It was as if every thunderstorm in the world had congregated in this station: to them, it was Hell on Earth.

A glimmer of light shone through the smog, leading the twins out of the station and into the freshest air they'd experienced since alighting. 'Come on,' Zena mouthed, taking hold of her sister's hand and heading directly towards a group of people. 'We go and ask someone how to get out of here...'

But for some reason, everyone they approached either ignored them or sprinted away. So they hoisted up their skirts and clambered over the wall adjacent to the taxi ranks. At last they had reached civilisation, their eardrums relaxing for the first time since arriving. Zena shouted, 'we get the taxi...' and waddled off to the waiting cars, thrusting her thumb in the air. Lenka waddled after her, struggling to keep pace under all those suitcases, fed up of being the pack-horse.

The line of black Hillman taxis drove off in a convoy the moment the women approached, with revving engines and screeching tyres. The sisters could only gasp for air, having been enveloped in a cloud of exhaust fumes and burning rubber. Lenka threw the suitcases to the ground with frustration.

Zena blew her nose and said, 'at least the Soviets, they speak to you, even if they only ever want to see your papers. But not one person has spoken to us since leaving the Manchester. The people in this country, they are *so* rude.'

Lenka unfastened the rusty brass buttons of her great-coat; 'it is as though the people, they are the frightened of us…'

'I wonder why?' Zena said. 'Come with me, I want to check something.'

'Check what?' Lenka asked, annoyed at having to lug all the suitcases again. She tramped after her sister, muttering and swearing.

Zena stopped outside a shop and examined her reflection in the window. She nudged her sister and said, 'even I am the frightened of me… Is *that* what I the look like?'

Lenka nodded her head.

Zena said, 'and you do not look any the better… Maybe we need to get the smartened up before we visit the sister.' She dragged a moistened finger across her cheek, removing the black soot and revealing the natural grime of her skin beneath. 'We also need to give the face the wash… Using the soap this time…'

Lenka sulked at the idea of having to use actual soap; even at home, the closest thing to soap she used was a scrunched-up leaf from a horse chestnut tree. She put her face to the window and examined her thick curly thatch, lifting up a section and picking out anything that had taken up residence. A shop assistant on the other side of the glass took one look at her and immediately flipped the sign on the door to "closed".

'We must go and find somewhere to wash the hair,' said Zena, folding her well-used handkerchief diagonally in half and swinging it onto her head to form a make-do headscarf, knotting the corners beneath her second chin. 'Viktor, he told me that such a place is called "The Toilet", but I do not the know where such a place can be found?'

Lenka said, 'the Policeman in Manchester, he says "The

The Dancing Barber

Trolleybus", it will take us to where we want to go. If we stand at something called "The Stop" we can ask to be taken to "The Toilet"...'

But after waiting at "The Stop" for half an hour, not one trolleybus stopped for them, many accelerating as they went by, even though Zena had extended her thumb and Lenka had revealed her flabby hirsute leg, wiggling it for all to see. 'Maybe,' Lenka said, 'the English men, they do not appreciate the beautiful women when they see them...'

'At least *one* does,' said Zena, 'and he is running this way, wearing the pointy hat and blowing the whistle.'

'I wonder what he the wants?' Lenka asked, waving at him.

'I have no intention in the finding out... Come on,' Zena said, taking hold of Lenka's hand. 'We shall go this way to find "The Toilet"... Quickly!'

'But the man in the pointy hat, he might know where to find "The Toilet"?' Lenka said, tramping after her sister. 'We ask him? No?'

'No!' Zena shouted, yanking her sister's arm. 'The man, he is from the Police, and I do not wish to speak with one of them again...'

'And what the blazes do you think you're doing?' shouted the irate washerwoman. 'This is a public lavatory, not a bleeding bathroom! Get out, out, out!'

With her left breast draped over her arm, Zena turned around and said, 'what is the matter? We are only having the wash!' With the energy of a carpenter sanding a block of wood, she continued to scrub away vigorously at the accumulated grime beneath.

The washerwoman struggled to dodge the blackened soapy water splashing all over her freshly cleaned mirrors and tiles. The putrid smell was worse than the abattoir on a hot day.

'We travel the long distance,' Lenka said, 'so we have to wash away the dirt!'

The washerwoman wished she hadn't turned around, because the additional sound of sandpaper on wood that she heard was actually a skirtless Lenka, scrubbing away energetically at her undercarriage with an extremely wet and awfully brown flannel. The smell of fish was sickening…

The washerwoman screamed, 'never in all my years have I witnessed such a disgraceful display!' She picked up her mop and prodded at the twins, 'get out of my lavatory you heathens or I'll call the Police! Out, out, <u>out</u>!'

'The vicious old cow,' Lenka said, running into the street, simultaneously pulling up her bloomers.

Zena agreed; she also found it terribly inconvenient to be chased out of "The Toilet" whilst half-dressed, with all those suitcases to carry and with such a large part of her anatomy bouncing around so much that it almost bashed her in the face. She dragged her sister around the corner and out of sight of the irate washerwoman who was still hot on their heels. She finally managed to insert herself into the hammock that was her brassière. Catching her breath, she said, 'we must find another "The Toilet": I still need to do the number <u>two</u>.'

'Look,' Lenka said, 'pointing to a row of houses in the distance with signs by their front doors marked "TO *I* LET". 'There are plenty of "The Toilets" over there…'

It was a pity they were private residences whose soon-to-be-evicted tenants cursed the local yobs for adding the letter "I" to their "To Let" signs. But they cursed Zena and Lenka even more upon discovering them squatting in amongst the daffodils. The headscarved housewives chased them away with their prickly yard brushes, whilst their flat-capped husbands cowered indoors, amazed that women actually existed on this earth who were more terrifying than their own wives…

'Surely not?' said the Park Warden, 'are my eyes deceiving me?'

His assistant sauntered over from the bench where he'd been dozing beneath his newspaper. He yawned, stretched and said, 'well, if your eyes are seeing two big troll women crouching in the flowerbeds then they aren't deceiving you.'

The Park Warden deliberated, 'you think they're gypsies or tramps?' He clicked his fingers, 'my money's on tramps.'

His assistant agreed and said, 'you reckon we should tell them

The Dancing Barber

to shift?'

'I think they're doing that already,' the Warden smirked. 'Oh,' he realised he'd misheard, 'you mean we should move them along?'

'And quickly,' said his assistant, 'before anyone sees them...'

Zena and Lenka were both busy and didn't appreciate being interrupted, especially due to their proximity to thorny rose bushes. 'What you want?' Zena asked with a straining voice, upon noticing two men staring at her.

The assistant said, 'look here, you're obviously foreigners...' He lingered over every syllable, 'but in this country, you're not allowed to dump in public!'

Lenka's eyes lit up, 'thank you,' she said, taking the newspaper from under his arm and putting the front sheet to good use. 'The British newspaper, it is so much more comfortable on the buttocks.'

'Yes,' Zena said, 'and The Sun, it is the best,' helping herself to the second sheet.

The Park Warden and his assistant stood there aghast, especially when the twins used a further two sheets each before they were satisfied. Although some of the roses were in bloom, their sweet scents were woefully insufficient to mask the stench the twins created. The Park Warden would have to instruct the gardener to ensure this additional fertiliser was properly forked in... the sheer quantity of it would probably do the roses the world of good.

Eventually the sisters pulled down their skirts and carefully waded out through the roses. 'Thank you for your kind use of the paper,' Zena said, shaking the men's hands.

'Yes, you have been the much hospitable,' Lenka added, also shaking their hands.

The Park Warden didn't quite know what to say, other than 'that's quite all right. But in future, please make sure you use a toilet. There are many signposted across the city.'

'Oh, we know,' Zena said, 'but they have the bad tempered women inside them.'

'The very bad tempered,' Lenka added, 'they hit you with the mop and also the brush... Very unfriendly... Worse than the Soviets.'

The Warden and his assistant could only stare at their stained palms, endeavouring to keep them away from their spotless overalls.

Zena pulled a crumpled piece of paper from beneath her clammy waistband and showed it to the Park Warden. 'Here I have the two addresses; both, they are close to The Great Horton Road. You give the directions, yes?'

The Park Warden was all too pleased to show them the way... he and his assistant desperately had to wash their hands. He said, 'follow Manningham Lane straight on and you'll eventually get to the city centre. Then walk up the road that goes to the right of The Alhambra Theatre. The addresses you are looking for are a mile up that road. Hope that helps... Bye...'

Running after the Warden, his assistant said, 'those women certainly bring a more literal meaning to the term "Cack-Handed", if you know what I mean...'

'You're telling me,' said the Warden. 'I'm sure it'll wash off... But the smell will be with me for days...'

'Where shall we go first?' Lenka asked, wondering why the two men sprinted away so quickly.

Zena narrowed her eyes and said, 'follow me... I know the way.'

After walking around in circles for two hours, scaring children and intimidating the most aggressive-looking skinheads, Zena said, 'here it is,' pointing proudly at a road sign, 'The Great Horton Road.'

'What do you suppose is so the "great" about it?' Lenka asked, staring at the ribbon of asphalt stretching up to the horizon. She was already completely out of puff, finding Bradford's undulating streets hard going after a lifetime of walking on the pancake flat Steppes of Chaplinka.

'And here is The Alhambra Theatre,' Zena said, 'does it not look the lovely? Those domes, they are the pretty... Even though they remind me of The Kremlin.' She looked up and admired the fluttering banner advertising *Swan Lake*, 'and look at our niece, is she not the beautiful?'

The Dancing Barber

But Lenka was completely sweltered and didn't have the energy to lift her head to look at the banner; salty perspiration ran into her eyes, making them sting. The sky had cleared and the spring sunshine was unbearably hot. It was nothing compared to Chaplinka in high summer, but at least there, she could dress like her Uncle Viktor. She wafted the flanks of her unbuttoned great-coat and said, 'we have all these empty suitcases; so why do we have to wear all the clothes we brought with us?'

Zena shook her head, 'have you the forgotten that we only have the *two* hands? Each of us can only carry the two suitcases, which is why each one contains four more, you know, like the *Matroshka Doll...*'

'But I am sweating like the pigs,' Lenka said, taking off her great-coat and draping the heavy garment over her arm. 'I will faint if I do not undress!'

Zena twitched her arms up and down, as if impersonating a chicken, listening to the squelching from beneath. 'The four smallest cases, they are the empty,' she said, clawing at the rusty locks with her yellow nails. 'I suppose we can try to squeeze some of our clothes into them?'

After a great deal of fumbling, both Zena and Lenka found just enough room in the smallest cases to accommodate their great-coats and cardigans. They had to make do with tying their heavy woollen skirts, jumpers, and woollen tights around their waists, leaving their "best" clothes slung between the suitcase handles, so as not to crease them any more than they already were.

Zena waddled over to a nearby bench and said, 'we shall sit here in the sun and evaporate the sweat before continuing. Then we shall put on the more presentable clothes. We cannot greet our young sister and niece looking like we have just come out of the river!' She peeled away the sodden vest from her skin and wafted it vigorously.

The warm sun and pleasant breeze soon got to work, rendering their garments with yet another set of brown and yellow tide marks. To passers-by, they must have looked like a pair of tie-died hippies in desperate need of a wash; and their evaporating odours meant there wasn't a living being within fifty yards down-wind of where they sat... The council sent an inspector to check if there had been a blockage in the sewer, but even he couldn't stand the stench...

Although *Swan Lake* hadn't even opened, The Alhambra was already preparing for next week's production, which appeared to be some kind of "summer pantomime". From the bench, Zena and Lenka watched the main actors flouncing around whilst their costumes and props were unloaded from an enormous lorry by a team of workmen, and carried through the stage door. They could have been a legion of giant ants carrying leaves to their nest...

'Would you like the sugared almond?' Zena asked, holding out the crumpled paper bag she'd "acquired" in Manchester.

Lenka didn't need to be asked twice, so took a handful and said, 'thank you.' She quickly set to work, rather noisily sucking off every last bit of sugar until only the almonds remained.

As she spat the bare almonds back into the bag, an officious looking man wearing a beret and carrying a clipboard jumped down from the lorry; putting both his little fingers into his mouth, he whistled at the twins.

Zena and Lenka looked at him with curiosity. For some reason, they had developed a habit of attracting the attention of every officious looking man they recently encountered. And they were fed up of it. They looked at each other and thought: *what have we done this time?*

The man skipped over to them and said with a lisp, 'you two are simply marvellous!'

Zena and Lenka stood up and said, 'we *are*? Why, thank you for the compliment!'

The man beckoned his actor friends over and announced, 'just look at our Ugly Sisters! Aren't they simply fantastic?'

Every actor nodded enthusiastically, and one said, 'they've even got the authentic stench! Foo, take a whiff at this one,' as he sniffed Lenka's armpit, 'what a stink bomb!'

A second actor asked of Zena, 'is that genuine stale sweat, or has it come from a can?'

'And the fleas in your beards, they look so real!' said a third actor, tugging at the strands clinging to Lenka's chin. 'Although I don't know why you bothered... The audience will never see them...'

A fourth actor couldn't help asking, 'and where did you get

The Dancing Barber

those awful dentures?' He peered closer at their craggy teeth, 'you must tell me, because I'd love a set of my own!'

The man with the lisp concluded, 'you method actors are simply wonderful. You really do look like a pair of Ugly Sisters!'

Zena looked at Lenka and said, 'first we are called the tramps, then we are called the women of the "business", and now we are called the ugly! I <u>fed up</u> of the insulting.'

'Shall we teach them the lesson?' Lenka asked.

'One they will never forget!' Zena said, clenching a fist and cracking each of her knuckles in turn.

Chapter 21

The City of Bradford, West Yorkshire, Northern England

'Aye, it were a bloke in a balaclava what done it,' said the lone elderly eyewitness, leaning on a pair of wooden walking sticks that only just managed to prevent him from falling over. 'This car, it drove straight into the motor-bicycle and the rider went flying off and landed where he is now.'

'Then what happened?' Klem asked, kneeling on the floor to check if George still had a pulse. But the man was so well dressed that neither his neck nor his wrists were readily accessible.

'Well, the feller in the balaclava, he got out of the car and pinched the rider's leather satchel, he then got back in the car and sped off. He were a weird looking feller, all dressed in black, and he had a most peculiar style of running, like a long gangly heron.'

Klem had finally peeled back one of George's leather gauntlets, and to his relief found a strong pulse at the man's wrist. He looked up to the sky and thought *thank you*. He was preoccupied with making George more comfortable, propping his head on a folded coat and trying not to become intoxicated with all those petrol fumes. Eventually, he looked up at the elderly eyewitness and said, 'did you say this man was dressed in black? And he stole his leather satchel?'

'Aye,' said the eyewitness, making way for the Ambulance men, 'he cut the shoulder strap with a knife and nicked straight off with it.'

'And did you see the car's number plate?'

'Afraid not, it was covered with mud; and even if it weren't,' he said, adjusting his heavy spectacles, 'me eyesight, it ain't what it used to be. But the car, it was red.'

'You think it was the Vlads?' Taras asked once he and Klem were safely barricaded in the attic, having given minimal information to the Constabulary.

The Dancing Barber

'Oh yes,' Klem said, 'it was them... However, they may have used a "representative", so to speak. That old fellow, he said the car that knocked off George was red. And who do we know who drives a red car?'

'Come on, there must be dozens of red cars around here.'

'Not that many; besides I have a feeling about this,' Klem said, twisting his horseshoe of a moustache back into position.

'The fact this man was wearing black... does that not worry you?'

'No... of course not... Gunter has no interest in my work...'

Taras wasn't so sure... there was no such thing as trustworthy Mafia...

'And didn't that old fellow say the man ran like a long gangly heron? Who does that describe?'

'But I thought your friend Gunter was dealing with Ivan?'

'He is,' Klem smiled, 'but obviously not quickly enough.'

Taras said, 'you don't seem particularly concerned with what's just happened. If the Soviets have all those articles, then you've had it, understand? And more to the point – as you're living in my house – so have I!'

Klem smiled broadly, 'I knew they might try to intercept my articles. And that is why they're still in my possession,' Klem laughed, tapping the envelope he'd extracted from yet another one of his desk's secret compartments. 'So when Ivan – assuming it is Ivan, which it is – hands the satchel he stole over to the Soviet swine that paid him to do it, they'll have nothing more than a stack of Felix the Cat cartoons to amuse themselves with!'

Taras smiled, 'you wily old – '

'I think it's our duty to make life as difficult as possible for dear Ivan. And this is just the start...' Klem narrowed his eyes, 'and with that in mind, I need you to do that little thing now more than ever... It won't take long, and just think of the good it'll do...'

Taras took a deep breath. He said, '<u>No</u>! I want <u>nothing</u> to do with it!'

Chapter 22

Singing the Ukrainian equivalent of *"Oh what a beautiful morning..."* Halyna rubbed her hands together so vigorously that the gold wedding rings on her fingers clicked together as if impersonating a cricket. Linking arms with Mrs Wiggins, she strode down Great Horton Road, breathing in the air of freedom, despite it smelling of exhaust fumes, pollution and her friend's cheap-and-nasty perfume. She said, 'Mrs Wiggins, do you think it would be goodski to go to Busby's first? By now, it shouldn't be as busy.'

'A splendid idea,' replied Mrs Wiggins, wiping her perpetually streaming nose with the first Kleenex of a new packet. After examining her appearance in a small mirror, she applied even more cherry-red lipstick, drawing on her lips a quarter of an inch wider than before. 'It's time us slave-driven wives pampered ourselves.'

'I quite agree,' Halyna said, resisting the urge to skip down the road. She knew her hair, disguised beneath the usual headscarf, was in desperate need of attention, as were her chipped fingernails. She looked at Mrs Wiggins and deduced that a woman whose stockings were entirely covered with ladders, surely needed to replace them. It was a pity the woman couldn't pay more attention to her clothes and less attention to her make-up. With her orange hair, pink cheeks and blue eye-shadow, she looked like a circus clown. In fact, she wore so much make-up that one day, it might just come away in one piece to reveal a perfect effigy of her face... how did the woman find the time to daub it all on in the morning? Maybe she used her husband's plastering trowel? And she smelled so strongly of cheap-and-nasty perfume that Halyna deduced she probably bathed in the stuff... It wasn't even nice smelling and reminded her of the cheap perfume favoured by Soviet women of ill repute. She shook the criticisms from her mind, reminding herself that it was Easter.

So the two women headed directly for Bradford's poshest department store on Manningham Lane. At the bottom of Great Horton Road, they passed The Alhambra's stage door, and

The Dancing Barber

wondered why a lisping man wearing a beret had a metal clothes rail wrapped around his neck as if it were an enormous bow tie. And why on earth were many other people having difficulty extracting their heads from various painted set backdrops? It looked to the women as if these people were posing to have their photographs taken on Blackpool promenade, their heads having been forced through castle walls, tree trunks and one even emerging from an elephant's rear end. And why was one unfortunate individual capable of sweeping the floor even if his hands were full?

Mrs Wiggins gasped at the destruction. She said, 'what do you think's happened?'

Halyna shrugged her shoulders; she didn't really care... so many strange things occurred in Bradford that nothing surprised her any more. She said, 'some sort of accident perhaps? Or maybe a disgruntled actor-type flipped his lid: you know how highly strung these people can be?'

Mrs Wiggins mused that Halyna would know more than most about highly strung actor types; the same rule applied to Ballet Masters... and *some* should be strung up higher than others...

Mrs Wiggins said, 'the old git's gone fishing today...'

'Has he?' asked Halyna, knowing Mrs Wiggins was referring to her husband. She was grateful she didn't call him by his real name, Stanley. She *hated* the name and would lose her temper at the very thought of it.

'Yes, he's gone all the way to a reservoir near Blubberhouses. Lord knows what sort of pleasure he gets from standing in freezing cold water up to his waist for half the day. Mind you, credit where credit's due, the old git catches plenty of fish, big ones too. Pity he ain't got a rod license.'

Halyna smiled, 'my Taras went fishing once. The only thing he caught was a cold...'

Striding past The Gaumont Cinema, its Art Deco styling making it look like The Alhambra's poor relation, the two friends only just dodged a bombardment of bird droppings, the black and white mess straddling where they'd been only a second earlier. Halyna cursed, 'the starlings seem to be rehearsing The Dambuster's Raid, and they're getting more accurate every day.'

Mrs Wiggins examined her coat, thankful she'd survived the raid unscathed. She said, 'only last week I was walking to the dentist, and suffered a direct hit right in the centre of my head! The smell was awful! The dentist had to wear three masks when examining my gums! And when I got back home, it took three goes with the Head & Shoulders to wash the stuff out!'

Halyna wouldn't have had such a problem: she never left the house without her headscarf. She smiled, 'all I'll say is... it's a goodski job that cows can't fly!'

'Yuck,' said Mrs Wiggins, covering her head with her hands, 'all that *stuff* landing on you don't bear thinking about.'

The starlings certainly were out in force, gathering in enormous screeching flocks high above the Town Hall, billowing as if they were enormous sails as they rose up, morphing into so many abstract shapes that Halyna could often find any image, ranging from a piglet or hen to Lenin or Stalin's face, depending on her mood. The clouds would then descend rapidly, swirling and turning in an unexpected direction when they would billow up again, their density so compact that they blotted out the sun with all the ominousness of an approaching storm cloud. Halyna pulled the knot of her headscarf tighter and Mrs Wiggins hoisted up her pink umbrella: this cloud didn't herald the arrival of rain, rather something quite unpleasant, a vast quantity of which had completely covered the Town Hall, whose elaborate Italianate architecture, inspired by the Palazzo Vecchio in Florence, was blackened, as was the majority of Mrs Wiggins' umbrella.

'That was a close one,' said Mrs Wiggins, gingerly peeking up from beneath the rim of her umbrella. 'If they'd have got me, I'd have had to go home for a wash: I couldn't set foot in Busby's in a soiled state!'

Halyna smirked. *No one would probably notice, they'd just think it was another one of your make-up experiments gone wrong.*

With the sky overhead clear, the friends turned a corner and walked past a pile of rubble on their way through Forster Square. Mrs Wiggins said, 'when do you suppose they're going to stop knocking down what's left of the city? If they carry on at this rate, in a few years there'll be nowt left except a great big pile of bricks!'

Halyna shrugged her shoulders, 'they do have a habit of

demolishing such nice buildings: at least the old ones had character, being made of proper sandstone, instead of nasty concrete.'

'The old git says that a good architect can give even nasty concrete some character... He says that cities have to modernise... They can't stay the same forever...'

Halyna cringed, 'to my mind, concrete buildings look far too Soviet. And that is never goodski.' She looked over to the newly-opened Fine Fair Supermarket, its uninspiring concrete façade gleaming in the sunshine. She said, 'I don't know *why* they built that place... such a monstrosity... And they sell such rubbish... I don't know why anyone would want to eat a meal they'd bought in a plastic pot... If this is the way things are going, people won't be cooking fresh food any more... Children will start to think carrots come out of a factory and chips grow on trees!'

Mrs Wiggins would have blushed had the skin of her cheeks not been covered with an eighth of an inch of make-up. She surreptitiously zipped up her handbag to hide the pre-packaged meat and potato pie she'd bought for tonight's dinner... She knew that if – by some miracle – the old git caught some fish, the game-keeper would make him throw them back. Besides, in her opinion there were "nowt" wrong with eating meals that came in plastic pots... she never did like cooking "proper"... it was too much of a faff.

'All I shall say is this,' Halyna concluded, 'at least on a normal day when the factory chimneys are spewing out all that filthy smoke, we won't be able to see whatever horrible things they eventually build... I've seen the drawings in the Telegraph & Argus... they look like Soviet municipal buildings... ghastly...'

Mrs Wiggins smiled, 'I can't understand why they would use white concrete in a polluted town like Bradford? Within a week it'll be as black as a coalminer's face after a shift down the pit!'

The friends whizzed up Darley Street and along Manor Row, weaving their way through the throngs of people that all seemed to be walking in every direction except theirs, some heading to the park, others to the train station, or simply out for a stroll. And they were all in their best clothes; men in smart three-piece suits, ladies in flowing dresses and white gloves. But the former still retained their flat-caps and the latter, their headscarves.

Across the country, shops were forbidden from opening on a Sunday, but in Bradford, one particular store was granted a special license to remain open over the Easter weekend... Shoppers had flocked from miles around to take advantage of Busby's Famous Spring Sale that had started on Good Friday and would end on Easter Monday. Halyna wondered why this holiest of days had not been treated as such, before realising that she was just as guilty as everyone else for not observing the sanctity of the day. She felt especially sorry for all the workers who had to break their Sabbath... Not even the promise of *double time* would induce her to work on a Sunday.

Manningham Lane was exceptionally busy, so the friends hopped onto the road to overtake the slow-moving crowd, being careful to dodge the heavy traffic... and more importantly, dodge The Gossipmonger and her Gaggle of mothballed old women. Halyna was surprised such a "high and mighty" woman would dare go shopping on Easter Sunday... then again, she was sure that even The Gossipmonger would find it impossible to look down her nose at herself... especially in light of her son's behaviour.

Busby's ornate façade soon loomed on the horizon, its soldierly flags fluttering in the light breeze. The closer they got to the department store, regarded by many as the "Harrods of the North", the more people they encountered, and so the slower their progress became. They could just make out the distant figures of the doormen, tipping their tall hats to even the scruffiest of customers.

'Are you enjoying playing the piano for my husband?' Halyna asked, hoping she wouldn't regret it.

'I can't lie to you,' Mrs Wiggins said, 'but I think your husband is the <u>rudest</u> man I've ever met. I don't know *how* you put up with him! The way he...'

'Oh I've had twenty years to get used to it,' Halyna interrupted politely, for she knew her friend was about to embark on a ten-minute rant. 'He's only like that because he's a perfectionist. And nothing is *ever* right for him.'

'You don't need to tell me that! The way he speaks to his students is simply unforgivable! He calls one girl a fat pig, and says others dance like elephants! And if anybody puts so much as a foot wrong, he canes them so hard that even I can feel their pain.'

The Dancing Barber

Mrs Wiggins rubbed her backside, 'it's a wonder he has any students left!'

Halyna couldn't disagree, 'but he is a good teacher?'

'Of course,' Mrs Wiggins said, blowing her nose so strongly that bits of Kleenex exploded in every direction. 'There's no denying that! Given the patience, I dare say he could mould anyone into an excellent dancer. It's just his methods I disagree with. He needs to realise that he isn't herding cows in a field! They aren't animals, they're children!'

Halyna smiled, 'to Taras that amounts to pretty much the same thing…'

Mrs Wiggins couldn't disagree.

'And anyway,' Halyna continued, 'Taras is *firmly* in the dog house as far as I'm concerned!'

'So you're still on strike then?' Mrs Wiggins asked, preparing to hoist up her splattered umbrella should a starling decide to fly overhead. 'Good for you!'

'Of course I'm on strike,' Halyna said with a smile, 'I've set my mind on making that man appreciate me: when he gets tired of washing and ironing his own clothes and eating honey and oat bran for lunch, then he'll <u>know</u> how much he's taken me for granted!'

'So he's doing all the housework then?'

Halyna smirked, 'he doesn't know one end of a vacuum cleaner from the other! And I know for a fact he's been wearing the same pair of undies for the last week!' She held her nose, 'if he ever bothers to take them off, they'll be going straight in the dustbin… they'll be *way* beyond washing!'

'You're a brave woman Halyna, especially with his temper…'

'Don't you worry; I know *precisely* how to control his temper,' Halyna said with a wry smile and a wink.

'But what about your plants: they won't last long if you leave him to look after them! He'll probably water them with samahon!'

'Don't worry about my plants: I've been feeding and watering them during the night. I couldn't let them suffer…' She sighed, 'they're like all the other children I couldn't have… And you're right: he *had* been watering my geranium with samahon… but I emptied the bottle and replaced it with water… Now every time he thinks he's killing my favourite plant, he's actually doing it goodski!'

'I'm so glad. It's always a joy to wander past your kitchen window and see what's in flower: it's like a miniature tropical jungle!' Mrs Wiggins recalled last year's display with all the flowering cyclamen in magenta and vermilion, pure white peace lilies and pink geraniums, and the beautifully glossy leaves of an enormous aspidistra, rubber plant and even the Mother-in-law's tongue that almost reached the top of the tall window.

Halyna waved a crafty finger, 'and he thinks he's harming my favourite geranium by blowing cigarette smoke at it... But Pavlo's immune to it; he's a strong little fellow.'

Mrs Wiggins smiled; her friend had named every one of her plants, and often spoke to them more than she did to her own husband. She mused that if Taras was her husband, she'd do exactly the same thing... either that or divorce the miserable git.

'And do you know what?' Halyna said excitedly, 'the three Pussy Willows the Priest gave me at church last week – you know, because it was Palm Sunday – well, they've actually rooted! I'd put them in water and talked to them every day: so my perseverance has paid off! My Mama always says that if the Pussy Willows take root, then it is a goodski sign that the rest of the year will be goodski!'

Mrs Wiggins hoped her friend's omen was right; the last few years had felt like she'd been wading through manure up to the waist; some good luck was long overdue...

The two friends joined the end of a millipede of people that eventually wound its way into Busby's, their feet constantly shuffling forward ever so slightly, yet the entrance never seeming to get any closer. They both waited patiently and Mrs Wiggins entertained herself by eavesdropping on the conversations of the people around her:

'*I caught him at it again, you know...*' said a wrinkled-stockinged biddy in front of her.

'*I saw three fellers going into her house... three! And none of them were her husband...*' said a chain-smoking woman behind, dressed in a cleaner's tabard, her hair still in rollers.

'*Well, after what I did to him, he wouldn't dare do that again...*' said the wrinkled-stockinged biddy.

'*Mmm... he'll have to sew them back on first...*' said a vicious looking woman with cauliflower ears, further down the queue.

They were only fragments of conversations, exchanged in the midst of a smog of cigarette smoke, but they certainly got Mrs Wiggins' imagination whirring. She asked Halyna, 'what do you suppose she caught him doing? What will he have to sew back on first?'

But Halyna was never interested in such depravity. 'Shhh,' she said, honing in on a distant sound, 'did you hear that?'

'Hear what?'

Halyna shrugged her shoulders, 'I thought I heard someone call our names?'

'I didn't hear anything…'

'And you wouldn't… you're too busy trying to work out what that woman was doing with three men in her house…' Halyna looked around, 'there it is again…' she said, 'I just heard someone call our names.'

Mrs Wiggins also looked around, but didn't see anyone she recognised in amongst the milling crowd. 'Maybe you're hearing things? You know what you're like with that tinnitus.'

'Mrs Halyna! Mrs Wiggins!' shouted the mysterious voice again, 'I'm over here!'

The women swivelled their heads around, as if they were a pair of barn owls, determined to see who was calling them. It was then when they noticed a slender figure jumping up and down in amongst the crowd as if on a trampoline, waving her arms as if communicating in semaphore and calling: <u>Hello</u>! I'm over here!'

'Good Heavens,' Halyna said, 'it's Natalka…'

'What *is* that silly girl doing jumping on that ankle?' asked Mrs Wiggins. 'Is she insane?'

When the crowds parted, Halyna was relieved to see the girl was only hopping on her good leg, yet still managing to leap four feet into the air. She had to hop so high, because she was stuck behind a pair of fat women who were each as large and as sessile as telephone boxes, refusing to get out of her way. Every time she moved to one side, they also moved; Halyna could see the infuriation in Natalka's face. Eventually a gap in the traffic opened up… Halyna and Mrs Wiggins watched Natalka dash across the road, finally able to pass the fat women. But the fat women were hot on her heels, determined to keep up with her…

Halyna then realised – especially after seeing the enormous cheap plastic suitcases, and smelling the distinctive whiff of farmyard on the breeze – precisely who the fat women were. She asked, 'are *those* your aunties?'

'Yes,' Natalka said glumly, 'and I drew the short straw so – sprained ankle or not – I've been showing them the sights for the last hour.' She then added, matter of factly, 'we've just been thrown out of the swimming baths.'

'Why?' Mrs Wiggins asked, blowing her nose as if it were a trombone, 'I've never heard of anyone being thrown out of the swimming baths!'

Natalka took a deep breath, 'unfortunately my aunties didn't wear swimming costumes, and after what they left behind bobbing around on the surface, the attendants had no choice but to evacuate the pool and trawl through the water with an enormous net.'

Halyna and Mrs Wiggins nodded at each other discretely. They thought now an opportune moment to bid Natalka farewell and re-join the queue, so as to avoid talking to her aunties… Regrettably, Mrs Wiggins made the mistake of smiling at one of the big women. So before they had chance to escape, both her and Halyna's right hands were encapsulated by the aunties' clammy bear grips, and shook so vigorously that their arms were almost torn off and catapulted across the road.

The aunties said in unison, 'it nice to meet niece's friends, we are to go to her house now. You know she live in Harewood House. It very big house!' Displaying bright white smiles, they said, 'Nice to see you!' They turned to Natalka, 'come on, it is time we went to house!'

Blessedly releasing Halyna and Mrs Wiggins' hands, they waved goodbye and dragged a worried looking Natalka over to the bus stop.

'What was that about Harewood House?' asked Mrs Wiggins, examining her crushed hand, checking no bones were broken.

When Halyna told her, Mrs Wiggins said, 'vanity, it is such a terrible sin, don't you think?'

Halyna used a wet-wipe to cleanse her soiled hand. She offered one to her friend and thought: *thank Heavens I told my mother the truth. The thought of her turning up and expecting to find us living in Bolling Hall would be too much for me to bear! At least now she'll know I'm simply the early morning cleaner, and not Lady of the Manor...*

She said, 'I'm sure Natalka's parents will think of a suitable lie to cover up all the others. They seem to be quite goodski at it.' She gestured towards the aunties' suitcases, 'what do you suppose they've got in there?'

Mrs Wiggins cringed, 'I dread to think... It's certainly not soap...' She'd finally scrubbed her hand clean, and cast the blackened wet-wipe into an adjacent litter bin.

'Nothing,' Halyna said, 'absolutely nothing!'

'But why?'

'They'll have come with a list. And they'll be expecting to fill those suitcases with every item on it.'

Chapter 23

'Remember,' Klem said to the motorcyclist at the back door, 'you must ensure this is delivered by three o'clock. And watch out for red cars, especially those being driven badly by men wearing balaclavas.'

'Righto!' said George's brother, sliding Klem's package into the inside pocket of his leathers. In less than ten seconds, the racing motorcycle was out of sight and on its way to Fleet Street, leaving a cloud of dust in its wake.

'Good news about George, isn't it?' Klem said to an uninterested Mister Pushkin. 'He's a lucky fellow to only have a bruised shoulder after his Superman impersonation…'

But the cat wasn't bothered. It never was, unless food was concerned.

'Come on,' Klem said, letting the cat lead the way. 'Let's go in for some tea.'

With Taras insisting on brooding in the shop, Klem and the Russian Blue scuttled up to the attic. While he waited patiently for the hob kettle to boil, Klem struck a Swan Vesta and lit the tall church candle in its brass holder that never seemed to get any shorter. He hitched up his trousers and knelt at his altar, placing his clasped hands onto the smooth leather cover of the Holy Bible that had been in his family for at least three hundred years.

He prayed: 'whatever happens next o Lord; I know it to be your will. Please grant me the strength to endure what is to come.' He then crossed himself in the Ukrainian Orthodox fashion, 'in the name of the Father, the Son and the Holy Spirit. Amen,' and kissed the Holy Bible.

The whiff of singed whiskers meant only one thing: Mister Pushkin had sniffed the candle flame again… But that didn't stop the cat from tracking the path of a pretty little blue tit that often visited the attic to feast on whatever breadcrumbs Klem left out for it on the balcony.

Blue tits had always been Klem's favourite birds, but this one in particular had a daring personality and would make light work of

The Dancing Barber

dodging Mister Pushkin's frequent pounces. He often held out a finger in the hope of the bird coming to perch on it, but it always refused. Occasionally, a robin would also visit: Klem didn't like this bird as much, but tried to remind himself that it wasn't its fault it had a *red* breast.

He'd read recently that cats could only see in blue and yellow... How lucky they were to live in a world painted in the colours of the Ukrainian Flag. They were doubly lucky, because they were also unable to see the colour red: a trait Klem wished he possessed.

'Ah, thirty years,' Klem muttered, 'thirty years of personal toil has just disappeared off to Fleet Street on the back of a 500cc motorcycle. I hope it was worth it.' He shook the thought from his mind, 'don't be so silly, of course it was worth it!' He stroked Mister Pushkin under the chin and listened to the cat purr like a tractor. 'Don't lose faith now, Klem.' He patted the cat on the head, 'and people told Klem that the power of the written word would never be enough!' He listened to the cat purr louder, 'what was that old saying about the pen being mightier than the sword? Klem will show them that it's true!' He stroked the cat more vigorously, 'yes he will... yes he will!'

Mister Pushkin emitted a slight growl and went to stare at the wall: there was only so much stroking and patting it could tolerate. The cat also found it unnerving that its owner was talking to himself again.

'Sorry Pushkin,' said Klem, 'I know people say it's the first sign of madness, but you and I know that I've been going mad for years! Are you surprised after what I've – after what *we've* – been through?'

But the cat continued to be transfixed by the wall, wondering if it'd get told off if it sank its claws into the pure white plaster and had a good scratch... The plaster looked so soft that it reckoned it could climb up the wall like "Spider Cat"... and maybe then wander around on the ceiling...

With the kettle taking its time to boil, Klem reflected that if it hadn't been for Voloshin's calming presence, Ukraine would have long ago found herself involved in an unwinnable war against the Soviet Union, the consequences of which were too horrific to contemplate.

Ask any Ukrainian who they thought their national hero was

and more often than not, Stepan Bandera would come top of the list. But Klem never did like Bandera... the man went completely against Voloshin's peaceful principles. His branch of the *Organisation of Ukrainian Nationalists* placed too much emphasis on guerrilla activities and appallingly poor-quality propaganda for Klem's liking. In Klem's opinion, Bandera's actions did far more harm than good, the legacy of which would take decades to rectify. And because of Bandera, the Soviets treated every partisan – peaceful or otherwise – in the same poison-tipped umbrella way. Bandera was hated so much that the Soviets even took his name as a synonym for "Enemy of the State"... something Bandera probably relished. Voloshin however, became a synonym for "Pain in the Other End"...

'Don't you dare,' said Klem, watching the cat's unsheathed claws poised to take a swipe at the wall. 'Taras'll do his nut!'

Mister Pushkin growled and hunkered down as if it were a mother hen, but it continued to stare at the wall.

Klem wondered whether it was possible for a cat to be depressed... It did a lot of staring – if not at the wall, then at the floor – and it never looked remotely happy...

Recognising the cat was obviously in a bad mood and wanted to be left alone, Klem went over to his desk and extracted a tatty file from a compartment concealed beneath the writing slope. It was the first time he'd looked at this file in months: if the Soviet Secret Police knew he had it, he'd be shot on the spot. He pulled out a selection of dog-eared, musty leaflets that were brown with age: ancient examples of Bandera's propaganda that encouraged Ukrainians to "liquidate" as many Soviets as possible, just as the – he hated the word – "Kulaks" were "liquidated" by the Soviets in 1933. He shook his head as he recalled telling Bandera at the time that such propaganda would reduce Ukrainians to the Soviets' level. But Bandera could only laugh in his face, telling him that he was too soft for his own good... Klem would rather be soft and alive, than hard and dead...

Klem had only ever been concerned with the truth, and was faithful to the fact that the <u>truth</u> would unshackle Ukraine. But as Voloshin once said, "truth without proof was useless." Back in Bandera's time, the truth was known, but unfortunately there was neither proof nor the will within the *Organisation of Ukrainian*

The Dancing Barber

Nationalists to find it. But over the last few years, Klem had independently collated plenty of proof and Voloshin was on the cusp of delivering the news to a soon-to-be horrified world. Klem felt a shiver down his spine, thinking that this time tomorrow, everyone will know that Stalin's Collectivisation policy, which led to The Great Famine, was his way of eliminating what he called the "Ukrainian Problem". And not even the mighty Khrushchev would be able to argue.

Before Klem put the file away, he examined the grainy images of another pair of partisans he utterly disapproved of: Ivan Mazepa and Symon Petliura. They, just like Bandera failed miserably and yet were regarded as national heroes. Even after all their efforts, Ukraine was still not independent: centuries of wars, battles and countless loss of life had achieved nothing but bitterness and despondency. But now the politics of the world were changing and Klem had faith in Voloshin to succeed where so many had failed.

Bored with the wall, the cat chased the blue tit out onto the balcony and up onto the roof, but had to admit defeat when the bird fluttered up onto the tall television aerial. Mister Pushkin could only sulk as the bird twittered mockingly before flying off, dropping a tiny pellet that only just missed the cat's furry nose. As if they were radar dishes, the cat's ears swivelled around, honing in on the sound of the hob kettle's piercing whistle. It was tea-time, which for the cat, meant a plate of delicious sirloin steak…

With the tea mashing in the pot, Klem tried to nibble one of Halyna's sturdy biscuits, before giving up and reaching for the Digestives… His nerves were shot to pieces and the sooner tomorrow was over, the better he'd feel. It was at times like these he used to reach for the wine. But now, his willpower was immense and the stresses and strains of the last few days would be easily soothed away with a cup – or three – of Peppermint tea. Surely, if the Vlads were coming for him, they'd have turned up by now…?

Chapter 24

'A fur coat!' Taras declared after several hours' intense deliberation. 'I'll get her a genuine fur coat... She's always wanted one! A good, <u>second hand</u> fur coat. Rabbit would be cheapest... I'm sure she'll understand...'

He counted the pennies in his till and decided there were probably just about enough. And if there weren't, he'd haggle as usual, maybe offering something from his clothes rail in part exchange. He liked it when he had a good idea; it made him feel all tingly inside... he should have them more often.

But then he slammed shut the drawer of his till: he remembered that decades ago, he'd bought Halyna a coat of what he'd called "stimulated fur" that looked just like the real thing... but the static electricity it generated was so great, it not only made her hair stand on end, but also the hair of anyone within a five foot radius! He also remembered that in the summer, it became infested with fleas and then began to malt. But worst of all: it somehow managed to confuse a male dog in the park... an experience that upset her so much that she had to throw it away; and who could blame her?

But what if he bought her a *proper* one this time, one made of *actual* fur...? Lightning doesn't strike in the same place twice... He reopened his till and counted out the piles of pennies. Besides, Halyna surely would have forgotten about the dog incident by now...

This was the best idea he'd had in a long time: and there were plenty more to come...

Decisively, he stubbed out his cigarette, declaring that from today, he was to be a 'modern man', resolving that he would no longer take his wife for granted. She would still have to clean the house and iron his shirts: a man of his status would never stoop so low as to do such menial tasks. But he thought it was acceptable for him to occasionally cook dinner...

So later this afternoon, he'd send Sofia to the Chippy at least two hours before they were to set off for The Alhambra. He'd serve the fish and chips on warmed plates and would even get

The Dancing Barber

some mushy peas. They might even use proper knives and forks, instead of the two-pronged wooden ones... *Ah!* He could already taste that crispy battered haddock and smell the mouth-watering aromas of chunky chips that had been lovingly fried in beef dripping, sprinkled all over with salt and vinegar.

He knew how to make Halyna happy and liked the idea of being a modern man so much that he lit another cigarette to celebrate, inserting it into a long black holder reminiscent of the one Klem's friend in Jamaica uses when in a creative mood... Klem had one of his signed first editions somewhere... and with two of his novels already made into films, its value would surely rocket... Feeling a surge of creativity coming on, he flipped open his ballet notebook, unsheathed a green felt-tip-pen and began refining the choreography he planned for *The Nutcracker*, populating page after page with complex hieroglyphics.

Just as he was getting into his stride, the doorbell's incessant ringing interrupted his creative flow; he frowned and screwed his cigarette into the ashtray. It was bound to be one of those pesky Urchins goading a reaction from him. He wished he knew where they lived, so he could go and tell their parents precisely what he thought of their parenting skills. One Urchin in particular – the one with the grubby bedsheet – thought it was funny to shout "Tar-Arse! Tar-Arse!" at him from across the street, whilst slapping his backside: he'd take a cane to him if he could...

So Taras swung his weight over to the door, determined to give the Urchins the largest piece of his mind he'd ever given. He might even give them an old-fashioned smack around the head, or maybe two. But what stared through the glass at him was anything but a pesky kid. Immediately, his rage diffused, and was replaced by a compost of fear and panic. Without even opening the door, he knew precisely who these men were, what they were and what they wanted. He prayed Klem would stay silently up in the attic, whilst he tried to get rid of them...

The goons stood with their arms folded, staring coldly at Taras through the glass. And yet the bell continued to ring.

With trembling hands, Taras unlocked and opened the door, but only wide enough to reach around to mute the doorbell by freeing the little white button that had become stuck through overuse.

Employing his politest voice, he said, 'good afternoon gentlemen, if you're here for a haircut, I'm afraid I'm not open today.' He began to close the door, wedging his size eleven foot firmly behind it.

One of the goons said, with a voice so deep that it made the ground tremble, 'Klem, we want speak to him.'

Taras shook his head, 'Klem, you say? Sorry gentlemen, but my name isn't Klem. In fact, I've never heard of a Klem.' He continued to smile politely while holding his breath... their halitosis smelled worse than nerve gas and was probably just as deadly.

The goons whispered obstinately to one another; fidgeting in awkward-looking suits that were the standard civilian uniform for members of their organisation. Their hostile and bloodshot eyes bored straight through to the back of his skull... 'You sure?' one of the goons said, 'we told the man called Klem lives <u>here</u>. And the information we have <u>cannot</u> be wrong.'

'Unfortunately gentlemen, it seems you have been given erroneous information.'

The goons' eyebrows wrinkled and met in the middle, giving the impression that long hairy caterpillars had taken up residence across the widths of their protruding foreheads.

Taras clarified, 'what I mean to say is, whoever told you this Klem – whoever he is – lives here, got it wrong. Now, if you'll please excuse me.'

He closed, locked, bolted and chained the door, backing his way into the shop. He went to his small desk and peered through the window, waiting for the goons to go. Once they had gone, he would sprint up to the attic and warn Klem that the Vlads had traced him to this address – undoubtedly thanks to Ivan – and sent some unsavoury looking goons to "arrest" him. Taras had never seen such tough and ugly goons in his entire life; compared to them, the Nazi guards in the labour camp were Sunday school teachers.

And it would be a pity, but Klem's poetry recital tonight would definitely have to be cancelled. The Bishop would have to be disappointed...

After five minutes of standing on the doorstep, grumbling to one another, the goons finally decided to wander off: but not far enough. Taras noticed they positioned themselves across the street and were, as American gangsters would say, "staking out the joint". If they were to look up from that position, they would easily see the attic window.

There wasn't a moment to lose...

Taras dashed to the foot of the stairs. After he'd only ascended three steps, there was a knock on the door so loud, he thought it was being kicked in.

He wiped the sweat from his brow and calmly went back, determined – whatever they might do to him – to stick to his story. He had a horrible feeling the goons had seen Klem standing by the attic window... Their pockets were probably filled with coshes, truncheons and knuckle-dusters and they would swiftly use them to punish him for deceiving them, before storming up to the attic to give Klem the same treatment... or worse...

Taras couldn't believe his luck... the goons were still across the street, drinking something strongly alcoholic and arguing with one another. But they kept their hostile eyes constantly trained on the odd-looking man currently hammering the shop door with his clenched, yet feeble fist.

Taras' relief was short-lived: having to deal with Soviet goons may have been frightening, but it was strangely preferable to the prospect of dealing with the durak now staring straight at him through the glass. This man had one of those faces that demanded punching; in fact it insisted on it.

Taras pointed to the "Closed" sign and gestured with his thumb for Ivan to clear off. But The Ginger Rasputin continued to hammer. Taras thought: *If this piece of work is here to repossess my house, I'll tell him to go to Hell! Hang on... he could just as likely try to wheedle his way inside, leading the Vlads straight to Klem... in which case, he can definitely go to Hell!*

Taras shouted, 'go away!' and began to pull down the blind. But Ivan didn't move, and hammered on the door even louder.

Taras then noticed a familiar silhouette loitering almost invisibly at the bus stop... Wherever The Ginger Rasputin went, the anonymous looking man was never far behind; and today was no exception. He wished the man would, this instant, come over and sort out Ivan; anything to make him stop hammering on his door and attracting unwanted attention. Taras shouted, 'clear off!'

and pulled down the blind even faster.

Ivan whimpered, 'listen Taras, I'm here to extend the hand of f-friendship.' He crouched so as to maintain eye contact while the blind descended as if it were the blade of a guillotine. 'It seems I o-o-owe you an ap-ap-apology.'

'Oh yes?' Taras said, halting the guillotine, wondering why Ivan's voice didn't sound as smarmy as usual. He thought it was worth hearing what the durak had to say, if only for the sake of entertainment. He shrugged his shoulders, before unchaining, unbolting and unlocking the door. He opened it by only a few inches. 'For what, exactly, are you apologising for? Could it be for ruining my reputation as a barber, by falsely accusing me of providing you with Imaac shampoo? Or could it be for inflicting your talent-less daughter on my ballet? Or perhaps you're apologising for your foul-mouthed mother? Or… now this is a good one,' Taras said, scratching his dyed hair, 'could it be for a certain car "accident" that occurred today? Mmm?'

'I know *n-n-nothing* of a c-c-car accident,' Ivan said, robustly shaking his head; what remained of his singed beard swaying in the breeze.

Taras always prided himself in being a good judge of character. He thought: *he sounds genuine enough... but he is a professional liar...*

'I think this feud has gone on for long enough, and I d-d-don't blame Klem for what he did; I *p-p-probably* deserved it.' Ivan couldn't believe what he was saying; and Taras' floating eyebrows suggested he couldn't believe it either.

Ivan felt the patchiness of his singed beard, 'so I think it's about time we buried the hatchet…' Carefully avoiding seeing his reflection in any of Taras' mirrors, he said, 'please, would you shave off what's l-l-left of my b-b-beard? I can't attend The Alhambra tonight l-l-looking like a l-l-leper?'

Taras smiled inwardly, thinking: *You are a leper in every other sense of the word, so why not look like one? And as for burying the hatchet, most people I know would like to bury it in the back of your skull!*

'All right,' Taras said, unwedging his suede shoe from behind the door. 'Come in and I'll scrape your chin.'

Ivan said, 'err… th-thank you and err… th-thank you also for

The Dancing Barber

forgiving me.' Completely ignoring Taras' expression of disbelief, he added, 'and if K-Klem's home, I'd like to a-a-apologise to him *personally*.'

Taras shook his head. *Here it is... the real reason for his visit...* He said, 'Klem's moved out. I don't know where he's gone. Nobody does.' Taras hoped his lie was believable... Everyone in the street knew Klem hadn't moved out... certainly not without taking all his Victorian furniture with him... shifting all that needed two removal vans and six strong men...

Ivan's expression remained impassive; and although Taras was thankful Ivan said no more about it, he was nevertheless curious as to the reason why?

Through the mirror opposite the window, Taras saw the goons watch with great interest as the sunburnt man lunged indoors, hung up his fedora and rain coat and sat in the chair. Taras believed they were waiting for Ivan to give a pre-arranged signal of some kind... so decided to watch his every move... He draped an unwashed cape over his customer's feeble torso, and fastened it tightly around his neck, resisting the urge to garrotte him.

An awkward few moments of silence came to an end when Taras unapologetically flung a boiling hot towel onto his customer's face... the resultant high-pitched scream making the dog in the back yard howl like the Hound of the Baskervilles. With the towel clinging to Ivan's face, Taras amused himself by thinking that it could have been Ivan's death mask...

Having recovered from his impromptu scalding, Ivan couldn't stop fidgeting in the sticky PVC chair, constantly rocking from side to side... he knew the creaking and squeaking was driving Taras mad, but he continued nevertheless. Eventually, he said, 'my m-mother and I are looking forward to seeing our Oksana p-p-perform. I know she's not the easiest p-p-pupil, so I th-thank you for giving her the op-op-opportunity...'

'I *beg* your pardon?' Taras said, checking the bluntness of his cut-throat razor by flicking the blade against his thumb, images of Sweeny Todd floating around in his head. 'As I remember it, you didn't exactly give me much choice?'

'That was unfortunate,' Ivan said, '*I* was only going to increase your m-m-mortgage r-r-repayments by a few percent to,' he reached up from under the unwashed cape and gently stroked his smooth scalp, 'to compensate for my sudden b-b-baldness. But it was my <u>mother's</u> idea to coerce you into casting Oksana as Odile, <u>n-n-not</u> mine.'

'*Really?*' Taras said, stirring an ancient pot of shaving cream that could have been filled with scrambled eggs… He couldn't imagine it being any other way… Ivan had always been a "Mummy's Boy" and The Gossipmonger had been a conniving cow ever since Taras had the misfortune of dancing with her in St Petersburg all those years ago. He hated her then, he loathed her now. When the French Army liberated her from the Nazi labour camp in 1945, she could have gone to America, Canada or Australia, but – as if purely to annoy him – she had to settle in Bradford. The woman was a spectre of criticism that followed him everywhere, along with the whiff of mothballs.

'Oh, by the way,' Ivan smiled, 'it wasn't your shampoo that caused this…' Again, he stroked his smooth scalp that showed only a few iron fillings of regrowth. 'It seems Oksana decided to play a little joke on me…' He tried to make light of the situation, but began to regret it the moment he saw the way in which Taras held the bone-handled razor. 'So you see, I could q-q-quite understand if you wanted to d-d-drop her from the d-d-dance… and I'll tell my m-m-mother – she hasn't got a clue about Oksana's antics – that I've decided to be l-l-lenient as a g-g-gesture of goodwill. It *is* Easter… What do you th-th-think?'

When Taras approached, aiming the blade at his customer's proffered throat, droplets of sweat oozed from Ivan's forehead, streaming down his face and under his collar…

If Taras allowed himself to get any angrier, superheated steam would explode from his ears and whistle louder than Klem's kettle up in the attic… which he hoped Ivan hadn't noticed. But sensibly, as he remembered who provided him with his mortgage, he resisted the urge to kick the fiend out onto the street. He hated bottling up his anger, but didn't have any option. And it was a wise decision… those Soviet goons were still watching the shop far too inquisitively, and drawing attention would certainly not be advisable.

With the steam of anger simmering from his ears, Taras daubed Ivan's patchy ginger face fungus with the minimal amount of scrambled egg.

The Dancing Barber

Ivan breathed a sigh of relief when Taras slotted the bone-handled razor back onto the rack; but gulped when he selected another, the size of a sickle...

Taras tested the weight of the razor by bouncing it gently in each of his hands, as if he was the knife-thrower from a travelling circus. *So it was <u>Oksana</u> who'd put Imaac in her father's shampoo: maybe the girl wasn't all bad?* Examining the edge of the razor, he stood menacingly beside Ivan's outstretched neck... He asked, 'and how long have you known that Oksana was the culprit?' He feigned laughter, 'I bet you've known for *days* and just used the situation to persecute me. Do you get some sort of pleasure from ruining a man's business?'

'Taras, p-please,' said Ivan, feeling the blunt blade scrape across his scorched neck. 'I came to t-tell you as soon as I found out: h-honestly. I'd caught her earlier t-today, p-putting I-Imaac in my bubble bath. It seems my d-daughter won't be satisfied until I'm *completely* b-balded.'

Shuffling over to scrape the other side of Ivan's neck, Taras saw for himself what had made the church choir nearly plummet from the balcony at the All-Nighter. Was this more of Oksana's handiwork? Had she used masking tape? Or was it sun block?

'Oksana must *really* hate you...' Taras said. *And who could blame her?*

'It seems so. It's all the f-fault of my m-mother... she sm-sm-smothers her t-too m-much.' Ivan flinched when the blade scraped down the full length of his chin. 'You see, she's p-planned out the girl's entire l-life.'

Taras thought: *what are you telling me for?*

Ivan continued, 'she expects h-her to be a b-ballerina, and yet f-feeds her so much that she'd be better off as a junior s-sumo w-wrestler!' Seeing Taras' uninterested expression, he said, 'but I suppose that's not your p-problem. Anyway, I am very s-sorry for all the g-grief: truly I am.'

Outwardly, Taras decided to laugh off the entire incident. 'Oh that's quite all right,' he said, 'I'm sure my ballet can only *benefit* from your daughter's presence. Besides it's too late to make any major changes now.'

'That's very decent of you! Especially after everything that's happened... Oksana is *so* looking forward to performing centre stage... It'll break her little h-heart if she were told she couldn't dance...'

Taras imagined that if Oksana had a heart, it certainly wouldn't be little, and would be covered with a layer of visceral fat an inch thick. He said, sternly, 'in that case, you'd better make sure your daughter concentrates tonight...' He pointed the razor at him, 'because if she makes a bullock of my ballet, I will hold you personally responsible!'

'Agreed. Let's not say any more about it.' Ivan stuck out his chin even more, 'so once you've shaved me, I promise to leave you in peace.'

'Mmm,' said Taras, remembering the anonymous looking man loitering at the bus stop, 'I'm sure you will...'

Ivan smiled, but only briefly.

Taras thought Ivan's sunburnt face made him look even more devilish, and the tiny horn-like bumps on his head (one from the collision with Klem's flask, the other from being dropped in the lavvy) made him wonder whether his customer also had cloven hooves and a tail, and perhaps kept a pitchfork at home.

'What do you know about motorbicycle despatch riders?' Taras asked, scraping Ivan's cheeks, pressing the blade harshly against the red-raw skin, endeavouring to inflict as much discomfort as possible.

'Absolutely n-nothing,' Ivan said, struggling to wriggle away from the razor, despite his head being firmly wedged into the chair.

'Are you sure?' Taras said, wiping the blade on a towel, preparing to shave the man's raw neck again...

'Yes, very s-sure,' Ivan replied. He spoke quietly, for Taras' blunt razor was scraping over his Adam's apple. 'Aw, be c-c-careful Taras,' Ivan screamed. 'Do you have to be so rough?'

'Terribly sorry,' Taras said, dabbing at the oozing blood, 'but I'm bound to nick you if you can't keep still...' He deduced that if Ivan was lying, he was doing it very well. But this man could say he was Sheila from Timbuktu and the needle on a polygraph machine wouldn't twitch...

When Taras had finished, he liberally smeared Ivan's swollen and bleeding face with half a bottle of his most stinging aftershave, causing him once more to scream like a scalded pig.

'If you're ready to forgive Klem,' Taras said, sharpening the blade on a well-worn leather belt, 'then you won't have any intention of telling the "Police" about him?' He looked Ivan squarely in the eyes, 'will you?'

Taras watched Ivan twitch at the mention of the word "Police".

'Of course n-not,' Ivan said, 'I was exceptionally angry after being incarcerated in your outside l-l-lavatory, so I had to let off some s-steam; surely you can understand th-that? I would never go to the "P-Police"... Klem can relax...'

Taras' eyes narrowed, 'and all this blackmailing business... has it come to an end?'

'Naturally,' Ivan said, crossing his fingers in his pocket. 'I behaved foolishly... I am sorry...'

'Mmm,' Taras said, 'I hope you're telling the truth. Because if you're not...' He tested the sharpened blade against his thumb...

'Of c-course I'm t-telling the t-truth.' Ivan perspired more than ever, 'all I want now is a q-quiet l-life. No more h-hassle, just a q-quiet l-life. I'm honestly t-telling the tr-truth. H-Honestly.'

Taras smiled, knowing that he'd just listened to a bucketful of steaming himno.

Bizarrely, Ivan refused to look at his reflection in the mirror Taras brandished before him. 'N-no, it's all right,' he said, 'I tr-trust you to have done a g-good j-job.' He levered himself out of the sticky PVC chair, a puddle of condensation remaining in the space between where his legs had been.

'Suit yourself,' said Taras, wiping the chair with the unwashed cape Ivan had thrown to the floor. He didn't blame Ivan for not wanting to see his reflection... his cheeks and neck were red raw... he'd been hiding beneath that beard for so long that being shaved was a tremendous shock for his delicate skin; and the massive dose of aftershave couldn't have helped. But in the time it took Ivan to pull his corduroys up to his chest and wrestle himself into that ancient misshapen mackintosh the local Urchins called his "flasher's mac", some of the redness had subsided to reveal not only lily-white skin, but also an enormous chin that looked remarkably like a boomerang. Gone was The Ginger Rasputin, only to be replaced by The Bolshevik Bruce Forsyth.

'Now, will that be all?' Taras asked, moving the dawdler towards the door. 'You know I'm not actually open for business today.'

'Oh, so you won't want p-paying then?' Ivan said cheekily, 'thank you very much. See you at The Alhambra!' He placed the fedora onto his bonce and lunged out of the door.

'That no good piece of – ' Taras said, watching his customer stride down the street and frighten passers-by. Even the Urchins ran away when they saw him…

Without wasting a second, Taras closed, locked, bolted and chained the door. He grabbed the cord of the window blind and prepared to pull it down… Then he noticed the goons were missing from across the street… perhaps they'd decided Klem wasn't at home after all? Yeah right, he knew they'd soon be back… On the positive side, the bus stop was also unoccupied… was Ivan finally going to get what he deserved…?

The Dancing Barber

Chapter 25

---------------------------------------✂---------------------------------------

'Oh my goodness, I cannot believe *so* many of my fruits are *so* badly damaged,' said John Street Market's *fruit 'n' veg* man. He batted a bluebottle away from his face, 'I am *so* very sorry.'

'Oh that's quite all right,' replied the grinning Gossipmonger, 'but don't worry, I will take them off your hands if you give me a big discount. I don't mind eating bruised apples.'

'It is *so* very kind of you madam,' said the man, '*so* very kind of you indeed.' He reached across his stall and took the few pennies from The Gossipmonger's hand, not noticing the apple skin beneath her thumb nail.

Hovering a few steps behind, The Gossipmonger's Gaggle was exchanging some of their own private gossip. 'I agree, the girl has her father's personality,' one of them whispered, 'but don't you think she's the spitting image of someone else?'

'Do you mean Billy Bunter or Fatty Arbuckle?' joked another.

'Imagine what she'd look like if she was thinner... who do you see?'

'But that's like imagining a thin pig... it just isn't possible.'

The Gaggle may have tried to hide their sniggering from their leader, but The Gossipmonger always knew when gossip was being exchanged. And she did not like being excluded. 'What are you talking about?' The Gossipmonger croaked, causing many of her Gaggle to almost choke on their dentures.

'Err,' said the sensible one, racking her brain, 'we were talking about, err, about Klem's new pet dog, and how it won't get on with that cat of his.'

The Gaggle all nodded their agreement. They were glad the sensible one had an imagination...

'Mmm,' said The Gossipmonger, 'I thought that was what you were talking about.' She knew perfectly well that it wasn't: she wasn't as stupid as she looked. She also knew there was probably truth in the actual gossip: her son was an excellent liar... he'd learned from the Grand Master. And if she discovered he'd been lying to *her* for all these years, she vowed to make his life even more of a misery than it already was.

The Gaggle thought it wise to continue with their diversion. 'And what a terrible name Klem gave that dog,' said the sensible one, 'it shouldn't be allowed.'

'Mmm, let's hope he never has to call for it in the park!' said The Gossipmonger. She put the clutch of damaged apples into her shopping bag next to the mothballs and chewing tobacco she'd bought earlier. She zipped it up and said, 'I need to go and buy a new headscarf. You can all come and watch me pick one…'

So with a shrug of the shoulders, the Gaggle did as they'd been ordered and marched begrudgingly behind their leader, wondering how much more of the day the old baggage planned to monopolise. And they were convinced their leader's senses were slipping: she'd never swallowed such an obvious "fob off" so easily before… so there must be truth in the gossip.

A few minutes' walk down Manningham Lane, Sofia imagined she was wearing the stunning auburn leather coat displayed on an excessively busty mannequin in the broad window of Busby's clothes department. She stood on her tiptoes so the reflection of her face replaced the plastic head of the mannequin and decided she wanted that coat more than any other thing in the world; she thought it was beautiful and it would make her look like Sophia Loren, or possibly even prettier. She adored the feel and scent of leather, but this coat – being slim-fitting at the waist – probably wouldn't look right when draped over her thighs. And it was far too expensive. She sighed when her eyes shifted their focus onto the reflection of the tatty old thing she was actually wearing: she knew she'd never have any decent clothes. But then she remembered what the nuns always said at school, so decided to be grateful for what she had: there were people far worse off in the world… But still, she couldn't take her eyes off that coat, not realising she was partially blocking the pavement, thus causing throngs of eager shoppers to grumble as they walked around her. Would her thighs always be so big? Probably not; they might get bigger…

Her nose started to twitch with increasing frequency: the

The Dancing Barber

approaching stench of mothballs signalled only one thing. And sure enough, she was soon engulfed by a Gaggle of gossiping old women, who stopped to admire the latest range of headscarves displayed on an array of severed mannequin heads in an adjacent window. So, sandwiched between The Gossipmonger's Gaggle and the milling crowds on Manningham Lane, Sofia had no choice but to listen.

And that was precisely The Gossipmonger's intention. Standing on her imaginary soap-box, she broadcast to her Gaggle:

'Can anybody tell me why we bother paying for our children and grandchildren to attend Taras' studio? The man is as bad a teacher as he is a barber!'

Her Gaggle all nodded enthusiastically, whether they agreed or not.

Sofia glanced at the old hag's reflection in the window and noticed she was staring directly at her... a vicious snake preparing to strike at its prey.

'My daughter, err granddaughter is so talented,' The Gossipmonger continued, chewing up a new piece of tobacco, 'but can Taras uncover her talent?'

Sofia really had to bite her lip.

The look of 'what talent?' rippling through the Gaggle made Sofia smile. However, the instant The Gossipmonger stared at any of them, they shook their heads so forcefully that several sets of rattling dentures were nearly ejected from their mouths.

'No. Exactly. Oksana has been practicing for weeks, but...' The Gossipmonger shrugged her shoulders, then spat out a bolus of sludgy tobacco, which splattered widely across the pavement.

The sensible old woman looked dismally at the brown sticky gunge that had landed only inches from her shiny brogues. She said, with the utmost diplomacy, 'what if Oksana lost a little of her weight? Maybe then she would find it easier to dance?'

The Gaggle winced and prepared to cover their ears.

The Gossipmonger swelled with rage, then barked, 'my daughter, err, granddaughter is not overweight!' She prodded the sensible one with her club hand, 'wouldn't you rather be "chunky" than starving to death like in The Great Famine!' She prodded again, 'have you forgotten how bad it was back then?'

The sensible one said, 'of course not, I'm very sorry.' She

knew that every one of the Gaggle somehow survived The Great Famine by eating leaves, grass and worms. But none of them were ever as desperate for food as The Gossipmonger.

The Gossipmonger tucked her club hand back in her pocket, 'that's quite all right.'

But the sensible one had more to say. 'If Taras is such a bad teacher, then how come our Natalka is doing so well? How come Taras is going to recommend her for the Royal Ballet? And how come all the top ballet critics in the country are coming to see his dancers – your Oksana included – at The Alhambra tonight?'

The Gossipmonger's face turned almost as red as her cut-price fingernailed apples.

Sofia smiled and quietly slipped away. She thought: *it's about time those women stood up to the old bag and realised that they had minds of their own. No wonder Oksana's such an unpleasant heifer, if she's got* that *for a role model. And good on Natalka's grandmother for defending Tato!* She turned the corner, but couldn't resist looking back to see a fierce handbag fight occurring; for women with an average age of almost eighty, they were *so* childish.

After a morning's pampering in Busby's, Mrs Wiggins stepped out onto the pavement, proudly wearing her new pair of stockings, deliberately hitching her dress higher so as to show them off to the full. The longest she'd ever worn a new pair before laddering them was three whole hours, so she was determined to enjoy their pristine condition while it lasted. She carried an enormous carrier bag, emblazoned with the famous Busby's logo, which only contained her old stockings (that she'd keep for emergencies). The bag had sharp little corners that tried their best to snag at her legs, so she held it in front of her, parading it down the street.

Halyna's transformation was far more radical. She'd entered the department store looking like a frustrated Margaret Rutherford, but now – after sessions in the makeup and hair salons – she wouldn't have looked out of place promenading along the French Riviera. And as the afternoon had turned out bright, hot and sunny, it wasn't too much of a stretch of the imagination.

The Dancing Barber

'Are you not too hot in that coat?' asked Mrs Wiggins.

'Only a little,' Halyna said flamboyantly, allowing the flanks of the expensive fur coat to flap in the breeze. It was the plushest, most expensive coat they stocked: its lusciously thick brown pile shimmered in the light, giving the impression that it was also deep purple and even silver in colouration. It smelled of quality: like an expensive musk perfume from Chanel. Halyna hoped everyone would be jealous of it. 'I've always wanted one,' she said, admiring its blue silk lining gleaming in the sunlight. 'But Taras never gets the hint, so I've saved up to buy it myself. And if he doesn't like it, then tough!' she said with a nod of the head.

'Good for you,' Mrs Wiggins said, slightly jealous of her friend's new look. 'With that new hairdo and manicure, and now with this beautiful coat, you'll do Taras proud at tonight's concert! You look every inch the glamorous wife of a famous *and rude* ballet choreographer!' She thought: *It's a pity you're still wearing the apron...*

Halyna smiled; she knew Taras wouldn't notice. He hadn't noticed in years...

Chapter 26

'So who did you say they were?' Klem asked, whilst using a miniature electroplated dustpan and brush to sweep up the tea-leaves he'd annoyingly spilt all over his tea-making table. He was fastidiously tidy most of the time, but especially so when a guest in Taras' newly refurbished attic: he didn't want to be evicted again. Taras wasn't listening, so he repeated his question.

'Well, err...' Taras stuttered, 'I didn't *actually* ask. But it was obvious who they were... so I knew I had to get rid of them as quickly as possible.'

'And they asked for me by name?' Klem said, pouring the tea-leaves back into the caddy, closing the lid with a satisfying click.

Taras nodded, 'they said...' he attempted to imitate their fierce accent, '..."Klem, we want to speak to him!" But they didn't look like friends of yours. They were big, mean-looking goons; not the sort to be messed with.'

'Yes, I know the type. It can only be the Soviet Secret Police,' Klem said calmly, pouring hot, but not boiling water into his teapot, only to realise he'd swept all the tea-leaves back in the caddy. He stopped himself from cursing and shovelled in a heaped teaspoonful; holding the teapot in his asbestos hands, he rotated it clockwise, then anticlockwise, thoroughly swirling the mixture around.

Taras smiled, 'I'm sure at least one of them is called Vladimir, and I'm also sure they'll be back!'

'I don't doubt it,' Klem exhaled slowly, 'but I won't let it worry me. By now,' he consulted his pocket watch, 'my parcel will have been delivered.' He chuckled, 'and some of my articles will already have been printed... Sorry, *Voloshin's* articles...' He smiled, 'millions and millions of copies of the truth! Isn't it wonderful?'

'Yes, wonderful,' Taras said, half-heartedly.

While waiting for the tea to brew – such a process could never be rushed – Klem went to admire an oil painting of the Steppes hanging on the wall above his desk. He imagined himself standing

The Dancing Barber

in the shimmering wheat field with his trouser legs tied with string so as to prevent rodents from climbing up them. To him, this field was like a golden sea, the scythe-wielding harvester, a man in a boat, rowing to the horizon...

It wasn't a particularly good painting, but at least it reminded him of home... he could almost smell the sweet fragrance of the crops...

In spite of the Soviet mismanagement of the land, Ukrainian crop yields were rapidly recovering and would soon be just as luscious as they were when this painting was completed, nearly fifty years ago.

After three minutes had elapsed, Klem decanted the perfectly-brewed tea into a pair of china cups from a height of precisely seven inches... the ideal height for optimal aeration of such superior tea. He said, 'I don't know what I believe least of all: the fact Ivan told the Vlads about me, or that they actually believed him?'

'But that's the interesting thing,' Taras said, 'when Ivan came for a shave this afternoon, he said that he hadn't been to the "Police"... it was just bluster, heat of the moment stuff...'

Klem's silver teaspoon clattered down on a bone china saucer, 'so he's been here, has he?'

Taras nodded, 'he came in for a shave.'

'Well, I hope you used a blunt razor...'

'The bluntest...' Taras smiled, 'it was actually Halyna's favourite kitchen knife...'

'Excellent... But I'm surprised he had much beard left after I'd incinerated it so well last night?' Klem looked introspectively at Taras, 'but the man could have shaved himself, couldn't he? Instead, he came to you. Why? So he could check I was still staying with you: that's why!'

'That was my initial thought, but actually, he didn't show much interest in your whereabouts. I asked him about the "accident" involving the red car and the motorbicycle, but he denied all knowledge. All he spoke about was Oksana and his mother... I thought he was in cahoots with the goons, but no... when he left the shop, they'd disappeared... It just goes to show, nothing is ever quite as it seems with a man like Ivan...'

'Let's hope Gunter sorts him out quickly...'

'Mmm, quicker than that...' said Taras, taking his first ever sip of Peppermint tea, unsure as to whether he could manage a second sip.

'Err... Taras...' said Klem, 'it would do Katya the world of good if you...'

Taras gave him *that* look.

Klem shrugged, 'fair enough, I won't ask again... *At least not today*... Anyway, I don't know why Gunter's taking his time? He's normally very efficient; a little *too* efficient.' He selected a Digestive from the tin, 'we can only assume that – regardless of what Gunter does – the Vlads will try to make their move on me tonight, so we must be vigilant. They'll do everything they can to stop the truth from getting out... And I suppose, if they poke enough people with their cyanide-tipped umbrellas, they could probably still accomplish it?'

Scraping out the gloop of soggy Digestive from the bottom of his cup, Taras said, 'they've got no chance of stopping Voloshin's articles from being printed. So if the Vlads come for you, you might as well tell them where to find Voloshin and maybe then, they'll leave you alone? Understand?'

'You know it is impossible for me to tell those swine where to find Voloshin. In any case, there really is nothing to worry about... I have the dog to protect me, and I have a backup plan of last resort, should the worst happen... which it won't... Here,' he said, giving Taras a fresh cup, 'have some more Peppermint tea to calm your nerves. Remember, if you have faith, then nothing can go wrong.'

Taras sighed... he wished he could believe it.

The Dancing Barber

Chapter 27

By the time Ivan got home, his face – having been soothed by the warm breeze – had finally stopped stinging, but his skin still felt terribly raw. The solid oak front door clunked behind him; he bolted it shut before putting his keys – which his mother had only entrusted him with last year – onto the French-polished table in the hall, throwing his hat and mackintosh to the marble floor.

'Here goes,' he said, having plucked up enough courage to look in the gold framed mirror hanging outside the drawing room door. He'd been hiding behind the beard for so long that he'd forgotten what his face looked like... He dragged his clammy fingers down his cheeks: *is my chin really so big? And look at the state of my skin... it looks like fragments of rotting chicken stapled together...*

Sighing deeply, he lunged into the ornate drawing room and wound-up the Swiss chronometer on the enormous carved marble mantelpiece. He didn't particularly want to go and see his daughter humiliate herself on stage, but his wretched mother was most insistent. It was such a pity Taras didn't jump at the chance of dropping her; but he knew best, it was too short notice. At least it was only two o'clock; so he had a few hours before he'd have to change into his evening wear... and raid his mother's make-up to do something about his face. And after the afternoon's exertions, he was in need of a rest...

So he strode into the glossy, minimalist kitchen and opened the refrigerator concealed behind a highly polished cupboard door. But it was so full of Oksana's pies, pasties, cream-cakes and chocolate that there wasn't any room for proper food.

So while he waited for his mother to return from town, and hopefully bring tonight's dinner, he strode back to the drawing room, poured himself a quarter of a pint of his mother's fruity sherry and relaxed to the military marching music blaring from the gramophone, whilst nibbling on a pickled gherkin. The few friends he had often told him that – with the exception of the seriously contemporary kitchen – the interior of his outwardly rather nondescript terraced house was like a "mini-Versailles".

And as he gazed at the gilded picture frames surrounding the opulent drawing room, shuffled his feet in the deep, plush carpet and listened to the loud ticking of that ridiculously expensive timepiece above the fire, he wished his mother showed more restraint with his money. Looking rich was bad enough, without having to rub people's noses in it.

In a few weeks, he'd be sixty-six years old, and reflected on what it felt like to have been a pensioner for almost an entire year. It didn't bother him too much, because he didn't feel like a pensioner: his only ailment was the stomach ulcer that was the result of all those years of worry. But after being on the run for so long, it was a relief to have finally been caught... Although he wouldn't have all the money tomorrow, he hoped the sight of a pile of cash would buy him a little more time... Gunter was a reasonable man... he'd understand... he hoped... But then he remembered, all too vividly, what happened to the last man who'd dared to double-cross Gunter.

Ivan's mood became deeply melancholic as he contemplated signing the sale documentation for his collection of sixty-six properties. Having to accept only half the market price was agonisingly painful, but being poor and alive was better than being rich and dead.

He closed his eyes to the world; conducting an invisible marching band, using the pickled gherkin as a baton, he allowed the music to relax his taut muscles and the sherry to warm him from within. He smirked; finally that tea drinking cretin was going to get what he deserved. Whatever *they* had planned for him, he hoped it would be long, slow and painful... He sank into the genuine leather sofa, knowing his reward for delivering Klem to *them* would more than make up for temporary hardship. He couldn't believe how good a businessman he was...

The instant he began to unwind, a stout knock on the solid oak front door brought him abruptly back to reality. He wasn't expecting anyone, so he begrudgingly lifted the gramophone needle and stood up. Quietly, he lunged over to the window, avoiding the creaky floorboard, and discretely peered through the net curtains. Whoever was knocking must have been stood very close to the door, because he could only see the outline of their large, curved back. Hesitantly, he strode over to the door and

The Dancing Barber

turned the key in the lock, all the while examining the person's enormous black silhouette in the small frosted window... it was Sunday, so it couldn't have been the postman... and the Jehovah's Witnesses knew never to call again...

He slowly unbolted the door and opened it by a few inches, peering through the gap. Before he'd properly seen who it was, the door was kicked in his face and he was steamrollered to the floor. Then everything went black.

The Vacheron Constantin chronometer on the mantelpiece bonged three times, inducing Ivan's eyes to creak open. But he couldn't see anything. He tried to speak, but he couldn't say anything. He tried to move, but was unable to. In fact, he was very uncomfortable, because his arms and legs had fallen fast asleep and his head throbbed tremendously. His outstretched chin, chest and stomach felt as though they were being crushed.

He groaned as loudly as he could, but it only made the pain worse. The strong smell of mothballs and the feel of plush carpet on his sensitive skin meant he was probably on the drawing room floor. And the approaching footsteps shuddering through his body told him he was not alone. He groaned again, but no-one came to his assistance.

After what seemed like hours, the blindfold was torn away and Ivan squinted at the bright light shining through the Georgian window and pouring into his eyeballs. Slowly, he took in his surroundings... He was lying on his front, in the middle of the drawing room floor, with his hands and feet tightly bound behind his back. He'd been gagged with carpet tape, again, and it tugged terribly on his raw skin.

There must have been a struggle, because the old brass bin, in which his mother spat her ghastly chewing tobacco, had been tipped over and the contents treaded deeply into the plush carpet. She would not be happy.

His bleary eyes focussed on the muddy, but polished army boots directly in front of his face. He looked up and saw pairs of legs, clad in cheap, badly fitting trousers made of what looked like nylon. The baggy trousers were six inches too short and revealed red socks, splattered with mud. Unable to crane his neck any higher, he dropped his head and groaned most miserably, his boomerang chin lancing the rough carpet.

'At least we know where the loyalties of the man lie,' one of his captors said in a deep voice that quaked through the floor.

'And his head will make the good football, no?' said another in a deeper and harsher voice that sounded distinctly Soviet.

'Better not,' said the first captor, observing Ivan's bleeding, bruised and peeling red-raw skin. 'It looks as though the man has been tortured enough recently…'

They stomped off to the kitchen, preventing Ivan from hearing their plans. But the sound of a kitchen knife being sharpened did not bode well, neither did the rasp of more carpet tape...

Ivan gulped. He knew precisely to whom these Soviet voices belonged. And he cursed himself for trusting the Colonel. He'd done everything asked of him, and more, yet he'd still gone back on his word. He could only assume the greedy Colonel wanted his fee for himself... He vowed to seek him out and give him a taste of his own medicine... if he ever escaped these goons alive...

Just as the chronometer bonged half past three, a rough hand that reeked of grime dragged the blindfold back over his eyes. With his ears also covered, he couldn't hear precisely what his captors were saying, but it sounded as though they planned to take him somewhere. He tried to force his tongue between his lips, and somehow dislodge the gag, but it was no use: the carpet tape was too sticky. If only he could cry out for help, then someone might come to rescue him... He doubted anyone would, but it would be worth a try...

The pain in his shoulders and pelvis was immense; the men must have been strong to lift him up by his hands and feet as if he were a heavy bag of shopping. He was sure his shoulders were on the verge of dislocating and he howled in pain. Then he heard the rasping of more carpet tape... it was added to the existing gag, encircling his head many times, muffling his cries.

His captors laughed and shoved him into what felt like a car boot, pressing his limbs into the minute space, wedging him right into the corners. It must have been a tiny car, because they had great difficulty closing the lid. Eventually it did close and he heard the click of the lock.

Now there was nothing but complete darkness and silence. He

tried to wriggle, but was unable to, and he noticed the air was already getting bad...

Sweat poured off his face and dripped onto the vinyl floor. He groaned pitifully. After all the bad things he'd done over the years, he thought there was little point in praying. But he prayed nevertheless...

Chapter 28

Through his half-moon spectacles, Klem inspected his two-pronged wooden fork and said, 'is a fish and chip dinner really the most suitable thing to eat before your performance?'

Taras looked very pleased with himself. He said, 'it is a special treat! I thought I'd cook dinner for once, so as to give Halyna a rest.'

Klem raised an eyebrow, 'I'd hardly call it cooking...'

'I paid for it, didn't I?' Taras said, arranging the salt and vinegar directly in front of him.

Sofia nudged open the door and weaved her way, backwards, into the kitchen. She couldn't look any sulkier if she tried. Plonking the four newspaper parcels onto the bare table, she said, 'I absolutely <u>stink</u> of fish and chips! And why hasn't anybody warmed the plates? And where's the cutlery?'

Klem and Taras held up their two-pronged wooden forks; Taras shrugged his shoulders and said, 'we will eat like the English: directly out of the newspaper!'

Sofia picked up some curls of her hair and put them to her nose. She shook her head and repeated, 'I *absolutely* stink! I'll *have* to have a bath... How can I go to The Alhambra smelling of fish fried in beef dripping...?'

'Oh <u>no</u> you won't,' Taras said, 'it is not Wednesday!'

Grumpily, Sofia unwrapped her dinner and stabbed at a few chips... it was a long time to wait until Wednesday. In all her life, she'd never had a proper bath. Her Mama and Tato had always used the water before her, and sometimes Klem and the cat too. And when her turn finally came, not only was the water cold and filthy, but it always seemed to coincide with one of the mothballed headscarves coming to visit Mama, or a drunken flat-cap coming to visit Tato. She hated sitting in that tin bath in the middle of the kitchen floor, with some old biddy watching as she scrubbed her back... And many a time, she emerged from the water filthier than before she got in. Why couldn't her Tato get a bath installed in the indoor lavvy? There was plenty of room... But no, he liked to

The Dancing Barber

bathe the "old-fashioned" way... But as her Tato said, it wasn't Wednesday: a bath of any kind was not permitted. So she'd have to content herself with a quick scrub with a flannel and then go out and stand in the wind for a while...

Twenty minutes later, father, daughter and lodger scrunched up their beef dripping infused newspapers with satisfaction, and used a Kleenex tissue to scour the grease from around their mouths, screwing up the tissue and adding it to the pile.

Klem smacked his lips together and said, 'that's the way all meals should be: delicious and with no washing up!' He licked clean his two-pronged wooden fork and put it in his waistcoat pocket.

Taras nodded his agreement, 'the chips were a bit soggy, but the haddock was so tasty, I could have eaten three...'

Beneath the table, Mister Pushkin meticulously cleaned its furry face with a moistened paw, paying just as much attention to its whiskers as its owner paid to his moustache. The cat enjoyed a few morsels of haddock and even a chip, but not the mushy pea Klem had managed to crush under his boot.

'Where *has* Halyna got to?' Taras asked, washing down his scrumptious meal with some milky tea. 'That's the last time I cook for her if she can't be bothered to turn up!'

Sofia shrugged her shoulders, 'Mama must be having a pleasant time with Mrs Wiggins; but don't worry, I've put her fish and chips in the oven, so when she returns, it'll still be warm.'

'Mmm,' said Taras, swigging the last of his tea before going down to the studio to collate his things for the short walk to The Alhambra.

Sofia emitted a very unladylike burp; the acidic taste of partially digested haddock and chips up-welling from her stomach. She knew it was the wrong sort of food for before a performance, and imagined that a proper ballerina such as Margot Fonteyn would be appalled at eating such stodge prior to dancing. Thankfully, indigestion never lasted long; but she could feel the molecules of fat floating through her bloodstream and settling at her thighs... she hoped she could still squeeze into her costume...

Ever since Sofia had witnessed her parents' ferocious argument surrounding this woman called Katya and these men called Vlad, she'd wanted to find out more. But neither of these people had been mentioned since, and the atmosphere at home – in spite of her Mama's seemingly unending strike – had been relatively calm.

Contrary to what curiosity did to the cat, Sofia couldn't help but conduct some investigations of her own…

With the exception of Klem sleeping-off his stodgy lunch in the kitchen, the house was empty for at least half an hour… so she lugged her overfed body up to the attic. While catching her breath, she stood on her pointes and reached up for the key Klem balanced in a certain place on the doorframe. She unlocked the padlock and swung open the hasp, keeping the padlock safely in her hand.

She'd known for a long time that most of her parents' arguments seemed to concern Klem, so she deduced the best place to look for evidence for who Katya and Vlad were would be in Klem's domain: specifically within his fancy desk.

Just like the key to the attic door, the key to Klem's fortress of a roll-top desk was balanced high above it, in the lampshade suspended from the ceiling. She was careful not to disturb the dust, and would be equally as careful to return the key to precisely where it had come from… Klem could always tell when his things had been disturbed.

Sofia slid open the desk's corrugated top to uncover the orderly chaos of the creative mind. The jumble of books and papers may have looked a complete mess, but Klem knew precisely where everything was.

She didn't really know what she was looking for, other than for any bits of paper that had the name "Katya" or "Vlad" written on them. But after ten minutes of methodically leafing through all his books and papers she had found nothing remotely relevant. There wasn't even anything hidden beneath his typewriter; she sighed sorrowfully and began to replace every item back to its exact position. She lifted a heavy pile of notebooks that were full of poems he was working on, but couldn't quite remember where they came from: there was so much stuff… it was so confusing... The heavy pile slipped from her hands, slamming harshly onto the mahogany writing surface. She swore, hoping that Klem hadn't heard…

But then she did swear, loudly. The impact of the falling books

The Dancing Barber

had broken Klem's desk, a panel above some tiny drawers had cracked open. The thing was an antique; it was his pride and joy and was worth a small fortune. She started to panic, wondering whether there was any glue in the house.

But then she took a closer look, and was relieved to discover the desk wasn't actually broken... Curiously, this panel was meant to open in such a way. It must have been some sort of secret compartment? She fully slid open the panel and delved inside...

Chapter 29

'That was lovely, Mrs Wiggins,' Halyna said, picking, with her thumb and forefinger, the final few crumbs of Victoria Sandwich from her earthenware plate, with the thoroughness of a wren on a bird table. 'But it's *me* who should be buying *you* the tea and cake for putting up with my Taras!'

'If it makes you feel better, you can buy it next time,' Mrs Wiggins said, gesturing for the waitress with the hair lip to bring the bill. She liked this café: it always smelled of freshly baked cakes, even though it was obvious today's Victoria Sandwich was baked last week. 'Besides I only have to put up with him five evenings a week, whereas you've got him all the time! I mean, has he *always* been *so* difficult?'

'Oh no,' Halyna said, 'when we met in the Labour Camp hospital in 1942, he was lovely, really lovely. He was so kind and considerate and he helped me recover from my shrapnel injuries.'

Mrs Wiggins sniffled with disbelief, muttering, 'kind and considerate…'

Beneath the gingham tablecloth, Halyna massaged her leg, where tiny pieces of metal were so deeply embedded that they were impossible to remove. 'After we married, things were goodski for many years,' she said with a smile, 'but eventually, Taras became more and more dissatisfied with his life in Bradford…'

'But surely, your life here is so much better than it ever was in Ukraine?' Mrs Wiggins asked, pouring the last of the tea from the earthenware teapot, which was still heavy despite being empty. She nodded her thanks to the waitress with the hair lip, and glanced at the bill that had what looked like strawberry jam smeared on it. She looked back at Halyna and said, 'so surely he should be grateful for his blessings?'

'I know he should, and <u>he</u> knows he should, but…' Halyna sighed. 'He was the best ballet dancer in Europe when he graduated from the school in St Petersburg in 1930. There was genuinely no one better. He had the pick of every top ballet

The Dancing Barber

company.'

Mrs Wiggins tried not to giggle; Taras was prone to excessive over exaggeration... The list of "celebrities" he knew personally ranged from Peter Ustinov and Jack Palance to Tino Valdi and Ken Dodd... And over the years, he'd claimed he'd danced with not only Anna Pavlova, but also Margot Fonteyn...

Halyna said dreamily, 'there aren't many people who can lose themselves in dance like Taras. He is so natural, so smooth and so intricate; when he dances, it's like electricity pumping through his veins.' She shrugged her shoulders, 'but because he was Ukrainian, regardless of his talent, he was ultimately destined for the Collective Farm or the Gulag. You see, he was a "Kulak", an intellectual, and the Soviets got rid of anyone who stood in the way of Collectivisation. He was damned lucky not to get shot like the rest of his family...'

'I had no idea,' Mrs Wiggins said, blowing her nose on the last Kleenex of the packet. 'He's never told me any of this.'

'And he wouldn't,' Halyna said, 'he rarely speaks to anyone about what happened... it is just too painful... At first, I didn't think it bothered him... you see, when we settled in Bradford in 1948, our existence was blissful, truly blissful. We had new clothes and plenty to eat. The only thing I didn't like was the concrete tenements, in which we had to live... they looked far too Soviet for my liking! But we both had goodski factory jobs, and for the first few years we saved as much money as we could by living in cheap one-room flats. Eventually, we saved enough money to buy the shop and Taras decided he would take care of my every need; back then, he earned enough money by cutting hair to make me a "kept woman". He was very proud of that. I thought that – just like me – he was satisfied with a simple life...

'All the while, we kept in touch with our friends in America and Canada, and at the time, we were doing comparatively well. But Sofia's birth coincided with his fortieth birthday and that was when things became far from goodski. You see, although his parents were rich, they still sacrificed *a lot* for him to go and study the ballet: they were not rich enough, and ballet school was very expensive... especially for a Ukrainian.' She cast her eyes to the ceiling, 'he knew they were watching, and he desperately wanted them to be proud of his achievements. But it dawned on him that he was too old to be a ballet dancer – even though, with the help of Ralgex, he still practiced daily – and that his time had passed. At that moment, it was as if a little of the spirit inside him had died.'

Mrs Wiggins was enthralled: in the decade she'd known him, Taras had always been a mystery, but at least now, his demeanour was beginning to make sense.

Halyna emitted the longest sigh yet. She said, 'he got terribly depressed and irritable, and the barbering business soon dwindled because of it. And his depression reached its lowest point when our friends across the Atlantic gained their degrees, and embarked on careers as doctors and lawyers, earning more money in a year than Taras earned in a decade! Was he jealous? Of course he was! So he started drinking too much, smoking too much and wallowing in plenty of self-pity. We were soon struggling to pay the bills – especially with Sofia to clothe and feed – and we even missed a mortgage repayment: things were getting very serious.

'That was when I'd decided <u>enough was enough</u>. And the next day I went back to work at Lister Mill and even had to take an early morning cleaning job at Bolling Hall... our savings had all but gone and *he* wasn't any use. I had to get him to snap out of this downward spiral, so told him that it was time for him to think about the ballet again. Not dancing it, but <u>teaching</u> it. It took him some time to get used to the idea, but soon enough the old Taras returned and was full of so much enthusiasm that he thought he could do anything! He fitted out our cellar with a sprung floor, second hand mirrors and *barres* made from broom-handles, and opened for business, taking advantage of some free advertising in the Telegraph and Argus that Klem managed to arrange. A week later, Taras was teaching a full house and loving every moment. And that was when he realised that teaching the next generation of ballet dancers and ballerinas was his ticket to fame and fortune! You see, a back street barber couldn't compete with a doctor or lawyer, but a famous Ballet Master and Choreographer could!' She looked up to the ceiling, 'and importantly, it would make his parents proud. The rekindled fire in his belly was soon a roaring inferno and things were goodski once again!'

Mrs Wiggins said, 'so that is why he's driven those dancers so hard...'

'Correct,' said Halyna, 'he wants them to dance at their full

The Dancing Barber

potential: <u>better</u> than their full potential! And tonight's *Swan Lake* is his way to prove to the world that he has talent worth seeing: both as a dancer and choreographer.' She smiled, 'I hope that if all goes well, he'll be much easier to get along with.'

'I can second that!' Mrs Wiggins said, knowing that if all didn't go well, everybody would have to take cover. She placed a few coins on the table and stood up, waving goodbye to the waitress with the hair lip. 'And with *Swan Lake* in mind, we'd better get going. I've got to make sure the orchestra are ready before Taras comes to inspect them: you know how much he hates listening to them tune up... And I don't want him to give me another headache with all his shouting!'

Halyna smiled. Tonight was the night Taras would probably shout the most; she just hoped he wouldn't burst a blood vessel.

The two women linked arms and decided to walk home through Manningham Park. 'I think we can treat ourselves to an ice-cream,' Halyna said, looking at the time on her old Sekonda wristwatch. 'Besides, I wouldn't bother rushing to check on the orchestra. Taras'll only check them again... even if he has to listen to the tuning up...' She whispered, 'he puts cheese in his ears if he can't stand the din...'

'In that case, why not! I'd *love* an ice-cream. And we've still got plenty of time before "curtain up"!' said a jovial Mrs Wiggins, who without taking "no" for an answer dashed off to buy two ice-cream cones from the Hilton's van and carried them over to the bench Halyna had selected. She also made a mental note never to eat any cheese Taras offered her...

Even though the children's rhyme of *"Hilton's ice-cream tastes like whipped cream"* rang true, both Mrs Wiggins and Halyna liked the taste of whipped cream, so it didn't matter. And the crumbly chocolate ninety-nines made useful scoops, despite melting far too quickly in the afternoon sunshine.

'Look at those blackbirds,' Halyna said, watching them dart across the lawn with their heads bowed and their beaks aerodynamically cleaving their way through the warm spring air like feathered darts. 'Do you think they're having a race?'

'Probably not,' said Mrs Wiggins, juggling an ice-cream cone in one hand and a snotty Kleenex in the other. She looked at the birds inquisitively, 'why are female blackbirds not called brownbirds?'

Halyna shrugged her shoulders, 'that's a question my Sofia always asks. But I have no idea... all I know is the boy ones have yellow beaks and a little yellow smudge under their eyes.'

Mrs Wiggins sneezed so loudly that all the birds in the vicinity scattered. And in the struggle to unravel a fresh Kleenex, she launched her ice-cream high into the air...

With surprisingly quick reflexes, Halyna caught the ice-cream, almost losing her own in the process.

'Thank you,' said Mrs Wiggins, whilst repeatedly sneezing and blowing her nose.

Halyna had known Mrs Wiggins for years, and in all that time, she'd suffered from a perpetual cold. The woman must have been allergic to something... probably that horrendous perfume she bathes in. Was she ever going to see the doctor about it?

'Your Sofia is a clever girl, so intelligent, so inquisitive,' said Mrs Wiggins, wiping her nose. 'Just the sort of daughter I'd have wanted for myself...' She shook her head, 'if only the old git's bits worked as they should...'

'What bits?' asked Halyna, quickly regretting it when Mrs Wiggins explained in unnecessarily excessive detail.

Mrs Wiggins smiled, 'but we've been on the fostering register for a few months... So I'm hopeful that any day soon...'

'Fostering is very admirable,' said Halyna, desperate to hand the cone of melting ice-cream back to her friend. 'Let's hope you get a nice one... Some of them can be real hooligans...'

'I quite agree,' said Mrs Wiggins, blowing her nose as if playing a trombone. She then attended to her false eyelashes... they'd meshed themselves together so tightly that she was unable to open her eyes. A couple of minutes later, she said, 'thank you for saving my ice-cream,' and took back the dripping cone, but only after admiring her combed pipe-cleaner eyelashes in a small mirror, ensuring they were equally spaced.

Halyna couldn't watch when her friend raised the cone into the air, bit off the end and proceeded to suck out the melted vanilla, slurping every last drop until only the ninety-nine remained,

The Dancing Barber

rattling in the cone. Until now, she thought watching Klem eat his Easter "sandwich" was the grossest thing she'd seen in three decades; but that was nothing compared to this...

'I'm not the brightest of women...' said Mrs Wiggins, licking her lips, 'but something you said earlier utterly confused me... it put me in a proper flummox...'

'What confused you?' Halyna asked, preferring not to ask what a "flummox" was.

'You said that Taras were forty when Sofia were born...'

Halyna shrugged, 'what of it?'

'Well, I've done my mathematics... If Taras is fifty-five now, when Sofia were born, he must have been forty-three...?'

Halyna didn't know what to say. She hadn't intended making the error, and was surprised Mrs Wiggins was astute enough to spot it... She took a deep breath, 'you are quite right... Taras *was* forty-three when Sofia was born...'

'I thought so,' interjected Mrs Wiggins.

'But three years before, I was pregnant with our first child...' Halyna's chin quivered ever so slightly, 'we were going to call him Stepan...' She looked up to the blue sky and crossed herself in the Orthodox fashion.

'I am sorry,' said Mrs Wiggins, 'I really am...'

'Even the midwife was surprised Stepan was still-born... I felt fit and healthy, and being seventeen years younger than Taras, there shouldn't have been any problems... But...' she shrugged her shoulders.

Mrs Wiggins blew her nose as if she were a one-woman brass band, 'I am sorry, really I am...'

'We had him cremated, and I sprinkled his ashes into the soil, in which my houseplants grow... so he's still with us, in a way...'

Now Mrs Wiggins understood why those plants looked so healthy.

'The doctors thought I'd miscarried because the stress of pregnancy was too much for my weakened body. I'd endured so much during The Great Famine, and later in the Nazi Labour Camp... I suppose it's understandable...? And they were adamant I wouldn't be able to have any children...' She smiled, 'but then Sofia was born... It was a miracle, a wonderful miracle...'

'A miracle is what it was,' said Mrs Wiggins, resuming her

slurping.

'And one day soon, I'm sure you'll have one of your own…'

'I hope you're right…'

'I am… the Lord works in mysterious ways…'

'I hope He does,' said Mrs Wiggins, 'I really hope He does!'

Halyna closed her eyes, angling her face to the warming rays of the sun.

'Did you hear that?' said Mrs Wiggins with a full mouth. She was sure she heard her name being called from somewhere behind the rose bushes. She looked around, but there was no one there. She shrugged her shoulders and thought nothing more about it. It was no use asking Halyna; with her tinnitus, she often could only hold a conversation by lip-reading. At least the blackbirds were back; the brown one was the winner of their little race and pulled up her prize of a juicy earthworm as if she were an Italian sucking up a strand of wriggly spaghetti.

'When I've saved up enough of my winnings,' said Mrs Wiggins, 'I'm going to buy the old git a pigeon loft. Now he's close to retirement, he quite likes the idea of pigeon racing.'

Halyna smiled, 'at least it'll keep him out of mischief…' She remembered when Taras bought some homing pigeons: they flew straight home the instant they were released… all the way back to Leicester… he never did get his money back… She was glad they went… they made a worse mess of her back yard than Klem's dog. She narrowed her eyes, '*winnings*: you said something about winnings?'

'The Bingo!' declared Mrs Wiggins, munching through her melting ninety-nine. 'Last week, I won more from the Bingo than I'd got from my regular jobs!'

Halyna cringed, 'when I went with you, I didn't win a penny! Besides, you know what The Good Book says about the evils of gambling…'

'But it's not gambling, not the way I do it: I've got a system,' Mrs Wiggins said proudly. 'I run several books at the same time and have been winning five and ten pound prizes every night; I've got a right pile under my mattress! But I tell you, you've got to be quick when they're calling out the numbers: scanning four or five books si-mult-aneously is a skilled business.'

Halyna licked at her remaining ice-cream; last week may well

The Dancing Barber

have been a profitable one for her friend, but how quickly the woman forgets about the months when she too didn't win a penny. She also wished Mrs Wiggins would have more discretion: announcing to the world that she's "got a right pile" under her mattress was never a goodski idea... especially with all those dishonest looking Urchins playing football close by...

Mrs Wiggins extracted the small mirror from her handbag and looked through the fingerprints at her reflection. Deciding her lips weren't quite wide enough, she quickly set to work with the cherry red lipstick, widening the upper margin of her top lip until it touched her nose. She said, 'you know, I think I have too much money under my mattress! And there's bound to be loads left over once I've bought the pigeon loft, so I was thinking... I might go to Busby's and get my hair done how they did yours? What do you think? And maybe also get what they call a facial...?'

Halyna could only smile; they'd have a lot of trouble washing out that terrible orange hair dye. And her friend's eyelashes were so thick with mascara that they looked like a pair of joke shop tarantulas hanging from her brow. She said diplomatically, 'or you could put the money into the Bank; you never know when it might come in handy?'

'Ooo no, I don't trust banks, and neither does the old git,' Mrs Wiggins said with a dismissive wave of the hand, her long false nails clawing through the air. Crunching through the wafer cone, she continued, 'what's the point of having money if you can't enjoy it? That's what I say.'

Halyna resisted the urge to shake her head. Mrs Wiggins was the sort of woman who'd never have any money: it would smoulder away in her purse until she spent it... why couldn't she have the sense to invest it somewhere safe and profitable?

Halyna contented herself in the knowledge that although Taras thought he ran the household finances, the money *she* earned paid the bills. Taras didn't even know she'd been regularly paying into a bank account to save for Sofia's future: if it were down to him, he'd waste it on more tramp clothes and poisonous cigarettes for his shop, and whatever remained, he'd smoke and drink away... And her mother in Ukraine had always been grateful for whatever she'd managed to send back home; she hoped all those dollars – and it *had* to be dollars, *never* pounds sterling – had been put to good use.

'I think someone's calling out our names,' said Halyna, looking around. 'I am sure I recognise that voice...'

Mrs Wiggins turned around so quickly that a blob of ice-cream clinging to the remnants of the wafer cone detached and plopped down the front of her dress. She cursed, trying to mop it up with a snotty tissue. But her efforts only served to rub it deeper into the abstract psychedelic nylon of her best dress, causing her to curse even more.

Halyna grinned, 'that's something you'll have to get used to if you're buying "the old git" a pigeon loft... You'll have to hoist up your umbrella each time you go through the back yard...'

'Very funny,' said Mrs Wiggins, licking off as much as she could, her cherry-red lipstick staining the multi-coloured dress, merging perfectly with the gaudy pattern. She looked around, 'I've been hearing someone call our names for ages... we can't both be imagining it... unless I've also developed tinnitus?' She shrugged, 'maybe I am, maybe I'm not... Anyway... I always forget to ask you... how come Taras decided on ballet instead of Ukrainian National Dancing? I mean Uki Dancing is macho, and much more Taras... whereas ballet is, well, you know...'

Halyna stroked the luscious fur of her coat. She shrugged, 'classical ballet was more in keeping with his background. You see, Uki Dancing was – for want of a better word – for the peasants... and Taras was *never* a peasant...'

Mrs Wiggins could believe it; someone so snobbish could never have come from a humble background...

'Mrs Halyna, Mrs Wiggins!' cried Natalka, limping over to the bench, 'I can't find those stupid women anywhere.'

'Natalka!' said Mrs Wiggins, 'I knew someone had been calling my name!'

'Sit down and take the weight off that ankle,' Halyna said, nudging Mrs Wiggins and her mountain of snotty Kleenex to one side. 'You should be resting. Tell me, what has happened?'

'It's all my mother's fault,' Natalka sobbed, 'if only she hadn't lied about where we lived and what my father did for a job, then there wouldn't have been a problem. But when those stupid women heard that we lived in what they called "the squalor" they were so disgusted that they wandered off in search of chips: and

The Dancing Barber

they didn't even take any money with them. I've been running around trying to find them for an entire hour, and,' she gestured to her extremely sore ankle, 'I think I've done it in *properly* this time. Mr Taras is going to do his nut, isn't he?'

'Don't worry about Mr Taras,' Halyna said, putting a comforting hand on the girl's shoulder. 'You leave him to me. I will make sure everything turns out better than goodski.' Although in reality, she knew precisely how Taras would react: badly or very badly. If only he could realise that Sofia would make a perfectly suitable lead dancer. But he wouldn't be told: he'd have to work it out all by himself...

'And as for those aunties of yours,' Mrs Wiggins said, 'you'll only have to follow your nose... you're bound to find them! Either that, or follow the screams of all the people they've frightened!'

Natalka smiled, 'you're right. I'm sure they haven't gone far.' She then noticed the commotion developing at the far end of the boating lake. She squinted her eyes and saw two troll-like women up to their knees in the water, trying to catch some fish to go with their chips. The furious Park Warden and his irate assistant weren't having any luck in coaxing them out...

'Looks like you've found them,' said Mrs Wiggins. 'Although if I were you, I wouldn't admit to knowing them...'

Halyna nodded, 'have they no shame?'

'Give me strength,' shouted the enraged Warden, 'why do these damned women come to my park?'

'Search me,' screamed his irate assistant, 'we should be grateful they haven't decided to fertilise the rose bushes!'

'But this is worse!' shouted the enraged Warden, 'at least then, they were fully clothed!'

Chapter 30

Ivan swallowed a couple of painkillers and collapsed onto the straw-covered stone floor of his office, a room reminiscent of Scrooge's counting house. Every single bone and muscle ached: he was no stranger to brutal treatment, but what he'd just experienced made a session with the Gestapo feel like a pillow fight. He wedged himself into the corner of the darkened room and tried to focus the whirring kaleidoscope of his mind. But try as he might, he couldn't remember the correct combination for his safe… it was a number he used every day; how could he have forgotten it? All he could do was stare at the calibrated dial, illuminated in a pool of shaky torchlight. He rotated the dial one way and then the other, before yanking the handle of the door that constantly refused to open…

He rubbed the scorched skin on his wrists and ankles; yet more scars to add to his battered body. While incarcerated in the miniscule car boot, he'd somehow contorted his arms to extract a box of Swan Vestas from his trouser pocket and had used every match to melt through the carpet tape. It was painful work, especially with his hands and feet bound behind his back: he hadn't smelled burning flesh for thirty years and was repulsed by the memories it conjured up. With his hands free, he forced open the lid of the car boot with surprising ease and fled as fast as he could down the alley before his captors had even noticed him missing. He only dared to look back once, astonished to discover he hadn't been locked in a conventional car boot; instead it was a trunk strapped to the back of what looked like a rickety vintage motorcar.

So Ivan blundered across town to the safety of his office. He couldn't believe the Colonel had broken his word; especially after everything he'd done for him. This was the final straw: Ivan wanted out. The experience had shown him, once and for all, that absolutely no-one could be trusted. And he didn't care how formidable an opponent the Colonel was, he had to be taught a lesson… even if it killed him…

The Dancing Barber

Ivan then planned to go where no one would find him: not even his daughter and certainly not his mother. And he didn't care what he'd promised the Mafia: they could whistle for their money...

But now, a simple eight-digit code was the only thing standing between him and his escape funds.

Across the street, a pair of expensive Leica binoculars poked through the net curtains, watching Ivan's every move. Behind the lenses, Gunter chuckled to himself so much that he struggled to keep his hands steady; in fact he'd been chuckling to himself for the past few hours...

He'd planned to deal with his deceitful former employee straight after he'd left the barber's shop. But it seemed – rather annoyingly – that another party had a similar idea. So he stealthily followed the goons that followed Ivan and wondered what they had planned for him. They certainly were not members of *his* Mafia... they had the distinctive appearance of Soviet Secret Policemen dressed in poorly fitting nylon suits that were meant to allow them to merge in with the general public, but actually had the opposite effect. And he was seriously impressed by the method they'd used to apprehend Ivan and vowed to try it out one day: carpet tape was much more secure than rope and so easy to apply.

But he was pleased Ivan escaped... he hated the Soviets muscling in. They would have to wait their turn.

So for the last quarter of an hour, Gunter had watched Ivan twiddle the safe's combination and try its handle time and time again... the classic behaviour of a man desperate to escape...

Gunter wished he'd hurry up... his bowels were doing cartwheels; how he cursed eating that dreadful curry last night. Dare he go to the toilet and leave his watching post? Would Ivan remember the combination, clear the safe and flit in the time it took him to relieve the imminent cataclysm?

Gunter focussed the binoculars onto his nemesis. Ivan was in a terrible state, weeping, banging his balded head against the wall and generally feeling sorry for himself. So he thought about risking it...

Chapter 31

With his chest stuck out and his head held high, Taras inspected the signed photographs of The Alhambra's most famous performers adorning the walls of the carpeted corridor leading to his dressing room. He knew that soon, his picture would be hanging alongside the likes of George Formby and his good friend, Ken Dodd…

Taras had such happy memories of this theatre and recalled taking Halyna to see Laurel & Hardy perform in 1952: how wonderful it was to see "thinny and fatty" in colour for the first time, even if they looked rather old and doddery… he still had their autographs somewhere…

Following the corridor around a corner, Taras was instantly captivated by an atmospheric photograph of Anna Pavlova, taken after her acclaimed performance of *The Dying Swan* in 1930. Taras remembered how happy he was back then; and it may have taken three decades, but that level of happiness was definitely returning. Further along the corridor there were faded photographs of past productions by The Royal Ballet, The Bolshoi Ballet and The Kirov Ballet displayed in frames that needed a good dust: Halyna would never let them get *this* filthy.

Taras then walked up to a signed photograph of the craggy toothed, messy haired comedian, Ken Dodd, above which one of his tickling sticks was nailed to the wall. And for a feather duster, it was itself in desperate need of a dust. Beneath the photograph was an inscription: "The Longest Pantomime in the History of The Alhambra – it lasted until Easter!" Ken Dodd was a funny man; he certainly had a funny face… it reminded him of someone… but who…?

Feeling overwhelmingly privileged to be treading the same boards as such illustrious people, Taras noted there was space for one more framed photograph – *Swan Lake* by The Taras Ballet! A tingle ran down the full length of his spine… maybe Klem could take a photograph on that expensive camera of his?

Taras strutted down the thickly carpeted corridor, searching for

The Dancing Barber

his dressing room. There was a chill in the air, so he fastened the gold buttons of his blazer and held the lapels together. The carpet beneath his feet became polished wood, and the polished wood eventually became bare floorboards, and the bare floorboards became dusty concrete... he didn't imagine Anna Pavlova's dressing room to have been in the cellar? He may have paid a discounted price to book the theatre for a week, but he expected at least a little luxury... At this rate he'd be walking on bare earth. But finally, there was light at the end of the tunnel...

Expecting to find a gold star on his door with his name etched onto it, Taras was disappointed to discover his name was actually scrawled in chalk on a small blackboard that looked like a fragment of roof tile hanging on a rusty nail. He didn't imagine the Palladium was like this...

But when he stepped inside, the light bulbs surrounding the mirror made him smile, as did the enormous bunch of flowers on the dressing table. He sniffed the multi-coloured lilies by plunging his nose deeply between the petals, inhaling the sweet nectar and staining his nose bright orange in the process.

Maybe things weren't so bad after all? He couldn't remember the last time he'd been so excited; tonight was the first step of his wonderful new life and he insisted on savouring every moment.

Taras picked up an ivory-white envelope that was laying on the table by the lilies, noting it was embossed *With Compliments of the Management*. He sliced it open with his thumbnail, discovering that it contained a small number of tickets to the adjacent Gaumont Theatre to see any film being shown in the next month. He liked films and would frequently go to the cinema, usually alone. *The Guns of Navarone* and *Lawrence of Arabia* were still being shown: he'd seen them both twice and didn't think they warranted a third viewing. But *Taras Bulba* certainly was worth watching again, even though he'd already seen it four times. Perhaps he should let Halyna choose? A ticket to see a film would be a perfectly good anniversary present: just so long as she didn't find out it was free. He could conceal it in a pocket of the rabbit fur coat he planned to buy her... Or maybe he could forget the coat; cinema tickets alone would make a perfectly good anniversary gift... He thought it was an excellent idea: a modern gift from a modern man!

Using a water jug as a make-do vase, Taras arranged the lilies artistically around the rim, alternating the colours, before placing the display on the small windowsill that looked to be at the end of a coal chute... Why was it that his ballet career always seemed to involve cellars in some way? At least the blooms would get a little natural light and benefit from the cool breeze from the alley above. He added a spoonful of sugar to the water to give the slightly saggy stems some much-needed nourishment, one of the few housekeeping tips Halyna had taught him that he'd actually remembered, making him feel even more like a modern man. He poked a moistened finger into the sugar and tasted the crunchy sweetness, smacking his lips together with delight before thoroughly rinsing out his mouth with water: he didn't want any more false teeth.

With only an hour to go before his dancers were due to arrive, he unpacked his small leatherette case, and hung his billowing white shirts methodically onto wire hangers: he'd need at least two for each performance, because the audience didn't pay to see a sweat-stained ballet dancer... thank Heavens Halyna washed and ironed them before going on strike. Next, he hung up his underwear and the dozens of pairs of white tights that were only around twenty inches in length, yet somehow stretched to envelop his long, muscular legs without tearing. And last, but not least, he placed his prized pair of ballet shoes behind the door before unpacking his stage makeup, arranging the various powders and paints on the dressing table.

Taras checked his dyed hair in the mirror and was satisfied all the greys had gone, at least for tonight. He then removed the cap from his Eiffel Tower-shaped atomiser and liberally sprayed his costumes. The concoction of leftover aftershaves it contained caused every housefly in the dressing room to tumble to the floor, gasping for air...

Knowing Mrs Wiggins could always be relied upon to check the orchestra was correctly assembled, he decided to begin his elaborate warm-up routine, but only after smearing his most troublesome muscles with copious amounts of Ralgex. For the next fifteen minutes he performed press-ups and sit-ups before moving onto chest exercises and squats, making sure he lingered over every repetition until his muscles screamed for him to stop. He'd then repeat the entire routine another twice.

The Dancing Barber

Whilst the old man pushed his body to do the seventieth consecutive press-up, the dressing room door opened wide enough for an arm to surreptitiously creep in, reach round and snatch what it was looking for. The hand at the end of the arm performed the two-fingered salute at the old man just before the door closed as quietly as it'd opened.

Taras was at his physical peak, even at the young age of fifty-five, his body was supple, energised and supremely strong. He doubted anyone else his age could do one hundred and fifty consecutive press-ups in three minutes? He put it down to his staple diet of honey and oat bran... if it was good enough for Chopin, it was good enough for him!

It was as though his whole life had been leading up to tonight, and nothing would stand between him and the success he not only craved, but also deserved. He moved a chair out of the way and went on to do five-hundred star jumps, followed by fifty more squats, keeping his back perfectly straight and then fifty more sit-ups, without ever taking a rest.

Taras knew he was just as talented as Rudolf Nureyev, if not a smidgen better. And as he watched himself perform twenty perfect pirouettes in the mirror, he hoped someday to dance with Peggy once again, but this time on the world stage. Ever since he saw her perform in *Giselle* in 1937, he knew she was destined to be the world's leading Prima Ballerina, even though she chose Margot Fonteyn as her stage name. Taras thought the woman had perfect physique, supreme muscularity and the best interpretive powers he'd ever seen, not unlike Natalka, who even bore a striking resemblance to a youthful Fonteyn. But with Natalka out of action, it was down to his own daughter and Oksana to support him as best as they could. He didn't have any option: cancelling the performance would be professional suicide. Deep down, he knew they would make him proud: *very* deep down.

After thoroughly drying himself off with a towel, he slung on his billowing white shirt and inserted his legs into his miniature tights... their stretchiness never ceasing to amaze him. Taras then applied his jet-black eye shadow, mascara and lipstick and admired his reflection in the mirror. 'Right,' he said, clapping his hands, 'show time!'

Considering his dressing room was somewhere beneath the stage, the cacophony of tuning instruments he hated so much was conspicuous by its absence... he skipped upstairs to investigate. But as he ascended the steep steps into the orchestra pit, he discovered – to his horror – his costume was incomplete. He dashed straight back down to his dressing room, sweating so much that his mascara produced zebra stripes down his cheeks. It was a terrible omen for such an important part of a ballet dancer's costume to have gone missing... He searched behind the door, but there was nothing to be seen. He tried not to panic, but under the circumstances, it was impossible.

With the exception of his prosthetic scalp-lock, which resembled a swimming cap with a ponytail growing out of the centre, his range of stick-on moustaches of every style imaginable and his fake noses that looked like a collection of misshapen carrots, Taras' small leatherette case was empty, and certainly didn't contain the most vital part of his costume. For some reason, he'd even brought the Charlie Chaplinka mask he wore in Character Ballets, until it was banned for giving the children – and some of the adults – nightmares. He tossed the mask – that resembled a satanic gnome – back in his small leatherette case and slammed down the lid.

'I don't know what to do?' Taras said, rubbing his face, smearing the black mascara across his cheeks. He clicked his fingers, 'the studio! I must go and check the studio!' He slipped on his outdoor shoes and sprinted home as fast as he could...

The Dancing Barber
Chapter 32

With half an hour to go before the dancers were due to arrive at The Alhambra, Taras locked up the studio, subsequent to his fruitless search, and darted up the stone stairs to the kitchen, cursing under his breath. It looked as though he'd have to improvise... and he hated improvising.

Avoiding Halyna's pans of chilled soup, he ascended to the landing and began turning the door handle; he stopped, put his ear to the kitchen door and listened. Nobody was meant to be in, yet strangely he could hear much laughter and noisy conversation. It didn't sound like Halyna and Mrs Wiggins... the voices were too deep, so he deduced Klem must have guests, despite being told to lock himself in the attic.

Taras pressed his ear closer to the door and listened to masculine voices accompanied by a peculiar bubbling noise akin to a cauldron of water on a rolling boil. He crouched down and peered through the keyhole, but couldn't quite believe what he saw. He rubbed his eyes and looked again... Klem was sat in the armchair drinking tea, nothing unusual there. But the tin bath, normally kept beneath the table, had been pulled out and was occupied by an enormous hairy man, who seemed to have no difficulty creating his own Jacuzzi.

Taras thought he must be overtired and hallucinating... maybe doing those last hundred press-ups wasn't such a good idea. He rubbed his eyes and took another look. Now there were two enormous hairy men; the second, wearing a towel that made him look like a Sumo Wrestler, was scrubbing the first one's back so vigorously that the loofah had started to wear away. Taras deduced Klem obviously knew these men, for they were laughing and joking, as if they were old friends catching up after not seeing each other for years. But Taras thought he knew most, if not all of Klem's friends... and he certainly wouldn't have forgotten these two...

Halyna was due any moment and he knew she wouldn't appreciate coming home to this improvised bathhouse. So he flung open the door and stepped straight in, determined to turf out Klem's "guests" and tidy up the kitchen before she returned. Immediately, the smell of farmyards shot straight up his nostrils and down into his lungs; gasping for air, he rushed to open the window as widely as possible, only to suffer a dose of astringent curry from the shop down the road...

'Hello Taras?' Klem said with surprise, 'I thought you were at The Alhambra?'

The two enormous hairy men slowly looked around, their beards dripping with soapy suds, giving them the appearance of a pair of Rip Van Winkles.

Taras was about to light a cigarette, but had second thoughts when the man in the bath continued creating his Jacuzzi, the methane fumes drifting dangerously close to the lighter. Taras held his breath and examined Klem's "guests", whose faces were so ugly he was sure he'd seen them somewhere before... From the neck up, they could have been the overweight distant relations of Ken Dodd, but – as the bubbles popped – the rest of them bordered on Neanderthal.

'Who are these men?' Taras demanded.

'Men?' Klem asked, 'what men? And what happened to your face? Is it camouflage paint?'

Taras shouted, 'don't get smart with me: I am not in the mood, understand? Now tell me, what do you think you're doing, bringing your hirsute friends home for a bath? Get these men shifted before Halyna comes home!'

The Sumo Wrestler in the towel nappy said pompously, 'first we are the tramps, then we are the women of the "business", then we are the ugly sisters and now we are the men! Why must we always have the insults?'

'Klem,' said the bather, 'will you please tell this stripy-faced durak that we are not the men! Is he the blind?' Scraping her tough fingernails through the encrusted grime along the bath's edge, the woman struggled to lever herself out of the blackened water. She then confirmed her gender far too clearly, wobbling her anatomy around as if she were a hessian bag filled with the largest melons.

'Good grief!' Taras shouted, 'that's the most disgusting thing I've ever seen! Cover yourself up at once!' He turned to Klem and

The Dancing Barber

barked, 'I am waiting for your explanation. And it'd better be good, understand?'

Taras had to drink a full glass of samahon before he regained a fraction of his composure, and even then, he still shook as if operating a pneumatic drill. He knew he was going to be woefully late for The Alhambra, but didn't care: he needed time to recover from *such* a shock.

Using both hands, Klem heaved up the last suitcase and prepared to haul it upstairs. He said, 'it'll only be for a few days. Promise.'

'Oh no!' Taras said, 'I forbid you to allow these "women" to sleep in the attic, my attic! You can tell them to go and find a hotel!' When Klem took no notice, Taras shouted, 'I'm serious! We do not have any room to accommodate these ghastly ape women! The floor won't stand the weight! You tell them to leave, now!'

'Come on Taras, I *can't* do that!' Klem pleaded, disappearing up the stairs, leaving the women sat slurping the cheapest PG Tips at the kitchen table, staring at Taras through slatted eyes, their bodies swathed in towels.

Instead of picking up their chipped mugs, Taras watched as the women lowered their mouths to the table and sucked up the tea as if they were animals drinking from a trough. He could only cringe and avert his eyes.

Taras slammed down his glass and chased Klem up to the attic: for someone who did little, or no exercise, Klem was very quick on his feet, especially as he carried such a bulky suitcase. Taras had to climb two steps at a time just to catch up. He demanded, 'and why can't you get rid of them? It's very easy, you just tell them to get lost!'

Klem disappeared through the attic door and said, 'listen Taras; you wouldn't ask Halyna to leave? Would you? So why should I ask them to leave?'

'What are you on about? I've never heard you talk such himno! All that tea must have brewed your brain!' Taras marched back downstairs and said, 'if you're not going to get rid of them, then *I* damned well will!'

Klem dropped the heavy suitcase to the floor and ran after

him…

'Oh my…' Taras cried when he saw Halyna lying in a heap on the kitchen floor. 'What's happened?'

Sofia knelt by her mother's side, wafting her pale face with the Radio Times, trying in vain to revive her.

'They did it!' shouted Mrs Wiggins, wiping her nose on her sleeve, having ran out of Kleenex tissues. 'As soon as Halyna saw them, she collapsed straight to the floor!' She shook her head, 'I thought Natalka's aunties were ugly, but these two…' She pretended to throw up.

Taras stared at the hairy ape women and demanded, 'what have you done to my wife?'

'We do the nothing,' said the marginally more intelligent one, while scratching beneath her armpit, then sniffing her fingers.

'All we say is the hello,' said the other one, shrugging her shoulders, 'and Halynochka, she the faint!'

Taras was speechless. He thought: *could these women be so ugly as to cause someone to faint? Maybe their stench overpowered her?* He held his breath. *It's certainly overpowering me…*

'Tato,' Sofia said, continuing to waft vigorously, 'I think I'd better introduce you.'

Taras screwed up his face, 'but I already know who these two are!'

'No you don't,' Sofia said. She pointed at the women in turn, 'this is Auntie Zena and this is Auntie Lenka.'

The two women smiled broadly at the mention of their names, bearing sets of teeth that resembled smashed up piano keyboards.

Taras stared at the women, struggling to comprehend what he'd been told. He looked back at his daughter through narrowed eyes, '*what* did you say?'

Zena interjected, 'she say that we are the sisters-in-love.'

'I *beg* your pardon?' Taras said. 'I won't allow any of *that* in my house!'

Sofia clarified, 'they mean they're your sisters-in-law!'

'Yes,' Lenka said, 'so you are the brother-in-love.' She smiled broadly, displaying her craggy teeth in all their splendour.

'Law,' Sofia clarified again, 'they mean you're their brother-in-law! Do you understand? They're Mama's sisters from Chaplinka. They've come to visit us... isn't that nice?'

Taras could only stare... He wasn't surprised Halyna had fainted. *Fancy this pair turning up after all these years; I'd forgotten they even existed.*

'Yes, we are the aunties of Sofia,' Zena said. She then looked at Sofia, 'but this girl, she does not look anything like the photograph of the niece Halynochka, she sent us in the Air Mail?'

'No, she does not,' Lenka added, 'and this house, it looks nothing like The Bolling Hall?'

Klem burst out in laughter and said, 'Bolling Hall?' He turned to Lenka and said, 'why would you think this house would look like Bolling Hall?'

'In the letters,' Lenka said, 'Halynochka, she told us that she lived in The Bolling Hall; she sent us many of the photographs of her wonderful house...'

Klem gave Taras *that* look, a look echoed by Sofia.

'And...' said Zena, holding out a photograph of Taras sat behind the wheel of a car, 'we cannot wait to have the drive in the car...' She looked at Taras, 'you are the very lucky man to have such a beautiful car!'

Taras didn't know what to say... The car in the photograph was just a random one he'd found parked in the street outside his shop... He'd tried the door handle, and when the door opened, he got behind the wheel and Klem took a picture on his Leica... Taras thought it was right that someone of his standing should be seen to own a motor car, but never imagined his deceptions would be uncovered...

Taras wished he could faint as conveniently as his wife. Or better still, be swallowed by a great chasm that opened up in the earth. He blinked his eyes energetically and tapped the sides of his head. No, this wasn't a dream: it was a nightmare.

Unable to deal with this on his own, Taras crouched to the floor and frantically tried to revive Halyna. He shook her, dowsed her face with cold water and even tried wafting smelling salts beneath her nose. But she was still out like a light.

He cursed his decades of snobbery, especially when Sofia's long-lost aunties pulled out bundles of Halyna's crumpled letters and showed Sofia the advertisements for *Swan Lake* with Natalka on the front cover, saying, 'but this, it is not our Sofia?'

'Wake up Halyna,' Taras pleaded, 'wake up!' If this was how she reacted after only *seeing* her sisters, what would she do when she realised Klem had moved them – bag and baggage – into the attic?

Klem always insisted on helping damsels in distress; and if they had a pretty face then so much the better. Neither Zena nor Lenka possessed faces that could be described as even remotely pretty and they certainly weren't damsels. But all those years ago, when Klem met Zena, she was definitely in distress, and he had to do something to help her. How was he to know she'd turn out to be Halyna's sister?

Klem noticed that Zena looked terribly concerned... Halyna was never very good with surprises, and she reacted even worse to shocks. He took the time to examine Zena's face and wondered what on earth had happened to her? She looked nothing like the Zena he remembered; and it hadn't been that many years since he'd last seen her, perhaps twelve at the most? Was life in Chaplinka so hard? Gone was the daintiness of her youth; she was now built like a Siberian bison and could probably survive in sub-zero temperatures for months on end without the need for clothes. And he certainly didn't remember her spending so much time foraging beneath her armpits, let alone foraging anywhere else...

'Get out of the way,' Taras shouted, shoving Sofia to one side. 'Wafting the woman with a magazine isn't doing any damned good!' He picked up his wife as if she was a rag doll, propped her up in a chair and desperately tried to revive her by shaking her and gently slapping her cheeks. It was then when Taras noticed there was something different about his wife today, but he couldn't figure out what? Maybe it was new lipstick?

Klem watched Sofia withdraw to the corner and cry into her handkerchief; she was only doing her best and Taras' attitude was inexcusable. Klem had always disapproved of the way Taras treated his daughter. She only ever wanted to make her father proud, but the poor girl's efforts were never good enough. It wasn't a secret that Taras had always wanted a son-and-heir, but he'd had twelve years to get used to having a daughter-and-heir

The Dancing Barber

instead, so it was about time he cut her some slack. Sofia reminded Klem of how he was at her age – full of dreams and ambitions – and he hoped the gifted young dancer wouldn't let her father criticise it all out of her…

Sofia stomped up to her bedroom to dry her eyes, fed up to the back teeth with her Tato's attitude towards her. She thought slyly: *very soon, you'll get what's coming to you… Mr Tar-<u>Arse</u>.*

Feeling guilty, she said a prayer and then had only the purest of thoughts.

As she raked the knots from her hair, she looked inquisitively at a musty old photograph of a fishing boat called "Katya" she'd found within the secret compartment of Klem's desk. It was in amongst a wad of papers that were all to do with the supremely tedious subject of Ukrainian politics…

She looked at it closely, wondering why her parents would argue about a fishing boat that spent all its time bobbing about on the Black Sea? For a fishing boat, it didn't have many nets, but it did have far more fishing rods than usual…

Chapter 33

With his lizard-skin briefcase brimming with white fivers, Ivan uncomfortably shoehorned his bruised and sore body behind the wheel of his red Volvo P1800S and set off on the fast road to Keighley. Moments earlier, while using a crow bar to prise the safe from the wall, he suddenly remembered the eight digit combination... he wasn't surprised he'd forgotten his own mother's birthday...

Changing up to fourth gear, he muttered, 'this is the last time the Colonel double-crosses me.' His right foot crushed the accelerator pedal to the floor, 'nobody messes with Ivan and gets away with it!' He could have sworn he heard laughter... but it was only imaginary laughter to match his imaginary courage...

Ivan wound-down his window, making a mental note never to park his car outside the curry shop again. Pity the shop wasn't one of his properties... he would close it down for polluting the atmosphere... The thought of eating such food turned his stomach; the most exotic thing he'd ever eaten was lamb with *mint* sauce, and even that was too much to bear... plain and simple was how he liked his food, attributes that also matched his taste in women.

The scents of an early spring evening soon refreshed the car, as Ivan weaved along the twisty hedge-lined lanes. More rain must have been predicted, because the asphyxiating stench of muckspreading soon made him wind-up his window. At least the smell of curry was gone. He enjoyed driving, even when under stress: to him, it was one of the privileges of wealth and an experience he found rather meditative. With marching music humming from his lips, he ran his fingers along the stitching of the leather steering wheel and relaxed into the comfortable oxblood leather bucket seat.

After three miles, he made a right turn and headed over to Brontë country, preparing in his mind precisely what he was going to say to the Colonel: it was never wise to visit *him* unprepared. Whilst steering the Volvo with one hand, he slid the lizard-skin briefcase under the passenger seat, opened the glove box and

The Dancing Barber

pulled out a crumpled old shopping bag, placing it on the oxblood leather seat beside him.

Eventually Ivan signalled left and turned up an overgrown track that led to a dilapidated farmhouse. Unfortunately, he still didn't have a clue what he was going to say: a very foolish strategy when dealing with someone as formidable as the Colonel.

Ivan parked the Volvo behind a privet hedge, then tied the carrier bag's handles with a double knot, placing the bulging bag where only he would be able to find it. He then strode to the boot to put on a jacket and tie: the jacket matched his corduroy trousers and the tie was clip-on, an added precaution after their last meeting. Making sure there was no one in sight, he plodded the familiar mossy gravel path to the old door, knocked in the usual way and waited, his feeble fists clenched behind his back.

A minute later, Ivan listened to the door being unbarred... the grating of rusty bolts and the clanging of corroded chains sounding more ominous than ever. The heavy door slowly opened... Ivan gingerly peered into the kitchen beyond that was cloaked in total darkness.

'Good afternoon,' said the commanding voice from deep within the room. 'Come in.'

Ivan did as he was told. He stood to attention and saluted his superior, despite being unable to see him.

'That's an interesting disguise,' said the Colonel, who'd never known Ivan without a ginger beard. 'Stick on chin, is it?'

Ivan said nothing.

'If it's real... I suggest you re-grow the beard...' Unable to laugh, the Colonel emitted a brief grunt. 'Anyway... Let's get on with the formalities, shall we?' he said, switching on the dimmest of lights and wasting no time in carrying out his usual checks.

The Colonel's minty breath was stronger than ever: he must have eaten an entire packet of Polos. Ivan surmised it was better to be addicted to mints than to booze or cigarettes...

Eventually, the Colonel was satisfied that Ivan was unarmed. He said sternly, 'you have broken with strict protocol by coming here in daylight.' He pushed Ivan to the wall so forcefully that much of the crumbling plasterwork in the dishevelled kitchen scattered to the stone floor. 'So you'd better have a good explanation for it.' He reached out to throttle him, 'because if you haven't...'

Ivan was pleased when the tie detached from his neck.

But the same could not be said for the Colonel, who was utterly taken by surprise. He examined the strange thing hanging from his hand, before using it to whip Ivan across the face as hard as he could.

But the Colonel was even more surprised when Ivan seized the long-awaited opportunity to turn the tables on his superior...

After punching the Colonel as hard as he could in the solar plexus, Ivan twisted the man's gorilla arm forcefully behind his back. He then slammed the man's enormous melon of a head down onto the scrubbed table, ramming his face into the splintering wood.

'Right then Colonel,' Ivan said calmly, 'you may well be annoyed that I have visited you at an unscheduled time, but recent events have made it most necessary. And before you ask, I came alone and made doubly sure that I hadn't been followed. So you are to be quiet and *you* will listen to *me* for once!'

'Very well,' said the Colonel, his free hand creeping stealthily towards his ankle. 'But you must understand my caution.'

Ivan batted the hand away and relieved the Colonel of the miniature pistol he kept for emergencies in a holster strapped to his sock. 'Don't be a durak!' he said, flinging the pistol into a corner, the weapon clattering against the stone floor. He watched the Colonel's face become paralysed with fear and knew that for once, <u>he</u> was in control of the situation. 'Right then,' said Ivan, 'I want to know why you sent those goons to beat me up and kidnap me? And I want the <u>truth</u>!'

'Goons?' the Colonel said. 'Kidnap? I know nothing of this?'

Ivan levered the Colonel's arm further up his back. 'Liar!' he shouted, 'you sent them to my home, where they knocked me out, tied me up like a slaughtered pig and bundled me into a trunk strapped to the back of an old car! And I want to know <u>why</u>!'

'Honestly,' the Colonel pleaded, 'I have no idea what you are talking about?'

'<u>Liar</u>!' Ivan shouted even louder, making sure the Colonel knew what it felt like to have a shoulder on the verge of dislocation.

'Listen to me,' the Colonel begged, 'I'm on <u>your</u> side! Who do you think stopped Comrade General from having you poisoned?

The Dancing Barber

Hmm? You know what he's like when people disobey him!'

'What rubbish!' spat Ivan, trying his best to dislocate the Colonel's arm. 'I have *never* disobeyed Comrade General!'

The Colonel tensed his muscles and began to resist Ivan's effeminate attempt at an arm lock. Calmly, he said, 'you were ordered to send that cassette tape straight to the BBC. Then Voloshin would have been instantly discredited before he could do any damage to the Soviet Union. But instead, you decided to blackmail Klem to satisfy your own greed for money: and you couldn't even do that right! Do you have any idea how hard it was to dissuade a man like Comrade General? He was angry enough to poison you himself, but I talked him out of it!'

'I don't believe you,' Ivan said, 'I made up for my mistakes by intercepting Klem's documents. So Comrade General should be pleased!' He twisted the Colonel's arm a little more before saying, 'but I know the *real* truth! You want me killed so that you can keep my payment for yourself! I may be a lot of things, but a durak is not one of them…'

'Oh yes you are!' the Colonel shouted, 'you're a complete durak. And Comrade General is not pleased with you! Why would he be?'

Ivan was confused, 'but I gave him exactly what he wanted…'

'No you didn't!' the Colonel interrupted, 'you gave him a stack of Felix the Cat cartoons! And Comrade General hates cats!'

Ivan's feeble grip on the Colonel's arm loosened. 'What?' he said, 'but I could have s-sworn…'

Before he knew what hit him, Ivan was shoved up against the wall again, shielding his balded head from the shower of crumbling plaster.

The Colonel foamed at the mouth, 'you've let yourself be outsmarted by Klem again, haven't you? That "tea drinking twit" probably expected us to steal the documents, and you played right into his hands!' The Colonel banged Ivan's shoulders repeatedly against the wall, 'so now we *neither* have the cassette tape *nor* the documents! And it's all your fault!'

'I can s-sort h-him,' Ivan said, gasping for air, the Colonel's thumbs pressing hard onto his trachea. His superior's mouth was so close that he could taste his halitosis: all those Polo mints were obviously not strong enough.

'<u>No</u>!' the Colonel shouted, 'I will "sort him" myself! And <u>tonight</u>! Our *Bureau of Intelligence* states that Klem is our only link to Voloshin. So if we apprehend Klem, we silence Voloshin! And that "tea drinking twit" will <u>not</u> outsmart me!'

The Colonel punched Ivan so hard in the solar plexus that he crumbled to the floor like a puppet with cut strings. '<u>Durak</u>!' the Colonel said, picking up his pistol, annoyed that it'd been scuffed on the rough stone floor. Upon hearing a noise outside, he looked over to the window, and narrowed his eyes...

Ivan pleaded, 'but C-Colonel, C-Colonel...'

'Shut up!' barked the Colonel, 'I think I heard something.' He rushed to the grubby little window just in time to see Ivan's Volvo disappearing down the track. All that remained was a cloud of dust hanging in the air. The Colonel turned to Ivan and said, 'your car has just driven off... I thought you said you came alone?'

'My c-c-car... No...? But I <u>did</u> come alone and I <u>wasn't</u> followed!' Ivan pleaded, 'there wasn't a single c-c-car behind me all the way here. <u>I checked</u>. It must have been stolen... I thought it was safe to leave the key in the ignition... It's so quiet around here...' He put his head in his hands and cried. He wanted to shoot himself, but remembered that Klem had even taken his pistol.

The Colonel looked down on Ivan's head and emitted the worst possible string of expletives. He slapped him hard on the back of his decorated skull and demanded, 'how long have you been walking about like this?'

'Like w-w-what?' Ivan asked, not appreciating being slapped by someone other than his mother for the first time since school.

Using a couple of fragments of broken mirror, Ivan was just as shocked as the Colonel when he saw the Soviet Hammer and Sickle drawn atop his head.

Oksana, he thought, *this time you've gone too far!* Then he remembered... when he was dozing in the park yesterday afternoon, he felt something crawling on his head... He ignored it, thinking it was only a spider... But it must have been his darling daughter being overly artistic with the sun block; she was going to be in *serious* trouble. *So that explains why all those old biddies were muttering about me in church... Why didn't someone tell me sooner...?*

The Dancing Barber

For the Colonel, seeing the Soviet flag drawn on top of Ivan's sunburned head was the straw that broke the camel's back. This durak was a serious liability. Stealing from the Mafia was stupid, but forgivable; bungling his duties for the Soviet Secret Police was moronic, yet acceptable. But there was no room for error when *his* organisation was concerned...

Ivan gulped when the Colonel clicked the miniature pistol's hammer with his thumb and carefully took aim...

Chapter 34

Halyna jostled for position in The Alhambra's overcrowded orchestra pit, trying to talk to her husband. But his mind, as usual, was elsewhere... She repeated, 'I said *thank you* for complimenting me on my new hair-do...' Sighing, she gave him a firm nudge on the arm...

'Hmm?' Taras replied, 'new hair-do? Ah yes, very nice indeed...' But he didn't look; he was too busy watching the audience filtering in, each person representing several shillings of much-needed income, which he'd use to extend his studio into the back yard, regardless of obtaining his wife's approval.

Halyna raised her nose. 'I knew you wouldn't notice; I told Mrs Wiggins you wouldn't notice and you haven't!' She examined the reflection of her new perm on a highly-polished trombone, patting several escaped strands back into position... she thought she looked like the Queen. 'It was about time I sorted out my hair... it's a pity I flattened half of it by lying on the carpet for so long.' She sighed again, 'but I couldn't think of anything else to do under the circumstances?'

'As I said, I think your hair looks *very* nice!' Taras scrutinised it for the first time, deducing Halyna did look a little younger tonight... but only a little... And she hadn't worn that string of cultivated pearls around her neck for many years: he'd forgotten how much they suited her... he hoped she wouldn't find out they were only ceramic beads... But there was something else different about her... but what? Either way, he was grateful she'd made the effort, especially in the wake of recent events...

'I must say,' said Taras, 'you're taking it all rather well! Your twin sisters turning up out of the blue, expecting to find us living in Bolling Hall is the sort of stress we can <u>all</u> do without.'

Halyna unfastened the catch of her delicately sequined handbag and extracted a small bottle wrapped in a plastic bag. She didn't care what Taras thought: she needed a drink and she was going to have one! And before Taras could protest, the small bottle was empty: the acidic samahon never even touched the sides. 'Ah!' she

The Dancing Barber

said, 'I needed that!'

'Give me strength, woman,' Taras said, trying to hide her from the gaping audience. 'What do you think you're doing? I have my reputation to think about!'

'Your reputation,' Halyna spat, 'never mind your reputation! And what have I told you about calling me "woman"?'

'That's right luv,' said the violinist, 'you put the old – in his place.'

'Too right,' said the man entwined in his tuba, 'good on you...'

Taras winced. He said, 'Halyna, I'm sorry...' He then turned to the insubordinate members of the orchestra and said something that not only forced an apology, but also guaranteed their complete cooperation for the rest of the evening. He was pleased he still had it in him...

Halyna huffed, 'do you have to be so awful? And for your information, I haven't decided what to do about Zena and Lenka... Heaven knows how we're going to break the news to them?' She looked squarely at Taras, 'and don't forget that it was your snobbishness that spun all these lies in the first place... So really you should be the one to tell them...'

Conveniently, Taras then decided to notice her fur coat. Caressing the thick fur between his thumb and forefinger, he said, 'is this *new*?' It certainly felt expensive... much more expensive than rabbit...

'Of course,' Halyna said, doing a little twirl, revealing a traditionally embroidered dress beneath; it was typical of him to change the subject at that precise moment. 'Wearing this coat is just like giving a piggy back to a bear cub. Do you approve?'

'Yes, it does suit you,' Taras said through gritted teeth, knowing he'd have to put his thinking cap back on when it came to choosing an anniversary present... would a cinema ticket to see Taras Bulba *really* be a satisfactory gift? Noticing her glistening temples, Taras asked, 'but won't you be rather warm greeting the dignitaries? Perhaps I could hang it in my dressing room?'

'Never mind all that,' she said, 'we have to decide who is going to tell Zena and Lenka?' She pointed her manicured index finger at Taras, 'and as living in Bolling Hall was a figment of your imagination...'

Taras immediately backed away, 'but I can't tell them the

truth…'

'And why not?' Halyna said, raising both eyebrows.

'Because… because,' Taras stuttered, 'because I just can't…'

'Because <u>you'll</u> be embarrassed and you've got your reputation to consider! Well tough,' Halyna said, 'as soon as we get back home, <u>you</u> are going to tell them the truth! I have decided and my decision is <u>final</u>!'

The tuba player smirked when Taras wasn't looking, then went back to arranging his sheet music.

'Now just a minute,' Taras pleaded. But Halyna had turned her back like a grumpy Mister Pushkin. Those ghastly women utterly repulsed him; there was no way he was going anywhere near them. They spoke like uncouth navvies and they looked just as bad, their grubby skins looked as though they'd never been washed and when he shook their hands it was as though they wore gloves made from sandpaper. And they smelled so earthy that he imagined they slept in a hole in the ground. And by all accounts, they had a fuse that was even shorter than his. But he knew Halyna's edict was mandatory… he was going to have to tell those women the truth… his pride would be gone, but then again, hopefully the troll twins would be gone too! He just hoped they didn't turn too nasty…

Halyna watched the rows of plush velvet seats slowly filling with people; she also watched Taras muttering to himself, clearly racking his brain for any excuse not to tell the truth. She thought: *if only I'd posted yesterday's letter sooner; then perhaps the first meeting with my twin sisters in thirty years might not have been so awkward… What must they think of me, first collapsing, then running straight out of the house without even saying hello? Well, it's all Taras' fault and he can sort it out!* She sighed. *When those two go back to Chaplinka, they will tell everyone that their young sister was a fibber. Oh, the shame of it… I hope my Mama will forgive me…*

'Have you seen the time?' Taras moaned, tapping his wristwatch so hard that he almost cracked the glass. 'The Wiggins woman only lives around the corner, so how come she's late?'

'Oh shut up,' Halyna snapped, 'Mrs Wiggins and I had a nice time in town this afternoon, so I don't want you upsetting her when she does finally arrive. Is that understood?'

Taras nodded, 'understood. But what I *can't* understand is why

The Dancing Barber

she makes her husband drive her such a short distance?'

Halyna shrugged her shoulders: at least "the old git" *could* drive, despite only having a battered Morris van... She recalled what happened during Taras' one and only driving lesson... the instructor was so scared of him that he daren't say anything critical... even after Taras crashed directly into the back of a parked Police car...

Taras craned his neck up to the Dress Circle and said, 'I think the VIPs are starting to arrive.' He looked at Halyna, 'remember, *best* behaviour.' He pulled up his tights and adjusted his billowing white shirt, releasing a gust of fly-repellent aftershave that had the same effect on Halyna. He then donned his fifty-shilling blue blazer with the ballet school logo embroidered onto the breast pocket, fastened the upper gold button and switched on his broadest smile.

Halyna shook her head, 'it is you who should be on your best behaviour!'

Taras winked, 'but I am always on my best behaviour.'

Halyna was thankful that he could still take a joke, sometimes... But the moment of levity was only brief...

Taras couldn't believe the orchestra hadn't organised themselves yet... apparently they were waiting for the conductor to arrive. Maybe next time, he'd hire a proper orchestra, instead of relying on a bunch of flat-caps from the Club... If all went to plan, he'd be able to afford it...

'Halyna, before I forget,' Taras said, 'take these.' He handed her a heavy wad of foolscap paper, 'I want you to give one of these to each of the critics. I've written their names at the top using a bright green felt-tip-pen. And remember, make sure you tell them to copy these reviews out word for word, understand? Word for word!'

Halyna shook her head. It wasn't illegal, but it was unethical... but that wouldn't stop him. 'Can't you do it...? I'd rather be in the changing rooms, checking the girls were properly attired in their leotards and tutus...' She also insisted on helping them with their stage make-up; left to their own devices they'd daub it on so thickly that they'd all end up looking like miniature Mrs Wiggins'.

'I don't have time,' Taras said, adjusting his tights again, 'I've got to sort out Klem.'

'Klem?' Halyna cried, 'but why have you brought him here?'

'He was *most* insistent! He said he wasn't going to let the threat of "arrest" prevent him from taking his place in the limelight. And quite frankly, I agree with him! Why should he hide in the shadows? Besides, he's probably safer here in the company of hundreds of people than he would be stuck at home with your hideous sisters!'

The Dancing Barber
Chapter 35

Zena used a stone to bash another rusty nail into the pristine white wall of Taras' beloved penthouse. She said, 'Lenka, hand me the other end of the washing line…'

Lenka bent down to pick up the washing line, in so doing emitting a loud rasping noise. 'Do you think Halynochka, she will mind us making the attic into the washetaria?'

'Of course not; I suppose this house, it is only the spare house.' Zena chuckled, hanging up the fifth washing line, checking the tightness by twanging it as if it were an enormous guitar string.

Whilst changing her underwear, Lenka said, 'we have the spare knickers, and our Halynochka, she has the spare house!'

'Yes, she is the very lucky woman,' Zena said, poking the next batch of stained undergarments into the pan of boiling water on the electric hob, turning the heat fully on.

'It the strange that she collapse when she see us,' Lenka said, plopping her soiled underwear into the brimming pan, and then searching for the pegs.

'Yes,' Zena said, 'and even more the strange when she run out of the house. But she is the busy woman… Maybe she will be the calmer when she comes back from the theatre, yes? Taras, he is the demanding husband.'

'It the pity he could not demand for us to be allowed to see the *Swan Lake*,' said a frowning Lenka. 'I would have liked to have watched our Sofia dance…'

'But how were we to know that none of our dresses were appropriate?'

'Oh well,' said Lenka, shrugging her shoulders, 'we will have to watch it on the film of the Cine. I sure it will be just as the good… I suppose.'

Earlier that evening, neither twin kicked up a fuss when they were refused entry to The Alhambra for lack of tickets and inappropriate clothing. Fortunately they were wearing numerous dresses, but the man at the door was not pleased when they started peeling them off one by one until they'd found an "appropriate" dress. And it didn't help when a lisping man in a beret chased them out onto the street, waving the remnants of his tubular steel bow tie, shouting, 'Thugs! Vandals! Hooligans!'

So the twins had to go back "home". Taras did not like them using this term: under no circumstances were they to get used to living in the attic.

And they agreed: they'd much prefer living at "The Bolling Hall" and couldn't understand why they hadn't been chauffeured there in Taras' limousine…

'Why you hang the brassière in such a way?' Zena asked, watching her sister pin up the fluorescent garment as if it were a miniature hammock.

Lenka smiled, 'the cat of Klem, The Pushkin, it finds it the comfortable place to sleep, so I give it as the present. Is the good idea, yes?'

'I suppose so, although you could have given it the wash first. I not sure that Klem would like such a dirty thing attached to the wall?'

'I *have* given it the wash: it is the whitest it has been in many of the years! And any way, it is not for Klem, it is for The Pushkin.' Lenka hollowed out the vast cups so the cat would have plenty of room to sprawl out. 'I think it looks nice… I want to make it up to The Pushkin for using its tray of the litter. The Pushkin, it still has not the forgiven me…'

Zena agreed with the cat: it was quite ridiculous for a grown woman to have crouched over that tiny box, and then covered up 'the doings', using her hand to shovel the litter. As she quested through the few cupboards in the attic, hoping to find space to stow away their suitcases, she said, 'the cat, I am sure will approve of the brassière hammock when it returns from the theatre… The Pushkin, it is not the fussiest of the cats.'

Lenka added a pair of grubby stockings to the left cup, one stuffed into the other and said, 'there, it will make the nice cushion… And this old vest, it will make the nice blanket.'

'Aha!' Zena declared with delight, 'look what I have found!' From the cupboard under the sink, she lifted out a box brimming with Halyna's distillation equipment, comprising of assorted glass tubes, flasks and bottles. She said, 'I think that maybe we should make some of the samahon for our hosts: we shall make it *Chaplinka-style.*'

Lenka immediately dashed out, and quickly returned with a crate of bruised plums she'd found beside a dustbin down the alley. After wafting away the swarm of bluebottles, she promptly de-stoned the fruit by tearing it apart with her thumbnails, lobbing the squelchy flesh into an old half-barrel. Then with stockings removed and skirts hoisted up, the sisters treaded the plums into mush using their bare feet, their fungal nails and encrusted toes adding to the flavour.

Half an hour later, the distillery had been assembled and clear samahon began dripping from what they termed the 'drippy end'. 'Quick,' Zena said, handing her sister a clean bottle, 'we do not want to waste any!'

Lenka moved fast, but not fast enough: some samahon had already dripped onto the floor, dissolving away the varnish...

After a few minutes, the first bottle contained a couple of inches of their tipple. 'Shall we?' Lenka asked eagerly, her mouth salivating, her hand poised to grab the bottle.

'Of course,' said Zena, insisting on having the first gulp. The moment the liquid entered her mouth, it felt as though her gums were on fire and her tongue was melting. As she swallowed, her throat smouldered until her stomach acid finally quenched the inferno.

Seeing her sister's contorted expression, Lenka thought twice before having a taste: surely it wasn't as bad as that? So she threw her glassful down her throat and quickly realised that it was worse... Gasping, she said, 'this is the sort of samahon Uncle Viktor, he says will put the hairs on the chest.'

Zena looked at her sister's appearance, deciding that in her case, it certainly did. Leaving the distillery to do its work, she said, 'come on, we cannot be sitting and drinking the samahon all day! We must get on with the laundry...'

Lenka begrudgingly stood up. The samahon may have tasted foul, but it was the best they'd ever made.

'My stomach the rumble,' Zena said after she'd finished festooning the washing lines with her grubby flannels, vests, knickers and socks. 'We should make the cooking. It will be nice for our family to come from the *Swan Lake* to the hot foods. You agree, yes?'

'But I use all the pans for the knickers,' Lenka said, shrugging her shoulders and gesturing to the fully laden hob that steamed with the stench of stale sweat, and other, much more unpleasant odours. There were even pans of underwear simmering in the oven and several brassières sizzling on the grill.

Zena clicked her fingers, 'Halynochka, she has more pans in the downstairs kitchen: I have seen them! Come, we shall go and make the cooking!'

So the twins trundled down the spiral staircase and began clattering around Halyna's fastidious kitchen, scattering pots, pans, tins and anything else they could find all over the floor…

The Dancing Barber
Chapter 36

Taras said, 'you *do* understand, no one's forcing you to recite your poems tonight?'

Klem replied, 'but I *want* to recite. I enjoy it, besides after tomorrow, who knows when I'll be able to recite in England again?' He smiled, 'now hand me my Thermos; I could do with some Peppermint tea... I've not been this nervous since the time I, err... never mind.'

'Here,' Taras said, handing him one of the two flasks Halyna had prepared, 'I don't know how you can drink that stuff?' He picked up his own Thermos flask to take to his dressing room, 'I prefer something a little stronger.' He contemplated having a snifter, but decided to save it for the interval.

Taras was pleased Klem had finally put on his unworn brown bespoke suit, baring the trademark blue and yellow pinstripes. It may have been slightly out of fashion for 1963 with its broad shoulders, wide lapels and tapered profile, but for once, Klem looked relatively well turned-out... Even his scuffed red boots had been polished and his moustache twisted to look as though he had a couple of pencils protruding from his nostrils. He knew Klem's immaculate appearance wouldn't last long... and he was proved right when he watched him spill Peppermint tea down the front of his embroidered shirt and waistcoat...

Taras handed him a cloth, then decided to skip up to the Dress Circle. It was time to greet the critics; and also to make sure they understood precisely what he wanted them to write in their official reviews. And if necessary, remind them of those little secrets in their pasts that he'd consider divulging to the press should they decide not to comply...

'Of course,' said the critic from The Ballet Chronicle in his usual flamboyant way, wafting around his perfume-soaked silk handkerchief before stuffing it up his frilly sleeve. 'Anything for you dear...'

'Don't worry your pretty little head, darling,' said the critic from The Pirouette Weekly, fluttering his eyelashes.

Taras cringed and said with his deepest voice, 'very good,' before rapidly excusing himself.

The instant Sofia poked her tiny, whitewashed face through the heavy curtains, her eyes became wider than dinner plates. It was the first time she'd seen The Alhambra's auditorium and was in awe of its elegance; she thought the gilded plasterwork, painted panels and velvet chairs were like something from a palace. And it certainly felt as though it was a State occasion: *everybody* was dressed up.

The ladies wore elegant, glittering frocks complimented by twinkly jewellery and stoles with the fox's head and feet still attached as if poised to leap from around their necks at any time... It was a pity they retained their headscarves... did they ever take them off? Whilst most of the men wore glossy dinner jackets, and would have looked like James Bond's doppelgangers if they weren't wearing their flat-caps, others would have looked quite Count Dracula-esque in their white tie and tails had it not been for their scuffed work boots. At least they'd all made the effort, which was more than could be said for Mrs Wiggins' husband, who dashed around backstage in his patched-up dungarees, moaning to himself that nothing seemed to be going right.

The expensive Chanel and Dior scents that Sofia recognised from Busby's perfumery department, when intermingled with the stench of mothballs and the sharp-smelling fog of tobacco gave the auditorium an intoxicatingly eerie feel. And the sounds of hundreds of conversations all merging into an indistinguishable cacophony reminded her of the jabbering of the birds and the bees in the sunny park where she'd gained her tan, which was now disguised beneath an inch of stage make-up.

But not everyone was engaged in conversation. Like a speck of amethyst in a chunk of granite, the Bishop sat in deep meditation, preparing to endure a ballet he was obviously completely and utterly uninterested in, purely to hear Klem's poetic declamation during the interval... He may have been asleep, but it was hard to tell, because he wore the darkest of sunglasses.

The distant slam of her Tato's dressing room door was the cue

The Dancing Barber

for Sofia to scamper backstage and resume her stretches with enthusiasm. She could tell he was on edge, and just like all the other dancers, she didn't want to do anything to upset him.

'Only half an hour until curtain up, understand?' Mr Taras shouted, strutting straight through the girls' changing room, leaving the scent of Ralgex in his wake, swooshing his cane through the clammy air as a reminder that discipline would be maintained. Every dancer turned to face him, standing to attention, shoulders back, and eyes facing forward.

'Right!' he said, raising his palms upwards, 'arms in third position, quickly!' He proceeded to parade up the long dressing room, scrutinising every aspect of every dancer's appearance. But he soon started tut-tut-tutting…

Sofia cringed when he gave a Bic razor to a girl, ordering her to the toilets to shave her armpits. How embarrassing for her, especially as he insisted on announcing for all to hear: 'there is no room for hairy ape-women in my ballet!' He moved to the next girl and said, 'and as for you, go and put some more white make-up under your nose: there isn't any room for moustachioed ballerinas either! You can shave it off when you get home!'

Then he methodically checked that every single costume was precisely the same shade of white: woe betide any girl whose mother had inadvertently washed her leotard alongside a dark coloured garment. Inevitably, his tut-tut-tutting quickly resumed: 'you,' he tapped a girl on the shoulder, 'and you… and you… and you. Go to Mrs Wiggins and get some new <u>white</u> tights! Your parents can pay for them later.' He clapped his hands harshly, '<u>move</u>!'

They didn't bother to argue; Mr Taras could spot even the slightest shade of pink, even in the dim light of the changing room.

But his inspection was incomplete: whilst puffing out plenty of cigarette smoke, he examined every girl's make-up in turn… any inconsistencies resulting in him screaming for Halyna to come and make corrections. And the more things he noticed that annoyed him, the more enraged he became… The light bulbs shook on the ceiling, the radiator pipes clattered against the bare brick walls and the false teeth were nearly spat from his mouth; one of the smaller dancers was so frightened that she almost had an accident. And worst of all, his perspiration caused his aftershave concoction to mix noxiously with the Ralgex, making the clammy air unbreathable.

Sofia hoped he wasn't going to burst a blood vessel: *why did he have to get so wound up? The audience wouldn't notice if a dancer's make-up wasn't quite right, they were sat too far away... And most of them only came because the tickets were cheap and there was nothing to watch on the telly...*

To her horror, she noticed one of the older girls wasn't even slightly intimidated by the ferocious Ballet Master: she may not have been, but it was never wise to show it. But this foolish girl was finding it difficult to resist the urge to burst into hysterical laughter. Sofia watched as her mouth curled up ever so slightly at the corners, before resuming a neutral position, only for the corners to curl up even more a moment later. And as Mr Taras approached, the more difficult it became for her to maintain her composure. Even beneath all that white make-up, it was obvious the foolish girl was bright red: her face looked as pink as some of the other girls' tights.

The moment Mr Taras came to stand in front of her, the foolish girl laughed loudly in his face... the more she tried to stop herself from laughing, the more she laughed...

Sofia covered her eyes when her father's lips screwed up and he tightened his grip on the knobbly handle of his cane. He glared at the foolish girl, his eyeballs bulging from their sockets, his jugular veins throbbing and his nostrils flaring. But that only made the foolish girl laugh even more; and as her eyes wandered down his body to the floor, she laughed with as much silliness as a tickled Stan Laurel.

Mr Taras grabbed the other end of the cane and flexed it, forming the usual hula-hoop. 'What is the matter with you?' he demanded, 'why are you laughing?'

But the foolish girl couldn't help it. The more she tried to ignore what made her laugh, the more she noticed it, so the louder she laughed...

The younger girls cried and wailed, huddling up to each other so as to achieve safety in numbers, while Mr Taras applied his usual brand of discipline to the foolish girl. He shouted, 'I will not be laughed at! Especially by one of my pupils, understand?' The foolish girl didn't dare laugh again: in fact, Mr Taras would be a dancer short, because she ran out into the night, never to be seen again.

'Does anybody else want to laugh at their Ballet Master?' he shouted, slicing the air into strips with the red-hot cane. His eyes quested the room, but not a single utterance was heard. 'Good!' he said, examining himself in the mirror, deciding there was absolutely nothing wrong with his appearance. For a brief moment, he regretted losing his temper and wondered whether his actions were truly justified?

'In precisely twenty minutes,' Mr Taras ordered, 'everyone is to go to their allotted places, understand?'

Every dancer nodded her understanding, praying that everything would go smoothly.

With the inspection over, Mr Taras made a swift exit, preferring to spend the least time possible in these changing rooms. Their heavy wooden doors, lack of windows and strange ventilation grates embedded in the floor reminded him too much of gas chambers.

With the old man gone, those girls who weren't crying or dabbing at their bleeding armpits subsequent to using the Bic razor, spent most of their time hopping from one bare foot to the other, attempting to swing on their brilliant white tights as quickly as possible... They'd soon learn to sit on the bench when getting changed: the stone floor was painfully cold to stand on.

'Phew,' said Natalka, 'I've never seen your Tato *so* wound-up before.'

'I don't think anybody has,' Sofia mused, 'I just hope nothing goes wrong tonight, otherwise he'll need sedating.'

Natalka smiled. *They'll probably need one of those tranquilliser guns they use for dangerous lions on the Serengeti.*

This evening – despite everything that had happened – Sofia's mood was higher than a kite. Her "Cygnet Number Eight" costume was consigned to the stores and she hoped she'd never see it again. She admired herself in the mirror wearing Odette's beautiful outfit: as expected, it was a little tight around her thighs, but she was comfortable enough. The golden crown of the Swan Queen hung on her arm like an enormous bracelet; she'd wait until the last moment before putting it on.

Seeing Sofia trembling with nerves, Natalka hobbled over to the mirror and said, 'don't worry Sofia, you'll be brilliant. This is your chance to prove to your old man just how good you really are.'

'Thanks Natalka,' Sofia said, stroking her white-feathered leotard, which from some angles, made her look like a deformed chicken. 'I *am* sorry about your ankle.' She truly regretted hiding Natalka's bandage in the park – although would never admit to it – and felt guilty that her friend's worsened injury was partially her fault.

Natalka shrugged her shoulders, 'it's not your fault... it's just one of those things,' she said, tapping the plaster cast with one of her NHS crutches. 'Running around searching for those stupid aunties of mine caused me to break a bone in my foot. Doctors said it'd be at least six weeks before the pot comes off... It's a bleeding nightmare: I won't be able to have a bath until June! And by that time, I'll smell as bad as my aunties! I don't know which one whiffs the worst: Auntie Lyudmila or Auntie Valentina? What is it about old Uki women: they all seem to reek of something awful? Bleeding hell, I hope I don't when I'm ancient like them...'

Sofia smiled... at Natalka's house, everyone was allowed their own fresh bathwater; they may only live in the "squalor" of a back-to-back, but at least their bathroom actually contained a bath. 'Here,' she said, holding out the bag of nuts her Auntie Lenka had given her as a good luck gift before the performance. 'Would you like one? They're almonds...'

'Ooo, yes please,' said Natalka, extracting a handful of nuts and munching away as if she were a squirrel. 'They're my favourites!'

Sofia mused that a few nuts wouldn't make up for what she'd done to her best friend; but it was a start. 'Here,' she said, after Natalka had eaten half the bag, 'you may as well have the lot...'

'Ooo thanks,' Natalka said with a full mouth, shuffling over to peek out at the audience through a gap in the heavy curtain. 'Bleeding hell, would you look at that: the auditorium's full! Your Tato's going to make a heap of money tonight...'

Sofia smiled. *Maybe, but it wouldn't take him long to drink and smoke it all away...*

In the cheapest seats down in the stalls, just behind the footlights, Natalka's parents sat with their arms folded, facing one

The Dancing Barber

way, whilst Natalka's aunties sat with their arms folded, facing the other way. Sofia smiled and said, 'are they still not talking?'

Natalka shook her head, 'they say they want to go home... and the sooner the better!' She – just like the rest of her family – wished they'd never turned up in the first place. 'Here you go,' said Natalka, holding out the bag, 'you can have the last one.'

Sofia accepted her friend's generosity, even though the almond tasted dreadful; but Natalka seemed to like them. After swilling her mouth out with water, she said, 'I suppose your father's happy?'

'Happy...? He's bleeding ecstatic! Trouble is, they don't have return tickets. So we're stuck with them until my father saves up enough money.' She sighed, 'so he'll have to do a lot more portering at the hospital.'

Sofia huffed, 'it seems my parents have precisely the same troubles... Mama's great big twin sisters turned up out of the blue this afternoon and are under the impression that we all live in Bolling Hall!'

Natalka shook her head. 'You're kidding... I didn't think your Mama was snobby... Mind you, your Tato bleeding well is... Will our parents *ever* learn?'

'Apparently not,' Sofia said, 'and it gets worse, because my old man sent them photographs of you, telling them that it was me! Can you imagine how it makes me feel? It's no secret he's ashamed of me, but how could he do such a thing?'

If it weren't at her friend's expense, Natalka would have thought the gesture was quite complimentary. She smiled, 'tonight's the night when you can prove him wrong!' she said, using her fingernail to extract fragments of almond from between her teeth.

'Mmm,' Sofia said, 'I'll certainly try my best.' *But will it be good enough?*

'Where are these aunties of yours?' Natalka asked, squinting as she surveyed the auditorium.

'They're back at home,' Sofia said, 'the man at the door wouldn't let them in.'

'Really? Why ever not?'

'If your aunties are the ugliest trolls in the world,' Sofia said, 'then mine are the ugliest trolls in the entire universe! And they smell quite badly of gone-off eggs.'

Natalka smiled, 'speaking of gone-off eggs,' she said, holding her nose upon hearing a formidable rasping sound that meant only one thing. She looked around at a relieved Oksana; 'I suppose it makes a change from cheese and onion crisps...'

Sofia and Natalka watched Oksana being shoehorned into her XXXL costume – a process akin to squeezing a watermelon into the finger of a glove – and trussed up with an entire roll of special black carpet tape, crosshatched for added support. The heifer couldn't help breaking wind, for her carpet tape corsetry compressed her bowel so much that the gas had nowhere else to go.

'I hope you've been to the loo,' Mrs Wiggins said, fixing the last piece of tape into place, 'because it's too late now!'

Oksana regretted drinking that last pint of Cola. Could she keep her legs crossed for three whole hours?

The Dancing Barber

Chapter 37

'Which durak was stupid enough to give him booze?' Halyna demanded, surveying the drunkard slumped between dusty boxes in a dingy storeroom beneath the stage.

Mrs Wiggins shrugged her shoulders, 'no idea.' She picked up Klem's Thermos flask, 'but this is full of it.' She smiled, 'it smells kind of nice, don't you think?' She took a small sip of the astringent liquid and remarked, 'it tastes kind of nice too...'

Halyna snatched the Thermos flask and sniffed the contents, 'I didn't put booze in his tea... This is not goodski, this must be sabotage!' Her eyes darted about the room, 'it'll be them; they've come to get him. I knew he should have stayed at home! I curse Taras for letting him come here!'

'Them?' Mrs Wiggins asked, wiping her nose with a snotty Kleenex, 'what are you on about?'

Halyna didn't need to worry about concocting an answer, because the characteristic sound of rupturing carpet tape echoing from the girls' toilet meant Mrs Wiggins had to urgently run to Oksana's assistance.

Halyna crouched down, endeavouring to keep her dress out of the dust. She gently slapped Klem across the face. When that didn't work, she slapped him harder still, leaving a clear print of her hand on his red cheek. She shouted, 'wake up!' and shook him forcefully, causing his head to wobble about. She cursed and slapped him again, watching his head flop backwards so strongly that she had visions of it detaching from his neck, falling to the floor and rolling around like a bowling ball with a moustache.

'Damn it!' Halyna screamed, 'wake up!' She looked at Mister Pushkin, who sat patiently by its master's side; the cat's heavy eyelids suggested it'd seen it all before...

But not even the dead could sleep under the stage once the orchestra started to properly warm up. The trumpets, violins and drums may have made an awful din, but at least they'd finally got themselves organised. Unusually, Halyna heard the sound of a bandura, its strumming giving Tchaikovsky a Ukrainian twang...

The din came to an abrupt halt; she could clearly hear the conductor call Taras something obscene, yet strangely accurate, in response to him reprimanding them for their ineptitude. Halyna smiled: she liked it when her husband was put in his place.

The deep trumping of a tuba drowned out anything else Taras could say, so he stormed off to shout at his dancers some more.

The blinds over Klem's drowsy eyes slowly twitched open and he looked at Halyna with the typical drunkard's grin. He said, 'I have some *wonderful* news!' He momentarily looked away and said to himself, 'unless it was a dream?' He looked determinedly back at Halyna, 'no, it *wasn't* a dream! I really do have some most *wonderful* news!'

'Not now Klem,' Halyna said, 'you can tell me later. Right now, you must drink plenty of water if there's even the *remotest* hope of you sobering up in time for your recital.' She tried to hand him a pint glass filled with tap water, but he refused to take it. 'Come on, now is *not* the time for stupidity... you *must* flush out your system!'

'Recital?' Klem said, blowing such a large raspberry that he'd inadvertently splattered Halyna's plastic framed glasses. 'You know what I think of the recital? I'll tell you... I think the recital should – !'

'Klem!' Halyna protested, drying her face with a perfectly ironed cotton handkerchief that she'd embroidered with a floral pattern in one corner. 'Language, *please*. There is a Bishop in the auditorium!'

Klem blew another raspberry, 'ahhh, Bishop S*mi*shop...' He turned and gazed dreamily into Halyna's eyes, 'but *I* am going to be married!'

'Not this again, look,' Halyna rolled her eyes to the ceiling, 'we've been through this. You know I think you're a very sweet man...'

'No, not you!' Klem slurred, examining Halyna's almost perfect beauty, 'although...' He shook the thought from his mind, 'no, I am to marry the most beautiful woman... I am to marry Zena!'

All the smelling salts in Boots weren't enough to revive Halyna after that shock.

The Dancing Barber
Chapter 38

---✂---

Gunter tore the lining from the empty lizard-skin briefcase. *I must be going mad... through my own binoculars I watched Ivan empty his safe into this case... so where have all those white fivers gone?* He checked again beneath the passenger seat, but there was nothing there. Apart from an old umbrella, a half-empty jar of pickled gherkins and a screwed up packet of cheese and onion crisps in the glove compartment, the entire car was empty. So he threw the briefcase to the floor and slumped into the comfortable oxblood leather seat. *There must have been another briefcase... but he went empty-handed to that ruined farmhouse?*

After climbing out of the car, he went to open the glass door to the boot; but the money wasn't there either. He checked inside the spare tyre, slicing it open with his Mafia-issue knife. Sadly, it only contained stale air.

Gunter decided not to worry about it: deep down, he knew Ivan would pay him in full tomorrow... the formerly Ginger Rasputin didn't have the courage to be even a penny short. As Klem frequently said, *"Who of you by worrying can add a single hour to his life?"* (Matthew, 6:27). Besides, being the proud owner of a nearly new Volvo P1800S made Gunter beam with happiness; such a beautiful car was wasted on a philistine like Ivan. He blew the dust of Ivan's peeled skin from the mahogany dashboard and decided the car was in need of an urgent valeting. It would also have to be re-painted: red just wasn't his colour. White would be better: then he could pretend to be Simon Templar. On second thoughts, black would be much more anonymous.

Although that disgusting curry – he now understood why it was called a vinda*loo* – gave him the most dreadful stomach-ache, the journey in the Volvo's rear foot-well – however cramped – was certainly worth it... He counted Klem as one of his closest friends and was glad to have heard – by eavesdropping at the farm house's window – that the Soviets planned to "sort him" tonight. He had always suspected Ivan was in league with the Soviets: and now he knew it. But he also knew Klem wasn't daft; he'd be lying low for the next few days, safely barricaded in his attic, where not even the most intelligent Soviet Secret Policeman could find him. And even if one did find him, the dog would be a valiant bodyguard.

After sliding back into the driver's seat, Gunter checked the time on the dashboard clock, turned on the engine and sped back to Bradford. He reckoned Ivan would be at The Alhambra, eager to watch his daughter blunder around the stage as if she were an elephant in a tutu... And if Ivan were there, so would be the Soviet Secret Policeman... but neither of them would know Klem wasn't going to turn up...

The Soviet Secret Policeman – the one Ivan addressed as "Colonel" – was most insistent on taking care of Klem "personally", so Gunter knew to look for an obnoxious man in a badly fitting nylon suit, probably going by the name of Vladimir. Using his thumb, he nudged the brim of his black hat higher up his forehead; he'd also need to pay close attention to people carrying umbrellas... any one of them could have a cyanide tip.

Gunter examined his appearance in the rear-view mirror: being dressed in black meant he wouldn't need to change into a dinner suit... And it was just as well, *Swan Lake* was due to start in fifteen minutes...

The Dancing Barber
Chapter 39

Halyna sprung to life like Frankenstein's Mother the instant Mrs Wiggins thrust a bottle of extra-strength smelling salts into each of her friend's nostrils. But the same treatment was useless on Klem, who'd slumped into an even deeper drunken stupor. Not even Mister Pushkin could revive its owner; the feline's efforts only served to stain Klem's favourite embroidered shirt a rather nasty shade of green.

Leaving Klem in a heap on the floor, Taras gently carried his wife to a nearby chair and watched her eyes roll around their sockets while she got her bearings.

Halyna slurred, 'if Klem wants to marry Zena, then how can I stop him? The drunken *oaf*, I bet he'll forget all about it once he sobers up! The silly fool! And why was he prattling on about a baby? Heaven help us if Zena's pregnant!'

'You know how he jabbers when he's had a drink,' Taras said, 'I can't imagine anyone wanting to marry *that*! Let alone breed with it!'

'Please Taras; it is not goodski to speak about Zena in such a way. Remember, she and Lenka are my sisters! I know they're not oil paintings, but I'd rather you weren't rude about them.'

Taras said, 'all right, I'm sorry.' He thought: *They might not be a Rembrandt, but could easily be a Pollock...*

Upon hearing the backstage buzzer, Taras immediately jumped to attention. He said, 'good Heavens, we've got to get a move on: curtain up in less than <u>ten</u> minutes!' He pulled out a small mirror from under the wide sash around his waist and checked his freshly applied make-up hadn't smudged. He then smiled and blew himself a kiss, thinking how dashing he looked: *not bad for a fifty-five year old*! He thrust the mirror into his wife's hand, 'tidy yourself up, and sort out that hair! Remember, *best* behaviour for the rest of the evening, understand?'

Halyna tried to keep a cool head. She said, 'of course dear,' as she tidied her hair and reapplied a dab of lipstick. She watched her husband continue to faff with his own makeup; even after all these years, she couldn't get used to a man paying so much attention to his own appearance... it was little wonder the ballet critics couldn't keep their eyes off him! But at least his costume was complete; it was typical of Taras not to have noticed his prized prop hanging on the hook behind his dressing room door!

'Right, come on Halyna,' Taras said, herding her out into the auditorium.

She pointed to the heap of pinstriped suit on the floor, 'but what about him?'

'Leave him,' Taras said with a dismissive wave of the hand. 'He'll sober up eventually. And if he doesn't, I'll have to do what I always do...'

With five minutes before curtain up, Taras plonked his wife in a private box high above the auditorium, where she could watch the performance in comfort. He screwed the cumbersome Cine camera he'd borrowed from a friend onto the heavy tripod he'd borrowed from another friend, and said, 'are you *sure* you're all right?'

'Yes, yes,' Halyna protested at his fussiness. She should have savoured the moment, because he hadn't fussed over her like this in years. But the sooner he went, the sooner the smell of Ralgex would go too.

'And you're sure you know how to use the camera?' he said, putting a perspiring hand on her shoulder. 'Remember, record the whole performance, understand?'

'Yes, yes, now go downstairs,' said Halyna, 'you're on stage in *three* minutes! The principal dancer can't be late for his own ballet.' Her shoulder felt wet... it wasn't like him to get so nervous.

Halyna let him kiss her on the cheek, and was careful not to smudge his freshly applied makeup. She said, 'goodski luck.'

'Thank you, Halya,' Taras said, blowing her a kiss as he passed through the privacy curtain. 'I'll need all the "goodski" luck I can get!'

Halya? He's not called me that in over a decade... But it'll take a lot more than that to release him from the doghouse.

The Dancing Barber
Chapter 40

Even the Bishop – who'd made no secret of his indifference to ballet by snoring loudly up to that point – sat up and watched the spectacular main scene of Act One. It was the lavish party at the Royal Court, where Taras' Prince Siegfried made a big show of not being particularly interested in any of the available young ladies...

Taras relished the experience and was pleased his choreography was being danced precisely as planned. Every *pirouette*, every *plié*, every *petit échappé* and every *jeté passé* was performed accurately, elegantly and perfectly... The extra rehearsals were worth it, as was employing Mrs Wiggins' husband to build the set and paint the backdrops: the man's talents were wasted on joinery, and if it wasn't for his loathing of "those pansy actors", he would be better suited to designing sets for West End plays. The man could transform the smallest stage into the largest arena: even Taras found it difficult to tell where the stage ended and the backdrop began.

As he pranced across the polished boards, Taras watched the dancers in the wings lining up obediently for Act Two. He noted – much to his surprise – they were all present and stood in the correct places, poised to flutter onto the stage in the manner he'd taught them the instant Mrs Wiggins gave the signal. And for the first time he noticed his Sofia in Odette's white-feathered costume and realised how foolish he'd been not to consider her for a leading role to begin with. He thought she looked handsome, resplendently wearing the golden crown belonging to the Swan Queen, and was pleased her tutu was wide enough to disguise her thighs. He was so filled with pride that he almost forgot to commence the twenty successive pirouettes that he knew would wow the audience.

Being principal dancer and choreographer was already taking its toll. Taras found it increasingly difficult to dance with perfection when he'd noticed, and could do nothing about, some of the cygnets playing around in the wings... they were only feet away from emerging on stage and ruining everything! He knew it was too good to be true for them to have been so obedient. But at long last, Mrs Wiggins scooped them out of sight, hopefully to give them a piece of her mind: he certainly would do the same, the moment he had the opportunity.

Once the excitement of the lavish party scene was over, the Bishop adjusted his dark sunglasses and instantly resumed his loud snoring, his fleshy lips vibrating as he breathed. Sat behind the Cine camera, up in the distant private box, Halyna wished someone would give the clergyman a nudge so as to shut him up... But there was no one close by... his shoulders were so wide that he also occupied most of the seats either side.

She tried to ignore the asthmatic walrus, but it wasn't easy.

Peering through the viewfinder at the distant stage, it puzzled her how the majority of the audience could be so enthralled by watching a middle-aged man in tights prance aimlessly around the stage, carrying a wooden crossbow during a ten-minute scene she thought was at least ten minutes too long...

Prince Siegfried was out hunting with his chums – and seemingly having a little difficulty with a certain part of his costume – when he came across a lake occupied by a flotilla of Swans. The ingenious use of mirrors in the background made it look as though there were hundreds, if not thousands of dancers, all paddling and flapping their wings in unison. And the stirring orchestral accompaniment – it certainly made a change from Mrs Wiggins' monotonous piano playing – of one of Pyotr Ilyich Tchaikovsky's most famous ballet scores mesmerised everyone except the Bishop. Down in the orchestra pit, the conductor gesticulated with a white church candle at the woodwind, string and percussion sections to ensure their efforts combined harmoniously... not a bad effort for an amateur. But Halyna wouldn't expect anything less from the Priest... and it was the first time she'd seen him out of his cassock; so he did have legs after all...

Up on the exclusive Dress Circle, Halyna watched the critics writing page after page of notes, their eyes never leaving the stage. As usual they were flamboyantly dressed in velvet suits and frilly shirts, with silk handkerchiefs sticking out of their frilly cuffs. Nevertheless, Taras thought very highly of them, but would curse if he saw them writing on the back of his meticulously prepared

The Dancing Barber

reviews.

But it was Halyna who cursed when she realised the Cine camera had followed her roaming gaze around the entire auditorium. She flicked the camera back to the stage, and dreaded what Taras would say when he discovered the film of his best performance in years had been ruined. To be sure nothing more was missed, she tightened the wing-nut on the tripod, ensuring the camera's telephoto lens would never leave the stage again. She shrugged her shoulders: at least she had another seven opportunities to record an entire performance... although it wouldn't satisfy Taras. Nothing ever did.

Studying Prince Siegfried through the viewfinder, she was glad Taras decided to leave the prosthetic scalp lock and stick on moustaches in his dressing room; and the less said about the Charlie Chaplinka mask the better. Her husband's creativity was often excessive, and his original idea of making Prince Siegfried into a Cossack would have been a step too far, let alone using that dreadful mask to transform him into a nightmare-inducing Satanic Gnome.

Taras was certainly putting every ounce of effort into his performance: the whiff of Ralgex he gave off whilst energetically dancing, leaping and prancing made the audience's eyes water. But there was something distinctly out of proportion about him. The billowing shirt, unbuttoned to the waist wasn't out of the ordinary, nor were the white tights and glossy ballet shoes. But the bulge, located at the confluence of his legs was far larger than normal. She shuddered to think what he'd shoved down this time? It had already attracted the critics' attention, especially as he kept repositioning it every few minutes. *Give me strength, Taras... Leave it alone!*

At long last, it was time for Sofia's Odette to make her big entrance. Halyna double-checked the Cine camera was focussed accurately and was facing the right way... She was so proud of her clever daughter for being able to take Natalka's place at such short notice. But it was unfortunate the Swan Queen's crown – made especially for Natalka – refused to stay in place atop Sofia's much smaller head, preferring to repeatedly drop down and bang onto the bridge of her nose, making it into the most ornate blindfold in history. And Sofia's smile frequently disguised a grimace when she danced on pointes: her bunions must have been terribly painful... the minimal cotton wool padding within the white leather shoes hardy did anything to alleviate it. At only twelve years old, it already looked as though she had six toes on each foot... and the bunions would only get worse as she got older.

Halyna dried her eyes; if Taras weren't proud of their daughter, then she certainly was. Sofia heeded perfectly her Tato's advice, making sure every step was acted and every action danced; the critics were utterly captivated by her, putting down their pencils for the first time since the performance began. Sofia phrased her movements to follow the soothing melody of violins, which combined playfully with the sweet sounds of flute and piccolo, together with the incongruous strumming of a bandura, as she proceeded to dance with the Prince.

Halyna noted Sofia's expert footwork and textbook pirouettes, her tutu rising like a frilly dustbin lid around her waist as she spun. Halyna was also supremely proud of the cygnets... they danced like little cherubs... and so they should after enduring months of rehearsals and Taras' bad-tempered rants and plentiful canings...

But Sofia's time in the limelight soon ended once the villain, Von Rothbart made his hideous crow-like appearance, accompanied by the sounds of clashing cymbals, thumping drums and coughing bassoon. Taras had been most insistent that Von Rothbart's music was not to sound like that of a pantomime baddie; but it seemed the orchestra weren't capable of playing in any other way.

In the corner of her eye, Halyna glimpsed Oksana's Odile waddle around the darkness of the wings, looking like a sack full of melons, ready to burst at the seams. She hoped the black carpet tape would hold... at least it couldn't be seen under all those black feathers. The heifer slouched, waiting for her cue, crunching noisily through another packet of crisps...

Halyna knew that Taras dreaded what the critics would make of her, and hoped they couldn't hear her crunching: how could that girl eat so much before performing? But she knew Taras was trying not to let it bother him: he concentrated on his dancing and traversed the stage as if walking a tightrope, placing each foot carefully in front of the other, following the line of the floorboards before exploding into another frenzy of pirouettes that sent the audience dizzy.

Later, when Von Rothbart deposited the least-likely Odile in history before Prince Siegfried, a great deal of muttering reverberated around the auditorium. Halyna continued to film, and even captured the moment when Oksana's Odile felt the need to extract her knickers from between her buttocks using both hands, in the process releasing a thunderous cloud of trapped wind that was so loud that it drowned out the blaring tuba. The audience thought this was hilarious... But the critics had other thoughts... they mopped each other's glistening brows after witnessing what they called such "brave" choreography, which was enhanced by the honky-tonk trumping of a single trombone accompanying Odile's every move. Halyna wondered whether the trombone was necessary... Oksana was more than capable of making her own music.

It may have been a spellbinding performance, but once again, Halyna's eyes soon began to wander. She noticed that every seat in the auditorium was occupied, except two. With the Cine camera whirring away, she examined her list and discovered that these seats were reserved for Ivan and The Gossipmonger. How awful it was for Oksana to dance her flabby little heart out and her family couldn't even be bothered to turn up. With those two as role models, it wasn't any wonder the girl was a menace.

Halyna then glanced at the purple blob that was the Bishop, and thought: *I bet he's asleep again under those sunglasses! I've never seen him without them – he even wore them at church – maybe he's a Roy Orbison fan?*

But she was surprised to discover that he wasn't asleep, because all of a sudden he lifted the sunglasses onto his brow and peered through a pair of antique opera glasses. His gaze was not at the stage, but at the audience. He must have been as bored as she was.

Halyna was so distracted by the Bishop's intriguing antics that she hadn't noticed Ivan and his mother slip apologetically into their seats, managing to annoy everyone they brushed past. Ivan wore a navy-blue dinner jacket beneath his old mac and retained his large hat once seated, much to the irritation of the people behind. Meanwhile, The Gossipmonger wore a hideous sequined dress that gave her the appearance of a Christmas tree, which rattled so much that Halyna could hear it from the other side of the auditorium... even her Gaggle couldn't tolerate the stench of mothballs it gave off. Halyna thought the dress was very Charleston-esque in appearance, therefore exceptionally unfashionable for 1963, augmented by a fan The Gossipmonger brandished that resembled an unfurled peacock in miniature that wafted the appalling smell of mothballs far and wide.

Halyna reflected on what a strange pair they looked. Although The Gossipmonger was ancient, she still looked younger than her son, to the extent that those who didn't know them would be forgiven for thinking they were husband and wife. Hilariously, The Gossipmonger made Ivan carry her handbag, despite it being more sequined than her dress, making him look the most foolish of fools.

One of Halyna's secret talents was her ability to lip read, even at a distance. It was a skill she found necessary to perfect since her hearing had been damaged by wartime air raids, coupled with decades of working in the noisiest of factories. Through the camera's long lens, she watched The Gossipmonger's cruel and shrivelled mouth utter: 'I couldn't care less what they did to you; all that bothers me is the state of my drawing room carpet! How could you let them tread all that dirt into it?'

And as Ivan no longer sported that ghastly beard, Halyna saw his reply: 'There wasn't much I could do about it; do you have any idea how uncomfortable it is being tied up like a dead pig?'

'But *I* wouldn't have let them tie me up like a dead pig; and I remember a time when you wouldn't have, either.'

'You'd have had no chance against the goons Gunter sent; clouting them over the head with your clubbed hand wouldn't have made any difference, they'd have probably bitten off your arm, chewed it up and spat it out.'

The Gossipmonger shook her head, 'and how do you know it was Gunter? You have so many other enemies... You collect them like a dog collects fleas.'

Ivan shook his head, 'I've been thinking... it could only be Gunter... It's a warning... he's giving me a taste of things to come if I don't pay up... Well, he can shove it! He's not getting a penny!'

'Shhh!' said several of the women sat in the row behind, 'if you want to gossip, go outside! You are spoiling our enjoyment of the ballet.' One of the women jabbed at Ivan's enormous fedora, 'and

The Dancing Barber

take that stupid hat off, it's blocking my view!'

The Gossipmonger turned to her son, who was tightly gripping his fedora with both hands. She whispered, 'not even Mick Pallo or Jackie McManus would dare tell someone like Gunter to "shove it", never mind a cowardly wimp like you! So if this is a taste of things to come, you'd better pay him... Otherwise...' She drew a line across her throat with her clubbed hand...

Halyna smiled: at last "he who cannot be named" was doing something about Ivan, and it was about time too. And how entertaining it was to have lip read such a conversation: if Klem hadn't incinerated the man's beard, she wouldn't have known half of what was said...

She cursed under her breath when she discovered the Cine camera was pointing to everything but the stage. She repositioned it quickly, but knew that – as Natalka would say – Taras would "do his nut". *Ah*, she dismissed the thought, *after the way he's been treating me, it'll do him goodski not to get what he wants for once. I've filmed Sofia's performance, and that's what matters.*

Once Prince Siegfried and Odile began their elaborate dance routine – comprising plenty of, as Taras would say, Batman and Enter-Shat – it wasn't long before members of the audience began whispering to each other. Halyna thought it was rather out of character for cultured ballet-goers; but she supposed it did look rather odd for the Swan Queen's doppelganger to be twice the size of the Swan Queen, and bear a striking resemblance to a befeathered Oliver Hardy wearing a tutu. Some people even started to snigger, especially when Sofia's Odette appeared in a high window and witnessed her Prince dancing with an obese swan: did the Prince need to go to the optician?

Gradually the whispers became louder and soon, noisy conversations sprung up around the whole auditorium. Other people began pointing and laughing. Halyna heard the critics' pencils furiously scratching away with even greater speed, accompanied by the occasional curse as one of their leads snapped, followed by the frantic use of a pencil sharpener.

Halyna automatically assumed it must have been something Oksana's Odile had done: had she ruptured her carpet tape corsetry and spilled her tsunami of a belly across the stage? Or had she bounded straight through the floorboards? Or had her excessive intake of Coca-Cola induced her to create a lake of her own? But no, in her attempts to deceive Prince Siegfried into thinking that she was Odette, Odile was dancing better than planned, in fact – much to Halyna's surprise – her performance was bordering on being goodski.

It was then when Halyna noticed Prince Siegfried's bulge had dropped down one leg of his tights. A moment later, it was back in position before it dropped down the other leg! Whatever Taras had used to augment his bulge must have escaped his truss and was going on a tour of his tights. For many in the audience it was the funniest thing they'd seen in a long time. But – much to their credit – Odile and the cygnets continued dancing as if nothing had happened, despite Prince Siegfried delving both hands down his tights, making the necessary adjustments…

Then – as if it had been deliberately choreographed – Taras' Prince Siegfried gracefully exited stage right, while an understudy Prince Siegfried entered stage left. Halyna panicked: she knew his understudy would only ever be called on in an emergency. As she ran down to find out what was the matter, she hoped the critics hadn't noticed that Prince Siegfried had suddenly developed breasts…

The Dancing Barber
Chapter 41

'Get this thing off, you stupid woman!' Taras barked, laying on his dressing room floor with his legs spread widely apart, his black hair dye and makeup streaming down his perspiring face and both hands rummaging around inside his truss.

'I am <u>not</u> a stupid woman!' Halyna protested, 'and what the hell's wrong with you? You've ruined your own ballet!'

Taras cringed with pain, '<u>please</u>,' he demanded, 'pull down my tights and help me take this truss off!'

'Why?' she said with disgust, 'take that ridiculous thing off yourself!'

'Damn it woman, didn't you see what happened on stage? There's something moving around inside my truss, understand? So help me get it out!'

'Certainly <u>not</u>!' Halyna folded her arms and turned around; she was fed up of him referring to her as "woman". And as for the thing moving around inside his truss, she imagined that one of his disgruntled students – of which there were many – had poured itching powder into it again, or maybe added a flea or two. It'd happened before and it'd happen again…

The instant Taras unhitched the strapping, Halyna jumped back several feet, as the monstrous codpiece skidded across the floor. A cascade of old socks, rolled-up underpants and stockings – she wondered where they went – spilled everywhere, as if someone had just tipped over the laundry basket. In amongst it all, she watched, as if in slow motion, something distinctly rat-like spring out, run straight for the skirting board and then disappear.

No one's ever put a rat in his truss before, Halyna thought with admiration. *It was a big one too; during The Great Famine it would have made a nice roast dinner.*

Taras fainted, his hair dye painting a black arc on the wall before his head hit the ground.

Halyna promptly asked for someone to fetch Mrs Wiggins and her smelling salts. The only problem was, Mrs Wiggins was currently on stage as Prince Siegfried…

'Hey, what's all the fuss about?' Klem staggered in, still exceptionally drunk. Even with his system diluted with half a gallon of Peppermint tea, he found it impossible to remain upright. 'Did I hear the word "rat" mentioned? Oh, oh, Taras doesn't like rats, does he?'

'Klem, you're not helping,' Halyna said, 'now go back to the storeroom and practice your poems. Remember, you're on as soon as Act Two ends!'

'I know these poems off by heart!' He tried to straighten the green ribbon on the collar of his embroidered shirt, but ended up undoing the knot. 'I did write the book…'

'You still need to prepare. Now go,' Halyna insisted, pushing him into the dusty corridor and slamming the door.

Klem saluted and said, 'yes m',' before staggering back to the storeroom, leaning on the wall, letting it guide the way. He only ever behaved so childishly after consuming the smallest drop of alcohol… the more he drank, the more childish he became. At least this time, it wasn't his fault: how was he to know he'd picked up Taras' Thermos flask by mistake and the tea within was augmented with a substantial amount of samahon. After the first sip, it was too late: the old alcoholic had been reawakened.

The fact he could stagger around suggested his own Peppermint tea was slowly getting to work… so at least his brain and voice would soon be able to function properly. But the same would not be true for his legs for another few hours. He fell head first into the storeroom, landing in a heap of dusty boxes.

Shaking the drowsiness from his head, he noticed for the first time the insalubrious room he occupied. It was filled with racks of musty old costumes and cardboard boxes filled with assorted props, stacked from floor to ceiling. He noted that all the cardboard boxes had a damp patch, six inches from the ground, and wondered how Mister Pushkin managed it, considering he'd never witnessed the cat drink anything.

The snow of dust from the ceiling intensified, coating his hair and jacket, making him cough and sneeze: it could only mean Oksana was bounding around the stage above. He dusted himself down, in an effort to look at least half presentable – he needn't have bothered putting on an unworn suit after all – and examined his moustache in an old mirror. Noticing it had drooped into a

The Dancing Barber

horseshoe, he twisted it back into place before searching his pockets for a comb with which to tidy his thatch of hair. It was then when he noticed the hard lump in his jacket pocket. He smiled mischievously as he took out Ivan's pistol and admired his trophy.

If the Soviet Secret Police came for him now, he'd certainly be ready for them: he may have been sozzled, but he could still aim. He spun the pistol around on his index finger, contemplating what to do if the worst happened. But for now, he helped himself to some more Peppermint tea and pretended to shoot at things across the room as if he were a cowboy...

Chapter 42

The posse of flat-capped old men yearned for burning torches and sharpened pitchforks, and possibly even a gallows, as they chased a petrified Ivan towards the fire escape. Ivan's enormous fedora still spun high above the auditorium, casting a shadow on the stage suggesting that an alien flying saucer was descending down the beam of the spotlight. And the woman who – fed up with the hat blocking her view of the stage – had pulled it from his head and launched it into the air, was still screaming like a banshee after seeing the hated symbol emblazoned on the balded head beneath.

One of the spotlights left the stage – giving Prince Siegfried's understudy the blessed opportunity to finally adjust her brassière – and followed the Soviet snooker ball as he clambered over the disgruntled audience to reach the nearest aisle, whilst trying to avoid being clouted by dozens of handbags and walking sticks.

Very soon, the entire audience – from the stalls to the upper circle – understood what all the fuss was about. They traced the path of the spotlight – the beam of which swirled with tobacco smoke – to the head branded with the hammer and sickle in the pool of light at the end. A second spotlight traced the path of the posse and as the pools of light converged, Ivan was booed and the posse cheered unanimously, as they rapidly gained on the hated villain. The Bishop remained stony-faced, his arms folded across his broad chest, his eyes, maybe open, maybe not, still disguised behind the sunglasses.

Ivan bounded out in his usual lumbering way, then disappeared deep into the night. The posse shouted out what they were going to do to him in so much detail that the Bishop cringed and the critics wafted each other with frilly handkerchiefs, saying, 'ooh, I say!'

Not even the fearsome headscarved old women could stop their husbands, even if they wanted to... they looked forward to what they hoped would be "a good lynching". Besides, they much preferred to clout The Gossipmonger around her head with their well-aimed handbags, crying, 'we always knew he was Satan! And

The Dancing Barber

now we *know* where his loyalties lie!' Bits of sequin detached from The Gossipmonger's dress, scattering small tap washers across the floor, the smell of mothballs swirling through the air. The Gossipmonger tried to fight back, but her clubbed hand was no match for all those swinging handbags.

The critics weren't interested in any of this. They only had eyes for ballet; and as the spotlight swung back to the stage after Act Two had ended, they contented themselves by sipping pink gin, dabbing perfume onto their necks and comparing their manicures, deducing this to be the sort of behaviour they'd expect from *common* people who could only afford the *cheap* seats in the stalls.

Instead of the safety curtain descending, a single spotlight remained, illuminating a patch of polished floorboards in the centre of the stage. Some of the remaining flat-caps in the audience were itching to go for a smoke, but the headscarves insisted they stayed put. And it was just as well, because the floorboards soon creaked open and the depressing announcer rose up through the hole in the stage as if he were a zombie rising from the grave.

'And now,' he droned, 'without further ado, I have pleasure in welcoming our favourite poet to entertain you during the interval! A round of applause, please, for Klem!'

'About time too,' mouthed the Bishop, unfolding his arms only to re-fold them the other way. He watched – along with the rest of the audience – as the spotlight swung over to where the heavy curtains joined...

The audience's enthusiastic applause persisted for at least a minute before petering away to silence, when it became clear the curtains weren't going to open any time soon. They knew that, as they were waiting for Klem, such delays were expected...

After five minutes, the flat-caps began standing up, pressing their hands to their bursting bladders and heading for the exits, muttering, 'sitting still for two hours is ridiculous!' This time, the headscarves thought it best to let them go, but woe betide if they came back smelling of alcohol and tobacco...

The shadowy figure in the private box at the highest point in the auditorium was getting impatient. How was he expected to do what he'd planned if the target wasn't on stage? He rested the rifle with the telescopic sight across his knees, put a Trebor mint in his mouth and decided to do the same as everyone else: wait...

When everyone had given up hope, the curtains finally parted, revealing Klem stood like a shop dummy behind a wooden lectern, with his poems stacked on the sloped surface in front of him. Mister Pushkin sat statuesquely by his side, the pair of them squinting at the single spotlight shining in their faces.
The audience gave a standing ovation the instant their national hero appeared. Many of the flat-caps ran back from the toilets without washing their hands; with toilet paper trailing from their heels, they re-joined their wives who immediately detected the alcohol and tobacco on their breaths. Even the flat-caps, who'd successfully chased Ivan off the premises had returned – massaging their bruised knuckles and looking exceptionally pleased with themselves – in time for the highlight of the evening.
The clapping ceased once Klem's right hand lifted, a little too Hitler-like, as if to say "thank you" and "shut up so I can begin". Hardly anyone noticed the colourless puppet string extending from his wrist to the ceiling, the taut string slackening a little too quickly, causing his arm to thud down onto the sheets of poetry, and almost knocking them to the floor. But instead of speaking, Klem stood motionlessly, peering through the lenses of his half-moon spectacles as though deep in thought.

Directly beneath the stage, Halyna whispered to Taras, 'oh for goodness sake, stick it in further!'
Taras did as he was told, ramming the steel knitting needle through the gap in the stage flooring and straight up Klem's trouser leg, until it lanced deeply into the thin calf muscle.
Instantaneously, Klem shouted: '<u>The grass</u>...' His eyes opened widely, 'it blew merrily, so merrily in the wind! The cows, they ate it steadily. On *that*, the farmer could depend!'
With his first poem finished – yes it really was just two lines – the audience gave another standing ovation. Many of the headscarves whistled their approval, much to the flat-caps' condemnation, especially when they started blowing kisses at their

The Dancing Barber

hero.

Beneath the stage, Taras shook his head.

'I know,' Halyna said, 'a child could write better poetry, or even a trained monkey...'

'And yet that lot out there seem to like it,' said Taras, looking out at the audience through a tiny peephole. 'Look,' he said, 'even the Bishop's cracked a smile for the first time this evening.'

'Let me see,' Halyna said, nudging her husband out of the way and putting her eye to the peephole. 'I know I shouldn't say such things about men of the cloth, but there's something about that man I just *can't* stand.'

Taras was inclined to agree, 'he's got one of those faces, hasn't he? But Klem said there were some real weirdoes at his Seminary... maybe this is one of them...'

Eventually the applause silenced, for the headscarves were all whistled out and didn't have the energy to blow another kiss. Klem's hand arced upwards again, the audience waiting on tenterhooks for his "keynote" poem.

The shadowy figure in the private box put the rifle's telescopic sight to his eye and rested his steady finger on the trigger, watching and waiting...

Another overlong silence prompted Halyna to look up through the gap in the stage floor... She discovered Klem's chin resting on his chest; his spectacles had fallen off and he was snoring deeply. He was even dribbling from the corner of his mouth, the droplets bouncing off Mister Pushkin's head.

The old women in the stalls began to mutter, 'looks like he's been at the samahon...'

'Yes, he's probably had the whole bottle...'

'Maybe an entire crate...'

'Yes, they must have trussed him up again. Look closely and you'll see the coat hanger beneath his jacket. It'll probably be tied to a broom handle that's been shoved up his trouser leg and under his waistband. That's how they did it last time.'

Even Natalka's aunties had a good laugh about it... it had been a long time since they'd seen such rubbish.

Taras was disappointed to hear such comments. He thought this year's "trussing up" was well camouflaged. So he rammed the knitting needle up again – harder than ever – and Klem burst into his recital:

> 'We Ukrainians will survive
> the Soviet oppression!
>
> But only if we are strong and
> don't succumb to depression!
>
> We will beat them without
> seeing any blood trickle!
>
> And Ukraine will be
> independent once more and rid
> of the hammer and sickle!'

Halyna smiled and Taras cringed as they witnessed several pairs of rather large knickers being launched from the stalls. The garments scattered in an arc on the stage around the lectern, one pair hooking onto the microphone, and another landing on Klem's head, giving the impression that he wore an ornate bonnet... Unfortunately, on closer inspection, it was a pair of Y-fronts. And a nice frilly pair came to rest in front of Mister Pushkin. Hopefully the thrower wouldn't want her garment returned, for the cat had claimed it as its own and had gone to sleep in amongst the frills.

The shadowy figure in the private box relaxed and smiled. He placed his rifle on the floor, and for the first time that evening, came out from the shadows and joined in with the standing ovation. He'd taken off his black leather coat to reveal a black double-breasted suit beneath, but retained the wide-brimmed black hat, worn at an angle to obscure most of his face. Although pleased the Soviet Secret Police hadn't acted, he couldn't help but worry as to the reason why...

He'd instructed his people to verify the identity of every person in the theatre, even down to the woman in the box office and the sweeper-up backstage, so he felt fairly confident there wasn't a single Vlad amongst them... but that could never be guaranteed...

As the curtains closed, he dismantled the lightweight rifle and fitted the barrel and telescopic sight into the polished ebony butt,

The Dancing Barber

slipping it into his pocket. But there was something – or should that be some*one* – he'd overlooked; he put the telescopic sight to his eye and re-examined every member of the audience...

Chapter 43

'This is the good idea,' said Zena, trying not to sneeze, despite clouds of feathers swirling around the kitchen. 'This meal, it will bring back the plenty of the memories for Halynochka, yes?'

'I *know* it will,' said Lenka. Having finished plucking the last pigeon, she positioned it on the chopping board and prepared to hack off its head and feet with Halyna's favourite kitchen knife. 'The street outside, it has the many of the wild birds. And they do not cost anything. With the pigeon each and the seagull, this will be the wonderful meal.'

Thankfully it had gone dark and the twins had drawn the kitchen curtains, because apart from an extra-large apron, neither of them wore anything else. Every article of their clothing had been bleached and boiled, and was draped over the washing lines in the attic, dripping onto Taras' new carpet, leaving enormous white polka-dots all over the fancy pattern.

'And look,' said Zena, 'out in the street, I found plenty of the herbs…' She bit off a few dock leaves and munched them around her mouth. 'Nice and bitter… and much tastier than the bunch I found at the base of the lamp-post…' But her preference was for the bright yellow flowers, and especially the delicate seed heads… they were lovely and sweet… unfortunately, they became stuck between every one of her craggy teeth, giving the impression she wore dental braces.

Lenka grabbed a bunch of stinging-nettle leaves with her bare hands, rolled them up into a ball and inserted them into her mouth. 'Mmm,' she said, 'the tasty, yes? Just like the spinach, but free of the charge…'

Zena sighed, 'who said the herbs were the food of the poor?'

Lenka shrugged, 'Halynochka, she is not the poor, but she will love them more than us, yes?'

'She will, if there are any left…' Zena said, slapping her sister's nettle-filled hands. 'Do not eat them all…' Zena then helped herself to a handful of soggy moss she'd scraped from a wall, most of it dangling from her chin like a goatee beard.

The Dancing Barber

Lenka sighed... Zena was much greedier than she was.

Having finished gutting the last pigeon, Zena slopped the offal into a bowl and said, 'all we need now is the rabbit... It will go nicely with the tinned meat I found in the cupboard.'

'But there are no rabbits around here,' Lenka said. 'Bradford, it is the big city... rabbits, they do not live in the city...' She clicked her fingers, 'but there are plenty of the *rats* though...' Her mouth began to water, 'shall I go catch some?'

'Yes, Halynochka, she will be the very pleased! I bet she has not eaten the rat in thirty years... It will remind her of home... And so will my borsch...' Zena stirred the beetroot-filled cauldron that looked as though it brimmed with blood. She delved a finger into the soup and licked off the viscous liquid, before adding three more heaped tablespoons of salt. She then plopped in the pigeon's heart, liver and kidneys to give the borsch some "meaty surprises". She said, 'I hope my Klem, he can also come to the dinner, because there is the *so much* to arrange!'

Baiting the snares she never left home without, Lenka said, 'but what is the rush: you still not have the divorce? You cannot even think about the new husband until you get rid of the old husband! Otherwise you will be the "Bigger Mist" and that is not the good.'

'True, but the wedding, it must still be the planned,' Zena said, adding even more rotten cheese to the snares, then fully opening the sharp jaws, being careful not to trap her fingers. 'So the next time we pay my old husband the visit, we must *try* to be the friendlier.'

Lenka shook her head, 'what you did to him was terrible! It was worse than terrible! It was <u>very</u> terrible! Even *I* did not think it was the good idea to tie him up like the dead pig and bundle him into the suitcase. I was amazed that we managed to fit him in! And he was the heavy piece of himno!'

'But you do not know him,' Zena said, bending down to pull up the red socks that perpetually concertinaed at her ankles. 'He can be the very dangerous: it best to have him under the control straight away! You cannot talk to him as an adult... in his head, he is still the child.' Standing up, she released a pungent hurricane of flatulence without noticing. She said, 'it the pity that the suitcase burst open and he escape, because all would be sorted by now!'

Lenka picked up the baited snares and prepared – very carefully

– to take them out to the alley. Sadly, they soon began snapping shut…

Zena mulled over a thought, 'I do not even know if he knew who I was? But he *would* have known if he saw the papers and he *would* have signed.' She clenched her fist, 'I would have *made* him sign! But getting the divorce, it is the easy,' Zena reasoned, 'however, making the durak understand that I want my daughter back will be the <u>less</u> easy.'

'Mmm,' said Lenka, with three snares already clinging to her bruised fingers, 'especially with his mother to hide behind: apparently she is as tough as four men!' She narrowed her eyes, 'but I suppose that depends on the size of the men?'

'I not scared of her!' Zena said, clenching both fists. 'It is the nothing to do with her! And remember, we are The Wild Boar Wresting Champions of Chaplinka! What is a club-handed old baggage to us?' She rolled her eyes to the ceiling upon noticing that every one of Lenka's fingers now had a baited snare hanging from it… why was her sister so stupid?

An hour later, Zena shook her head so vigorously that she made a snowstorm from her plentiful dandruff. 'This <u>no</u> good,' she said, staring at the cooker. Four of Halyna's largest pans, crammed with carcasses were stacked on the hob, with all four gas rings turned on full blast. 'This will not the cook, even if it is left for the whole year…'

Lenka shrugged, 'what do you suggest we do?' She'd only just finished bandaging every one of her fingers. 'Soon, they will be back from the theatre…'

'Move the table,' said a frustrated Zena, 'and I will go collect the firewood…'

Lenka smiled, 'yes, the old-fashioned way, it is the best! Why would anyone use the gas cooker? They are so silly.'

Zena shrugged, 'I do not know? But Halynochka, she must like it…' She retrieved an axe from her suitcase, testing its sharpness by flicking the blade against her thumb, instantly drawing blood.

'I cannot think the why? These English cookers, they are too small,' said Lenka, dragging the table into the corner, its legs juddering across the carpet. 'What shall I do with the tin bath?'

With a distant horse chestnut in her sights, Zena said, 'leave the

The Dancing Barber

bath there... why use seven pans when one big pan is better... you can fill it with the meat, yes?' Wearing only her apron, she ventured outside...

Lenka clicked her bandaged fingers, 'the <u>good</u> idea! In this bath, we shall cook the feast! Just like old times!'

Less than ten minutes later, the tin bath was suspended from a tripod of tree branches above a roaring inferno built directly on top of the kitchen carpet. Smoke quickly filled the room and would have stained the ceiling had Taras' tobacco not done so already...

'Good,' said Zena, opening and closing the door in order to ventilate the kitchen. 'Cooking over the open fire, it always makes the food taste the best.'

Lenka stirred the "stew" with the handle of Halyna's yard brush, gripping it with both hands as the concoction gradually thickened to the consistency of tar.

Zena sighed, 'the aroma, it is *wonderful*... It brings back so many of the memories...'

'Err, Zena,' said Lenka, dancing on the spot, 'I do not wish to give you the worry, but I think the floor, it is on fire...'

Chapter 44

Taras waved goodbye to the Ambulance, watching it speed off with its siren roaring and its blue lights flashing on its way to the Infirmary, cleaving its way through the traffic, leaving the smell of burning rubber in its wake. He was completely inconsolable, and all Halyna could do was put a fur-clad arm of comfort around him and try to reassure him that things weren't quite as bad as he imagined.

'After all my efforts,' Taras snivelled, 'the evening has turned into a <u>complete</u> disaster. I must be cursed!'

'Don't be silly,' Halyna said, 'the ballet was a genuine success! From what the critics told me, their reviews are going to be even better than the ones you'd written for them! And both Sofia and Oksana danced beautifully! They were the stars of the show! As for the incident with Ivan, it has already been forgotten; and not many people will have noticed the principal dancer's wandering bulge!'

'Maybe you're right,' Taras sobbed, 'Sofia and Oksana were both excellent. You must remind me to thank them, and also remind me to thank Mrs Wiggins for taking my place before the interval... But it's what happened to the Bishop that will overshadow everything! Can't you see? The papers won't report on my ballet, but on the fact that the Bishop was almost killed! And in such a *terrible* way...'

Taras put his head in his hands and cried. But then he heard the approaching jingle jangle of Klem's golden watch chain. Without looking up, he said, '<u>where</u> do you think you're going?'

Klem stuttered, 'err, I thought it best to go home...'

'Oh no,' Taras said, 'you're going <u>nowhere</u>: we need to have a <u>serious</u> talk!'

Klem swallowed, but the lump in his throat remained... if anything it got bigger. He looked down at the Russian Blue and saw it shaking its furry little head with utter disapproval. 'But how was I to know?' he asked the cat that immediately raised its nose and turned to look the other way.

The Dancing Barber

It was strong black coffee all round at the Uki Club bar, even for Klem.

'Right then, Klem,' Taras demanded, while Halyna and Sofia listened, 'you still haven't told me where you got that pistol?'

'From Ivan,' Klem said matter-of-factly, pushing the cup of ghastly coffee away: he tried tasting it, but the aroma *didn't* appeal. 'He threatened me with it; so I took it off him, just before I strung him up in the lavvy. Halyna knows *all* about it!'

'Oh does she now?' Taras turned to his wife.

Halyna stared at her husband and said, 'don't look at me in that tone of voice!' She held out her hands, palms facing upwards. 'He gave me the gun, and when he wasn't looking, I took out all the bullets.'

Klem looked at her as if to say, *'did you?'*

'But I forgot there was one in the barrel, but as all the others were blanks...' She shrugged her shoulders, 'I assumed the remaining one would be blank too, so I didn't let it worry me. It never crossed my mind that it might have been real; Ivan must have wanted to play "Russian Roulette"?'

Taras shook his head, 'never mind confiscating the bullets, woman, you should have confiscated the pistol too. You know what he's like! Have you forgotten what happened last time?'

'But he's only like that when he's drunk,' Halyna said, whipping off her plastic frames glasses and glaring at her husband. 'And *whose* fault was that? Fancy pouring all that samahon into a flask of perfectly good tea.' She almost growled, 'you should never have brought him here in the first place... You should have locked him in the attic!'

Taras took a deep breath; he was about to release some steam, when Klem interrupted.

'I was drunk as a skunk,' Klem slurred, still giving off enough alcoholic fumes to knock out a horse. 'I was just minding my own business under the stage, mucking around and pretending to shoot the "Injuns", like they do in the Cowboyski films.' He extended two fingers, 'Bang! Bang! Bang!' He frowned, 'how was *I* supposed to know that a pair of legs were going to come crashing through the ceiling? Hmm? I was in so much shock that I fell backwards and the pistol went off. Bang it went! And then there were blood and buttocks all over the place! And if things weren't bad enough, it wasn't just anyone I'd accidentally shot, but a *Bishop*!' He glared at Taras, 'what was the man doing on stage in the first place, hmm?'

Taras said, 'it's not my fault the Bishop decided to give a speech of thanks for inviting him to the ballet.' He scratched his head, 'although I don't actually recall inviting him in the first place? He also wanted to thank you for, as he called it, your "wonderful recital". I told him you were busy... how could I say you were three sheets to the wind? And after he'd given his speech, he decided to show off his version of a pirouette – it wasn't half bad for a man his size – but after his second spin, he crashed straight through the damned trapdoor!'

Halyna couldn't help but see the funny side. From her private box she witnessed the six-foot tall Bishop shrink to half his size in an instant, his purple cassock bunching up on stage as his legs went through the floor and his broad torso wedged firmly in the trapdoor. And from what Klem told her of what he'd seen from the storeroom beneath the stage, the Bishop and traditional kilt-wearing Scotsmen had a lot in common... she wondered whether the Archbishop had approved of this unorthodox attire, or should that be, lack of? She tried desperately, if unsuccessfully, to disguise her grin.

'I don't know what you're laughing at, woman?' Taras snapped, 'it's a very bad thing to shoot anyone, especially a Bishop, and particularly there!'

'You address me as "woman" once more,' Halyna said sternly, 'and I'll make you into one!'

Sofia almost wet herself with laughter, while Klem looked at Halyna with tremendous satisfaction.

'I'm sorry Halyna,' said Taras, 'but I'm still very upset!' He turned to look at Klem, 'but I tell you this: if my reviews are himno, I'll be blaming you, understand?'

Act 4

Easter Monday

> 'Therefore I tell you, whatever you ask for in prayer, believe that you have received it, and it will be yours.'
>
> *Mark 11:24*

Chapter 45

The kitchen was a sauna. Condensation dripped from the blackened ceiling, streamed down the window and misted-up all the framed photographs of Taras' varied ballet exploits that lined every square inch of every wall. And for once, Halyna wasn't the slightest bit bothered: if Taras wanted his frames wiping, he'd have to do it himself... She hoped they all rotted: at least then she could redecorate without having to paint around hundreds of nails.

And much to her delight, her most hated photograph, that of Taras wearing the Charlie Chaplinka mask, whilst performing his ballet entitled *The Insane Elf*, had become so warped with moisture that it surely would be destined for the bin. And about time too: the thing gave her the creeps... as usual, it's eyes stared at her, anticipating whatever creative answer she could formulate to her twin sisters' inevitably awkward question.

As she waited for "dinner" to be served, she rested her palms flat on the table and tried to calm her mind. But it was anything but calm; she fidgeted, lifting her hands off the plastic tablecloth, only to realise they'd adhered themselves firmly with the perspiration of worry. And the other diners around the table also perspired, not because of worry or guilt, or the ferocious heat of the kitchen, but at the prospect of eating a meal that looked completely and utterly inedible.

'A-hem,' said Klem once Zena had plonked a Pyrex dish full of what could only be loosely described as "food" in the centre of the table. He waited for the cheap Chinese pendulum clock to finish its midday chimes before clasping his hands together and closing his eyes. But it was only when Halyna, Sofia and the twins did the same that, begrudgingly, Taras followed suit; even the cat held its paws together beneath the table. Klem continued, 'Oh Lord, for what we are about to receive,' he glanced dubiously at the bubbling contents of the Pyrex dish, 'let us be truly grateful. Amen.' He then crossed himself in the Orthodox fashion, permitting Zena to, as she would say, 'the dish it up.'

After everyone replied with a unanimous, 'Amen,' and made

the sign of the cross, Zena slopped out the "food" with the refinement of a school dinner lady at the wrong time of the month.

'The tuck in,' Zena said, 'while it is still hot, yes?'

'And if there is not enough,' said Lenka, 'we have a bath-full left over...'

Taras smiled, not thinking for a second that she meant it literally.

Halyna shuffled her feet, wondering why the carpet felt strangely rubbery. She poked the plastic tablecloth out of the way, and looked to the floor. With curiosity, she said, 'who bought the new rug?'

Zena and Lenka looked at each other shiftily.

Lenka opened her mouth; but then howled, upon feeling a sharp pain in her shin. She glared at Zena, 'err... we buy it; you like it, yes?'

Halyna peered at the rug through her plastic framed glasses. She said, 'it's not what I'd have chosen... But, I suppose, modern styles are changing all the time...'

'Good,' said Lenka.

Zena added, 'we knew you would the like it.'

Neither twin dared mention that the rubbery rug was actually the underside of the scorched carpet they'd found upon clearing away their bonfire. In desperation, they'd sliced out a circle of charred carpet and flipped it over, hopeful Halyna wouldn't notice... And as the steam cleared, they desperately hoped she'd blame the sooty walls on Taras' cigarettes. Maybe they should have persevered with the gas cooker after all?

While Halyna debated what to do with the contents of her plate, she was – for once – grateful for Taras' foul mood. His temperament always dictated the atmosphere of the house, and as long as he sat there simmering like a pan on the hob, no one would dare to speak, nor would the cat dare to purr. Halyna counted a full ten minutes, when the only sounds in the kitchen were the scraping of cutlery against crockery, the ticking of the pendulum clock and frantic digging as Mister Pushkin went to excavate a trench in the downstairs litter tray.

Even though Taras glared at him, Klem said, 'this salad looks nice.' He pointed to the bowl of assorted leaves by his elbow, 'what's in it?'

Lenka smiled, 'nettles and dock leaves... you like, yes?'

Sofia cringed, 'you mean *stinging*-nettles?'

Lenka laughed, 'they do not sting...' She scrunched up a handful and shoved it into her mouth, 'see, there is no sting...'

Halyna tapped Sofia's wrist and shook her head. She whispered, 'don't bother... they *do* sting.' She turned to Lenka and asked, 'where did you pick them?'

'From the street,' said Lenka, 'there is plenty at the bottom of the lamp-posts...'

'I see,' said Halyna, who now knew what was causing the smell...

Klem continued, 'Zena, where *did* you learn to cook so well?'

Halyna mused that if anyone had dared to eat any of their meal, they'd have probably just choked on it. She didn't know how Klem could say such a thing while keeping a straight face: for a man who hated lies, he was certainly proficient in telling them.

'Thank you my darling,' said Zena, fluttering her sleep-encrusted eyelashes. 'I learned the cooking from my Mama...' She looked at Halyna, 'just like our Halynochka, she will be teaching Sofia, yes?'

Both Halyna and Sofia feigned a smile.

'Of course,' said Halyna.

'Definitely,' said Sofia.

Halyna remembered her own Mama's cooking; it certainly wasn't anything like this, whatever *this* was? And as for teaching Sofia how to cook... she was happy to leave that to the nuns at school, during lessons on domestic science.

Sofia had already witnessed the deterioration of her own Mama's cooking, largely because of Mrs Wiggins' influence. Healthy Ukrainian fayre based on cabbage and potato had been replaced by various things fried in vast quantities of lard, much to the woeful detriment of her thighs; it also made her clothes smell so appalling that the girls at school thought she lived in a "greasy spoon café". Although her Mama's cooking was bad, it was infinitely more palatable than the brown amorphous sludge her Auntie Zena had slopped into her plate: it looked and smelled like slurry, and the flavour probably wasn't much better, with its slimy

The Dancing Barber

texture and earthy aftertaste.

Halyna and Sofia discretely scraped a portion of their respective plates clean, giving the impression they'd eaten more than they had, which was difficult considering they'd actually eaten absolutely nothing. The morsels they'd tasted had been furtively spat out and dropped to the floor, where they were duly sniffed and rejected by an intelligent Mister Pushkin.

Halyna could see the dread in Klem's eyes when Zena turned to him and said, 'when we are the married, I will make sure you eat like this <u>every day</u>!' She then noticed the corner of Taras' mouth curl ever so slightly upwards: he undoubtedly thought a lifetime of eating nothing but Zena's "cooking" would be suitable punishment for ruining his ballet. Klem smiled, continuing to chew thin air... Halyna then noticed him surreptitiously shovelling blobs of "stew" into a saucer on his lap, presumably to be disposed of later. Even the bluebottles that regularly buzzed around the kitchen refused to linger over the Pyrex dish... and who could blame them?

With the next exhausting performance of *Swan Lake* only a few hours away, Sofia knew she had to eat something, so decided to risk another bowlful of her aunties' blood-red chunky borsch: the only source of vegetables they'd prepared. Everything else was pure meat, but Heaven knows what kind... Strangely textured burgers occupied the centre of the Pyrex dish, which – despite six platefuls already gouged from it – was still brimming with meat. Her aunties had also produced what looked like a large selection of various game birds, and piles of unidentifiable body parts, which had been simmered in a sauce so thick that it could have been used to fill a crack in the wall.

Sofia had never seen her Mama look so worried; why couldn't she just tell the twins the truth about Bolling Hall? Maybe then they'd insist on going home like Natalka's Lyudmila and Valentina? Sofia wished Zena and Lenka would hurry up, and just ask their inevitable question...

The atmosphere around the dinner table hadn't been this tense since the time her Tato came home with lipstick on his collar... lipstick that wasn't one of his usual shades.

Not one pair of eyes met with another... Everyone, other than the twins, wondering how to get rid of their slurry without causing offence. Klem's lap was already full of slurry, and neither Sofia, nor her Mama knew what else to do, other than scrape the stuff around their plates to give the impression they'd eaten at least some of it.

Sofia watched her Tato and Klem mould their meals into interesting shapes that would have given a psychiatrist plenty to talk about, whilst her aunties Zena and Lenka wolfed it all down as if it was the best thing they'd ever eaten. She couldn't take much more of this... The pendulum clock chimed half twelve; she wondered what she was missing on the telly? Staring longingly at the prized Bush television set in the corner, Sofia watched the reflection of the room in the domed screen that gave the impression they were all starring in a silent movie.

That twenty-inch screen was a member of the family, so paying the man from British Relay was a higher priority for Mama than buying anything, but the most essential of groceries. The kitchen's focal point was no longer the fireplace... gone were the depressingly silent evenings when everyone would count down the minutes to bedtime... there was never enough to talk about and no one was ever interested in playing board games.

Right now, all Sofia wanted to do was flick the switch and see what was on... it was bound to be good... after all, today was a Bank Holiday.

Sofia hoped they'd repeat yesterday's *Sunday Night at the London Palladium*: it was her highlight of the week. She hoped Norman Rose would invite Cliff Richard to sing his latest record: Natalka said it was his best yet... and she wished she was going on a *Summer Holiday*... Watching *Sunday Night at the London Palladium* was the only time her Tato allowed "Pop Music", which – with the exception of the *Singing Nun* – he called "Musical Himno" to be played in the house. At other times she had to content herself with sneaking up to the attic to listen to Klem's little radio when he was out; her Tato's in the shop was so old that it may have been steam-powered and was far too complicated to fathom.

The smell of stale eggs drifted across the table; Sofia looked at her aunties, but neither of them owned up to it. *Please, someone, say something... Anything... Otherwise I'm going to go nuts!*

She placed her fork onto the side of the plate, as silently as she could, and reached across to switch on the television set. There

The Dancing Barber

was bound to be a nice comedy, or the News, or maybe even *Danger Man* to watch... Tato never missed an episode. But before her hand was even half way to the switch, the silence of the room was shattered...

'Halynochka, why you no like the dinner?' Zena asked, after watching her sister conceal a burger-sized portion beneath a slice of stale bread. 'It may be, how you say, the overcooked...' She shrugged her shoulders, 'but we did not know you would be so late coming back from the ballet...' While licking her own plate clean, she said, 'throwing the food away, it is the sin... if the food, it is not good, Lenka and I, we shall eat it...'

'Mmm,' said Lenka, 'I like it. It is, how the French, they say *Cordon Bleugh...*'

Klem couldn't agree more... With emphasis on the *Bleugh...*

'Oh no, the dinner is goodski,' Halyna said, chewing some imaginary food, 'but I don't have much of an appetite.' She gently put down her knife and fork. 'Yesterday was a bit too eventful for me. I suppose it's the shock of seeing you and Lenka again after all these years...' She thought for a moment and decided to correct herself, 'maybe *shock* is the wrong word,' she smiled genuinely, 'what I meant to say is that it's a truly *wonderful* surprise!'

Zena also smiled and said, 'ah, we knew you would be the pleased to see us!' After refilling her plate, she shovelled a heaped tablespoon of the "stew of the meat" into her mouth, allowing some of its gloopy brown gravy to spill out of the corners and dribble down her chin. She chewed for a moment, shovelled in some more and said, 'so when are we to go to your real house?'

Halyna's heart skipped a beat. Out of the corner of her eye she saw the photograph of Charlie Chaplinka burst into fits of uncontrollable laughter as if it were the famous animatronic clown at Blackpool Pleasure Beach. She stared at her husband, but the coward didn't make eye contact, preferring to rearrange the food on his plate, sculpting it into the thing that sprang from his bulge the other night, before ceremonially cutting it back up again.

Everyone around the table watched as the gravy that had clung to Zena's downy beard slowly drip, drip, dripped onto the tablecloth, forming a brown puddle that she plunged her elbow straight into, while uncouthly slouching at the table. That was the final straw. Everyone, apart from the twins was now completely put off attempting to eat any more of their "food": four sets of cutlery clattered down onto four plates that were simultaneously pushed into the centre of the table.

Zena and Lenka waited expectantly for their question to be answered, both eagerly glaring at their young sister. They couldn't wait to go to "The Bolling Hall" and live like the Tsars for a little while... but given their current surroundings, neither twin could understand why their sister needed a big house when this one was so luxurious? With carpets on every floor, cold and *hot* running water, two toilets that flushed away normal amounts of himno and electric lights: this house was better than the one owned by the richest man in Chaplinka.

They assumed it must have been Taras' influence, because Halyna had never been "the show-off". They knew that, beneath all the finery, their young sister had barely changed in thirty years; she may have worn expensive clothes and spent a lot at the barber's, but underneath, she was still a peasant. Those gnarled hands were the give-away, even if they'd been manicured.

They remembered from her letters that behind "The Bolling Hall", their young sister had cultivated a fabulous kitchen garden, undoubtedly maintained by several gardeners to produce fresh vegetables all year round: they couldn't wait to see it and looked forward to doing some planting of their own, if they were allowed.

And it was obvious to them that Halyna hankered to get her hands dirty again... But why did she just sit there, staring blankly into space? Could she have fallen asleep with her eyes open: was that even possible? Zena coughed loudly and said, 'The Bolling Hall? When are we to go there?'

Dismissively, Halyna said, 'oh, we can talk about that later,' racking her brain for an alternative subject. She couldn't just blurt out the truth – she didn't know how they'd react – Natalka's aunties went ballistic when they found out they'd been lied to for decades. Before the twins could say another word, Halyna turned to Klem and said, 'when you were drunk, you said the funniest thing,' she smiled, 'you said something about Zena having a *baby*?'

Taras couldn't help but laugh: Klem announcing to the world that he was going to marry Zena was funny enough, but for a

The Dancing Barber

woman like Zena to be having a baby was hysterical. He laughed a little too much, and grimaced when he aggravated his rat-induced injuries.

Even the dog in the back yard joined in the laughter, barking and howling like the Hound of the Baskervilles, making the picture frames rattle against the walls... It had been howling ever since they'd sat down to dinner... what *was* the matter with it today?

'It's true,' Klem said, dislodging a lump of meat from his throat with half a gallon of tea. 'Zena had a baby twelve years ago,' he looked dreamily at his wife-to-be and said, '*our* baby...'

Now Halyna burst out laughing, 'very funny – but it's not *April Fool's Day* – how can you have a baby without being married? Who'd ever heard of such a thing?'

But Zena's screwed up lips informed Halyna that she was certainly not joking.

Halyna had wanted to direct the conversation away from Bolling Hall, but this was ridiculous. She said, '*no*, I *cannot* believe it.'

From beneath a furrowed brow Sofia said, 'but the nuns at school taught us that such a thing is a most terrible sin. They said the parents would go to hell and the child would be a b –'

'That's enough Sofia,' Halyna interrupted, 'I need to talk to your Auntie Zena in private.' She pointed to the door, 'go and find out what's causing that dog to go crazy...'

'*Mama*...' Sofia pleaded. But it was no use, and she was promptly thrown out. She didn't mind, because she was glad to leave that vile concoction her aunties called "the stew of the meat"... She could think of a much more appropriate four-letter word to describe their "stew"...

The dog howled so much that Sofia found it impossible to eavesdrop at the door. So she tugged the salivating beast to the far end of the yard, its claws ploughing the concrete as it struggled to stand its ground. She tied its leash to the straining gatepost, before scuttling back, hoping she hadn't missed too much. She put her ear to the cold door and listened...

Chapter 46

Once she was sure the back door was closed, Halyna took a deep breath and tried to compose herself. She turned to her sister and said, 'now listen to me Zena, how dare you speak of such ungodly things in the presence of Sofia's young ears! It is not goodski for her to hear such things!'

'I give the apologies,' said Zena, 'but it is the important that the truth is told...' She glanced briefly at a nodding Klem, 'although Klem and I, we are not yet the married, we *do* have the daughter...'

Halyna could only stare. 'So, err... Who, err... Does she live in Chaplinka...? Mama never mentioned her in her letters?'

Zena shook her head. 'This is where the trouble is. You see, Ivan, he thinks he is her father.'

'Ivan?' said Halyna, 'but... no... you *can't* mean Oksana?'

Zena nodded.

'Halyna, please,' said Klem, 'you don't need to pull such a face. From what I know, Oksana is a *nice* girl... underneath...'

Taras erupted in a fit of coughing, 'what did you say?' He cleared his throat with some cold coffee, '*Oksana*? But how can *she* be your daughter?' He stared at Zena, who was making a crude demonstration, 'no, I don't mean it like *that*!'

Halyna said, 'more importantly, why does Ivan think she's his?'

Zena said matter-of-factly, 'because Ivan and I are the husband and the wife.'

Without warning, Halyna's stockinged feet appeared at the table as she fell back in her chair, her head hitting the floor with a thud, almost crushing the cat.

Taras shouted at Zena, 'you stupid woman! Now look what you've done. I think this bad joke of yours has gone on for long enough!' He crouched down and gently lifted Halyna from the floor, placing her on a chair as if she were as light as a rag-doll. Gradually she came round, helped in part by some of Mrs Wiggins' smelling salts that Taras had kept for emergencies.

Zena was most apologetic, 'it was not the plan to tell you in such a way. But it *is* the truth, and I feel all the better for telling it!'

Taras said, 'I'm glad *you* feel better...'

Zena was the first person Halyna saw when her eyes creaked opened. She said, 'tell me; are you truly Ivan's wife?'

Zena nodded, 'Halynochka, please, do not look at me like that: it is not as though I married the devil...'

Taras, Halyna and Klem all raised their eyebrows.

Lenka said, 'even then, he was a durak! In fact, calling him a durak is an insult to duraks!'

Zena ignored the comment, 'it may be the hard to believe, but Ivan, he swept me off my feet! He had the money, he had the charm and I was the young and the stupid...'

Taras thought: *you're not young any more but you certainly are stupid!*

Zena continued, 'he promised me the best: more land for us to farm, the new house, the motorised automobile car, the fancy clothes...' She sighed, 'but I was the secret wife; not even his club-handed mother knew about me... and she probably still does not. Ivan, he was the strange husband, he liked to tell me all his woes; and he had many of the woes. So I would listen and let him prattle on...' She reached for Klem's hand, 'but I am a woman with *needs*...'

Klem smiled, ignoring her sandpaper grip, hoping she didn't have *needs* any more... He looked at Halyna and shrugged.

Halyna could only hope all this was a bad dream... She pinched herself... No, it was really happening...

Taras looked at Zena and said, 'who'd have thought it, eh?' He stared at Klem, 'and for all this time, everyone thought Ivan's wife was a figment of his imagination. It had even been said that Oksana had been brought by a stork, just like Dumbo... it must have been a *big* stork...'

Halyna's cogs turned very slowly; all these revelations were too much for her to take all at once. Yesterday was stressful enough: was it too much to ask to have a quiet day today? Being told that her own sister was married to the local villain was bad enough without an extra-marital affair and an illegitimate child to deal with! How was she supposed to brush a scandal as big as this under the carpet? She said to Zena, 'so you were "friendly" with him,' she gestured towards Klem, 'while you were married to

Ivan?'

Zena nodded, 'technically, I am still the married to Ivan.' She fluttered her sleep-encrusted eyelashes at Klem, 'and yes, we were the *very* friendly.'

Klem looked away, winding his watch the usual seven times, even though he didn't need to.

'Mmm,' Halyna said. She stared at Zena and Klem, 'so you two are Oksana's parents? Oksana's Mama and Oksana's Tato?'

Give me strength, thought Taras, *haven't you understood yet? He stopped himself from saying anything. The revelation certainly explained why Oksana didn't have a single ginger hair on her head... And The Gossipmonger's Gaggle had suspected it for years...*

Zena nodded with embarrassment. She knew the name the nuns at Sofia's school had for women like her and men like Klem. It was a pity they couldn't make allowances for women who'd been conned into marrying such disrespectful, manipulative, ginger-bearded men...

'Do you know how serious this is?' Halyna said, sitting upright with her arms folded. She was barely able to look at Klem. 'You and him have *sinned* most terribly...'

'Please do not the judge us,' Zena said, 'Klem was the brave Cossack who came to rescue me. It was the pity he could not have stayed; his work, it called him away... and that was the much more important.'

Klem looked at Zena sympathetically, 'and someone in my position *didn't* need the scandal.'

'It okay,' Zena said, 'I understand; it the pity I could not find you when Oksana was born. I wrote many of the letters and asked many of the people, but no one could find you...'

Klem maintained a neutral expression... *Not being found was the general idea...*

Zena bowed her head, 'I know we have the sinned.' She looked at Klem with a tear in her sleep-encrusted eye, 'but it was meant to be... I should have married Klem in the first place.' She shook her head, sprinkling more dandruff onto her shoulders, 'marring The Ginger Rasputin was the biggest mistake of my life...'

You don't say... Thought Taras.

'Mmm,' said Halyna, believing marriage was a lifelong

commitment, even if husband and wife despised each other. There had been many times when Taras had completely and utterly infuriated her, but he was her husband and that was that. 'I assume Ivan doesn't know about your, err...' Halyna couldn't bring herself to say the word, 'affair?'

Klem couldn't believe how long it was taking for Halyna to understand. He said, 'of course he knows about our affair: that's why he's been blackmailing me! But he doesn't know the *truth* about Oksana... and he definitely is not her father!'

'Oh, I see,' Halyna said, 'now I know why you didn't tell me any details...'

Relieved the penny had dropped, Klem said, 'Ivan was going to tarnish my reputation, tell everyone that I was an adulterer. You know what people think about a Priest – even a retired one – committing adultery... But at least now, it's all out in the open.'

Halyna said, 'but why have I never been told any of this? Hmm? And why did you decide to tell us on the holiest day of the year? It is *Easter Monday*, remember?'

Klem shrugged, 'I suppose, the truth has to come out sometime...'

'Mmm,' said Halyna.

'Halynochka,' said Zena, 'Mama, she never did approve of Ivan...'

Lenka interrupted, 'and who could the blame her?'

'Thank you Lenka,' Zena said. She looked back to Halyna, 'I married Ivan because he was the rich man; but after a year of his nastiness, the money, it no longer seemed important.'

'He was the evil,' Lenka added, 'everyone knew he had the fingers in the many bad pies.'

'Bad pies?' Halyna asked.

Zena clarified, 'she means Ivan associated with Soviets and other criminals... Where do you suppose he got all his money from? Hmmm? And do you think I would have married him if I had known?'

'He is also the violent man,' Lenka said, clenching her fist, 'he hit Zena on the head...'

Halyna and Taras were surprised anyone would dare strike such a fearsome woman.

'But only the *once*,' Zena confirmed, 'he caught me off the guard.' She smiled and said proudly, 'but when I punched him on the chin, I loosened many of his teeth!'

'You should have told me,' Halyna said, 'I could have helped you.'

Zena shook her head, 'Mama, she was the letter writer. She did not want to tell anyone that such nastiness happened in the family... you know how the Soviets, they read *everyone's* letters... And I did not want to burden you with my troubles... you have the hands full here with The Bolling Hall and Taras and Sofia. Anyway, while Ivan was in the hospital, I packed the suitcase and left! I was not going to stay with the man who did not treat me with the respect!'

'But he did not like it,' said Lenka, 'he thought that he was the big boss man! And the big boss man was not going to let Zena leave him and take away his unborn child, even though the unborn child, it was not his...'

Halyna couldn't believe what she'd heard. She said, 'you mean, Ivan hit you when you were pregnant? The man was more evil than I'd ever imagined.'

Zena nodded with excitement, 'I have been trampled by the herd of wild boars and got up unscathed: a weakling like Ivan could never hurt me!' She beat her chest like Queen Kong, unleashing the nauseating stench of stale sweat from her armpits.

Lenka said, 'but Ivan, he had disappeared by the time Oksana was born... Apparently he steal many of the thousands from some very nasty people – people nastier than him, if it was possible – and he went on the run with his club-handed mother.' She smiled, 'we thought we had seen the last of him...'

'But sadly not,' Zena said, 'because when Oksana was the six months old, she disappeared from the cot in my room in the middle of the night. I awoke to discover a note from Ivan saying that he had taken what was his and he had gone to England. Oh how I cried... all I had to remember her by was a nappy full of himno.'

'And from that moment on,' Lenka said, 'we <u>had</u> to find Oksana and bring her back to Chaplinka, where she belongs.'

Zena dried her eyes on her sleeve, 'it took nearly ten years to save the money to come and see you, but we did it! The dollars you sent us came in the very handy: they buy a lot more than the Soviet Coupons. And when we realised that Ivan lived in the same town as our Halynochka, we wasted no time booking the tickets. Viktor, he knows many of the pilot men who were more than the happy to help.'

Halyna said, 'and – regardless of what happened – we are *so* pleased you came,' she looked at Taras, '*aren't we?*'

'Oh yes,' Taras said, '*overjoyed!*'

Halyna turned back to Zena, 'if you need any help to sort out this ungodly mess, all you need to do is ask...'

Both twins nodded their heads in thanks, whilst Taras looked on with despair.

Zena gestured to "the stew of the meat" congealing in the Pyrex dish and said, 'please, let not this news affect the appetites. You all will have more, yes?'

Taras and Klem gripped their empty stomachs, insisting they were too full to eat another morsel.

Halyna said, 'no thank you... Err, forgive my asking, but how do you know Ivan isn't Oksana's father? You can't know for certain?'

Klem grinned and said to Zena, 'you tell her...'

Zena picked up a pair of pink *Pysanky* that were left over from yesterday. She said, 'I shall make the demonstration. You see, it is impossible for Ivan to be Oksana's father, because...' She squeezed both eggs together in the palm of one hand and sprinkled the resultant fragments of hard-boiled egg and shell onto her plate.

Taras cringed, Halyna grimaced and Lenka looked on with pride.

'So you see,' Zena said, 'it will be the very easy to get the divorce. And if that was not enough,' she showed the tattered birth certificate to Klem, 'here it proves that Oksana is ours, not his!'

Klem admired the certificate and said with excitement, 'this is the first time I've seen it...' He looked at Zena, who was picking bits of egg white and yolk from in amongst the fragments of shell, 'it's a bit dog-eared though...'

Klem frowned when he saw that the Registrar had entered the father's occupation as "Peasant"... technically, he was a Priest at the time... He then handed the smelly document back to his wife-to-be, realising why it smelled once he discovered where she kept it.

A couple of questions had been nudging at Taras' brain. He

turned to Klem and asked, 'so have you known all along that Oksana was your daughter?'

'Of course,' Klem said, 'I knew the moment I saw her, but what could I do about it?' He shrugged his shoulders, 'I had no proof.' He straightened the green ribbon at his collar and pulled his embroidered cuffs from his jacket sleeves, 'but now things are different...'

'One last question,' said Taras, 'when you first met Zena, did you know she was Halyna's sister? Because it all seems rather coincidental to me that you happen to be living in your future sister-in-law's house when your future wife turns up out of the blue.' He leaned forward to examine Klem's face: he knew when he was lying.

Klem said, 'I didn't have a clue. I first met Zena in 1932, when Halyna was only a child.' He looked at Halyna, 'you've changed a lot since then... there was no way I could have recognised you... not after all that time.'

Taras believed him.

But Halyna seemed offended, 'what are you saying? I haven't changed that much? Have I?'

'Of course you have,' said Lenka, 'you were only seven in 1932!'

'Now, who wants more of the stew of the meat?' Zena asked, stirring around the congealed sludge with a finger that had just been somewhere exceptionally unpleasant.

Halyna shuffled in her seat and said, 'it looks as though divorcing Ivan will be easy, but I can't imagine him handing over Oksana,' she clicked her fingers, 'just like that?'

Zena winked, and said loudly, so as to be heard over the howling dog in the back yard, 'do not the worry, I know *exactly* how to deal with him...'

'You'll have to find him first,' Taras said. 'From what my friends at the Club told me, I'd be surprised if he's still alive...'

Klem smiled at Zena, 'a-ha, now that *would* be a happy outcome! There's no need to divorce a dead man!'

'And what does our Mama think about this dreadful ungodly mess?' Halyna asked, pushing her plate of "the stew" even further away.

Zena said, 'we shall discuss the Mama later.' She thrust what looked like a chicken wing into her mouth, sucked off the meat and then used the sharp bones as a toothpick.

Halyna said, 'I'd rather discuss her <u>now</u>.' She knew her mother was the strictest Ukrainian Orthodox, who quite rightly believed the institution of marriage was sacrosanct, and would have positively disapproved of such scandalous goings on.

Halyna watched as Zena picked at the plentiful dirt that collected beneath her fingernails, presumably hoping that if she ignored the question, it would go away. She was exactly the same when she was younger, but it was a much less endearing quality now she was a fully-grown woman.

Halyna repeated her question, and watched as both Zena and Lenka looked the other way, desperately trying to think of an alternative subject…

'Well, well, well,' Sofia said to herself, unsticking her ear from the door, 'we all thought Oksana had an illegitimate nature, and now we know why…' She rubbed her hands together with glee, before scuttling out of the yard and down the alley to spread the wonderful news far and wide!

Chapter 47

'No, it <u>can't</u> be true!' Oksana's cries echoed down the alley, 'you'd only say such a thing to get back at me for all the nasty things I've said and done to you!'

'But I'm *not* lying,' Sofia said, '*everyone's* saying you're illegitimate!'

Natalka smiled, 'I didn't doubt it for a minute…'

The second she'd heard the news, Sofia simply had to go and tell Natalka. And after they'd had a good laugh about it, they scuttled off to tell everyone they met in the street. What luck that they happened to bump into Oksana. Sofia enjoyed giving the heifer a taste of her own medicine, watching her face go tomato-red and tears stream from her piggy eyes behind those milk bottle glasses. Sofia savoured every moment.

The heifer ran as quickly as she could, crying, 'I'm going to tell my Grandmother on you!'

Sofia and Natalka could keep up with her by walking briskly. Sofia said, 'go ahead and tell her. I mean, why would I make up such a thing? Hmm? Because if it's true, then it makes us related. And I don't want that any more than you do!'

'It is *quite* a detestable thought,' Natalka added.

'Extremely,' Sofia said. 'Worse than detestable… Repulsive!'

Oksana stopped in her tracks and wiped her eyes on her sleeve, sniffling the descending strings of fluorescent snot back up into her nostrils. It seemed the girls had finally hit a raw nerve; she turned around with the grace of a juggernaut and accelerated towards them, putting her chins to her chest and bracing herself for the crushing impact.

Sofia instantly crumpled to the cobbles and was smothered by Oksana's bulk, while Natalka toppled over as soon as the NHS crutches were kicked from under her, and landed in a dazed state in amongst the whiffy alleyway litter.

There was just enough room for Sofia to sock the heifer in the face, taking great delight in making her nose bleed, giving her a little Hitler moustache that suited her rather well. But Oksana

The Dancing Barber

didn't budge... it was as though her subcutaneous fat absorbed the blow, the heifer was seemingly immune to pain. Sofia shouted for help, but the sound was muffled. She felt as though she was being slowly swallowed by the bulk of the heifer's body, never to be seen again...

Natalka may have had a broken ankle, but it didn't stop her beating Oksana relentlessly with her NHS crutches. But after two minutes, Natalka was exhausted, Oksana was still laying into Sofia and the crutches were deformed beyond use...

Chapter 48

Zena discretely kicked Lenka on the shin. She stared at her in a way that said, 'Shut up! Let me do the talking!'

Lenka looked at her sister and shrugged. She wondered why her shin tickled. She was also confused as to why she was not allowed to talk about her own Mama?

Zena then turned to Halyna and noticed that she was tapping her fingernail on the plastic tablecloth with the speed of a sewing machine's needle. There was no point in lying… Halyna wouldn't be happy until she'd heard the *real* truth.

Halyna's finger was a blur with tapping. 'Well?' she said, letting the word taper into silence.

Zena shuffled in her seat, rehearsing in her head what she would like to say.

Lenka opened her mouth, but then her shin tickled even more... was it fleas?

'I'm waiting…' said Halyna, her brow deeply furrowed.

Zena gulped, 'the reaction of our Mama, it was not how you think… She never wanted me to the marry Ivan. She knew he was the bad, and the way he treated me did not surprise her. But her advice was, as the English say, "the put up and the shut up". And she made herself forget what happened between me and Klem…' Zena noticed Halyna hadn't blinked once.

She continued, 'and when Ivan, he stole Oksana, our Mama, she felt that it was the Lord's punishment for my infidelity; she did not suspect that Oksana could not possibly be the daughter of Ivan… But again, as the English say, "the cloud has the silver lining", so although I lost my Oksanochka, I was also blessedly rid of The Ginger Rasputin…'

Halyna still hadn't blinked.

Zena continued, 'but as the years, they went by, our Mama, she could see how the upset I was over losing my daughter. And it was her final wish that I came here to the Bradford to bring my Oksanochka back to where she belongs! And at the same time,' Zena gazed longingly at Klem, 'to marry the man I should have married in the first place, and for us all to be the happy family!' She looked back at Halyna and Taras, 'oh, and *of course* coming to see all of *you*... I cannot forget that!'

The furrows had disappeared from Halyna's brow, and were replaced by an enormous chasm. Although she still hadn't blinked, her eyes had narrowed to the thinnest of slits. She took off her plastic framed glasses and looked squarely at Zena. 'You said our Mama's final wish?'

'Did I?' Zena stuttered, 'I, err...'

Lenka interjected, 'yes, it *was* her final wish. It was the last thing our Mama, she said before...' She gazed up to the blackened ceiling.

'What?' Halyna cried, 'you mean our Mama has... But when...?'

'Thank you very much, Lenka,' Zena said, hitting her sister hard on the shoulder, 'I wanted to pick my moment to break the news gently! Not for you to the blurt it out! Sometimes I wonder whether your head actually contains the brain.'

Lenka hit her sister back, almost knocking her off her chair. 'But you let the cat out of the bag to spill the beans, didn't you? It is not the fault of me! It is you who the blurted it out! You said the words "final wish"... Not me!'

'Oh shut up,' Zena snapped, 'I told you to let me do the talking... why do you *never* listen?'

Taras could see his wife swaying, so he rapidly thrust the bottle of smelling salts under her nose.

'I don't need that!' Halyna shouted, grabbing the bottle and throwing it at her husband. She glared at her argumentative sisters and shouted, 'be quiet, the both of you! And tell me what happened to my Mama!'

Taras shrank away, never before seeing his wife exhibit so much aggression... But she had just heard some incredibly devastating news...

Klem also couldn't believe what he'd heard; neither could he believe how many times Mister Pushkin sneezed after sniffing the spilled smelling salts.

Lenka was about to speak, but after Zena gave her *that* look, she fastened her lips with an imaginary button.

Zena took a deep breath, 'it was almost a year ago. Our Mama, she went to bed alive, and in the morning.' She shrugged her shoulders, 'Uncle Viktor, he discovered she was the dead!'

'A <u>year</u> ago!' Halyna cried, 'and you've only decided to tell me <u>now</u>!'

Zena said, 'it is the sort of news that should be told sensitively the face to face, and not in the letter...'

Taras frowned. While lighting a cigarette, he said, 'yes, and you delivered the news *very* sensitively, didn't you?'

Zena ignored him; in any case, she was glad that she could no longer see him behind the plumes of tobacco smoke. She turned to Halyna and said, 'remember, our Mama was the ninety-two. As the English say, she had the "good innings", but the old age, it catches up with everyone, eventually. And after all the hardships she endured, I think she did the very well. To the very end, she was just as active as Lenka and me. In fact, she was as active as Uncle Viktor still is!' She reached out to give Halyna a hug, but Halyna flinched away. 'Like everyone who survived The Great Famine, our Mama, she made the most of every day. She also wanted to come and visit you, but it took so long to save all the money...' Zena shrugged her shoulders, 'travelling by the sky plane is not the cheap...'

Lenka rummaged in the depths of her handbag and retrieved a small package. She said to Halyna, 'our Mama, she wanted you to have this...'

Halyna looked at the parcel that Lenka placed into the palm of her hand. 'What is it?' she said, perching her plastic framed glasses on the bridge of her nose.

Lenka gestured for her to open it and find out, hopeful Halyna would appreciate the gift.

Halyna unfastened the yellowish string, and carefully removed the musty newspaper – a 1933 American edition featuring a defaced photograph of the hated Stalin – that was the make-do, if rather inappropriate wrapping paper.

Inside, was the most beautiful embroidered headscarf Halyna had ever seen. She unfolded it and laid it on the table, holding down the edges with her hands, smoothing out the gridlines of creases. Embroidery was like handwriting, and Halyna knew instantly this headscarf was created by her own Mama. Through her tears, she examined the intricate needlework, each tiny stitch being smaller than a grain of sand: no wonder her Mama's eyesight failed at such a young age. There was so much detail, that to her, it wasn't a mere headscarf, but a miniature tapestry. The cloth was rough to the touch and the embroidery silky smooth; it may have been a strange notion, but holding the item was as if her Mama was actually present in the room.

She recognised the thatched homestead, the well, the fields of wheat, the horses, cows, goats and pig as they looked prior to 1933. Her Mama and Tato, wearing traditional costumes were depicted hauling water from the well, while the twins began the harvest, using scythes to cut corn before it was bundled up to be taken to the barn, and a tiny girl stirred a cauldron of borsch suspended over an open fire... Halyna burst into uncontrollable tears.

Lenka said, 'our Mama, she was going to give it to you when you returned to Chaplinka, but,' she shrugged her shoulders, 'you never did...'

'But I wanted to!' Halyna cried, 'you know that when they released me from the Collective Farm, I planned to go straight back home.' Her glasses had slipped down her nose, so she pushed them back into position, 'but it took a long time to scrape together the money... Chaplinka was many weeks travel from the farm they sent me to.'

Zena nodded towards Lenka and said, 'but *we* the managed to get back to Chaplinka; and we weren't sent much further than you? Our Mama, she thought that perhaps you did not *want* to come back?'

'At least you two were together. And you had our Mama! I was alone and I didn't have any papers: you have no idea how frightened I was!' Her glasses began to slip down her nose again, so she took them off, placing them on the table.

The twins realised the experience must have been frightening for their young sister... even though being frightened was an emotion neither of them had ever truly experienced.

Halyna continued, 'eventually, I somehow ended up at that small jewellery firm close to Kyiv: the money was good, I got to work with my hands and the people were friendly... they were happy years... But as soon as I'd saved enough money for a ticket home, the Nazi swine arrested me and the other workers and sent us all to a Concentration Camp in Germany. It was only when I'd finally convinced them that I was Ukrainian Orthodox that they released me to work as an "Ostarbeiter"... As for my colleagues, they were sent to the gas chambers. The Nazis took all the money I'd saved... from then on, I knew I might *never* see Chaplinka again... and began to think maybe this was how it was meant to be.'

Zena and Lenka looked away, annoyed with themselves for upsetting their sister.

'Will you please excuse me,' Halyna said, failing to hold back the tears, 'but I'd like to be left alone.' She darted upstairs, clinging onto the precious headscarf as if it embodied the Mama she would never see again, at least in this life...

When he'd heard Halyna's bedroom door slam and the bolt slide across, Taras clapped at the twins, 'well done!' He got up to go after her, 'the last time she got herself into such a state, it took me a *whole week* to coax her out!'

Klem hated to see Halyna upset. He said, 'leave her be: she'll need time to digest all this traumatic news...'

'Don't tell me what to do,' snapped Taras, 'I know my wife better than you do!'

Klem raised his eyebrows, and looked the other way.

Lenka said, 'but we have the *more* to tell...'

Zena kicked her on the shin, harder than ever. She mouthed, 'not now!' Gingerly, she looked at Klem and Taras, grateful neither of them had heard Lenka's little outburst.

The telephone rang; and Taras wasted no time excusing himself from the table to go and answer it. 'Hello,' he said, standing by the window and watching the Alsatian in the back yard straining at the leash, desperately trying to get indoors. He pulled back the net curtain and looked around the yard, wondering where Sofia had gone.

'Yes, this is Mr Taras,' he said to the well-spoken gentleman at the end of the line, 'of course... Thank you... The dancers and I would be delighted... Our run at The Alhambra lasts for a week, so we'll be available after that... Yes, I know the YTV studios on

The Dancing Barber

Kirkstall Road... Yes, we're performing tonight... I can leave a ticket at the Box Office for you... Yes I understand... Thank you... Thank you very much... I look forward to your call.'

Slowly, he replaced the receiver, and turned back to the table, not quite believing what he'd heard. Klem and the twins were still dumbfounded by how their news had affected Halyna. And although he knew it was inappropriate, he simply couldn't contain his excitement.

'Yippee! We've finally made it,' he sang as he danced around the kitchen, 'do you know who that was? It was the producer of a television programme on YTV called "Showtime", and he wants us to perform live on the TV, understand? *Live* on the TV! He's going to call back later today to tell me how big my fee is going to be! At last! We've finally made it! Yippee! Yippee!' He continued to dance around the kitchen with all the energy of a small child who'd discovered his mother's secret tin of sweets.

'That's wonderful,' Klem said, smiling beneath his frown of a moustache. 'I'm pleased for you.'

The twins shrugged their shoulders, not understanding anything Taras had just said. To them, the Ukrainian language he spoke was completely different to their own...

Taras danced around, jumping and clicking his heels. 'One of the critics from last night works for YTV, and he recommended my ballet for the show! Can you believe it?' Taras scratched his head, 'funny thing though, he referred to my version of *Swan Lake* as a "comedic ballet"! Whatever could he mean? *It doesn't matter*... And he thought the ballerina dressed in the fat suit was hilarious...' He scratched his head again, 'but none of my ballerinas were dressed in a fat suit...'

'Yes, that's wonderful,' Klem said, standing up, 'but if you'll excuse me, I need to go and see how Halyna is.' He turned to the twins, 'and perhaps you two could go up to the attic and tidy away some of your washing? I don't particularly want my current accommodation to resemble a circus tent festooned with bunting made from your stained knickers! Neither do I want you pinning any more of your brassières on the wall. And whatever you've got bubbling on the hob smells like it went off long ago, so throw it away and wash out my pans! And don't get me started on those buckets you keep by the window...'

'Hey Klem,' Zena said, 'why you in the bad mood all of the sudden?'

Klem snapped, 'why do you think?' before storming upstairs.

Taras was so excited that he dashed outside, in the quest to find someone, anyone, to brag to.

But when he looked down the alley, the first thing he saw was two people engaged in a vicious brawl. He marched closer, determined to break it up, and shouted, 'stop fighting <u>at once</u>!' But they completely ignored him, and continued to kick and punch each other. 'I said stop fighting!' he shouted. Looking closely, he was horrified to discover the aggressor was his own daughter! Sofia was slapping Oksana's face with both hands; the fat girl's cheeks and chins rippling with each impact, as if made from suet...

Taras strode purposefully through the litter, rolling up his sleeves. After effortlessly parting the brawlers, and holding them by the scruff of the neck, he demanded, 'which one of you is going to tell me what all this is about?' He didn't even notice Natalka sat in amongst the litter, holding her bent NHS crutches, worrying about what she was going to tell her own father...

Oksana didn't need any encouragement to tell the truth, which for her was quite an achievement. She blurted out the full story, chapter and verse, and sounded so plausible that Taras had no choice but to believe her.

'I am <u>extremely</u> disappointed with you, Sofia,' Taras said, looking down at his black-eyed daughter. 'That was a private conversation and you had <u>no</u> business to eavesdrop! Understand? And you certainly had absolutely no business telling Oksana, especially in the way you did! You are a disgrace to the family!'

'Oh, so I'm a disgrace, am I?' Sofia said, struggling to escape her father's grip. 'This fat heifer has bullied me at school every day for two years! And <u>I'm</u> the disgrace for getting my own back?'

Taras said, 'that's enough...'

'<u>No</u>, it isn't,' Sofia interjected, 'if she spoke to you in the way she spoke to me, you'd cane her for three hours solid! And it may interest you to know that it was <u>her</u> who put Imaac in her father's shampoo and let you take the blame for it! She did it on purpose... just so she could force herself into the ballet and ruin it for everyone!'

The Dancing Barber

Taras tried to tell Sofia that he already knew this, but she hadn't finished...

'And it was her who put one of the school hamsters I'm supposed to be looking after in your ballet underpants! What a barbaric thing to do to poor little Brenda!'

Taras screamed, 'I thought it was a rat, and it was a *hamster*? Either way,' he cringed, 'its teeth were *very* sharp!' He stared at his daughter, 'I never gave you permission to bring such a thing into the house? Does your Mama know? Of course she doesn't... she would have told me! Oh Sofia, how could you do it, especially after what happened last time?'

'The nuns didn't give me any choice,' said Sofia, 'it was my turn to look after them and that was that!'

'*Them?*' Taras cried, 'you mean there's more than one?'

Sofia nodded, 'originally, there were two... But even if I'd asked your permission, and you said "no"... it wouldn't have made any difference: not even you could argue with those nuns! But that is all irrelevant, because Brenda and Audrey were safe enough in the coal-shed until she,' Sofia sneered at the grinning Oksana, 'stole one and put it in your ballet underpants!'

Taras turned around and stared angrily at Oksana. The thought of being her uncle made his blood curdle, but what she did with that hamster made his blood boil! He released the grip on his daughter and pulled Oksana closer to him, holding the heifer's plump shoulders between his hands. He shouted with so much anger that the whites of his eyes turned red, 'is this true?' And when she nodded proudly, he shouted with more anger than ever before, 'you unpleasant fat pig! How could you concoct such a thing? I could have been seriously injured!'

'Good,' Oksana said, 'I hope it bit a big chunk out of your,' she smiled, '*pride!*'

That was it. Taras was not going to be spoken to in such a way. Much to Sofia's pleasure, he dragged Oksana down the alley, through the yard, past the sleeping dog and into his studio. As if he were a knight unsheathing his sword, Taras released his cane from the hooks that kept it hanging menacingly on the wall, and whipped it as far back as possible.

'Do not dare to hit my daughter,' Zena shouted, catching the cane and preventing its forward trajectory.

But Taras whipped the cane out of his sister-in-law's hand and belted Oksana harder than ever.

In an instant, the heifer's bravado was gone and she whimpered pathetically, much to both Taras' and Sofia's satisfaction, especially after the seventh and eighth lashes. Taras whipped back the cane for the ninth lash, but Zena grabbed it again, this time with both hands and in one effortless movement, snapped it in half and then in quarters. She then pushed Taras out of the way, and with outstretched arms, sought to comfort her estranged daughter, unleashing the full pungency of her hirsute armpits.

Taras shouted, 'you won't be so quick to defend this girl once you realise what she's capable of!' He then picked up the fragments of his cane and wondered whether it could ever be mended; it was as if a part of his body was smashed to pieces...

Zena said, 'and what do you expect, with <u>Ivan</u> as the father figure? The girl, she has picked up the bad habits from him and his club-handed mother.'

Lovingly, she looked at Oksana and stroked her head with a filthy hand. She said, 'there, there my baby, your Mama is here to protect you...'

But Oksana couldn't escape Zena's putrid clutches quickly enough, 'get off me you smelly old troll!' She shouted, 'there's no way *you're* my mother!' She felt sick at the thought of it, 'I'm going home to tell my Grandmother all about you... then you'll be in trouble!' She kicked Zena on the shin and ran out of the door.

Sofia was impressed, 'that's the quickest I've ever seen her move!'

Even with the stump of a cane in his hand, Taras was frightening. He took hold of his daughter's arm and said, 'all this is your fault: how dare you bring hamsters home without permission!'

'But Tato,' Sofia said, struggling to release her arm from the tourniquet of his grip, 'as I said, the nuns *made* me bring them home over Easter. Nobody can argue with them! You can try if you want... but I wouldn't recommend it. And remember, if it weren't for that fat heifer, then they'd still be safely tucked up in the coal-shed. So what happened was <u>all</u> the fault of Oksana, your *wonderful* new niece!' Sofia added, 'in any case, Oksana hates you so much that she'd have put anything in your ballet underpants...

The Dancing Barber

you should be grateful it wasn't the flea circus again...'

Taras squirmed at the thought of those biting fleas... He said, 'I'm sorry,' releasing his daughter's arm, 'it's been an eventful and exhausting few days... I must go and lie down.' He shook his head with dismay, 'and before you go back to school, we'll have to visit the pet shop and buy a replacement. Do you remember what this "Brenda" looked like? I wonder if the price has gone up since last time?'

Sofia said, 'but we still have Audrey! And she's been very busy making many more baby hamsters: they're a bit pink at the moment, but they'll soon grow! The nuns will be upset at losing Brenda – *or should that be Brenda_n_* – but there were at least *three* new ones in the cage the last time I looked... And Audrey was still heaving!'

'More... There's more...' Taras stammered, his body almost wilting to the floor. 'Well, you make sure that cage is closed, locked and bolted! I don't want them escaping! Understand?'

Zena stomped her foot angrily, almost cracking the floorboards, 'my long lost daughter, she calls me the smelly old troll, and all you two can talk about is the silly rats! You make me the sick! And to think that Lenka and I spent all the afternoon of yesterday skinning and gutting those rats, and none of you had the courtesy to eat the delicious stew of the meat! Do not worry, it will not go to the waste; Lenka and I shall finish it off. We think it is the delicious; we are the grateful for such delicacies!'

Taras glared at the big woman, hoping he'd misheard...

'No,' cried Sofia. She ran out to the coal-shed, 'you disgusting heathens!'

Chapter 49

'Bon appetite,' said Klem, watching the dog chase the metal bowl, piled high with Pedigree Chum around the back yard, the medallion on its collar jingling against the bowl's rim like an unseasonable sleigh-bell. The metal disc bore the dog's name, "Mykola", but it was a pity the beast never responded to it.

After patting the dog's coarse fur, Klem immediately returned to the kitchen to wash his hands; and when he ambled back out to the yard, the bowl had been licked completely clean.

The dog looked up at its master expectantly, hanging its long, salivating tongue from its mouth and wagging its tail as if it were a feather duster attached to a windscreen wiper. Klem shook his head and reached, once more, for the can opener...

The dog was finally satisfied after three heaped bowlfuls of "Duck and Kidney" Pedigree Chum, and quickly fell to a flatulent sleep in the corner of the yard. Holding his nose, Klem couldn't help thinking: *Dog food smells as bad out of the can as it does after passing out of the dog!*

He collected the half-dozen empty cans and took them to the metal dustbin, keeping them at arm's length. He lifted the heavy dustbin lid, then – for some mischievous reason – deliberately clattered it to the ground, inches from the dog's sleeping head...

"Mykola" was even grouchier than Taras after being woken up abruptly. It bared its three-inch fangs and snarled, bubbling saliva stretching between its jaws, then dripping to the ground...

Luckily for Klem, the beast was still tethered to the gatepost.

Once the dog had settled down, Klem was surprised to find the dustbin entirely filled with empty cans of Pedigree Chum; how on earth could one dog eat *so* much? The animal's stomach must have been a bottomless pit. All the thing did was eat, sleep, bark and break wind; and despite its obvious aggression, and all the training it'd been through, he doubted it would have the intelligence to cope with a Soviet Secret Policeman.

But it didn't matter. Klem knew the Vlads would have struck by now if they were going to... he had an instinct for these things, and knew he was right. Gunter was due to collect the beast next week, which would undoubtedly please Halyna... it'd been giving her some rather peculiar looks whenever she wore her new fur coat...

Klem inhaled a lungful of fresh Bradfordian air... He liked it when the factories were closed, because the atmosphere became remarkably clear. When he went for his regular morning constitutional, it was the first time in months when he didn't see a yellow cloud hovering above Leather's Chemical Works...

Still breathing deeply, Klem looked at the golden hands of his bulky pocket watch: Voloshin's news would have hit the headlines in Moscow three hours ago. He tugged at the green ribbon at his collar and smiled at the scene he imagined currently taking place in the Kremlin...

He wouldn't want to be in the boots of all those Comrade Generals, who'd bragged to him about what they did thirty years ago... He smiled even wider, because he knew they'd surely be sent to the Gulags they themselves had built.

And the Soviet Secret Police wouldn't dare to seek revenge on either him or Voloshin, because – no matter how accidental they could make it look – it would be an obvious sign of their guilt.

After winding his watch the usual seven times, he slotted it back into the silk-lined pocket of his pinstriped waistcoat and looked up at Halyna's bedroom window. He wasn't surprised the curtains were still drawn. He couldn't help feeling partially responsible; but it wasn't his fault Zena had kept the terrible news to herself for so long and saw fit to break it in such an insensitive way... Zena never used to be so stupid. If he'd known, he'd have insisted Zena told her straight away. But what's done was done, he supposed. When he'd knocked on Halyna's door half an hour ago, the lack of a reply suggested she had sunk into one of her depressions again... but from past experiences, he knew she'd soon claw her way out of it... so long as the twins didn't drop any more bombshells.

Heading indoors, Klem looked down and noticed the dog's stinking gift just before he stepped on it. He reached for the shovel he'd bought expressly for this purpose, scooping it up and lobbing it over the wall into the alley, where it only just missed a sleeping tramp, wrapped in his cardboard duvet, who emitted a torrent of obscenities.

Klem scuttled across the yard, but was taken by surprise when

Sofia emerged from the coal-shed looking completely and utterly distraught. She cried, 'they've all gone now; there's no more left!' She ignored his attempts to find out what was troubling her and ran off to her room with tears streaming down her cheeks. He wondered what Taras had done this time?

As Klem ascended the stone steps to the kitchen, he heard an almighty thud echoing from Taras' shop. He froze, putting a steadying hand onto the cold stone wall. It sounded as though someone was trying to kick down the door... And with such a flimsy door, it wouldn't take very long. He knew he'd put the "mockers" on it by thinking the Soviet threat was over... it was such an idiotic thing to do...

Mister Pushkin head-butted his ankle, giving him the courage to go and investigate. 'All right,' he said, 'I'm going...'

Daring not to reawaken the dog, he walked calmly through the kitchen, but stopped by the door leading to the shop. Despite every fibre of his being telling him it was a bad idea, he put a hand on the door handle and slowly turned it until the latch clicked open...

He listened to a further three thuds, each one getting progressively louder... His perspiring palm began to slip off the door handle... he knew there'd be a gang of Vlads waiting in the shop, ready to "do him in". He supposed it was about time he confronted his enemies face to face... He'd dealt with Ivan, so he could deal with the Vlads... *Tell yourself you can do it, and you will!*

Klem made his free hand into the shape of a gun, by extending his index and middle fingers, and put it into his jacket pocket. After another head-butt of encouragement from Mister Pushkin, he flung open the door, crouched down and aimed his pocketed gun at the intruders. He shouted: 'Right! Stay where you are! One wrong move, and I'll shoot!'

But his words echoed back at him: there wasn't a soul in the shop and to his astonishment, the door was undamaged. He left his pretend gun in his pocket and dried his hands by wiping them on the seat of his trousers. He looked around the shop and didn't notice a single thing out of place; the compost heap of hair clippings in the corner was undisturbed, the rack of tramp clothes was untouched and the awful smell of stale tobacco still hung in the air. Surely he couldn't have imagined hearing all those thuds?

The Dancing Barber

He hoped he wasn't developing tinnitus...

The remaining tension in his shoulders melted away the moment he looked at where the doormat used to be...

It seemed as though the newsagent had delivered his entire stock of newspapers: *The Times*, *The Telegraph*, *The Express*, even *The Sun*, as well as many less well known titles. Realising how silly he'd been, he rubbed his hands together and scooped up all the newspapers into a pile a foot thick, deliberately avoiding reading the headlines until he and the cat were safely tucked up in the attic. His friends in Fleet Street had never let him down...

Before leaving the shop, Klem placed – with great relief – the latest copies of *The Ballet Chronicle* and *The Pirouette Weekly* onto Taras' little desk. The reviews of *Swan Lake* – at least at first glance – seemed better than expected... Thankfully, the Bishop incident wasn't mentioned anywhere, although there were a couple of lines concerning the "witch hunt" that occurred before the interval, but the critics thought this to be an entirely successful addition to what was dubbed a "comedy ballet with audience participation". Taras may have been an aggressive, impatient and rude *so-n-so*, but he nevertheless deserved some good luck for once...

Klem scampered up the spiral staircase, steadying the heavy pile of newspapers under his chin, with the excitement of a child on Christmas Day morning...

Chapter 50

An hour later, Zena and Lenka were busily creating their next gastronomic delight that involved reheating various leftovers, along with more of the tinned meat with the "wolf" on the label they'd found in the cupboard. They thought it was delicious and wished it was available in Chaplinka: Uncle Viktor would love it.

Having visited the Fish Market, the twins fried some herring and mackerel, preferring to use Halyna's new Morphy Richards electric iron instead of the frying pan.

And while they cooked, they watched the Cine film of *Swan Lake's* opening night, projecting the shaky image onto a stained bedsheet they'd nailed to the kitchen wall. Cringing, Zena said, 'our Halynochka, she is not the good maker of the films…'

'She is worse than the terrible,' said Lenka, 'Hitch-Cock, she is not; it makes me go the dizzy just to look.'

Zena shook her head, 'why can she not hold the camera still?'

Lenka groaned, 'and we have not yet seen the dance of Sofia…'

Zena frowned… Sofia was certainly not in her good books… 'It is the pity,' Zena said whilst peeling potatoes with her thumbnail, 'that Sofia, she had to tell my Oksanochka about me and Klem…' She sighed, 'I wanted to tell her myself.'

'Now you cannot,' snapped Lenka, 'so *stop* going on about it. You are giving me the ache in the head!'

'I sorry,' said Zena, 'I will not mention it again… I suppose Sofia, she was so excited to have the new cousin that she could not wait to tell her!'

'Maybe…?' Lenka said, scraping flakes of burnt fish from the formerly shiny base of the electric iron. 'But from what I hear, I do not think the two girls, they like each other much. In fact, I have been told that Oksana, she is the nasty piece of work…'

'I know… some people, they call her the heifer… But what do you expect? Hmm? Ivan, he is the nasty and his mother, she is the worse. So it goes without the saying that Oksana, she will be the *horrible* child!'

Lenka gazed over to the bed sheet cinema screen and said, 'at

The Dancing Barber

last! Halynochka, she has finally held the camera still!'

Zena briefly looked up from the gloopy concoction she was stirring around the pan and said, 'it is the pity the camera films the audience, and not the stage...'

'But this is the much more interesting,' Lenka said, pointing with a wooden spoon that dripped with all manner of inedible leftovers. 'Look at this durak, why does he swing his stick around?'

Zena shrugged, 'maybe he is trying to knock off someone's big hat, like that woman did to Ivan?' There was something vaguely familiar about this man, but she was too fed up to think about it. Zena had seen enough, and went back to stirring around her gloopy concoction. She said, 'I do not the care... This is the rubbish... turn it off and put the sheet back on Taras' bed.'

Lenka did as she was told, but only after helping herself to an entire fillet of ironed fish. Spitting the plentiful bones to the carpet, she said, 'maybe later in the week, we will be allowed to see the *Swan Lake*? I am sure Taras, he can arrange it, yes?'

But after what they'd done to the man with the lisp, neither twin believed it...

As per Taras' instructions, the back door had been left on the chain, ventilating the kitchen, whilst also keeping out any unwanted visitors, which included the dog, driven wild by the smell of their cooking... which wasn't surprising, considering they were cooking Pedigree Chum. But the little chain wasn't strong enough to keep out The Gossipmonger: one nudge of her shoulder snapped it easily, and she stormed into the kitchen brandishing her clubbed hand as if it were a truncheon.

'Just look at what you've done to my poor Oksana,' she shouted, thrusting the fat girl into the kitchen, as if she were a prized pig at market. 'She's distraught with all the lies you've been filling her head with. Distraught! Just look at her!'

So Zena stopped stirring her gloopy concoction and did precisely that. To her, Oksana looked just like *she* did when *she* was twelve... although Oksana was *much* plumper. She looked back at The Gossipmonger and said, 'the girl, she is probably the scared of you. And who could the blame her? Of all the wild boar I wrestled, none have been as the nasty as you!'

'I beg your pardon?' The Gossipmonger said, polishing her club with the palm of her hand. 'I may be nastier than a wild boar, but at least I don't *look* like one!'

Oksana smiled. Her grandmother's only good quality was her ability to effortlessly insult anyone, and in the most offensive way.

'I should say not,' said Lenka, rolling up her sleeves. 'Do not insult the wild boars! You are as *ugly* as the rear end of *the wart hog*!'

'At least I don't *smell* like one!' shouted The Gossipmonger.

Zena's eyeballs bulged and her nostrils flared; her face pumped with so much blood that all her blackheads could have burst in unison. She rolled up her sleeves and cracked each of her knuckles in turn…

With a couple of hours before he was due at The Alhambra, Taras sat contentedly in the shop with his feet propped up on the little desk, and Tchaikovsky fluttering from the radio. He conducted an imaginary orchestra, using his cigarette as a baton, whilst sipping samahon and revelling in *Swan Lake's* glowing reviews… Halyna was right: the critics had written much better reviews than he'd expected… he'd have to send them a crate of pink gin as a gesture of thanks.

But the shouting in the adjacent kitchen was getting louder, and was beginning to annoy him. He ignored it; turning up the volume on the radio and rereading the papers… Both *The Ballet Chronicle* and *The Pirouette Weekly* had the same attention-grabbing headline:

<u>**THE DANCING BARBER**</u> **TRIUMPHS AT THE ALHAMBRA**
COULD THIS BE <u>THE NEXT NUREYEV</u>?

The next Nureyev? But I am <u>far</u> better than Nureyev… He shrugged his shoulders, letting the cigarette smoke hiss from between his teeth. And he wasn't sure he liked being referred to as "The Dancing Barber", but supposed it was a unique title… and they could have called him many other things, especially after the

The Dancing Barber

exploits of his bulge and the incident of the Bishop…

The shouting in the kitchen was getting unbearably loud. He thought: *what are those stupid women doing?* He threw down his copy of *The Ballet Chronicle*, screwed his cigarette into the overflowing ashtray and marched into the kitchen, flinging the door wide open. He hollered, 'what is going on in here?'

'You're a liar,' screamed The Gossipmonger, taking a swing at Zena with her clubbed hand. 'Don't you think my own son would have told me?'

Zena laughed, dodging the swinging club with ease. She looked to be enjoying herself, deliberately waiting until the last possible moment to dodge the fearsome club.

'The damned Gossipmonger,' Taras said upon discovering the hated woman gesticulating in his kitchen. He glared at Zena and Lenka, 'which one of you two idiots let her into this house?'

Lenka pointed to the broken door chain, 'she let herself in…'

'You're not his wife,' shouted The Gossipmonger, 'and even if you were – which you're not – he'd be too embarrassed to tell anyone he'd married such a *hideous* monstrosity!'

Taras couldn't believe The Gossipmonger had dared to force her way into his house… 'Hey you,' he shouted, 'shut your face and listen to me!'

The Gossipmonger ignored him, preferring to take another swing at Zena. She sneered, 'and if you're Oksana's mother, then I'm a monkey's uncle… A *disgusting* woman like you could never produce such a *beautiful* daughter!' She looked at the pan of simmering stew, 'you even *eat* himno as well as *talk* it!'

Taras parted the two women just before Zena succeeded in punching the false teeth from The Gossipmonger's mouth. Lenka restrained her sister, while Taras turned his attention to The Gossipmonger. He said: 'that is enough! Why don't you ask Ivan to tell you the *real* truth…? About why he abducted a child that wasn't his?'

The Gossipmonger dragged Oksana to the door, 'come on… I do not have to listen to this.'

'Yes you do,' said Taras. 'Can't you see there isn't the slightest family resemblance?' He pointed at Oksana's face, 'she may be growing a beard, but it isn't a *ginger* one!'

The Gossipmonger said nothing. But the voice of doubt started chattering in the back of her mind... especially when she noticed Oksana scratching her backside in the same uncouth way as the Zena woman. She sighed... hadn't Ivan caused her enough shame? The next time she saw him, she'd put him across her knee... She turned to Taras, 'but you cannot *prove* any of this is true... Can you?'

Zena held out the tattered birth certificate and said, 'the see for yourself... If you can read.'

The Gossipmonger snatched the certificate, examining it through her reading glasses, peering through the lenses without unfolding the arms. Even she was educated enough to realise it wasn't a forgery. She snapped, 'how much did it cost you to bribe the official, hmmm?'

'Do not be ridiculous,' Zena said, 'go to Chaplinka, and you will find the same information on the official records. This is the fact!'

'Look here,' said The Gossipmonger, 'both you and I know that all officials can be bribed! They all have their price!'

Zena shook her head, 'not everyone in this world is the criminal.' She said matter-of-factly, 'I do not the care what you the think: I *know* that Ivan, he *cannot* be the father of Oksana.'

'You're talking himno again,' barked The Gossipmonger. 'If you are his wife, then Ivan must be Oksana's father! This is the fact!'

Taras picked up a pair of eggs and handed them to Zena.

The Gossipmonger looked on with curiosity, while Zena made her demonstration.

Zena said, 'see, Ivan, he cannot be the father of *anyone*!'

The Gossipmonger was dumbfounded. She said, 'rubbish... I don't believe you! You are in for it when I tell my son about the *evil* lies you've been spreading about him!' She threw the certificate onto the table, grabbed Oksana's chubby hand and dragged her straight out, almost throwing her down the stone steps to the yard.

'What was all that with the eggs?' Oksana asked, stumbling to the gate, nearly tripping over the grouchy dog.

'Never you mind,' The Gossipmonger snapped, clubbing Oksana over the head, causing her to cry out in pain.

The Dancing Barber

'I'll tell my Tato what you do to me!' Oksana shouted, even though she knew he wouldn't care.

'Good!' screamed The Gossipmonger, 'because then I can do the same to him! In fact, when he crawls back, I'll do much worse! Now come on!'

'Zena, leave her be,' Taras advised, preventing his sister-in-law from charging out after them. 'The Gossipmonger will need time to accept the truth. She may be a lot of things, but stupid isn't one of them...'

Zena watched as The Gossipmonger kept Oksana in line by clubbing her on the backside until her protests were replaced by more tears. She shook her head, 'the poor girl, she is the terribly unhappy with that old cow!' She looked at Taras, 'it has taken me the long time to save the money to come here, and I am not going back to Chaplinka without my daughter!'

Taras said, 'but Oksana will also need to get used to all this, understand? It cannot be rushed.'

'Maybe you are right... I shall just have to wait and hope The Gossipmonger does not beat my Oksana to death in the meantime.' Zena wiped her eggy hands on her rump. She said, 'but please, give me the *hard boiled* eggs next time!'

Taras smiled; he never could tell the difference. He sniffed the air... All the aggravation had caused Zena to sweat more profusely than normal... he couldn't retreat fast enough from the spreading cloud of her bodily odours...

It was common knowledge The Gossipmonger thought Oksana was the daughter she never had; there was no way the "old cow", as Zena referred to her, would give her up without a fight. At least the law was on Zena's side, but that never mattered to The Gossipmonger...

Chapter 51

Sipping a steaming cup of Camomile tea, Klem sat at his cluttered roll-top desk in the cool shade of the attic with Mister Pushkin purring on his lap, completely oblivious to the rest of the world. He'd just finished talking to his Fleet Street friends on the telephone, relaying Katya's gratitude for all their help... The editor of *The Times*, one of his oldest friends, requested to meet Katya one day and maybe take her for dinner. Klem declined on her behalf; Katya wasn't one for eating...

While listening to the enchanting song of his blue tit visitor, he fanned out the broadsheets in front of him and carefully read each front page in turn, checking that his words had been faithfully reproduced:

THE TIMES

UKRAINIAN HOLODOMOR – "MURDER BY HUNGER" OF 1933
PEASANTS ATE GRASS WHILE GRAIN LEFT TO ROT

THE TELEGRAPH

SOVIET UNION RESPONSIBLE FOR GENOCIDE
SIX MILLION INNOCENT UKRAINIANS STARVED TO DEATH

THE DAILY EXPRESS

THE DELIBERATE GREAT FAMINE OF 1933
STALIN'S ANSWER TO HIS "UKRAINIAN PROBLEM"

PRAVDA

THE PEACEFUL PARTISAN LIVES!
VOLOSHIN PROVES THAT SOVIETS CAUSED HOLODOMOR

'By now,' Klem said to a purring Mister Pushkin, 'the world is learning the truth!' The cat briefly lifted its head, allowed him to stroke under its chin, before nodding off back to sleep.

Klem's stomach groaned much louder than the cat could purr.

The Dancing Barber

It had been three hours since he'd consumed his delightful lunch... and he could still taste every disgusting flavour, despite only swallowing one mouthful of "stew". He'd have to send Zena to Cookery School, because there was no way he was going to eat such rubbish for the rest of his life... although the School might not allow her into their kitchen for "hygiene reasons"... and who would blame them?

The blue tit fluttered out and across the road, landing on a distant chimney pot. Klem waved goodbye and flicked on his Roberts radio, taking the time to admire its green leather cladding... the only one Busby's had in stock. For some reason it was tuned in to Radio One, and he never listened to that infernal station, especially the "Musical Himno" purveyed by those mop-headed Liverpudlians... He switched to Long Wave and twiddled the chromium knob to Radio Kateryna, 1933 kHz, and was immediately absorbed by a fabulous Ukrainian folk song about a sheep wearing an apron. He liked the tune so much that he tapped away to it with his Pelikan fountain pen, stopping short of conducting an imaginary orchestra, as a certain other person frequently did.

He sipped his fragrant tea, being careful not to wet his moustache, and even dunked in a Sweetmeal Digestive biscuit to settle his stomach. For the first time in his life, he understood what it meant to have a weight lifted from one's mind. It'd taken him thirty years, but his work was actually complete: the Soviets were finally being accused of genocide... not even the Kremlin could brush the testimony of so many serving Soviet Generals under the carpet... and they certainly couldn't all be perforated by cyanide-tipped umbrellas.

A tingle ran down his spine as he remembered the fate of his mother and father, his sisters and brothers, his aunts and uncles; because they refused to work on the Collective Farm, they were left to starve to death even though there was plenty of food for everyone. He recalled how the Soviets barged into his home, bundled the dead bodies into sacks, tied them off with rope and slung them onto a waiting cart: a scene replicated thousands of times across Ukraine... The Soviets didn't care about giving people a proper Christian burial.

And as the death toll mounted, Stalin went on shaking the hands of Presidents and Prime Ministers, bragging at the success of Collectivisation, showing them photographs of fully-stocked shops and happy workers: how well he deceived the world. But now, those responsible would be punished for their crimes: he hoped Khrushchev choked on his lunchtime caviar.

Klem closed his eyes, clasped his hands together and said, 'thank you Lord for giving me the courage to achieve justice for Ukraine. Please grant the diplomats infinite strength so they can secure a peaceful future for my beloved Ukraine. Amen.' He crossed himself in the Ukrainian Orthodox fashion and exhaled slowly.

He recalled one of his favourite Biblical quotations: *"Consider it pure joy, my brothers, whenever you face trials of many kinds, because you know that the testing of your faith develops perseverance."* James 1:2,3. He muttered, 'how true that was...'

Confident that his life was no longer in danger, Klem slipped off his red leather boots to reveal a pair of psychedelic blue and yellow socks, through which his big toes protruded via well-worn holes. He put up his feet and leaned back in his creaky chair; he decided that, at last, he could relax and plan for the future. He looked up to the bright blue sky and allowed the swirling clouds of starlings above a distant mill soothe his mind...

With the melodies of Dmitri Shostakovich – the only Soviet composer he could tolerate – booming from his Roberts Radio, Klem decided he would marry Zena in a traditional ceremony in Ukraine – assuming he could find someone to officiate – and then move back to Chaplinka for good.

He'd had enough of city life, and longed for the country... it was the little things he missed, such as being awoken by the wondrous chorus of birdsong at dawn, the creamy milk, fresh from the udder and even the sweet smell of manure. He doubted he'd ever feel nostalgic about belching factory chimneys and traffic fumes.

He would then reopen the Chaplinka parish church and become the village's first Ukrainian Orthodox Priest in thirty years: it was an exciting prospect to do what he originally trained for.

And Klem knew that, eventually, Oksana would want to know her real family... both he and Zena looked forward to the day when they could liberate her from The Gossipmonger's clutches.

The Dancing Barber

With the cat purring contentedly on his lap, Klem lost himself in his dreams: he simply couldn't believe all his wishes were coming true... And before long, he fell asleep...

The bright sun had moved around and now flooded into the attic, reflecting off the white walls and scattering fragments of blue and yellow light from the Fabergé Egg that occupied pride of place on the polished copper mantelpiece.

Abruptly, Mister Pushkin's purring ceased and its deep yellow eyes sprang open, its ears then pricked up and rotated like radar dishes towards the sunlit balcony. The cat jumped to the carpet, jabbing its sharp claws into Klem's bony thighs, and scuttled out to the sunlight. As Klem flinched at the pain, the cat emitted a guttural growl.

'What's the matter?' Klem asked, squinting at the bright light. 'Damn it, these are new-*ish* trousers,' he said, examining the material for any loosened stitches. 'What's up with you now?'

But the cat continued to growl, louder than ever.

'Silly cat,' he said, 'you must be going dotty in your advancing years...'

All thoughts of the cat's erratic behaviour exited his head, when he was distracted by the glittering Fabergé Egg... only the genuine article would twinkle so beautifully in the sunlight. He decided that when it was sold, he'd have enough money to buy something he'd always wanted... it may have been rather an eccentric dream, but he'd always aspired to own the Askanya Nova Nature Reserve, located close to Chaplinka... he'd be quite content spending his days exploring it... but transforming that dream into reality was many years away... and he'd have to dismiss the incumbent Ranger... he never did trust him...

The cat was no longer growling... it was hissing and roaring... whatever was the matter?'

Klem then noticed the loud, inefficient engine of a car that had parked by the roadside, the wisps of black smoke emanating from its exhaust rising up to the balcony and beyond. He sniffed the unmistakable stench of burning oil that never failed to irritate the back of his throat. Swinging his feet to the floor, he went to investigate, crouching low, then carefully peering over the balustrade so as not to be seen from the street...

His bowels felt extremely loose when he realised his instincts had been right: the loud engine belonged to a black Zil automobile. He knew this type of car all too well; its presence was always the harbinger of doom. The thing must have weighed more than three tons and was well over twenty feet long. The horrendous noise came from the eight-litre V8 beneath the vast bonnet. It had parked up over a minute ago, yet its leaf-spring suspension meant it still wobbled like an enormous jelly; no wonder, because such automobiles were made in a Moscow factory alongside refrigerators and trucks, undoubtedly sharing many of the same cumbersome components. And Gunter told him that an automobile such as this was once discovered with thirty bodies crammed in its boot... Klem tried to swallow, but couldn't.

He peered curiously over the balcony and watched as two goon-like men lunged out of the front seats. 'The Vlads,' said Klem, 'the bloody Vlads!' One strode to the shop door, while the other opened the car's rear door and assisted an elderly gentleman onto the pavement.

The elderly gentleman looked like some form of sorcerer, wearing a black cape that brushed the ground. He walked with such a pronounced stoop that the conventional ebony walking stick he held appeared to be longer than a shepherd's crook. It was a pity the man's hat obscured his face, but Klem imagined it to be just as ugly, if not uglier, than the faces of the goons that assisted him.

Klem sat on the ground, keeping out of sight, while the cat stuck its head through the balustrade and growled like the MGM lion. 'Shhh,' Klem pleaded. The cat reluctantly quietened down, but only after it had raised its tail over the edge of the balcony...

Down in the shop, the doorbell rang incessantly for almost a minute, before it was blessedly muted. Klem wondered whether Taras would ever get it mended. Although he could hear a conversation, he couldn't quite discern what was being said... But there was no need to worry...

He knew Taras would tell them he'd never heard of a "Klem", and would insist they went away. He also knew that, although Taras was still angry with him for almost ruining his ballet, he would never do anything silly...

So he ambled back to his chair, sipped at his cold Camomile tea and once again immersed himself in the headlines, feeling the weight of the newspapers, and letting the newsprint blacken his fingers. There were millions of copies of Voloshin's articles in circulation. And not just in England, but also in America, Canada, France and even Russia: in fact, all countries with a Ukrainian diaspora... Not even the mighty Soviet Union had the ability to seize every copy. He didn't know how to thank his friends in Fleet Street: the usual cup of Earl Grey would be insufficient this time.

He smiled: the goons downstairs were probably just going through the motions to keep their "Comrade General" happy. They wouldn't try too hard... by this time tomorrow, they knew their beloved General would be languishing in a Siberian Gulag... if they had any sense, they'd go AWOL...

Soon enough, Klem heard the shop door slam, the sound of marching footsteps across the pavement and then the doors of the Zil banging closed. 'Thank you Taras,' he whispered, 'I knew you'd get rid of them.' He prepared to resume his daydreaming, 'that's the last we'll see of them...'

But Mister Pushkin refused to relax... standing with an arched back, its ears folded flat and growling louder than the Zil's engine, which oddly, was still silent...

Klem soon realised what troubled the cat... He cried, 'I don't believe it,' as he listened to the sound of footsteps ascending the spiral staircase to the attic. 'The durak has let in the bloody Vlads! Thanks a bunch, Taras. I won't forget this...'

Scattering the newspapers all over the floor, he looked over the balcony and saw the two goons sat alone in the Zil, blowing as much smoke out of the open windows as had billowed from the car's exhaust. But where was the sorcerer? He scampered over to the door and listened; he was sure the tapping of a walking stick punctuated the footsteps winding their way up the spiral staircase. Klem's hands started to shake: he knew all about these ex-Gestapo types who'd joined the Soviet Secret Police in 1946 so as to avoid the Nuremberg Trials... some of them were so heinous that even the Stasi didn't want them. This man may have looked like a crooked old codger, but Klem knew this would be far from the truth... Now Klem's entire body trembled...

The footsteps were getting louder, the getaway car was poised, and at the highest point in the house, Klem was cornered, with nowhere to flee and no one to help him. He gasped, realising that Taras probably didn't have any choice but to let this man in, and could only hope that Taras regained consciousness and came to his aide before it was too late...

So without a moment to lose, Klem slung on his red leather boots, quietly locked and bolted the attic door and hid in the cramped space beneath his desk. Where were Zena and Lenka? To them, a Soviet assassin was nothing when compared to wrestling a herd of wild boar: they'd tear him limb from limb...

'Mrryaw!' cried Mister Pushkin, head-butting Klem hard on the shin.

Klem said, 'Shhh!' and gently closed the cat's mouth. 'You can have your sir-a-loin later, but now is the time to be very <u>quiet</u>.'

The cat grumbled, before sulkily going to stare at the wall.

Klem counted the footsteps and knew there were ten, nine, eight remaining until the assassin ascended to the small landing and thumped on the door, demanding entry. He knew the man would kick the door down if there were no answer. And once he was inside, he'd soon find him cowering beneath the desk and wouldn't waste time extracting the required information as painfully as possible. Then there would be a quick 'pft' from the silenced gun, and it would all be over. If that happened, he hoped Halyna would be kind enough to look after Mister Pushkin. He shook his head and thought: *pull yourself together Klem! Don't be so defeatist!*

The heavy footsteps stopped, and there was a loud bang on the door.

'Klem!' a baritone voice called out, 'I know you're in there!'

Klem thought: *Stay quiet and he'll go away. If only I could reach the pistol...* The pistol was balanced on the cluttered mantelpiece beside the Fabergé Egg, but he was too afraid to move... in any case, it wasn't loaded.

The assassin hammered on the door again, rattled the door handle and repeated: 'Klem, are you in there?'

He's not going away, is he? Come on Klem: you're a sitting duck – you must do <u>something</u>! But what? His eyes moved repeatedly from left to right as if scanning through an invisible list of options. Unfortunately, the options he saw really were invisible.

'<u>Klem</u>!' the man shouted louder than ever. He hammered on the door with such force that his fists almost broke through the

The Dancing Barber

chipboard. 'I <u>know</u> you're in there!'

That's it! Here's what I'm going to do! When he breaks down the door, I'll make a lunge for <u>his</u> gun. Then I'll twist his wrist, the gun will fall from his hand and – hey presto – I'll have the situation under control!

Who am I trying to kid? The Vlads weren't shooting people any more. That ebony walking stick probably has a cyanide-coated tip: one stab in my leg and it'll be curtains. Or maybe it was a sword-stick – like the one Steed uses in The Avengers – No, that would be too messy. It'd be the cyanide, I'm sure. And don't forget about the two goons in the car... even if I dealt with the assassin, I'd still have them to contend with...

'Klem! Are you going to let me in?' the man cried. 'Are you all right?'

What does it matter to him if I'm all right?

'<u>Klem</u>! Are you going to let me in, or am I to stand here for the rest of my life? It is I, <u>the Bishop</u>!'

'The Bishop?' Klem said. He looked at Mister Pushkin – who'd jumped up to sit in amongst the clutter on the polished copper mantelpiece – shaking its furry head at its owner's groundless paranoia. Klem felt his heart thumping beneath his embroidered shirt: thank Heavens it was only the Bishop!

Once he'd crawled out from under his desk, and straightened his concertinaed body, it occurred to him that this could still be a ploy... the Vlads were prone to lie! So he turned to fetch his pistol, and watched in horror as Mister Pushkin jumped from the mantelpiece and dislodged the weapon with its hind legs. The pistol – as if moving in slow motion – tumbled into the fire and disappeared amongst the flames. He whispered angrily, 'thanks a bunch Pushkin...'

The cat flicked its tail in the air and wandered off to stare at the wall.

Extending his index and middle fingers, Klem placed his hand in his jacket pocket... it was better than nothing... Just so long as the "Bishop" didn't call his bluff...

'Klem,' the man pleaded from behind the door, 'will you <u>please</u> let me in!'

Chapter 52

'Do <u>not</u> dare to argue with me again!' The Gossipmonger ordered, with a clout of her clubbed hand. 'You are coming with me and that is <u>final</u>!' She threw another heavy Louis Vuitton suitcase onto the marble floor by the front door and dragged herself back upstairs to fill another one.

'But I don't want to go,' Oksana cried. 'I want to stay <u>here</u>! And what about *Swan Lake*? If I don't turn up, I'll be in <u>a lot</u> of trouble...' Her buttocks throbbed in anticipation of the cane.

'What did I just say?' The Gossipmonger stomped her foot. 'We are leaving today! Your Tato has brought great shame on this family and we <u>cannot</u> stay!' She recalled the Zena woman's demonstration with the eggs and wondered whether "Tato" was the best name for him? And if it wasn't, she knew precisely what that made Oksana.

Oksana realised there was no point arguing with her grandmother: once the old hag's mind was made up, there was no changing it.

So much had happened in the past few hours that Oksana's head whirled with confusion...

Her Tato wasn't her Tato, and that made her a little sad... now she knew why they never got on. That also meant her grandmother wasn't her grandmother, which was the most joyous news she'd heard in her entire life!

So why did she have to go anywhere with this old hag, if she wasn't related to her? And, actually, where were they going?

She'd often wondered what her mother was like... Zena certainly wasn't how she'd imagined...

And then there was the identity of her real Tato to consider.

Oksana asked, 'but is that smelly troll *really* my mother?'

'Of course not! How could she be?' The Gossipmonger said, listening to the Swiss chronometer in the drawing room strike four o'clock... she wondered whether she could squeeze it into her largest Louis Vuitton suitcase.

'But why did she say she was?' Oksana asked, scratching her

armpit.

'Because she's a <u>liar</u>! There are many liars in this world... You will soon learn that! Now, come on, the taxi will be here in three hours and we have *a lot* of packing still to do!'

'Yes,' Oksana said, thinking that Zena didn't sound as if she was lying. 'And what about Tato...'

'What about him? He is one of those liars I have just spoken of. He isn't to be trusted either. You can only trust <u>me</u>. No one else but me, is that clear?'

'But why?' Oksana asked, wondering if anyone told the truth any more.

The Gossipmonger brandished her clubbed hand, 'because I said so, <u>that's why</u>!'

Chapter 53

With both feet wedged firmly behind the door, Klem peered through the narrow gap and scrutinised his ecclesiastical visitor. The man that had looked so decrepit down on the street, didn't look that decrepit any more, despite having such a pronounced stoop... In the dimness of the landing, Klem noticed the outline of a biretta atop the man's enormous head, and dark sunglasses were perched securely across his nose. The man's fleshy lips slowly parted, 'what are you waiting for?' He displayed his crucifix and chunky amethyst ring, 'see, I <u>am</u> the Bishop! Don't you recognise me from last night?'

'Your Grace,' Klem said courteously, inviting the clergyman to hobble into the attic, '*of course* I recognise you.' He didn't recognise his face... but he'd probably recognise his other end... but the less said about that, the better. 'I am honoured that you have taken the time to visit *me*, a lowly poet...' He guided him to a hard wooden chair, 'please, take a seat?' He knew what he'd said, the moment the words left his lips.

'Thank you,' said the Bishop, extracting an inflatable rubber ring from the folds of his black cape. He inflated it with one lungful of air and placed it on the chair. He then sat down with all the care of a hen on eggs and said, 'the doctors removed the bullet, but it made a dreadful mess... I have to sit on this thing until it's healed.' He sighed, 'I wish I knew who was responsible... But it looks as though I'll never know...'

Saying nothing, Klem placed the kettle on the hob, and went to close the adjoining door to the twins' end of the attic, which was still festooned with their stained underwear. The cat remained curled up in front of the fire, undoubtedly warming itself with the additional heat emitted by the molten pistol... but its deep yellow eyes never left the Bishop. Klem asked, 'can I offer you some tea?'

'Thank you, a cup of tea will be *most* wonderful,' said the Bishop, unfastening his black cape, allowing it to fall away from his broad shoulders and tumble to the floor. Admiring the sun-drenched balcony, he said, 'this is certainly a nice place to live! It is so much better than my official residence... What a view... you can see for miles...'

'You certainly can,' Klem said, shovelling the exact amount of tea-leaves into his special Minton teapot, 'but I think Kyiv is a far more beautiful city than Bradford.'

'Ah, but beauty is in the eye of the beholder,' the Bishop replied, tapping his sunglasses. He then wafted his full length purple cassock, allowing the cool breeze from the balcony to ventilate his perspiring legs. Why did Klem have to light a fire on such a warm day? But he knew all poets had their eccentricities...

The Bishop watched his host monitor the temperature of the kettle, using a special glass thermometer protruding from the spout... he'd never witnessed such a palaver for making a simple cup of tea. But the delay gave him time to properly take in his surroundings...

The attic was obviously the residence of a devout Christian, if the small altar, Byzantine icons and background whiff of incense was anything to go by. It was also the home of a prolific writer: the shelves were brimming with Klem's published books, and one wall was a shrine to his journalistic endeavours, completely covered from floor to ceiling with framed newspaper front pages, some dating back several decades. The yellowing front page of the 1935 "Chicago American" caught the Bishop's eye... its headline read:

```
SIX MILLION PERISH IN SOVIET FAMINE
     PEASANTS' CROPS SIEZED,
  THEY AND THEIR ANIMALS STARVE
```

The headline was similar to this morning's newspapers, many of which the Bishop had read with his breakfast caviar. And he noted that these very newspapers, and many more, were littered about the floor by his feet. He shuffled on the inflatable rubber ring, so as to read more of the headlines, making humorous creaking noises in the process. He asked, 'I expect you're wondering why I'm here?'

The question had certainly crossed Klem's mind... he thought: *what if he knows it was me who shot him up the... are some Bishops likely to hold a grudge more than others?* He checked the temperature of the kettle and shrugged his shoulders.

The Bishop smiled briefly, 'I didn't get opportunity to congratulate you on your exquisite declamations yesterday. After the, err... incident, no one had any idea where you were, so – as I was in the neighbourhood – I thought I'd come and congratulate you in person.'

'That is very kind of you,' Klem said, noticing the thermometer's mercury had risen to almost ninety-nine degrees centigrade.

'Tell me,' the Bishop said, tilting his head so as to read the vertical book titles on a nearby shelf, 'how long have you made a living from your poetry?'

'I haven't really. I earn most of my money by writing freelance for a few newspapers.' He arranged his blue and yellow teacups on a tray, 'poetry is just a hobby of mine...'

'But you must be doing pretty well if you can afford such a luxurious ornament?' the Bishop said, nodding in the direction of the bejewelled egg on the mantelpiece. He compared the amethyst of the ring on his finger to the blue and yellow stones of the jewel. 'Fabergé, isn't it?'

Klem hated lying, especially to a Bishop; but his instincts made him do it. 'I wish it was real, your Grace, but sadly it is a mere glittery trinket.'

'May I hold it?' the Bishop asked, preparing to stand up, the inflatable cushion creaking even more...

'I'd rather you didn't,' Klem said, clattering a teaspoon. 'It may be valueless, but it is extremely fragile.'

The Bishop seemed disappointed, yet continued to admire it inquisitively.

The hob kettle whistled so loudly that it startled Mister Pushkin; the cat leapt from in front of the fire and straight onto its favourite chair... It was a pity the Bishop was presently occupying this chair. And he did not like his cassock being covered in fur, nor did he appreciate it when the cat's kneading claws pulled out many of the intricate stitches from the hand-made purple fabric. For the sake of politeness, he said, 'what a delightful cat. It's a Russian

The Dancing Barber

Blue isn't it?' He tried to stroke the cat on the head, but was fearful of being bitten or scratched, for it pulled a most unfriendly expression.

'That's right,' Klem said, setting the freshly filled teapot to one side, where it would brew for precisely forty-nine seconds. He admired the cat and said, 'he's my best friend.'

'Ironic, don't you agree, that you chose a <u>Russian</u> Blue cat as a pet?'

'Not at all,' Klem shook his head, 'as you know, a cat chooses its owner, and not the other way round. And anyway, I prefer to think of him as a <u>Ukrainian</u> Blue, because he was born in Chaplinka and is a descendant of the cat I owned as a child... the *purest* of pedigrees...'

The cat was so displeased with the purple thing occupying its favourite chair, that it arched its back, and did what it always did, before jumping to the floor and heading for the food bowl.

'I'm <u>so</u> sorry,' Klem said, handing a cloth to the Bishop. 'You should be honoured... it means he likes you...'

Mister Pushkin had done a wonderful job of dowsing the Bishop's entire face. The green liquid ran down his forehead, over the lenses of his sunglasses and along the bridge of his bulbous nose, before dripping down onto the front of his formerly pristine cassock.

The Bishop was clearly disgusted, but remained calm and collected, as was required of a senior clergyman. The corners of his mouth bent upwards, slightly, and he said, 'don't worry about it, these things happen.' He took off his sunglasses, placed them on the desk in front of him and wiped his face with the cloth until it was meticulously dry.

'Wouldn't you like to wash your face properly?' Klem asked, nodding to the sink. 'There's soap and water over there...'

'That will not be necessary,' replied the Bishop. 'Thank you.'

'Are you sure?' asked Klem.

The Bishop said nothing.

Klem was shocked to discover that the Bishop's sunglasses weren't a fashion accessory... The clergyman's left eye was heavily bloodshot, which wasn't surprising after what the cat had just done, but his right one... Klem could barely look.

The Bishop picked up his sunglasses and breathed on a lens,

prior to polishing it with a fold of his cassock. Klem couldn't help staring at him... As a result, the tea in the pot had brewed for a previously unheard of *fifty* seconds... that extra second would ruin the brew... he hoped the Bishop wouldn't notice...

Without looking up, the Bishop said calmly, 'a mad peasant attacked me during the troubles of 1933,' he shrugged his shoulders, 'and the eye was lost. As a temporary measure, I used a marble – it was the only thing available at the time – but I can't get it out, hence the sunglasses. A Bishop can't go around with the eye of a reptile, can he?'

'I suppose not,' Klem said, surprised the man had seen him staring at him. The clergyman must have had excellent peripheral vision in his good eye.

Klem tried not to think about the Bishop's horrific face, but it wasn't easy... He picked up the teapot containing the over-brewed tea, and placed it on an electroplated silver tray along with the blue and yellow teacups. He said, 'some dreadful things happened thirty years ago: being a clergyman back then was a dangerous occupation.'

The Bishop grunted affirmatively, whilst perching the sunglasses securely back in position.

'Any way,' Klem said, decanting the tea into the cups from the usual height of seven inches, thus aerating the over-brewed tea, and enhancing the spoiled flavour, 'thankfully, things are sure to improve in Ukraine now that Voloshin's back.'

Once again, the Bishop grunted affirmatively. He gripped the rim of the cup of strong Camomile tea in his enormous hand, and took the smallest of sips. He asked, 'don't you have any milk?'

'Milk?' Klem said, 'err, of course, but it'll have to be the *long-life* variety. I don't drink much of it, especially not with Camomile tea...'

The Bishop said 'thank you,' as he snatched the carton and glugged a generous amount into his cup. He took a slurp, 'that's a little better,' he said, setting the cup down on the desk's polished surface, instead of back on the saucer.

Klem raised his eyebrows; he'd never known anyone drink Camomile tea with *milk* before. But then again, he'd never met anyone with a marble eye before...

'May I,' the Bishop asked, pulling a hefty tome of poems from

The Dancing Barber

an adjacent shelf, and slamming it carelessly onto the desk in front of him.

'Of course, please, make yourself at home…'

Having felt the weight of the book, the Bishop said, 'you certainly have been busy.'

'Indeed,' said Klem, watching the Bishop flick through some of the Ukrainian poems, rhymes and short stories, licking his thumb and adhering it to the top corner of every page he turned.

'You know,' the Bishop said, 'many "Kulaks" were sent to Siberia in 1933 for writing things like this.' He closed the tome with one hand. 'The crime was termed "Anti-Soviet Agitation"! I notice this book was published at around that time… so being a "Kulak", how did you avoid the same fate?'

Remembering that he was addressing a Bishop, Klem tried to remain calm… 'I'd rather you didn't use such an offensive term; besides, surely you were also branded in such a way?'

'Oh no,' said the Bishop, 'I have never been called a "Kulak".' He thumbed through the pages of another musty book and said, '"Intelligencia" then, is that better? Either way, the writer of this,' he strummed his fingers on the tome's front cover, 'would have been lucky not to end up in a Siberian Gulag. It gets to minus fifty in those forests. Imagine cutting down trees from dawn until dusk with nothing but a bit of old bread to eat all day. I wouldn't have liked it, but many people thought it quite effective.'

Klem shook his head, 'only the idiot Soviets would think mass murder was "effective"… Anyhow,' he gestured to the cascade of newspapers on the floor, 'the butchers responsible will soon be held to account.'

'Quite,' said the Bishop, trying to sip more of the milky tea. He shoved the book back onto the shelf, between leather-bound volumes written by Voloshin.

'Voloshin is a very brave man,' said Klem, stroking his moustache. 'He has achieved so much for Ukraine… As the Good Book says: *"…we also rejoice in our sufferings, because we know that suffering produces perseverance; perseverance, character; and character, hope."…* Romans, 5:3,4…'

'Suffering,' muttered the Bishop, 'there's nothing like it…'

Mister Pushkin glared at the Bishop. The intelligent cat folded its ears flat and arched its back, its tail swelling to a fox's brush.

'Don't be silly Mister Pushkin,' Klem said, carefully arranging some meat on the cat's gold-rimmed china plate. 'Come here and have some more sir-a-loin…'

'Sir-a-loin!' the Bishop laughed, 'your moggie eats better than I do!'

'Only the best will do for Mister Pushkin,' Klem said, placing the plate onto the dining mat, garnishing the meat with a sprig of dill. He stroked the cat's luscious fur, 'bon appetite.'

For the next ten minutes, the Bishop seemed to enjoy reading through many of the first editions Klem was lucky enough to possess. They weren't just his own and Voloshin's, but also those of Taras Shevchenko, Ivan Franko and Lesia Ukrayinka, some of which were signed. The latter three were Ukraine's most famous poets; but as many of their original books were destroyed by the Soviets, who sought to eradicate all evidence of Ukrainian culture, very few first editions remained. Klem knew that when Ukraine gained her independence, they'd be worth a small fortune, even though the paper was mildewed and some pages had a slobbery thumb print in their top corners...

Klem decanted his third cup of Camomile tea, whilst the Bishop was still sipping his first: at this rate the tea would evaporate quicker than the Bishop could drink it. He tried not to think about it, but the Bishop's horrific face still haunted him… Eventually, he plucked up the courage to ask, 'your Grace, I cannot believe someone could do something so barbaric to a man of the cloth. And for an attack to be so vicious for you to lose an eye…'

The Bishop closed the book he was reading – Shevchenko's famous "Kobsar" – and slotted it back onto the shelf. He took off his sunglasses and placed them onto the desk, allowing Klem to take a long, hard look at his face.

Klem cringed. If the green and black eyeball wasn't bad enough, the man's right eyebrow and cheekbone were hideously defaced with parallel deep silver scratches that made it look as though he'd been clawed by a lion.

The Bishop said, 'when this happened, I wasn't a clergyman…'

'Really?' Klem said, 'but I was told that you were at the Seminary at the same time as me?'

'No, no, no, you must be mistaken; I had a different job before

The Dancing Barber

joining the Church.'

'Really?'

'Mmm,' said the Bishop, glancing once more at the glittery trinket on the mantelpiece. 'In fact, this is only my *third* day as a Ukrainian Orthodox Bishop.'

A deep furrow appeared between Klem's eyebrows, 'I didn't think you attended the Kyiv Seminary... I'd have remembered...' He gasped, 'you weren't originally a *Catholic*, were you?'

The Bishop shook his head, '*certainly* not.'

Mister Pushkin stopped eating, sat up and looked squarely at the Bishop.

'Ah, so you were a peasant then?' Klem said, placing his teacup neatly onto its corresponding saucer. Suspecting the Bishop hadn't had a cultured upbringing, he said, 'it must have been hard to get into the Church later in life?'

'Certainly not: I have never been a peasant.'

Mister Pushkin's tail swelled so much that it could have been used as a draught-excluder. The cat folded its ears flat, bared its teeth and hissed so much that fragments of sir-a-loin sprayed across the floor, the smell of partially digested meat filling the air.

Klem looked at his cat, 'don't be so silly,' he said, 'go and finish off your sir-a-loin.' He turned back to his guest, 'you must excuse my cat, your Grace; he does have a tendency to behave rather oddly at times...'

The Bishop smiled, as he watched the cat continue to hiss. He said, 'Mister Pushkin seems fearful of his own kind.'

'Whatever do you mean?' Klem asked, swallowing the last of the Camomile tea.

The Bishop laughed, 'but perhaps his breed should be renamed "Soviet Blue"?'

Klem felt the delicate glaze of his favourite bone china cup crack, as he slammed it onto the saucer. He said, 'that is a terrible thing to say!'

And Mister Pushkin agreed, for it launched itself three feet into the air and landed on the Bishop's broad chest, sinking its hind claws deeply into his purple cassock. The cat ignored Klem's commands and frantically scratched at the Bishop's tanned cheeks, leaving four parallel cuts, oozing blood.

The Bishop lashed out with his arms, and flung the cat to the floor, in so doing, severing the chain of the austere crucifix that hung around his neck. The crucifix clattered to the floor, and was lost in the pattern on the carpet.

The cat landed on its feet, darted beneath the sofa, and glared at the Bishop through the slits of its molten eyes.

The Bishop's fleshy lips parted, allowing his corpulent tongue to emerge and lick away the dribbles of blood that ran down his cheeks.

'I don't know what's gotten into him,' Klem apologised, 'he must have taken offence at being called a *Soviet* cat?' He stared at the Bishop, 'and who could blame him?' He crouched by the sofa, trying to coax the cat out with a piece of sir-a-loin. But the cat wouldn't budge. He said to the Bishop, 'but <u>why</u> did you make that remark? Saying such things isn't appropriate for a Ukrainian Bishop...'

Klem's ears pricked up at a familiar double-clicking sound.

He didn't have time to turn around, let alone dive out of the way, before he heard an almost silent, 'pft...'

A blizzard of feathers exploded from his favourite embroidered cushion...

The Dancing Barber

Chapter 54

---------------------------------✁---------------------------------

'I can't believe it,' Taras sang, skipping his way to the Club, still dressed as Prince Siegfried, following an early evening performance. 'I can't believe it, I can't believe it, I can't believe it!'

In so doing, he worried many of the headscarves he'd passed, who'd never, ever seen him happy before.

He sang, 'another standing ovation! The applause, the whistles... and thankfully no knickers!' He repeatedly sang, 'I can't believe it!' so quickly that all the words merged into one. Unfortunately, the other thing he repeated was his sisters-in-law's "stew of the hamster"; not even super-strength Listerine could take *that* taste away... but he wasn't going to let it spoil his day any more than it'd done already... He didn't imagine Rudolf Nureyev ever danced when suffering such chronic indigestion. Nevertheless, the performance – even without his over-sized Odile – was sensational...

He was in no rush to return to the den of depression that was his house. All Zena could do was sit moodily in a corner and bite people's heads off. Halyna still hadn't emerged from her bedroom... and he didn't look forward to the atmosphere when she eventually did. Sofia meanwhile was in a depression all of her own: understandably so, after discovering her delightful aunties had butchered the school pet and its offspring and served them up for dinner. And discovering Oksana was her new cousin didn't help either... at least it didn't affect her performance... her Odette danced better than ever.

But worst of all was when Lenka decided to eat an orange: after peeling it with her filthy thumbnail, she crammed the entire sphere into her mouth, chewing it around until every drop of juice was swallowed. She then spat the resultant pithy mess onto a plate, before repeating the process with a further four oranges, thus creating a pith mountain, the sight of which made Taras queasy.

It was only Klem who was happy, having evaded the looming threat of Soviet assassination, and was probably still enjoying a thoroughly ecclesiastical discussion with the Bishop at this very moment. Never before had Taras met such a friendly Bishop… especially after suffering such a horrific injury in such an unfortunate place…

Hopefully, by the time Taras got home, everyone would be in bed; he could then sneak in regardless of the state he was in… because now was a time for celebration!

So he jumped and clicked his heels as if he were Danny Kaye – a fellow Ukrainian – and delighted in the fact that he was finally going to be rich and famous, and it was about time too! The man from YTV had called before he'd left for the theatre, and Taras had already decided how he was going to spend the fee: it wasn't a fortune, but it would be the first time he'd be properly paid for doing what he loved most of all. And hopefully this would be the first of many pay cheques! So in a few years he could *buy* Bolling Hall, rather than pretend to live in it. With the evening bathed in golden sunshine, and sweet pollen swirling in the air, Taras swung himself around each lamp-post he passed, thinking how beautiful life truly was…

For the past few weeks, the Uki Club bar had been a sombre place, where flat-caps would come to wash away their worries and escape the perpetual nagging of their headscarved wives. But Taras was astounded to discover that this evening, the bar was a hive of celebration. Ukrainian folk music blasted from the windows, and there was singing and dancing abound. Many flat-caps danced the "Hopak", while others devised their own medleys of whatever traditional Ukrainian dancing steps they knew: arms waved, bodies squatted and legs kicked in all directions. The younger flat-caps tried to impress the young ladies by limbo dancing beneath ridiculously low broom handles while balancing glasses of samahon on their foreheads, whilst the older ones persuaded many of the headscarves to join in with the jollity. It was the first time Taras had seen the old women without their headscarves: he'd imagined they slept and bathed in them! But the plethora of permed and dyed hairdos was an interesting sight to behold, especially when the women's husbands flung them around the impromptu dance-floor, agitating the air with the whiff of mothballs.

The Dancing Barber

The community's reaction to the resounding success of *Swan Lake* brought tears to his eyes. He pulled the creases from the blue blazer he wore over his costume, scraped the dyed hair back into place across his head and prepared to make his grand entrance. He anticipated that as soon as his friends saw him, they'd cheer, maybe sing the Ukrainian equivalent of "for he's a jolly good fellow..." and pick him up like the champion he was, carrying him to an improvised throne that would be a stool placed atop the bar. They'd ply him with any drinks he wanted for the rest of the night and would treat him with all the respect he deserved.

With this in mind, Taras flung open both doors, walked in and took a long bow. But his friends were so busy carousing that they didn't even notice him. He went back outside and made his grand entrance for a second time, flinging the doors open so hard that they bounced back and almost struck him in the face. But not one person noticed him. He then coughed, as if he suffered from chronic bronchitis and emphysema, but again not one person noticed him. His shoulders slumped. He tried coughing loudly once more, but it was a waste of time; the party continued and he wasn't included... how could they ignore the star of the show? He thought nothing about why dozens of newspapers were strewn all over the place, nor why the photograph of Stalin that permanently resided on the dartboard, had been perforated with several kitchen knives and a meat cleaver.

Taras dragged his feet over to the bar and squeezed himself into the only remaining space, between the spreading posteriors of Natalka's aunties Lyudmila and Valentina, and ordered himself a drink. The inebriated barman with the Robert Mitchum eyes was so far gone that he'd walked off before Taras had chance to pay for his pint... and didn't even bother to congratulate him on his performance. Taras looked at the glass and noticed it was half-filled with froth: that was the <u>final</u> straw. He hammered on the bar with his fist, making the empty glasses clatter, and shouted: 'excuse me everyone, I want you all to know that I'm here!'

A flat-cap looked over his shoulder and said, 'so you are... what of it?'

'What do you mean?' Taras said, 'I am here and everyone is ignoring me!'

'You're not the centre of the universe, you know...'

Taras looked at him sternly.

'Haven't you seen the papers?' a particularly merry flat-capped man shouted from across the bar. 'It's Voloshin: he's back!'

Every flat-cap cheered boisterously in response, and sang, 'Voloshin! Voloshin! He's back! He's back! He'll go and tell Khrushchev that he's a durak!' They flung their caps into the air to reveal bald heads and comb-overs.

'And we've just heard on the radio,' the merry flat-cap continued, 'that he's going to meet with Khrushchev to discuss how the Soviet Union will compensate the victims of The Great Famine! I know that money will never come close to replacing what we lost, but it's a start...'

Another flat-cap said, 'I never thought I'd see the day the Soviets would admit that Stalin deliberately murdered our countrymen! And now those murderers will get what they deserve!' He poured another glass of samahon down his throat, and promptly refilled it, before deciding it would be more efficient to drink straight from the bottle.

'Yippee,' shouted yet another flat-cap, '<u>and</u> he's going tell Khrushchev that Ukraine wants her independence. And for <u>good</u> this time! And <u>he</u> won't take "no" for an answer!'

'And the UN have agreed that Voloshin's evidence is genuine, so have summoned the Soviet Foreign Minister to New York for an urgent meeting... I bet his pants are full of himno!'

'You wait thirty years, and nothing happens,' said the merry flat-cap. 'Then suddenly everything happens!'

Once more, every flat-cap cheered, waved their arms in the air and spilled even more samahon onto the squelchy carpet. Radio Kateryna was turned on full blast and there was so much dancing and merrymaking that Taras' own news no longer seemed particularly important, not even to him.

He ordered another free pint of froth and went to sit down, reflecting that he couldn't have wished for better news to overshadow his own: it made an already wonderful day truly monumental. And how pleased – and surprised – he was that all Klem's efforts had actually succeeded! The best he expected was a column or two in the *Mail* and the *Express*, but to have complete coverage was unbelievable: this Katya of his must be very well connected. But it was still a dangerous business, and he was glad

The Dancing Barber

he wasn't involved.

At last, the history books would have to be rewritten to include the atrocities of The Great Famine. Taras felt a shiver down his spine: it was as though the victims of 1933 were pleased not to have been forgotten. He raised his glass and drank a toast to their memory.

Just as Taras was getting up to demonstrate to the flat-caps how a "Hopak" should be danced, he felt a gentle tap on his shoulder. He turned around but didn't notice anyone there.

'Could I speak with you for a moment?' asked an anonymous looking man. 'Perhaps we can go somewhere quieter?'

Chapter 55

Klem shouted, 'what the Hell's wrong with you? Have you gone stark raving mad?' He watched the white feathers settle to the carpet like snowflakes. 'My Mama embroidered that cushion!'

The Bishop grinned as he clicked the next bullet into the chamber concealed in the shaft of his ebony walking stick.

Klem knew of several Bishops who'd suddenly – as Mrs Wiggins would say – "flipped their lids", but this was ridiculous. 'A-hem,' he said, 'but what do you think you are doing?'

The cat's head poked out from under the sofa, and 'pft', the Bishop pulled the trigger once more. The bullet ploughed its way through the air and embedded itself in the carpet where the cat's paws once rested. The cat squealed and immediately fled downstairs, dragging its blue and yellow leash behind it.

'Drat,' the Bishop said, 'missed again!' He looked at Klem, 'you know, I hate cats, especially when they piss on me!'

Klem was stunned; the only people he truly disliked were ailurophobes, especially those who were cruel to such beautiful creatures. He said, 'have you got a screw loose? You wait until the Archbishop hears about this!'

'Nuts to the Archbishop!'

'I *beg* your pardon? Well, I've never heard such…'

'Perhaps we can get down to business,' the Bishop interrupted, reloading his walking stick. 'I haven't been truthful with you, and I know you don't like liars.' He extracted a tube of Polo mints from a pocket in his cassock and, one-handedly, peeled back the silver foil, levering off a single Polo.

Klem gulped… He thought: *So the Bishop did know it was me who'd shot him up the… a-ha, that's why he blew up my cushion…*

The Bishop sucked the mint loudly for a few seconds, the air whistling through the hole, before he said: 'now I'm not one for beating about the bushes, so I'll get straight to the point. You and your friends downstairs will be unharmed – you have my word on that – if you tell me where I can find Voloshin. And before you say that you don't know where he is, rest assured that I have it on

The Dancing Barber

good authority that you <u>do</u> know!'

Klem felt the sweat dampening his shirt. He thought: *Voloshin? What does the Bishop want with Voloshin?*

'And as an incentive,' the Bishop stroked his deeply tanned chin, 'if you haven't told me after one minute, I will shoot you in the left foot. And, if after the second minute, I am still none-the-wiser of Voloshin's whereabouts, I will shoot you in the right foot.' The Bishop smiled sadistically, 'and after the third minute, I will proceed to more vital areas…'

Klem had a horrible feeling that his original suspicions were correct… Why didn't he listen to his instincts? Even Mister Pushkin tried to warn him… Why didn't he listen?

'A-hem,' Klem said, edging ever so slightly closer to the door, 'you said you were going to be truthful… I assume I'm not addressing a *real* Bishop?'

'This is true,' the Bishop laughed, emitting the minty scent that masked his horrendous halitosis, 'I am a Colonel of the Soviet Army, and have been tasked in locating and arresting Voloshin and his accomplices, of which <u>you</u> are one. It came as quite a shock to the Kremlin when Voloshin was all of a sudden reincarnated, and Comrade President does not have the time for such distractions.' The man's Ukrainian accent and pronunciation were gone, replaced by harsh Soviet Russian intonations. 'Be assured that I have a one hundred percent success rate with this kind of thing, so please make it easy on yourself and tell me of your own volition before I have to induce you to talk. I know you are an intelligent man, so please make the intelligent decision.'

Klem remained silent. Why didn't he listen to his instincts: a Ukrainian Orthodox Bishop would never be chauffeured around in a Zil automobile? Nor would he drink Camomile tea with milk, and hold a teacup in such an uncouth way. Just as the Nazis parachuted into England dressed as nuns, it wasn't such a leap of imagination to have a Soviet Secret Policeman masquerading as a Bishop…

'The first minute has just begun,' the Colonel said with enjoyment, sucking away at the Polo Mint, aiming the end of his walking stick at Klem's left foot. 'Tick-tock, tick-tock, tick-tock…'

Chapter 56

Leaving Lenka to clatter about the kitchen, Zena waddled out to sit on the doorstep for some much needed peace and quiet. And she would have got it, had it not been for the busses and juggernauts hurtling up and down Great Horton Road, and the teddy boys on their revving Lambretta scooters, shouting at the tops of their voices. She delved her hand between what unkind people called her udders and hauled up the old wedding ring that hung around her neck. As she rotated the tarnished metal band around the top of her smallest finger, she fantasised about how much better her life would have been had she married Klem, instead of Ivan, all those years ago…

But as far as her Mama was concerned, Klem's name had been mud ever since the Soviet soldiers discovered his stash of Voloshin's propaganda leaflets hidden in their homestead in the autumn of 1933…

So when Klem came to rescue her from Ivan's evil clutches, eighteen years after that fateful day, his name was still mud and her Mama promptly sent him packing. It didn't matter to her that Klem was a Priest… she never forgot that it was his propaganda that sent her husband to his death in the Siberian Gulag.

After everything that had happened, Zena thought it was a genuine miracle that her husband-to-be was lodging with her wealthy young sister: it was as if the strands of her life were finally coming together like an enormous plaited loaf.

Her thoughts were briefly interrupted when Lenka decided to make even more noise in the kitchen: what was she doing in there? Rearranging the furniture? Playing skittles with the pots and pans? But Zena soon resumed her daydreaming; she looked at the state of Halyna's tiny back yard that was half concrete and half bare earth, patchily covered with dock-leaves and dotted with the smelliest dog dirt. But she knew the gardens at The Bolling Hall were much better than this… she wondered if she'd ever see them…?

Beneath all her finery, it was clear to Zena that Halyna retained the peasant genes: she knew her young sister wouldn't have

The Dancing Barber

forgotten how to work the land, grow crops and could probably even remember the intricacies of animal husbandry. But she didn't have the time or space – in the back yard at least – to do what came naturally. She reckoned that Halyna hankered to get back to her old life, to get her hands dirty and work with the soil again in the great outdoors. She knew the manicured fingernails, fancy clothes and expensive hair-do were only to please Taras.

An almighty clatter echoed from the kitchen followed by the worst kind of cursing. Zena threw the ring back into her vest, stood up and stormed into the bombsite of a kitchen. She stared at a harassed looking Lenka and said, 'what is the up with you? And what have you done to the kitchen?'

'Have you got the list?' Lenka asked, 'I have looked *everywhere...*'

'You know I have!' Zena said, removing it from beneath her clammy waistband, and passing it to her sister, 'here!' She surveyed the bombsite, 'this mess, it will need to be tidied... Halynochka, she has enough to the worry about...' She pointed to the crumpled paper, 'but first, remind me of what we need...'

Lenka felt more foolish that usual; she was sure her memory was getting worse; it was probably because of too much samahon. She hooked on her reading spectacles that were a pair of magnifying lenses tied together with twisted copper wire. Holding the dishevelled piece of paper at arm's length, she read out aloud: 'we need the Dee-odour-ants, the Talc-um powder, the San-it-arry towels, the Au-de-toilet, the Minis-kirts and the Leather hands-bag for me and you.'

'And for Uncle Viktor?'

Lenka turned over the sheet and read, 'he wants the Tracks-suit and the Trainings-shoes and also the new Waste-scoat, oh and some more of the Ray-zorblades.'

'Not much then...' Zena said, wondering whether after ninety-two years, she could finally get him to wear underpants if she were to buy him a pair. 'We will also need some more of the Stock-kings, the Bubbles-bath, the Teeth-paté and the Sham-poo!'

'Do we have enough of the money?'

Zena shook her head, 'they know we are the poor, but I will make it sound as if we are even poorer than that. <u>They</u> can afford it! They have The Bolling Hall <u>and</u> this house; they must be rolling in the plenty of the money!'

Lenka said, 'with all their money, they could buy every house in Chaplinka!'

Zena chuckled, 'and Askanya Nova too! And even then, they would have the money left over!'

Lenka laughed, 'I bet they could use the pound notes sterling to wipe their other ends...'

Zena sighed... to her it was the epitome of luxury...

'This may sound like the silly question,' Lenka said, 'but do you actually understand the words that come out of the mouth of Halynochka?'

'Not really; her pronunciation, it is not always, how you say, "normal..."'

'I am glad you have the noticed; I was worried that my hearing, it was going... You know, with the, how you say, Tin-It-Us... I think Halynochka, she speaks the different Ukrainian to what we do. And the same with Taras and Klem... And as for Sofia... I do not know what they teach her at the Ukrainian School?'

'I suppose they all spent so long speaking the English that now they speak the "Ukrainish"!'

Lenka laughed as she peeled off her cardigan and unleashed a roomful of nerve gas from her armpits. 'Ukrainish,' she said, 'you have just invented the new language!'

The smell from Lenka's armpits was so bad that even Zena noticed. 'Here,' she said, lobbing over a tall aerosol can, 'use this to give the underarms the better smell.'

Lenka snapped off the lid and aimed the nozzle at the thick bushel of black, curly hair beneath her arm. She gave it a good long squirt and remarked, 'this smells the very nice,' as she inhaled a deep lungful of the scent that made her sneeze so violently that she nearly spat out the few teeth she still had. She looked at the label and said, 'Silvikrin Hairspray – we must buy some more of this, it is the very good!' She then liberally squired the other armpit...

Zena added it to the list. 'Ah,' she said, 'we must also buy more of the sponges that Taras, he gave us: they cleaned my skin the very well! What were they called?'

Lenka reached for the packet and read out, 'they are called the Brillo Scouring Pads...'

The Dancing Barber

Zena wrote it down. She said, 'we shall buy every packet in the shop!'

'What was that?' Lenka asked, looking up to the ceiling.

Zena said, 'I did not hear anything?' She gouged a chunk of wax from one of her ears, adding it to the pile she intended to make a candle with. 'Maybe you have the Tin-It-Us...?'

'Do not be the silly,' snapped Lenka. 'Who is upstairs with Klem?'

'Only the Bishop,' Zena said, surprised by her sister's aggression. 'He came to congratulate the "poet-in-residence" on the recital of yesterday. Klem, he must be the very honoured.'

Lenka said, 'but that was *hours* ago... The Bishop, he cannot *still* be here?'

'He must be...' said Zena. 'I never saw him leave?'

'Well, I am sure I just heard the shouting.'

'The shouting?' Zena said, 'that is not the shouting. You remember how sometimes Klem, he gets the carried away when he declaims, especially when it is a poem he feels the passionately about. The Bishop, he is probably being the very well entertained up there!'

Lenka shook her head, 'but the shouting I heard, it was the *angry* shouting... the *very angry* shouting!'

The door from upstairs creaked open, prompting both sisters to turn around. To their astonishment, it was Halyna: she was out of breath and rather flustered. And unusually, Mister Pushkin followed her, encircling her ankles, dragging the blue and yellow leash behind it, almost tripping her up. 'Zena,' she said, 'I think there's big trouble in the attic...' She held out her trembling hand, '*this* came through the ceiling and embedded itself in my bedside table.'

'Is that what I think it is?' Zena said, picking up the mangled piece of metal, rolling it inquisitively between her thumb and forefinger...

Chapter 57

Klem felt the sweat running down the sides of his nose and soaking into his moustache that now drooped like a horseshoe over his mouth. After he'd counted fifty seconds, he mustered the confidence to say, 'very well, I will agree to your terms.' He pulled the embroidered cuffs out of his jacket sleeves, 'I don't *seem* to have much choice?'

The Colonel's grin bisected his face. Like all Soviet soldiers, he was unaccustomed to smiling, his facial muscles quivering with the effort.

Klem continued, 'a-hem, but I will only agree if we make it official by putting it in writing!' He unclipped his Pelikan fountain pen from his top pocket and held it out for the Colonel.

'You think me to be a durak?' the Colonel's grin was replaced with a sneer, 'you expect the thing to explode in my face, don't you? Well, you may have read many espionage books, but I am a Colonel of the Soviet Secret Police and I know about all these tricks!'

'If one of us is a durak then it certainly isn't *me*,' Klem said, unscrewing the cap and pushing it onto the end of the long green barrel. 'See, it's just an ordinary pen...' He held it in his outstretched hand, 'go on... take it.'

The Colonel reached out and took the pen with his left hand, never breaking eye-contact, nor moving the walking stick's aim from Klem's foot. The pen was heavy and looked as if it had a solid gold nib: not even Comrade President had a pen as good as this one... in the old days, he'd have presented it to him once his mission was complete, but this time, he'd keep it himself...

'I suppose there's no harm putting it in writing,' the Colonel said, intending to incinerate the note the moment his mission was completed. 'Where's the paper?' he demanded, questing through the desk drawers, nearly yanking half of them from their runners.

Daring not to move, Klem said, 'you'll find some notepaper in the *centre* drawer...' He didn't want the Colonel stumbling across any secret files, especially the one crammed with old

The Dancing Barber

propaganda...

'Very well,' the Colonel said, yanking open the drawer. He slammed a sheet of paper onto the leather-topped desk and began to write. But the pen merely indented the paper, leaving no trace of ink. The Colonel screwed up his face with annoyance and shook the pen vigorously up and down. When it still wouldn't write, he extended his corpulent tongue and licked the iridium-tipped nib, cringing at the ink's sour taste. After a lot more scribbling, the ink began to flow; he didn't care that his scrawled sentences were being smudged as his left hand traversed the page... after all, it was only for show...

Klem wondered why he didn't have the foresight to impregnate the ink with cyanide; that would truly be "poetic justice". Nevertheless, he was pleased with his handling of the situation so far. Nearly four minutes had elapsed, so by now, had it not been for his delaying tactic, both feet and his more "vital areas" would have had it; and he shuddered to think what would have been next. But he couldn't help cringing as he watched his pen's delicate golden nib bend and flex as the Colonel pressed on far too hard, scratching deeply into the notepaper, as if he were a mason carving into a tombstone.

Klem said, 'err... be sure to state that no harm will neither come to me nor any of my friends, once I have divulged to you the location of Voloshin...'

The Colonel grumbled. 'What do you think I'm writing? Now shut up... I'm trying to concentrate!'

'And,' Klem added, 'make sure it states clearly that this agreement lasts forever.' He raised his index finger, 'so that neither you nor your successors can go back on it.'

The Colonel grumbled once again. 'Is that it?' he snapped, 'or do you want me to copy out *War and Peace*?'

'No, I think that's everything,' Klem said, watching the pen continue to write; he muttered, 'unfortunately...' The barrel must have contained more ink than he'd thought... he'd looked forward to refilling the pen... it would have given him opportunity to squirt ink into the Colonel's good eye... And he could see the Colonel was a professional; neither his gaze nor the aim of his walking stick faltered for even a moment.

With the pointless task complete, the Colonel slammed the pen onto the desk and pushed the paper over to Klem. 'Check it – <u>quickly</u>!' he snapped, 'then tell me where Voloshin is. Time is precious and I am getting impatient.'

Klem pretended to search his pockets for his reading glasses.

'You may be interested to learn,' the Colonel said whilst wiping his fungal growth of a nose with a Bishop's purple handkerchief, 'that I had second thoughts about assassinating you at the theatre; I'd loaded my gun, took aim and rested my index finger on the trigger.'

Pretending not to be bothered, Klem said, 'so what made you change your mind?'

'Surely that would be obvious to a "Kulak" like you?'

Klem shrugged his shoulders, refusing to react to name-calling again. Of course it was obvious to him; he was merely surprised to discover a Colonel actually thought it wise to attempt an assassination in such a crowded place and expect to get away with it. In any case, the argument produced another useful delay in proceedings...

The Colonel's cheeks puffed out as he exhaled, 'if I did, then everyone would have known that I was the assassin; the British Police can be very troublesome to deal with...'

'Really?' said Klem, rolling his eyes. 'The thought never occurred to me.'

The Colonel gestured to the note and said, 'enough with this charade of searching for your reading glasses, I know you only wear them to make yourself look intelligent! Check your note and do it quickly!'

Klem slowly picked up the notepaper and began deciphering the smudged scrawl. Naturally it was written in Russian, and judging by the lack of refinement in the language used, lack of any punctuation, and the scruffiness of the handwriting, this Colonel was certainly not an educated man.

The Colonel coughed then strummed his fingers impatiently on the desktop.

But only when he was ready did Klem say, 'yes, it all seems in order.' He blew on the ink to make sure it was properly dry, then neatly folded the paper in half, marrying the corners up precisely, and placing it into his inside pocket.

'Well?' the Colonel demanded brusquely.

The Dancing Barber

'My pen,' Klem gestured to the desk, '...if you please.'

The Colonel grumbled again and threw the pen at him.

Klem somehow caught his prized possession, wrapping both hands around it. He immediately took out an ironed handkerchief and wiped away the greasy Soviet fingerprints, before screwing on the golden cap and clipping it safely in his pocket.

'Damn it Klem!' the Colonel snapped, 'you're doing this deliberately to annoy me!'

Yes I am... and it's working... Noticing the man's finger tightening on the trigger, Klem said, 'you're going to be surprised when I tell you where you can find Voloshin...' He swallowed, 'very surprised...'

The Colonel ever so slightly edged closer, the inflatable cushion creaking humorously beneath him. 'Well, go on then! Tell me!'

Klem opened his mouth, then closed it again so quickly that he almost bit his tongue. He remembered Taras' advice... but would he be able to live with himself if he saved his own skin at the expense of everything else? He didn't have much time to think about it... the Colonel's trigger finger was getting increasingly twitchy... His mouth hesitantly reopened, but no matter how hard he tried, no sound came out.

The Colonel's inflatable cushion squeaked and creaked even more as his buttocks moved closer to the edge of the seat. 'Tell me, tell me...!'

Klem stuttered, 'you'll be surprised, because Voloshin is...'

The Colonel was almost salivating, 'go on, go on... Voloshin is... where?'

Klem gulped, 'Voloshin is... Voloshin is...'

The instant the attic door flung open, Klem let out a sigh of relief that could have blown out a candle made from his wife-to-be's ear-wax. A concerned-looking Zena occupied the entire doorway. She said, 'what is the going on up here?'

'And what is *that*?' the Colonel said, staring at the big woman as if she were something unpleasant he'd stepped on. 'Klem,' he demanded, 'get rid of it, whatever it is. Now!'

'"That"?' Zena said, 'did he call me "that"?'

Klem nodded, 'he called you "it" too!' He needn't say anything else, so sat back and watched the wild boar wrestler in action...

Zena effortlessly cleaved a path straight for the man she thought was a Bishop... she was unable to tolerate rudeness from anyone, especially from those who should know better. She said, 'I am fed up with the insults,' and lobbed a chair out of the way as if it were made of matchsticks.

Klem dived for cover when a coffee table flew overhead and collided with his tea-making table... He watched helplessly as his favourite moustache cup disintegrated as if made from icing sugar...

Zena tore the walking stick from the Bishop's hand, pulled the purple biretta from his pale bald head and picked him up by the neck before he had chance to utter a single word. 'What kind of the Bishop are you? Hmm?' She shouted, 'how dare you the speak to me like this? I am the <u>fed up</u> of always having the insults!'

With the tourniquet of Zena's hands around his neck, the man struggled to breathe. And when he could take a gasp, he was instantly gassed by Zena's halitosis, which made his own smell like Eau de Cologne.

And the feeling was mutual, because even Zena – the queen of bad smells – couldn't cope with his appalling over-boiled cabbage breath... it must have been thirty years since she'd smelled anything so vile.

Finally, Halyna and Lenka had made it up the spiral staircase. 'Zena!' Halyna exclaimed, 'what do you think you're doing? Put that Bishop down!'

'But he is the insulting man,' Zena said, crushing the man's neck until his face turned the colour of an aubergine.

'Surely not,' Halyna said, '*please*, let him go. You cannot treat men of the cloth in such a way...' She looked at the swollen Bishop, 'I am so sorry your Grace, please forgive my sister...'

Zena begrudgingly complied, allowing the rude Bishop to drop two feet back onto the chair. 'Aw!' he cried when his buttocks made contact with the hard oak, the inflatable cushion now on the floor, subsequent to the struggle.

Halyna demanded, 'Zena, how could you do such a thing to a Bishop?'

The Bishop coughed, spluttered and gasped for air: the pain in his buttocks was nothing when compared to the pain in his lungs. Zena's boa constrictor fingers had left indelible marks on the man's tree-trunk of a neck that only gradually faded as the blood drained from his head. He threw his dog-collar to the floor, loosened his top button and enjoyed the feeling of being able to breathe again. Only then, did he try to locate his walking stick...

'It's just a misunderstanding,' the Bishop said, resuming his somewhat strained, if near-perfect Kyiv accent, 'nothing for you to worry about.' As the purple hue receded from his head, he said, 'Klem and I are in the midst of an important discussion.' He picked up his dog-collar and simultaneously scooped up the walking stick that was laying by his feet. He glared in Klem's direction, *'aren't we* Klem?'

Uneasily, Klem said, 'yes we were in a discussion... *of sorts.*' He turned and looked at the women, 'but you're more than welcome to stay...'

'Err,' the Bishop said, discretely pointing the end of his walking stick at Klem's foot, 'actually I have some ecumenical matters to discuss with my good friend Klem, which aren't for the ears of women.'

Halyna said, 'say no more, your Grace, we quite understand,' and began following Lenka down the stairs. The Bishop was such an authoritative man that she'd completely forgotten about the bullet... She noticed Zena continued to stare aggressively at the Bishop, 'Zena, you come too...'

Zena grumbled and mumbled on her way to the door. She could tell by Klem's strained expression that something was definitely wrong... whatever was being discussed was certainly not ecumenical. She stopped and looked curiously to the floor: there was an object lying on the carpet by her feet. She crouched down to pick up an austere-looking crucifix on a tarnished chain and examined it inquisitively. She stared at the Bishop, and demanded, 'I not go until I get the apology! No Bishop has ever spoken to me like this!'

Lenka thought: *no Bishop has ever spoken to you. Full stop.*

'I really am terribly sorry if I offended you,' said the Bishop, 'but Klem and I do have some *very* important matters to discuss... and we did not appreciate the interruption.' He glanced at the crucifix in Zena's hand and said, 'that's mine... it must have fallen off when you were trying to kill me...' He pretended to laugh and held out his enormous hand.

Zena took another close look at the crucifix, before dropping it into his hand. While watching him put it on back to front, she grunted, 'and you call yourself the Bishop!'

'Zena,' Halyna nudged her sister and whispered, 'what about the *bullet*?' She couldn't believe she'd forgotten all about it... But if there was only an innocent Bishop in the attic with Klem, then this mangled piece of metal may not have been a bullet after all... but what else could it be?

'Not now,' Zena whispered, stomping back downstairs, insisting Halyna did the same.

Halyna didn't know whether to be confused or frightened. She reached around to close the door and noticed Klem's petrified expression. She also noticed the white feathers from his prized embroidered cushion scattered all over the floor by the sofa. She said, 'Klem, are you *sure* everything's all right?'

'Of course Halyna... everything's fine,' Klem said. 'But you *can* do me a favour... Make yourself useful and bring the dog in for his dinner...'

The Dancing Barber
Chapter 58

The Village of Chaplinka, Khersonska Oblast, South-eastern Ukraine

'Leave that knob alone,' Viktor shouted. 'It is already set to the correct frequency.'

'Maybe if I pull this out some more,' said his neighbour, extending the wireless' aerial to its full length.

'Leave it alone!' Viktor snapped.

His neighbour sat down in a huff and poured himself another generous glass of samahon, adding some slithers of garlic.

Viktor hated people polluting perfectly good samahon in such a way; and adding slithers of garlic was a terribly Soviet thing to do.

'I said leave it alone!' shouted Viktor, when he caught his neighbour's hand creeping over to the tuning knob like an oversized spider.

His neighbour grumbled and chewed on his drink. But Viktor was right – he usually was – and a moment later, Radio Kateryna was back on air, and both men leaned in closer to the crackly speaker, and turned up the volume.

As Voloshin's long awaited words danced into the room, Viktor gazed wistfully out of the window, which was an old Land Rover windscreen set into the clapboard wall, and admired his golden field of maturing wheat shimmering in the breeze. He was wholeheartedly grateful to God for providing the ideal amounts of sunshine and rainfall, as well as for blessing his land with the fertile *Chornozem*, and for giving him the enduring strength to farm it.

In the short time that passed since the land was redistributed to the peasants, Viktor had expertly ploughed and tilled his field to make it as productive as it'd been before Collectivisation. And when the horse tired of dragging the plough and tiller, his nieces were more than willing to take over... Although they were more costly to feed, and mucking them out was far more unpleasant.

The Soviet destruction of the Steppes – at least on his farmstead

– had been undone; the land was happy again. So this year, there would be plenty of wheat to sell, allowing him to meet all his expenses. Several sacks would be bartered in exchange for cured salami, cheese and other delicacies, as well as animal feed and the all-important ingredients for making his special samahon. And there would be plenty of wheat left over for milling into flour: Viktor never tired of the aroma of fresh bread, even the kind Zena and Lenka baked, augmented by tussocks of their shed hair.

Viktor reached over to the wireless, and turned up the volume a little more... He couldn't quite believe the Soviets had actually let Voloshin expose one of their worst kept secrets... They must have run out of cyanide... Or umbrellas... Either way, he was grateful, knowing the truth would bode well for Ukraine. But he was also deeply fearful...

The little voice inside his head refused to be silenced: life was actually quite bearable now, so he hoped Voloshin's actions wouldn't over-antagonise the Soviets. He also hoped there wouldn't be mass protests on the streets of Kyiv... he sighed... they always ended in the same brutal way...

Viktor's neighbour turned up the wireless' volume to maximum. He shook his head, 'how did Voloshin manage to interview that piece of himno Captain and resist punching his lights out?' Using his impeccably clean thumbnail, he picked the garlic from between his teeth, 'if it was me, I'd string him up by his...'

Viktor interrupted, 'a Peaceful Partisan doesn't go around punching people's lights out... Nor does he string people up by their... Now shush, I want to listen...' He found it curious that this Soviet Captain spoke so freely about his crimes. In fact, the sadist sounded proud of them...

"In my opinion, Collective Farms not only fed our factory workers, but they also purged the land of the troublemakers."

"Who were these troublemakers?" asked Voloshin, undoubtedly disguised and pretending to be a journalist.

"Who do you think?" slurred the Soviet Captain, obviously saturated with vodka. *"Those who called themselves "Ukrainians" of course! They never cooperated: they were only ever interested in owning their silly little postage stamps of land, where they'd keep mangy animals and grow pathetic crops. Such stupid people*

The Dancing Barber

never did understand Stalin's genius in devising the Collective Farm system! However, I, along with the other Captains, were under strict orders to make sure they did not stand in the way of progress!"

"Progress?" asked Voloshin, "if it was progress, then where are the Collective Farms now? Why didn't your President Khrushchev keep them going? Could it be that the system was flawed, and your Stalin wasn't the genius you thought he was?"

"What sort of questioning is this from The Times of London?" A glass was refilled, and the Captain took a noisy slurp. "The system was perfect, but there is only so much that can be done with so many uncooperative peasants... we gave them bread and water in exchange for their labours, and were they happy? No! Instead, they stole from the State and had to be punished!"

"Would _you_ be satisfied with bread and water after working a fourteen hour day? Especially after all your land, crops and livestock had been seized by force... and all you were left with were the clothes on your back...?"

"What a _stupid_ question! I am superior to the "Ukrainians"! I am not a good-for-nothing layabout! Purging the land of these useless people was the best thing Stalin ever did... but..." There was the sound of chinking glasses, "I can rely on your discretion to keep what I have just said, err... how you say, err... off the record?"

Once the interview was over, Voloshin concluded: "He who has ears, let him hear...! I have collected far more evidence just like this, having interviewed dozens of Captains, Colonels and even a General! These interviews are printed in all the good newspapers, and have been endorsed by the United States and the United Nations as being an exact record of what was said! Let us all stand together and sing the National Anthem..."

'You think it's really him?' Viktor asked, touching his scarred left ear, a lasting reminder of this most dreadful time. Upon hearing the dirge-like opening chords of the Ukrainian National Anthem, he stood up and saluted, insisting his neighbour did the same.

'Sounds like him,' said his neighbour, wondering whether Viktor ever wore clothes. He took another enormous swig of samahon, 'sure, he sounds older, but then again, we all do. Let's hope he has more success this time... although the odds are stacked against him.' His neighbour hoped it was Voloshin: the man was quite a celebrity in Chaplinka in the thirties... but it was a pity he was unable to stop the Soviets sending all the "Kulaks" to Siberia.

Viktor said, 'what use was a Peaceful Partisan in a violent world. But times, they are a-changing...'

'Let's hope you're right.' Viktor's neighbour shook his head, 'I can't believe that Soviet Captain had the nerve to call the Ukrainian people stupid!'

'He did sound a little tipsy...' Viktor said to his equally tipsy neighbour.

'He probably was... Fancy saying all that to a journalist and expecting him to keep it quiet? What a durak!'

Viktor thought that, for a state "official", his neighbour was too pro-Ukrainian for his own good. The man was in a privileged position, being head of Khersonska Oblast's sprawling Nature Reserve at Askanya Nova, known to many as "The Gem of the Tavrian Steppes"... it would take only one eavesdropping Vlad to catch him speaking a single derogatory word against the Soviet Union... and he'd be sent straight to the Gulag...

Viktor often wondered how an ordinary peasant could achieve such high status, especially because it wasn't that long ago when he too languished on a Collective Farm. Rumour had it that his family were acquainted with the Nature Reserve's founder, Baron Friedrich Falz-Fein, a man who enjoyed collecting so many animals that Tsar Nicholas II remarked, *"it's an amazing sight, a scene from The Bible when the animals left Noah's Ark."* Viktor had only ever seen a few deer and a horse, he wondered what became of the antelope, kangaroos and ostriches...? But with a rifle in his hand, his neighbour rarely missed...

Viktor's neighbour was still ranting, completely drowning out every verse of the National Anthem.

'Shhh,' Viktor said, sitting down once the National Anthem had ended, to listen to Voloshin's next instalment:

"Across the Steppes, there were tens of thousands of steaming heaps of rotting grain! I have photographs and sworn testimony to support my claims, many of which you will see printed in today's newspapers. The Soviets would rather the spare grain was

The Dancing Barber

left to rot than to "waste" it on feeding the Ukrainians, because that would only extend what they called "the Ukrainian problem". And I witnessed cartloads of grain being tipped into the sea when, only feet away, Ukrainians were dying in droves. But don't take my word for it... the photographs are in the newspapers. See for yourselves... make up your own minds...

"I pledge to all Ukrainians in Ukraine and abroad that I, Voloshin, will ensure every single perpetrator, whether they are a Private or a General will be held to account for their crimes! And I will not rest until – "

The station crackled and then went dead.

A tear ran down Viktor's wrinkled cheek. On the site of the very barn where he was to store his winter food, the Soviets built an enormous compost heap of grain, just as Voloshin described. Unprotected from the cold and damp of winter, the grain soon started to rot: he remembered how it steamed, giving off a ferocious heat even when the ground around it was under eight feet of snow. The Soviet soldiers showed such appalling brutality to any 'peasant' who took even a handful of the most rotten grain: what happened to those poor individuals was seared into his memory...

But the spring of 1934 was the worst of all... when the snow melted, tens of thousands of bodies were revealed. They were exceptionally well preserved, because after months of starvation, there was little flesh left to decompose; many of the faces were recognisable, yet contorted with anguish. A tear ran down Viktor's other cheek as he recalled how the Soviet soldiers raked up the corpses and pushed them into enormous mass graves as if they were failed crops being ploughed back into the earth.

Viktor often thought that Ukraine, once famed for being the "Breadbasket of Europe" would have been more aptly termed the "Death Casket of Europe". And those who thought that cowering to the Soviets and working on a Collective Farm was better than starvation were soon proved wrong... What those sadistic soldiers did to those innocent peasants, he wouldn't wish on his worst enemy...

More tears ran down the deeply etched wrinkles on his face. But these were tears of happiness; not a day went by when Viktor didn't take the time to thank God that – against all odds – he and most of his family had survived such an ordeal, which at the time seemed as though it would never end... A pitchfork may have been no match for a machine gun, but good would always triumph over evil.

Viktor turned to his neighbour, 'how long do you think Voloshin'll last, now he's in the public eye again?'

'Oh, I would imagine the Soviets are loading their guns as we speak; or should that be filling their umbrellas with cyanide?' Viktor's neighbour gave a dismissive wave of the hand, 'Voloshin will never get to meet with Khrushchev, you mark my words: never in a hundred years!'

'I wish you'd have more faith, my friend,' said Viktor, nodding over to the wooden cross above the stove. 'You will be surprised by what can happen if you have faith.' But he knew his neighbour only had faith in samahon.

Viktor's scruffy dog emitted a pungent cloud of gas as it ambled past and went to recline in front of the fire; it yawned and fell to an instantaneous sleep. Even after all these years, Viktor's neighbour couldn't help but consider how much edible meat the animal could provide. But the dog was scrawny: it would only be sinew and gristle and wouldn't be worth the effort. Not like the wolf he once caught with Lenka's help...

She hit it on the head with a stone the size of a loaf of bread, killing it instantly: remarkably, she'd thrown the stone from ten yards away and still hit her target! They roasted the skinned and gutted carcass in an underground pit filled with hot stones for an entire day, spending much of their time wafting away the smoke so as not to draw the soldiers' attention.

Neither he nor Lenka felt any remorse for killing what some people called a majestic wild animal, a species he was now employed to look after on the Askanya Nova Nature Reserve; in fact the fewer of these predators that were allowed to prowl around back then, the better. Left to their own devices, they'd frequently be seen eating corpses that lay by the roadside, and even hunting in packs, targeting the weakest peasants who hadn't a hope of defending themselves.

He still had the lusciously soft pelt at home, which made a wonderful additional blanket for his bed in the wintertime. And although he knew it was wrong, the sight of Viktor's dog – even in

The Dancing Barber

these times of relative plenty – made his mouth water.

He shook the thought from his mind, took a big swig of samahon and said, 'but tell me Viktor, is it true that one of your nieces had, err...' he nudged Viktor on the arm, 'with Voloshin a little while ago?'

Viktor shook his head and gestured to the man's empty glass, 'I think you've had a little too much of that? Don't you think?' He thought: *This man drinks more than any of the Partisans I fought with during the War... and some of them were so drunk that they spent most of their time shooting at each other... especially the one with the droopy eyes.*

'Oh no,' said Viktor's neighbour, reaching for the bottle, 'you can *never* have too much!'

Viktor was about to confiscate the bottle, but as it was nearly empty, there seemed little point. His neighbour had travelled three miles to listen to Voloshin on the radio, and as usual he'd drunk everything alcoholic in the house. And he certainly was an inquisitive soul: ever since he'd arrived, he never stopped looking around the simple homestead, examining every nook and cranny. He reminded him of one of those Soviet soldiers during The Great Famine, checking everywhere for secret stores of grain... many of which they themselves had hidden.

'Have you still got one of these?' asked Viktor's neighbour, picking up a miniature copy of the Holy Bible from Viktor's otherwise sparse mantelpiece, which was a shelf nailed above the stove.

'Of course; and I still read it every day... even with *my* eyes.' Viktor lit a yellow candle by holding the wick against the flames of the fire, then fixing it in the centre of the table with a few blobs of melted wax. He said, 'it gives me hope.'

'I remember when Stalin was around; anyone with one of these in their house would have been sent straight to the Gulag... I should know...'

'This one – I think – was printed in St Petersburg and shipped secretly to Odessa and then overland to Chaplinka and beyond. There were millions of them,' Viktor stroked the scuffed leather cover, 'this must be one of the few from that era that remain.' He placed the precious book by the candle, the faded gold cross on the cover glowing in the flame.

'You get it from Voloshin, did you?'

'Where else... You know, he's done so much for Ukraine... I wish I could shake his hand.'

'I did, once,' said Viktor's neighbour, holding out his hand. 'He's got a grip like a vice...'

'I'd heard he's a big fellow...' said Viktor.

'Speaking of big fellows,' said Viktor's neighbour, 'do you remember that horrible ginger man that used to live down in the valley?'

Viktor ran his fingers along the top of his scarred left ear, 'how could I forget? He was the cause of so many of my woes.'

'The last time I saw him, he was in a Soviet uniform, and proud of it. His ginger mane was hidden beneath one of those bearskin hats with the big furry ear-flaps, but I knew it was him... He had a chin like the tusk of an elephant...' Viktor's neighbour examined the white knuckles of his clenched fist, 'I'd do anything to get my own back.'

'Well I wouldn't,' said Viktor, 'and I hope I never see him again.'

Viktor's neighbour hiccupped and emitted a burp that lasted half a minute. 'Ah, that's better,' he said, tapping his chest with the palm of his hand. 'I've been meaning to ask you... how do you suppose Halyna will take Zena and Lenka's news?'

Viktor moved the candle away from the man's flammable breath. He said, 'I expect they'll pick their moment, but I can't imagine there'll ever be the right time to tell Halyna that her mother is no longer with us.'

'Her mother?' said his neighbour, 'no, I mean the other news...'

'I didn't know you knew about Oksana?'

'Oksana? Who is Oksana...? I mean the *other* news, the news about...'

'But there is no other news,' Viktor interrupted, 'what do you mean?'

His neighbour smiled and said with a wink, 'you know...' before passing out.

Viktor wasn't one to worry, but now he couldn't help it. His neighbour couldn't possibly know about the other news: Zena was the only person alive who knew this most secret of secrets...

The Dancing Barber
Chapter 59

The City of Bradford, West Yorkshire, Northern England

'Before we were so rudely interrupted,' said the Colonel, 'you were going to tell me where I could find Voloshin...' He gripped the walking stick's handle, his index finger whitening as it applied pressure on the discrete trigger, 'and I am losing my patience!'

Klem chose to say nothing. He put his right ankle onto his left knee and, with his fingers, tapped out the tune of the Ukrainian National Anthem against his polished red leather boot.

'Damn it,' the Colonel shouted, striking the desk so hard that the typewriter jumped from the surface. He held the ebony shaft of the walking stick in his other hand, as if taking aim with a shotgun, and screamed: '<u>Tell Me</u>!'

'Do you know,' Klem said, crossing his legs the other way and settling comfortably into his chair, 'you lot were responsible for murdering <u>14 million</u> people. That's like wiping out the entire urban populations of Moscow and St Petersburg!'

'Is that all,' said the Colonel, 'I thought it would have been more?'

Klem continued, '7 million were murdered during what you called "the liquidation of the Kulaks" and the other 7 million perished during The Great Famine...'

The Colonel smiled, 'yes, it truly was a *great* famine!'

Klem clenched his teeth and slowly exhaled before saying, '3 million of those were *innocent children*. How can that be something to be proud of?'

'Because they were "Ukrainians", of course! Such simple people only stood in the way of Comrade Stalin's wonderful plan. The sooner they were liquidated, the better! Such lazy, disobedient people have no place in the Soviet Union!'

Klem knew that to this butcher, a human being was only a component of a machine: if the component didn't function as was required, it would be discarded and replaced. He wondered how many people this Colonel had put to death, either personally or by issuing orders. A shiver ran down his spine... the Colonel would have seen it as a service to society, or more accurately, a service to the Soviet Union and that *durak* Stalin.

Klem sneered, 'I should have known you were one of Khrushchev's cronies... A Bishop would never have driven around in a Zil automobile. Nor would he speak so rudely, and with such a phoney accent. And he certainly wouldn't attend the theatre without wearing trousers...'

Colonel Stanislaw laughed, '*I* do not report to that weakling Khrushchev! Do you think *I* would take orders from a man who believed *cooperation*, rather than *coercion* is the best way to deal with the filthy peasants?' Behind the sunglasses, he squinted his good eye and thought: *How does he know I wasn't wearing trousers?*

Klem snorted. 'If you don't report to Khrushchev, then who *do* you report to?'

The Colonel smiled. He said, 'you and Voloshin have been on my *List* for years: the pair of you are like a disease, poisoning the people against the greatness of the Soviet Union.' He settled into the chair, forgetting the pain in his buttocks, 'and if you are the disease, then I am the cure. *I* will ensure my beloved Motherland makes a <u>full</u> recovery and never falls ill again!'

Klem glanced surreptitiously at the time, hoping Halyna had remembered what to do. He looked back at the Colonel, 'I asked you a question... <u>who do you report to?</u>'

The Colonel smiled even more. He looked up at a yellowing newspaper article, which hung in a frame on a nearby wall, and started to laugh. The photograph was of well-fed and happy workers on a Collective Farm. He gestured to it with his thumb, 'see, even you have evidence that Collectivisation was good for my beloved Motherland!'

Slowly, Klem closed his eyes. He opened them and said, 'if you were able to read, you would realise those "well-fed and happy workers" were actually actors and the Collective Farm was an elaborate stage set. It was all a big lie! Stalin fooled every visiting dignitary, even managing to pull the wool over Sidney and Beatrice Webb's eyes and conning the likes of George Bernard Shaw!'

The Dancing Barber

The Colonel shuffled pompously in his seat, 'they seemed happy enough with what they saw at the time...'

'But they'd have quickly changed their minds if they'd have seen what was *really* going on.'

'But they didn't? Did they?' the Colonel said, smugly.

Klem shook his head, 'and don't I know it... So many reporters risked their lives to photograph the mass graves overflowing with skeletons, the bleached bones of your victims lying on the roadside and the piles of rotting grain that could have saved so many lives... But not many photographs made it to the West, and for those that did, the Kremlin laughed them off as "meaningless propaganda" created by "radical partisans". Now the West realises those "radical partisans" were not radical at all: they were telling the truth! Not even the Kremlin can laugh off the testimonies of some of their own most senior Generals!'

'Mass graves,' the Colonel laughed, 'you *show* me a mass grave... But you can't, because there aren't any!'

'Then how do you explain all those human bones that keep washing up on the shores of the Black Sea?'

The Colonel shrugged, 'obviously, they are victims of shipwrecks... Come, come, you are clutching at straws...'

Klem shook his head, 'we've had them analysed: most of these people died of woeful malnutrition. Then there are the skulls caved in with blunt objects: probably Soviet gun butts... Just a few hundred of the millions your lot butchered...'

A little of the Colonel's bravado had gone. It had been his idea to temporarily dam the Chaplinka River, enabling his Privates to excavate the riverbed by fifty feet. Once the hole had been filled in and the river allowed to resume its natural course, no-one would ever know what lay beneath... Obviously he had been wrong: the riverbed had eroded quicker than anticipated...

'Come, come,' said the Colonel, 'it is obvious this so-called "evidence" has been manipulated to make it suit your own agenda!'

'Don't assume the rest of the world operates as unscrupulously as you! I gathered my evidence with the help of the Americans: *they* can vouch for its authenticity. Who will the world believe, hmm? The honest Americans or the lying Soviets?'

'You are talking out of your other end! Everyone knows the

Americans are the biggest con merchants on the face of the planet!'

'Like I said: don't assume everyone is as unscrupulous as the Soviets!' He folded his arms, 'and you still haven't answered my question...' He narrowed his eyes, 'I bet you work for one of those Generals who'll soon be sent to the Siberian Gulag...'

The Colonel grinned, 'you have no idea... but you will... you will...'

Klem suspected the Colonel wasn't an ordinary Vlad... and that made him much more dangerous... He looked at the time again: *come on Halyna, where are you?*

The Colonel tried to stay calm. He said, 'I do not know why I am letting you annoy me. There is no *genuine* evidence that a famine ever occurred! But there is *plenty* of evidence to support the success of Collectivisation: according to my figures, crop yields were better than ever in 1933!'

Klem couldn't be bothered wasting any more breath on this *durak*. His own figures stated unequivocally that during Collectivisation, Ukraine suffered a disastrous collapse in agricultural production. And the simple reason: the Soviets sent all the successful farmers to the Gulag, perceiving them to be "Kulaks", where they took their detailed agricultural knowledge to the grave... And yet the "Intelligencia" residing in the Kremlin continued to impose unachievable crop quotas, punishing the peasants, because of their own stupidity.'

'What?' said the Colonel, 'are you not going to argue with me...?' He stroked his pale bald head, 'it goes to show, deep down, even you know I'm right...'

'Whatever you say,' said Klem. 'Whatever you say...'

The Colonel became very excited when he noticed a familiar object glinting from beneath Klem's four-poster bed, 'is that what I think it is...'

Klem nodded, 'a souvenir... would you like to see it?'

'Pass it to me... *Carefully*... No sudden moves,' said the Colonel, tingling with excitement. 'I used to wear one just like it when I was a Private...'

'Here you are,' said Klem, holding out the old Soviet Army helmet, being extra careful to keep it upright. 'Why don't you put it on...?'

The Dancing Barber

'I could...' said the Colonel, chuckling. 'For old-time's sake...'

Klem maintained a neutral expression; Lenka had filled it to the brim.

'No,' declared the Colonel, 'I will not allow you to delay me any longer.'

Klem's shoulders slumped; it would have been too good to be true for the Colonel to have tipped the stinky contents all over his head... Never mind... He checked the time again and listened for the sound of footsteps... but there weren't any...

The Colonel verified a round was in the chamber, reached across the desk and pushed the end of the long barrel against Klem's foot. 'No more stalling... Where is Voloshin?'

Klem tried to speak, but couldn't. He stared at the end of the man's walking stick and knew that at such close quarters, most of his foot would be gone should the trigger be pulled. He had to say or do something, but what?

The Colonel grunted like a wild boar and began counting down, 'ten, nine, eight, seven...'

Klem remembered the wording of the signed agreement nestled in his pocket: assuming the Colonel was to be believed, he and his friends were safe. The trouble was, he knew that all Soviets were liars.

The trigger creaked as the Colonel began to squeeze, 'three, two...'

'All right,' Klem cried, 'I'll tell you.' He watched with relief as the Colonel's trigger finger relaxed.

The Colonel became increasingly agitated. 'Well?' he demanded, leaning forward in eager anticipation, resting the gun barrel on the edge of the desk.

Klem opened his mouth as if to speak; then – in an unprecedented display of athleticism – kicked the stick out of the Colonel's hands and watched it clatter to the floor, well out of reach. The Colonel was completely taken aback – the shock on his face was a joy for Klem to behold – this must have been the first time he'd ever been outsmarted by a lowly poet.

Klem scampered over to pick up the heavy walking stick, while the Colonel struggled to stand up from behind the desk. With a hand on each end, he tried as hard as he could to snap it in half. The ebony began to crack and split, but because the shaft contained a long steel barrel, he could only bend it by the smallest amount. But bending it was sufficient: it would never fire again.

'That was foolish!' the Colonel shouted, once he'd finally stood up. '<u>Very</u> foolish! Whatever you do will be utterly futile: need I remind you that I have a one hundred percent record and have <u>never</u> failed my Comrade Generals!'

'Well, there's a first time for everything,' Klem said, holding his breath, noticing the Colonel's mints had worn off. 'If you come any closer, I'll clout you around the head with your own walking stick!'

'I'd like to see you try,' the Colonel sneered, lunging forward with the speed of a scalded rhinoceros.

Klem twisted his body back as far as it would go, before swinging the stick forward as if he were a golfer teeing-off. The stick's metal handle pounded into the Colonel's face, ejecting blood from his fungal growth of a nose, which only narrowly missed splattering Taras' pristine white walls.

Refusing to wait for the inevitable backlash, Klem struck the Colonel again, pulverising his nose further.

The Colonel staggered about like a drunkard before he fell to his knees as if in prayer – a truly alien concept for a man like him – and tore off what was left of his shattered sunglasses. The Colonel clutched his bleeding nose with both hands, and groaned miserably...

Klem couldn't help himself; he took another enormous swing and *whack*, the stick's handle struck the Colonel's rear end, causing him to squeal loudly before passing out, slumping to the floor, his bleeding nose cushioning his landing.

Scuttling to the attic door, Klem shouted, 'Halyna!' his voice echoing down the stairs... He kicked the purple carcass in the ribs and watched it wobble like an enormous jelly. He hadn't a clue what to do next; he thought about tying up the Colonel and calling the Constabulary. But then there were the goons to consider: he didn't relish dealing with them on his own...

As he searched for a ball of string, he noticed it'd suddenly become very dark; but the weather wasn't set to be stormy and dusk wasn't for another hour... He turned around slowly... but all he could see was purple. Then the palm of his hand burned as the walking stick was snatched away. Before he realised what was

The Dancing Barber

happening, his body flew through the air, coming to rest on the smashed coffee table on the other side of the attic.

'You can't outsmart a Colonel of the Soviet Union,' the Colonel said, examining the damage to his beloved stick. 'We are the <u>real</u> Intelligencia!'

Once the room had stopped spinning, Klem realised how foolish he'd been to have turned his back for even a moment. He thought: *Come on Halyna, where the hell are you?*

While the Colonel tried to work out how best to straighten the stick, Klem noticed the Roberts radio lying on the floor by his feet. He reached across and picked it up, examining the green leather case. 'Look at that,' he protested, 'you've scuffed it!' He proceeded to use his handkerchief to polish away the blemishes; then he realised what time it was. Whilst the Colonel put the ebony stick across his knee, pressing down on both ends with all his strength, Klem rotated the radio's "on" switch and turned up the volume, allowing Voloshin's voice to fill the room as he led his listeners in reciting the Lord's Prayer...

Just as Klem joined in with the prayer, bits of plastic, electrical wire and solder scattered everywhere. With satisfaction, the Colonel watched the smoke rising from the end of his walking stick...

Klem couldn't believe the gun still worked; he wished he'd had the strength to bend it properly... Zena would have tied it in a double knot, probably around the Colonel's neck...

'And this,' the Colonel shouted, 'is for your uncooperative behaviour!' He pulled the trigger another twice: Bang! Bang!

Klem looked at the smoking holes in the carpet that were only an inch from his toes. He felt immensely relieved. Mopping the sweat from his brow, he said, 'thank you for your leniency...'

'What leniency?' the Colonel shouted, going back to sit behind the desk. 'I missed! And I never miss...! You have destroyed the accuracy of this fine weapon!'

'Have I?' Klem sounded surprised, 'oh, what a pity...'

The Colonel's face went beetroot red as he tried to reload, fumbling with the little switch that was concealed beneath the ornate metal handle, cursing that it was stuck.

Klem rubbed his hands together. Smiling, he said, '*now* you're in trouble!'

Without looking up, the Colonel said, 'no I'm not; I won't need to *shoot* you to obtain what I want! I am more than capable of using *other* methods. In fact, I think I might...' The Colonel contemplated utilising the tried and tested techniques he'd used during the War; he briefly reminisced at the joy he had in those dark, damp dungeons. But his happy thoughts were quashed when he looked up and noticed that Klem wasn't alone.

The Colonel scoffed, 'you think I'm scared of your fleabag mongrel? Does it piss in people's faces too?'

The dog growled and bared its fangs. Strings of bubbling saliva descended from its cheeks and formed puddles that wouldn't soak into the carpet.

The Colonel commanded: 'call off your mongrel, or I'll shoot it!'

'No you won't,' Klem said confidently, 'that gun of yours is useless...'

'In that case, I'll strangle the mongrel with my bare hands!' the Colonel said, putting down the walking stick. He held his hands in front of him and strangled an imaginary neck.

Klem said calmly, 'you really are a complete Bastard!'

The Colonel laughed, 'what? Resorting to name-calling now are we? How very childish...'

Klem clicked his fingers and the dog responded instantly, diving beneath the desk and plunging its head straight up the Colonel's cassock.

Without wasting a second, Klem grabbed the walking stick and flung it straight into the fire, where the ebony veneer ignited most satisfyingly.

The Colonel cried out, 'call off your fleabag mongrel!' The pitch of his voice was a semitone higher, '*Please...*'

Klem shook his head, 'just like Mister Pushkin, Bastard is a pure pedigree. And calling him a "fleabag mongrel" will only make him bite even harder.'

The beads of sweat that formed on the Colonel's pale scalp now ran down his tanned cheeks, disappearing beneath his collar. He tried to edge away, but there was no escape...

Halyna peered through the small pane of glass in the attic door; she'd followed Klem's instructions by "bringing the dog in for its dinner", but couldn't see the beast anywhere... All she could see was Klem looking exceptionally relieved, and the Bishop howling with pain. What on earth was happening?

She tried to focus on the crucifix hanging around the Bishop's neck, wondering why it had rattled Zena so much. She whispered, 'it might be on back to front, but I'd need to see it close-up to be sure.'

Zena said, 'it *is* the back to the front! But that is not all I have noticed...'

Lenka also peered through the window, steaming it up as she breathed heavily. She said, 'the Bishop, he is making the howling noises... Listen... And his head, why has it turned the same colour as his cassock...?'

'Shhh,' said Zena, 'talk the quietly, otherwise they will hear you...'

But it was too late...

The door creaked open and Klem looked down at the three eavesdropping women. He said with a smile, 'I thought I could hear you skulking around.' He looked lovingly at Halyna: 'I'd almost given up hope of the dog coming to the rescue... glad you remembered the code-phrase!' He opened the door wider, 'why don't you come inside for some tea? And then you can help me decide what to do.'

'About *what*?' Halyna asked.

'About our guest,' said Klem, revealing the whimpering man sat behind his desk.

'What *have* you done to him?' Halyna asked once she and her sisters had stepped into the attic, all of them wondering where the dog had gone.

Klem shook his head, 'I bet you all think this man's a Bishop?' He shook his head, 'you are looking at a Soviet Secret Policeman; and a *Colonel*, no less!'

Zena barked, 'I knew he was no Bishop!'

Klem twisted his moustache back into position, 'and I suspect he's no ordinary Secret Policeman... He's been saying some *very* strange things...'

'But he's dressed as a Bishop?' Halyna said, 'and he was at the All-Nighter and at The Alhambra? If he was an imposter, then surely someone would have noticed?'

Klem said, 'and when was the last time any of us ever saw a Bishop...? Exactly...' He tapped his nose with a finger, 'often the most innocent disguises are the most effective.'

Zena said, 'and that would explain why he wears his crucifix the back to the front: the Vlads, they do not know anything about the religion.'

'And look at that eye,' Klem said, pointing to the reptilian marble. 'A Bishop wouldn't have an eye like that?'

'The good Heavens,' said Zena, 'the eye...'

Klem picked up the packet of Polo Mints on the desk and threw three into the Colonel's panting mouth. Holding his nose he said, 'this man has the worst case of over-boiled cabbage halitosis I've ever known... we should be grateful he never conducts confession! His breath is even worse than Zena's fart!'

Halyna didn't think such a thing was possible until she smelled it for herself.

Whilst Zena and Lenka went to examine the back to front crucifix, in the process comparing their own gaseous emissions to those of the Colonel, Halyna looked around the room with bemusement. She asked, 'I sent the dog up for its dinner, as you asked, but where did it go? Is it out on the balcony?'

Klem smiled broader than ever. He said, 'have a look under the desk.'

Halyna peered between the ornately carved mahogany drawers and saw the dog's furry tail emerging from under the Colonel's purple cassock. 'Good grief,' she said, 'what *is* that dog doing?'

'It's Gunter's preferred method for controlling an aggressor. Quite effective, don't you think?' Klem straightened the green ribbon at his collar, 'you control the man's weakest part... you control the man!'

Halyna felt queasy. 'Please, tell me the dog hasn't bitten off his...'

'Oh *no*, of course not...' Klem smiled, 'but the dog does have a *firm* grip...'

Halyna wished she didn't have such a vivid imagination.

Klem said, 'so it turns out old Bastard came in useful after all: you see, the Colonel wanted me to tell him where to find Voloshin... which, as you know, is *quite* impossible... And he was going to do some *quite* nasty things to me if I didn't tell him. I had

The Dancing Barber

no choice *but* to use the dog.'

As the dog growled and the Colonel whimpered, Zena was deep in thought, staring at the Colonel, studying his scarred face, sniffing his strangely familiar over-boiled cabbage halitosis and examining that hideous eye…

'How low will these Soviets stoop,' Halyna said, 'it is not goodski for one to come disguised as a Bishop! Is nothing sacred to these people?'

'It appears not,' Klem mused, 'but now we have to think quickly about what to do with him. It won't be long before those goons waiting in the car outside start wondering why their Colonel is taking so long. And if they come to investigate, we'll be in *real* trouble…'

'Of course,' Zena declared, clicking her fingers.

'No, don't do that,' Klem protested.

Zena clicked her fingers again, 'I know <u>exactly</u> who this swine is!'

But it was too late; Klem could only close his eyes…

The dog growled ferociously, and the Colonel cried out: 'Ahhh!' before his head slumped to one side…

Chapter 60

'I'm sure they'll all be *delighted*,' Taras said, extracting his cigarette case from the inside pocket of his blue blazer. 'Who *wouldn't* want to rent their house from the Mafia?'

The anonymous looking man cringed; he looked around the bar, relieved that no-one had heard. From beneath the wide brim of his black hat, he said, 'please, less of the "M" word. I am a *legitimate* businessman. In any case, I'm sure the tenants would prefer me as their landlord... anything is better than The Ginger Rasputin...'

Taras smiled, 'I suppose so... Cigarette?' he asked, holding out his leatherette case.

'No thanks; Klem's finally put me off smoking. With all his nagging, it was only a matter of time...'

'He's not put me off!' Taras said, striking a match and igniting his twenty-eighth cigarette of the day.

Watching the smoke rise from between Taras' lips, the anonymous looking man said, 'I'd have thought a physically fit man such as you would have given up long ago...'

'Oh no,' said Taras, 'meditation is for Buddhists, as smoking is for me, understand? I simply couldn't function without my cigarettes.'

'But what about the risks: cancer, emphysema? And the stained teeth and fingers?'

Taras smiled, 'most of my teeth are false, and as for stained fingers, I find washing my hands does the trick... and when at home, I've taken to using one of those cigarette holders.' He sucked in another deep lungful, 'besides, my grandfather smoked enormous cigars all his life... sometimes *ten* a day... and it didn't do him any harm. He was well into his eighties when...'

The anonymous looking man knew that whatever killed Taras' grandfather, it certainly wasn't cigars...

'Any way,' said Taras, 'I'm interested to know what you did with Ivan...? I've neither seen hide nor hair of him since the concert!' He grinned, 'rumour has it he's at the bottom of the River Aire, wearing a pair of those concrete shoes your lot specialise

The Dancing Barber

in...'

The anonymous looking man cringed again, 'please, we don't do that sort of thing anymore. But Ivan won't be giving anyone grief for a <u>very</u> long time. He knew the consequences of not paying me back in full. Now he's experiencing the consequences...'

'So it's nothing to do with rivers and concrete shoes?' Taras asked hopefully.

The anonymous looking man shook his head.

'Pity...' Taras was genuinely disappointed.

'Hey Taras,' shouted one of his neighbours from across the bar, 'you opened up a butcher's shop in your house, or something?'

'Of course not,' Taras replied, 'what makes you say that?'

The man hiccupped, 'because it looks like someone's butchering a pig's carcass up in your attic. I wasn't being nosey, it's only what I saw from the alley.'

Taras wouldn't put anything past Zena and Lenka. He just hoped they weren't making too much mess. How could they afford an entire pig's carcass? At least pork was better than rat or hamster. And his nosey neighbour was rarely wrong: he'd probably used his binoculars again.

'What was all that about?' asked the anonymous looking man, sniffing longingly at the smoke drifting from Taras' cigarette.

Taras took a sip from an imaginary glass.

The anonymous looking man nodded and said, 'as a newt'.

'So come on then,' Taras leaned forward, 'are you going to tell me what you've done with dear old Ivan?'

'Let's just say I have finished off what Oksana had started...'

'What does that mean?'

The anonymous looking man shook his head, 'that is no concern of yours.'

'It may not be <u>my</u> concern, but it is Klem's. You see, he wants to marry one of Halyna's older sisters – the one called Zena – but unfortunately, she's still married to Ivan.'

'So Ivan actually did have a wife! Who'd have thought anyone would be stupid enough to marry someone like him?' The anonymous looking man lifted the brim of his hat, 'Zena, you say?'

Taras nodded, 'Zena.'

'That's not one of those trolls that got kicked out of The Alhambra, for undressing at the Box Office, is it?'

Taras nodded, 'I'm afraid so.'

'But *why* would Klem want to marry *her*? She reeks of stale sweat!'

'Amongst other things… The point is, he can't until she's divorced Ivan.'

'Oh, that's easy,' said the anonymous looking man, rummaging in his lizard-skin briefcase. 'I presume Zena has the papers ready to sign?'

'Yes, she brought them from Chaplinka…'

The anonymous looking man walked his nimble fingers through various foolscap folders, searching for one in particular. He said, 'then all you'll need is Ivan's signature?'

'Well, I suppose…'

'Here you are,' the anonymous looking man placed a heavy bundle of property deeds in front of Taras. 'Ivan's signature is on the back page. You can copy it onto Zena's papers and all will be well.' He closed the lid of the lizard-skin briefcase, clicking down the locks. 'And by the way, you can keep those deeds when you're finished with them…'

Taras examined the musty deeds; they looked as though they were made from vellum and were covered in lavish copperplate handwriting and seals of red wax. He put on his reading spectacles and checked the address. He gasped, 'but these are the deeds to my house!' He looked up, but the anonymous looking man had gone…

The Dancing Barber
Chapter 61

The Village of Chaplinka, Khersonska Oblast, South-eastern Ukraine

Viktor's snoring was so loud that it woke his neighbour from a rather pleasant dream he was having that concerned roasting a dog on an open fire. He yawned and stretched, then his eyes settled on the silent radio... he switched it on, but the station was still dead... he wasn't surprised.

It seemed his body had recovered after consuming all of Viktor's samahon... He felt energised and alive... who said samahon was bad for you?

He had always been jealous of Viktor's simple life. Being your own boss had its virtues, but he wouldn't enjoy living quite so austerely... and wearing so few clothes... Despite the blood stains, the only object of value in the entire homestead was an ancient embroidered icon of the Madonna and Child, hanging above the stove. He wondered whether it would ever again be used as the centrepiece on The Feast of Our Lady... That sad day in the autumn of 1933 would always be remembered as the day the Soviets cleared the last peasants from Chaplinka... But he often wondered what would have happened if Zena hadn't acted so quickly?

While Viktor and the scraggy dog snored, he went out to his ancient Jeep to fetch something he thought Viktor would be interested in... He opened the Jeep's door, which was adorned with the word "RANGER", and reached inside for a heavy oblong case and a large drawstring bag that was almost as heavy.

For many years he'd worked for the neighbouring private Nature Reserve at Askanya Nova and the automobile and the contents of the heavy case and bag he carried were perks of the job; as was an endless supply of venison, although he never told his superior of this. He had to drag the heavy oblong case across the dusty yard and into the house, its corners scraping parallel tracks in the ground.

'What on earth is this contraption?' Viktor asked. He'd awoken to find his home filled with enormous black boxes that emitted a horrendous humming sound, and long wires curling all over the floor, trying their best to trip up the sleepy dog as it headed outside to drink from the trough and then relieve itself against it.

'This is my televisual set,' Viktor's neighbour said proudly, plugging the strange-looking device into a battery bigger than one of Zena's suitcases. 'I thought it would be interesting to see if Voloshin has made the televisual news headlines yet? I can get British Broadcasting Co-operation on this televisual set…'

'Oh,' said Viktor, filling two tin cups with strong black tea from his samovar. He approached the apparatus and stared inquisitively at the black box. 'I've heard of such a thing; but I've never seen one.'

His neighbour smiled, 'you really have no idea about the new-fangled technological things, have you?'

Viktor glanced at him blankly before going back to stare at the black box.

'Perhaps,' said his neighbour, 'it would be better if you watched the *screen* and not the battery pack?'

It didn't make any difference; to Viktor, it all looked the same. And why would a Ranger need such a thing?

As the men sipped their strong tea, a ghostly black and white image emerged from the static haze of the flickering five-inch domed screen. The men leaned in closer to watch a group of protestors, numbering many thousands gathering outside the government offices in Kyiv, and at the permitted distance from the Kremlin in Moscow. The protestors waved banners with Voloshin's name and brandished placards bearing enlarged photographs of just some of the millions of innocent victims of The Great Famine.

'What do you make of that?' Viktor asked, swigging the last of his tea, the regular consumption of which had stained his remaining teeth black.

'If it wasn't the British Broadcasting Co-operation, I wouldn't believe it.'

'Nor would I,' said Viktor. 'I just hope the Soviets don't get too annoyed…'

The Dancing Barber

'They're always annoyed... you should hear how my boss speaks to me... he's a Muscovite... they're the worst...'

Viktor said, 'I can believe it...'

'But I wonder how Halyna is taking the twins' news: to her, it will be much more important than all this about Voloshin.'

Viktor shrugged his shoulders, 'other than the sad news about her mother and Oksana, the twins have *nothing* else to say.'

'I see,' said his neighbour with a wink, 'well, I think Halyna will be happily overjoyed!'

'I don't know what you mean?' Viktor said, going to get some more tea, only to discover that the samovar was empty. 'There really is *no* other news.'

But his neighbour had passed out again: the exertion of setting up the new-fangled televisual set must have been too much for him. He was a good man, but like so many, depended on too much samahon to get through the day...

The little voice in Viktor's head had reawakened: how could his neighbour possibly know of the twins' other news? But then it dawned on him: his neighbour did – indirectly – work for the authorities...

AC Michael

Chapter 62

The City of Bradford, West Yorkshire, Northern England

'Here you go, Zena,' Klem said, unfastening the rusty chain from around the Colonel's thick neck. 'Have a closer look.' He placed the crucifix into his wife-to-be's grimy palm. 'You were right, he was wearing it back to front...'

Zena collapsed onto a creaky wooden chair, the force of the impact nearly destroying it. 'I cannot the believe it,' she said, 'I really cannot the believe it!'

'What can you not the believe?' Lenka asked.

'This,' Zena said, dangling the crucifix in front of her sister's eyes, as if trying to hypnotise her.

Lenka looked inquisitively at the crucifix, watching it swing to and fro. She shrugged her shoulders, 'so what?'

'Do you remember when the men of Chaplinka, they used oak to repair the roof of the church? And some of it was left over, yes? And with that, they made themselves the crucifixes. Remember?'

Lenka shrugged her shoulders again, 'not really.'

Halyna said, 'I remember... they all carved their own patterns. But that must have been in what: 1927?'

'That is the correct,' said Zena, 'and do you remember the pattern our Tato carved on his crucifix?'

'Of course I remember,' Halyna said, drawing an imaginary cross with her finger. 'It was fluted around the edge, and in the centre he carved an intricate fish scale pattern... it was very beautifulski. But from the front, the crucifix was plain... our Tato carved the pattern on the back so only *he* could enjoy looking at it.'

Zena dangled the Colonel's crucifix in front of Halyna's eyes and said, 'it looked very much like this one, yes?'

'Let me see,' Halyna said, taking hold of the crucifix and examining it through the lenses of her plastic framed glasses. 'I think you're right... our Tato used his sharpest cobbler's knife to carve with, and he always carved with his left hand, see... look at

The Dancing Barber

the fish scales... they all point this way.'

Lenka screwed up her face, 'if that is the crucifix of our Tato, then why does the Bishop have it?'

Zena rolled her eyes to the ceiling, 'but he is not the Bishop, he is the <u>Colonel</u>!'

'Sorry,' Lenka said, 'I the forgetful.'

'You the stupid,' muttered Zena.

Halyna said, 'the last time I saw this crucifix, it was torn from our Tato's neck by one of the soldiers that sent him to Siberia...'

Lenka looked accusingly at Zena, 'and I remember <u>why</u> our Tato was sent to Siberia. And I remember whose fault it was!'

'Here we go,' said Zena, 'you seem to have the selective memory; how many times do we have to go over the same thing, hmm? You saw the Soviets hide that bag of grain! We were all the done for: finding that propaganda did not make any of the difference!'

'Of course it did,' said Lenka, 'had it not been for the propaganda, our Tato, he would have been sent to the Collective Farm with us, instead of being sent to Siberia to die!'

'You talk the twaddle,' said Zena. 'Tell me, how many of the men did you see on our Collective Farm, hmm? <u>None</u>! That's how many! And another thing...'

'Oh shut up, the both of you,' said Halyna, 'I am fed up of you arguing. What is done is <u>done</u> and nothing can change it!'

'I sorry,' said Lenka, 'I know I should not rake over the old ground. But the question is yet to be answered: if this *is* the crucifix of our Tato, then how come the pig-faced Colonel has it?'

'When he comes round,' Klem said, 'you can ask him. But I don't know how long that'll take?' He flung the Colonel's inflatable cushion to the floor, sat down behind his desk and slumped his shoulders. 'And because he destroyed my radio, I've missed Voloshin's broadcast...'

'But you knew what he was going to say,' Halyna said, 'you wrote it for him...'

Klem grumbled, 'I know, I know, but I wanted to hear it "live on air" at the same time as everyone else.' He looked to the floor and noticed Mister Pushkin had stepped into the centre of the inflatable cushion and was settling down to take yet another nap... It was a pity the cat kneaded the cushion with its claws... air slowly began hissing out...

'And err, when the Colonel does come round,' Halyna said, 'have you come up with any goodski ideas about what you're going to do with him?'

Klem stood up, strode over to the balcony and peered discretely down to the street. The black car was still there, and so were the goons. He looked at his watch and said, 'it's been nearly two hours, so I reckon we'll have another hour at the most before those two come to investigate what's taking the Colonel so long...'

Halyna put a comforting hand on his shoulder. She asked, 'what do you suppose they'll do?'

'That is a question you won't want answering... Now leave me to think for a few moments. I must think!' He snatched himself away and went back to his desk. Sighing, he took out his watch again and wound it the usual seven times before clicking open the back and observing the intricate Swiss mechanical movement dance and turn through the sapphire crystal. He narrowed his eyes, focussing his mind on finding a solution.

Halyna and Lenka plodded downstairs and returned after a few minutes, lugging the enormous black and white rented television as if they were Laurel and Hardy delivering their infamous Music Box, panting and lathered in sweat. The sisters placed the heavy box on the edge of the desk, plugged it in, switched it on and waited for it to warm up.

'Why have you brought *that* up here?' Klem asked, closing his watch, sliding it back into his silk-lined pocket.

'You'll see...' Halyna said, 'but bear with me while I fiddle with the aerial.'

Klem was a firm believer that television decayed the mind, so would rarely remain in the same room as one. The only programme he'd ever watched was *The World in Action* when Kennedy and Khrushchev were at loggerheads over the Cuban Missile Crisis... And all Taras could say at the end of it was that if the two Presidents were in a wrestling ring, his money would be on Kennedy... thus proving cerebral decay was already setting in...

Klem looked sulkily at his treasured newspapers that, after the lengthy scuffle, were now strewn across the floor, torn and crumpled. He was planning to frame the front pages, but now most

The Dancing Barber

of them were ruined.

The television's twenty-inch screen displayed its usual snowstorm, accompanied by an infernal crackling noise that went straight through Klem's head, killing off any solution he could think of before he'd even thought of it... As Halyna performed her usual dance with the coat-hanger aerial, Klem turned to Zena and said, 'you okay?'

'I the suppose so,' she said, shrugging her shoulders. 'But how was I to know that the clicking of the fingers, it was the signal for the dog to snap its jaws shut?' She didn't mind a good punch-up, but couldn't stand anything gruesome; she'd seen far too much of that during the war.

Klem put his hand on hers and gave it a little squeeze; her skin was so rough that a match could be struck against it. 'Don't worry,' he said, 'I clapped my hands just in time... the dog released its grip before too much damage was done.' He laughed, 'the Colonel must have fainted with the shock... beneath all that bravado, he's a weakling. And you slapping him around his face probably didn't help...' He recalled how Zena tried to revive the Colonel by slapping his alternate cheeks with so much force that his false eye popped out and lost itself on the floor.

'Nearly had it then,' said Halyna, standing on one leg, holding the aerial in an outstretched hand. 'I'll get it in a moment... All will soon be goodski...'

Klem doubted it. He turned back to Zena; she looked contented and obviously looked forward to questioning the Colonel when he woke up... he hoped she wouldn't be too rough on him. Although she'd announced that she knew exactly who "this swine" was, as yet, Klem was none the wiser.

Lenka – as usual – seemed excessively interested with her armpits, and Klem wasn't shocked when she plucked something from amongst the plentiful hairs and examined it close to her eye. He watched her crush it between her thumb and forefinger, listening for the tell-tale cracking of the carapace, and then carefully checking to see if it was dead. She was taken by surprise when the flea leapt across the room and disappeared... the dog soon began scratching frantically.

Klem shook his head; at least Zena wasn't as uncouth as her twin. But his heart sank when he watched her pick her nose with both index fingers before wiping what she'd extracted down the nearest wall. He would have to have a serious talk with her...

He waited for Halyna's *Dance of the Aerial* to come to an end, thinking that perhaps Taras could choreograph it into one of his ballets...?

But all these distractions weren't helping him formulate a solution to his problem...

Much to Halyna's relief, the snow on the television screen receded to reveal a BBC newsreader wearing a bow tie and sporting excessively Brill-creamed hair that made it look as though he wore a plastic wig. Halyna made a few more adjustments to the aerial, which was balanced on the lampshade, and the crackling mercifully faded to allow the man's plummy voice to fill the room:

"It seems there's somewhat of a revolution occurring in the Soviet city of Kyiv, where protestors loyal to the so-called "Peaceful Partisan" have descended on government buildings to demand the Soviet Union admits responsibility for an alleged genocide that occurred thirty years ago.

"Their leader, a secretive man going by the name of Voloshin, demands the Soviet President formally apologises for the alleged atrocities of 1933, when seven million innocent Ukrainians were deliberately starved due to the Stalinist policy of Collectivisation. A further seven million also allegedly perished during the Liquidation of Intellectuals whereby anyone standing up to Stalin was eliminated before they could cause trouble.

"According to unconfirmed sources, this Voloshin will also be discussing the prospect of Ukraine's future independence with President Nikita Khrushchev. The Kremlin has declined to comment..."

For the first time in over an hour, the Colonel started to stir... he looked through his eye on a topsy-turvy world... The last thing he remembered was the ugliest of the hideous twins clicking her fingers; he felt a searing pain, then everything went black... His eye quested his surroundings but he couldn't work out where he was. Everything looked so strange...

For some reason his face felt terribly numb. He wanted to touch

The Dancing Barber

it to discover how swollen it was, but he couldn't move his arms. They weren't tied together, but – try as he might – he was unable to lay a hand on his face. His whole body felt strange, almost saggy in quite a peculiar way, and his hands could easily feel his stomach, chest and lower back, but couldn't reach his waist.

As the world around him spun, he discovered the feeling re-entering his legs; but they were very cold. The kaleidoscope of his vision eventually slowed and the room before his eye came into focus. But there was something not quite right.

The idiot poet and those women were watching a television while that ghastly dog snoozed by the fire where his treasured walking stick still smouldered. He was disgusted to see the BBC television news was all about Voloshin! Although he last came face to face with him in 1929, the troublemaker hadn't changed a bit, apparently still wearing a fancy suit and sporting that ridiculous moustache... although the photograph used in the report looked to be at least fifteen years old...

He tried not to make a sound, which was difficult because he couldn't help laughing: it was typical of these "Ukrainians" not to notice that the television they were watching was upside-down! These peasants were so stupid that they didn't deserve to have their own country.

Only then did the Colonel realise that it wasn't only the television that was upside down, but everything else was too! He contracted his powerful stomach muscles and strained to look at his feet. But he couldn't see them, for they were mummified beneath a vast amount of carpet tape. He followed the track of the carpet tape as it wrapped itself around a roof beam: he was hanging from the ceiling like a pig's carcass! His bare legs looked terribly pale and as he looked along them, he noticed a great deal of bandaging around his middle. The bandages were stained brown, but it wasn't the right shade for dried blood. It was the brown of iodine. And the tell-tale stinging from beneath the bandages confirmed it. He then discovered the reason why he was unable to touch his face: the lower portion of his purple cassock, though still tied at the waist, had been pulled up and tied extremely tightly at his neck, ensuring his arms were trapped like snakes in a sack.

He hung limply, conserving energy and mulling over his options. He'd have around fifty minutes before his Privates came to his aid; but he didn't want them to see their commanding officer in such a humiliating position. He knew how much shame he'd bring on the Soviet Union if – after all his promises – it were discovered that his mission had been thwarted by a lowly poet and some smelly peasants. As leader of his organisation, he had to be strong and courageous, otherwise there would be no organisation.

As his fingers quested the folds of his cassock, he could feel the shape of his folding knife, but couldn't locate the pocket's opening. Jabbing his thumbnail deep into the material of his cassock, he managed to unfold the knife's blade, which satisfyingly clicked into place. Slowly he slid the blade to and fro until the weave of the fabric gradually parted and the sharp blade poked through.

The peasants were so engrossed with their television that they didn't notice a thing. So, with the knife now in his hand, the Colonel set to work cutting his way out of his chrysalis...

The Dancing Barber

Chapter 63

Taras double-checked there was nothing coming before he stepped out onto the road. He then checked again, just to make sure, for he knew to be extra careful after consuming so much free whisky, brandy and gin; and not forgetting all that samahon. When the truth about The Great Famine appeared on the BBC News, the barman single-handedly drained another bottle of whisky, thus rendering himself completely comatose... So by the time Taras and his friends had finished – with the exception of the three gallons contained within the perpetually sodden carpet – there wasn't so much as a molecule of alcohol left in the entire bar. And there was so much merrymaking that for the first time, the headscarves became so rowdy that their flat-capped husbands had to take them home, dancing and singing all the way... There'd be a lot of sore heads tomorrow morning...

But drinking too much always gave Taras a dry throat: a cup of Klem's refreshing tea was what he needed. Perhaps he'd have some Darjeeling, or some of that Chinese stuff Klem seems to enjoy so much...

He dropped both feet onto the tarmac and began sauntering across the road as if he was John Wayne, holding his knees closely together and thrusting out his chest.

The evening was becoming chilly, so he pulled together the lapels of his blue blazer... maybe he should have changed out of his costume before leaving the theatre? He ignored the Urchins who thought it humorous to parade along the pavement, imitating his bulge by shoving their cloth caps down their trousers... Something would have to be said... but it would have to wait until he was sober...

He pressed his arm against his side and felt the bulky envelope beneath his blazer that contained the most valuable pieces of paper he'd ever owned. He vowed never to say another word against the Mafia: some of them were true gentlemen.

As he weaved his way over to the white line in the centre of the road, he imagined the look on Halyna's face when he presented her with the deeds. It'd mean she could finally leave that awful factory and become a full-time housewife. Oh how she'd enjoy waiting on him hand and foot every single day!

And when the money started rolling in from his performances in theatres and on television, Halyna could have a fur coat for every day of the week. And as for Sofia, she would be sent to a good private school, or maybe he could buy her a place at the Royal Ballet... now there's an idea? There certainly was a great deal to look forward to.

But he couldn't share the wonderful news unless he got home; and he wasn't getting very far dawdling in the middle of the road like an alcoholic. So he continued putting one foot in front of the other and meandered in the general direction of the distant kerbstones.

Without warning, a taxi screeched around the corner so fast that it almost knocked him to the ground, and the precious deeds very nearly slipped out from beneath his arm. Through the cloud of burning tyres, he shouted, 'you should learn how to drive! <u>Durak</u>!' It was then when he recognised the silhouettes of the passengers: it was The Gossipmonger and Oksana. He wanted a word with that fat pig: how dare she go AWOL from *Swan Lake* without permission... and where on earth were they going in such a hurry?

The Dancing Barber

Chapter 64

---✂---

'Wasn't that Mr Taras?' Oksana asked, straining to look through the rear window.

'No,' The Gossipmonger snapped, 'it was just some drunkard. Now turn around and have another packet of crisps.' She thrust a packet of Golden Wonder into Oksana's chubby hands and said, 'be quiet. I am fed up of hearing your voice!'

'But that was the first thing I've said since we left home,' Oksana pleaded as she pulled open the packet and released the comforting aroma of her favourite cheese and onion. 'All I said was that I thought that man was Mr Taras and you started shouting at me. You're always shouting at me...'

'Shut up!' The Gossipmonger tried not to reveal too much anger, because the driver's beady eyes were watching her every move through the rear-view mirror. 'I need to think! And I can't think if you persist in talking!'

Oksana's hand moved faster than the needle of a Singer sewing machine as she rapidly ate up all the crisps. She knew it had been Mr Taras who'd very nearly been run over; and for the first time, she was truly concerned about him. Only yesterday she wouldn't have given two hoots if the old man had been killed, in fact she'd have jumped for joy... But knowing that she'd never dance in his studio again made her feel strangely nostalgic for his cruel words and stinging cane. She realised Mr Taras only wanted her to reach her full potential, which was more than could be said for her own father, let alone her grandmother... assuming they were who they said they were. She felt terribly guilty about what she'd done with Brenda the hamster and was actually going to miss the old bully...

As she contemplated what her grandmother had in store for her, she straightened the edges of the packet and poured the remaining fragments of crisps into her mouth. She let them melt on her tongue, before meticulously picking off any crumbs that had missed her mouth and had clung to the frayed fibres of her duffel coat and downy fluff on her chin.

'Driver,' said The Gossipmonger, 'how much longer until we

get to the aerodrome?'

Aerodrome? Oksana thought. She imagined they were going to stay with relatives in Leicester or Manchester? She didn't want to go abroad; she went once and didn't like it... there weren't any televisions abroad, and she never missed an episode of *Take a Letter* with Robert Holness. But she dare not question her grandmother.

The driver said, 'that depends on traffic; but we should be there in about half an hour.' From beneath the brim of his black hat, he surveyed the woman's severe reflection through the rear-view mirror and surmised that she was likely the ghastliest woman he'd seen in a long while... and he'd seen some real dragons over the decades... He then examined the sulky face of the fat girl next to her, who obviously wanted to be anywhere else but here.

'Don't you know how to drive quicker?' The Gossipmonger snapped.

'Sure, if you're happy to pay my speeding fine,' said the driver, 'and assuming I can avoid hitting any innocent pedestrians...'

The old woman grumbled and stared out of the window, resting her warty chin on her clubbed hand.

'Going on holiday, are we?' the driver asked. He hoped it'd be somewhere windy, because the woman's smell of mothballs was overpowering. He was amazed she didn't gas herself.

'It's none of your business!' The Gossipmonger snapped again. 'Now get on with your driving!'

Charming, the driver thought, *I'm only trying to make conversation...*

'But where *are* we going?' Oksana asked, screwing up the empty crisps packet and throwing it to the floor. She looked out of the window at a landscape littered with slag heaps and mine shafts...

'I told you to be quiet!' shouted The Gossipmonger. She would have struck Oksana with her clubbed hand, had the driver not been watching her every move through the rear-view mirror. The Gossipmonger smiled at his reflection and said, 'I apologise for my rudeness, but I have a lot on my mind. If you must know, we are going to Kyiv for a little while to visit some relatives.'

'Oh yes, I know Kyiv *very* well,' said the driver. 'It's in Ukraine, isn't it?'

The Dancing Barber

The Gossipmonger shook her head, 'the Soviet Union!'

'Oh,' said the driver, 'of course it is...'

The Gossipmonger grumbled, but said nothing.

The driver asked, 'whereabouts in Kyiv do your relatives live?'

The Gossipmonger thought for a moment, 'well, err... they've only just moved there.' She said vaguely, 'they live somewhere in Kyiv.'

The fat girl's furrowed brow and scrunched up mouth confirmed to him that the old woman was lying. He straightened his black hat and indicated that he was turning right. There was no oncoming traffic, so he rotated the steering wheel and turned off the main road...

Chapter 65

'Where's everyone gone?' Sofia said, skipping into the uninhabited kitchen. Since coming back from *Swan Lake*, she'd been in her Tato's shop listening to Cliff Richard on BBC Radio One. Singing along to *"Summer Holiday"*, she'd completed as many thigh-slimming exercises as she could, squatting, lunging and star-jumping herself to exhaustion... But even after all that, her thighs didn't seem to have got any thinner...

As life was too short to worry about what the nuns were going to say about those hamsters, she decided to watch a bit of television before dinner... *Rawhide* was about to start: so if no one was about – Mama never did like "Cowboyski" films – she might manage to watch the entire episode uninterrupted...

She also had to apologise to Klem for running away from him earlier... she was too distraught to speak to anyone. But neither he, nor Mister Pushkin were anywhere to be seen... the house was like the Marie Celeste; even the dog had disappeared...

The little mound of fungal toenail clippings beside Lenka's seat still looked fresh, the half-drunk cups of tea were still slightly warm and the fetid stench of her aunties hung in the air like mustard gas... had they been abducted by extra-terrestrials? But why would extra-terrestrials want them? Hopefully they might put them off invading Earth...

To her horror, the television had disappeared – so much for *Rawhide* – the only evidence it'd ever been there was the rectangle of dust that accumulated beneath. Maybe it was the extra-terrestrials?

Apart from the ticking of the cheap Chinese pendulum clock on the mantelpiece, the only other sound in the room was that of frantic scratching coming from behind the door that led from the attic. When Sofia opened it, Mister Pushkin bounded into the kitchen and uncharacteristically began encircling her feet in a figure of eight, looking up at her and repeatedly head-butting her ankles and meowing, rendering her white socks with a plentiful coating of blue fur.

The Dancing Barber

'What's up with you?' Sofia asked, noticing the blue and yellow leash was still attached to the cat's collar. 'Where's your owner?'

But the cat could only meow and head-butt her ankles again and again, looking up at her with those deep yellow eyes.

Through the crack in the door, Sofia noticed the stairway light had been left on, and much to the cat's delight she crept slowly upstairs. She stopped and listened: her mother and aunties were shouting at each other up in the attic… so much for her theory on extra-terrestrial abduction.

The shouting was getting louder, accompanied by bangs, crashes and thuds, too numerous to count. She knew Zena and Lenka got on her Mama's nerves, but surely she hadn't lost her temper?

She couldn't hear what they were saying, so crept further up, being careful to avoid the creaky steps. Mister Pushkin went first, beckoning her to hurry up...

Chapter 66

'Himno,' Taras cursed when he realised he'd dawdled a hundred yards down the wrong street. He said to himself, 'you've not had that much to drink! Pull yourself together!' He looked around and tried to get his bearings, but deduced that once you've seen one street lined on both sides with terraced houses, you've seen them all.

Eventually, he stumbled across a short cut through an arched snicket between the houses and impressed himself by walking down it in an almost straight line, only knocking over one dustbin, scattering the rats...

He then ambled through a homogenous maze of cobbled alleys in the general direction of home, looking forward to painting the most enormous smile across Halyna's face when he presented her with the precious deeds. He knew it was probably his fault she didn't smile as much as she used to, but recently there hadn't been much to smile about. But his luck was finally changing and soon there would be plenty to smile about... even though he hated the press calling him *The Dancing Barber*.

He and Halyna would soon relive the happiness of their younger days when the intoxicating cocktail of hope and ambition got them through the harsh "Ostarbeiter" lives they led when they first met. Halyna had been hospitalised following an accident in a Nazi munitions factory and Taras – because of his pre-war career as a dancer – was forced to work as assistant to the physiotherapist in the Labour Camp hospital. He didn't mind: it kept him away from dangerous work and gave him the opportunity to help people get better, even if it was only to allow the Nazis to exploit them further. And it was there where he met Halyna on a stormy day in 1943; despite their wide age gap, they were married the same year thanks to a mutual acquaintance who was a priest. Twenty years had passed, but it seemed much longer.

He honed in on the distant glow of his attic window at the other end of a dustbin-lined alley... everything looked normal to him... maybe his nosy neighbour was imagining things?

The Dancing Barber

Looking up to Heaven, he thanked God for all his blessings: for Halyna and for Sofia, for his talent as a ballet dancer and choreographer, and now for owning his home outright.

Fame and fortune would enable him to wear better clothes and circulate in higher echelons of society, but he knew they would never distract him from what mattered in life. As Klem used to say, quoting Timothy, 6:8, *"But if we have food and clothing, we will be content with that."*

Chapter 67

'Hey, what is happening?' The Gossipmonger protested as she watched a glass panel slide up behind the taxi's front seats, clunking into position. She pulled the door handle, but the door was locked. She just about managed to stretch across the bulk of her granddaughter to pull the other door handle, but that too wouldn't budge; and much to her dismay, the windows were also locked. Braying on the glass panel with her clubbed hand, she shouted, 'what is happening?'

Ever since the taxi sped into the darkened garage, the driver had remained motionless. All The Gossipmonger could see was the silhouette of the man's wide-brimmed black hat... she began to wonder whether he was there at all? Or had there been some kind of magic trick whereby he'd been replaced by a shop dummy?

Oksana welcomed any delay in reaching the aerodrome... she ripped open another packet of cheese and onion crisps and munched away merrily. She listened to her grandmother have quite a tantrum, which only got worse when the driver got out of the taxi and locked the door behind him with a resounding clunk. She couldn't believe her grandmother knew so many swearwords... even she didn't know what some of them meant... Then the garage doors slammed shut behind the taxi, and the garage was plunged into total darkness.

The Gossipmonger cried and howled and shouted and swore as she tried to smash the window with her club in order to be able to reach out and pull the outside door handle. She then lay on her back and used both feet to try to stomp through the window. But her stout brogues were no match for toughened glass. It was only then when she realised something was missing. This was just an ordinary taxi, not a limousine, so how come she'd been able to recline on the back seat? She quested the passenger compartment with her hand and realised there was something missing: Oksana! The faint whiff of cheese and onion crisps and a seat littered with crumbs was all that remained of her beloved granddaughter. 'Oksana... my darling Oksana... where are you...?'

The Dancing Barber

The Gossipmonger was startled by a knock at her window. She looked up and saw a demonic man staring directly at her. His face was illuminated by torchlight from beneath to reveal a thin nose and thick eyebrows. He waved at the old woman who still struggled to sit up from her reposed position. The torchlight receded from the man's face and then illuminated somebody else... Oksana was stood next to him; she looked terrified and struggled to get away, but the man had tied her up...

'Hey! You can't kidnap my daughter, err granddaughter!' cried The Gossipmonger. 'Bring her back and let me out!'

But the man said nothing, and with a click, turned off the torch. A slit of light flooded briefly into the garage prior to the doors clunking shut again, this time with several bolts grating into position.

The man had gone and so had Oksana. The Gossipmonger, left all alone in the darkness, cried for the first time in thirty years.

Chapter 68

Taras stumbled into the desolate kitchen. He hiccupped, then shouted blurrily, 'hello everyone, the Ballet Master's home!'

Half way up the stairs, Sofia shook her head... By the sounds of it, her Mama was already in a dreadful mood, so she'd go ballistic when she discovered her Tato was so drunk...

'Hello everyone!' Taras hollered louder than ever, 'the Ballet Master's home! Where is everyone? Halya, are you home? Your husband is here! I have a *wonderful* surprise for you!'

When Taras got no response, Sofia heard plenty of cursing; then the door to the shop slammed shut, shaking the entire house. Why did he have to be so bad tempered?

She looked down and noticed Mister Pushkin's ears had pricked up and its nose quested the air flowing from the attic. Then all of a sudden, she was alone... the cat bolted down the stairs, the blue and yellow leash dragging in its wake.

But Sofia wasn't alone for long, for the Alsatian suddenly appeared, like a big furry stampede, taking up the full width of the stairs. Sofia hauled her thighs onto the banister and narrowly avoided being bowled over as the animal careered past her down towards the kitchen. And with the attic door now open, her mother's and aunties' voices were clearly audible:

'Calm down,' said her Mama, her voice trembling. 'I think you should let the authorities deal with him.'

'I agree,' said her auntie Lenka, 'you will only get yourself into the trouble!'

'I do not the care!' shouted her auntie Zena, 'this son of the lady dog, he is the murderer! I knew it the moment I saw the eye! I have waited the thirty years for the revenge and you cannot stop me!'

Sofia sprinted up the stairs, determined to find out what had made her auntie Zena so furious.

The second she put one foot into the attic, an extremely flustered Klem pushed her straight out and closed the door behind him. He called to her Mama, 'Halyna, this is no place for Sofia. Please send her downstairs...'

The Dancing Barber

'Down you go, Sofia,' said her Mama, peeping around the door, her face glistening and her hair ruffled. 'Go and put the kettle on... we'll all be down in a few minutes for a nice cup of tea.'

Klem went back inside and the attic door was closed and bolted. Her Mama then pulled the curtain across the little window. But Sofia wasn't going downstairs until she'd discovered what was happening. Did Zena say the word *murderer*?

And it looked to her as if Klem was in a lot of trouble... and it worried her. He was her godfather and she felt closer to him than she did to her own Tato. Klem was always cheerful, and even if he weren't, he'd always have a friendly smile for her. And that smile would often be the only smile she'd see all day, especially if it was during the school holidays and she'd been trapped in the house... it was such an antidote to the frowns perpetually adorning her Mama and Tato's faces.

'Here you are, my little one,' Klem would say, giving her a bag of her favourite fudge sweets, 'this is for doing so well at school.' And if her examination results were good, he'd always treat her to a cream bun: they were delicious but didn't help in reducing the size of her thighs. He was always the one who'd shown most interest in her academic achievements and had attended her school parent's evenings so often that her teachers thought he was her father! It wasn't that Taras didn't want to go, but Klem's grasp of the English language was as fluent as Taras' was pigeon.

Sofia had to return Klem's kindness and be there for him in his hour of need... Whatever was going on, must have been something to do with Vlad and that fishing boat... But what could *she* do? She pressed her ear tightly to the door and listened... there was another voice in the attic, an unfamiliar voice, a man's voice... Could he be called Vlad...?

Chapter 69

The fierce bruises on The Gossipmonger's clubbed hand told her that trying to smash the glass was futile. Instead, she decided to make as much noise as possible, in the hope of attracting someone's – anyone's – attention. So she ranted and raved, louder than ever. But after almost an hour of constant screaming, her voice had worn out and her throat was dry and sore. Unable to utter another syllable, let alone another word, she became resigned to the fact that she'd likely be incarcerated in this smelly taxi for a very long time...

She propped herself up in the seat and heard the familiar rustle of a packet of Golden Wonder beneath her shuffling backside: *Oksana's last meal*, she sobbed. What a dreadful thing to have happened... why was everything going wrong? Her Gaggle of mothballed old women would say, "what goes around, comes around..." The two-faced set of...

She reassured herself that – contrary to popular belief – she was not a stupid woman: she knew precisely what was behind this kidnapping and would do everything in her power to stop that hideous troll and that tea-drinking poet from taking her beloved Oksana from her. But she couldn't do anything unless she escaped this damned taxi...

All of a sudden, she felt a gust of cold air come in through the taxi's door and was immediately buried beneath a heavy hessian sack. The thing was damp and smelly and she couldn't get it off her fast enough.

The strip-lights on the garage ceiling flickered on and The Gossipmonger squinted at the sudden brightness. Being surprisingly strong for such an old woman, she heaved up the smelly sack and dropped it into the foot-well: *how dare someone throw a sack of rubbish at me...?* She looked out of the window but could only see the three brick walls of the garage, with the pair of closed wooden doors in the fourth wall behind. There were no windows and the roof was solid. Escaping the taxi was one thing, but escaping the garage was going to prove equally difficult...

The Dancing Barber

She was about to resume screaming for help when the sack in the foot-well began to move. She looked at it with curiosity and gently poked it with her club, causing it to emit a high-pitched groan. She knew that sound. 'Oksana!' she cried, what have they done to you! Oksana!' When she tried to undo the knot, she noticed her hand was stained red: the sack was soaked with blood...

Chapter 70

It was typical, Taras thought, that most of the time there were people constantly under his feet, annoying him and interrupting his concentration, but when he wanted people to talk to, when he actually had something to tell them, there wasn't a soul about!

He flung the precious deeds onto the small desk in the corner of the shop and sat down, completely missing the seat, thus banging his coccyx on the linoleum floor. He lit his last cigarette, but only after charring the end of his nose with two matches...

After picking himself off the floor, Taras hoisted up one of the blinds and looked out of the broad window. Across the street, the horrible little children were playing a rowdy game of football. He expected them to give him the usual rude gestures of the two-fingered and occasionally one-fingered variety. But this time they all stood with smiling faces and waved at him. He waved back and watched as they resumed their game. He knew the little blighters were plotting something; they'd never been friendly before. Nevertheless, his heart was momentarily warmed.

But his elation was short lived when he realised the imposing black car was still parked in front of his shop; surely the Bishop couldn't still be with Klem?

The Bishop's assistants looked to be getting impatient... the pyramid of cigarette ends outside the front passenger window suggested they'd been waiting for hours...

All of a sudden, Taras became rather suspicious of the quietness in the house...

The Dancing Barber
Chapter 71

The Gossipmonger couldn't undo the knot fast enough; it was formed from the stiffest rope and had been tied unbelievably tightly. But finally, after many frantic minutes of pulling at what turned out to be a triple-knot, using her one working hand and her dentures, it finally began to loosen.

'Don't worry Oksana,' she cried, 'you'll soon be free.' The high-pitched groaning from the sack was getting too much for her to bear.

Gingerly, she peeled open the hessian, trying to cause minimal discomfort. But as it had stuck to Oksana's delicate skin with copious quantities of dried blood, she couldn't help but cause even more pain. And the high-pitched screams continued, getting ever louder as more of the sacking was pulled away from the tender skin.

'Oh my God!' The Gossipmonger cried, 'what have they done to my beautiful Oksana!' The contents of the bag were too much for her to bear; every last part of Oksana's skin was stained red with blood. From that moment, she knew this wasn't the work of Zena and Klem: this was down to the vengeful Mafia, and all because of her thieving liar of a son... words couldn't express how much she despised him.

'Mama?' said the voice from the sack. 'Is that you, Mama?'

'Yes, it's your Mama,' she said, 'it's your Mama!' How pleased she was that Oksana had called her *Mama*!

'Mama?' the voice sounded different. 'M-Ma-M-Ma?'

She thought she was hallucinating... She peeled away more of the sacking to reveal the head and shoulders. She rubbed her eyes with her club and blinked hard. But the image remained.

She sniffed her fingers, expecting the horrible iron-smell of dried blood. But the smell was sickly-sweet, and reminded her of her time at Lister Mill.

'Mama?' repeated the voice, 'is that you?'

'Oh my God!' cried The Gossipmonger, pushing the sack away from her. She was repulsed by what she saw and said, 'I didn't expect to see <u>you</u> again!'

Ivan pulled himself out of the foot-well, wrapped the sack around his almost naked body, and sat beside his mother.

The Gossipmonger said, 'not that I'm even the slightest bit bothered, but what the hell have they done to you?'

Ivan said, 'this is Gunter's favourite punishment for traitors...' He rubbed at his bare arms, 'they soaked me in a vat of red dye for a day, and dunked my head in and everything, so that wherever I go, people will know what I am. Apparently the dye will wear off in a few months... although sometimes, it *never* wears off... I suppose it's better than being tarred and feathered like last time.' He feigned a smile, 'and at least it's disguised the hammer and sickle on my head...'

The Gossipmonger had experienced such a concoction of emotions that she didn't know what to do or say. Only seconds earlier, she thought she was unwrapping the mutilated remains of poor Oksana. But now, she was face to face with Ivan, her liar of a son. And what a state he looked, with his dyed-red birthday suit wrapped in an old sack. He was redder than he'd ever been, even after having too much sun: a pointy-chinned, sixty-five year old beardless and bald-headed lobster! And with those lumps still resplendently swollen atop his head, he certainly lived up to another one of his nicknames, "The Devil".

'I suppose at least you're not injured,' she said unfeelingly. 'When I first saw you, I thought all this red stuff was blood.' Although she didn't want to, she crossed herself in the Orthodox fashion and said the shortest of prayers.

'Beating people up isn't Gunter's style, although I wish the same was true for those thugs that chased me out of The Alhambra... my dinner jacket is ruined.' Ivan sounded almost happy, despite his mouth being full of loosened teeth, 'Gunter is the "nice" Mafia. Besides, all I did was steal from him; it's not as though I'd done anything serious...?'

The Gossipmonger shook her head, 'but you said Gunter <u>gave</u> you that money.'

'I'm afraid that was a lie,' Ivan looked at his red feet. His toenails had grown so long that they were beginning to curl... he wondered when his mother would cut them for him... 'I'm sorry, but it was all just sitting there, *waiting* to be taken, *asking* to be

The Dancing Barber

taken, *demanding* to be taken! I couldn't resist! I didn't think Gunter would miss it... he's richer than Khrushchev!'

'And that's not the only thing you've lied about, is it?'

Ivan looked puzzled, 'what do you mean? I haven't lied about anything else; you know I would never lie to you...'

The Gossipmonger shook her head, 'but what you have just said is a lie.'

'No it wasn't!' Ivan said, 'I'm telling you the truth!'

'Ah!' said The Gossipmonger, dismissively waving her clubbed hand, 'you deserve another beating!'

'What do you mean, Mama?'

The Gossipmonger sighed, 'I know all about Zena, the wife you never speak about! And having seen – and smelled – her I can understand why you've never mentioned her! But why didn't you tell me that Oksana wasn't yours? I brought that girl up as if she was my own, and all along, she was Klem's daughter! I mean Klem of all people!' She glared at him, 'you've got some *serious* explaining to do!'

'What are you on about?' Ivan said, 'of course Oksana's mine! I'd like to know who told you these lies!'

'Please, please, please,' said The Gossipmonger, 'that's enough amateur dramatics: I've seen Oksana's real birth certificate...'

'But I'm n-not l-lying,' said Ivan, 'I've always k-known ab-ab-about Zena and Klem, but I *know* O-Oksana is m-my d-daughter!'

'Lies, lies, lies!' shouted The Gossipmonger. 'Zena told me that you couldn't be anybody's father!'

'Don't talk himno, of course I'm her father!'

The Gossipmonger socked her son in the jaw with her clubbed hand, loosening a few more of his teeth. She screamed, 'do not raise your voice to me! And do not swear! And do not lie!'

'I'm telling you... I'm n-n-not l-l-lying!'

The Gossipmonger tore away the hessian sack, and confirmed that the Zena woman hadn't lied about what she did to him...

'Get off!' shouted Ivan. 'What's the matter with you?'

'The matter with *me*...' grunted The Gossipmonger. 'You are a pathetic eunuch!'

Covering himself back up, Ivan turned to look out of the window. He said, '*eunuch*? Who are you calling a eunuch?'

The Gossipmonger grumbled, but said nothing.

Ivan tied the sack securely around his waist. He said, 'and as far as I'm concerned, if Klem wants to claim Oksana as his own, then it's *fine* by me!'

'What?' said The Gossipmonger, 'how can you say that?'

'She's a waste of space, so I say "good riddance"!'

The Gossipmonger's clubbed hand responded eloquently on her behalf...

The Dancing Barber

Chapter 72

---✂---

Despite the Colonel tensing every one of his formidable stomach muscles, Zena's fists relentlessly pounded through him like a steam hammer, bending his body in half. He groaned, pleading for her to stop… but she pounded all the more. When he eventually straightened up, he was punched in the stomach with so much power that his head flicked downwards and collided heavily with Zena's upward thrusting knee. His fungal growth of a nose was completely obliterated, ejecting blood in all directions…

He panted for air, exhaling his over-boiled cabbage breath and pleading for mercy. 'Enough! Enough! I can't take much more of this!' It had been a long time since he'd met such a tough peasant… It was as though the woman had unleashed decades of pent-up anger… Even in peak condition, he doubted he could defeat someone as strong as her.

Zena shouted, 'shut the face *Stanislaw*, you murdering son of the lady dog!'

Clutching his oozing nose, the Colonel sneered, 'but how do *you* know my name is Stanislaw?'

'Do not speak to me, you pile of himno!' Zena shouted, forcing his arms behind his back and binding his wrists with copious amounts of carpet tape. Spinning him like an enormous wooden-top, she unravelled yard upon yard of rasping tape, wrapping it around his torso, aiming to mummify him completely.

'Full of insults, aren't you?' the Colonel said, getting dizzier by the second. He licked the blood from his lips, enjoying the nostalgic taste of rust.

Zena shouted, 'I said for you to shut the face!' She kicked the backs of his knees, causing him to crumble to the floor, where she continued her work with the carpet tape.

She said, 'you are Captain Stanislaw, the man who terrorised Chaplinka in 1933! I would never forget a face like yours or the stench of your breath!'

The Colonel said, 'I'm surprised that someone as ugly,' he twitched what was left of his fungal growth of a nose, 'and smelly as *you* would dare insult anyone, especially an Officer of the Soviet Army!'

He soon regretted making the comment... Zena's kick was well placed... 'Okay, so my name is Stanislaw,' he said after his eyes had stopped watering, '<u>Colonel</u> Stanislaw... what of it?'

'What of it?' Zena said, glancing at her sisters. She tut-tutted and glared at the Colonel, 'I will tell you "what of it"... Thirty years ago, it was <u>you</u> who hid the bag of the grain in our homestead, just so you could send me, my sisters and our Mama to the Collective Farm! But you were not satisfied... I tried my best to stop you, but you still sent our Tato to Siberia!' She dangled the carved oak crucifix in front of his bloodshot and bleary eye, 'did you keep this as some sort of the trophy? The men like you, they disgust me!' She spat directly into his face.

'But I have never been to Chaplinka... I don't even know where it is...' pleaded the Colonel. 'And I have never seen *you* before.'

Zena clenched her fist, 'I am the surprised you do not recognise the woman responsible for your false eye?'

The Colonel looked up, and said, '*what?* That was... that was *you?*'

'Shut the face,' Zena said, punching him on the chin. 'I hate you! And I hate the sound of your voice!' She spat all over his swollen and perspiring head. She punched him repeatedly on the chin, never seeming to tire, shouting, 'son of the lady dog!'

Halyna said, 'all right, that's enough.'

'No it is not,' Zena said, 'I will decide when it is the enough!' And she punched him another twice on the chin, knocking him out cold.

Klem was still trembling with shock, 'I can't thank you enough, Lenka... if you hadn't heard him creeping up behind me... he'd have slit my throat with that knife.'

'I am as the surprised as you are,' Lenka said, examining the Soviet Army pocket knife. 'I cannot believe he freed himself without any of us hearing.'

'Nor do I,' Halyna said, 'how can someone so heavy move so silently?'

'Because he is the professional,' Zena shouted, while binding the Colonel's ankles with what was left of the carpet tape. 'The Soviets, they train their murderers well,' she said, looking hatefully

The Dancing Barber

at the Colonel.

Lenka said, 'I still cannot believe that we are the face to the face with the Stanislaw... he should have died the long time ago!'

Halyna grimaced, 'I think he'll soon wish that he had...' A noise behind the attic door caught her attention, but when she went to investigate, there was no one there... She looked at the bulk of purple cassock piled on the floor: Stanislaw was the only person she truly hated. As a Christian, she should forgive him, but after what he'd done, forgiveness was not only impossible, but utterly unacceptable.

The Colonel's eye opened as he slowly regained consciousness... It wouldn't be long before his Privates came to the rescue... He'd enjoy watching the peasants die for what they'd done to him... He wasn't bothered if his Privates saw him in such a weakened condition... promoting them to Sergeants would certainly buy their silence...

Zena rasped another long strip of black carpet tape from the roll... and by the time she'd finished, only the Colonel's swollen face was visible. She stared at him and said, 'this is only the beginning of the revenge!' She spat, 'you murdering son of the lady dog!'

'Help!' the Colonel cried in the direction of the balcony. 'Help! Help me!'

Zena shook her head. 'Pathetic,' she said before ramming several screwed-up sheets of newspaper between the Colonel's bleeding gums and fixing them in place with the last piece of carpet tape. 'When it comes to the crunch,' she sneered, 'you are just the big coward.'

'Well, what do we do now?' Klem said, making a rather good impersonation of a headless chicken, hoping the cries hadn't been heard by the goons in the car.

'This man, he sent our Tato to his death, and starved us into working on the Collective Farm.' Zena spat in the man's face, the green phlegm crawling down his cheek. 'Our Mama, she would still be alive if it was not for him: all those years of eating the leaves and the worms, it was not the good for her, it was not the good for any of us.' Zena held back the tears, 'so I think we should allow him to experience what starvation feels like...'

Klem's ears honed in on the sound of heavy car doors slamming shut. He dashed to the balcony and swore loudly. He looked down to the street and swore again, 'oh hell! Now we really are in trouble!'

'What is it, Klem?' Halyna asked.

'Those goons have just got out of their car,' Klem said, trying not to panic. 'They're heading for the front door and I'm sure they're armed!'

Zena wrenched the screwed-up newspaper from Colonel Stanislaw's mouth. She demanded, 'how do we get the goons to go away?'

'Go hang yourselves!' said the Colonel.

Zena grabbed him by the neck and cracked his head against the wall. 'Tell me, or I will call the dog!' She looked over her shoulder and began to shout, 'B – !'

'No,' Halyna protested, 'please, don't involve the dog again; the poor beast is traumatised enough.'

Colonel Stanislaw said with determination, 'call it if you want! See if I care!'

Exasperated, Zena turned to Klem. She held out her hand and said, 'the pen...'

'What?' Klem asked, 'you mean my pen? My Pelikan fountain pen?'

'Give it to her,' Halyna said, waiting for Klem to comply, albeit begrudgingly.

Zena unscrewed the golden cap by gripping it between her craggy teeth and rotating the green barrel with her spare hand. Much to Klem's horror, she spat the golden cap to the floor and then examined the pen's pointy italic nib that was inlaid with platinum and delicately etched with an *Art Nouveau* pattern.

'You going to write your will?' scoffed Colonel Stanislaw. 'I didn't think filthy peasants like you *could* write!'

Zena's death grip at the Colonel's throat became tighter and his face took on a distinctly purple hue. 'You will tell me how to get rid of the goons or I will have your other eye!' She held the pen's pointy nib only a fraction of an inch from his bulging eyeball.

'You wouldn't dare,' said the Colonel. Two floors down, he could hear his Privates kicking in the door. *Keep your nerve... You'll soon be rescued...*

Zena said, 'I may not have the sickle like the last time, but the

The Dancing Barber

pen, it will be the just as effective...' Her prayers had been answered on that fateful autumn day in 1933... Lying on the floor beneath the embroidered icon of the Madonna and Child was a gift from Heaven: a small sickle, which had been thrown to the floor by the vandalising soldiers. She'd tried her best to fight off the Captain, hacking at his face with the sharp blade, hoping to injure him sufficiently so as to make him leave them alone. Sadly, her efforts were futile, and made matters much worse... Her Tato still went to the Gulag, while those who remained were scattered to the most punishing Collective Farms...

The Colonel gulped. He remembered all too well the pain he'd endured at the hands of this sickle-wielding peasant that fought tooth and nail to stop her scrawny, flea-ridden father from being sent to the Gulag. She wielded that sickle like a Kendo Master... it was the only time in his life when he'd been properly frightened. And it was definitely the same smelly peasant that was now in front of him: such ugliness was hard to forget. He focussed on the blurry image of the pointy nib that could easily do its damage with a quick slip of this gormless peasant's wrist. He gulped again and, pressing his head deeper into the wall, said, 'all right, I'll tell you. Go to the balcony and shout down to the street "Vladivostok", and make sure you use a deep voice so they'll think it's me!'

Zena squinted as she said, '*Vladivostok?*'

'Yes,' said the Colonel, 'even someone like you should know that it is the terminus of the Trans-Siberian railway, a port city on the Sea of Japan.'

'I know where it is!' Zena snapped, banging his head against the wall, 'but why use this as the code word?'

The Colonel twitched a shoulder, 'why not?'

'If you are the lying...' Zena twisted the end of the pen's barrel and squirted the smallest amount of ink at the Colonel's good eye.

The Colonel screwed up his face and blinked madly, his eye watering with inky tears. 'I'm not lying,' he said, 'now go quickly! They'll soon smash in that flimsy door!'

Klem was at the balcony, looking down at the goons braying on the shop door. Using his deepest, most sinister Soviet voice, he emulated the Colonel rather well as he shouted out the code word.

The goons must have been trained with the efficiency of Pavlov's dogs... the instant they heard the code word, they turned on their heels, marched in step to the black car and drove away without signalling or turning on their headlights, even though twilight was descending and Great Horton Road was busy with traffic.

'Phew,' said Klem, 'that was a close one!' He collapsed to the floor, and retrieved the golden cap of his pen, checking for teeth marks.

The Colonel cursed his weakness. If only he'd had the courage to give the *emergency* code word, then he would have been freed by now... Until he was sent, inevitably, to the Gulag for Gross Incompetence, Criminal Insubordination and anything else General Borodov could think of. But that sharp nib got dangerously close...

With his Privates called off, it was down to him to complete the mission alone, whatever the cost. Comrade General knew he had a one-hundred percent success rate... nothing in the world would make him fail. He wasn't even slightly worried, because he knew he'd soon regain control of the situation... his old nag of a horse was at least twice as intelligent as this Zena woman...

After a brief moment of calm, Halyna looked at Zena and said, 'what do we do with him?'

Zena looked at the whimpering Stanislaw and said, 'how long do you suppose he will last without the food?' She then looked at her young sister, 'three, four weeks?'

'Maybe longer,' Halyna said. A deep furrow appeared between her eyebrows, 'why do you ask?'

'I think it would be the interesting to find out,' Zena said, hoisting the mummified Colonel onto her shoulders as if he were as light as a baby wild boar...

Taras had never prayed so hard in his entire life; he vowed that, from now on, he would attend church every week without fail, even if it were raining and he were hung-over. He couldn't thank God enough for helping him in his hour of need... he peeked gingerly over the windowsill just in time to watch the black car disappear into the twilight, forcing its way into the busy traffic and incurring much angry hooting of horns...

The Dancing Barber

Those goons had almost knocked a hole through his door with their fists; and when no one answered, they set about picking the mortise lock. They'd succeeded, but the strong bolts at the top and bottom of the door had thankfully thwarted their entry... Taras had prepared to defend himself by tightly gripping his old metal dustpan thinking it might make a useful bullet-proof shield... To disorientate them, he was going to throw hair-clippings in their faces, then clout them with the dustpan as hard as he could. Thankfully, none of this was necessary...

Bizarrely, he heard one of them shout "Vladivostok" and then both goons disappeared! The entire experience seemed surreal and he began to wonder whether the excessive booze he'd consumed at the Club might have made him hallucinate – it had happened before (he never did catch that six-foot chicken) – but the picked lock and the damage to the door proved otherwise. At least it was all over... He'd sweated so much that most of his hair-dye ran in zebra stripes down his face, and he was sat in a puddle on the linoleum floor.

'Tato?' Sofia called, running into the shop as quickly as she could. She immediately noticed her Tato curled up under the window... 'What's happening? I heard all the banging on the door: are you okay?'

'Come here Sofia,' Taras said, hugging his daughter for the first time in years. 'Nothing is happening... it was just some people who'd been given the wrong address.'

Even though her Tato stank of tobacco and booze, and was damp with perspiration, she hugged him tightly. Whoever those people were, they certainly spooked him... his entire body still trembled. She'd never seen him scared before – she thought he were afraid of nothing – but at least it proved he was human.

'Tato,' Sofia said, but he wasn't listening. She looked at him and saw that his eyes had glazed over and his eyelashes were damp with tears. 'Tato!' she repeated, tugging at his sleeve, 'I <u>must</u> tell you something...'

'What?' Taras said. He narrowed his eyes, 'you've not got any more hamsters have you?'

Sofia shook her head and said, 'listen... this is serious... Mama, Klem and my aunties are in the attic, and they are shouting at someone called Stanislaw... Who is this Stanislaw? Because he's making them very angry... and it sounds as if they're throwing the furniture at each other.'

Taras deposited his daughter on the floor, stood up and without saying a word, stumbled out of the shop and clambered up the stairs... He remembered all too vividly what happened the last time that name was mentioned...

'Hand him over to the authorities?' Zena shouted, 'are you the crazy?'

Klem said, 'of course I'm not "the" crazy! You want justice to be done, don't you?'

'Pah, you are going the soft in the head,' said Zena, 'the authorities, they will only send him to Moscow and that durak Khrushchev, he will probably give him the medal!'

'I doubt it,' said Halyna, 'even the Soviets don't reward failure.'

Klem agreed, 'I'm sure Nikita Khrushchev will send him to one of those Gulags he refuses to shut down in Siberia. At least there, this Stanislaw can get a taste of his own medicine.'

Zena shook her head, 'that cannot be guaranteed... I have the better idea.' She cast her eyes up to the small square hatch, behind which was the dusty loft, 'do you suppose I could fit him up there?'

'Up there?' Halyna said, 'but *why*?'

Zena didn't bother answering her young sister. She checked the carpet tape around the man's mouth, wrists and ankles, making sure there was no room for movement. And before anyone could stop her, she effortlessly thrust his torso through the hatch; stepping onto a creaking chair, she shoved again, and the man's legs disappeared into the darkness of the loft.

'There,' she said, rubbing the dust from her hands, 'he can stay there until he becomes as the hungry as we were...'

Halyna said, 'but if Taras finds out, he'll do his nut!'

'Let him do his nut,' said Zena, 'let him do both his nuts!'

'Halyna's right,' said Klem, placing his hand on Zena's bristly arm to try to prevent her from closing the loft hatch. 'It's illegal to hold someone against their will in this country!'

'Pah!' Zena spat, 'I do not give the toss! In my book, the laws of the country should not apply when punishing the criminals! Now get the hand off me, I know what I am the doing!'

Taras dreaded what he was going to see. The last time the name "Stanislaw" was mentioned, Halyna became so distraught that the doctor had to come and sedate her. Even Mrs Wiggins had to refer to her husband as "Mr Wiggins" or "the old git" in front of her, because his Christian name of "Stanley" was too similar to "you know who".

Ascending the stairs, he just knew one of those idiot twins had said what they weren't supposed to and had upset Halyna again. He hoped the doctor was on call and had plenty of tranquillisers in his bag...

But Taras' fears were groundless... when he and Sofia entered the attic, they were met by the epitome of calmness. Klem was sat at his roll-top desk, reading poetry to an engrossed Zena, who rested her bristly chin on her clenched fist, absorbing every word; while Lenka and Halyna were sat cross-legged on the carpet, rolling a marble at each other in the vain attempt to coax Mister Pushkin to be even the slightest bit playful. As usual, the cat only watched the marble going to and fro, while the women had their exercise. And the dog, which had followed him up from the kitchen, went to stare at its own reflection in the window... it probably thought it was another dog, constantly trying to sniff the reflection's derrière, but – annoyingly – never able to reach it.

Taras looked down at Sofia and said from the corner of his mouth, 'I thought you'd heard a lot of shouting and furniture being thrown about?'

'I did,' Sofia said, 'honestly.' Something certainly smelled fishy, and for once it wasn't just her aunties.

'Oh hello Taras,' Klem said, setting his book down on the desk, marking the page with the handle of a silver teaspoon. 'How are you? Isn't it delicious news about Voloshin?' He gestured towards the television, 'he'd even made the BBC News.'

Sofia said, 'so that's where the telly went...'

Taras narrowed his drowsy eyes and examined the attic – *his* attic – looking for something, anything – other than the television –

that looked out of the ordinary. And to his surprise, everything looked suspiciously tidy: there wasn't a washing line or an article of women's underwear to be seen... the pans, which had previously simmered with all manner of filthy garments had been cleaned and put away... even the carpet had been vacuumed, and the litter in Mister Pushkin's tray, changed...

'You know,' Taras said, holding the lapels of his blazer as if he were a barrister, 'a man at the Club said the strangest thing: he said he saw a pig's carcass being butchered here in *my* attic. Why would he say such a thing?'

Klem shrugged his shoulders, 'was he drunk?'

'Of course,' Taras said, 'but he always is.'

Mmm, Halyna thought, smelling the alcohol on her husband's breath, *as indeed you are*. She said, 'and what was he doing snooping through our window in the first place?'

Zena smiled, 'maybe he is the peeping tom?'

Lenka said, 'the next time I take the bath, I will give him a lot to peep at!'

Both twins laughed hoarsely, while Taras cringed at the memory of their last bath time.

Looking up to the ceiling, Taras noticed the smallest amount of black tape stuck to one of the roof beams. 'And what is this?' he asked, recollecting all too vividly the sight of Ivan in the outdoor lavvy a couple of days ago.

Zena stood up and examined the fragment of tape with fascination. 'This is what we used to hold up the washing lines.' She scraped it off with her soiled thumbnail, 'I will throw it in the bin... yes?'

Taras snatched the tape and said, 'I am quite capable of throwing it away myself!' And before anyone could stop him, he stamped on the pedal with his foot, the bin's chromium lid springing open, revealing its contents. He crouched down inquisitively and asked, 'why have you thrown away all these newspapers?' He looked at Klem, 'I thought you were going to frame them? Besides, *I* haven't seen any of them yet.'

Klem pulled the embroidered collar away from his neck. 'Err,' he said, hoping Taras wouldn't notice the blood stains, 'when I read my articles in print, well I err... got a little carried away...' He tried to smile, but all he could do was grimace.

The Dancing Barber

Halyna added, 'I think we *all* got a little carried away with excitement. But it doesn't matter, because the newsagent will bring some fresh copies around later. Won't he?' She looked in Klem's direction, giving him a discrete wink.

'Mmm, indeed he will,' Klem said, casually leafing through his book, making a mental note to telephone the newsagent as soon as possible.

'I see…' said Taras; he'd never known Klem get so frequently carried away in such a short space of time. Stringing someone up by his feet with his head down the toilet was bad, shooting someone else up the backside was worse, but for Klem, desecrating the printed word was the most deplorable act of all. He deduced there must have been a lot of samahon still swilling about in his system…

But the man at the Club wasn't in the habit of making things up: he simply didn't have the imagination. So if he saw a pig's carcass being butchered in the attic, then that's what it must have been; or at the very least something that looked like a pig's carcass.

'At last!' Halyna and Lenka said in unison, once the cat had finally decided to intercept the marble and whack it against the skirting boards as if the room was an enormous pinball machine.

'Hey, watch it!' shouted Taras, dodging out of the way of the high-velocity marble.

Even Klem didn't know what had come over his ordinarily rather sessile cat. The marble ricocheted from skirting board to skirting board, denting the wood and flaking off blizzards of white paint. The cat crouched low with its chin brushing the carpet, its eyes tracking the marble as it approached. Then with a bob of the head and a wiggle of the bottom, the cat scooped up the marble with its paw and batted it straight across the room with the power of a Soviet shot-putter. Taras jumped out of the way as the marble continued on its final trajectory before disappearing in amongst the dog's fur. The canine almost jumped out of its skin as the marble lodged itself firmly under its tail.

'That's enough,' Taras shouted, lunging for the cat, determined to shoo it out of the way. 'Are you going to let your Cooking Fat destroy my attic?'

The cat didn't linger… it launched itself through the open window and up onto the safety of the roof tiles. Meanwhile, the dog stood up, hobbled around and sniffed at the offending marble.

Sofia was getting fed up with all these distractions, so stomped her zippy boots impatiently and tugged at her Tato's tobacco-scented sleeve. She wasn't surprised when he ignored her: he obviously cared more about the condition of his skirting boards than he did about the strange goings on she'd told him about. She tugged his sleeve again, but he snatched his arm away.

Taras crouched down and picked up the marble. He said, 'I'm confiscating this before it does any more damage.' He placed it in his blazer pocket, from where it promptly dropped through a hole and bounced to the floor: with Halyna on strike, sewing up holes in his pockets was another menial task he was unwilling to do for himself. So again, he picked up the marble and placed it into another pocket; but it was soon bouncing along the floor, worrying the dog.

Halyna smiled; annoyances such as these would soon make Taras appreciate her...

Sofia yanked her father's sleeve and said, 'ask them about the *shouting* I heard. *Go on*, ask them!'

'What shouting?' Halyna said, looking inquisitively at her daughter. 'There hasn't been any shouting.'

Taras said, 'apparently, Sofia heard a lot of shouting going on up here. She said it was about someone called...' He braced himself, '...Stanislaw?' Closely, he examined his wife's expression, 'can you shed any light on that?'

Zena and Lenka looked at each other, as did Klem and Halyna, each forming the expression of a trout and shrugging their shoulders. Zena said, 'no, we never said a thing about a "Stan-is-law..."' She raked her fingernails through her greasy hair, creating a snowstorm of dandruff, 'what is a "Stain-is-law"?'

Now Taras was worried; how come Halyna hadn't gone ballistic? Maybe it was a delayed reaction?

Sofia could smell a liar a mile off; and there were four of them in front of her. She said, 'but I *distinctly* heard you shouting at someone called Stanislaw! And I'm sure I heard a man's voice up here... I'm sure of it!'

'Oh, I know what you heard,' Zena said in the same deep tone Oksana used when she'd concocted a suitable lie to cover up her latest misdemeanour; she was about to click her fingers but

The Dancing Barber

remembered what happened the last time... 'I was discussing with Klem what sort of the house we should have when we go back to Ukraine. He says that he wants the tall city house with the many floors, but I says I want the nice "bung-a-low". So when you thought we were talking about the "Stan-is-law", we were actually talking about the "bung-a-low"!' She looked at Sofia, 'your hearing, it is not so good... maybe the ears, they need to be the cleaned, yes?' She looked at her sisters, who nodded their agreement, eventually.

Sofia said nothing. *How dare that woman tell me to clean my ears when her own produce enough wax for a decade's supply of candles...*

'Not bad,' said Taras, clapping slowly, 'that's quick thinking... even for you.'

He turned to Sofia and said, 'please, go to the kitchen and put the kettle on; we'll all be down in a few minutes and we'd like some tea before dinner. And here,' he handed her the marble, 'go and put this in the jar with the others.'

In a huff, Sofia did what her Tato wanted; she muttered, 'make the tea, make the tea, always make the bleeding tea...' She huffed even more when she was unable to eavesdrop... her Tato waited for her to go all the way downstairs and out of ear-shot before closing the attic door and continuing his inquisition.

'Now this time,' Taras said, turning back to the three sisters, 'let's have the truth.'

Zena said, 'but the truth, it has already been spoken!'

Taras shook his head, 'I know who this Stanislaw is and what he did: Halyna told me long ago and I have not forgotten.' He found it strange the name had been said several times and Halyna hadn't so much as flinched. 'And I think it's a bit of a coincidence that all this talk about Stanislaw occurs on the same day Voloshin springs to life and a pair of Soviet goons very nearly kick down my shop door...'

'Goons?' Klem said, 'when was this?'

'Come on,' Taras said with increasing impatience, 'you must have seen that enormous black car parked outside my shop? A few minutes ago, a pair of goons came out of it and tried to kick down the door. Come on, you <u>must</u> have heard.'

'Did you hear anything?' Klem asked the women, who promptly shook their heads.

'Well I heard them!' Taras shouted, 'and I know you're all lying to me! And I'm getting fed up of it!'

'Perhaps,' Halyna said, smelling the alcohol on her husband's breath, 'you may have imagined it all? You know how you imagine things when you've had too much to drink...'

'It seemed real enough to me,' Taras said, remembering the six-foot chicken. He thought for a moment and scratched his head, the black hair dye staining his fingertips, 'but maybe you're right? Maybe I did imagine it?'

'Why don't you sit down?' Halyna said, 'and take the weight off your feet: you've been under a lot of stress recently and you need to take the time to relax.'

'Yes, I suppose I have,' Taras said. He hitched up his trousers and sat down, putting his feet onto the coffee table.

'Oh, it's always doing that,' Klem said after the hastily reassembled coffee table collapsed beneath Taras' feet. 'Don't worry about it.'

But Taras didn't even notice. He lit a cigarette and settled into the chair. Narrowing his eyes, he turned to Klem, and said, 'how did your meeting with the Bishop go?'

Klem held his breath so as not to breathe Taras' fumes, 'oh fine, it went fine. He didn't stay long; you know how busy Bishops are.'

'Exciting meeting, was it?' Taras asked, blowing enormous smoke rings whilst searching for an ashtray.

Klem moved away from the fumes that irritated the back of his throat... under the circumstances, he dare not tell-off Taras for smoking in his presence. He said, 'not particularly; he congratulated me on my declamation, read a few poems and went.' He checked the fire and noticed the walking stick's ebony veneer had burned off, revealing the molten gun barrel beneath, glowing bright orange. Without panicking, he repositioned himself so as to hide it from Taras.

Taras asked, 'didn't the Bishop arrive in a big black car? It was a Zil, wasn't it?'

'I think so,' said Klem, 'but he left *hours* ago...'

'Did the Bishop say anything about his, err...' Taras gestured to

The Dancing Barber

his rear end.

Klem shook his head, 'thankfully not.' He watched Taras drop his ash onto a particularly exquisite Minton saucer. 'I think it was a sensitive subject.'

Inhaling another lungful of smoke, Taras muttered, 'I couldn't have imagined goons trying to kick down my door... I couldn't have... could I?' Things weren't making much sense for him at the moment. And for a man with a constantly clear mind, it was quite an odd feeling. Then he remembered the damage to the shop door, or did he imagine that as well? It was then when he noticed the cigarettes within his leatherette case were the Benton and Wedges; now he knew why they tasted of almonds... He stubbed out his cigarette onto the saucer, not noticing Klem's cringing expression.

All of a sudden, there was a loud thudding noise from above. Taras swivelled his eyes to the ceiling and asked, 'what on earth was that?'

'What was what?' Klem said, 'I didn't hear anything?'

'Shhh!' Taras said, 'listen...'

Zena, Lenka and Halyna waited on tenterhooks, hoping the noise they pretended not to hear wouldn't get any louder.

'There it goes again,' Taras said, 'listen...' He cupped his ears in the palms of his hands and tried to locate the source of the noises. He stood up, pointed to the loft hatch and said, 'I'm sure I can hear movement up there...'

'Oh that...' said Klem, 'it's only Mister Pushkin promenading on the roof tiles! He's probably gone to spray your chimney-stack!'

'Who are you trying to kid, hmm?' said Taras, 'I've never known a Cooking Fat make so much noise! What's it got on its paws: clogs?'

'Honestly,' Klem said, crossing his fingers in his pocket, 'it was Mister Pushkin who made those noises, look...' He pointed to the cat that was now balanced on the windowsill. 'You can't hear the noises now, can you? That proves it *was* Mister Pushkin.'

Taras stared at the cat and shrugged his shoulders, 'maybe it was the Cooking Fat; but it needs to be lighter on its paws, I don't want any cracked tiles.'

Klem could feel the sweat beneath his arms soaking into his shirt; and he, just like the sisters, hoped the Colonel up in the loft didn't move another muscle.

Sofia stared at the steam billowing from the whistling kettle, fed up more than ever with the way her Tato treated her. He had been so nice after the performance, but now he was back to his normal self: ordering her about as if she were his servant. So if he wanted tea, he could come downstairs and turn off – as Natalka would say – the bleeding gas himself! She was more than happy for all the water to boil away and for the flames to burn through the base of the kettle…

She looked at the stupid marble he'd given her: it wasn't even a nice one, all black and green, rather like a lizard's eyeball. So she chucked it into the jar with all the others and shook it about so it was properly mixed in.

She went back to stare at the steaming kettle… Watching the clouds accumulate at the ceiling, she wondered how long it would take for the wallpaper to start peeling.

Words couldn't express how fed up she felt… She never did discover what all the shouting was about on Saturday morning… the identities of Katya and Vlad were still a mystery… And now this "Stanislaw" was the subject of yet more shouting. Who would they be shouting about tomorrow? It was so frustrating: if trouble was brewing, why didn't they tell her? She might be able to help?

Through the mist, she watched the pendulum of the cheap plastic clock swing for eight full minutes before the thunder of footsteps inevitably descended the stairs… She braced herself for a serious telling-off…

When Halyna flung open the door, it looked as though a steam engine had parked in her kitchen, transforming it into the stickiest of saunas. Condensation was everywhere, streaming down the window, running down the framed photographs and beginning to make the wallpaper peel away at the edges.

The photograph of Charlie Chaplinka had curled up like ancient papyrus beneath the misted glass. But as Zena would say, she "didn't give the toss"… it'd be in the bin first thing tomorrow morning, just in time for the dustmen to take it away. By the time Taras noticed, it would be too late…

The Dancing Barber

'What do you think you're doing?' Halyna shouted over the piercing whistle of the kettle. She'd discovered her daughter sat amongst the steam, 'why have you made my kitchen into a Turkish bath?'

Typical, Sofia thought, *he's sent Mama to make the tea instead of making it himself.*

But it was never her intention to annoy her Mama. She said, 'sorry... I must have dozed off...'

'Dozed off?' said Halyna, 'with all this noise... don't be ridiculous... you've done it on purpose, haven't you...?'

Sofia shrugged.

Halyna wrapped a nappy tea towel around her hand, gripped the kettle's red-hot handle and lifted it from the flames. Even with her tinnitus, it was a relief when the whistling ceased. 'Well... I'm waiting...'

Sofia looked at her Mama. Remembering how she and her aunties lied about "Stanislaw", she said, 'noise...? But what noise would that be?'

AC Michael

Act 5

The Sunday of St Thomas

> 'Then Jesus told him, "Because you have seen me, you have believed; blessed are those who have not seen and yet have believed."'
>
> John 20:29

The Dancing Barber
Chapter 73

---✂---

Taras could do nothing to stop his body slipping from the harness. As he watched the floor getting further away, he wished he'd spent those few extra seconds making sure the straps were secure.

All he could do was try to maintain his composure and hope he didn't slip any further: easier said than done.

And it was obvious – even to him – that contrary to Sofia's made-up smile, her body was also slipping from her own harness. But at least she had those jodhpur thighs to slow down the process; and if they failed, he still had a firm grip of her hand. But to his horror, even that was starting to slip.

The closer he ascended to the electric winch, the louder it squeaked: he desperately hoped it would not be heard. He'd insisted on it being oiled on the opening night, yet a week later, it squeaked louder than ever, as if it were a baby bird desperate to be fed. The floor may have been getting further away, but the gantry hovering high above the stage was getting tantalisingly close: only a few more feet to ascend before he could reach out to safety.

Despite his precarious situation, he couldn't help but notice the Cine camera up in the private box, swinging around in every direction except at the stage. Why couldn't Halyna leave it alone? He dare not criticise her: he was fed up with wearing unironed shirts and hoped her strike would soon come to an end.

He sighed: his memories, along with a few black and white photographs, would be the only record he'd have of this monumental run of performances. But then the harness slipped a little further, nipping him in a very uncomfortable place and reminding him that he had more important things to worry about.

As far as the audience was concerned, the spirits of Prince Siegfried and the Swan Queen had almost ascended to the Heavens after the most elaborate drowning scene Taras had ever choreographed for the stage. In the rim of his vision, he watched the hideous crow-like corpses belonging to Von Rothbart and Odile languishing in the lake dozens of feet below, around which ballerinas danced joyfully. Special indoor fireworks boomed and hissed, the fountains of colour celebrating the death of the evil sorcerer; the spell that transformed the ballerinas into swans and cygnets having finally been shattered.

But the rickety gantry was still impossibly out of reach and Taras' perspiring grip now only held on to the very tips of Sofia's fingers, her fingernails digging into his flesh, only millimetres from drawing blood. He didn't blame his daughter for swearing under her breath, for he was doing the same thing and using much stronger words.

The squeaky winch jerked and stalled, making his and his daughter's body flick harshly to one side; the audience gasped... they thought it represented the spirits' jubilation at entering the Heavens and spending an eternity together. Little did they realise how close the stars of the show were to plummeting to their actual deaths...

Taras' nose twitched, he'd detected the smell of burning. He looked up... the electric motor was spewing out smoke and squeaking an octave higher; it also emitted the occasional spark. And to his horror, the rope passing from the pulley was fraying; the kelp like strands waving in the air, narrowly avoiding being ignited by the errant sparks. Taras said, 'come on,' willing the winch to speed up and for those damned curtains to close. But the winch crawled at a snail's pace, as if deliberately trying to annoy him; the rope becoming thinner with every passing second...

Taras foolishly looked down; the lake in the centre of the stage could have been a cup of water, Von Rothbart and Odile, dead houseflies floating on the surface. He stopped himself from screaming and – with one hand – made a desperate lunge for the gantry... but it was still inches from his grasp... Thankfully, the audience's clapping was so loud that it masked the squeaking and swearing, but also completely drowned out Tchaikovsky's thunderous finale music.

Then came the noise Taras dreaded hearing most of all: the winch's mechanism snapped with the violence of a gun being fired. All of a sudden, he and his daughter were suspended in mid-air from a slackening rope; time standing still before the inevitable happened...

It may have been a rather hackneyed notion, but Taras' life really did flash before his eyes. Not his entire life, but only the last four hours. It wasn't because of momentary amnesia, but because the performance that had taken place at The Alhambra that evening amounted to the sum total of his life's work. If he were to plummet to his death, at least his life had been worthwhile... But there was no way he would let his Sofia plummet with him, not with such a bright future ahead of her...

Only minutes earlier, he'd watched Sofia's Odette swirl in the vortex of Swan Lake for the final time, her small body descending to the darkening stage accompanied by the orchestra's booming drums. Taras had to pinch himself: it was as if he'd just watched Anna Pavlova all over again. Sofia had come such a long way in the last week, her movements refined, her poise magnificent: not bad for a girl with jodhpur thighs. And thanks to a carefully folded piece of cardboard, the Swan Queen's golden crown had not spent the entire performance covering her eyes, but was still perfectly balanced on top of her head: it was the mark of a true professional to maintain dignity to the very end.

As the rope slithered down Taras' spine on its journey to the distant stage, he could only pray for a miracle. He promised to renounce his selfish ways, if only – somehow – he could be saved. No longer would he take his Halyna and Sofia for granted: he'd cook a proper dinner every night – never again would he cheat by buying fish and chips – and he'd happily wear a flowery apron to do the housework, not caring if his friends laughed at him. And this time, he meant it.

He looked down again and saw the hard floorboards starting to accelerate towards him. He quested the stage for something soft on which to land, but there was nothing in sight... where was Oksana when he needed her?

Just as he'd closed his eyes to the inevitable, his arm snagged on something; it jerked so much that it almost snapped. His body was flung upwards towards the rattling Meccano set that was the gantry; he wrapped the sweaty fingers of one hand around the rusty railings, which blessedly took his weight. His heart was pumping so hard that it hurt, but at least he was safe. He used his sleeve to wipe the tears from his eyes, only to discover his face was blackened with running hair dye.

Despite dangling by one hand, fifty feet above the stage, he still found the time to catch his breath. Using his free hand, he released the tourniquet of his harness, allowing it to plummet to the stage and splash into the lake...

But why did he have a free hand? Had he dropped something...?

All the blood drained from his face... Only moments ago, he'd promised to renounce his selfish ways, and yet he'd just committed the most selfish act of all. He dare not look down through the mesh of his eyelashes to the stage, for fear of what he might see...

His eyes were so tearful, that the whole world had gone blurred and his chest felt so tight that he struggled to breathe. At least the curtains had swished closed, their velvety shroud concealing the carnage below. What was he going to tell Halyna? How could he have saved himself at the expense of his own daughter?

'You all right?' said an exhausted voice from above.

'What do you think?' Taras sobbed, 'I can't believe what I've done!'

'What have you done?' said the voice. 'If you've broken wind, then don't worry: your farts are like Chanel Number Five compared to my Auntie Lenka's!'

Taras looked up, not quite believing what he saw. He said, 'Sofia! But... How did you get up there?' His daughter had her thighs clamped tightly around the gantry's railings, with one arm by her side, and the other reaching down for his.

'Are you all right?' she repeated, knowing he was anything but.

'Yes, I'm fine,' said a tearful Taras. 'I thought I'd lost you; I thought...'

'Don't worry about me, Tato. Here,' she held out her hand, smiling though the pain. 'Grab a hold and I'll help you up...'

If he had bothered to ask whether she was all right, he'd have discovered that her left arm hung lifelessly by her side...

With his feet firmly on solid ground, Taras watched one of the old women use a diagonally-folded headscarf as a make-do sling, supporting Sofia's left arm, making her as comfortable as possible... at least until a doctor could be found. Sofia was smiling, grateful for the help, but was also trying not to be asphyxiated by the overwhelming stench of mothballs while the

The Dancing Barber

woman laboriously tied the sling behind her neck...

He couldn't believe how brave his daughter had been to have swung those thighs up to the gantry, anchored them around the rickety railings and then reached down, almost tearing off her own arm in the effort to save her father. She must have been the only ballerina in the world who could dance like Anna Pavlova, yet possess the strength of Mick McManus...

Taras put a hand to his chest, wondering how much longer the tightness would continue... it had never been this bad before... He examined the frayed rope coiled at his feet and the burnt-out motor that had been unbolted from the gantry... never again would he include anything acrobatic in his dances.

'Bleeding hell,' said Natalka's Tato, inspecting Sofia's injury. 'It appears to me that your *humerus* has dislocated from your *scapula*.'

Mrs Wiggins' husband shrugged his shoulders. He said, 'sorry Taras, but he were the closest thing to a doctor I could find.'

Dismissing Mrs Wiggins' husband back to his duties, Taras said, 'he'll have to do.'

He turned to Natalka's Tato and, pressing his hand to his tightening chest, said, 'can you fix it?'

Natalka's Tato raised his hands and backed away. He said, 'you know I'm not a doctor.'

'But you work with doctors; you must know what to do in such a situation?'

The hospital porter pushed back his chequered flat-cap and scratched thoughtfully at the comb-over concealed beneath. 'Yes... But...'

'Well, get on with it,' ordered Taras. 'Can't you see my Sofia is suffering?'

Natalka's Tato didn't need telling twice; he took a deep breath and unfastened the headscarf sling, holding it as far from his nose as possible. 'Time to be a brave little girl,' he said, carefully manoeuvring Sofia's elbow into the relocation position... a procedure he'd only ever watched once before. 'Now look the other way; this won't hurt half as much as you might think...'

Sofia could hardly see Natalka through her tears... She'd never seen her best friend look so concerned; realigning bones was a delicate procedure, and not one to be attempted by a hospital porter, even if he was a wannabe doctor.

Natalka retreated into the shadows of the wings, unable to watch.

No matter how much pain she was in – even when her butcher of a dentist had ripped out her canines without anaesthetic – Sofia never screamed. But after she'd endured Natalka's Tato's knee in her ribs as he yanked and twisted her delicate bones, grinding and scraping them until the ball of the humerus was firmly back in the socket of the scapula, she screamed louder than a scalded cat. She turned to the hospital porter and said, 'you were right…'

Natalka's Tato nodded and said, 'thank you.'

Sofia continued, 'it didn't hurt *half* as much as I might think…'

Natalka's Tato shook his head and said, 'no?'

'No!' shouted Sofia, 'it hurt *twice* as much!'

'Pain is good,' said Natalka's Tato, 'it means there hasn't been any nerve damage.'

Slowly and carefully, Sofia rotated her arm, the pins and needles in her fingers gradually receding, although the pain in her shoulder was excruciating.

Taras gave the hospital porter a nudge, 'you say pain is good? So why does my chest feel so tight: I feel *so* short of breath.'

The hospital porter exhaled slowly, as if he were a workman about to deliver an estimate. He said, 'muscle strain, probably. Or maybe indigestion: Natalka's told me all about your sisters-in-law's "cuisine". Here,' he tapped out a large white pill from a small brown bottle he'd retrieved from his pocket. 'This is a calcium carbonate tablet; chew it, swallow it, the pain will soon go.'

'You sure?' Taras asked, placing the sour pill on his tongue.

The hospital porter said, 'of course, it'll just be indigestion: you've had a stressful week.' He winked at his own sisters-in-law who were stood with their mouths open, scrutinising his every move. He said, 'I may not be a doctor, but at least I know what to do in an emergency…' He watched them grumble to each other and – satisfied with what they'd seen – waddle back to their seats.

'It's working already,' said a smiling Taras, taking some deep breaths. 'So it was indigestion all along; and I was worried it might be a heart attack?'

The Dancing Barber

Natalka's Tato smiled. He said, 'heart attack? No... You're the fittest fifty-five year old in England! Your indigestion was brought on by worry and stress: stay nice and calm and you'll be fine.'

'I expect you're right,' Taras said, fanning his perspiring brow with yesterday's Times. 'I'll need to sleep for a week to recover from the last few days...' His eyelids felt heavy, '...maybe even a month.' He yawned, settling down in his chair, determined to rest his eyes for a few moments...

When Mrs Wiggins' husband gave the signal for the dancers to assemble for the first encore, Taras rolled his eyes to the ceiling and groaned for half a minute... He shook his head, mouthing, 'not yet...'

Even though the curtains had been tightly shut for some time, he could still hear the audience's applause, anticipating the first of several encores. And on account of them helping themselves to most of the post-performance Champagne – which was actually fizzy white wine with a fancy label – the orchestra were playing Tchaikovsky's fabulous music decidedly off key. But Taras didn't mind.

After a few minutes, Mrs Wiggins' husband noticed that Taras hadn't moved, so he repeated his signal so forcefully that he almost gave himself a hernia.

Taras shook his head, he wasn't ready. 'Not yet,' he said, 'not yet...'

His exhausted eyes settled on a lithe figure perched on a chair in the shadows of the wings, her leg propped up on a stool. Although he wouldn't have minded Oksana reprising the role of Odile, her disappearance – which according to Klem's theory, was because The Gossipmonger and Ivan had kidnapped her – necessitated a suitable stand-in to be found.

Natalka didn't need much of an excuse to do what she enjoyed, especially as it meant escaping her Aunties Lyudmila and Valentina. So despite having a broken leg, she danced a simplified routine, keeping her Plaster of Paris cast hidden beneath a specially made full-length tutu that swept the floor as she traversed the stage, rising up as she performed a pirouette, encircling her waist and continuing to camouflage the heavy cast she'd somehow found the strength to hoist into the air. For consistency, Odette's costume was identical, and so wonderfully disguised Sofia's thighs.

Taras hoped Natalka's experience hadn't set back her recovery too much: important ballet examinations were looming and the girl looked completely exhausted...

At least the colour had returned to Sofia's cheeks; she stood and began gently manoeuvring her arm to stop it from seizing up. He'd insist she gave it the ice-cream treatment as soon as she got home; he couldn't afford to have his new protégé injured for too long, especially with what he had planned for her in the coming weeks...

Just as Taras mustered the strength to think about standing up, he observed the beret-wearing Stage Manager on the warpath; lisping the filthiest words and pointing to the damage Mrs Wiggins' husband's fireworks had done to the formerly pristine varnish of the stage. Taras couldn't believe the little twit was so concerned about a few singed floorboards... the man was worse than all the ballet critics he knew, combined. He really didn't have the patience to deal with him now...

The Stage Manager continued to lisp a repertoire of the most appalling language, fanning his brow with an invoice for re-varnishing the stage and gesticulating so flamboyantly that he almost slapped himself in the face with his flaccid hands.

Taras took a calming breath and said, 'hey you, come here.'

The man skipped over, and with his hands on hips, resumed his lisping rant at an increasingly nonplussed Taras.

Taras showed him the burnt-out motor and frayed rope, and explained how two people had almost died because of them... Immediately, the man gulped, tore up the invoice and scuttled away, never to be seen again.

Taras got to his feet and clapped his hands, ordering the dancers to assemble for the encore. He watched Mrs Wiggins grumble as she took her place, having spent the last few minutes re-feathering her costume, subsequent to most of it being ignited by her husband's pyrotechnics. The scene reminded Taras of the inferno that was the Priest's cassock at the All-Nighter that seemed such a long time ago. She also had a sore head... when he dropped the harness from the gantry, how was he to know she was directly beneath it?

With Mrs Wiggins' husband's finger hovering over the "Curtain

The Dancing Barber

Open" button, Taras made a final adjustment to his greying hair, shifted his bulge back into position and forced a smile across his exhausted face. Never did he imagine becoming bored with applause…

Chapter 74

The Gossipmonger spat to the taxi's floor, not the least bit caring that most of it had splattered all over her own foot. Her clubbed hand flopped to the dirty seat beside her; she groaned until her lungs were empty. She said, 'how much longer do you think Grunter is going to leave us to fester in this stinking garage?'

Ivan twitched a shoulder, 'I've already told you: I don't *know*. I suppose it could be for a day, or for a month, or for a year... It depends on how fed up he is.' He peered depressingly at his vermilion skin, 'and considering what he's done to me...'

'Brilliant,' said The Gossipmonger, staring at the six deep scratches she'd made on the door frame, one for each day of her incarceration. She tore out her false teeth and threw them into her lap. Taking a deep breath, she then used the pointy end of a nail file to nimbly pick out the accumulated fragments of chewing tobacco from between the stained ceramic molars, the largest pieces of which she rolled into a ball and put back into her mouth, muttering 'waste not, want not.'

She shook her head, Ivan had given her nothing but trouble for sixty-five long years; she often fantasised about how much better her life could have been had she drowned him in the river like she'd planned. The only ginger baby in the village: he was such an embarrassment. She thought he'd redeemed himself by bringing Oksana into the world, but that turned out to be the worst embarrassment of all.

The Gossipmonger sighed, 'I hope Grunter has gained his satisfaction and comes to let us out soon.' She shuffled from side to side, 'because if he doesn't, I'll be sat on a damp seat...'

Ivan didn't care: his seat was already damp.

Each time she looked at her disgrace of a son, she couldn't stop shaking her head... His beacon of a skull illuminating intermittently by the flickering strip-lights high on the ceiling, combined with his pointy chin, made him look like a flashing red comma. She knew the red dye would wash off after a good scrub with her roughest loofah: he must be the only sixty-five year old in

The Dancing Barber

the world who's still bathed by his mother... She said, 'I know that *you* aren't bothered, but are you sure Grunter won't do anything to harm my dear Oksana?'

Ivan fidgeted inside his hessian sack: he was sure it crawled with fleas. He said, 'Grunt... Gunter likes children; he wants to give them all the opportunities he missed out on when he was a child. He has an orphanage in Kyiv and even has a private hospital, just for children.' He looked reassuringly at his mother, 'Oksana couldn't be in safer hands.'

'Hmmm,' said The Gossipmonger, hoping that if Oksana did end up in an orphanage, it wouldn't be like the other Mafia-run orphanages she had first-hand experience of. A shiver ran down her spine.

Even in the flickering gloom of the taxi, Ivan could see his mother had more goose pimples than a pimply goose: why did he have to mention orphanages? But he knew that of all the Mafia he'd encountered, Gunter was the only good guy. He regretted stealing from him and cursed his greed... If only he could turn the clock back...

The Gossipmonger placed her upper and lower sets together and held the grinning dentures up to the taxi's window. Utilising what little light there was, she meticulously checked that every last fragment of chewing tobacco had been removed; extracting any bits she'd missed by using a strand of her grey hair as dental floss.

She amused herself by opening and closing them as if they were a set of wind-up chattering teeth from a joke shop. Then, much to Ivan's dismay, the teeth proceeded to have a conversation with their reflection in the taxi's window....

'He's behind you...'

'Oh no he isn't...'

'Oh yes he is...'

She could see in the corner of her eye that Ivan was twitching away with annoyance, so she persisted with her dental Punch & Judy show for quite some time, wondering how long it would be before he snapped...

Eventually she became bored with her childish antics and gave her dentures a final polish by rubbing them vigorously on the sleeve of her overcoat until they were so white that they could have been plucked from Mr Edd's mouth. She slotted them back onto her gums, making the clicking sound that never failed to make Ivan cringe. She said despondently, 'I don't know what possessed you to marry,' she could barely bring herself to utter the name, ' *"Zena"* in the first place?'

Ivan stared at his mother, 'why do you say that?'

The Gossipmonger raised her eyebrows and said, 'why do you think? Because she's uglier than a wart hog's backside, and smells worse than the stuff that comes out of it! That's why!'

'No,' Ivan said, shaking his head, 'that *can't* be Zena. She is an attractive girl: when I last saw her, she had plaited hair and freckles.'

'That must have been a *long* time ago... Now she has greasy hair and blackheads! And she and her equally hideous twin sister have *absolutely* no dress sense! When I saw them, they both wore badly fitting nylon suits and scuffed army boots: that's no way for ladies to dress! They looked like a pair of goons! And they wore red socks! They couldn't even be bothered to wear headscarves. At least a headscarf would stop the grease from their hair dripping onto their shoulders: they produce enough between them to fry several portions of chips in!'

'Army boots?' Ivan said, recollecting the pair he'd seen while tied up on the drawing room carpet. 'Red socks?'

'So as far as I'm concerned, the sooner you divorce that horrible woman, the better! Give her whatever she wants! Give her half your money, give her all your money: if there's any left?' She said with a nod, 'just make sure you are rid of her for good!'

Ivan muttered, 'army boots... Red socks... So that was *her*?' He sighed: it seemed he might have to apologise to the Colonel, if he ever had the misfortune of seeing him again. He thought: *but why would Zena treat me so roughly? Surely she should know that I would never harm her again...* He crossed his legs... *what she did to me last time was more than a sufficient deterrent. But what if – even after all these years – the woman was as thirsty for revenge as she was for samahon?* His eyes watered at the prospect.

Having only just cleaned her teeth, The Gossipmonger was determined to dirty them again; she rummaged in amongst the clutter within her handbag and pulled out her last packet of chewing tobacco, inserting a chocolate bar-sized chunk between her dentures.

The Dancing Barber

Ivan tried to close his mind to the cringe-worthy sounds of his mother's clicking teeth and squelching mastications, averting his eyes from the camel beside him who moved the saliva-soaked substance around her mouth as if she was chewing the cud.

And he didn't need to look at her to know what she was going to do next: without a spittoon, she slid open the overflowing ashtray affixed to the door and spat in its general direction. Ivan knew she'd miss – she always did – so it didn't surprise him when he felt the slimy phlegm creep like a slug down his bare leg. She didn't even apologise, and did it another twice, before stuffing more of the ghastly substance into her mouth. He couldn't look further away from her if he tried.

After what seemed to Ivan like hours of chewing, The Gossipmonger went through the rigmarole of cleaning her dentures again. At this rate, every square inch of the taxi's interior would soon be coated with her slimy tobacco. And if – as he feared, deep down – this taxi was to be their home for the next few months, the sooner the old hag treated it as such, the better.

Once again polishing her dentures on her sleeve, she sighed, 'you were such a wonderful child...' She then cleared her throat, missing the ashtray as usual, 'and you'd do *everything* to please your Mama...' She shrugged her shoulders, 'what went wrong?'

Ivan rolled his eyes and thought: *here we go again.*

'I'll tell you what went wrong! You were too greedy for your own good.' She hawked up another mouthful and spat to the floor, 'I didn't mind it when you were disloyal to Ukraine: there was no point in being a poor Ukrainian when you could just as easily become a rich Soviet.'

'Mama,' Ivan tried to interrupt, but his mother wouldn't let him.

'I even turned a blind eye to your betrayal of that innocent family in Chaplinka: they were decent people, stubbornly standing up for what they believed in and suffering terribly because of it. And why did you betray them? To line your own pockets!' She poked him with her club, 'that's why! Oh the shame of it!'

'Hang on a minute! Not even Stanislaw thought he'd find a stash of Voloshin's propaganda leaflets in their house! As you know, their harsh treatment was entirely their own fault! There was nothing I could do about it, even if I'd wanted to.' Ivan crossed his legs the other way... Zena had enacted her own brand of revenge when – years later – she'd discovered that he was one of Stanislaw's Privates... Never before had he suffered such pain.

'I don't believe a word you say,' said The Gossipmonger. 'And I no longer wish to speak to someone who is stupid enough to steal money! How dare you not tell me where it came from?'

Ivan glared at his mother. He said, 'don't call me stupid, you old hag! You were never bothered where the money came from, just so long as it kept coming!'

The Gossipmonger screamed, 'how dare you speak to me like that!' She put her sixty-five year old son across her knees and smacked him viciously until she ran out of energy.

Neither of them noticed the faint sound of laughter coming from a hatch in the wall.

'But it's true,' said Ivan, ignoring the stinging pain in his buttocks. 'You said it yourself... You *didn't* care where the money came from!'

Ivan regretted answering his mother back when she smacked him harder than ever, using the leather straps of her handbag as a make-do whip. He was at least grateful that nobody was watching.

The Gossipmonger was soon exhausted with all the effort. After a brief pause, she gave him a few more lashes for good measure. 'If we ever get out of here,' she screamed, 'I <u>never</u> want to see you again!'

Ivan scrambled away and hid behind the hessian sack, shielding his head from the onslaught of his mother's handbag and swinging club. He stopped himself from crying. He said, 'so what if I stole it? Gunter p-promised that money to me, but when one of his schemes went belly up, he refused to p-pay me, even after all the risks I'd taken. I only took what I was owed... not a p-penny more.'

'Grunter doesn't seem to think so,' The Gossipmonger said, massaging her sore club. 'Otherwise we wouldn't be held prisoners in this stinking taxi, would we?' She spat to the floor.

Ivan waved his hand dismissively at his mother and looked away. He muttered, 'it wouldn't be h-half as s-smelly if you'd stop s-spitting all over the place!'

The Gossipmonger was about to spit in her son's face when suddenly the ground began to move violently from side to side.

The Dancing Barber

'What's happening?' she said.

'I don't know?' Ivan said, watching the garage walls tremble and the taxi wobble about on its bouncy suspension. 'It feels like we're having an earthquake...? But they don't have earthquakes in this country...?'

Then all the lights went out.

Chapter 75

After the curtains had closed following the second encore, Mr Taras exhaled a calming sigh of relief... he desperately hoped the audience wouldn't want a third... His back was in agony from the harness and despite Natalka's Tato's calcium carbonate, his chest still felt exceptionally tight... he'd had indigestion many times before, but it had never been as bad as this...

He looked down on his daughter and said, 'thank you Sofia, I am very proud of you!' He kissed her gently on the forehead just before the cardboard gave way and the crown clouted the Swan Queen's nose for the first time since last Sunday.

That instant, Sofia experienced a feeling she'd never had before... she thought it may have been happiness... *He said thank you... He said he was proud of me...* But it didn't last long... the sharp twinge in her freshly relocated shoulder swiftly brought her back to reality... she couldn't wait to go home.

Mr Taras placed Sofia's crown gently back in position and then turned to face the other dancers, who remained in their three neat rows, stood in height order as required, some stretching their exhausted backs, others massaging their sore bunions. He smiled genuinely, 'thank you for all your hard work: the success of *Swan Lake* is as much down to your perseverance as it is to my talent for choreography.'

Not one of the dancers blinked: *was that a compliment from Mr Taras?*

Mr Taras' smile was even broader, 'and now, I have a <u>special</u> surprise for you!'

The older girls were very worried when he slipped his hand inside his bulge and rummaged around. Thankfully all that emerged was a folded sheet of paper, saturated with plenty of sweat.

'Here is a cheque for *fifty* pounds,' he announced proudly, displaying it for all to see, being careful not to smudge the ink. 'This is the advanced payment from the television people for agreeing to appear on "Showtime" next month.' He looked

The Dancing Barber

lovingly at the piece of paper, 'isn't it wonderful?'

'"Showtime",' screamed one of the girls.

'That's my favourite programme,' cried another.

'I never miss it! And we're going to be on it?' shrieked yet another.

'Indeed you are,' said Mr Taras, permitting the interruptions on this occasion. 'Didn't I tell you that if you worked hard, you'd be rich and famous? And this is only the start of things to come!' He hid the cheque in amongst the rolled up socks. 'As a gesture of appreciation, I plan to divide this money equally between us all!'

The girls gasped with amazement: this wasn't the Mr Taras they were used to. Had aliens abducted him and replaced him with an impostor? No, only the real Mr Taras would wear a bulge of such epic proportions.

Sofia tugged at her Tato's billowing white sleeve, 'who'll get Oksana's share?'

'Err,' said Mr Taras, 'I will put it to one side and will give it to her if, err... when I next see her.'

The dancers hoped the heifer would never return; and if she didn't, they knew precisely what would become of her share of the money.

'So as a special treat,' Mr Taras said, rubbing his hands together gleefully, 'you can all have tomorrow morning off! But...' He waited for the cheering to stop, 'rehearsals for *Sleeping Beauty* start at five pm sharp!'

The gasps of amazement were instantly replaced by groans of the deepest displeasure. The dancers knew they'd spoken too soon: this *was* the Mr Taras they knew. The remainder of the Easter holidays weren't going to be holidays after all... It would have been nice to give the bunions a rest.

'Don't give me that look,' said Mr Taras, upon discovering nearly all of his dancers' upper lips had creased upwards, as if imitating Elvis. He said, 'don't forget that it was me who convinced the Priest to let you off attending church this morning! He was most angry – it being St Thomas' Sunday – but he agreed, just so you could have a lie-in before the final performance.'

'And we're very grateful,' said Sofia. She looked at the other dancers, 'aren't we, girls?'

They all gave the briefest of nods, muttering, 'yeah...

grateful...'

Natalka hobbled over on her crutches and asked, 'Mr Taras, who was St Thomas? And why is today his day?'

Mr Taras said, 'please Natalka, it's not good to show your ignorance...'

Natalka bent down to Sofia's ear and whispered, 'he doesn't know, does he?'

Sofia smiled, 'of course not...'

Mr Taras was about to dismiss his exhausted troupe when Mrs Wiggins' husband shouted: 'Not yet!' gesturing behind the curtain, 'they want a third encore!'

So the three lines of dancers all linked hands and curtseyed lingeringly in front of rapturous applause that sounded as if it would never end. Mr Taras, of course, was the only one who took a bow... The tightness in his chest returned when he bent to the floor... but now it was more than tightness... it was pain.

Across the auditorium, only two figures didn't stand up; there was a circle of empty seats surrounding them. Although Mr Taras was glad the Stage Manager had forgiven Zena and Lenka for tying a metal clothes rail around his neck, and had allowed them to enter the theatre, he was surprised to find that he'd positioned them on the front row of the exclusive Dress Circle, where – in their usual attire – they seemed to have spent the whole evening sucking the sugar from sugared almonds and spitting the slobbery nuts back into the paper bag.

Natalka had been watching this disgusting display; she hobbled over to Sofia, stooped down and asked, 'that bag of almonds you gave me? Where did you say you got it from?'

'Why do you ask?'

Natalka pointed at the two sucking and spitting machines up on the Dress Circle. She said, 'please tell me they *didn't* come from your aunties...'

Sofia squirmed, 'but how was I to know they'd already sucked them?' A furrow appeared across her brow, 'I wondered why they tasted funny?'

Natalka muttered, 'bleeding hell,' before she hobbled to the lavatory, feeling extremely unwell.

Once the curtains had closed, Mr Taras pranced over to Sofia

The Dancing Barber

and asked, 'what's up with her?'

'I'm afraid its Zena and Lenka; they've upset her…'

'I quite understand,' said Mr Taras, 'the sight of them makes me feel unwell too. But they'll be going home soon. I hope.'

Sofia truly felt sorry for her best friend: Natalka had devoured an entire bag of those sucked nuts. She hoped Natalka hadn't caught anything nasty… Zena and Lenka probably harboured bacteria that had yet to be discovered by medical science. Her Tato was right: the women should have been put in quarantine before being let loose on the streets of England, or better still, they should have been sent straight back to Chaplinka.

Mr Taras turned to his dancers. But they'd already disbanded, heading straight for the changing rooms for a blessed sit down; and in the case of the older girls, a much needed cigarette on the fire escape. He clapped his hands sharply, stopping them in their tracks.

They turned lethargically to face their Ballet Master, hoping that whatever he had to say would be brief and didn't involve taking up any more of their holiday.

With the broadest of grins, Mr Taras said, 'as a special thank you, I invite you and your families to my house for a meal of celebration, understand? Once we've all got changed, we shall head up the road for a feast to remember!'

Although appreciative of Mr Taras' uncharacteristic act of kindness, the dancers would have much preferred to have gone home… they were sick of the sight of him.

Sofia smirked: she knew her Mama had read his note instructing her to prepare a celebratory meal. She also knew that her Mama had screwed it up and thrown it in the bin, insisting she was still on strike. It certainly would be a feast to remember...

With most of his things already packed up, Taras only had to get changed out of his costume before leading his triumphant troupe to their well-deserved banquet. He draped his billowing white shirt and tights over the changing screen, humming a jolly tune. And with much relief, he unstrapped his bulge and also hung it over the changing screen, from which it promptly fell to the floor with a thud.

He wondered what Halyna had prepared for them: whatever it was, it would be a treat, especially after all that fish and chips and "stew of the meat". He scooped up his costume, squeezed it into his leatherette case, put on his blue blazer and skipped out of the door.

Catnip is to cats as Taras' bulge is to hamsters. For unbeknown to him, Brenda the hamster, after spending days scurrying around beneath the stage, had decided to revisit the nice warm nest it had occupied after that fat girl had taken it from its cage... It had crawled in, curled up in amongst the rolled up socks and fallen asleep...

The Dancing Barber
Chapter 76

'*Na zdorovya!*' Halyna said, raising her steaming cup of Lapsang Souchon.

'And the same to you,' said Klem, clinking his cup with Halyna's.

Klem held the cup to his nose and wallowed in the delicate aroma, despite the tobacco fog of the Uki Club bar. His pencils of a moustache looked as though they belonged to Salvador Dali, almost pointing to the ceiling, which wasn't surprising, considering the source of his new pot of moustache wax... Did Zena have *any* idea about hygiene? He'd have to have a serious talk with her... if he dared...

He smiled at Halyna, and couldn't believe how happy she looked. He said, 'I bet you're glad it's finally all over...'

'Pardonski?' asked Halyna, leaning in closer, allowing Klem to repeat what he'd said. 'Glad?' she said, 'that's an understatement... I'm overjoyed! But as you know, this is only the start...' She sipped her delicious tea, still finding it impossible to detect the delicate pinewood smoke flavour Klem always went on about. 'At least Taras' attitude is improving, slowly. But there's no way I'm ending my strike yet: I want to know how dirty and hungry he has to be before he starts fending for himself... Only *then* will he realise how hard I work around the house!'

'Good on you,' Klem clinked cups again. 'And let's hope all goes well with "Showtime", because if it doesn't...' He raised his eyebrows and sipped his tea.

'I'm sure everything will be goodski,' Halyna said, crossing her fingers. 'He wanted fame, and now he's got it.'

Klem knew that Taras found fame once before, and when it came to the crunch, he hated being centre of attention. Only time would tell if history was set to repeat itself... Klem's stomach started to groan; looking hopefully at Halyna's handbag, he said, 'I don't suppose you've got anything to munch?'

Halyna shook her head, 'sorry, food is the last thing on my mind... I've had such a terrible stomach ache today. It's nothing to worry about, it just happens sometimes.'

'I didn't think you still suffered from stomach problems?'

'Afraid so... Recently, I've had a lot of trouble with my digestion.'

Klem raised his eyebrows, and said 'a-ha...'

Halyna shook her head, 'no, it's nothing to do with Zena and Lenka's "stew"... I hardly ate any of it.'

'Have you seen a doctor?'

Halyna nodded, 'for what good it did... He said there was nothing that could be done... It's not the sort of thing that can be reversed. Reducing the amount of roughage I eat is about all I can do to alleviate it.'

Klem exhaled loudly through his nostrils, his pencils of a moustache quivering before his eyes. He said, 'those Germans didn't have a clue about what they were doing...'

'It wasn't their fault; my doctor said the operation was very common in the forties...' Halyna shrugged, 'it was a pity they had to remove so much of my stomach...'

'Mmm,' said Klem, 'perhaps you're right... if anyone's to blame, it's the Soviets. If it wasn't for them, you wouldn't have had to eat leather and tree bark for all those years.' He clenched a fist, 'what they did makes me so angry...'

'Forget it,' said Halyna, 'it's time to stop living in the past.'

Klem nodded, albeit reluctantly. He'd been living in the past for so long that he didn't know what to do in the present, especially with Zena now back in his life.

Halyna swigged the last of her tea, smacking her lips together with satisfaction. She said, 'at least I ate something back in 1933, even if it was only leather and tree bark.' She shook her head, 'it's more than can be said for our prisoner up in the loft...'

Klem shuffled in his seat. 'If it was up to me, Stanislaw wouldn't still be there... But as you know, it isn't...'

Taras couldn't understand why the house was in complete darkness? Why wasn't Halyna in the kitchen making the finishing touches to the post-performance meal of celebration: surely she'd got his note? He'd used nice words and even signed off "with love

The Dancing Barber

and kisses", placing it prominently on her dressing table. Surely she couldn't still be on strike?

So while the millipede of dancers and their families waited outside, kicking their heels and muttering to one another, he went indoors to investigate. Cursing, he unlocked the door to the cold kitchen, the stench of lunchtime's "stew" lingering in the air. The woman's silly strike had gone on for long enough... punishing him privately was one thing, but humiliating him in front of his dancers was not acceptable. He would have to put his foot down! And he still hadn't forgiven her for throwing away his beloved photograph... it wasn't that badly damaged... but she never did like Charlie Chaplinka... And whatever Halyna didn't like, she always got rid of...

And all the business that occurred last Monday with the mythical Stanislaw and the goons was still troubling him. If – as Halyna had alleged – he'd imagined his shop door being kicked in, then why did he have to pay Mrs Wiggins' husband to repaint it and replace the lock that had been picked? He hated being fobbed off... and bizarrely, none of the nosey neighbours saw a thing... not even him with the binoculars. Neither Halyna nor Klem had ever lied to him before, so it must be Zena and Lenka's bad influence... if he ever got to the bottom of it, there'd be trouble...

And if Sofia heard them shouting at a Stanislaw, then that was who they were shouting at... why would she lie? He didn't believe Zena's story about a bungalow. And then there was that fragment of carpet tape stuck to the roof beam, not forgetting the peeping tom's testimony about a pig's carcass being butchered in the attic.

For some reason, he had the word "Vladivostok" in the back of his mind... He must have heard it recently... But where?

As Sofia said, something smelled fishy, and for once, it wasn't only Zena and Lenka...

The twins waddled up alongside him and stared at the cold oven. 'What is the problem?' Zena asked, still out of breath after the brisk walk up the mountain that was "The" Great Horton Road. 'Your dancers, they are hungry for their foods and you are not letting them in?'

Taras ignored her. How was he supposed to prepare a meal on his own? He couldn't even find Sofia to help him... And to make matters worse, the Chippy was closed...

'The surprise...' said Klem, tapping his fingers contemplatively on the table. 'If only I could find the surprise...'

'Not this again,' said Halyna, refilling their cups from a chipped earthenware teapot, 'you've been going on about it for days.' She sipped her tea, finally detecting the faintest hint of burning wood. 'Go on then,' she said, 'tell me your thoughts.'

'Every Fabergé Egg has a surprise... It was Karl's trademark... So mine must have one too... If only I knew what it was meant to be?'

Halyna looked on inquisitively, listening to the expert speak.

'The first one contained a tiny golden chicken, another had a golden model of the Imperial State Coach and another still had a miniature portrait of Alexander III... They were all Easter gifts for his Tsarina, decorated with various shades of gold, each of them exquisitely delicate...'

'It looks like you'll have to do some more research...'

'Mmm, I think I might... Gunter lent me some of his books... I thought I knew everything about the Imperial Easter Eggs. But this one's not mentioned anywhere? It's as if it never existed... But it's definitely genuine... No doubt about it...'

Halyna rested her chin in her hands and settled into her seat.

'You see,' Klem continued, 'when you twist the two hemispheres of my egg in opposite directions: the northern sapphires clockwise, and the southern yellow diamonds anticlockwise, my egg expands to reveal a rose gold collar, inlaid with baguette cut emeralds. But you see, there's a circular space that suggests something is missing. The recess is too deep for a portrait, and why would there be a screw thread? No, it has to be something else... And I just can't think what it could be?'

'It could be a great big diamond... what better gift for a Tsarina? But don't ask me,' said Halyna, 'you're the expert.'

'Of course,' said Klem, 'a diamond...' He straightened the green ribbon at his collar and pulled out the embroidered cuffs from the sleeves of his pinstripe jacket by exactly half an inch. 'If it were complete, and depending on the quality of the diamond, a Fabergé Egg with its provenance would be worth ten times as

The Dancing Barber

much... Maybe up to one hundred thousand pounds... And that would make a real difference for Katya, wouldn't it?'

'It would make a real difference for *all* of us,' Halyna said, remembering Klem had promised her some of the proceeds.

Klem's pocket watch emitted its orchestral chimes, signalling the top of the hour. He said, 'drink up Halyna, it's time to go. We don't want to be late for our meal.'

'Meal?' Halyna asked, hoping Klem hadn't booked a table again. Even without The Gossipmonger, the Gaggle would still enjoy devouring anything that had the remotest chance of being scandalous, even if it was – in her mind at least – perfectly innocent.

'Yes,' said Klem, clearing away the tea things, 'Taras invited everyone home for a meal of celebration now that *Swan Lake* has ended... I wonder what he's cooked.'

'Oh, that...' Halyna grinned. Even with that paycheque burning a hole in his bulge, she doubted he could afford to buy fifty portions of fish and chips...

So it was beans on toast all round, accompanied by a mug of the weakest PG Tips mixed with condensed milk. Being absolutely famished, the dancers were grateful for the meal, especially as the apron-wearing Ballet Master had actually made it himself. And for a first attempt, it wasn't that bad; the white sliced bread was singed in places with the mouldy bits having obviously been pinched out, and he'd somehow managed to burn the beans, but it was edible.

The dancers were glad they came... if not for the food, then certainly for the entertainment... Mr Taras just about had the situation under control, but Sofia's twin aunties tried their best to annoy him... Mr Taras went ballistic when the one called Lenka put Mrs Halyna's new Morphy Richards electric kettle on the roaring flames of the gas hob, and watched it melt faster than one of her ear-wax candles... And after listening to the upstairs toilet flush a dozen times, Mr Taras couldn't believe that the one called Zena had washed her feet in it... Those women were like something from a zoo, picking off each other's fleas, scratching and farting... they couldn't even drink a cup of tea without spilling most of it down – as Natalka referred to them – their udders. Were these women truly related to Sofia?

'Where have you been?' Taras asked when he noticed Sofia and Natalka discretely joining the back of the queue. With the former's arm in a sling and the latter leaning on crutches, it looked as though they'd just returned from battle. He barked, 'why are you late? I *desperately* needed your help! I've had to do this all on my own! Me... a cook!'

Sofia said, 'Natalka and I went to get my Aunties Zena and Lenka a nice present...'

'Oh, I see,' said Taras, 'if you think it's necessary...'

Although she knew precisely what was troubling her Tato, she asked, 'is everything okay?'

Taras threw the wooden spoon into the remaining burned beans and said, 'have you seen your Mama?'

Sofia nodded, 'she's in the Uki Club bar with Klem; they're having some Lapsang Souchon together.'

'Are they now?' Taras said, narrowing his eyes. He thought Klem had stopped having secret tea drinking sessions with Halyna: surely now, he should be drinking tea with Zena? Words would have to be spoken...

But judging by Zena's irate expression, she may well speak to Klem herself. She clenched her fists... the conversation was unlikely to be pleasant...

The next two cremated slices of bread clattered up from the old Breville toaster, prompting Taras to juggle them onto a flat plate, slop some beans on top and serve it to the next girl in the queue. He feigned a smile and said, 'I hope you find it delicious... If you don't, then tough, that's all you're getting! Understand?'

The girl looked at her ration and – despite neither liking toast nor beans – thanked the Ballet Master, who to her was more intimidating than Mr Bumble from Oliver Twist.

Because – much to Zena and Lenka's displeasure – everyone refused unanimously to go anywhere near what was left of the "stew of the meat", those who were still hungry were expected to be grateful for some slices of stale *Paska* and a boiled egg. Taras tried toasting some slices of *Paska*, but they became stuck in the slot so tightly that it took two forks and several minor

The Dancing Barber

electrocutions to extract them. And once they'd been extracted, they were only fit to be used as artist's charcoal. He deduced that cooking was harder than it looked; and warming salami in the toaster slots was far from a good idea... as was boiling eggs in the melted remains of Halyna's electric kettle.

As per tradition, the cook only sat down to eat once every guest had been fed: so accompanied by the background noises of steel scraping against earthenware, Taras finally kicked off his shoes and dropped gratefully to his chair. There weren't any clean forks in the house, so he decided to put the two slices of toast together and crunch his way through a baked-bean sandwich. It always amazed him how delicious such simple food tasted... especially when famished...

He looked up at the depressing void on the wall and sighed: throwing away his Charlie Chaplinka photograph was unforgivable. But at least he still had the mask; Halyna would never throw that away, especially now that it'd been hidden in such a secret place that not even he knew where it was... he just hoped it hadn't been hidden in the dustbin... He glanced at the time on the cheap Chinese pendulum clock on the wall and wondered when Halyna would bother to come home?

He also wondered what possessed Sofia to waste money on buying Zena and Lenka a present; unless it was a vat of industrial strength soap, they needn't have bothered.

He shouted over to his daughter, who was one-handedly chasing a baked bean around her plate, 'have you put ice-cream on your shoulder yet?'

'Just doing it now,' Sofia replied, reaching for a Fresh Fair bag of frozen peas; it would be much less messy.

Taras delved into his pocket, expecting to find the little strip of paper that was his biggest ever paycheque. After a brief panic, he remembered the precious cheque was in his ballet underpants... a place where it was perfectly safe. He took another bite from his bean sandwich, feeling the charcoal grate down his throat. He was fed up of eating rubbish... if only he'd remembered their wedding anniversary...

He also regretted promising to split the fee amongst his dancers: it could only be put down to overexcitement. He had a much better use for the money; besides, those silly girls would only waste it on

Beatles records and mini-skirts.

He checked the time on the cheap Chinese pendulum clock on the wall, and wondered how much longer the dancers and their families were going to stay. They'd finished their meals ages ago, so why were they still hanging around? Short of ordering them to go home, he had no idea how to get rid of his guests politely? Perhaps a more subtle approach was needed... Zena and Lenka had eaten so many beans that it was only a matter of time before the stench in the kitchen became unbearable... hopefully that should do the trick...?

And didn't those girls chat such utter rubbish? Why couldn't they discuss the ballet, instead of the usual subjects of boys, bras and Beatles? He really worried about the intelligence of the next generation. At least his Sofia was different: she always preferred Chopin to popular music... she wouldn't dream of polluting her ears with the dreadful noise purveyed by those mop-headed Liverpudlians, or that white-toothed Cliff Richard. And it was this sort of music that put off Taras from watching "Val Parnell's Sunday Night at the London Palladium". The programme was in desperate need of an injection of culture... therefore, providing his dancers did a good job on "Showtime", it was to be his next target. He rubbed his hands together at the thought of earning even more *proper* money.

When Halyna and Klem ambled in from the yard, Taras inhaled a deep lungful of cool night air: the smells of cremated toast, burnt beans and sweaty ballerinas, not forgetting their mothball-infused entourage and the twins' pungent flatulence were all too briefly refreshed before the door closed again.

He watched as Halyna bid Klem good night and went straight to bed, choosing to ignore the mess in her kitchen. She also ignored her husband, even though he'd called after her, and said, 'thank you *so* much for preparing tonight's meal of celebration...' a fact that hadn't gone unnoticed by the headscarves.

Taras tore away the idiotic apron, throwing it to one side: what more could he do to make Halyna happy? Surely giving her the deeds to the house was better than a normal anniversary present; but did she appreciate it? No! All she'd said was, 'I see...' before wandering off without bothering to thank him. Searching for his cigarettes, he knew precisely who caused his wife's uncharacteristic behaviour. Something would *have* to be said... but maybe not tonight. He yawned... it was too late, and he was too tired for an altercation.

He watched as Klem went to sit next to Zena and – holding his breath – whispered something in her waxy ear. Occasionally, Klem pointed to the ceiling and seemingly made several suggestions, each of which Zena turned down, shaking her head so vigorously that dandruff scattered far and wide.

The cheap Chinese pendulum clock struck midnight, and much to Taras' delight, the dancers and their entourages were ready to leave. With the kitchen door wide open, the air was blessedly clearing...

On their way out, the headscarves muttered amongst themselves, looked at Taras, then muttered some more. They then looked at Klem and "the Zena woman", disgusted by all the gossip they'd heard, the source of which was probably their own imaginations. But they certainly didn't imagine the sound of smashing glass... the twins' distillery having exploded in the attic, the ancient equipment unable to cope with their demanding production schedule... They'd already drawn up a contract to supply the inebriated barman with the Robert Mitchum eyes (for his own personal consumption).

Taras smirked... the headscarves may have disapproved of "moonshine" production, on account of it being illegal in England, but they all recognised the sound of an exploding distillery quickly enough... A Ukrainian household without an illicit distillery was akin to an English household without a kettle.

But this was only a minor distraction... the headscarves soon resumed their gossip:

'Fancy Halyna not saying "good night" to her own husband...'
'She completely ignored him, didn't she?'
'Something's not right...'
'It was only a matter of time...'
'They'll be divorced before you know it...'
'And he'll only have himself to blame.'

Paying no attention to the gossiping headscarves, Taras said good night to Klem and Zena – who were still arguing at the table – and poured himself a glass of samahon. When they ignored him for the second time, he went up to his bedroom, taking the bottle with him.

The washing up could wait until morning, if he could be bothered... It never failed to amaze him how his wife's attitude could ruin an otherwise perfect day.

'I want to know where you have the been all this time?' Zena said, somehow folding her arms across her flabby bosom. 'I expected you back the two hours ago.'

Klem felt as if he'd just been reprimanded by the Headmistress. He said, 'a-ha, so it's going to be like this from now on, is it? You always questioning my whereabouts?'

'The wife, she must always know the whereabouts of the husband,' Zena said, unfolding her arms and hammering the tabletop with her index finger. 'I will not be making the same mistakes with you as I made with The Ginger Rasputin. When we are the married, I am the boss!'

'A-ha, I see: *you* will be the boss.'

'Correct,' Zena said with a nod. 'And from now on, if you want to go and drink the tea with anyone, you drink it with me!' She extended the third finger of her right hand and thrust it in front of Klem's face. She said, 'see this? Halyna, she has the ring on this finger. That means that she should be drinking the tea with Taras. And when you buy me the ring for the finger, you will only ever drink the tea with me!'

Klem breathed out harshly through his nose. He said, 'you make it sound as if "drinking tea" was some kind of euphemism... Well, it isn't – I assure you – I simply like to meet my friends to have a good conversation over a delicious cup of tea. And once we're married, that will not change.'

'We shall the see,' Zena said, trying to fold her arms again, wondering what a "You-Femism" was.

Klem wound his pocket watch the usual seven times, the clicking of the ratchet calming his mind. He'd planned on heading into town tomorrow in search of a suitable wedding ring. But now he decided not to bother. He didn't mind being told what to do, but the tone of Zena's voice really bothered him. In fact, quite a lot of things she did bothered him... he had a type-written list pinned up next to his desk. Just as he thought she'd stopped talking, her mouth reopened once again...

'Where could that horrible man have taken our Oksanochka?' Zena said for the hundredth time today, whilst continuing to pick various ghastly things from up her nose, lining them up on the kitchen table.

So for the hundredth time, Klem sighed, 'I've asked my friends to keep an eye out for her: I'm sure she won't have gone too far. Remember, neither Ivan nor The Gossipmonger have passports... it's only a matter of time before they turn up.' He looked at the table and cringed, 'do you have to do that?'

'Do what?' she said, arranging her pickings into neat ranks.

'It doesn't matter,' Klem said, thinking there'd soon be enough pieces of snot to make an entire chess set. 'Have faith, Oksana won't have gone far. All we can do is wait...'

'But I am fed up of the wait,' said Zena, brushing the snots to the carpet with one sweep of her hand. She stormed up to the attic, grunting and muttering...

Mister Pushkin shook as if he were a dog emerging from a river, the fragments of green snot that hadn't adhered to his blue fur, flicking away in every direction. The cat made a mental note never to sit near that woman again.

'Waiting is all you can do,' shouted Klem, running after Zena, leaving Lenka on her own at the kitchen table, where she examined her armpits with far too much interest.

Sofia and Natalka had just waved goodbye to the last dancer, closed the door and immediately set their sights on their target.

'Auntie Lenka,' Sofia said with a glint in her eye, 'would you like one of my chocolates?'

Lenka gave up trying to understand why the hair beneath her arms felt so firm, even after copious use of that most wonderful "de-odour-ant" called Silvikrin Hairspray. She turned to her niece and said, 'I would very much like the chocolates; thank you! It will take away the disgusting taste of Taras' burnt bread and mushy beans...'

Sofia smirked... at least the hatred of each other's "cooking" was mutual...

Natalka nudged Sofia on the arm and asked, 'are they what I think they are?'

Sofia nodded, 'super strength.' She put a finger to her lips, 'don't say a word.'

Lenka liked the chocolates so much that she took a further nine bars up to the attic. With an overfull mouth, she said, 'Sofia, you can the buy me as many as you want: the chocolates, they are the delicious!'

Natalka narrowed her eyes, 'how long do you think it'll take?'

Sofia shrugged her shoulders, 'the woman's got the constitution of an ox; so I reckon it'll be a few hours. But when she goes off, it'll be spectacular…'

Natalka giggled, 'let's hope they don't have to evacuate the street…'

The Dancing Barber

Act 6

✂

A Normal Day

> 'See how the farmer waits for the land to yield its valuable crop and how patient he is for the autumn and spring rains.'
>
> James 5:7

Chapter 77

Stanislaw didn't know why his people still used chains and handcuffs when carpet tape, at a fraction of the price, was just as impossible to escape from; especially when used to bind a prisoner's ankles and wrists behind his back...

The tape the Zena woman had used may have been stickier than fly-paper and stronger than steel, but after a great deal of tugging and twisting, not only were his wrists able to rotate freely, but they were also painfully plucked of all their hair. However, any attempt to stretch the tape so as to wiggle a hand free only served to roll it at the edges and make it as sharp as cheese-wire. The damp feeling and the smell of rust told him to stop struggling; he didn't want to wear away any more skin. He was utterly despondent, and repeatedly bashed his chin on the wooden joist, the week's stubble grating harshly on the rough-sawn wood.

It was so dark in the dusty loft that he'd completely lost track of how long he'd been there; day and night were indistinguishable. And without his analgesics, he couldn't think clearly, the pain exacerbated by his sore rump being wedged against a hot water pipe that never seemed to cool down. He was dangerously close to giving up, but somehow found the strength to persevere...

Those smelly peasants didn't know who they were messing with. They thought he was a Colonel of the Soviet Secret Police... but he never pledged allegiance to that idiot Khrushchev. Everyone had forgotten that the delightful "Comrade President" was himself a Ukrainian, so would obviously sympathise with his own people. The Motherland did not need such a weak president... but that would soon change. His organisation was much more powerful than the so-called "Vlads" and was poised to overthrow the Kremlin when the time was right. And Voloshin's unexpected reincarnation would prove useful... When his organisation succeeds, where Khrushchev and the "Vlads" failed, it will demonstrate to his fellow Soviet citizens precisely who should be running their beloved Soviet Union... But without its leader at the helm, his organisation's apparatus could only stall. And he

The Dancing Barber

was painfully aware that none of his people knew where he was, and even if they did, they wouldn't be able to do anything to help him.

"Give him a taste of his own medicine" were the Zena woman's words... he knew he was to remain in this dusty loft until he was starving like the Ukrainians were during The Great Famine. But he wasn't a feeble peasant: his entire body was like a camel's hump, he could survive for months without eating... Nevertheless, after only a week, he felt ravenously hungry... all he could do was drift in and out of consciousness, and dream about occupying the Presidential office in the Kremlin...

Stanislaw awoke to the sound of stomping footsteps in the attic below, followed by the juddering of a table being dragged across the carpet until it was positioned directly beneath the loft hatch. A pair of heavy feet slammed, one by one, onto the tabletop followed by the rasping sound of breaking wind. He reckoned it was the Zena woman come to check he wasn't dead.

His suspicions were confirmed when a gorilla paw thrust open the hatch and crawled towards him. The light flooding in through the square opening was so bright that he squinted his eye... But then darkness slowly descended when the Zena woman hauled her ample bosoms, one by one, into the loft, agitating the dust into swirling clouds that would have made him sneeze, had his nose and mouth not been covered with tape.

As the dust settled, he took the time to assess the geography of his surroundings. He noticed the loft was about the size of a bivouac tent and he was lying on a board that bridged the gap between two chunky wooden joists. Insulating material was spread out in the gaps between the joists, beneath which he believed, would be the ceiling of the attic rooms below: as a last resort, he planned to roll into one of these gaps and fall straight through the ceiling... but he couldn't guarantee what he'd land on... He observed the apex of the roof, hopeful of spotting an alternative escape route, but decided that even if he was able to sit up, there wasn't the room to... He considered head-butting the rafters and trying to dislodge enough roof tiles to create a hole for his body to squeeze through; but then he'd be stranded on the roof with a forty-foot drop down to the street... No, there had to be a better way...

As the woman's enormous gorilla arm reached towards him, he hoped she was going to remove the gag from his mouth. He could then practice his acting skills by pleading for her mercy: he knew the woman was soft in the head... after listening to him whine, she was bound to release him... and when she did, he'd strike...

But instead, she shoved the sharp point of a knitting needle deeply into a most unfortunate place, making him squeal like a scalded pig and confirm to her that he was indeed still alive.

'The pity,' she said, before slamming a small glass of water onto the joist in front of him. She hawked up a mouthful of phlegm and spat in the glass, the green frogspawn floating disgustingly on the surface. She said, 'the drink, Soviet swine!'

She laughed, perforated him with the knitting needle once again, and then, after unwedging her bosoms, disappeared through the hatch. But the loft hadn't plunged back into the darkness he'd expected: the hatch was still slightly open... if only his hands were free...

Being trussed up like a hog roast, he could only watch as the liquid he craved so much – regardless of the frogspawn – evaporated slowly and even claimed the life of a moth that had drowned in it. The insect floated on the surface with its legs in the air; he wondered what it tasted like? He reminded himself to be patient... soon enough he'd know how to escape...

After a while, he noticed a long, thin, glistening object in front of him. He focussed his eye and realised the Zena woman had dropped her knitting needle: how stupid those peasants were. If only he could reach it, he'd be able to use it to pierce the carpet tape and would be free in minutes...

He tried to wriggle closer to the hatch, shuffling his stomach and chest alternately from side to side, as if he were an enormous purple manatee. But no matter how slowly he moved, the joists creaked louder than ever. So as silently as possible, he rolled onto one side and waited until the Zena woman left the attic... *Hurry up and go!* He'd never heard a woman burp and fart as much... And although she was probably combing her hair, it sounded more like leaves being raked up...

Stanislaw tuned his ears into the sounds on the roof tiles above. But it wasn't the usual tap-dancing crows; this animal was lighter on its feet, or should that be paws?

He sneered when he realised the poet's cat was paying him another visit, squeezing itself through the smallest of gaps in the darkness of the eaves... *So that's how it gets in...* The cat then padded its way across the joists, placing one paw in front of the other, its ears folded flat, its tail hoisted up in the air and its molten eyes fixed on its target. Stanislaw closed his eye just before his face received a thorough dousing as the cat zigzagged its stream from his cheek to his forehead and back, three times.

Hopeful the cat had gone away, his eye re-opened cautiously... Unfortunately, the cat's furry behind was all he could see: and it delivered a perfectly aimed squirt. At least none of it got into his mouth: he may have been thirsty, but he would never be *that* thirsty.

Satisfied with its work, the cat sauntered off with its nose in the air. It stopped and examined the gap in the loft hatch, sniffing at the air rising through it. It listened as the Zena woman lumbered downstairs, each step creaking under the strain. The woman then exchanged several angry words with a man, who'd skipped upstairs, prompting her to break wind discontentedly, which in turn prompted him to call her a 'human stink-bomb'.

Stanislaw watched the cat place a careful paw on the hatch, checking if it would take its weight. He tried to shoo it away, but as usual, it ignored him. When a second paw made contact with the hatch, Stanislaw could only curse when the cat disappeared with a loud, 'Mrryaw!'

'Cooking Fat!' bellowed an authoritarian voice from the attic below. 'Is there nowhere in this house where I can have some peace?'

Taking advantage of the tumult, the purple manatee wriggled over to the hatch. Squinting at the bright daylight, he saw a grey-haired man repeatedly shout 'Cooking Fat' at the animal that had landed on his head and clung on with all four of its paws; it reminded Stanislaw of his favourite Captain's hat with the furry ear flaps. The cat then leapt to the floor, its claws almost tearing the carpet to shreds as it scuttled downstairs.

Stanislaw allowed himself a little chuckle, especially when the grey-haired man prattled on and on: 'I come up to <u>my</u> attic for a snooze, and what happens? The ceiling falls on me and I get mauled by the Cooking Fat again! The sooner Klem and those women leave, the happier I'll be!'

Stanislaw thought: *Where have I seen this man before... His voice is so familiar...* He leaned out further for a closer look, *No... it can't be? The Dancing Barber...?*

He then glimpsed the Fabergé Egg, which Klem had insisted was fake, sat twinkling on the cluttered mantelpiece. He knew it was real and was determined to add it to his collection... it was one of the few he didn't already own, and hoped it was complete...

When he saw the grey-haired man pick up the loft hatch, he wriggled quickly into the shadows, listening as the table juddered across the carpet and two feet thudded onto the tabletop.

Holding the knitting needle firmly in one hand, he wondered whether the time to escape was *now...*

The Dancing Barber
Chapter 78

Taras could barely look at his dishevelled reflection in the bedroom mirror... He'd worn the same shirt for three days, its collar, singed from his failed attempt at ironing it; its cuffs, stained with tobacco; and its armpits, luminous with sweat. His trousers looked like he'd slept in them – which he had – and his underwear didn't bear thinking about.

His face may not have been wrinkled, but it looked a little gaunt... He hadn't had a decent meal in over a week, refusing to class beans on toast as anything approaching a *decent* meal. And his hair was greyer than ever; he dare not risk dying it without Halyna's assistance, unless he felt like auditioning for the *Minstrel Show*.

And to top it off – thanks to that Cooking Fat – his scalp was covered with scratches...

Because he wasn't used to getting up before sunrise, he'd sneaked up to the attic for a half-hour snooze after returning from his clandestine trip to town. Snuggled up on his reproduction Eames chair, his feet resting on the matching PVC-clad footstool, he calmed his whirring mind, and felt exceptionally pleased with himself.

He'd only just nodded off, when the loft hatch came crashing down, the cat riding it as if it were a surf board, before leaping straight at him, landing on his head, kneading his hair with its sharp claws. He hated that Cooking Fat: it was determined to give him a heart attack... and one day it'd succeed. He also hated heights, so was glad to have nailed the loft hatch back in place without falling off the rickety table. It didn't bother him that the loft reeked of over-boiled cabbage... in fact, the whole attic was rather whiffy, with an ailing Lenka still curled up in bed, rumbling away beneath the sheets. At least Zena had the courtesy to get out of his way... He told her to go and rake her greasy hair outside, and was most insistent she wiped her oily comb on something other than his artificial silk curtains...

With his walls perforated with rusty nails, his pristine carpet polka-dotted with bleach, and his curtains smeared with hair grease, his only possession that hadn't been ruined was his beloved PVC-covered Eames chair. But even that wasn't comfortable enough to fall asleep on...

Desperately needing some proper shut-eye, he had no choice but to go back to his own bedroom with its grimy pyjamas and unwashed sheets...

So after an hour of relatively restful sleep, Taras awoke, hopeful that it would have done him at least some good... But his dishevelled, gaunt and greying reflection suggested otherwise... He couldn't look at it any more.

Taras slid open his wardrobe's mirrored door, and sighed at the solitary hanger on the rail. What was the world coming to when the baggy-sleeved sky-blue shirt and yellow tights – his costume for tomorrow's performance of *Sleeping Beauty* – were the only clean clothes he possessed? At least he'd look like Prince Charming, despite feeling like a dirty tramp...

Now he realised why all those concerned-looking people in the street gave him money on the way back from town first thing this morning. He didn't mind: the three pounds, four shillings and sixpence would go towards his cigarette fund...

He'd braved the fetid stench of the abattoir, which in Bradford was the harbinger of a fine afternoon, to purchase two wonderful gifts, paying an extra shilling to have them professionally gift-wrapped. He imagined the joy on Halyna and Sofia's faces when they eventually opened their eyes after their well-deserved lie-ins and found his gifts placed lovingly by their beds...

Squinting at the bright morning sunshine flooding into his cobwebbed bedroom, Taras knew his gifts would not only coax Halyna back to the housework, but would also prove to Sofia how proud he was of her... Sofia must have been devastated when she found out he'd been pretending Natalka was his daughter, and yet she still chose to save his life yesterday... He would never forget it.

After using a Remington electric shaver to grind the stubble from his jaws, he slapped on a generous amount of aftershave from the Eiffel Tower bottle, combed his greying hair into place and

The Dancing Barber

inserted his pearly-white dentures that gave him the smile of Gene Kelly. He would have spent longer admiring his improved appearance, but Lenka had obviously used his mirror when squeezing her plentiful pimples, thus splattering it thoroughly with yellowy-green pus... In her pathetic attempt to wipe it clean, she produced her very own hômage to Jackson Pollock. From now on, he'd be locking his bedroom door.

When the nine am chimes from the cheap plastic pendulum clock in the kitchen echoed up the stairs, Taras decided he was finally ready to face the day. So – wearing yesterday's clothes, which he'd laid under his mattress in a half-hearted attempt to press out some of the creases – he stepped onto the landing and stumbled straight into the wicker washing basket, knocking it over and cascading grimy clothes down the stairs. Cursing, he picked up the basket and scooped up the musty clothes. They were all *his* clothes... He dangled a dead fish of a sock in front of his nose, immediately cringing away... what were they all doing in there? He plonked on the wicker lid and kicked the re-filled basket to one side.

Cursing as he stomped downstairs, he noticed the sound of high-pitched sneezing getting louder as he approached the kitchen.

When he opened the door, a blue flash of fur shot under the kitchen table, rear end first. Mister Pushkin sneezed again, re-emerging and reversing straight into its plate of *Kit-e-Kat*, tipping chunks of jelly-covered meat all over the carpet. The cat hadn't caught a cold, nor had it developed hay fever, but it did regret sniffing around the dusty ornaments on the sideboard: at least it gave the house mice something to laugh at...

'*Na zdorovya,*' said Taras, before he too had to fight off the urge to sneeze. There was a film of dust covering every surface, and it – just like his hair – was getting greyer by the day. When he blew across the sideboard, a thick cloud of dust billowed up, before settling back onto the ornaments. He knew that dust was made from fragments of dead skin... although most of this was likely to be Zena and Lenka's plentiful dandruff... he cringed at the thought of bits of those grubby twins being sucked up his nose...

Covering his nose and mouth with a well-used handkerchief, he shooed the sneezing cat out into the yard, from where it promptly returned and hid beneath the sofa, still petrified of Gunter's dog, and hopeful – as everyone was – that the beast would soon be gone.

Taras couldn't stand living in filth any longer; he unbuttoned his tobacco stained cuffs, rolled up his creased sleeves and went in search of Halyna's cleaning cupboard...

It didn't take him long to wipe down the surfaces with a wet cloth and steer the Hoover around the carpet, only once sucking up the cat's tail, inducing it to emit the loudest 'Mrryaw!' he'd ever heard.

There, he thought, wringing out the cloth, *this cleaning lark is a doddle; I don't know why Halyna makes such a fuss?*

Inspired by his sudden enthusiasm, he made light work of doing all the washing up, putting every cup, plate and pan back in its rightful place once it'd been dried meticulously.

To hell with it, he thought, marching upstairs for the washing basket, *if I clean my clothes, maybe Halyna would iron them for me? A bit of compromise, that's all that's needed...*

Taras knew that Halyna always did the laundry in the tin bath... but he didn't anticipate having to scrape out a large quantity of "stew" before being able to use it... the stuff reeked... if Lenka was eating this, no wonder she was so ill...

Half an hour later, he'd wiped out the tin bath and put away the mangle, his gleaming laundry pegged out in the yard, fluttering in the breeze. It wasn't even ten o'clock and he felt as though he'd already done a day's work. But that was still to come...

Taras donned his smock and swivelled the shop sign from "Closed" to "Open", hopeful the new day would be profitable in more ways than one...

But then he looked out of the window and saw the mound of litter outside his shop door...

Where does it all come from – bits of old paper, ring pulls, sweet wrappers and old cans as well as quite unspeakable things that should never be found in the street – and why does it congregate outside my shop?

He may have moaned, but he didn't really mind having to sweep it up. He was getting used to menial work and found it

The Dancing Barber

strangely therapeutic, so long as it didn't become a habit.

With a yard brush in one hand, he unlocked the door to what he hoped would be a busier day. With his fame from The Alhambra spreading, he had two <u>paying</u> customers on Saturday: not only were they eager to meet *"The Famous Dancing Barber of Bradford"*, but also they wanted a "short back and sides", which in addition to a "crew cut" and the occasional "basin cut", was the only hairstyle he was capable of creating. So today he hoped for at least three paying customers; but there was no hurry... first of all, he planned to put up his feet and recover from all that housework. Besides, he was eager to tune in to Radio Kateryna, interested to know whether Voloshin had met with Khrushchev yet, and indeed whether Voloshin was even still alive. But he knew neither were actually possible.

Whistling *Singin' in the Rain* and spinning the yard brush cheerfully in his hand, Taras wasn't going to let anything spoil this bright and wonderful day...

But the moment he stepped out onto the pavement, the steam of anger whistled from his ears. He flung the brush to the ground and stood with his hands on his hips; the smell of the abattoir had been replaced by the stench of Esholt Sewage Works... Taras vowed that if he ever caught one of those canine defecators, he'd ensure their creations were put firmly back where they came from! And if the owners had a problem with it, he'd apply the same treatment to them!

'Hey you!' Taras shouted at a passing boy, who cuddled a grubby bed sheet as if it was the most precious thing he owned. 'What do you know about all this? Hmm?'

'Nowt! It weren't me,' said the boy, who often called him "Tar-Arse" whilst slapping his backside. 'But it must've just appeared, 'cause I've only just been t' shop to buy me Mam some cigs and it weren't there five minutes ago. Honest!'

'So where's it all come from?' Taras said, tiptoeing out in amongst it all.

All of a sudden, an enormous dollop collided with the pavement, splattering widely. Taras darted out of the way just in time, holding his breath... *Singin' in the Rain*, Taras thought, *not even Mrs Wiggins' umbrella was strong enough to repel this stuff.*

The boy – who, to Taras' mind had the appearance of a

Victorian street urchin, being dressed in rags, with a face dirtier than an ashtray – said, 'maybe it's from some sort of bird, or something?'

Taras shook his head angrily, 'and how many birds do you know of that produce stuff *that* big?'

'Maybe t' cows have started to fly?' said the Urchin jovially before toddling off down the street to present the cigarettes to his mother. Cuddling his blanket, he turned around and shouted, 'my Mam, she saw you at T' Al'ambra t' other night! She said she was very impressed with you! And even though my Pap forbids it, she wants me t' learn t' ballet and be as good as what you are! So I'll be coming to your next class!'

'Oh?' Taras said, 'right… err… thank your "Mam" for her kind compliment, and I suppose I'll see you *next* Monday, five pm sharp! Lessons cost ha'penny a day, paid a week in advance.'

'But Tar-Arse, I thought your rehearsal was *tonight* at five? 'cause when you perform on t' "Showtime" programme, me Mam, she wants me to be on t' telly too! She wants me to be a famous Ballet Prancer, just like you!'

Taras smiled, 'only me… err *my* senior dancers will be appearing on "Showtime". It might take you a little while to reach their standard…' He thought: *all eternity wouldn't be sufficient time to teach a thicko like you…* 'But very well, come along tonight and we'll see how much potential you have… But leave that dirty bed sheet at home!'

'Thank you Tar-Arse, a quick learner is what I am!' the boy shouted as he walked backwards down the street, bouncing off several lamp-posts. 'All me teachers, they say I'm as clever as two short planks!'

'Yes, I can see their point!' Taras waved, thinking *hurry up and go!* He watched the Urchin disappear down the road and couldn't help wondering whether it was just another ruse to annoy him… he hoped it wasn't, because it would be useful to have at least one male dancer other than himself, even if it was the local hooligan, whose "Pap" spends all day in his string vest and whose "Mam" thinks it appropriate to send a child to buy her cigarettes.

'And the next time you dance t' Duck Lake,' shouted the Urchin, 'I want to be t' Prince Sigmund, so then I can dance with your So-fear… Even though the boys call 'er Saddlebags, I think

The Dancing Barber

she's wonderful, and I want to marry 'er when I'm old enough…'

'Over my dead body!' shouted Taras once the boy had disappeared around the corner. He shook his head and muttered, '*Duck* Lake! Prince *Sigmund*! Saddlebags…?'

Taras went to fetch a carrier bag, a trowel and some bleach, only to feel something disgustingly soft beneath his foot. He looked down and cursed: *there's another pair of suede shoes ruined!* To make matters worse, another two gargantuan dollops splattered down only feet from where he stood. He looked up to the sky and was sure he saw the briefest flash of yellow over the rooftop, before dodging another massive dollop that landed at his feet.

Leaving his shoes on the doorstep, he marched back indoors…

Chapter 79

Taras swung open the attic door and stormed straight in, immediately witnessing the most appalling of sights. Lenka's rear end hovered above a yellow bucket, while Zena lobbed the contents of another bucket over the balcony. By this time, the bucket beneath Lenka was full, so Zena adeptly slid it from beneath her squatting sister and quickly replaced it with the empty one. Bending her knees, Zena lifted the full bucket onto the balustrade and was preparing to tip out its contents when Taras shouted, 'what do you think you're doing, you stupid woman?'

But it was too late, Zena upturned the bucket and a moment later there came a great deal of cursing from the street below. Angrily, Zena turned to Taras and said, 'why do you call me the stupid woman?' She shouted over Lenka's thunderous flatulence, 'I am not the stupid woman!'

Taras pressed a well-used handkerchief over his nose and mouth as the stench began to engulf him. He said, 'only a *stupid* woman would empty faeces out onto the street! We're not in Chaplinka now!'

'Fee Shies?' Zena said, 'what is the Fee Shies?'

Taras shouted, 'your himno!'

'And what else am I supposed to do with it? Hmm? Tell me this?' Zena set the bucket down on the stained carpet and folded her arms, cradling her bulbous bosoms.

'Who told you to do it in yellow buckets? We *do* have toilets in this house!' Taras pressed the handkerchief even tighter over his nose as the stench slowly but surely permeated the cotton fabric. 'There's a toilet in the bathroom and there's a lavvy out in the yard!'

'We know,' Zena said, 'but my sister, she blocked them both!' She presented Taras with a pair of rusty loo chains, 'see, my sister, she try to flush it away but no matter how hard she pull, it does not go. In fact, now the dirty water, it has flooded all over the floor!'

'You've done what?' Taras cried, 'that linoleum was only put down five years ago...'

The Dancing Barber

Zena shrugged, 'now you will need the wellie-boots to go to the bathroom!' She said proudly, 'there is Fee Shies everywhere...'

'You stupid, stupid woman! Are you determined to ruin my house?'

'And what does it the matter, if we do?' asked Zena. 'You have The Bolling Hall! We will go stay there: it is the much nicer! Err, not that this house is not the nice,' she smiled, 'you know what I am the meaning, yes?'

'Never mind the damned Bolling Hall, I want to know why she,' he glared disdainfully at a heaving Lenka, 'seems to be generating more himno than an entire herd of cows? I mean, is this normal for her?'

'No, it is not the normal,' Lenka said with a strained voice. 'Yesterday, Sofia, she gave me the most delicious chocolates... I eat every single one, thinking how nicely they taste. But... All through the night, the stomach, it churns, the bowels, they throb and then when I get up, boom, it was like the bomb going off!'

'What chocolates?' Taras said, remembering Sofia and Natalka saying something about buying Zena and Lenka a present. But chocolates couldn't upset someone's stomach so much, could they?

'Here is the wrapper,' Zena said, pleased she didn't eat any. 'It is called the *"Chocolax"* and my sister, she eat ten *whole* bars!'

Taras looked at the wrapper closely and said, 'but these are *laxative* chocolates! You only need to eat one little chunk and it'll send you running!' He looked at Lenka as if she was the most stupid thing on the face of the Earth, 'and you've eaten ten whole bars!'

'The laxative?' Lenka said, contemplating whether it was safe for her to stand up and pull down her skirts. 'Is that not what we give the cow when she gets the hardening of the stools?'

Zena nodded her head and said, 'at least you are the empty now.'

'Uh-oh,' Lenka said, making a lunge for the bucket, 'not yet...'

With loo chains in hand, Taras escaped and went to investigate what these heathens had done to his toilets. But the moment he set one foot in the bathroom, the dampness of his stocking feet informed him that himno had now ruined his socks as well as two pairs of suede shoes. *Brilliant.*

He peered gingerly through the seat, noticing the water was far from clear. He reckoned he had the strength to shift the blockage, so reattached the rusty loo chain and gave it a firm yank.

The resultant tidal wave chased him all the way down to the kitchen, where he wasted no time telephoning for Mrs Wiggins' husband to come and bring his plunger. If Halyna awoke to discover her bathroom and hall carpet was smeared with her sisters' slurry, he worried about what she'd do...

'Why should I help you?' shouted Mrs Wiggins' husband down the telephone. 'You asked me to do the fireworks at the Theatre... And now that lisping Stage Manager knocks on my door with a bill to re-varnish his stage! How is it my fault if he used sub-standard varnish? Besides, *Swan Lake* were your performance: so <u>you</u> should foot the bill! And as for your blocked bog, you can buy your own plunger and shove it you know where!'

Taras hung up. He knew Stan wouldn't let him down... He ambled over to the back door and, a couple of minutes later, let him in.

The Dancing Barber
Chapter 80

After so long in bed, Sofia's body may have felt stiff and numb, but at least – for the first time in months – she was well rested. She snuggled luxuriantly into her feather-filled pillow, pulling the duvet comfortingly up to her chin.

She couldn't remember the last time a lie-in had been permitted to such a late hour, therefore – even though the sunlight was shining through the thin curtains – she hadn't any plans to get up for at least another hour, or maybe two.

She turned over to face the other way, pins and needles tingling through the arm and leg she'd spent the entire night lying on. Her hand was fast asleep; she wiggled her fingers briskly, pumping the blood until the feeling returned. And before long, she began to drift down the long tunnel of sleep...

But it was no use; she couldn't settle on her sore shoulder, and her body knew the time to wake up was long overdue. So she opened one eye and gazed blearily at the smiling clock on the wall that informed her it was ten past ten.

After stretching out fully beneath the duvet, Sofia yawned widely, deciding that twelve hours in bed was probably long enough... she knew her Mama had been up for ages, hoovering the carpets and sloshing the washing around the tin bath. She'd been awoken a couple of times by the sound of laundry being scrubbed against the washboard and the high-pitched squeaking of the mangle as her Mama squeezed out the water between those tight wooden rollers.

Sofia sniffed the air, thinking she could smell drains; but it was probably the stench of the abattoir drifting in through the window...

The stench was so appalling that she was surprised her Mama had hung the washing on the line: there was nothing she hated more than clean clothes smelling of rotten meat, or worse. And it must have been the first time the dog hadn't given her any trouble... perhaps it had got used to the sight of her fur coat?

Sofia rubbed the encrusted sleep from her eyes and wallowed in another luxuriant stretch, extending her body so her fingertips and heels hooked over both ends of the bed. She contracted her stomach muscles and slowly sat up, feeling her vertebrae click and grind, preparing her mind to perform the morning exercises that were doing wonders for her thighs.

Very soon – she hoped – she wouldn't look completely ridiculous in a mini-skirt and the boys would stop calling her Saddlebags.

She rubbed her eyes again and blinked, her eyelids flickering up and down: was she still dreaming?

When her eyes finally focussed, she discovered a most wondrous gift waiting by her bed. The sunlight reflecting off the golden wrapping paper scattered onto every wall, making the room look as though it was filled with sparkling treasure. She flung away her duvet and, in her bare feet, scampered excitedly over to examine this unexpected gift.

She wondered what it could be. It was neither her birthday nor Christmas, yet this gift had the promise of being better than anything she'd received before. She recalled that for her last birthday, the itchy charity shop jumper she'd received had been wrapped in the same paper that had covered her previous year's present. And at Christmas, she had to appear grateful for receiving a Satsuma: a sour one, full of pips! So this gift had the potential to be better than all the other gifts she'd ever received, combined.

Natalka got presents like this all the time, and it always made Sofia incredibly jealous. She shook with excitement as she contemplated what it could be: something so expensive must have been from Klem, a reward for coming top of the class at school… Who else could it be from?

But then she remembered her teachers had taught her never to judge a book by its cover, no matter how glittery that cover may be: those nuns always knew how to put a damper on things. They even managed to depress Klem: "The Nuns of Doom" is what he called them upon his return from last week's Parents' Evening.

Sofia sat on the edge of the creaky bed with the disappointingly light box on her knee. But the golden paper was the thickest, most expensive type; it had the aroma of freshly mown grass and wouldn't rip, no matter how hard she tried. And the iridescent blue ribbon that divided the box in quarters looked like it was made of

The Dancing Barber

the finest silk.

She pulled open the ornate bow and let the ribbon slip away. She wound it neatly around her fingers, then slotted it into her 'best box' along with the other trinkets she liked to keep, such as shiny pennies and a collection of Mister Pushkin's old collar bells. She then unpicked the sellotape, which came away surprisingly easily, leaving the paper undamaged.

But disappointingly, beneath the fine wrapping was the tattiest cardboard box, the corners of which were crushed and the staples holding it together so rusty that they'd stained the surrounding cardboard the colour of Irn-Bru. It looked as though "The Nuns of Doom" were right...

In the centre of the lid was an old-fashioned Busby's logo depicting the red-coated, bearskin-wearing soldiers that were the store's famous mascot. And whatever the box contained was certainly not new: an ancient receipt sellotaped to the lid stated *Lady's Garment, two Guineas, date of purchase - April 1933.* She angled the receipt to the light and discovered it had long ago been crossed out, the ink faded with age... She flipped over the receipt and found an inscription, written in felt-tip pen, that stated:

> *To my darling Sofia, a daughter full of surprises!*
> *Not only are you a talented dancer,*
> *But you're the cleverest scholar in your year,*
> *And a very brave little girl!*
> *I know this is something you've always wanted...*
>
> *Tato X*

It's from Tato? "The cleverest scholar in my year": so he did *read my school report.*

She scratched at her curly hair. *How odd to have received a present from him... Maybe Mama's strike is working? "Something I've always wanted"... but how did he know about that leather coat?*

Then she realised Natalka had probably told him; it was no

secret that the auburn leather coat was the object she coveted most of all in the entire world. She examined her reflection in the mirror and decided that she'd have to change her hairstyle... a perm wouldn't suit a coat befitting Sophia Loren. Cliff Richard nodded his approval from the inside of the wardrobe door she'd forgotten to close before going to bed. She smiled, and said, 'thank you.'

Impatiently, she lifted off the lid and cast it to the floor. She imagined the wonderful garment nestled beneath the musty tissue paper and hoped her Tato had picked the correct size. She sighed deeply, allowing the intoxicating feeling of anticipation to remain for as long as possible, preparing herself to be bathed in the wonderful scent of the finest leather the moment the garment was unveiled...

In the bedroom next door, Halyna had been snoring so loudly that she'd managed to wake herself up. With a grunt to clear her throat and a snort to clear her nose, she sat up and fumbled for the glass beside her bed.

She put her fingers into the water and fished out her clean dentures, clicking them into position.

The room quickly came into focus once she'd slotted on her plastic framed glasses; she looked at the time and thought: *goodski Heavens, I've slept in!* But with relief, she examined the calendar and discovered that for once, sleeping in was allowed. She yawned, making her mouth as wide as a hippopotamus' and swung her legs out of bed. She cursed when her stockinged feet banged into something that was stood next to her slippers.

With curiosity, she peered at the enormous brown cardboard box that seemed to occupy the entire floor: it wasn't there when she went to bed, and she couldn't remember the last time she'd received a gift from Father Christmas...

She hoped it weren't a gift from the twins... the thought of it made her skin crawl... it would almost certainly be something unpleasant such as a selection of candles made from their ear-wax, or a taxidermy wild boar to remind her of Chaplinka. In the latter case, she'd keep it pride of place in the kitchen... but the instant they went home, it would go the same way as Taras' photograph of

The Dancing Barber

Charlie Chaplinka. Knowing them, it could just as likely be a carcass of some unfortunate animal they'd expect her to skin and butcher... She peered through the net curtains to check the dog was still in the yard. Fortunately, or unfortunately, it was. And it appeared to have hung out the laundry... she knew that nobody else in the house would bother to do it... unless she'd been sleep-walking again...

On inspection of a neatly-written note sellotaped to the top of the box, she knew that neither Father Christmas nor her sisters would use felt-tip pen...

Happy (belated) Anniversary Halya,
And you thought I forgot our twentieth anniversary?
Here's something you've always wanted...

Taras XXX

She put her fingers beneath her hairnet and adjusted the rollers that had moved out of position during the night. She thought: *Something I've always wanted?*

Hmm... he knows I've only <u>ever</u> wanted a fur coat, so he must have bought me another one! And judging by the size and weight of this box, it must be a warmski one for winter!

Pleased her strike had worked, she smiled, *oh Taras! All is forgiven!*

She tore open the top flaps and peered inside...

Sofia's shoulders slumped once she'd peeled back the rustling tissue paper to reveal a pink leotard, a pink tutu, a pair of pink tights and a brand new pair of pink ballet shoes with pink laces. There was even a big bag of pink cotton wool for packing around the toes: it may have looked like candyfloss, but it was vital for pointe work, especially for dancers with bunions as big as hers.

The box contained nothing else, certainly not a leather coat. She shook her head and muttered despondently, 'something I've always wanted...'

But then she had second thoughts: this was actually quite a charming gift to have received from her Tato. And it boded well for her dancing career, because this was not the costume of a supporting dancer, it was the costume of a *Prima Ballerina.*

She slipped on the tutu over her nightie and admired her reflection in the mirror. As she worked through her ballet positions she noticed that it complimented her physique perfectly, making her thighs look almost normal.

She scampered to the wardrobe door and curtseyed before her poster. She was sure Cliff gave her a wink of approval. Was it her imagination, or did her thighs really look thinner today?

As she unfolded the pink leotard, a long white envelope fluttered to the floor; she bent down to pick it up and noticed it was addressed to her. It looked official, the postmark had Friday's date and it had come all the way from London, first class.

It didn't surprise her that it had been opened: her Tato had always censored what little mail she ever received. The whiff of tobacco smoke confirmed it when she extracted and unfolded the thick headed notepaper and observed the typewritten text.

She gasped when she discovered it was from the Royal Ballet in London. *What are they doing writing to me?*

```
Dear Sofia,

On the recommendation of your
esteemed father, I have pleasure in
extending you the invitation to
attend a selection interview for
admission to our School in January
1964...
```

Selection interview? But I'm nowhere near good enough for the Royal Ballet? She shrugged her shoulders: the letter must have been intended for Natalka... she was his protégé after all.

As her Tato had a habit – whenever he disagreed with an examiner's judgement – of changing the grades on even the most official of ballet certificates, she angled the letter to the light to see whether it had been tampered with...

The Dancing Barber

'The cheeky – ' Halyna said, kicking the box into the corner of the room, denting the side and toppling it over. 'If he thinks I'm going to end my strike because he's bought me a <u>Hoover</u>, he's got another thing coming!' She stood up and said, 'I'll tell him what he can do with his Hoover! And it will <u>not</u> be goodski!'

She imagined smacking Taras around the head with the appliance, and maybe throttling him with the extendable hose that, according to the words on the box, was for those "hard to reach places".

She couldn't believe he'd dare buy her such a gift: how could he have forgotten what she did to him when he'd bought her a sack of horse manure a few Christmases ago, expecting her to spread it onto the small flowerbed in the back yard with her bare hands. She smiled as she recalled the expression on his face when he realised she'd soaked his truss in paraffin and set it alight! It was even more humorous considering he was wearing it at the time!

She wrenched the curlers from her hair, slung on the comfortable nylon dress she'd had since before the War and picked up the Hoover, brandishing it as if it were a Neolithic club. As she opened her bedroom door, her darling husband shouted up from the kitchen: '<u>lunch is ready</u>!'

Halyna thought: *Did he just say <u>lunchski</u>?* She checked the time on her tarnished wristwatch... it had just gone eleven o'clock. *It's far too early for lunchski...* She sighed, *I couldn't eat fish and chips at this time of day...*

But even that would be infinitely preferable to Zena and Lenka's "stew of the meat", some of which remained in an old saucepan in the attic beneath an inch of green mould. For some reason they refused to throw it away, even though it was teeming with so much life that it could probably walk itself to the dustbin.

But the aroma in the house was neither fishy, hamstery, nor Pedigree Chummy... in fact it didn't smell of cooking at all. She sniffed the air, hoping the sewer under the street hadn't backed up again.

When she stepped out onto the landing, she realised she was walking on newspaper: but it didn't feel scrunchy, but squelchy.

She looked at her cream-coloured sheepskin slippers and cursed. Her nose twitched more and more, her eyes tracing the newspapers' path...

Her ears tuned in to a great deal of grunting and heaving coming from the bathroom; dreading what she'd see, she peered through the door and witnessed Mrs Wiggins' husband thrusting away with the biggest plunger she'd ever seen, the gurgling and squelching water splashing up and staining his boiler suit. He cursed, using the coarsest language, muttering how much he hated Taras taking advantage of his good nature and how those heathen women should be kept in a zoo... He could only have meant Zena and Lenka.

'Excuse-ski,' said Halyna, walking carefully into the bathroom, breathing as shallowly as she could. 'But can you tell me what has happened?'

'What has happened?' said Mrs Wiggins' husband, hanging his head out of the window, gasping for air. 'Your sisters is what's happened... Never in my life have I seen so much – !'

'*Please*, watch your language in this house,' interrupted Halyna. But when Mrs Wiggins' husband told her about everything the twins had done, the strength of her language surprised even him...

The Dancing Barber

Chapter 81

Steaming piles of enormous *Varenyky* awaited Halyna and Sofia as they sauntered into the kitchen, neither of them quite believing what they saw.

The aromas were so delicious that Klem wondered whether Halyna had ended her strike early… But the ferocious expression adorning her face suggested otherwise… She'd told him about the Hoover, and what she planned to do with it. She also told him about what Lenka had done… At least the toilets were unblocked and a new hallway carpet had been ordered.

Still wearing a flowery apron beneath his blue blazer, Taras used a serving spoon to point at three earthenware bowls containing the filled dough parcels. He said jovially, 'here we have potato, cheese and sauerkraut. And there's plenty of fried onions, butter and *Smetana* for everyone!'

Halyna was flabbergasted, 'have you made all these *yourself?*' She was so surprised that she momentarily allowed the ferocious expression adorning her face to slip.

'Of course,' said Taras, 'while you were asleep, I have been busy…'

'Makes a change,' muttered Halyna, 'normally it's the other way round…'

After tasting them timidly at first, Halyna deduced the *Varenyky* were genuinely delicious: the dough was snow white and silky smooth, the mashed potato was Heavenly soft, the cheese was creamy and the sauerkraut was as expected. As for the fried onions, they were cremated, but that was how everyone liked them, and the tangy *Smetana* – home made of course – left that characteristic furry coating on her teeth and dried her mouth so much that it felt as though she had a cactus for a tongue… but strangely she could never truly enjoy *Varenyky* without it.

Zena tucked in with her usual gusto, inserting three *Varenyky* at a time into her mouth. But Lenka – still worse for wear since the *Chocolax* incident – could only manage a nibble and was poised to flee to the yellow bucket should the need arise.

'Well done Taras,' said Klem, mopping up a puddle of melted butter with his last potato-filled *Varenyk*. 'I never knew you possessed the ability to cook so well.' He narrowed his eyes, 'are you sure you made these all by yourself?'

'Naturally,' said Taras, 'it just goes to show that you can do anything if you put your mind to it...'

'I quite agree,' said Klem. He picked up a curly strand of brown hair from the edge of his plate and compared it to an identical one he'd plucked from Lenka's head. He narrowed his eyes again, 'then how do you explain <u>this</u>?'

Taras grinned and shrugged his shoulders. He said, 'I may have had *some* help...'

'*Some help?*' Lenka said sarcastically.

Zena added, 'it is we who made the dough, the fillings and the everything else!' She looked at Klem, gesturing to Taras with her dirty thumb, 'all *he* did was smoke the cigarettes!'

'I thought so,' muttered Halyna, 'he can't even boil an egg!'

'I boiled an egg once,' Taras protested, folding his arms pompously. He thought for a moment, 'how was I to know that it'd already been boiled?'

Halyna shook her head, 'I would have thought you'd have noticed that it was a *peeled* hard-boiled egg? How many chickens have you seen that lay eggs without a shell, hmm?'

Klem couldn't help adding, 'or lay eggs that are hard-boiled?'

Taras looked away. He said, 'at least I tried! If that's how you're going to be, I don't think I'll damned well bother in future!' The twins were going to make *Varenyky* regardless of his intervention, but <u>he'd</u> made sure they scrubbed their hands with soap and water before they touched any ingredients. He even ensured they scraped all the filth from beneath their fingernails, creating a pile so big that he could have planted a potato in it.

Halyna sneered. She knew her husband's efforts around the house would never last... It was a pity, because he had a natural talent for dusting and vacuuming, and even for scrubbing the most unspeakable stains from underwear... the laundry was whiter than white, but it still fluttered on the line in the yard... she hoped the starlings would leave it alone.

'Halynochka,' said Zena, her mouth crammed with fried onion, 'Lenka and me, we cannot understand how you can be on the

The Dancing Barber

strike...?' She shrugged, 'it is not correct for the wife of the house to be on the strike...!'

Halyna placed her fork calmly on the edge of her plate. After swallowing her food, she said, 'it is *perfectly* correct if the husband of the house is too lazy to earn enough money for his family, yet expects his wife to cook the meals and clean his house, clean his shop *and* clean his studio as well as having *two* jobs!'

Taras shook his head glumly.

'Two jobs?' asked Zena, her mouth fuller than ever. 'Apart from the Lister Mill, where else do you work?'

Sofia couldn't resist being a little mischievous. She said, 'Mama is also a cleaner at a great big enormous house...'

Taras thought: *Is she?*

'That's enough Sofia,' interrupted Halyna. She looked back at Zena, 'every penny helps; I like to keep busy...' She glared at her daughter: now was not the time to tell the twins that the "great big enormous house" she cleaned was "The" Bolling Hall... And Taras didn't know about this extra job either... how else could she afford the fur coat?

'The strike?' Lenka said, shuffling uncomfortably in her seat, 'does that mean you can go outside and burn your brassière like the firemen?'

'No,' said Halyna, 'they burn braziers... that is something quite different...'

The smell of farmyards engulfed the table as Lenka excused herself, running for the yellow bucket, but not quite making it.

Taras went to open the window, while Klem opened the door, wafting it so as to clear the air.

Sofia thought her Mama was being very unfair on her Tato; at least he'd helped make lunch in his own small way. And it was infinitely better than greasy fish and chips, regardless of the fact that every *Varenyk* she sliced into seemed to contain at least one strand of curly brown hair embedded somewhere inside it. She was worried that some of these hairs were too short to have originated from her aunties' heads, and could only hope the thorough boiling had killed off the nastiest germs.

Her Tato looked so glum, grinding the same piece of fried onion between his molars for the last few minutes. Was it any wonder? He'd tried so hard to get back into her Mama's good books, and all she could do was sneer. He'd cleaned his own shop and studio; he'd done all his own laundry and even done the washing up without being asked. Her Mama's devious plan had worked to perfection – he was becoming a house-husband and he didn't even know it – and yet her Mama was still in the foulest of moods.

And the reason for her mood was currently perched on a yellow bucket in the hallway, groaning and heaving like a navvy. Sofia had no idea *Chocolax* was so potent. It took Mrs Wiggins' husband almost an hour to unblock both toilets, explaining in the most colourful language how this was the last time he'd ever help Taras, insisting those two curly haired heathens should go and dump in the park like all the other animals... a comment which prompted Lenka to attempt to tip a freshly filled bucket squarely on his head.

Her Tato was grateful that Lenka stood up for him, even though it meant he'd be without a pianist... Unless Mrs Wiggins decided to ignore her husband's vow to ban her from attending the Ballet Studio... but everyone knew she never paid any attention to "the old git".

'Tato,' Sofia said, determined to lighten his mood. 'Thank you very much for my wonderful gifts!'

'Do you like them?' her Tato asked, his face lighting up as he unfolded his arms and looked lovingly at his daughter. At least she was polite enough to thank him, unlike his ungrateful wife... that Hoover was expensive!

'Of course I do,' Sofia said, reaching across to give him a big hug. 'You've made me very happy!'

Taras nodded his appreciation, 'I knew it was what you wanted more than anything else.' He put his hands flat on the table, 'I've done my bit... The rest is up to you...'

Halyna looked at him inquisitively, trying her best to ignore Lenka's fumes that seeped beneath the door. She asked, 'what did you buy her?' She thought: *it'll be a feather duster or an iron...*

But when he told her, Halyna pursed her lips and said, 'and why didn't you consult with me before arranging an interview for our daughter at *The Royal Ballet* of all places?'

'*The Royal Ballet?*' said Klem, 'oh well done Sofia, I'm sure you'll do very well: congratulations!'

Sofia said, 'thank you Mr Klem,' accepting one of his fudge

The Dancing Barber

sweets with a picture of a cow on the wrapper: his standard reward for any success.

Taras looked at his wife and shrugged, 'I thought you'd be pleased? It will be good for Sofia's future career...' He glanced at his daughter, 'she seems happy enough with it, don't you think?'

Sofia nodded enthusiastically and said, 'as Tato said, it's up to me to impress them at the interview.' She clasped her hands together, holding them to her heart, 'for me to attend the Royal Ballet would be like a dream come true...'

Halyna thought: *don't over-do it, Sofia. I know you're not that bothered about ballet...* She glared at Taras: *And it's you who doesn't think, Taras! If you send Sofia to London, I'll be stuck here on my own with you!*

'Besides,' Taras said, knowing he shouldn't say what he was about to. 'I don't need to ask your permission, woman!'

'"Woman!"' Halyna shouted, going to fetch the Hoover. 'What have I told you about addressing me as "woman"?'

Chapter 82

Taras' head throbbed so much that it felt as though that mop-headed Ringo Starr was thumping it with drumsticks. He cursed: *Oh how I hate those Beatles... "Please, Please Me"... It'd please me if you'd all shut up!*

But for once, his headache wasn't caused by modern popular "music", nor was it due to excessive samahon. This afternoon, the culprit was the Hoover that collided squarely with the side of his head, after Halyna had swung it at him as if it were a Neolithic club.

Rubbing the red and swollen lump, he thought: *Why does the woman not like being called "woman"? She is one, isn't she? And what does she have against Hoovers? She didn't even thank me for obtaining the deeds to the house... it was as if she wasn't bothered... What's wrong with the woman? Maybe she's going through The Change?*

And why does she hate the idea of Sofia attending the Royal Ballet so much? How dare she threaten to divorce me if she was accepted! Not wanting to be left alone with your husband is insufficient grounds for divorce, especially for a Ukrainian.

Am I really so bad to live with? I don't think so... Maybe it is an excuse, especially as she's recently developed more of an appetite for tea...

After Taras had singlehandedly done the washing up, all he could do was take his tablets and sit at the kitchen table with a chilled pork chop balanced on his head. As meat juices ran down his neck and soaked into his clean, yet unironed collar, he relished having the house to himself for a little while... For once, he was grateful his shirt was unironed; ever since Zena and Lenka had used Halyna's Morphy Richards electric iron to fry herring and mackerel, everyone's clothes reeked worse than a fishmonger's apron...

His headache was just starting to fade when the idiot twins barged in, scraping the walls with their baggages of Heaven knows what, coughing, snorting and emitting their usual gasses. Taras closed his eyes, hoping they'd go away. But it didn't work.

'Hello Taras!' shouted Zena.

'Hello Meat Head!' Lenka shouted with much laughter, 'Taras is the Meat Head!'

Taras sighed. 'I can see you've been shopping,' he said, surveying the long bundles of assorted salami Zena and Lenka had thrust beneath their festering flea-ridden armpits; at least – being wrapped in brown paper – the salami shouldn't be contaminated.

'Yes, we have been to the market,' Zena said, struggling to put down her load without dropping it. She thrust a piece of paper into Taras' palm and said, 'here is the bill: I told the man that you would the pay him.'

'Just a minute,' said Taras. He peeled off the pork chop and wiped his glistening head with a towel that was one of Sofia's old nappies. He stared at the extortionately large bill and asked, 'why didn't _you_ pay him?'

'Pay him with what?' Lenka asked, 'we do not have the money!' She slammed the bundle of salami onto the kitchen table, wedging it with an old shoebox she'd been carrying, so as to stop it from rolling to the floor.

Zena said, 'but we made the small contribution: I took the old wedding ring to the Prawn Broking shop, and he gives me the _two_ shillings! Ivan, he told me it was the gold, but the Prawn Broker, he says it was only the copper!'

'_I_ could have told you that,' said Taras. 'Even I know gold doesn't go green!' He was surprised the copper ring was worth as much as _two_ shillings... He rubbed his head and stared with disbelief at the mountain of food occupying the entire table. In addition to salami, there were boxes burgeoning with potted meat, pickled eggs, gherkins, bunches of wilted dill, loaves of Ukrainian rye bread and an enormous bull's heart the twins planned to stuff with sauerkraut and serve for dinner... He said, 'did you really have to buy _so_ much? It'll take us years to get through all of this!'

Lenka smiled; it would only take her a couple of days.

Zena said, 'we want to make ourselves the useful while we are the guests. We want to treat you, so we buy you the presents! Is the nice idea, yes?'

'Mmm,' said Taras, 'but the recipient of a present doesn't

usually have to pay for it?'

'But who else would the pay...? Tell me this...?' Zena said, making Lenka laugh so much that she nearly had to waddle over to the yellow bucket.

'It doesn't matter,' said Taras. He couldn't be bothered explaining... At least – in addition to wrestling wild boars – the twins had found something else they were good at... Pity it was spending other people's money.

'You want the nibble, yes?' Lenka asked, with an over-filled mouth. She displayed several strings of chipolata-sized salami sausages hanging around her neck; she ripped off another one and chomped it in her open mouth.

Taras thought the chipolatas looked remarkably like strings of cat turds... 'Certainly not,' he said, trying not to notice the masticated mess of mangled meat between her craggy teeth.

'The suit the self...' Lenka said, burping with satisfaction.

Taras observed the overabundance of long packages on the table in front of him, but one was much longer and thinner than the others. 'What type of salami is this?' he asked, separating it from the rest.

Lenka said proudly, still with a full mouth, 'it is not the salami.'

'No,' said Zena, 'it is the special present for you!'

'For me?' Taras said, holding the package in both hands.

'Yes,' said Zena, handing him another bill she'd extracted from a very unhygienic place.

Taras' gift was wrapped in so many sheets of brown paper that he began to wonder whether the *paper* itself was the gift and there was nothing inside...

The sisters watched eagerly as Taras peeled away the last layer, knowing he was sure to appreciate their gift: it was the most expensive in the shop.

Taras gasped when he realised what it was. He said, 'you mended it... But how?'

'No, not the mended,' said Zena. 'This is the brand new!'

Taras smiled, admiring the remarkable implement.

Lenka said, 'you like, yes?'

Taras tested the new cane by whipping it through the air a couple of times, making the most satisfying of swooshing noises. He smiled with approval as he flexed the six-footer between his

The Dancing Barber

strong hands; easily making it into a hula-hoop that sprang straight back the moment it was released with twice the power of his old one.

'This is an excellent cane,' he said, admiring it as if it were a work of art.

Zena and Lenka said in unison, 'we knew you would the like it. And you do, yes?'

'Oh yes,' said Taras, 'I like it very much!' With reluctance, he re-wrapped the cane with the brown paper and placed it resolutely back on the table.

The twins looked at each other with some confusion.

'Maybe he lie... Maybe he <u>no</u> like it,' muttered Lenka.

Zena tutted, 'it is the last time I buy him the present.'

'But I *do* like it... however, it will have to go back to the shop...' said Taras, not quite believing what he was saying. 'As nice as it is, I've decided I won't be needing such an implement from now on...' Over the last few days, the rehearsals for *Sleeping Beauty* had gone perfectly well... even if he'd had a cane, he wouldn't have had to use it.

Leaving Zena and Lenka to find space to put away all the things they hadn't paid for, Taras went out to the yard to have a quiet word with Halyna.

She was sat on the doorstep, cradling a cup of cold PG Tips in her hands...

The treadle-powered Singer sewing machine had been wheeled outside, but she didn't have the energy to operate it, let alone select a bobbin of brightly-coloured thread, with which to stitch together a new cushion cover...

So for the past half an hour, she'd stared at the dog that stared at her with *that* look in its eyes...

The smell of Taras' aftershave signalled his approach. Immediately, she turned to face the mossy sandstone wall with the stubbornness of Mister Pushkin.

He may have been – as Zena put it – in "the house of the dogs", but he was determined to make her listen to what he had to say...

'Those damned sisters of yours are costing us a small fortune,' Taras said, sitting down alongside his wife and thumbing through the sizeable pile of bills Zena and Lenka had presented him with.

'They say they're buying us presents and yet <u>we</u> are expected to pay for them...! You should see the heap on the kitchen table...'

Halyna nodded to the dry washing, muttering, 'how long are you going to leave it there? Maybe until the starlings have plopped all over it perhaps?'

Taras took in a calmingly deep breath. 'In a minute,' he said, 'but first, I want you to look at these bills...'

Begrudgingly, Halyna put down the cup of congealed tea, the earthenware scraping harshly against the sandstone of the doorstep. She scrutinised the bills through her plastic framed glasses and said, 'but this isn't a small fortune, it's an *enormous* fortune; they've spent nearly fifty pounds!'

'And how did they manage to persuade the shopkeepers to agree to be paid later?' Taras shrugged his shoulders, 'especially that salami man...'

'Come on Taras,' Halyna said, arranging the bills in order of magnitude, 'you should know by now that Zena and Lenka can be *quite* persuasive.'

'Aggressive is a more appropriate word; not even Mick McManus would dare argue with them... they'd hammer him into the ground as if he were a tent peg.'

'Good grief,' said Halyna, 'have you seen this?' She held up a piece of dog-eared paper that was mixed in with all the bills. 'It seems they're going to cost us a whole lot more... Oh, this is *not* goodski.'

Taras snatched the paper and examined the long list of their demands, scrawled in barely readable pencil. He said, 'they want us to buy them all this?' He threw the paper angrily to the ground, 'well, they can go – '

'Taras! Language, *please!*' Halyna shouted, picking up the paper and straightening it out. 'But they are *so* poor-ski...'

'Poor-ski?' said Taras, 'we'll be the ones who'll be poor-ski! Even though we don't have to make any more mortgage repayments, it'll still be tight this month...'

'Yes,' said Halyna, wondering why he'd taken such an interest in the household finances all of a sudden. 'I'm sure it will...' She didn't know what to think about the subject of the mortgage: she and Taras may hold the deeds, but there was no escaping the fact they'd been stolen. And she didn't believe Taras' quasi-logic that it was acceptable for a thief to steal from another thief... two wrongs don't make a right.

She had a feeling that when Ivan eventually turned up, not only would he demand the return of the deeds, but also all the arrears. And for that reason, she'd be putting aside a little more every month just in case...

And she still didn't understand why the divorce papers failed to mention dividing up Ivan's assets? Surely as his wife, Zena would be entitled to half of everything... including the remaining equity of this house? Then again, Ivan might not have any assets of his own... whatever didn't belong to his mother was probably stolen. And no-one seemed remotely bothered that by forging Ivan's signature, the divorce papers were legally worthless...

But Halyna chose to keep her concerns from her husband; he'd only say she was worrying over nothing. Slowly, she stood up and ambled over to sit behind her Singer sewing machine. She opened a small wooden drawer and selected a bobbin of bright blue thread. The more money she could save by "making do and mending", the better. Working the treadle with one foot, she began sewing when the needle's speed was just right... she enjoyed sewing outdoors, regardless of what the neighbours thought... she waved at the man with the binoculars, smiling as he almost dropped them from the window he was leaning out of.

'In any case,' she said, turning her attention back to the bills, 'my sisters can't get any of this in Chaplinka. And let's face it, they desperately need all these things...'

'Deodorants!' Taras said, 'there won't be enough in the shop to cover up the smells they create! And as for razor blades, a hedge-trimmer wouldn't be able to cope with their hair!'

'Don't be silly,' Halyna said. She twitched her shoulders, 'I suppose all these things aren't *that* expensive? Besides, they *are* my sisters... and it's the least we can do after everything they've done for us...'

Taras narrowed his eyes. He said, 'but what have they done for us?'

Come to think of it, Halyna didn't know either. But it didn't matter: she had missed her sisters – odours and all – and was determined to show them as much hospitality as she could afford, even if it meant taking her beloved fur coat back to Busby's.

Chapter 83

Klem rushed to the shop door the moment he recognised the silhouette of a wide-brimmed black hat in the window. He flung open the door and shouted over the noisy doorbell, 'hello Gunter! Wonderful to see you! Would you like to come in?' He straightened the green ribbon on the collar of his embroidered shirt, 'I've got some fresh tea in the pot...' With the twist of a finger, he unstuck the doorbell's button, blessedly muting the hive of angry bees. 'Phew,' he said, tapping his ears, 'that's better...'

Gunter looked left and right to check nobody had heard his name being blurted out. With no one in sight, he tipped his wide-brimmed black hat and said, 'thank you, but no. I haven't the time, I only came to collect Mykola.'

'Mykola?' Klem said, scratching his head. 'A-ha...!' He stopped himself from clicking his fingers, 'you mean B – '

'That's the one,' said Gunter. 'Such a pity he wasn't needed, because I could tell he desperately wanted to sink his teeth into some *real* work...'

Klem tried his best not to laugh, his quivering mouth disguised behind his horseshoe of a moustache.

Gunter waved his hand dismissively, 'never mind. You know, I still find it strange the Soviets left you alone...' He smiled, displaying his tobacco-stained teeth, 'they obviously didn't believe a word Ivan told them. Either that, or they realise Voloshin's got them by, as the English say, the "short and curlies"...'

'It was better to be safe than sorry,' said Klem, trying desperately not to laugh. 'In any case, the dog was nice company for Mister Pushkin...' He nodded through to the kitchen, 'are you *sure* you won't have some tea? I've got some nice Lapsang – '

Gunter raised both hands and said, 'no, thank you. I've just come to collect the dog.'

Before Klem could say another word, Halyna trotted through the shop, dragging the dog behind her, its clammy paws squeaking across the shiny linoleum floor. She said, 'hello Mr Gunter, I understand you've come to collect the dog?' She yanked at the leash, and encouraged the hairy beast out onto the pavement with her feet, 'so here he is!'

'Thank you,' said Gunter, being careful to keep the malting dog away from his pristine black trousers. He took a firm hold of the leash and said, 'come on Mykola, time to go.' But even he struggled to drag the beast in the direction of his car. His nose twitched… why did the dog smell so strongly of mushy peas?

Halyna was glad the dog was going; she hated the way it stared lustfully at her when she wore her fur coat. Thank Heavens it had been tied up; she didn't want a repetition of *that* incident.

'Oh,' said Gunter, 'I almost forgot…' He reached into his pocket and unveiled a circular tin containing a Cine film. He polished it against the lapel of his black jacket and displayed it in the palm of his hand. 'A present,' he said to a curious Klem, 'the contents of which I am sure will come in useful in the future…'

Klem picked up the tin that had the aroma of boot polish, and examined the label through his half-moon spectacles. He smiled from ear to ear. '*Ivan gets smacked*, that's an interesting title…'

'So if he ever decides to blackmail you again,' said Gunter, 'this film will be a wonderful deterrent. It's very entertaining, especially when you see who's doing the smacking…'

'I bet it's his mother…' Klem said knowingly. 'Rumour has it, she still bathes him once a week…'

Gunter winked discretely from beneath the wide brim of his black hat. 'Be sure to keep it safe: it's the only copy I have.'

'Don't you worry,' said Klem, preferring not to ask how Gunter obtained such a film. 'This is cinematic gold: I'll put it where no one will ever find it.' He slid the tin into the inside pocket of his pinstriped jacket, patting it reassuringly with his hand. 'I don't know how to thank you: sorting out Zena's divorce, giving Taras the deeds to this house and now this film… I'll be forever in your debt…'

Halyna cringed. Being in the debt of the Mafia was never goodski.

Gunter smiled. 'Nonsense! It's the least I could do after everything you've done for me. Really, it's *me* who is in *your* debt!'

Halyna didn't believe it for a second.

'Any way,' Gunter said, trying to ignore the smell of mushy

peas being emitted by the dog, 'aren't you going to ask me what became of Ivan and The Gossipmonger?'

Klem shrugged, 'I assumed they'd ran off with Oksana?'

Gunter shook his head, 'they're not with Oksana. I decided Ivan was in need of some *re-education*, if you know what I mean... And I sent his mother along for good measure...' He winked again from beneath the wide brim of his black hat, 'it'll do them the world of good.'

Klem gave a knowing nod of the head. The Convent was a frightening place; the canes they used made Taras' seem like a toothpick. A *re-education* was just what Ivan and The Gossipmonger needed... and if they survived, they'd certainly have learned the error of their ways...

Gunter gave the leash another tug, but the dog refused to move an inch.

The watch in Klem's waistcoat pocket chimed one o'clock and emitted a brief rendition of the opening bars of the Ukrainian National Anthem. He pulled it out and wound it the usual seven times, rotating the fluted crown with panache.

Gunter was pleased his friend still used this expensive gift every day: such quality was not meant to be left to tarnish in a box... The same was true for that beautiful Fabergé Egg...

The dog still refused to move, even after several kicks of encouragement from Gunter's polished black leather boot. 'Come on,' he said with a sigh, yanking at the leash with all his strength. He shouted, 'please, come on!' But the obstinate animal didn't budge.

He looked at Klem and said, 'any ideas?'

Klem shrugged, 'he'll move when he's ready...'

'Will he?' said Gunter. 'I wish he'd hurry up! Anyway, while we're waiting, I may as well tell you... I was listening to the Home Service on the way here... Apparently the biggest crackpot in the Soviet Army escaped from The Asylum last month: he strangled ten guards with the straps of his strait-jacket, tore steel doors from their hinges and swam across an icy-cold moat before escaping out into the tundra wearing only his socks.'

Klem thought nothing of it... Crackpots were always escaping from The Asylum...

'How dangerous is he?' asked Halyna, 'and did they say why he

The Dancing Barber

was there?'

Klem looked at her without blinking. He said, 'I'd imagine he's very dangerous, don't you think? And as for why he's there... I should think it was obvious... he's a crackpot isn't he... the place is full of them!'

Halyna elbowed Klem in the ribs, 'don't be cheeky...'

Klem smiled, 'sorry...' He looked at Gunter, 'do you reckon they'll catch him?'

'The Kremlin insists he's frozen to death, but I'm not so sure... they refused to confirm whether or not they'd found the body... Such crackpots are indestructible, they're like machines... Apparently this one is hard as nails, although he does have a bizarre penchant for wearing women's dresses.'

'A lot of them do,' said Klem, 'there are more cross-dressing psychopaths in the Soviet Army than anywhere else in the world...'

'True, but this one's a real nutter,' said Gunter. 'He's so detestable that not even Khrushchev can stand him... And that's saying something.'

Halyna said, 'but The Asylum is a thousand miles from anywhere, in the far north of Siberia... I'm sure the wolves will have already picked clean his bones...'

Gunter smiled, 'you're probably right. All that'll remain will be his false eye... Anyway,' he looked down to the dog, 'it's time we were off... come on...' But the dog dug its claws into the cracks in the pavement, sniffing at the sandstone as if it were the most fascinating thing it'd ever sniffed.

Halyna gave Klem a nudge, 'do you think...'

'No,' Klem said confidently, 'there are loads of false-eyed crackpots in the Soviet Army...'

But Halyna wasn't so sure...

'I said <u>come on</u>!' Gunter yanked the leash with all his strength and the beast sprang forward, almost knocking him off his feet. 'Thank you,' he said, 'it doesn't hurt to be co-operative once in a while, does it?' Dragging the dog to the car, he called over to Halyna, 'oh, could you please let me have whatever Pedigree Chum is left? The stuff is expensive, and I like to ration it...'

'Sorry,' said Halyna, 'but it's all been eaten...' She decided not to say by whom, 'so for breakfast, the dog ate leftover potatoes and some of Zena's pea soup...' She then promptly disappeared through the shop, into the kitchen and out to the yard to resume her sewing.

Gunter said, 'but I gave you a <u>month's</u> supply!' Shaking his head, he glared down at the dog, 'you greedy glutton!'

Klem shrugged his shoulders, 'I guess body-guarding is a hungry business...'

'It must be for him,' Gunter said, wondering whether it was even possible for one dog to get through thirty cans in only a few days.

'He'll eat anything,' said Klem. 'Those potatoes and peas looked like proper pigswill, but he gobbled up the lot!'

Holding his nose, Gunter dragged the dog the final few yards to the car, being careful to keep its malting fur away from his trousers. He shouted, 'by the way, what do you think of my new transportation?'

Klem cringed when he saw the bright red contraption. 'Not very "anonymous looking", it is? And *why* did you have to buy the same sort as The Ginger Rasputin?'

Gunter shook his head, 'I didn't buy it... it was more like "compensation"...'

'I see,' said Klem, knowing that most of Gunter's property had been confiscated from various villains that lived to regret crossing his path. He doubted Gunter ever bought a thing in his entire life.

Gunter nodded, 'such a fine automobile was wasted on a durak like Ivan! She's much happier now *I'm* her owner... Although I'm going to get her re-sprayed a nice shade of black.'

What else? Klem thought. He could never understand the appeal of owning such a contraption. He said, 'I hope you've had "her" cleaned. You don't know what's been festering in there.'

'Don't worry... she's spotless,' said Gunter, shuddering at the recollection of all the appalling things he found concealed beneath the floor of the luggage area...

Klem narrowed his eyes and noticed the shadow of someone sat in the passenger seat. He asked, 'who's your friend?'

'All will be revealed in a moment,' Gunter said mysteriously, unlocking the car's rear door. 'This is someone who has come *especially* to see you... But first...' He looked the dog in the eye, then pointed at the compact luggage area that was lined with

The Dancing Barber

yesterday's newspapers. He ordered the dog to jump in, but it could only look at him obstinately as if to say, "Make Me."

Gunter clapped his hands harshly and shouted, 'get in there!' The dog had no choice but to comply, especially after the encouragement offered by his steel toe-capped boot. He said 'thank you,' being careful not to trap its tail when the flimsy glass door clicked shut.

'Someone to see *me*?' Klem said, approaching the car. 'But who?'

Gunter walked casually to the frameless passenger door and opened it using the polished chromium handle.

Klem watched the car's suspension rise by several inches once the figure stepped out onto the pavement, the enormous body only just squeezing through the tiny door. The skin-tight clothes that were always on the verge of rupturing had been replaced by a sensitively tailored dress and coat. But it was a pity the milk bottle glasses and smell of cheese and onion remained.

Gunter smiled, 'after hearing all about Ivan's villainy, she wants nothing more to do with him or his hideous mother.' He looked to his side, 'do you Oksana?'

Unexpectedly, Oksana lunged forward and hugged Klem with all her strength, crushing the packets of crisps she'd deposited in every pocket. 'I am sorry for the way you have been treated,' she said, lifting up her milk bottle glasses to wipe a tear from her cheek. 'Mr Gunter has told me how Ivan and his mother took me away from my real Mama – Mrs Zena – and that you are my real Tato…'

'Indeed I am,' said Klem, noticing for the first time how striking a resemblance the unfortunate Oksana bore to her mother.

Klem waved goodbye to Gunter, who'd sped away in his "new" car. He was left standing on the pavement with his estranged daughter and her bulging PVC suitcase. He didn't know what to say, other than, 'please, come inside… your Mama can't wait to see you… Do you like tea?'

Chapter 84

'And who are the *horrible* people with Natalka?' Lenka asked, standing by the back door, picking her nose and flicking green snots over the yard wall. 'They are such ugly women!' She squinted her eyes as if to zoom in on them, 'are they the women? They could be the men dressed as the women?' She looked at Sofia, who stood by her side, 'some of the men, they do that, you know: there was one in our village that – '

Halyna, who sat at her treadle-powered Singer sewing machine in a beam of sunlight at the end of the yard, shouted, 'I don't think Sofia needs to know about things like that...' She then continued embroidering the new cushion cover she'd been working on for months, wondering whether it would ever be finished.

'The apology,' said Lenka, convinced the horrible people with Natalka were friends of that man in the village. 'Ugly is not the word...'

Sofia couldn't help smiling, thinking that maybe Lenka should look in the mirror more often, and then dodge the shattering glass? She said, 'they're Natalka's aunties and they're going back to Ukraine today. They're called Lyudmila and Valentina.'

Lenka said, 'so they *are* the women? Who would have the thought it? They look more like the gorillas in the overcoats! Such people, they should be kept in the zoo!' She scratched energetically beneath her skirt, 'they shouldn't be allowed in the public!'

Sofia almost burst out laughing as she waved goodbye to her best friend and her aunties, watching them trudge down Great Horton Road towards the train station. It seemed the four suitcases they'd brought with them had reproduced, the women resembling packhorses with two bulky suitcases in each hand, and one wedged under each arm. Even Natalka, despite her crutches, was expected to drag an enormous suitcase behind her. Sofia wondered whether there was anything left in Natalka's house...

Having seen enough, Lenka waddled into the kitchen and over to the sink. She decided to wash her hair using plenty of green

The Dancing Barber

Fairy soap and a Brillo pad. This time, she'd try not to get her head stuck under the taps...

When Sofia followed her in, she noticed an old shoebox with the word *SOFIYA* scrawled on the lid stood in the centre of the kitchen table. It wasn't written in felt-tip, so it couldn't have been from her Tato. 'Who is this from?' she asked, looking at it closely, noticing the lid had holes punched through it.

Zena was sat in the armchair with her left foot resting on her right knee, filing away half an inch of desiccated skin from the sole of her foot. She said, 'it is the present from us to you.' She handed Sofia the scrunched-up bill, before brushing her filings all over the carpet, giving the disgruntled cat a substantial dusting of icing sugar.

With soaking wet hair, Lenka added, 'yes, this present, it is to replace the ones that we cooked...'

'Hamsters?' Sofia said excitedly as she lifted the perforated cardboard lid to release the familiar musty smell. She peered in amongst the shredded newspaper and sawdust, not believing what she saw. She said, 'but these aren't hamsters? They're far too furry and large! And since when did hamsters have tails like pipe cleaners?' She stared at her aunties, 'are they guinea pigs?'

'No,' said an offended Zena, 'these are not the pigs of the guinea! The man in the shop, he says they called the Chi-Chi!'

Lenka had rubbed green Fairy soap all over the bird's nest that was her hair, giving herself a big green afro. She said, 'no, they are the Chi-Chi-Nillas!'

Sofia looked puzzled, 'there's no such things as Chi-Chi-Nillas?' She thought for a moment, 'you must mean *chinchillas*? But why would you buy these instead of hamsters?'

'We prefer these,' said Zena, 'they are the meatier.'

Sofia cringed, 'but my teachers entrusted me with <u>hamsters</u>! How am I supposed to explain that they've turned into chinchillas over the course of the Easter holidays?'

'The magic?' Zena said, levering her body out of the armchair and releasing an enormous pocket of gas she'd been incubating.

'I go to a Catholic School,' Sofia said, wondering why Zena was heading her way with a strange look in her eye. 'They don't believe in magic...'

Zena shrugged, 'it was worth the try...' She hawked up a

mouthful of phlegm, making the most repulsive of noises, and spat into the palm of her hand.

Sofia flinched away just in time. She said, 'what do you think you are doing? Get away from me!'

Zena had prepared to smear the slimy green saliva all over a tussock of hair she thought was out of place on her niece's head. She said, 'what is the problem?'

'That is disgusting,' Sofia said, scampering well out of the way.

'What is the disgusting?' Zena said, hawking up more phlegm. 'I only want for you to look the best.'

Every time Sofia thought she'd witnessed the worst of her aunties' habits, one of them always did something even more revolting. But smearing someone's head with spit was nothing when compared to what Zena had used to fix a loose window pane... it certainly was not putty.

Zena stared at her phlegm-filled hand... she didn't like wasting perfectly good spit...

'Oh Zena...' Klem cooed, tottering in from the shop, 'I've brought someone to see you...'

'To see *me*?' Zena said, hoping it wasn't the man from the salami shop: he was far from happy when she and Lenka took half his stock without paying for it...

While Lenka struggled to free her half-rinsed head from beneath the kitchen sink's taps, Zena checked her reflection in the mirror to make sure she looked sufficiently presentable to receive visitors.

To Sofia's mind, such a thing was impossible: she recalled one of Natalka's more colourful sayings, "you can't polish a turd..." But it certainly wouldn't stop Zena from trying...

Zena had somehow managed to spot some hairs out of place in amongst her big curly thatch, so she smeared the offending strands with plenty of the saliva festering in her palm until they merged in with the rest of the greasy mess.

Satisfied with her appearance, Zena pulled the underwear out from where it crept several times a day, readjusted the positioning of her bust in the hammock of her brassière and said, using her poshest voice, 'who is it dear?'

Once the door from the shop opened, Sofia thought she may have been watching a cow being reunited with its long-lost calf as Oksana lunged onto Zena, the two masses colliding with a

The Dancing Barber

resounding thud. They hugged each other so tightly that Sofia was relieved the room contained no naked flames.

Klem tried to look on with pride... his "little" family was together at last. And very soon, once he married Zena, Oksana and that dog would have nothing in common, apart from a furry face.

Sofia decided it was best to leave them to their tea and reminiscences; especially when the cow and calf hugged Klem so tightly that his eyes bulged, and they threatened to do the same thing to her... She also preferred to keep a safe distance away from Lenka who, with her head still stuck in the sink, rumbled like a dormant volcano, the remaining *Chocolax* taking it's time to work through her system. If flatulence ran in the family, she hoped it had skipped her generation.

And she wondered if she'd ever get used to that crisp-eating heifer being her cousin. They may have shared the family genes, but at least Oksana got all the ugly ones...

Sofia took the shoebox containing her "Chi-Chi-Nillas" out to the yard to show to her Mama, who laughed so much that she nearly stitched her finger to the cushion cover. She said, 'now Taras would know if he had one of *those* in his truss!'

Chapter 85

Stanislaw's throat was desperately dry, his belly was bloated and he felt almost unbelievably weak. He didn't care if he never ate another steak nor drank fine wine again: just a handful of grain and a cup of water would do. *So this is what starvation feels like...?*

He personally was responsible for starving tens of thousands of Ukrainian peasants into working on the Collective Farm. He even issued the order for millions of tons of grain to be left to rot, because it was preferable to wasting it on the peasants. How could he have been so cruel? And actually, what was the point of it all: wasn't the Soviet Union big enough?

Cracking his head against the hard wooden joist, Stanislaw thought: *Snap out of it! Stay strong! Of course the Soviet Union isn't big enough! It will never be big enough. And it'd be a lot bigger if it wasn't for people like Klem and Voloshin...*

He was slowly going mad... He had to escape... All he could say – over and over again – was, 'I want that egg, I want Klem dead and I want a closer look at the grey-haired man's head...' Easier said than done, with the loft hatch nailed shut.

Keeping his eye tightly shut, he muttered, 'Joe... Joe... Please help me... I don't want to let you down... Please give me the strength to succeed... I know you want me to succeed!'

With added determination, he forced his tongue between his tightly closed lips until the very tip made contact with the sticky underside of the carpet tape covering his mouth. The adhesive tasted like concentrated honey, but left an aftertaste more akin to petrol. The more he pushed with his tongue, the more the tape stubbornly refused to let go of his skin, gripping it as if it had claws. He then tried to lower his jaw as much as he could, but as the tape had mummified his head, the effort was pointless.

He pressed his ear to the joist, being careful to avoid collecting any more splinters, and listened to the happiness and laughter emanating from the room below. How dare they have fun when a man lay starving to death above their heads? He had a good mind to roll off between the joists, fall straight through the ceiling and

The Dancing Barber

squash them all flat. He wished he could hear what they were saying...

Stanislaw listened so intently that he hadn't noticed the poet's cat paying him a visit, squirting him liberally on the back of his head before sauntering off into the shadows of the eaves.

Down below, he could hear the deep voices belonging to those hideous twins fussing around what sounded like a female child, as if they were mother hens, clucking around an egg. And that reminded him... how did a durak like Klem come into possession of a Fabergé Egg? And if his memory served him correctly, this was no ordinary Fabergé Egg...

The object was worth much more than the stones it contained and had been feared lost during the "Turning Treasures into Tractors" fiasco when the Kremlin was desperate for cash. This egg would be the perfect addition to his burgeoning collection... a collection worthy of the next Tsar...

He listened again. He was sure he heard the hideous twins mention the name "Ivan", followed by a great deal of hawking and spitting... did Ivan have any friends?

And why hadn't Ivan come to rescue his superior... surely he still wanted paying? Or could it be that Ivan wasn't quite as loyal to the Soviet Union as he'd said he was?

The hideous twins then went on about someone called "Taras" being ungrateful for something. He muttered, 'Taras...? That's it... the grey-haired man is called Taras... The Dancing Barber! I knew I'd seen him before...!'

'And they told me I was mad...' Stanislaw whispered to himself. 'It's *them* who are mad, not *me*! They should send themselves to The Asylum! As for me, I'm the sanest person on the planet. And they'll soon realise it when I show the stupid "Ukrainians" how misplaced their faith in Voloshin really is... And as for Klem, I'll do everything to him that he and that hideous Zena woman did to me!' He narrowed his eyes, 'from where could I obtain a dog with sharp teeth?'

Stanislaw stopped himself from laughing. All his plans were worthless unless he could escape... 'My organisation may only have one member, but what a member he is! Isn't that right, Joe...? I'm glad you agree.'

Stanislaw's fungal growth of a nose started to twitch. The

aromas of cooking in the room below had filtered through the ceiling and filled the loft with a humid fog. *Smells like a delicious stew*, he thought, his stomach groaning and his mouth salivating.

The moist, meaty smells had got into his nose along with some of the dust from the woolly insulation. He couldn't help but sneeze so loudly that he banged his bruised ribs harshly against the joist... he whimpered with pain, instantly knowing he'd made too much noise.

The voices in the room below suddenly fell silent; the female child declaring that it'd heard something "up there". But they soon resumed their happiness and laughter; one of the women blamed the noise on the poet's cat trying to catch a pigeon. At least the Zena woman now knew he was still alive... and soon enough, she'd know just how alive he was!

Stanislaw continued to listen... he was sure they were planning to leave after they'd eaten, and they spoke excitedly about wearing something called a "mini-skirt". At least then, the attic would be empty and he could make as much noise as he wanted.

Then followed the sound of food being chiselled from a pan, one of the hideous women saying, "eating the mould is the good for you: the greener it is, the better!"

Stanislaw twitched his nose, realising that all the moist, meaty air had got behind the carpet tape covering his mouth and caused it to peel away. Using his tongue, he levered the gag down onto his chin and stretched his mouth widely in all directions, relishing the wonderful freedom of movement for the first time in days.

He rubbed his dry tongue against his teeth, discovering that one of them was loose... the hideous woman must have hit him harder than he'd thought. He couldn't resist wobbling it to and fro, the action focussing his mind as he planned his escape...

A gust of cool air whistled through his ears, drawing his attention to the "cat flap" in the shadows of the eaves... But before he could do anything, he had to free his wrists and ankles... So with added enthusiasm, he firmly gripped the knitting needle and recommenced his task of repeatedly perforating the thick layers of carpet tape, until he could break free...

The Dancing Barber

Chapter 86

Halyna and Taras found it difficult to keep a straight face when Zena insisted that Klem went to hire a car that was to be her and Lenka's personal transportation for the afternoon. But keeping a straight face was completely impossible when Klem parked his chosen hire car outside the shop and displayed it for everyone to admire. At least the presence of this bright pink automobile gave Taras the opportunity to persuade plenty of passers-by to come in for a haircut and to buy some of the shabby clothes occupying his rack, while they waited for the spectacle to unfold...

The car may not have been as miniscule as a Bubble Car, but considering the load it had to carry, it might as well have been, especially as Oksana had also decided to go along for the ride, together with a picnic hamper the size of a large wardrobe.

Zena and Lenka squeezed through the shop door brandishing their shopping list as if it were a precious scripture. They wore their least-filthy clothes, their pockets stuffed with everything except money. But they could only gawp at the toy car Klem had brought them...

Halyna snorted, but somehow managed not to smile; the three women combined took up more space than two of these cars... and there wasn't even a roof-rack for the hamper...

Zena stomped her foot, almost fracturing the paving stone. She said, 'how do you expect us all to fit into that? Have you gone the mad?'

'He must have gone the mad,' said Lenka, clutching her yellow bucket, as if she were a child heading for Blackpool. 'I could not even fit one of the buttocks into this car!'

Klem frantically twisted his moustache between his fingers until it zig-zagged in all directions. He said, 'look, it's all they had, okay? It was either this bright pink Mini or we would have to travel by bus!' He opened the passenger door, tipped forward the PVC-covered seat and said, 'right, who's going to sit in the back?' He watched as the troika of enormous females looked at each other in disbelief... as did Taras' crew-cutted customers, many of whom were clad in threadbare jumpers and frayed overcoats with mismatched buttons...

Half an hour later, Halyna and Taras waved goodbye to the Mini with the crushed suspension, sparking exhaust and crunching gears... Klem obviously struggling to change up to second due to Zena's thigh spilling onto the gear stick. And he certainly couldn't see through the rear window, because Lenka and Oksana, not to mention the picnic hamper, were crammed onto the back seat, their bodies pressed up against the windows like over-risen dough in a glass bowl.

Halyna could only cover her eyes as the Mini surged in front of a Ford Anglia, causing it to swerve and plough straight into a Triumph Herald.

She grabbed Taras' arm and dragged him into the shop the instant the crumpled cars' drivers jumped from behind their wheels to exchange large pieces of their minds. The Mini, meanwhile, disappeared up Great Horton Road, leaving fountains of sparks in its wake.

'Listen to this,' Taras said, rattling the pockets of his smock. 'Today's been the best day since... I can't remember!' He whispered, 'and I've even sold half those rags on my rack too... And it's not even two o'clock!'

'Mmm, it seems my sisters are quite the tourist attraction,' said Halyna. 'What will people think when they see them in town? I can't imagine the doorman letting them into Busby's...'

'When they come back,' Taras said, 'and your delightful sisters decide to put on those mini-skirts they're threatening to buy, you make sure I'm not around. *That* is something I do not wish to see!'

'And do you think I do?' said Halyna, looking over the top of her plastic framed glasses. 'We can only hope they don't have their size!' She smiled, 'I shouldn't worry... I don't think it likely that any shop will stock a range of XXXL mini-skirts...'

Reclining on a picnic rug on a sunny afternoon in Manningham Park, Klem quietly munched a cucumber sandwich made with rye bread, nibbled the occasional chunk of leftover Easter salami and

The Dancing Barber

washed it all down with his favourite variety of green tea.

All he wanted was a few minutes to himself to recover from the shopping expedition he'd had to endure without uttering a single word of criticism. He didn't even complain after Zena and Lenka decided to try on every pair of bloomers Busby's stocked, thus bringing a literal meaning to the term "shop soiled".

The twins then sent him to an expensive tailor to purchase a waistcoat for Uncle Viktor; but instead of measurements, they provided him with a photograph of Viktor in his usual attire... That was the first – and last – time Klem had ever been thrown out of a shop...

The women then decided they were hungry and were desperate for sustenance... So while Oksana munched through her usual Golden Wonder, Zena and Lenka devoured several packets of Smith's Crisps, chewing and swallowing the sachets of salt they contained without noticing.

If that wasn't bad enough, Klem was then ordered to drive them to "The" Shipley Glen, where they insisted on visiting the quaint little fairground at the top of the Victorian funicular railway. The troika of females all decided to clamber onto the carousel, its tired motor nowhere near strong enough to cope with the heavy load, its gears crunching and grinding before spewing out plumes of blue smoke. Lenka had a go on the seesaw, requiring ten small children to sit opposite her, and only just counterbalancing her weight. When she jumped off, she nearly sent them all into orbit. Zena then decided she wanted to "make up for the old times" by giving Oksana a push on the swings, snapping every chain in the row before the attendant pleaded with them to leave. But before they went, Oksana insisted on going down the tubular slide, predictably getting stuck a third of the way down, necessitating the Fire Brigade to be summoned to cut her free.

So Klem thought he'd keep them out of trouble by taking them to Manningham Park... But things were set to get much worse. He'd never witnessed such a deplorable display of gluttony in his entire life. It was bad enough when Oksana replaced the cucumber in her sandwiches with cheese and onion crisps, but when she and her mother decided to have an eating contest which involved them somehow inserting every sandwich the picnic basket contained into their already full mouths, Klem didn't know where to look. People on afternoon strolls would stop and marvel at this uncouth behaviour, wondering how the little man in the pinstriped suit and a pet cat on a lead had managed to persuade these gorillas to dress in human clothes?

Lenka then decided she liked the look of the moorhens, which were quietly minding their own business on the banks of the boating lake, pecking randomly at the tiny insects wandering around on the manicured lawns. She thought these wildfowl were "the little black chickens" and in less than ten minutes, the poor little creature she'd caught had been garrotted, plucked, gutted and placed on a roaring bonfire she'd created using dry reeds, surrounded by a trench she'd dug in the aforementioned manicured lawns.

With black feathers still raining down on him, Klem could barely watch as Lenka took it upon herself to throw the Park Warden and his Assistant into the boating lake as if they were as light as pebbles, all because they poured water on her gourmet feast and told her she was banned from ever coming to Manningham Park again.

And if that wasn't bad enough, Zena and Oksana then proceeded to sing "Ta-Ra-Ra-Bum-Di-Yey" at full volume, breaking wind exceptionally loudly each time they sang "Bum", causing all the ducks on the boating lake to scatter immediately with fright. As indeed did Klem...

The Dancing Barber

Chapter 87

The cheap plastic pendulum clock on the kitchen wall chimed quarter past three.

From her seat in front of the television, Zena glared at Taras and said, with a yawn, 'how can you find this the interesting?' She continued combing her curly hair with what appeared to be a miniature lawn rake, the wiry implement frequently getting entangled in amongst the many greasy knots, scattering dandruff and fleas far and wide. 'This *Danger Man*, it is like watching the paint dry.'

'How *dare* you?' Taras protested, leaning forward to turn up the volume. He whispered, 'this happens to be my *favourite* programme.' He put a finger to his lips and said, 'now shush: I'm trying to listen!'

Zena folded her arms, cradling the melons of her bosom and fidgeting pompously from side to side. She was unable to get comfortable on the hard wooden chair Taras insisted she sat on, the sheet of newspaper protecting the thin cushion, scrunching and ripping. She said with a frown, '*Danger Man, Smanger Man*... it is *worse* than the rubbish!'

'No one's forcing you to watch,' Taras snapped, straining to hear the dialogue, 'if you don't like it you can – !'

'Taras!' Halyna shouted, whilst carefully placing a stack of dirty plates into the kitchen sink. 'What have I told you about your language?'

'Yes, yes,' Taras said, shuffling his chair closer to the television, eager not to miss how Patrick McGoohan's character was to thwart yet another of his sinister enemies. He'd hoped Klem would have kept the trolls out of the house until much later. But he had no such luck; they returned after less than two hours, hauling their mound of acquisitions, minus Klem and minus the hire car, offering no explanations for the absence of either.

Zena narrowed her eyes and said, 'what is this "uck" that Taras, he always says?'

'That is *not* a word for you to know,' said Halyna, rasping the last of the Fairly Liquid from the crushed bottle into yet another sink full of washing up. She didn't want her sisters going back to Chaplinka corrupted by Taras' bad language; and was glad Taras hadn't used the worst of the four-letter words.

Halyna said, 'Taras! You should be grateful that I have not only filled the sink with water, but also added the Fairy Liquid! You do realise that I'm still on strike! So now it's up to you to do the washing up... And you'd better do it goodski!'

Taras snapped, 'I'll do it tomorrow... I don't have time now... And when *Danger Man* finishes, I've got an hour's rehearsal for *Sleeping Beauty*, after which I must go to town to collect something I've bought. Now shush... I'm watching this...'

'Never mind your stupid *Danger Man*! You will do the washing up now!' said Halyna. 'I won't tell you again!'

'I said when this finishes... and I won't tell you again!' Taras' nose twitched, 'and tell your reeking sister that it's time she learned to control her bowels!'

Halyna was about to lob the washing up brush at him, but had second thoughts. She always knew Taras wouldn't change his ways for long... and to think, she'd almost succumbed to doing his ironing.

Zena turned to Halyna, 'I cannot believe that you have such a *rude* husband! And if he tells me that I smell once more...' She clenched her fist, 'I do not know what I will do...'

Taras was now so close to the dome of the television screen that the static electricity made the tiny hairs on his nose stand on end. He said, 'will everyone *please* be quiet; it's just getting to the good bit!' Despite his proximity to the screen making the image look like a cubist painting, he could just about follow what was going on...

'It is the okay, Halynochka,' Zena said, struggling to stand up, 'I will go and see Lenka. I know when I am not the wanted!'

The moment Zena stood up, her hefty buttocks ripped straight through the material of the mini-skirt she'd miraculously inserted her body into, displaying the most stained pair of bloomers Taras had ever seen. And oblivious to the fact that her entire hind quarter was displayed for all to see, she waddled out to the yard, curious to find out what Lenka was doing with those chinchillas...

Taras shook his head and said, 'the *stupid* woman,' as he

The Dancing Barber

watched the mini-skirt snag on the doorknob and dangle like an enormous sleeping bat while Zena waddled outside in a state that might hopefully get her arrested.

'What did you say?' Halyna screamed, slamming the washing up brush into the sink, a fountain of white suds rising into the air. 'What have I told you about addressing me as "woman"?'

'I meant <u>her</u>!' Taras pointed outside, '*she's* the stupid woman, not you!' The lump on his head was still throbbing from the Hoover, and he did not want a repeat performance. But to his horror, Halyna was already brandishing a rolling pin and heading his way...

Chapter 88

'Lenka, what *do* you think you are the doing?' Zena said, storming into the yard, her stained bloomers glowing in the late afternoon sunshine. She hoisted the drenched chinchillas out of the bucket by their furry tails and watched them wriggle and shake themselves dry. 'The things, they are the exhausted... if you leave them any longer, they will be the drowned!' Through the slits of her eyes, she examined Lenka's sly expression, 'unless that was the plan?'

Lenka looked away, busying herself with something inside her new, yet exceptionally scuffed handbag that she hid behind the dented dustbin.

Zena said, 'these are <u>not</u> the food! They are the pets! Remember, we buy them to stop the nuns from getting the cross with Sofia... The nuns, they can be very nasty when they get the cross...'

Lenka's bottom lip quivered ever so slightly, 'can I not just eat the *one* of them?' She picked up the fattest chinchilla, sniffed its musty fur and hooked a finger around its neck. She looked at Zena from under her brow, contemplating doing the same thing to the rodent as she'd done to the moorhen in Manningham Park. 'Please?'

'No!' Zena said, snatching away the unfortunate animal that hadn't a clue about how close it had come to death. She squeezed the chinchilla through the tiny cage door and watched as it went to snuggle with the other one in amongst the sawdust and shredded newspaper. 'And do not pull that face: you are <u>not</u> the child!'

Lenka continued to sulk, cradling her bosoms in her folded arms. 'I cannot the help it... they look so delicious...' She nudged her scuffed handbag further behind the dustbin, thinking Zena hadn't noticed.

Zena sniffed the air, but couldn't pinpoint the source of a *very* familiar smell.

'But I only wanted the *one* of them,' Lenka said, fidgeting her bosoms. 'I am sure that with all her money, our Halynochka, she could buy Sofia another Chi-Chi-Nilla... It is the fact that

The Dancing Barber

Halynochka, she could buy the hundreds of them and we could take them to Chaplinka and open the special Chi-Chi-Nilla Farm: we could sell the fur, we could sell the meat, and then we could afford to build our own The Bolling Hall in Chaplinka. The idea is the good, yes?'

'Sometimes Lenka, I really do think you have the screws loose.' Zena thought for a moment, 'and that reminds me... I wonder why Halynochka, she has not taken us to The Bolling Hall yet?'

Lenka pursed her lips, 'I think she is the embarrassed of us... They all are... They do not eat our stew, they spray the perfume wherever we have the been and even Klem, he runs away from us in the park, leaving us with the silly little car that we could not the drive: no wonder it end up in the lake...'

'Embarrassed?' exclaimed Zena. 'What is to be the embarrassed about?' she said, reaching beneath her bloomers and giving her backside a good scratch, regardless of the fact that she was in full view of a couple of dozen passengers on the upper floor of a double-decker bus waiting in traffic on the main road. She then used a hair-clip to remove what had collected beneath her stout fingernails, wiping it on her bosom, then slotting the clip back in amongst her greasy thatch when she'd finished. 'I think Halynochka, she has just been too busy to take us to The Bolling Hall... She is so busy that she has not even got the time to break the wind.'

'Fortunately,' Lenka said, '*I* do not have the same problem!' She emitted a rasp so loud that pigeons scattered for miles around.

Zena sniffed the air again, her nose twitching like a pig's snout. Intermingled with the scents of traffic fumes and flatulence, she'd realised precisely where that familiar smell was coming from. She picked up the bucket that had previously contained the chinchillas and put it to her nose. She stared at her sister, 'Lenka...' She took a sip, declaring instantly, 'this is the <u>samahon</u>! Why are you letting the Chi-Chi-Nillas swim in the samahon?'

Lenka smiled, 'how you say, it is the *marinade*! There was so much samahon left over, and I ran out of the bottles... I thought it would make the Chi-Chi-Nillas taste even better... Yes...?'

'I have never heard of anything so the stupid! You cannot *marinade* the living animal! Now come on,' Zena said, grabbing the bucket of samahon in one hand and Lenka's scuffed handbag in the other. 'The samahon, it is the too good to waste! In the time it takes you to filter off the fur, I will find some more bottles.' She looked at the yellow bucket and sighed, 'did you have to use this one? I wondered why the samahon, it was a little brownish...' She shrugged, 'the never mind...'

'I will take that,' Lenka said, reaching out for her scuffed handbag.

'It okay,' said Zena, 'I have it.' She stood still, wondering why Lenka was so keen to carry a bag she didn't particularly want to buy in the first place. She put down the bucket. Noticing the handbag felt rather heavy, she tore open the zip and was woefully disappointed with what she found hidden inside...

Lenka gulped and looked at her sturdy feet.

Holding open the bag, Zena said, 'and *how* did this get in here? You *cannot* steal from the future brother-in-love! You are to put it back before he realises it is the missing!'

Lenka bowed her head, 'but it is so the beautiful, do you not the think?'

Zena pointed angrily up the stairs, 'it is not yours!'

'But I was not going to the steal it! I only like the looking at it...' She sighed, 'I can imagine myself to be the Tsarina...' She curtseyed, then gave a bow. Noticing Zena's expression showed no sign of thawing, she trudged back upstairs and did what she'd been ordered to do.

The Fabergé Egg was the prettiest thing she'd ever seen... if only she could break it in half... she could then turn it into a pair of ear-rings... Klem wouldn't mind... She wrapped a hand around each half and had another go...

The Dancing Barber
Chapter 89

'Forget the tea,' said a flat-cap, 'have a <u>real</u> drink for once!'

'<u>No</u>, thank you,' Klem said, sitting at his table at the Club, trying to get some peace. He'd rolled his moustache between his thumbs and forefingers so much that it zig-zagged in all directions, resembling bunches of pipe cleaners protruding from his nostrils. He turned away and looked out of the window, hoping the flat-caps would realise he wanted to be left alone.

Another flat-cap asked, 'did he say thank you?'

'I think he did,' said the first flat-cap. And before Klem could protest, he was presented with a pint of beer, the froth of which overflowed the sides so much that it made the glass look as though it was wearing a curly white wig.

Klem looked down at the glass of brown swirling liquid and said, 'it's very kind of you, but you know I <u>don't</u> drink booze…'

The first flat-cap shook his head, 'you were a wino, weren't you?' He pointed at the glass, 'but this is different, this is <u>beer</u>!' He smiled broadly, as if he was the serpent in The Garden of Eden.

'Ah-ah,' Klem said, waving his finger, 'I was an alcoholic, so neither can I drink beer.' He lifted his teapot and poured what was left of the strong tea into his cup, 'I'll stick to my Earl Grey…' His pocket watch chimed half past three… he always thought that drinking alcohol in the afternoon was inappropriate, and the preserve of the lower classes.

'But you haven't been an alcoholic for years,' said the second flat-cap, pushing the frothy beer closer to Klem's hand. He said, 'go on, it won't do you any harm to just have this one… You deserve it… Go on…'

'<u>No</u>, thank you,' Klem said sternly, pushing the glass away. 'Why don't you drink it yourself?'

'We've got our own,' said the flat-caps, clinking their glasses together, each then taking a big slurp. 'We want to toast your good health and the good health of your, *beautiful* wife to be and your *adorable* daughter,' they said, trying not to sound too sarcastic. 'So go on…' They pushed his glass back over, 'just have this one...'

Seven pints later, Klem's entire body had turned to jelly and he flopped to the floor in a crumpled pile of pinstriped suit. Mister Pushkin – who'd seen it so many times before – rested its chin on its paws and dozed off, knowing that it'd be hours before its master sobered up... possibly even days...

Even though the seat of his pinstripe trousers had soaked up plenty of the spilled beer contained in the carpet's thick pile, the damp cloth clinging uncomfortably to his skin like a well-used nappy, Klem still managed to sing every verse of the Ukrainian National Anthem at the top of his slurring voice until he couldn't utter another syllable. At that point, the two flat-caps continued from where he'd left off, striking a harmonic melody as their baritone voices combined, while Klem re-lubricated his vocal chords with yet another pint.

He'd developed a taste for beer... he wasn't especially keen on the flavour, but it did help him block out some of the misery of his life, past and present. And strangely, even after eight pints, he still didn't want to go to the toilet...

Mister Pushkin had already inched as far away from its owner as it could, reaching the full radius permitted by the blue and yellow leather leash. But now it had no choice but to jump onto the table to avoid the spreading puddle emanating from beneath its owner... Cats always choose their owners, and Mister Pushkin thought it was about time for a change...

The inebriated barman with the Robert Mitchum eyes had fallen off his stool again, so the flat-caps dashed behind the bar to help themselves to as much samahon as they wanted, even daring to drink the proper vodka straight from the optics.

'You looking forward to your forthcoming nuptials?' asked the first flat-cap, meandering back to the table and thrusting a glass brimming with crystal clear samahon into Klem's wilting hand.

'Of course,' said Klem despondently, hauling his limp body back onto a chair. 'I simply can't *wait* to walk her down the aisle.'

The second flat-cap smirked and said, 'I hope the aisle will be wide enough, otherwise you might have to walk behind her!'

'True,' said Klem, thinking that if he did have to walk behind her, then how on earth would he see where he was going? And she'd probably gas him with all her flatulence.

'And where will you buy the wedding dress?' asked the first flat-cap. 'You'll need a lot of material to cover all of that!'

The second flat-cap smiled and said, 'I know a fella from the circus who could lend her his tent...'

Klem looked glumly at the samahon before throwing it down his throat, feeling it burn its way to his stomach. When the flat-caps went on to make several crude comments relating to reinforced bedsprings, Klem dropped the glass on the carpet and commandeered a whole bottle...

After only a week, his enthusiasm for marrying Zena was waning rapidly; in fact it was largely non-existent. How could a woman develop so many deplorable habits in only twelve short years? How could he even think about marrying someone who thought it was appropriate to eat dog food and throw faeces out of a top floor window? And then there was the smell: if it wasn't rotten cabbage, it was mouldy cheese, and if it wasn't mouldy cheese, it was gone off fish. The more aware of these things he became, the less time he wanted to spend with the woman, and the thought of marrying her made him feel exceptionally ill.

At least he didn't need to worry about obtaining a wedding ring... When Mrs Wiggins' husband came around to fix the perpetually blocked lavvies, he brought his toolbox with him, inside of which Klem discovered a wonderfully shiny brass ring – a plumber's olive – that looked as if it were made of rose gold. Mrs Wiggins' husband was kind enough to let him have it for "nowt"; Klem was most grateful, because – although he was ashamed to think it – a gold wedding ring would be wasted on a woman like Zena. He only hoped it was wide enough to fit onto her finger...

But Zena and Oksana's performance in Manningham Park was the final straw: he cringed as the tune to "Ta-Ra-Ra-<u>Bum</u>-Di-Yey" repeatedly played in his ears. He contemplated telling Zena about her ceaseless scratching and picking, flatulence and bodily odours, nerve gas breath and caster sugar dandruff, but he knew it would only make her cross. And his eyes watered at the thought of what she did to Ivan when he made her cross that last time...

Klem watched the flat-caps amuse themselves by balancing beer mats and bottle-tops all over an increasingly annoyed Mister

Pushkin, wagering how many it'd take before the cat clawed them. He shook his head as he watched the drunker of the flat-caps run directly to the toilet with his gashed hand raised high above his head. The silly fool shouldn't have tried to balance that last bottle-top on Pushkin's nose. The cat had already been decorated with eighteen bottle-tops scattered all over its back, not to mention a small house made from beer mats... No wonder it unsheathed its claws and went ballistic...

'That must be a record,' said Klem, knowing the two flat-caps always enjoyed a wager that somehow involved antagonising the cat. 'How much have you won?'

'A whole pound!' said the other flat-cap, turning to face Klem, yet continuing to stroke the simmering cat. 'Assuming he,' he nodded towards the toilet door, 'won't need to use the pound note as a bandage...'

Klem knew his friend shouldn't have taken his eyes off the cat. He held out a handkerchief and said, 'here, you'd better have this.' He winced at the bleeding wound, 'I've seen worse... Pushkin was only playing... You'd have known about it if he'd *really* meant business...'

'I suspect the cat's as annoyed as you are at having to go back to Ukraine,' said the flat-cap, tying Klem's blue and yellow chequered handkerchief around his index finger, staining large parts of it dark red. 'It can't be much fun over there these days...' He sighed, 'it wasn't much fun back then...'

Klem sat up straight. He pulled the embroidered cuffs too far out of his jacket sleeves and then attempted to straighten the green ribbon at his collar, yet only managed to undo the knot. But maintaining an upright posture was too much effort, so he slid lower into the chair. He slurred, 'that's not true, I *am* looking forward to going back to Chaplinka! It will be nice to live in the countryside again, after spending so many years in this polluted city.'

The flat-cap smiled and was about to say something, but changed his mind at the last moment.

'What is it?' Klem asked.

The flat-cap smirked, 'I was just thinking; if you ever become nostalgic for pollution, you'd only have to go and smell your wife-to-be...'

The Dancing Barber

Klem agreed, but he didn't think it was funny. He said, 'but maybe you're right about Pushkin... maybe he *is* annoyed at having to go back to Ukraine, especially if it means living with Zena... I don't think they get on... In fact, I think he hates her...'

The flat-cap nodded, 'it's understandable... and don't forget, a cat's nose is so much more sensitive than your own... To Pushkin, Zena will smell worse than... well, you know...'

'I quite agree...' said Klem, 'and maybe worse than that...' He racked his brain for something positive to say. 'But at least in Chaplinka, I'll have more time for writing poetry... *proper* poetry, not the nationalistic stuff... That is something I will look forward to.'

He checked the time on his pocket watch; it had only just gone quarter past four... He couldn't remember the last time he'd been so drunk so early in the day... Oh yes he could: how else could he have produced Oksana...?

'And Voloshin...' slurred the flat-cap, 'will you miss him?'

Klem shook his head, 'I'll never be rid of Voloshin.'

The flat-cap smirked; he knew just as well as everyone else that Klem and Voloshin were inseparable...

'I wonder if the Ukrainian Orthodox Church would let me back into the Priesthood. Then once Chaplinka's church is rebuilt, I could be the village Priest...' Klem rubbed his hands together, 'and then I'd be able to go on a nice sabbatical to the Saint Sofia Cathedral in Kyiv... I have missed the serenity of the place...' He looked at the flat-cap and said, 'what about you... do you ever dream about going back to Ukraine?'

But the flat-cap had fallen into a snory sleep, his chin resting on a beer mat, and his hands hanging down to the damp carpet...

Klem shook his head. He said, 'the drunkard...' before helping himself to even more samahon.

Chapter 90

'Just look at the state of that,' said a headscarved old woman, tut-tutting and shaking her head as she watched Klem weave his way around the lamp-posts, holding an empty bottle of samahon as if it were a trophy and humming the tune to the wedding march. He almost fell over when his leather-soled boots slipped on the mossy sandstone pavement.

'And I thought he *never* touched the stuff,' said a second headscarf.

'You obviously didn't see him at The Alhambra last Sunday,' said a third headscarf.

'So he was...' said the second.

'...As a pond full of newts,' said the third, 'and trussed up like a life-sized puppet.'

'Once an alcoholic, always an alcoholic,' said the first headscarf, the most sensible member of the whole Gaggle, who held the ambition to become The Gossipmonger's successor. 'But unlike my husband, Klem doesn't insist on staying until chucking out time...' She checked the time on her old NHS fob watch, 'it's only just gone half past four.' She then looked pitifully at Mister Pushkin, 'I don't know how he'd get home without the cat's help...'

'Mmm,' said the second headscarf, 'then the cat can come back in a few hours to guide Taras home...' She shook her head as she watched Taras struggle into the bar, wrestling an enormous cardboard box in his arms.

The sensible one smiled, 'it doesn't matter what time of day it is, there's always someone from that household lounging around in there...' She sighed, 'I hope Sofia doesn't follow their example...'

'Mmm,' said the third headscarf, 'of all of them, Sofia is by *far* the most intelligent...'

The sensible one said, 'but at least I shall get some peace this evening. My husband will definitely not be leaving the house...' She laughed, 'the list of jobs I've given him should keep him occupied until bedtime!'

The Dancing Barber

The other two were jealous... if only they could control their husbands as easily.

The old women watched as Mister Pushkin tugged at the leash each time Klem veered off in the wrong direction. The sensible headscarf said, 'surely it would be better if Klem wore roller-skates; then the cat would only have to tow him home...'

The Gaggle wandered into the Club, deciding that they'd done quite enough gossiping for one day... Even though The Gossipmonger had been gone for over a week, her influence, like the smell of mothballs, was difficult to shake off. But gossiping was no longer the Gaggle's primary activity, as the heavily laden handbags they carried would suggest...

'Do we really need to lug all this stuff?' asked the second headscarf.

'It weighs a tonne,' said the third, 'my arms are getting longer...'

'Of course,' said their interim leader. 'It'll all be worth it in the end...'

Chapter 91

'Ey-Up Mister Tar-Arse!' declared the Urchin, trotting into the Uki Club bar with a crate full of rattling empties. 'How's it hanging?'

Taras placed his full glass of vodka onto the warped coaster. He said, 'how is *what* hanging?'

'Nowt in a literal sense,' said the Urchin, shrugging his shoulders. 'It's just a figment of expression... know what I mean?'

'No, I most certainly do not,' said Taras. 'Now go away! The bar is no place for a child.'

'Keep your hair on, Mister Tar-Arse... I'll go when I get me money! I'll get a shilling for this lot, I will.' He heaved the crate onto the bar and shouted: 'service!'

Taras smiled, 'I wouldn't bother... Robert Mitchum's asleep in the cellar.'

'Is he?' said the Urchin. 'In that case, I'll run and tell me Pap that the booze is free!'

'Your "Pap" isn't a member of this Club,' said Taras. 'It's for Ukrainians only.'

'But we is what you call "honorary" Ukrainians,' said the Urchin, 'on account of me attendin' your studio, ain't we?'

Although Taras couldn't stop him running to fetch his "Pap", he was at least grateful the boy referred to him as the more formal, "*Mister* Tar-Arse", instead of just "Tar-Arse".

And the Ballet Studio would never be the same again: from the moment the Urchin turned up at the rehearsal, wearing his "Pap's" stained long johns and his "Mam's" dirty canvass pumps, none of the ballerinas seemed able to keep their eyes off him. What was it about this scruffy boy they found so fascinating? It certainly wasn't his "suntanned" face... Zena and Lenka soon made sure it had been thoroughly wiped clean, bringing a whole new meaning to the term *spit and polish*.

At least his Sofia hadn't fallen under the Urchin's spell, despite him making every effort to impress her with his constant supply of wilting dandelions. But by his own admission, the Urchin was "as clever as two short planks", so it would take a long time for him to

The Dancing Barber

"get the message", as Natalka would say when fending him off, frequently using an NHS crutch to reinforce her message.

Taras' feet shuffled on the squelchy carpet... it seemed damper than usual, and smellier. He raised his feet onto the cardboard box to keep his suede shoes dry. From the corner of his eye, he noticed a troika of headscarved old women parade into the bar, lugging their enormous handbags over to their preferred table. Whatever they were up to, they certainly looked much happier without The Gossipmonger's overbearing presence.

In the time it took Taras to drink his well-deserved glass of vodka and watch a squadron of starlings bombard the window through which he gazed, the Urchin had gone home and fetched his "Pap". Taras cringed when he watched the rotund string-vested layabout saunter behind the bar and drink beer directly from the tap, spilling most of it down his front, decorating his face with a beard of froth worthy of Father Christmas.

'Ey-Up Mister Tar-Arse,' shouted the Urchin, helping himself to the shilling he reckoned he was owed from the till. 'What's your surname? No one knows what it is?'

Taras watched the Urchin scrawl a note onto the back of a cigarette packet and wedge it in between the empty bottles in the crate. At least he was honest; unlike his belching "Pap". Taras coughed, 'if you must know,' he said hesitantly, 'my surname is Panas...'

'What?' screamed the Urchin, 'you mean that your name is Tar-Arse Pan-Arse? That's a lot of Arse for one name... Wait until I tell me Mam; she'll wet 'er knickers!'

Taras knew he shouldn't have told him. 'It happens to be a very distinguished name,' he sipped at his second glass of satisfying vodka, 'like Chamberlain would be in this country.'

The Urchin smirked, 'more like chamber pot...'

Taras didn't let it rile him too much: today was one of his "good mood" days, and he was determined not to let anything or anyone spoil it. He'd even managed to stay calm when the absent-minded coal man tipped several barrows full of coal down into the studio only half an hour before the rehearsal was due to commence. And what a rehearsal it had been... He reached into the inside pocket of his blue blazer and extracted his dog-eared notebook, each page adorned with green ticks from his felt-tip pen. It was hard to believe that not one dancer put a foot wrong… it seemed the carrot of fame was much more of an incentive than his cane ever was…

'I danced right good, didn't I?' said the Urchin, pirouetting across the soggy carpet, flicking globules of spilled beer all over the place…

'I suppose you did…' Taras said; it was a fact that surprised everyone.

From behind the bar, the Urchin's Pap shouted, 'what do you think you're doing? You look like a complete pansy poofter! And I'm not having any of *them* in my family!' He shuffled over to the next tap and proceeded to empty another barrel of stale beer, not noticing when his son raised both his middle fingers at him, sticking his tongue out for good measure.

Taras would have said something… he believed all children should behave respectfully towards their parents… but he didn't think this "Pap" was worth respecting. 'Keep up the practice,' he said to the Urchin, who despite wearing scuffed hobnail boots was pirouetting remarkably accurately. 'Because practice makes perfect!'

'Thank you Mister Tar-Arse Pan-Arse! I will!' said the Urchin, prancing over to the door, once again displaying his middle fingers to his slurping Pap. 'See you at tomorrow's re'earsal!'

'Goodbye,' said Taras, glad he was finally leaving.

Walking backwards, the Urchin banged into the door frame, 'and this time, I'll make sure I wash me face proper; I don't want them fat Ken Dodd women fleggin' all over me again…'

Taras smiled. The Urchin may have been common, but he was quite funny. Maybe it was a good thing he attended the studio… perhaps then, some of the other local boys would realise that ballet wasn't just for the "pansy poofters".

The Urchin ran out onto the street and immediately collided with Sofia and Natalka who were coming the other way. When Sofia smiled and said "hello", the Urchin's face went redder than a beetroot… he scampered away before Natalka had opportunity to chastise him… or hit him with her NHS crutch…

Taras couldn't believe his eyes… Sofia had no business *smiling* at the Urchin… He knew how Urchin's minds worked… something would have to be said… And he was supremely disappointed that Sofia had chosen to emulate Natalka by wearing

The Dancing Barber

the minutest mini-skirt... something would *definitely* have to be said... there was no way his daughter was going to be seen in public dressed like that... it would only give the Urchin and his ilk "ideas"...

'Sofia!' Taras shouted, hammering the table with his index finger, 'come here, <u>NOW</u>!'

'Yes Tato,' said Sofia, tiptoeing across the squelchy carpet, wondering why the bar smelled like the outdoor lavvy.

'Your aunties may dress like trollops, but you certainly will <u>not</u>!' Taras took off his blue blazer and draped it over her shoulders, 'you are to wear this until you go home and change into something more appropriate... Understand?'

'But *Tato*...' Sofia said, sliding her arms into the sleeves of the tobacco scented blazer. The blazer was so long that the hem wicked moisture from the carpet... and it was more than just the usual spilled beer.

'Don't *Tato* me,' said Taras. 'If you have any hope of being accepted into the Royal Ballet, then you must look respectable! Would Margot Fonteyn dress like this? No! What about Anna Pavlova? Certainly not! So neither will you! Understand?'

When Sofia saw the jugular veins on the sides of her Tato's neck bulge and pulsate, she daren't utter another syllable.

'Go and sit in the corner while I finish my vodka,' said Taras, refilling the glass from the bottle. 'Then we will all go home together.'

For the first time today, the tightness in Taras' chest subsided after the burning liquid descended to his stomach... it was as if the vodka had dissolved away the pain... Once the "Showtime" performance was over, he vowed to see a proper doctor... he hadn't eaten anything all day, so it couldn't be indigestion... He held his left arm closer to his side... pressing his ribs seemed to alleviate the pain, for the time being, at least... And he could do without Sofia adding to his stresses.

Sofia's shoulders slumped... She'd only dared to leave the house wearing the mini-skirt, because, for the first time ever, she was confident her thighs no longer looked like a pair of baggy jodhpurs. And as Natalka frequently said, "if you've got it, flaunt it"... And finally, she had "it"! But flaunting it was only possible if your Tato wasn't called Taras Panas...

'Sofia! Natalka!' shouted a voice from the door. 'Why didn't you wait for me?'

The girls' eyes rolled to the ceiling when the out of breath Oksana stumbled into the bar, her chubby face glistening with perspiration.

Taras narrowed his eyes: 'it was my understanding that you three were going to be friends from now on...?'

Looking at the carpet, Sofia and Natalka murmured their excuses...

'Go and get Oksana some cheese and onion crisps,' Taras said, giving his daughter a shilling. He whispered, 'and remember, be <u>nice</u> to your cousin...'

'Yes Tato,' Sofia said, crossing her fingers. As the inebriated barman was nowhere to be seen, and the only other person behind the bar was an unconscious string-vested drunk, Sofia pocketed the shilling and helped herself to several packets of cheese and onion, which Oksana proceeded to devour in record time.

With fragments of crisp fountaining from her over-filled mouth, Oksana said, 'Sofia, it's lovely to be living at your house...'

'Yes,' Sofia said, 'lovely... although I could think of other, more accurate words...' Looking directly at Oksana, she said, 'have Zena and Klem mentioned when they were thinking of going back to Chaplinka?'

'Hey Natalka,' said Oksana, 'how come your ankle mended so quickly?'

'Ignore me, why don't you...' muttered Sofia.

Natalka smiled, 'my ankle might not have been as badly injured as I'd first thought...' She rested her crutches against the table, 'actually, I don't need these any more...'

Oksana brushed the fragments of crisps from her downy beard. She said, 'so you weren't faking it, then? Just so Sofia could play Odette?'

'Oh *no*, of course not,' said Natalka, the corners of her mouth turning ever so slightly upwards. 'But it all worked out *beautifully* in the end.'

Sofia agreed... she knew there was a reason why Natalka was her best friend... She'd also noticed Oksana had inherited Zena's skill for dodging questions. She said, 'Oksana, so when *are* you going to Chaplinka?'

The Dancing Barber

'Yes,' Natalka said hopefully, 'are you going soon?'

Knowing it was rude to speak with her mouth full, Oksana crammed in as many crisps as she could...

Taras had forgotten how nice it was to drink proper Russian vodka for a change. Although it cost a fortune, it was much tastier than Halyna's samahon and by comparison, Zena and Lenka's moonshine was paint-stripper. He swirled the remnants around his glass and shuffled his feet contentedly on the large cardboard box he'd lugged all the way from town. Admiring his brand new suede shoes, he listened to the sounds of Chopin flowing from the radio behind the bar and was instantly transported to his student days in St Petersburg.

Today had been a good day: the weather had been fine and warm, the rehearsal for *Sleeping Beauty* had gone so smoothly that they were finished in less than an hour; and now even Oksana was making friends with his two best dancers. Things couldn't be better.

He was as happy now as he'd been in St Petersburg. But back then, fame and wealth were abruptly and brutally replaced by poverty and notoriety. The poverty he could deal with, but the notoriety had resulted in too many encounters with cyanide-tipped umbrellas... Klem was always much better at dodging them than he ever was.

Gazing out of the window, Taras relaxed and enjoyed having a pain-free chest. Judging by the darkness of the clouds and the silence of the songbirds, the day would surely end with a thunderstorm. And some heavy rain was needed, because a second squadron of starlings had bombarded the window... it would undoubtedly amuse Halyna to discover how many days it would take for the rain to rinse it away.

He shuffled in his seat; his chest may not have hurt, but his lower back was in terrible pain... Having to lift Oksana without the aid of a winch should come with a health warning. He still didn't know why he'd let Zena persuade him to cast Oksana in the lead role? *Sleeping*, she had no problem with; but she was certainly no *Beauty*... He'd already heard mutterings that the ballet should by renamed *Kipping Fatty*... unkind, but accurate...

In any case, Oksana would soon be leaving for Chaplinka... and as a result, he'd be lacking the comedic aspect of his comedic ballet. Perhaps in time, the Urchin could fulfil this role?

If all went well with *Sleeping Beauty*, YTV promised to let his group reappear on "Showtime" and dance some scenes from *The Nutcracker*, a ballet he planned to perform at The Alhambra at Christmas. It was a pity Oksana wouldn't be around, because her input would have been appropriate given what she'd done with that hamster... And that reminded him...

Crossing his legs the other way, Taras discovered he'd foolishly forgotten to take off the bulge he'd worn for the rehearsal... It was easily done, because – although it was a little tighter – this new one was of much more modest proportions, and also did not remind him of hamsters. He couldn't bear to wear the old one again... prior to putting it on, he was horrified to discover it was carrying a passenger that had begun gnawing through the treasured YTV paycheque he'd hidden there to supposedly keep it safe.

At least Sofia's nuns would be pleased that, in addition to two marinaded chinchillas, the hamster known as Brenda would also return to the safety of the classroom for the summer term. With any luck, Sofia would never again be entrusted to look after the school pets...

With a sigh, he lifted his feet lethargically from the cardboard box and placed them gently onto the squelchy carpet; unfortunately, the time had come to go home... a place where there were more interlopers in residence than there were members of his own family. And with the weight of all those fat women living in the attic, he hoped the floor could take the strain... Lenka rolled out of bed last night... he had nightmares of her crashing through his bedroom ceiling, crushing him dead.

'The Three Stooges,' Taras called over to the girls, 'time to go home, understand?'

Neither Sofia, Natalka nor Oksana liked being referred to as a "stooge". Sofia mused that her perm would make her Larry, Natalka's black hair would make her Moe... so that left Oksana to be big fat Curly...

The girls completely ignored him, and continued their conversation:

'What *have* you done to your thighs?' Oksana asked, squinting at Sofia through her milk bottle glasses, thinking that perhaps she might have to visit the opticians again...

'Careful diet and exercise,' replied Sofia, flexing her toned muscles.

Natalka added, 'you should try it sometime, Oksana...'

Oksana clutched her belly in her arms as if she were a baker with an enormous pile of dough. She said, 'I'll need more than diet and exercise...'

'True,' said Natalka, 'you've got enough fat to start your own pork scratchings factory...'

Sofia shook her head, 'please be nice Natalka. Oksana can't help being fat.'

'Fat?' Natalka said, 'she's <u>obese</u>!'

'Stop it,' said Sofia, remembering her Tato's instructions. She turned to Oksana, 'if you're serious about losing at least some of your fat, I could show you some exercises to do?'

Oksana nodded enthusiastically, 'as long as they're not too strenuous...'

'And,' Sofia said, removing the half-eaten packet of cheese and onion crisps from Oksana's chubby grip, 'you can't have any more of these!'

'What?' Oksana cried, 'but I'll starve!'

Natalka raised an eyebrow.

'Are you three deaf?' shouted Taras, 'I said that it's time to go!' He clicked his fingers, 'Oksana, Natalka, you carry my box... Sofia, keep my blazer fastened!'

Had Taras not been pre-occupied with watching the inebriated barman ejecting the Urchin's "Pap" for draining several barrels of his best beer, he'd have seen Natalka click her heels and salute, mouthing, 'Heil Mein Herr...' Taras decided to keep the bottle of vodka and the glass... he'd pay the barman later, if he remembered.

With bended knees, Oksana and Natalka heaved up the unbelievably heavy box, almost giving themselves quadruple hernias. Sofia read the label on the box: *Twinkle-Toes Ballet Supplies*. She looked up at her Tato and asked, 'Tato, what have you bought?'

Taras swallowed. He said, 'I thought some new costumes were needed for *Sleeping Beauty*... I plan to distribute them tomorrow... your Mama will make them all fit... she's good at that.' He looked at Oksana, 'and I've bought you something you're sure to appreciate... a proper whale-bone corset to squeeze in and smooth out all that flab...' He poked her in the stomach, 'there's a waistline under there somewhere...'

'*Thanks*,' said Oksana...

Taras didn't feel the slightest bit guilty at spending the YTV paycheque; it was wrong to have promised it to the dancers in the first place. Besides, if they looked the part for *Sleeping Beauty*, more paycheques would follow. They'd understand when he explained it to them; and if they didn't like it, then tough.

On his way out, he waved goodbye to the headscarved old women sat around their table. They briefly stopped gossiping to wave back at him; they even pretended to smile. He knew they'd be tut-tutting about Sofia's skirt the moment he was out of ear shot, not to mention the fact he'd gone outside without wearing his blazer... What was the world coming to?

Taras skipped back home with the Three Stooges, planning to rope them in to help him prepare dinner. He'd decided to cook one of Mrs Wiggins' recipes: Toad in the Hole (not Zena's version containing amphibians) and maybe, if he had time, some Tapioca pudding (not Lenka's version that actually was frogspawn).

The Dancing Barber
Chapter 92

'You know, Oksana is living in Taras' house now,' said the most sensible of the headscarved old women, who was pompously sat in The Gossipmonger's chair at the head of their table in the Uki Club bar.

'And do you know what I heard?' asked the second headscarf, pouring out the over-brewed tea into several cups, anticipating the imminent arrival of the rest of the Gaggle.

'Well, what?' asked the other two, leaning in so as not to miss a syllable.

'Apparently,' the second headscarf lowered her voice, '<u>Klem</u> is her real father...'

'No...' said the other two, 'it can't be true...?'

The second headscarf nodded, 'and apparently, Ivan abducted Oksana when she was very young and has been pretending for all these years that she was his!'

'It doesn't surprise me,' said the third headscarf, blobbing gold-top milk into each cup and swirling it in with a spoon that was in desperate need of a scouring pad. 'We all know what Ivan's capable of...'

'Let's not start spreading gossip,' said the sensible one. 'We don't really know if it's true?'

'I do,' said the second headscarf.

'And – come to think of it – so do I,' said the third. 'We both heard it from the mouth of the horse... Although I couldn't believe it at first...'

The sensible one asked, 'which horse?'

The other two puffed out their cheeks and displayed their own sets of wonderfully crooked teeth, while scratching their armpits, with one hand and their backsides with the other.

'Which one?' asked the sensible one, 'Zena or Lenka?'

'Zena,' said the second headscarf, 'because *she* is the wife of Ivan... Until she gets the divorce...'

The third headscarf added, with a great deal of tut-tut-tutting and shaking of the head, 'rumour has it that she and Klem had an *affair*... Oksana was the result.' She covered her mouth with her cup, so as to hide the fact she was giggling, especially when she recalled Zena's demonstration with the eggs. But she didn't want to lower the tone by telling this to the Gaggle.

'An *affair*... Really?' said the sensible one. 'It must be true if you heard it from the horse's mouth.' She tut-tutted, 'and Klem is such an esteemed poet... he shouldn't be getting up to such mischief!' She shook her head, 'disgraceful, truly disgraceful! And that'll be why he's no longer a Priest... I bet he was de-frocked!'

'I wonder what *she* makes of it?' asked the third headscarf.

'*She's* obviously embarrassed,' said the second headscarf, 'that's why no one's seen her for days. Who'd have thought such a scandal would tarnish *her* family name, eh? So her precious granddaughter was a b – , err, illegitimate all along! I bet she'll never show her face again!'

'It would appear so... I don't know what's worse?' said the sensible one, 'the extra-marital hanky-panky or the fact that Ivan turned out to be working for the hated Soviets?'

The three women slurped their milky teas and pondered the thought, accompanied by plenty more tut-tut-tutting and shaking of heads.

The sensible one looked at her old NHS fob watch. She wondered what was keeping the rest of the Gaggle... they weren't usually this late...

The second headscarf said, 'and the mouth of the horse also told me that Ivan was wanted by...' she looked from side to side before whispering, '...the Mafia.'

'Really?' said the sensible one. She whispered, 'what did he do to upset *them*?'

'Thievery,' said the second headscarf. 'He stole a lot of money. How else could he have afforded to buy all the houses we used to rent from him? But now,' she whispered, 'the Mafia, have seized the lot.'

The sensible one frowned, 'what do you mean: *all the houses we <u>used</u> to rent from him*?'

'Did you not get the letter?' said the third headscarf, extracting a long brown envelope from the zipped side pocket of her overfilled handbag.

The sensible one shook her head, 'what letter?' She slid on her

The Dancing Barber

horn-rimmed reading spectacles and examined the letter in detail. She said, 'oh that's good... our rent payments have halved! My husband will be pleased!'

'But have you seen *who* our new landlord is?' asked the second headscarf, pointing to the name at the end of the letter.

The sensible one looked closely at the name. She said, 'but isn't that Klem's friend? The little man with the black hat, the one *she* calls Grunter?'

The third headscarf nodded, 'yes, he's also the head of the Uki Mafia... so we'd better make sure the rent is always paid on time, or else...'

The sensible one shrugged, 'he seems such a nice little man... But I suppose it's the nice little men that are often the worst.'

The remainder of the Gaggle soon ambled into the bar, crowding towards the best seats around the table. 'Sorry we're late,' one of them said as they all took off their unseasonably thick overcoats, unleashing a stench of mothballs so strong that it instantly knocked out the barman who'd only just come back in after expelling the Urchin's "Pap".

'The bus driver refused to let us on with all this stuff...' another one said, shaking the contents of her overstuffed handbag. 'But we weren't going to let him push us around...'

'At least you're here... finally,' said the sensible one. 'We've only just poured the tea; sit down and take the weight off your feet.'

Soon, dozens of chairs creaked under the weight of dozens of bulbous old women, who fidgeted and wriggled as they greeted one another with all the emotions of long lost relatives, even though it'd been less than a day since they last saw one another.

'Oh how wonderful,' said another latecomer when she spotted the sensible one had a large piece of unfinished embroidery unfurled on her lap. 'I'm so glad we're reprising the Embroidery Circle, oh how I've missed it.'

'So have I,' said another, sipping her milky tea.

'My needles have gone rusty since *she* hijacked our Circle,' said yet another headscarf. 'So I hope she <u>never</u> returns! I never could stand her, always prodding at things with that clubbed hand and spitting her chewing tobacco all over the place. She was an awful woman!'

The sensible one said, 'I'm sure we hope nothing unfortunate has happened to her...' She paused to allow the Gaggle to grumble, 'but I must admit life has been better without her. I was talking to the Priest this morning and he said how wonderful it was to perform his entire Service on Sunday without being distracted by all her gossiping.'

Seeing the Gaggle had unravelled their individual pieces of embroidery, the sensible one rubbed her hands together and said with a smile, 'remind me, who was doing what?'

The Gaggle displayed their own semi-finished pieces of embroidery for the others to admire. Each clutch of headscarves announcing in turn:

'We are doing the Viking ancestors,' said one headscarf, showing her group's depiction of Ukraine from the times the horn-helmeted Scandinavians invaded the land.

'We're doing the Cossacks,' said another headscarf, showing her group's illustration of a Yul Brynner Cossack thrusting his sword into an invading Pole.

'And we are doing Mazepa and Bandera...' the remaining headscarves said with much disappointment, knowing they'd have difficulty depicting the cyanide-tipped umbrella.

'Good,' said the sensible one, 'in that case, I shall make a start on Voloshin...'

The others all stared enviously at the sensible one... Why did she get to do the best bit...?

'Bleeding hell! Quick, about turn,' said a flat-capped man, the instant he whiffed the scent of mothballs drifting on the air. 'We'd better use the other entrance'. His wife had ordered him to decorate the spare room, so he didn't want to be caught out boozing...

'That were a close one,' said a second flat-capped man, who was also skiving from the task his wife had ordered him to do. 'Do you think they saw us?'

'No, they're too busy knitting that tapestry of Ukrainian history they started a decade ago,' said the first flat-cap. 'I doubt they'll ever finish it? Mind you, they look happier without *her*... don't you think?'

The Dancing Barber

'Mmm, they're as happy as we are without *him* as our landlord!'

'I wouldn't go that far... I think it's a bit "out of the fire and into the frying pan", so to speak. I reckon that even though we haven't got a crook for a landlord, somehow I don't think the bleeding Mafia will be any better... They know how much money a hospital porter earns, but it won't stop them putting up the rent in a few months... it's always the same...'

'But this fella's a mate of Klem's,' said the second flat-cap, leading his friend through the other door to the bar. 'Klem says he's not one of the dodgy ones.'

'There's no such thing... Mafia is Mafia,' said the first flat-cap, 'they're all dodgy.' He gave his friend a nudge, 'look!' he said, pointing to the unconscious barman, 'it's free booze day again...' He rubbed his hands together gleefully, 'time to celebrate getting rid of Lyudmila and Valentina... And let's hope they never return...!'

'Did you see what I just saw?' asked the sensible headscarf, watching a pair of flat-caps ducking down behind the bar.

'Of course, we all saw them,' came the resounding reply.

The most aggressive of the headscarves cracked her knuckles and said, 'the skiving little toad won't know what's hit him when I get home...'

'It'll probably be your rolling pin,' muttered the sensible one.

Every headscarf took pride in keeping her flat-cap on the tightest of leashes. Today was Embroidery Circle evening, so every flat-cap was under orders to finish the domestic tasks he'd been allocated. It was only five o'clock, and none of them should be finished yet.

The aggressive one stood up and said, 'give me a minute... I'll make sure he goes back home with his tail between his legs and my boot up his – '

'Let them have their fun,' interrupted the sensible one. 'There's no point getting upset about it. Everyone deserves a rest sometime, don't you think?'

'*She* wouldn't agree,' said the aggressive one, sitting down, reluctantly unfurling her clenched fist.

'But *she* isn't here,' said the sensible one, smiling. 'And she hardly has the right to pass judgement when you consider the antics of her own husband... Anyway, shall we get on...? We have a lot to do this evening... I have arranged for our tapestry to be displayed next week at Cartwright Hall, so we mustn't waste any more time...'

The aggressive one was as excitable as she was aggressive. She asked, 'you don't mean the art gallery in Manningham Park?'

The sensible one nodded, 'there will be an entry fee to view our,' she shuffled pompously in her seat, '*Exhibition!* And all proceeds will be sent to Voloshin! If what I heard on the radio is correct, he wants to be the first elected President of an independent Ukraine... so he'll need all the money he can get...'

'But do you think we'll get everything finished for next week?' asked a perspiring headscarf. 'We've done Mazepa, but haven't even thought about Bandera, let alone those fiddly umbrellas...'

'Of course we will,' said the sensible one. 'And when we're finished, Halyna will stitch them together on her sewing machine... I think it'll look fantastic!'

'Yes, it'll be nice for Halyna to join us again... we've all missed her company...'

With a renewed sense of urgency, the headscarves began stitching accurately and quickly, the only sounds in the otherwise empty bar were the tapping of needles against thimbles and the slurping of milky tea; and behind the bar, the sound of a crate of bottled beer being slid from beneath the unconscious barman's nose, the flat-caps working with the stealth of a pair of commandoes.

The excitable one peered at the sensible one's embroidery. She said, 'but how do you know what Voloshin looks like? Nobody has seen him in years... He's almost as mysterious as this G*r*unter.'

The sensible one smiled, 'before I married the hospital porter, Voloshin and I were rather good friends...'

The Dancing Barber

Chapter 93

---✂---

Mister Pushkin led its owner home with ease, but unfortunately was unable to unlock the door for him. It emitted a piercing *Meow* and watched Klem fumble the key into the lock, scratching huge gashes into the flaky paint as he constantly missed the keyhole.

For what was ordinarily a ten-minute walk from the Club, the cat had twice heard the quarterly chimes of its owner's pocket watch and was supremely grateful for finally reaching the cosy comfort of the attic, even though Klem insisted on walking backwards up the spiral staircase.

Klem landed face down on the bed, his damp and smelly suit ruining the duvet cover.

With its owner snoring away, the cat visited the litter tray, happy that for once, the troll women hadn't filled it. It then had a thorough wash and jumped into its brassière hammock…

Mister Pushkin reflected that having a drunkard for an owner was an exhausting business, so decided to wash its paws of him: the quest was on to find a new, *sober* owner…

At five o'clock, Klem awoke to the tune of the dirge-like Ukrainian National Anthem – *"Ukraine Is Not Dead Yet!"* – chiming from his pocket watch. His throat felt as though it were lined with sandpaper and his body felt stiffer than ever. He groaned and tried to work out where he was…

Rolling onto his back, Klem fell straight off the bed, thudding to the floor.

He focussed his bleary gaze onto the cat, curled up fast asleep in one of Lenka's stained brassières, its paws twitching as if it were dreaming about catching mice… It must have been a good dream… he'd never heard a cat snore before… and for such a lean animal, it sounded like an asthmatic walrus…

Klem groaned again and put his hands to his throbbing head, imagining that Ringo Starr was bored of Taras and had decided his head made a better drum… but used mallets instead of drumsticks.

With a lingering groan, he performed a more laboured sit-up

than usual, hooking his arms around his knees and locking his hands together so as to remain upright... Suddenly, he felt very cold, yet his skin perspired and his stomach churned; thank Heavens one of Lenka's yellow buckets was close to hand...

After a thorough wash, shave and change of clothes, Klem began to look human again, even though he didn't feel it. He examined his verdant face in the mirror, twisted his moustache into place and pulled down his eyelids, discovering his eyes to be entirely bloodshot and bulging from their sockets as if they belonged to a toad.

He glugged out some of Taras' aftershave from the Eiffel Tower bottle and smeared it all over his face; it was so stinky that it killed houseflies at ten paces, so it would hopefully keep Zena at bay...

Yet another suit was consigned to the dry-cleaning basket; he was disgusted by how much of a mess he'd made of the trousers and knew his tailor would turn in his grave... Thankfully, there were another three suits in the wardrobe, still in their original wrapping... but at this rate, they probably wouldn't last the week...

Absolutely famished, he munched through half a packet of Jacob's Cream Crackers while waiting for the Earl Grey to brew, deciding once and for all, never again to go near booze. He couldn't believe he'd let those idiotic flat-caps talk him into drinking that first pint... he told them he was an alcoholic, but they just kept pushing...

Mister Pushkin's snoring ceased; the cat yawned widely, displaying a set of white fangs, before it turned to scowl at its owner.

'I'm sorry, Mister Pushkin,' Klem said, watching the cat lift its nose into the air and look the other way. 'I don't know why you put up with me?' He muttered, 'I'm surprised I put up with myself...'

Kneeling at his altar, he prayed for God's forgiveness, for not only succumbing to the temptation of the demon drink, but also for all the negative thoughts that had taken over his mind in recent hours. He'd loved Zena once, so would learn to love her again. He would have to, because she was the mother of his child, a child

The Dancing Barber

he would also learn to love, eventually...

He prayed that he be granted patience and tolerance, together with the courage and tact to persuade Zena to wash more than once a year.

He also prayed that Zena wouldn't do anything excessively barbaric to the man who still shuffled around up in the loft... Stanislaw may have been a butcher, but violence was never the answer. He prayed Zena would come round to the idea of handing Stanislaw over to the authorities... if not to the current ones, then certainly to the ones that would soon be elected...

Klem stood up, and after a little wobble, meandered over to the mantelpiece to reposition his beloved Fabergé Egg that — despite his edict that nobody was allowed to touch it — was laying on its side. He picked it up, but its surface was so greasy that he nearly dropped it to the alabaster hearth... he juggled the slippery egg between both hands, before thankfully putting it back into its rightful place.

Emitting a sigh of relief, he extracted a crisply ironed blue and yellow chequered handkerchief from his pocket; holding a corner between thumb and forefinger, he unravelled it with the flick of a wrist...

After three whole minutes of polishing, the egg gleamed brighter than ever, each expertly faceted sapphire and diamond twinkling in the light. He narrowed his eyes... he had a horrible feeling that Lenka had been rolling it across the carpet, in the vain hope of Mister Pushkin batting it against the skirting boards with its paw... Did that woman respect anything?

Gripping one of the egg's hemispheres in each hand, he attempted to open it, but it must have been twisted the wrong way, and therefore badly over-tightened...

Applying a little more pressure, he tried to loosen the egg. 'Gently does it,' he said, 'don't force it... don't force it...' All of a sudden, the egg twanged open. Thankfully, it was undamaged... and from now on, he'd keep it out of everyone's reach.

Sighing with relief, Klem picked up his glued-back-together moustache cup, filled it with delicious Earl Grey and went to sit behind his desk... the best place from which to admire his Fabergé Egg...

Sipping his tea, he was endlessly transfixed by the deep circular recess between the two halves of the de-shelled egg. He mulled over the possibilities: *If it wasn't for a miniature portrait, then what was it for? Halyna thought it could be for a diamond? But a diamond to fit this space would cost more than the Koh-I-Noor...*

A little more research was in order...

So Klem reached across to a nearby shelf and extracted a heavy reference book on Karl Fabergé. Gunter had given it to him years ago, but he'd never had the time to read it in detail.

Heaving the book onto his empty desk, Klem immediately turned to the chapter devoted to the Easter of 1887:

```
The Third Imperial Easter Egg

A 3¼ inch rigid yellow gold egg,
nestled on a gold tripod pedestal with
chased lion paw feet. It was crafted
by Chief Jeweller August Holmstrőm in
St Petersburg and presented to Maria
Feodorovna as an Easter gift by
Alexander III in 1887.

The only evidence of the egg's
existence is Holmstrőm's original
drawing, which sadly lacks detail
regarding the "surprise".
Interestingly, this rigid yellow gold
egg was commissioned as a last-minute
replacement for an earlier egg, which
was rejected by Karl Fabergé himself.

This earlier piece, referred to
informally as Imperial Easter Egg 2½
was one of the most beautiful of the
entire series. It was almost
spherical in form, with the upper half
pavé set with one hundred and fifty
princess cut sapphires and the lower
half pavé set with an equal number of
exceptionally rare princess cut and
flawless yellow diamonds. Only a
rough sketch, believed to have been
made by Holmstrőm, exists of this
```

The Dancing Barber

> unknown masterpiece, and once again, no details are given regarding the "surprise"; but the opening mechanism was said to be exquisite, the egg expanding when the upper and lower halves were rotated in opposite directions.
>
> It is believed that both eggs were sent to the Kremlin Armoury in 1922 where the Special Plenipotentiary of the Council of People's Commissars arranged for them to be sent to New York to be sold at auction. As the true provenance of both of these pieces was unknown, it is thought they will have been melted down by the unidentified buyers, and the stones sold off individually.

Klem already knew all of this; it was common knowledge that Karl Fabergé rejected the original egg, because the chosen colours were deemed woefully inappropriate for a gift to be given to the Tsarina of the Russian Empire. But upon turning the page, he read something that, for a moment, made his heart stop beating:

> Many experts believe the Third Imperial Easter Egg was hinged along its equator. And when opened, it revealed a *Vacheron Constantin* watch with a white enamel dial and openwork diamond set gold hands.

For half an hour, Klem could only stare at the page, letting his tea go cold and repeatedly re-reading the paragraph to check his eyes hadn't deceived him. Just because the exterior was rejected, didn't necessarily mean that the surprise was too... He couldn't believe the object that could increase the value of "Imperial Easter Egg 2½" tenfold had been in his pocket all along...

With the cat still snoring and twitching, and twanging one of the stained straps of its brassière hammock with its paw, Klem stood up and meandered over to the drawer where Taras' dreaded Charlie Chaplinka mask was hidden. Taras may have allowed Halyna to dispose of the warped photograph, but she would never be permitted to discard the actual mask. So a compromise was reached whereby the hated item was concealed somewhere in the house and hopefully forgotten about, forever... But only Klem knew where it was. He slid open the drawer and lifted out the pile of mini-skirts Zena had bought in anticipation of ripping her way out of every one of them, despite the triple stitched seams and sack-cloth material. He then extracted a plain cardboard box, the kind that once contained a very expensive shirt and shuffled off the lid.

Klem had forgotten how frightening Charlie Chaplinka was... and he hated how it laughed at him like a demonic *Punch* from a *Punch and Judy Show*. No wonder it was banned from Taras' ballets: if it frightened a fully-grown man, it almost certainly would give small children the worst of nightmares. And he believed it was the inspiration for the villainous character a friend of his in Jamaica was adding to his first children's book... something to do with a flying car...

He peeled the mask out of the box, shielding his nose from the sweaty stench of decomposing rubber. For the first time, he had the courage to put a hand into its slimy cavity, his fingers poking through the eye holes, his thumb through the mouth. The mask's protruding nose and chin quivered in his shaky hands, sending a shiver down his spine. Unable to look at it any longer, he flipped it over and opened up the back...

Klem knew that if he wanted to hide anything, inside this mask would be the perfect place... it was safer than a bank vault... Firstly, he inserted the original cassette tapes and transcripts of Voloshin's interviews with the Soviet Generals. As trusting as he was of the Americans, he refused to let them "keep them safe" for him: the Americans often suffered from bouts of selective amnesia, especially if the White House signed any agreements with the Kremlin, thus necessitating various "deals" to be done. In such a situation all his carefully collated evidence would be conveniently misplaced and the few paragraphs The Great Famine occupied in the history books would be erased forever. So Charlie Chaplinka

The Dancing Barber

was now the custodian of the truth. The mask also contained – amongst other things – the Cine film Gunter gave him... Woe betide Ivan if he dared to blackmail him again...

With yet another sigh of relief, he placed the heavy box back into the drawer and covered it with the not-so-mini-skirts. As an added precaution, he draped an embroidered towel over the front of the whole chest of drawers. He twisted his drooping moustache back into position over his smiling mouth: not only were his prized possessions safe, but his horrendous hangover was blessedly diminishing...

Checking his much more human appearance in the mirror, he noticed his eyes looked bright and healthy... Earl Grey really was the elixir of well-being. He watched the reflected image of the cat stretch and yawn, following what must have been a restful catnap. He said, 'was that a nice sleep?'

But Mister Pushkin ignored him and rolled out of its brassière hammock. It stretched again, extending its front paws and arching its back.

'Aren't you talking to me?' Klem asked, watching the cat amble out to the balcony and leap onto the balustrade. 'I said I was sorry,' he pleaded, but the cat was more interested in the red breast of a robin fluttering onto the roof. And following a running jump, the cat's rear paws fired like pistons, propelling its sleek blue body up onto the roof tiles.

Klem shrugged, 'I said I was sorry...' He knew he had a lot of making up to do with the cat; usually a large chunk of sir-a-loin would do the trick, but this time he wasn't so sure it would be enough...

Klem listened to the cat's claws scraping across the roof tiles... He hoped that if it caught the robin, it wouldn't bring it indoors... Zena would probably cook it...

After checking the attic was tidy, Klem gave his leather boots a quick polish using one of Zena's fishy cloths and prepared to skip down the spiral staircase for his dinner. All of a sudden, he heard an almighty thud above his head, before a flash of blue fur whizzed down past the balcony... 'Mmmrrryyyaaawww!'

Chapter 94

The Gossipmonger used her hairclip to scratch the door handle for the seventh time, the black paint flaking away to reveal silver metal beneath. She sighed, then turned lethargically to stare at her son. She said, 'I've been a prisoner in this rattling taxi for a week... and when you reach my age, that might be all the time you have left...'

She lifted her clubbed hand to give the door another whack, but didn't have the energy. Instead she reached for the bottle of water she'd been sharing with her son, but she'd drank the last drop that morning. Neither of them were strangers to being dreadfully hungry, but even during The Great Famine there was always plenty of water to drink, even if it were downstream from the Soviet latrines.

So in desperation she ate what was left of the chewing tobacco and then made a start on the foil wrapper. Her stomach churned like a cement mixer, but at least it was a distraction from her hunger. Experiences like these always helped put things into perspective; she'd forgiven her son's lies three scratches ago, and even chose to ignore his appalling attitude towards Oksana.

The foil wrapper was soon gone, so she considered chewing on the taxi's PVC seats, and then scraping up some of the dried bits of tobacco she'd spat out earlier. Although she was comfortably into her eighties, she was far too young to die...

Ivan had no such problems; he sat motionlessly, conserving whatever energy remained in his exhausted body. Although he knew release was impossible, he never gave up on the idea of being able to escape, somehow. And when he did escape, he would go directly to the farmhouse to retrieve the carrier bag full of money hidden in the dry-stone wall.

This money was all he had... it would be enough for him to move to America, where he wouldn't be recognised once his ginger mane grew back; he might even dye it a different colour. The Kyiv Mafia's influence didn't extend across the Atlantic and not even the Soviet Secret Police would go that far to look for him.

The Dancing Barber

Although it was against his better judgement, he wouldn't forget his mother: he'd give her enough money to rent a basement flat in Manningham... but he knew she wouldn't be grateful.

One thing he knew for sure: Zena wasn't going to get a penny. And he certainly wasn't going to divorce her... she didn't deserve to get half of whatever money he had left.

But all of this was irrelevant; he'd long ago come to terms with the fate Gunter had planned for him... So he closed his eyes and stayed calm... and he wished his mother would do the same...

'Why is the ground still shaking?' screamed The Gossipmonger. 'I can't stand it anymore! Why can't it be still? If it's not an earthquake, then what is it? And why is it getting so hot?'

Ivan said nothing. The constant rumbling wasn't an earth tremor: it felt man made, mechanical. He turned to his mother, 'you said you passed through a mining area before the taxi drove into this garage?'

'What's that got to do with it?' snapped The Gossipmonger. 'I saw plenty of slag heaps... You'd know all about slags, considering the thing you decided to marry...'

Ivan closed his ears to his mother's words. He said, 'I wish you'd stop being so irritable.'

'This isn't irritable,' she screamed, showing him her clubbed hand. 'I'll show you irritable!'

Ivan ignored the old hag; she was already on the verge of insanity, so he dreaded what she'd do when she discovered they were currently several miles below ground and going deeper every second...

The Gossipmonger pulled off her headscarf and used it to mop her perspiring brow. She said, 'how much longer do you expect your mother to put up with this?' She scratched at her flattened hair that had moulded itself into the shape of the headscarf she hadn't taken off in a week. 'This is ridiculous! I don't know what I'm going to do? And you're no use, just sitting there like a great big pile of – !' She struck the seat with her clubbed hand, a cloud of dust billowing up, 'I can't stand it any longer!'

Ivan's ears remained closed.

The Gossipmonger delved deeply into her handbag and couldn't believe her luck when, in amongst the accumulated fluff, she'd located the familiar shape of a Mint Imperial. She smiled for the first time in days. After eating all that tobacco, a mint was just what she needed... but her conscience nagged her to remember that her son was just as hungry and as thirsty as she was, maybe even more so.

She looked at the miserable soul out of the corner of one eye: his face and head, although still bright red, had been perforated by the spiky regrowth of his ginger hair that looked rough enough to strike a match against. He looked pathetic and she felt sorry for him, but reminded herself of whose fault it was for their terrible predicament. She rotated the precious minty sphere between her fingers, deliberating whether to share it.

The Gossipmonger gave Ivan a firm nudge, almost knocking him off the seat. She said, 'I asked you how much longer do you expect your mother to put up with this?' She discretely popped the Mint Imperial in her mouth, wedging it between her dentures and tongue.

Ivan said, 'I have no idea... we can only hope Gunter rediscovers his compassionate side.'

The Gossipmonger grumbled, 'such men do not have a compassionate side.'

Ivan knew that having to spend a month miles underground in the ferocious heat and pitch dark was Gunter's way of emulating Hell, a penance for his enemies and a taste of what awaited them for all eternity should they not change their ways. The last man that double-crossed him ended up at the bottom of a uranium mine, and was never seen again. Thankfully the mines in Yorkshire were merely for coal: so if they escaped, they would be black with coal dust, but at least they wouldn't glow in the dark.

All Ivan had to do was persevere, hopeful that Gunter possessed even the dimmest flicker of compassion. But then he watched his mother eject a mothball from her mouth, the tiny white sphere ricocheting off the window and landing in his lap. When she began spitting everywhere, he began to think this really was Hell on Earth...

'Stop doing that you old hag!' Ivan shouted, 'you dare criticise Zena when you have so many uncouth habits of your own!' And when she spat in his face, he spat directly back at her, taking her completely by surprise.

'Now you've done it,' she screamed, brandishing her clubbed

The Dancing Barber

hand. She prepared to put her son across her knee again, but then the ground began to shake even more violently from side to side, the taxi's suspension squeaking as it wobbled around.

The taxi then lurched over to the left, momentarily balancing on two wheels before thudding down with so much force that it dislodged the dividing screen behind the driver's seat. Before Ivan knew what was going on, his mother hitched up her skirts, clambered over into the driver's seat and immediately yanked at the door handle…

'Damn it,' she said, 'it's locked!' She slammed her clubbed hand repeatedly against the steering wheel, sounding the horn as if she were an irate motorist. Out of the corner of her eye, she watched as a red hand crept across and pulled up a small button on the edge of the door-frame.

'Now try and open it,' Ivan said smugly.

Much to The Gossipmonger's relief, the door opened instantaneously and she stepped out onto the shaky garage floor, finding it difficult to stay upright, even in her stout brogues. She heard the sound of laughter, so turned to glare at her son; she must have imagined it, because he was silent.

She looked up and noticed the faintest slit of a flashing light high up on the wall; with the garage doors firmly locked, this tiny gap was their only chance of escape. 'Come and look at this,' she said, waiting for her son to struggle out of the taxi wearing the hessian sack as if he were an ascetic Julius Caesar.

'I'm not climbing all the way up there,' he said when he saw what his mother was pointing at. He knew this faint slit of light would not be daylight; instead it would be the light bulbs that illuminated the mineshaft. So even if they could escape the confines of this "garage", he couldn't imagine his mother being capable of shimmying up miles of steel cable to reach the surface; he doubted he could either.

But when his mother was in this sort of mood, there was never any point in arguing with her. So in bare feet, he clambered – at the double – onto the taxi's ice-cold roof, struggling to maintain his balance as it lurched in every direction. He cried, 'I think I'm going to fall!'

'Shut up you big wimp,' said The Gossipmonger, 'and tell me what you can see!'

Ivan put his hands against the brick walls and stretched up as far as he could. The bricks were warm to the touch and were smoother than expected, and the texture of the mortar was identical. He also noticed the light was shining through what turned out to be the top edge of a ventilation hatch; he put his eye to the slit, but could only see the jagged edges of rough sawn timber. He tried to prise the hatch open with his fingernails, but it wouldn't yield. He tried again until it felt like his fingernails were being wrenched away.

'Hurry up,' shouted The Gossipmonger. 'Are you so useless that you can't even open a little hatch? You are a pathetic, useless, embarrassing, ugly pile of the worst kind of himno!'

Just as he was about to tell his mother to shut her face, the hatch fell away to reveal a window a square foot in size. He was instantly blinded by the brightest light...

'Good Heavens,' he said, squinting his eyes, 'I can't believe it...'

The Gossipmonger said grumpily, 'what can't you believe?'

He repeated, 'I can't believe it,' as he watched the world speeding by.

'Well?' screamed The Gossipmonger, denting the taxi's bonnet with her clubbed hand. 'What can't you believe?'

Ivan cleared his throat. He said, 'come up here and look at this!'

'Are you mad?' cried The Gossipmonger. 'How do you expect an old woman to get up there?' But curiosity soon persuaded her to climb up and join her son on the taxi's roof, her stout brogues denting the thin metalwork. 'I don't need your help,' she snapped when Ivan outstretched a helping hand.

Ivan muttered, 'suit yourself... I hope you stumble and break your neck...'

'Good Heavens,' she said when she peered through the window, the shock causing her to almost fall from the taxi's roof. 'What is this: some kind of trickery?'

Ivan shook his head. He was pleased that his theory was wrong. But then he began to worry about the nature of the alternative fate Gunter had planned for him...

'Does this garage have wheels?' said The Gossipmonger, hanging her head out of the window, the wind blowing through her permed hair. 'How can it be driving along a road?'

The Dancing Barber

Ivan said, 'I should think it's obvious by now that we're not in a garage. We're on the back of a truck that – from the inside at least – has been made to *look* like a garage!' He tapped the walls, 'listen, these are wooden and painted up to look like bricks...'

'On the back of a *truck*!' said The Gossipmonger, scratching her scruffy hair with her clubbed hand. 'So what I thought was an earthquake was actually the noise of the *road* rumbling beneath us... But we've been juddering for a week... we could be *miles* away!'

Ivan looked for some indication of their location, but the road signs whizzed past quicker than he could read them. But he did notice the truck seemed to be overtaking plenty of cars, many of which were Ladas and Trabants. And on the horizon, he thought he saw the silhouette of a building that looked remarkably like the Saint Sofia Cathedral. Suddenly, the mineshaft seemed much more appealing...

'Hello,' said a laughing voice, 'how are my passengers enjoying their trip?'

'Did you hear that?' Ivan asked his mother.

'Yes,' she said, 'it came from over there.' She pointed to the far end of the "garage" that was still in shadow.

A tiny oblong window slid open behind what was the truck's cab, the road ahead clear to see through the windscreen beyond. The silhouette of a man wearing a wide-brimmed hat appeared in the window...

'Hello Ivan,' said the familiar voice, 'are you pleased to be back home?'

'Back home?' Ivan said, watching the famous Golden Gate of Kyiv whiz past the window. He swore under his breath... 'Why couldn't it have been the mineshaft?'

'Yes, the Golden Gate is beautiful,' said the voice, 'built in the eleventh century by Yaroslav the Wise – a good Christian – who would have dealt severely with someone like you who broke the Commandment "Thou Shalt Not Steal"!'

Ivan smirked and shook his head. He jumped to the floor and slowly approached the tiny oblong window. He said, 'and I suppose *you* have never broken that particular commandment yourself?'

'That is irrelevant,' said the voice, 'the point is you did; and you stole from people you should never steal from! And that cannot go unpunished...'

The Gossipmonger also clambered to the floor, gripping her clubbed hand menacingly. She said, 'listen to me Grunter, if you don't release us immediately and reunite us with our darling Oksana, I will put you across my knee!'

The man behind the window laughed, 'Grunter... is that what you call me? That's funny... And as for putting me across your knee: I'd like to see you try...'

Ivan grabbed his mother's arm, preventing her from marching to the window. He said, 'please, you'll only make t-t-things w-w-w-worse.'

She polished the rounded end of her clubbed hand and glared at her son. 'Very well... so be it. You got us into this mess, so you can get us out of it!'

'Your mother is very sensible,' said the voice. 'You should listen to her, otherwise she'll put you across her knee again... That was *so* funny to watch... I made a nice Cine film of it... I'm sure all your enemies would love to see it...'

Ivan heard the sound of a rustling carrier bag, the man behind the window fanning his face with bundles of what appeared to be paper money. 'What h-h-have you g-g-got there?' Ivan demanded.

'It took a bit of finding,' said the man, proudly, 'and we are grateful you wrapped it up so carefully in a carrier bag... it kept it nice and dry for us. These white fivers, they really are attractive to look at... Don't look so upset... remember, it wasn't yours in the first place... Besides, where you're going, you won't need money...'

'Now l-l-look h-h-h-ere,' said Ivan, knowing he'd do just about anything to get that money back. 'W-what are you p-p-planning to d-d-do with us? Before you make your decision, please remember that I can be very useful to you...'

The Gossipmonger grunted, 'you're as useful as... as something useless...'

Ivan said, 'ignore her. Look, you know me... you know I have made mistakes... but you can trust me... I know how to get you even more money just like it!'

The man at the window laughed again, 'the details haven't been decided yet. But you have upset so many of our dear friends that

The Dancing Barber

we feel compelled to dissuade you from doing so ever again. You see, it's not just about the money, it's about your conduct and morals and the way you treat other people! We think a *re-education* is long overdue... For both of you...'

The window slid closed before Ivan had got half way to it, 'Gunter... wait... don't go...'

Ivan then turned and leapt onto the taxi's bonnet and clambered onto the roof. He knew his body wouldn't fit, but it didn't stop him from attempting to escape through the hatch. The old hag could look after herself: he was getting out, and quickly... there was no way he was ever going back to The Convent. He pushed his arms and head out into the cold dusk air...

The truck – as if on purpose – lurched sharply to the left, knocking The Gossipmonger to the floor. She was almost crushed when the taxi leaned over and balanced precariously on two wheels, before thankfully falling back onto its bouncy suspension.

'What does he mean by *re-education*?' shouted The Gossipmonger, struggling to get onto her feet.

Ivan was stuck firmly in the hatch, the splintering wood sawing into his chest and back.

'I asked you a question,' shouted The Gossipmonger. 'What does he mean by *re-education*? Answer me!'

'You'll soo-soo-soon find out...' said Ivan, trembling.

It seemed his time had finally come... The truck pulled in to a familiar curved driveway that led to a secluded house he hoped he'd never see again...

Chapter 95

'But *why* can't I keep some of these photographs?' Halyna asked, whilst taking her time to leaf through Zena's battered and scuffed album on the kitchen table, 'you seem to have *plenty* of them...' It was more of a scrapbook than an album; photographs were stuck into it with what Halyna surmised to be various unmentionable substances.

Watching her sister's constipated expression, Halyna said, 'it would be nice to have at least one photograph of our family, you know, like we used to be?'

Zena huffed, 'but the photographic, they are the very delicate...' She held out her hands to take back the album, 'I think it best they all stay together, yes...'

'I understand,' Halyna said, moving the album fractionally away from her sister. 'These photographs are precious to both of us; which is why I would like to take one of them to a goodski shop in town that can make me a copy. They could make you a copy too, a big one that you could frame? You could take it back to Chaplinka and give it as a present to Uncle Viktor?'

Reluctantly, Zena said, 'okay, but you must look after it; I do not want it damaged.' She reached out for the album again, but Halyna moved it further away.

'Do not worry,' Halyna said reassuringly as she extracted a grainy image of her family posing outside their thatched homestead. 'I will keep it safe...'

Zena grumbled, folding her arms across her enormous bosom.

The photograph was yellow around the edges and even smelled of Chaplinka, but it was full of character and Halyna loved it. She could just about remember the travelling photographer taking it on his enormous plate camera, with its black cloth and exploding flash bulb. They had to stand still for what felt like hours, which is why Lenka's arm appeared blurred; as usual she was unable to resist giving her backside a scratch. Her Mama was furious, but she couldn't afford to have the photograph retaken; and once the Soviets installed their roadblocks, no one ever saw another

The Dancing Barber

travelling photographer again. Although there was a brave journalist who sneaked past the Soviet soldiers to photograph the piles of rotting grain and mass graves in 1933... But no one ever found out what happened to him... though she had a pretty good idea...

Halyna examined the tattered photograph closely through a magnifying glass held against a scratched lens of her plastic framed glasses. She saw that her Mama wore the only dress she owned, in addition to her trusty apron and headscarf; her tall Tato wore his collar-less embroidered shirt and a waistcoat with a watch chain strung between the pockets, but without a watch at the end of it; her sisters wore clothes that were made from several old curtains; and the scraggy dog sported one of her Mama's old headscarves for a collar. She felt the weight of tears on her eyelashes when she saw her eight year old self, posing next to the well, wearing a dress made from one of her Tato's old jumpers, tied at the waist with a length of frayed string. She closed her eyes and imagined the happy scene playing in her mind; why did it have to end?

She wanted to put down the photograph, but it had stuck firmly to several of her fingers. With great care, she peeled it off, only to discover it'd stuck to her other hand... she hoped the adhesive was tree resin, but it looked more like ear-wax...

Halyna decided an enlarged copy of this photograph would fit perfectly on the mantelpiece between photographs of her wedding to Taras and Sofia's christening; she may even find space for it on the wall now the photograph of Charlie Chaplinka had been consigned to the dustbin.

Allowing Zena to seize back her precious album and hug it to her bosom, Halyna slid her chosen photograph into a used manila envelope and put it somewhere safe. She then wiped her unbelievably sticky fingers down her apron, only to watch them adhere firmly to the nylon material.

All the while, Zena held the crucifix she'd taken from Stanislaw, which now hung around her neck, repeatedly tracing the carved edge with her grubby fingers. Noticing Halyna's glass wasn't empty, she said, 'you like the samahon, yes?' topping up their glasses to the brim, not spilling a drop.

'It's a bit strong,' said Halyna. 'I can feel it dissolving my dentures.'

Zena's lips pursed so much that they almost disappeared into her cheeks.

Quickly, Halyna said, 'err... but the samahon is very goodski, very goodski!' She took another miniscule sip, 'mmm... delicious...'

Zena smiled broadly. She said, 'I knew you would the like it,' throwing the eighth consecutive glassful down her throat as though it was only water. 'This is the authentic Chaplinka-style samahon, sweetened with plenty of the *Slyna*!'

'*The Slyna?*' said Halyna, immediately putting the glass back onto the table, hoping she'd misheard.

'Have you forgotten the tongue of the mother?' Zena shook her head, 'you must have gotten the used to speaking the "Ukrainish" after the twenty years of living in the Bradford.' She smiled, filling up and instantly emptying her ninth glassful. 'The *Slyna*! You know, the spit from the mouth!'

'I know what it is,' Halyna said, pushing the glass as far away as possible. 'It's your spit, I assume?'

Zena nodded, 'and from Lenka and Oksana... we add a little every day, stirring it in... It is the family recipe! The *Slyna*, it gives the samahon the nice sweet taste, yes?'

'How delightful,' Halyna said, now realising why she'd detected the subtle flavour of cheese and onion crisps. Spit wasn't part of the recipe she remembered; thank Heavens she only had the smallest of sips.

'There is the plenty more in the attic... Help yourself! Have as much as you want... we are still making two or three bottles every day! It will put the hair on the chest!'

Halyna feigned a smile. She said, 'thank you, but I've had *quite* enough for the moment and I certainly don't want any hairs on my chest. Besides, it's rather early in the day for such hard drinking, don't you think? We haven't even had dinner yet?'

Zena shrugged her shoulders before draining her tenth glass, burping with satisfaction. She said, 'who needs the dinner, when you have the samahon?'

Halyna thought: *Not you, obviously...*

The rubbery rug beneath Halyna's feet constantly gripped the soles of her slippers and was beginning to annoy her. She knew

The Dancing Barber

the rug was a gift from the twins, but it didn't mean she had to like it. Poking the tablecloth out of the way, she looked down and noticed the rug had moved out of place...

Zena tried to stop her, but it was too late...

'What...? No...?' Halyna said, upon realising the 'rug' was the inverted charred remains of her old carpet... 'Zena, what has happened here...?'

Zena recounted the tale of her indoor bonfire, then said, 'at least we did not ruin the kitchen in The Bolling Hall... *It would be nice to see it one day...*'

Halyna sighed. Now she knew why the ceiling was blacker than usual. She added a new kitchen carpet to the lengthening list of repairs, and chose to ignore the comment about "The" Bolling Hall.

After persuading Zena to hand back the album, Halyna leafed through to the end, enjoying seeing photographs of the Steppes and of neighbouring Askanya Nova. The album certainly was a comprehensive archive of life in Chaplinka. But there was something, or rather some*one* missing... She asked, 'you know, I haven't seen a single photograph of Uncle Viktor?'

Zena shrugged her shoulders; 'he is the very shy of the photography.'

Halyna raised an eyebrow, muttering, 'Viktor...? Shy...?'

'Yes,' said Zena. 'Viktor and the camera are never in the same place.'

That didn't sound anything like the Uncle Viktor Halyna remembered...

Zena glanced out of the window. She was conveniently distracted by a flash of blue fur whizzing down, accompanied by a lingering, 'Mmmrrryyyaaawww!' She said, 'what was *that*...?'

From out in the yard, Lenka emitted a string of the worst expletives, many of which she'd learned from Taras. She stomped into the kitchen gripping Mister Pushkin by the scruff of the neck. She said, 'only in the Bradford does it rain the cats!' She looked at the dangling cat, eyeball to eyeball, her nose only just out of reach of the cat's slashing claws, the cat growling and hissing with its sir-a-loin-infused breath... 'I was minding my own business when the Pushkin, he lands on my head, digging every claw into the scalp and tearing out tussocks of the hair... Look,' she pointed at her hair, 'I am the baldy!'

The instant the wriggling cat was released, it wasted no time in running back out to the yard to find a quiet corner, in which to recuperate from its traumatic ordeal.

Halyna thought the cat was too surefooted to fall from the roof... maybe its fear of crows had finally got the better of it? Either way, at least it landed on something soft.

Zena watched as Lenka stared at the album on the table with her usual childlike curiosity. She closed her eyes, hoping Lenka wouldn't say anything she shouldn't...

Lenka smiled at Halyna and said, 'you like the photography, yes?'

Halyna nodded, 'but apparently there aren't any photographs of Uncle Viktor... It's a pity, because I would have liked to have seen what he looked like after all these years...'

Zena's eyes remained closed. She prayed Lenka wouldn't say and do what she knew she was about to say and do...

Lenka declared, 'but I have one!' And before Zena could stop her, she thrust a photograph of Uncle Viktor at Halyna. 'He is the handsome man, yes?'

Halyna picked up the photograph – it could have been of a scarecrow in a field of wheat – and looked at it closely. She said, 'why isn't he wearing any clothes?'

'He never does in the summer,' said Lenka, 'but at least you cannot see the dangler...'

'Thank you very much, Lenka,' said an irritated Zena, 'you can go back to whatever you are the doing.' Her eyebrows wrinkled and met in the middle, 'what *are* you the doing?'

'I teach Sofia's Chi-Chi-Nillas to swim...' Lenka said, waddling back out to check the rodents hadn't drowned in the bucket of water she'd plopped them in to.

Zena hoped her sister had used actual water this time: she was fed up of picking bits of fur from her samahon. She also hoped it was *cold* water, half imagining Lenka suspending the bucket over a bonfire and boiling the poor creatures alive.

'Zena?' said Halyna, after examining the photograph with her magnifying glass, this time taking off her plastic framed glasses and holding the thick lens close to her eye as if she were Margaret Rutherford's Miss Marple.

The Dancing Barber

Zena felt her clammy palms stick to the plastic tablecloth. She thought: *Trust Lenka to give her the photograph... Why could she not wait until the proper time like we agreed?*

'I remember Uncle Viktor when he was younger,' Halyna said, 'he was a short, rather podgy man.'

'True,' said Zena, 'but that was before The Great Famine. He lost plenty of the weight, just like the rest of us. I remember that it was possible to see every one of his ribs and every bone of his spine.' She looked at Halyna, 'and even you were thinner than the skeleton.'

'But Uncle Viktor was *very* short; even shorter than our Mama...' Halyna propped up the photograph against her full glass of samahon and examined it from a distance. 'He couldn't possibly have grown by two *whole* feet? Besides, this looks nothing like him...'

Zena shrugged her shoulders, 'you know how the time, it can play the tricks on the mind...'

Halyna picked up the photograph again; apart from the height difference, something else had caught her attention... She asked, 'does Uncle Viktor still wear his crucifix when working in the field?'

'Not usually,' Zena said, 'he does not want to lose it in the furrows.'

'Mmm...' said Halyna. 'He tans well, doesn't he?' She pointed at the photograph with her stout nail. 'Because it still looks like he's wearing a crucifix even though he isn't. If I look closely, I can see the outline of a large Ukrainian Orthodox crucifix, a bit like the one you're wearing around your neck.' Halyna placed the photograph on the table, feeling the rough edges with her fingers and looking unblinkingly at Zena...

'Oh yes, he tans the very well,' Zena said. She tried to swallow, but her throat was unbelievably dry.

'How big is Uncle Viktor's crucifix?' Halyna asked.

'It is the usual size, made of the silver,' Zena said, holding her thumb and forefinger half an inch apart.

'I see,' said Halyna, 'so that big cross-shaped mark on his chest couldn't have been made by his tiny silver cross, could it?' She narrowed her eyes and watched her sister's twitching face, 'Zena, what aren't you telling me?'

'It is time the truth, it was spoken,' Zena said, grabbing Halyna firmly by the shoulder and squeezing tightly. 'What I am about to tell you is the most secret of the secrets: you must never tell anyone... the promise!'

'Zena, you're hurting me,' Halyna tried to wriggle her shoulder free, 'please, let go.'

'I am the sorry,' said Zena, releasing her grip, 'but the truth, it is the very serious!'

If the "truth" Zena alluded to was what Halyna thought it was, it would be as difficult to digest as "the stew of the meat". She said, 'I won't tell anyone; you can trust me. The promise.'

'You are right,' Zena said shakily, 'the man in the photograph, he is not Uncle Viktor.'

'No?' Halyna said, feigning surprise, 'then who is he?'

Zena tried to swallow, but was still unable to. She said, 'he is... he is...'

Halyna's eyes settled onto the carved wooden crucifix hanging around Zena's neck. She said, 'he's our Tato, isn't he?'

Zena gasped, not knowing what to say. After a moment, she tapped her nose with a finger and said, 'you are the *very* clever...'

'Not really,' Halyna said, 'Tato's crucifix was unique! He wore it in the fields throughout the summer, and the shadow it cast on his chest – especially when he was splayed out sunbathing – branded him permanently... he may as well have been tattooed...'

Every muscle in Zena's body relaxed. She said, 'I have been scared out of the wits about how to tell you the news... It is the relief that you finally know the truth.' She relaxed so much that the kitchen was engulfed by a cloud of rotten eggs.

Breathing shallowly, Halyna said, 'you must tell me: when did he come back home to Chaplinka?'

Zena said, 'our Tato, he was put on the train bound for Siberia, yes? Well, the train, it was only ten miles from the Gulag when the boiler, it cracked because of the cold; the train, it stops and does not move for three days, waiting for the repair. In this time, there was much heavy snow, and many "enemies of the state", they die because of the cold and the soldiers, they throw them to the ground and leave them for the wolves to eat... But our Tato, he pretends to be the dead so they throw him to the ground with the corpses... He lay there all day and all night, not moving a muscle even when

The Dancing Barber

the wolf comes and bites the chunk from his ear. But he okay, and just before it gets light, he takes as many warm coats as he can from the dead – they did not need them any more – and he slips away...'

Halyna was so transfixed by what she was being told that she almost forgot to breathe; she became so light-headed that her body began swaying and she nearly fell from her chair... But not breathing was a good idea... Zena's emissions were much more pungent than usual...

Zena continued, '...years later, after walking across Siberia, living from the fruits of the forest, fish from the rivers and eating the bread he scrounged from the Nomads, our Tato, he finally gets back to Ukraine. Of course, by this time, it is the middle of the World War Two, so he hides up in the hills, eating the goats and drinking the fresh mountain water, waiting for the Partisans to tell him when it is safe to go back. But many of the Partisans, they are the stupid and they forget all about our Tato: he was up in the hills many more years than he needed to be...'

Halyna believed her sister... Zena didn't have the imagination to concoct a story such as this using her own brain...

'Then one day, when Lenka and I were working the land the authorities allocated to us after the Collective Farm was broken up, this hairy wild-man, he came to us with the beard that reached his waist, the dirty skin and the long broken fingernails. He was crawling with the fleas, looked a thousand years old and stank to the high Heavens. Lenka and I, we were the frightened: we knew there were many of the dangerous men in the woods who came and attacked the women in the night... so we picked up our axes and chased him away. He went, but the next day, our Mama she saw him watching from a distance, so I chased him down and wrestled him to the ground, determined to get rid of him for good! In a weak voice, he shouted, "Zena, it is your Tato! Look at me, it is your Tato!" So I stopped myself from punching him in the face, looked at him and saw that it *was* our Tato! Underneath all the dirt and the hair, his eyes, they stared at me: I'd know his eyes anywhere!'

Halyna said, 'why did you not tell me sooner? Did you not think that I had a right to know our Tato was still alive? For three decades, I thought he'd died in a terrible way...'

Zena shook her head, 'how could we have the told you? In the letter?' She laughed, 'you know how the Soviets, they censor all the letters. If they had found out about our Tato, he would have been sent straight to the Gulag. Remember, the Soviets, they have the lists! Our Tato, he is the wanted man!'

Halyna said, 'I expect you're right...' A tingle ran down the full length of her spine. She smiled and said, 'our Tato, is he well?'

'Of course,' said Zena, 'inside his head, he is still the twenty years old!'

'I'm glad,' Halyna said, smiling at the photograph of her naked father. 'But what happened to the real Uncle Viktor?'

Zena shrugged her shoulders, 'he was one of "the disappeared", but we kept his papers and gave them to our Tato... Because there is no photograph of Uncle Viktor, the Soviet soldiers, they do not have a clue.'

Halyna was surprised she hadn't collapsed; perhaps she was getting used to dealing with shocks... she'd certainly had plenty of practice in the past week. She'd never stopped mourning the loss of her Tato and thought about him every day... She neither knew what to say, nor how to feel: the happiness of knowing her Tato was still alive was overshadowed by her anger with Zena for keeping the news from her for so long. What an eventful few days: she may have lost a Mama, but she had also gained a Tato.

'Halynochka, are you the okay?' Zena asked, watching her sister's eyes glaze over. 'Do you want the tea or the coffee? I can set fire to the kettle?'

'Never mind tea or coffee... and keep that electric kettle off the hob! Give me <u>samahon</u> and plenty of it!' Halyna didn't care about the *Slyna*... 'Then we are to telephone Chaplinka; I must speak to Uncle... to Tato!'

The Dancing Barber

Chapter 96

---------------------------------------✂--

Stanislaw eavesdropped from behind the kitchen door, still breathless after lugging such a heavy weight down all those stairs from the attic... And he couldn't believe what he'd overheard...

'How can Viktor still be alive?' he whispered. 'It isn't possible... I put him on the Gulag train myself...?'

Dangling from a coat hook, a concussed Klem could only groan, the blood from his swollen nose soaking into the paintbrush of his moustache. He groaned louder and tried to wriggle himself free.

'Be quiet,' whispered Stanislaw, 'I'm trying to listen!' He put his ear against the door again, the flaking paint scraping his skin. When the conversation in the kitchen had ended, he said, 'Viktor was the last man from Chaplinka that I sent to the Gulag: he was brave, but a real pain in the other end. And now I discover that not only did he escape, but he is still *alive*. I hate it when people evade justice... don't you agree?'

Klem grunted.

Stanislaw breathed slowly from his open mouth, engulfing the air at the foot of the stairs with the stench of over-boiled cabbage. He forced the tip of Zena's misplaced knitting needle a little further into Klem's side, 'I said: <u>don't you agree</u>?'

Klem groaned angrily, if only he could speak...

Satisfied, Stanislaw retracted the knitting needle and resumed his eavesdropping.

Klem's head was a spinning top... The last thing he expected was to find Stanislaw waiting to ambush him on the balcony, subsequent to flinging the cat over the balustrade... He hoped Mister Pushkin had survived the three storey fall... but judging by the language Lenka had used, the cat had certainly landed on something soft...

And how did Stanislaw manage to cut his way out of all that carpet tape, let alone punch a hole through the roof tiles to escape the loft? Taras would do his nut when he saw the damage... And where did he get that knitting needle from?

And for a man incarcerated and starved for a whole week, Stanislaw seemed to have plenty of energy... Klem couldn't believe he'd been knocked out with a single punch, and then mummified with one of the twins' washing lines so meticulously that only his bruised head and bright red boots were visible.

Klem felt the washing line biting into his skin; it was so tight that his hands and feet were fast asleep. And if a rolled-up pair of Zena's clean-ish underpants weren't wedged in his mouth, he'd have shouted for help long ago... he doubted his taste buds would ever recover... But all he could do was groan; and the louder he groaned, the deeper Stanislaw perforated his side with the knitting needle.

Stanislaw obviously had a plan... he wasted no time hauling Klem downstairs and hanging him on a coat hook, all the while repeating 'The Dancing Barber,' so quickly that all the words rolled into one... it was as though the man was obsessed...

Klem watched Stanislaw's bloodshot eyeball pulsate, its pupil fully dilated, his cesspit of a mouth salivating as if he was suffering from rabies... The instant he'd overheard Halyna and Zena's conversation, thus discovered Viktor's true identity, all thought of The Dancing Barber was forgotten... The man had a new obsession...

Fortunately, Klem knew Stanislaw wouldn't have the upper hand for much longer...

Right on cue, the beautiful orchestral chimes of his pocket watch signalled six o'clock, with an apt rendition of the Ukrainian National Anthem...

For the first time ever, Klem saw panic in Stanislaw's face... especially as there was no way the watch could be silenced, not beneath all that washing line.

And panic became sheer fright when Zena swung open the door, expecting to greet her husband-to-be with one of her halitosis kisses and body-odorous hugs...

But upon discovering the escaped prisoner, Zena clamped her hands around Stanislaw's thick neck and squeezed so hard that his eyeball almost popped out.

Klem dangled helplessly as if he were an oversized pupa, and watched Zena effortlessly dodge Stanislaw's repeated stabs with the knitting needle. She squeezed even harder, her fingers disappearing into the flesh of his thick neck just as the knitting needle lanced completely through her muscular arm...

Zena admired her piercing and smiled; then using both fists, she repeatedly pounded Stanislaw's fungal growth of a nose... his loose teeth tinkling to the floor and his lips rupturing.

Klem watched Halyna dash out to the yard to fetch Lenka... He wished he still had the dog... He closed his eyes; it had been decades since he last saw someone killed...

While Stanislaw staggered around like a drunkard, Zena gripped the bulbous end of the knitting needle between her craggy teeth and slowly dragged out the blood stained spear from her arm. She examined the holes; thankfully, the needle had only passed through a fold of skin in her forearm, and there was hardly any bleeding. She considered inserting the knitting needle into the Colonel, but instead, tied it in a knot and threw it to the floor...

Stanislaw laughed raucously. 'You can't outsmart me, filthy peasant!'

Klem's eyes remained closed. He imagined Stanislaw enjoyed receiving pain as much as Zena enjoyed inflicting it....

Zena grabbed Stanislaw's ears and pulled his head down onto her upward-thrusting knee, repeating the action three times. Amazingly, he remained conscious.

Klem could see that Zena was enjoying herself too much... especially when she changed her mind about what to do with the knotted knitting needle...

Try as he might, Klem couldn't wriggle his way off the coat hook, nor could he snap it from the wall. He looked out to the yard, but could neither see Halyna nor Lenka... both of them would be needed to restrain Zena, and quickly. Klem watched Zena punch and kick the Colonel, her fists working with the speed and force of steam-hammers. The Colonel's eyelids quickly swelled to the size of plums, whilst his nose streamed with blood...

Stanislaw numbed his mind to the bombardment of punches; the Zena woman may have been strong, but she was certainly not clever. It was time he regained control, so in a gap between the punches, he used all his strength to head-butt the Zena woman in the centre of her face...

Zena was stunned, her body quivering as though it were a building during an earthquake, swaying forwards and backwards, before THUD! She crumbled to the floor.

Klem thought Zena was indestructible... maybe he was hallucinating? No, it was really happening... Come on Halyna, come on Lenka... where are you?

While Zena lay face down on the floor, Stanislaw shook the concussion from his brain and went to pick up his teeth, placing them in his cassock pocket...

He then stepped over the heap of Zena's unconscious body and reached for the telephone, proceeding to dial a seemingly endless number. While the telephone rang, he shook around the jar of marbles sat on a nearby shelf. He selected a bright red one, polished it on his cassock and inserted it between his swollen eyelids. The new eye was a little too small, but it would do...

Having relayed the correct code word to three levels of security personnel, he said, 'put me through to Comrade General Borodov, Head of the Soviet Secret Police... What do you mean he doesn't want to talk to me...? Tell him I have news of an escaped Enemy of the State and I need him to mobilise our operative in Askanya Nova. Now! I *beg* your pardon? Don't you realise you're addressing a Colonel!'

Lenka marched straight up to Stanislaw and tore the telephone receiver from his hand, simultaneously ripping the cable from the wall. She head-butted him in the nose and said, 'and *that* is for assaulting my sister! Soviet swine!' Watching him stagger around, she demanded: 'this operative in Askanya Nova, who is he?'

Stanislaw sneered, 'what makes you think I'll tell someone like *you*?'

Lenka knew that only the Ranger lived in Askanya Nova, but she didn't believe he could be in league with the Soviets? 'You will tell me,' Lenka said, thrusting her constricting hand up the man's cassock, 'and you will tell me the quickly...'

'It's too late,' replied a squirming Stanislaw, 'this "Uncle Viktor" is as good as dead! No-one escapes the Gulag... especially at his age!'

Lenka said, 'I do not the think so.' She smiled, 'you know, in my hands, I can easily crack the walnuts...'

Stanislaw didn't doubt it; but he didn't want to experience it. It was a pity the Zena and Lenka women were not Soviet; they'd be useful additions to the interrogation department in the dungeons of the Secret Police... curare and sodium pentothal need never be used again...

Lenka said, 'you will make the telephone call and cancel the order, yes!' She emphasised the importance of the matter by twisting as well as squeezing.

'Go hang yourself,' screamed Stanislaw, his voice an octave higher. He doubted Comrade General Borodov had even accepted his order... but the Lenka woman needn't know that...

Lenka began pulling as well as twisting and squeezing...

Stanislaw squeaked, 'okay, *okay*, I'll do it! *I'll do it!* But they won't believe it's *me*, unless you *let go...*'

Contrary to her better judgement, Lenka released her grip, but her hand remained firmly in position. She said, 'no messing...'

Stanislaw picked up the receiver and dialled the number; resting the receiver on his shoulder, he waited to be prompted to enter the security codes.

Lenka turned to Klem and smiled, 'see, I am not as the stupid as people think!'

Klem tried to warn her, but it was too late... In one swift movement, Stanislaw swept Lenka's hand from under him, and pushed her to the floor, striking the back of her neck with all his strength. 'Now it's my turn,' he sneered, searching for anything with which to tie up the ugly woman.

Sensibly, Lenka pretended not to see Halyna sneak up behind the Colonel, brandishing her heaviest Pyrex dish. But she couldn't help but cheer when the dish collided with the back of Stanislaw's skull, indenting it deeply and causing him to crumble to the floor in a heap of purple cassock.

'The thank you,' Lenka said, wiping her oily brow. 'Stanislaw, he got the better of me.'

Halyna said, 'he got the better of both of you... Zena's out like a light.'

Lenka pulled the face of a trout. 'Nothing has ever knocked her out before... Zena, she must be getting the old...'

But Zena soon regained consciousness when Lenka poured a bottle of super-strength smelling salts into each of her sister's nostrils, causing her to sneeze continuously for ten whole minutes.

'For your information,' Zena said, 'I am not getting the old...' Seeing the surprise on Lenka's face, she added, 'you think I did not the hear you...? You think he the knock me out...? Well... he did not, I was only resting the eyes!'

Still dangling from the coat hook, Klem emitted his loudest groan, desperate to be released.

So while Lenka unwound the yards of washing line that had cocooned him, Halyna went to observe what she'd done to Stanislaw...

Klem stared despondently at his crumpled suit, every pinstripe now cross-hatched with a crease from the constricting washing line. Prior to Easter, he'd worn the same suit every day for almost a decade... now, only three remained that hadn't been ruined. And if that wasn't bad enough, his mouth – even after gargling with the strongest Listerine – still retained the taste of Zena's russet underpants... Nothing would ever taste the same again...

'Is he alive?' Halyna asked, holding the Pyrex dish covered with congealed blood.

'Unfortunately...' Klem sighed, 'I think he might be... Remember what Gunter said about Soviet crackpots being indestructible machines...' He crouched down and removed the white cardboard strip from around Stanislaw's neck, unfastened the small button on his collar and wondered where to start looking for a pulse on such a muscular neck. After a couple of minutes of prodding with his fingers at the man's stubbly skin, he deduced things didn't look good. He shook his head, 'maybe he wasn't indestructible after all...'

The Pyrex dish clattered to the floor, and would have been closely followed by Halyna, had Lenka not caught her in her strong arms.

'If he's dead,' Halyna said shakily, 'it makes me just as bad as him... The Holy Bible teaches you to turn the other cheek...'

Lenka said, 'but the Holy Bible, it also says "the eye for the eye" and "the tooth for the tooth", yes?'

Halyna screamed at the pile of purple cassock, 'I hate you for what you made me do!' She kicked Stanislaw in the stomach and uttered the most shocking of words. She then burst into uncontrollable tears and refused to be comforted by anyone, not even by Klem...

Zena sniffled... her nose was bruised, but not broken... she blew it on her sleeve. She could not believe a head-butt from a man

The Dancing Barber

like Stanislaw was enough to knock her out... She turned to Klem and said, 'this operative in Askanya Nova... is he the problem?'

Klem shrugged, 'from what I heard, Stanislaw had tried to get through to Comrade General Borodov, but Borodov refused to speak to him... I think Stanislaw was told to get lost!' He straightened the crumpled ribbon on his embroidered collar, 'and as far as I'm aware, there hasn't been an operative in Askanya Nova in years...' He laughed, 'it wouldn't at all surprise me if Stanislaw was the one Gunter told us about... you know, the one that escaped from The Asylum...'

'But that is goodski,' said Halyna, reconnecting the telephone. 'If he is a known crackpot, then they'll know I acted in self-defence...'

Zena snatched the telephone from her sister's hand and slammed it back on the cradle. 'This is not the matter for the Police of Yorkshire...' She looked at Klem, 'you agree, yes?'

Klem shook his head, 'this has gone far enough... look at the state of us... it's time we let the authorities handle it.' He looked at Zena's swollen face, 'besides, you need to see a doctor... that nose of yours might be broken...' He picked up the receiver and began dialling...

Zena snapped, 'you <u>will</u> listen to your future wife and <u>do</u> what she says!'

Klem said, 'not when she talks such himno!'

'Himno!' screamed Zena, 'I do not talk the himno!' She turned to Halyna, 'do you think I talk the himno?'

'Keep me out of it,' said Halyna, taking hold of the receiver, preparing to ask the operator to send the Police and an Ambulance.

'How nice,' Zena huffed, 'even my little sister, she thinks I talk the himno...'

While the argument intensified, the heap of purple cassock on the floor began twitching... and the bruised eyelid slowly opened...

AC Michael

Chapter 97

The Village of Chaplinka, Khersonska Oblast, South-eastern Ukraine

Viktor's bony body collided repeatedly with the hard plastic dashboard as he struggled to fasten the seat belt. He asked, 'what's the hurry? You could have given me chance to put on my trousers before bundling me into this contraption…'

But Viktor's neighbour was in deep concentration, weaving his Jeep along the winding track to Askanya Nova, trying to avoid the worst potholes. He drove so quickly that the landscape behind was completely obscured by the dust kicked up by the Jeep's chunky tyres, making it appear as if they were being chased by a whirlwind.

Having given up trying to fathom how to fasten the clasp of the seat belt, Viktor grabbed both ends and tied them in a double knot. He may have been tethered securely to the seat, but his body still juddered with every contour, and his remaining teeth rattled in his jaws.

'Sorry Viktor,' said his neighbour, hurtling the Jeep along a straight part of the track. 'But there's been an urgent telephone call for you from Kyiv…' He scrutinised the clock on the dashboard, then pressed his foot harder on the accelerator, 'and they're calling back in *twenty* minutes!'

'Urgent call?' said Viktor, 'from Kyiv?' He thought: *Could it be the Embassy? I hope Zena and Lenka haven't been arrested…*

His neighbour reached behind the seat and dragged out the pair of soiled dungarees he wore when checking the Nature Reserve's boundaries. 'Here,' he said, 'put these on…'

Viktor looked at the filthy garment, and said, 'do I have to?'

The telephone was already ringing when the Jeep slalomed along the winding track to the Ranger's Office, flinging grit at the annoyed horses grazing in the bordering fields.

'Hello,' Viktor's neighbour said, panting after his sprint to pick

The Dancing Barber

up the receiver, 'yes, he's here; just a minute...' He balanced the receiver on his shoulder and turned around to find Viktor ambling in, fiddling with the straps on the dungarees, unable to work out how to stop them falling down. 'Hurry up,' he said, 'it's for you!'

'Hello?' Viktor said, holding the receiver upside down and talking into the speaker. 'Hello? Hello...?' He shrugged his shoulders, 'but there's no one there?'

'Oh,' said Viktor, once his neighbour had turned the receiver the right way round. With the speaker now at his ear, he said, 'hello, this is Viktor... Yes... And who am I talking to?'

Viktor's neighbour dashed to the adjacent kitchen to make a cup of tea. He silently picked up the telephone extension and covered the mouthpiece with his hand...

The moment the person on the line introduced herself as "Halyna", Viktor tried to speak, but was unable to utter a single sound, let alone a proper word. He sat down on a rickety chair, feeling the ill-fitting dungarees creep up to somewhere uncomfortable, and listened. How could he be sure this was Halyna's voice? She was only a young girl the last time he saw her; the voice on the line could have been *anyone*...

The main telephone exchange was in Kyiv, and so were the Soviet Authorities: what if they'd discovered his secret? It was just the sort of trick the Soviets would pull in order to trap him...

After a long silence, Viktor stuttered, 'yes... I'm still here... Oh, I'm fine...' It was then when the person purporting to be Halyna called him "Tato" and blurted out that she knew all about his escape from The Death Train and that he wasn't really Uncle Viktor...

Dirty sweat leached from his skin as he contemplated the likelihood of whether this was an elaborate ruse to trick him into confessing his identity. His neighbour may have been a friend, but it was a little known fact that he also used to work for the government: an occupation very few people ever leave. And the rumble of a boiling kettle was conspicuous by its absence. But Viktor hadn't survived undetected for thirty years to be caught out by a person on the end of a telephone wire he couldn't even see: they weren't going to send *him* back to the Gulag! He thought carefully before saying, 'Halyna, are Zena and Lenka with you? I'd like to speak to them... No... Can you go and get them?'

He had a hunch "Halyna" wouldn't be able to find Zena and Lenka, thus confirming it was a trap. While he waited, he turned and shouted towards the adjacent kitchen, 'is the tea nearly ready?' He smiled when he heard his neighbour stumble and knock something over, the sounds from the kitchen echoing down the telephone wire and into his ear...

His neighbour shouted, 'err... it'll be another few minutes.'

Viktor shook his head as he listened to the kettle being filled from the tap: from now on, his neighbour could drink his own samahon... And it certainly explained all that business with the slithers of garlic... only a Soviet would pollute his samahon in such a way. And it also explained why his neighbour had asked those questions about the 'other' news Zena and Lenka were to tell Halyna. A shiver ran down his spine; he hated these two-faced "officials"...

After waiting several minutes, Viktor knew he'd outsmarted the idiot Soviets and prepared to place the receiver back onto the cradle. He then had to decide what to do about his neighbour... The man will have heard "Halyna" talk of his escape from The Death Train, and call him Tato... Although he didn't say anything incriminating, the fact that he didn't deny what "Halyna" had said, would not have gone unnoticed... And to make matters worse, the office door had been locked and the windows were all barred... It was only a matter of time until this "official" wheedled the truth out of him...

'Viktor?' an angry voice bellowed down the line. 'What do you the want? Do you not think we are the busy?'

Viktor immediately recognised Zena's deep voice. 'How are you?' he asked, listening to the unmistakable sound of her nails scratching against her bristly chin, and the unique rasp of flatulence only she could create.

'I good and so is Lenka. But we are the very busy now! We have just made another batch of the samahon... Yes, plenty of the *Slyna*... Now we are preparing the stuffed heart of the bull for the dinner... What...? Yes, I have the signature... Taras, he gets it for me... No trouble... Yes, Oksana she knows... Klem and I are the very happy... especially now that he knows never to disobey me! But you can the talk to me <u>later</u>!' Zena shouted so loudly that it made Viktor's ears hurt: 'Lenka! Stop spitting... the samahon, it

The Dancing Barber

does not need any more of the *Slyna*! Go and get Halynochka! Now!'

Viktor found it hard to believe his hunch was wrong; was he getting paranoid in his old age? But he reminded himself that paranoia was the key to survival in Soviet occupied Ukraine... And although Zena's unique aggressiveness and rasping flatulence was impossible to imitate, there was still a chance he could have been speaking to an actor...

'Oh Viktor,' Zena said, 'I almost forget... *Kapusta*, remember Viktor, *Kapusta*...'

'What about it?' he asked, but Zena had gone. Then he remembered the word's usage when the girls were young... he hadn't heard it spoken in such a context since 1933. Zena was right to be cautious, especially in the light of his neighbour's eavesdropping. At least it confirmed without any doubt that Zena was actually Zena.

'It is wonderful to speak to you,' Viktor said after being handed back to Halyna. 'Yes, it will be lovely to see you again after all these years... When are you planning on – '

The telephone bleeped three times, then went dead.

'What happened?' Viktor asked his neighbour, who'd sauntered in with a samovar of black tea.

'The money must have run out,' he said, plonking the heavy samovar onto the rickety table. He sauntered back to the kitchen to fetch some cups, 'the exchange will have closed by now... so I'm afraid they won't be calling back today...'

As his neighbour slurped his black tea, Viktor allowed his own to go cold. He couldn't believe he'd spoken to Halyna – his youngest, and possibly favourite daughter – for the first time in thirty years, and she actually knew who he was! He hoped it wouldn't be long before they could meet... he was so excited. But he dare not look happy, not in front of his potentially deceitful neighbour.

'Your nieces had a good trip?' Viktor's neighbour asked, not especially enjoying his black tea.

'Hmm?' said Viktor, 'oh yes, a *very* good trip! At long last, Zena's family are together... And Oksana, she sounds an *interesting* character...'

'I am pleased,' said Viktor's neighbour, stopping himself from adding slithers of garlic to his tea. 'And Halyna, what does she think about her Uncle Viktor turning into her Tato? Is she excited?'

Viktor slammed the cup onto the table so hard that the handle broke off in his hand.

'What's the matter with you?' Viktor's neighbour took a deep breath, 'that was my best cup; it came all the way from St Petersburg.'

'Where else?' muttered Viktor. He said, 'I'm *sorry*, it slipped... Now, tell me: what are you talking about? I haven't "turned into" anyone! You <u>know</u> my name is Viktor.'

Viktor's neighbour smiled, 'of course I do...' He slurped his unpalatable tea, 'that's because you've been illegally using his papers... a very devious – *and dangerous* – thing to do...' He put his cup down on the saucer, 'you may be surprised to learn that I've known the truth for a long time...'

Viktor's expression was unyielding: *So much for this being the most secret of secrets... how the Hell did <u>he</u> find out?* Viktor stared at the key to the Jeep that was next to the telephone. Did he have the courage to take it and – despite being unable to drive – steal the Jeep and flee, before the soldiers inevitably came to arrest him? He examined his surroundings: the barred windows, the locked doors, all those cupboards...

But what if the soldiers were already here... there were plenty of places for them to hide... they could be waiting in the kitchen?

Maybe his time had finally come? Evading capture for three decades was an impressive achievement... but nothing lasts forever.

'Don't look so upset... Besides,' Viktor's neighbour gestured to the cross-shaped patch of light skin on Viktor's deeply tanned chest, 'you wore that old crucifix for so long that the sun branded your skin... especially after all the sunbathing you did when you were younger... And I know that, of all the men who helped renovate the old church, you were the only one who had the skill to fashion a proper Ukrainian Orthodox crucifix out of that piece of oak. You were so proud of it that you never took it off.'

'If what you say is correct, what will you do?' Viktor said. He fixed his eyes on the key to the Jeep, wondering whether he'd be able to grip it in his sweaty hand...

The Dancing Barber

'*Do?* What do you mean?' Then his neighbour realised, 'listen Viktor: surely you know I haven't worked for the government for quite some time... Relax, I'm happy your family is to be reunited.' He crossed himself in the Ukrainian Orthodox fashion... 'See,' he said, 'you have my word.'

Viktor said nothing. He knew that if his neighbour possessed a new-fangled televisual set, then he would also possess a new-fangled machine that would record everything he said... He folded his arms and kept his mouth shut. Kapusta.

'Relax; you've been listening to too much scare-mongering on Soviet radio! The Kremlin doesn't care about someone who escaped the Gulag thirty years ago. *Thousands* of people have done so and there are tens of thousands still to escape!' He drained the last of his black tea, 'yuck! No wonder you haven't drunk any,' he said, looking at Viktor's full cup. 'I must remember to clean out the samovar once in a while... Anyway, have you ever wondered why I stopped working for the government?'

Viktor shrugged, 'it is none of my business.' He shuffled to the edge of his seat, the dungarees still trapped somewhere exceptionally uncomfortable. 'To be honest, I thought you still did... Working in Askanya Nova would be the perfect "cover" for an operative of the Soviet Secret Police... Don't you agree? You could get on with all your secret work undisturbed...'

'No, that's not true! As my old Captain used to say, "You are talking out of your other end"... When I did work for the Soviets, I also worked for the Partisans... they called me a "double agent".' He looked seriously at Viktor, 'why do you think you were left up in the hills for so many years after the war had ended...? Because I knew it wasn't safe for you to return to Chaplinka until Captain Stanislaw went back to Moscow, when the Soviets – in their immense wisdom – made him a Colonel... Is that the action of a Soviet "operative"...? No!' He lowered his voice, 'and I'll tell you something else: just like you, I'm posing as my own brother.'

Viktor laughed, 'of course you are.'

'It's true, I tell you. I escaped the Gulag just like you. But I was much further north... that's where they sent Soviet soldiers who helped the so-called "Enemies of the State"... So just like you, I hid up in the hills with the Partisans during the war...' Viktor's neighbour rolled up his sleeve, 'how else would I get these scars?'

Viktor observed the familiarly indented skin, the teeth and claw marks having turned silver with age. He asked, 'how many?'

'Four in total... they attacked me when I was asleep. The wounds were so badly infected that it was a miracle they healed.' Viktor's neighbour rolled down his sleeve, 'so you see, I'm glad your family knows who you really are. At least you still have a family. Because all mine...'

Viktor cursed his suspicious mind. His neighbour was a brave man, being a "double agent"... And being attacked by four wolves must have been a horrific experience. He gestured to the broken cup, 'I am sorry about that; I'll try to mend it.'

'Don't worry, it was only a worthless piece of junk...' Then, as if by magic, Viktor's neighbour unveiled a pair of glasses and a bottle of proper vodka. 'Here,' he said, filling the glasses to the brim, 'let us drink to your future!'

'*Na zdorovya!*' declared Viktor, immediately draining his glass with one swig. 'You're right about the Soviets... they don't care about the likes of us, especially now they've got Voloshin to worry them.'

'True,' said Viktor's neighbour. 'And they make *excellent* vodka!'

Regardless of how sincere the man sounded, Viktor still refused to admit anything... And as he watched his neighbour add several slithers of garlic to his vodka, the little voice of paranoia in his head kept shouting <u>Kapusta</u>! He'd listened to that voice for thirty years, and it had never let him down...

The Dancing Barber

Chapter 98

✂------------------------------------

The City of Bradford, West Yorkshire, Northern England

If Sofia tripped on the increasingly dirty hem of her Tato's blue blazer once more, she vowed to take it off and fling it into the biggest puddle she could find... then she'd jump up and down on it until it was completely wet through. It was only a short walk home, so why couldn't she be seen wearing her mini-skirt? It was dark outside and it wasn't as though her thighs wobbled half as much as they used to...

But this was only one source of frustration. She looked up at the smug face of the other source, prancing along the pavement beside her, and said, 'Tato, did you *really* have to spend all the YTV money on more costumes? Surely we already have enough?'

'Think of it as an investment,' said Taras, balancing along the cracks in the pavement, placing one foot in front of the other as if on a tightrope. 'By looking like professionals, we shall dance like professionals and so command the *fees* of professionals, understand?'

Natalka and Oksana couldn't walk any further; their arms were two inches longer than they used to be and their burning biceps screamed for some rest. Dropping the heavy box on a nearby garden wall, Natalka said, 'Mr Taras, you cannot promise to do something and then not do it.'

'I agree,' added an out-of-breath Oksana, 'you should have given us our money... It was the least you could do after all the stress you've put us under!'

Sofia shielded her ears, anticipating her Tato's deafening reprimand for them daring to "answer back". But he was too busy plucking a bunch of bright yellow daffodils from someone's garden, plunging his nose deeply into the flower's egg-yolk coloured trumpet, inhaling the delicate, yet intensely sweet fragrance.

'Ah,' he said, ignoring the increasing tightness and pain in his chest, 'beautiful...' He threaded a single stem through the buttonhole of his blue blazer... he thought the sodium streetlights really brought out the intensity of the yellow petals.

Sofia shrugged her shoulders, as did Natalka and Oksana.

Taras tapped Sofia on the head and said, 'come on, dinner won't cook itself.' Skipping along the pavement, he called to Natalka who, with bended knees, was preparing to lift the heavy box again, 'there'll be plenty of food, so you are more than welcome to join us...'

'Thank you,' said Natalka, 'I am truly honoured...'

Taras nodded his appreciation for her gratitude, but didn't see the face she pulled when he wasn't looking...

Following one of Taras' labyrinthine shortcuts – that were anything but short – the foursome became predictably lost down yet another unfamiliar alley. But it didn't deter him from leading the way, marching between the dustbins and piles of litter, scattering the rats and frightening the cats. He reassured the girls that – contrary to appearances – he wasn't lost, but going via the "scenic route".

'He hasn't a clue where he's going,' said Oksana, wedging the box on the shelf that was her belly.

'Never has,' said Natalka, her arms now three inches longer.

Sofia turned around, 'Mama told me that it once took him two hours to get home when he'd had a "skin-full"...'

'She lies,' said Taras, clutching his chest... the pain shooting along his left arm and also down to his stomach. 'It was an hour and a half... But it often takes Klem over three hours... Longer, if the cat doesn't help him...'

Again, the three girls shrugged: they didn't like it when Mr Taras was happy... it really worried them. He may have been skipping down the alley, but he didn't look well... his complexion was getting paler by the second... He then stopped skipping and started marching.

But Taras' rate of marching soon slowed and then ceased entirely, causing Sofia to bump into him.

'Tato?' said a frantic Sofia, 'what's the matter?' His face was contorted with pain, his perspiring skin, ice cold to the touch.

'Good Heavens,' said Oksana, 'he's gone as white as a sheet...'

The Dancing Barber

Clutching his chest, Taras' knees gave way and he crumbled to the litter strewn cobbles. His precious bottle of vodka clattered down, but did not break. 'The pain,' he said, 'I can't pretend any more... it's unbearable...'

'Bleeding hell,' said Natalka, dropping the box... the full weight was too much for Oksana, so it fell to the cobbles and crushed the heifer's toes. 'I think he's having a bleeding heart attack...'

'What do we do?' Sofia asked, supporting her Tato's head and mopping his increasingly perspiring, yet freezing cold brow. 'I don't know what to do?'

'Well?' thought Natalka, 'my Tato would call an ambulance... I'll run to find a telephone.'

'Wait...' said Taras, grabbing Natalka's foot. 'I am *not* going to hospital. I hate hospitals!'

'But Mr Taras,' begged Natalka, 'you're having a heart attack... You need help!'

Sofia massaged her Tato's muscular shoulders. She said, 'don't worry, everything will be okay... I know it will...'

'This is ridiculous,' declared Natalka, 'I am going to get help whether you want it or not!'

But Taras refused to let go of her foot; if anything, his grip became tighter. 'Give me a minute,' he said, 'I'll feel better in a minute... But if I don't, *then* you can get help...'

Begrudgingly, Natalka agreed, counting down the seconds in her head; Oksana sat on the box of costumes, endeavouring to squash it flat, while Sofia prayed relentlessly...

'...fifty-eight, fifty-nine, sixty. Right,' said Natalka, snatching her foot away. 'That's a minute... I'm off...'

Slowly, colour returned to Taras' cheeks, accompanied by an unusual gurgling sound emanating from deep within his torso. He opened his mouth as if to speak...

Sofia hugged him, 'don't worry,' she said, 'everything will be okay...' She turned to Natalka and said, 'wait... he's trying to say something...'

'We best listen,' said Oksana, 'these could be his last words...'

Natalka slapped her, 'shut your cake-hole you stupid heifer!'

Taras' mouth opened even wider, the girls anticipating his words...

But instead of speaking, he emitted a thunderous burp that seemed to go on forever.

The girls hugged one another, shocked by what was happening.

After a while, Taras said, with much relief, 'by heck, that's better...' He then burped even louder, for several more seconds, 'by heck, that's even better!'

Natalka thought: *By heck? He's never said that before...* Despite the stench of partially digested food assaulting her nostrils, she still managed to smile. 'So my Tato was right! It *was* indigestion!'

But Sofia wasn't so sure. She watched her Tato's face turn, once again, paler than ever and his cheeks quiver and balloon... Then, much to everyone's surprise, from his mouth, he ejected a golf ball of matted hair that bounced along the cobbles and rolled in amongst the litter.

'What the – ,' Taras said, spitting to the ground to rid his mouth of any remaining fibres, before ejecting another, much larger one...

Natalka picked up the projectile and examined it in the sodium haze of a streetlight. 'Bleeding hell,' she said, 'I thought only cats could get fur balls?'

Taras stared at the balls, observing the brown curly hairs, from which they were composed. He said, 'fur balls...? Is that what they are...? Give me strength... and all this time, I thought I was having a heart attack... It must be Zena and Lenka's cooking... I don't know how they manage to shed so much hair into our food?'

'At least that's all it was,' said Sofia, thanking God most sincerely that it hadn't been a heart attack. 'Maybe you should examine your food more closely next time... I counted thirty-one hairs in the two *Varenyky* they served me last night... But you ate thirty of them... so you'd have swallowed over *four hundred* hairs! No wonder you've got fur balls!'

After washing out his mouth with vodka – what a terrible waste – Taras said, 'I'm not eating anything they cook *ever* again!' Using his thumbnails, he prised apart each of the balls and unravelled one of the hundreds of hairs.

Natalka muttered, 'you'd probably eat less hair if you licked a malting cat...'

The Dancing Barber

Chapter 99

After another half an hour of random wandering, Taras finally stumbled onto the way home… And after stopping to rest another three times, he led the exhausted girls triumphantly through the yard. He didn't bother to hold open the gate, which duly smashed into Oksana, almost knocking her over. He said, 'hurry up, dinner won't cook itself…'

Natalka muttered, 'no, we'll bleeding well end up cooking it for him…'

'Or it could be fish and chips again,' said a salivating Oksana, forgetful of the fact that she was supposed to be on a diet.

'That's odd,' said Sofia, 'our washing line is gone.'

'Oh yeah,' said Natalka, for once not having to stoop to walk across the yard.

'Who'd want an old washing line?' said Oksana. She looked in the corner of the yard, 'at least they left the bag of clothes-pegs behind. And a bucket full of something weird…'

Sofia approached the yellow bucket with caution, expecting to see the usual appalling quagmire… But when she peered over the rim, she witnessed the pair of chinchillas splashing around, panting with exhaustion… thankfully it was only full of water. 'What does bleeding Lenka think she's doing?' she said, lifting the sodden rodents from the water and drying them on her Tato's blue blazer. The creatures were so much smaller when wet, but their fur fluffed up wonderfully after a gentle rub with the blue blazer.

Sofia gasped when she realised what she'd done, 'oh I am sorry… I didn't mean to swear…' But her Tato hadn't noticed; he was much more interested with whatever was going on in the kitchen. Realising that it could have been the damp blazer that annoyed him, she repeated, 'I said, I'm sorry, Tato… and I'm sure your blazer will be dry by morning…'

'Shhh…' said Taras, raising his hand so the girls didn't follow him up the stone steps. 'Do not make a sound.' He leaned over the wrought iron railings that flanked the steps leading to the kitchen door, being careful to keep his clothes away from the flaking paint.

Looking through the kitchen window, he weaved his gaze between Halyna's windowsill jungle and muttered, 'what the – .' He rubbed his eyes and looked again...

Halyna and Klem were sat far too closely together at one end of the table, whilst Zena and Lenka sat like *Tweedle-Dum* and *Tweedle-Dee* at the other end, each baring the expression of a constipated hippopotamus. And in between, there was seated a most peculiar bald-headed man dressed entirely in purple, who's steady hand held a heavy aluminium pan above what looked like Klem's glittering *Pysanka*.

Taras wished Klem would stop inviting his weirdo friends to the house. What were they doing, playing one of those strange parlour games?

There was something vaguely familiar about the bald-headed man, whose solitary eye constantly scanned the room... he was sure he'd seen him somewhere before. Taras ducked down when the man's gaze drifted across the window, before it lingered once more on Klem's twitching face. Still holding the bunch of daffodils and the bottle of vodka, Taras leaned over a little more to get a better look, in-so-doing clattering the glass bottle against the railings. He cursed, hoping it hadn't been heard. Unfortunately, the bald-headed man was staring through the glass, directly at him.

Taras ducked down, hopeful that if he moved quickly enough, he might not be seen.

It didn't work, because the bald-headed man called out, 'Voloshin, please come in! We've been waiting for you...'

Voloshin... thought Taras, *did he call me Voloshin?* <u>No</u>, *I must have misheard...* He turned to the girls, 'wait here and do nothing...' He had second thoughts, 'actually, it would be better if you all hid in the coal-shed.' When the girls didn't move, he said, 'Go!'

Sofia and Natalka protested, 'what? You mean *Oksana* too...? But we'll never *all* fit in there!'

Taras said, 'do <u>not</u> argue!'

He waited until Oksana had breathed in sufficiently for him to be able to close the flimsy wooden door... 'And you are to stay here until I personally come to get you, <u>understand</u>?'

'But why?' pleaded Sofia, her face butted up against the chicken-wire window, gasping for air.

The Dancing Barber

'Yes, *why*?' demanded Natalka, her head wedged between the cobwebbed brick wall and Oksana's erupting posterior.

'Do not argue,' repeated Taras, checking the coal-shed door was closed, but leaving it unbolted. He turned to march up the stone steps to the kitchen, still holding his bottle of vodka and bunch of pilfered daffodils. As he marched, he struggled to understand why the bald-headed man had called him Voloshin? He must have been drunk, which would certainly explain his dishevelled appearance.

Sofia's little voice was screaming at her... Although she didn't know what was going on, the petrified look on her Tato's face informed her that whatever it was, it wasn't good... And she was sure she heard a deep voice in the kitchen call her Tato something that sounded like "Voloshin". If it was meant to be a joke, it wasn't very funny. She was equally sure the voice belonged to the man she'd heard in the attic... the one everyone denied existed... the one she was sure was called Stanislaw...

Natalka said, 'did someone call your Tato, "Voloshin"?' Even though politics didn't particularly interest her, it was impossible to escape the news of the mini-Revolution occurring in Kyiv, led by Voloshin, the Peaceful Partisan... a mysterious man, who despite being interviewed on the radio and on television, no-one had actually seen for three decades...

'That's what I heard,' said Oksana, fidgeting, unable to get comfortable.

Holding her breath, Natalka said, 'I'm surprised you can hear anything over the sound of your trumping... Why can't you control your bowels?'

'Shhh!' said Sofia, 'I think we all heard correctly... I think Stanislaw did call my Tato Voloshin...'

'Stanislaw?' said Natalka, 'who the bleeding hell is Stanislaw...?'

'I know,' said a bloated Oksana, 'my old Tato used to talk about him a lot... he's some sort of Soviet Colonel... a real nutter...'

'A Soviet Colonel?' said Sofia. 'Now that *is* interesting...'

The pieces of the jigsaw that were Stanislaw were slowly arranging themselves in Sofia's mind... the shouting in the attic; the thudding in the loft; her Mama's obvious denials; the Bishop that visited Klem, but never left; and then there were the articles she'd found hidden in Klem's desk... they were very similar to the articles that had been in every newspaper last week... And she remembered it had been a Captain Stanislaw who'd treated her Mama so brutally in Chaplinka, a time her Mama only ever spoke of once... And the Vlad her parents were arguing about must have been a Soviet Secret Policeman... why didn't she realise it sooner? The only thing she still couldn't place was the purpose of this Katya fishing boat...?

And Klem's articles were full of accusations... this Stanislaw was a butcher, a criminal, an implementer of Genocide... he and men like him caused The Great Famine... And instead of being in prison, this Stanislaw was currently sat in her Mama's kitchen... Her imagination was out of control. *Don't be a durak, Sofia... why would that Stanislaw come to Bradford? It's a common Soviet name... there must be millions of them...* Although it all sounded too far-fetched to be true, she decided there was only one way to find out...

'Oh no you don't,' said Natalka. 'Your Tato told us to stay here, and here we shall stay!' She gripped Sofia's arm, 'I don't know what's going on in your head, but there's no way I'm going to let you upset your Tato. We are all staying put!'

And just to make sure, Natalka shoved the majority of Oksana in front of the coal-shed's door, entirely blocking it, much to Sofia's increasing annoyance...

The Dancing Barber

Chapter 100

'Did you hear that?' said the sensible headscarved old woman, turning down the wireless' volume knob so forcefully that it almost came off in her hand. 'It just *can't* be true.

The aggressive one skewered her embroidered likeness of the hated Stalin with her thickest needle. 'He's only been back a few days; how could the Vlads have got him *already*?'

A third headscarf said, 'it'll be one of those cyanide-tipped umbrellas again…'

'But it didn't work last time, did it?' said the aggressive one, plunging another needle into the hated Stalin. She added, 'I reckon it'll be much more *gruesome*… especially as he's stirred it up properly for the Soviets this time.'

The sensible one had a feeling that it was only propaganda… the Soviets could claim to have assassinated the Queen of England and the President of the United States, and their citizens would believe it… Unfortunately, so too would most Ukrainians…

One of the other headscarves plucked up the courage to say, 'before you married the hospital porter, you said that you and Voloshin were rather good "friends".' She narrowed her eyes, 'how good?'

Every headscarf leaned in closer, eager to hear the sensible one's answer…

The sensible one swallowed, 'well… not as good as you all think…'

The headscarves groaned with disappointment. They still had a taste for a juicy piece of gossip, even if it was about a member of their own Gaggle.

The sensible one pulled the knot of her headscarf. She said, 'but we were good enough friends for my intuition to tell me that nothing bad has happened to him…' She smiled, 'and that same intuition tells me that my husband will enter the bar any second now…' She listened for the thunder of hobnail boots…

The flat-caps darted up from the cellar, two steps at a time. They'd been helping themselves to several bottles of beer and so were somewhat unsteady on their feet. After stumbling over the inebriated barman's carcass, they summersaulted into the bar, determined to share the awful news with anyone there. Even if it was only their ferocious wives...

'It sounds like Voloshin might be dead again,' announced the first flat cap, not in the least bit caring that his wife now knew he'd been skiving from his domestic duties.

'We've just watched the BBC News on the telly in the cellar...' said the second flat cap. 'It was a cyanide umbrella right up the...' he gestured with his finger, 'right up there.'

And despite the glare of his own wife, the first flat-cap added, 'did any of us really think he'd ever get to speak to Khrushchev?'

The aggressive old woman looked for something to break, but had to make do with inserting another needle into a very specific part of the hated Stalin's anatomy. She seemed disappointed that Voloshin's latest assassination wasn't more gruesome. She said, 'but without Voloshin to help us, everyone will soon forget The Great Famine... And as for independence, it's just been flushed down the lavvy...'

The sensible one said, 'we don't actually know he's dead, do we? And since his latest reincarnation, has anyone actually seen him in the flesh?' She glanced around the table of shaking heads. 'When a body's found, then we'll know for sure. You can't believe anything the Soviets tell you... Remember, as Voloshin says, truth is *nothing* without proof!'

She turned up the wireless' volume, but all she heard was a static hiss... so she tried to re-tune the wireless into another one of Radio Kateryna's frequencies. 'That's odd,' she said, turning the knob so the red marker was positioned at 1933 kHz, 'the station's completely dead?'

'It will be,' said her hospital porter husband, 'the BBC also reported a fishing boat had sunk in the Black Sea... A boat called Katya...'

The Dancing Barber
Chapter 101

'Voloshin! We meet at last,' said the bald-headed man in purple, his smile bisecting his face. As Taras was still dressed as Prince Charming, wearing his billowing blue shirt and yellow tights, he added, 'you needn't have dressed for the occasion... Please, take a seat!'

After counting to ten, Taras said, 'I do not need permission to sit down in my own house! And I would appreciate it if you stopped calling me Voloshin! Understand?'

The bald-headed man laughed. He said, 'you are funny. And you look funny too without that luxuriant Cossack's moustache clinging to your upper lip... It was so much more impressive than your successor's horseshoe...'

'I don't know who you are,' said Taras, 'but you're starting to get on my nerves!' He shielded his nose from the onslaught of over-boiled cabbage emanating from the bald-headed man's mouth. 'So I suggest you leave before you make me really cross!'

The bald-headed man laughed even more, 'charming as ever...'

Taras allowed the vodka bottle to slip in his hand, he gripped it by the neck, squeezing it tightly. After that bizarre comment about moustaches, he knew this was no parlour game... And he noticed Halyna and Klem didn't have any choice but to sit closely together, being bound so tightly that the former's trembling body made the latter's horseshoe of a moustache wobble. And the full length of a washing line had also been wrapped around Zena and Lenka, nipping their bodies at regular intervals, the resultant escaping flab giving the impression they were close relations of the Michelin Man.

This time, Taras counted to twenty. Judging by the shape of the man's head, it could have been the Bishop... he was wearing a rather ragged purple cassock and that distinctive amethyst ring on his finger... and having such a badly bloodshot eye would certainly explain those sunglasses he wore at The Alhambra. But this was very strange behaviour for a Bishop... maybe he was having some kind of a breakdown? As Klem said, the Seminary in

Kyiv churned out some real weirdos... Taras sighed when it was obvious the man had no intention of moving... he watched him settle comfortably into his chair, still holding the dented aluminium pan. Gripping the vodka bottle's neck even tighter, Taras said, 'I won't tell you again... Get out!'

The bald-headed man couldn't laugh any more. He wheezed, 'what... is *this* how you treat your old friends? Don't you recognise me?' He stuck out his chin and smiled, 'how about now?'

'I recognise a durak when I see one,' Taras said, tightening his grip on the vodka bottle even more. The sooner he got rid of this crackpot, the better... he genuinely didn't have a clue about who he was. He asked, 'why are you holding that pan of stinking gruel over that glittering *Pysanka*?'

The bald-headed man wiggled the heavy pan of gruel, the contents squelching as they slopped about. He said, 'gruel? But this happens to be a rather nice stew... underneath all the mould.' He transferred the pan to his left hand when his right one wouldn't stop shaking under the strain. He picked out a large chunk of Pedigree Chum, and placed it onto his corpulent tongue. 'Delicious,' he said, before helping himself to a further two chunks, the latter luminous with bacteria.

Even after counting to thirty, Taras was unable to calm down. He said, 'I don't give a toss who you are! And I haven't the patience to play whatever game you're playing, so get the hell out of my house or else I'll throw you out!'

The bald-headed man said, 'there's no need to be *so* aggressive... remember, you are the *Peaceful* Partisan...' He sighed, 'as you persist in pretending not to know who I am, I will do the courteous thing and introduce myself formally...' He coughed, dislodging the chunk of Pedigree Chum stuck in his throat, 'my name is Colonel Stanislaw, the future *Tsar* of the Soviet Union!'

In the corner of his eye, Taras watched Klem's head shake despondently, while Zena and Lenka retained the look of chronic constipation, and Halyna continued to tremble as if she were operating a pneumatic drill. He muttered, 'Colonel Stanislaw...' He remembered all the rubbish Zena had spouted about "bungalows", and that stench of over-boiled cabbage he'd smelled

The Dancing Barber

in the loft...

Stanislaw continued, 'and I cannot tell you how pleasurable it is to be face to face with the famous Voloshin, the celebrated Peaceful Partisan and saviour of "Ukraine" for the first time in what... thirty years? Of course, we've never actually met, but your face was on so much Partisan propaganda that I knew you better than I did my own family.'

Klem's head continued to shake. He said, 'I wish you'd shut up... you've been talking nothing but himno for the past hour. You're a nutcase, crackpot, insane fool, and I'm sick of hearing your stupid voice!'

Taras stared at Klem... it wasn't like him to lose his temper... He thought: *Nutcase, crackpot, insane fool... I'll have to remember that one!*

Halyna closed her eyes, knowing precisely what was going to happen.

'Tut, tut,' said Stanislaw, dropping the heavy pan. 'Oops...'

Everyone's eyes closed; but Klem's remained open.

'Ha!' Stanislaw said, catching the pan when its charred base only just touched the uppermost sapphire of the twinkly egg. He lowered his voice, 'you dare speak out of turn again and it'll be the last you see of your precious Fabergé Egg!'

Klem said nothing, but thought everything. And after nearly witnessing scrambled Fabergé for the second time, his perspiring body trembled even more than Halyna's.

'A little greyer perhaps,' said Stanislaw, looking back at Taras, 'but it's undoubtedly you.' He strummed the fingers of his free hand on the plastic tablecloth, 'so why don't you admit it?'

Taras turned to Klem, 'what's up with him? Surely he knows I'm not Voloshin?'

'Oh yes I do,' said Stanislaw, 'and I can prove it!' He extracted a well-worn foolscap folder from within his cassock, fanning out the pages it contained. 'See,' he said, 'look at all these photographs of Voloshin...' He stared at Taras, 'be truthful, and admit who you are.' He then examined Klem's pained expression... he truly enjoyed smashing up the poet's desk... and all the illicit Voloshin and Bandera propaganda he'd found confirmed he was right all along... Well, almost right... he always knew that Klem was the voice behind Voloshin, but never did he imagine *The Dancing*

Barber to be the man himself...

He turned back to Taras, 'now the question is, what should I do with you?' He grunted, 'I may not have a cyanide-tipped umbrella this time, but no matter. It is better you are captured alive... an imprisoned Voloshin makes a much more powerful statement to the stupid Ukrainians than a dead Voloshin ever did...' He glanced at the plastic pendulum clock, 'by now, Khrushchev will have announced your assassination... but it doesn't matter, because you turning up alive will make him look even more incompetent, and so pave the way for the new Tsar... Me!'

Zena snorted, 'if Taras, he is Voloshin, then Ivan, he is the Santa Claus!'

Lenka also snorted, 'please, do not tell any more of the jokes... you will only make me the laugh... and when I the laugh...' Her emission was so smelly that even she had to hold her breath. Sat a little higher, she said, 'I think it was more than just the gas...'

Ignoring the stench, Stanislaw said, 'I have seen it all before, and I have heard it all before. Those who know the Enemy of the State always deny his true identity... But please, go on... your performance amuses me.'

Halyna examined her husband's unyielding expression. Although she knew relatively little about his background, she couldn't believe he was Voloshin; even thirty years ago, the thought of him being a *peaceful* partisan was preposterous. He had never shown the slightest interest in politics and would switch off the television the instant Harold Macmillan appeared.

'For the last time,' said Taras, 'I am <u>not</u> Voloshin!' He shrugged, 'how can I be? I've lived in Bradford since 1945! And before that, St Petersburg. I'm not a Partisan, I'm a Ballet Master!'

'You can't fool me,' Stanislaw winked with his good eye, 'I am cleverer than I look...'

Klem raised an eyebrow, 'that's a matter of opinion...'

'What did I tell you...' snapped Stanislaw. 'Do you want me to smash your egg?'

Klem lowered the eyebrow, 'even you're not thick enough to smash such a valuable object... You've been telling us endlessly how it will so wonderfully compliment the collection of the new Tsar...' He smiled, 'and that reminds me... I've been meaning to ask you... what are you planning to call yourself: "Tsar Stanislaw

The Dancing Barber

the Dense"?'

Halyna shut her eyes again. Why couldn't Klem stop antagonising the crackpot? What a waste of ten thousand pounds...

'Stanislaw the *Dense*...' said the Colonel, thoughtfully. 'That has a nice ring to it... thank you for the suggestion.'

Klem raised both eyebrows; he didn't detect any sarcasm in Stanislaw's voice and mused that if this fool did somehow overthrow Khrushchev and install himself as the new "Tsar", the Soviet Union would crumble within a week. Suddenly, cooperating with this crackpot became a hypothesis worthy of consideration...

Examining his reflection in the glass of a framed photograph, Klem desperately wanted to straighten the green ribbon on the collar of his embroidered shirt... it was in a ragged mess, and he couldn't stand it any longer... But at least the photograph behind the glass was pretty... and much nicer to look at than Charlie Chaplinka ever was... He was glad Halyna had an enlargement made of Zena's precious photograph... that old homestead in Chaplinka was one of his most favourite places in the whole world. Little did anyone realise that less than a year after it was taken, the heinous Captain Stanislaw would destroy everything.

At least Taras was playing it cool: the last thing this situation needed was for Taras to lose his temper... Klem turned to the Colonel and said, 'so, when you become the new Tsar, what will you do with all that authority and power?'

Stanislaw scratched the fungal growth of his nose with the aluminium handle of the pan, flecks of dried blood sprinkling to the table. He said, thoughtfully, 'I will rename St Petersburg... *Stanislawgrad* has a much better ring to it, don't you think? And it will make a beautiful new Capital for the dynasty of "Stanislaw the Dense".' He narrowed his eye, 'dense... it means solid, does it not?'

'It does,' said Klem. He muttered, 'amongst other things...'

'Good,' said Stanislaw, 'because I will be a dense Tsar.' He rested his elbow on the table, in so doing, moving the pan fractionally away from the egg.

'Indeed you will,' said Klem, blowing on his drying moustache. 'But you won't be able to kick out Khrushchev on your own?'

Stanislaw smiled, 'I have a plan... And my organisation is

poised to carry out that plan the moment I give the word!'

Klem was pleased... the crackpot was relaxing... So long as everyone else stayed quiet, he felt confident that he could persuade him to untie them, and maybe even divulge the details of his plan, and the nature and scale of his organisation...

Taras had been looking at the egg. Before Stanislaw reopened his mouth, he said, 'and for all this time, I thought it was only an ornament? I had no idea it was a genuine Fabergé...'

Stanislaw said, 'that is why I am the future Tsar and you are a Partisan, masquerading as *The Dancing Barber*...'

Klem's shoulders slumped. Why couldn't Taras stay quite? It had been a long time since he was in such a situation... crackpots like Stanislaw had to be handled in a very specific way.

Klem closed his eyes; Taras hadn't finished...

Taras said, 'but we can discuss the egg later... because I'm sure we're all interested in hearing your plan...' He hitched up his trousers and sat down. Gesturing around the table, he said, 'this all looks rather elaborate...'

'Elaborate, yes,' said a somewhat confused Stanislaw, 'very *elaborate*...' He smiled. 'If you must know, I plan to present you to Comrade General Borodov. He will be so pleased that he'll help me throw Khrushchev out of the Kremlin like the alley-cat he is... We can then show the Soviet people how much of a liar *you* truly are...' He chuckled, 'I plan to have you hung, drawn and quartered... literally!'

'Thank you,' said Taras. 'You're too kind...'

Stanislaw smiled, 'it will be my pleasure... So all I have to do is get you to Moscow, and then – '

Taras interrupted, 'how?'

Klem's eyes remained tightly shut.

'What do you mean, *how*?' said an annoyed Stanislaw.

Taras look a deep breath, '*how* are you planning to get me to Moscow?'

'You'll see,' said Stanislaw, transferring the pan back to his right hand. 'My plan is fool-proof.'

Taras flicked a speck of dust from his trousers. He said, 'you realise old Borodov will be disappointed, don't you?'

Klem opened his eyes; maybe Taras hadn't lost his abilities...

Stanislaw shook his head, 'Comrade General will <u>never</u> be disappointed with me...'

'Well, if you're sure,' said Taras, admiring the man's deluded confidence. 'But he will certainly be angry when he realises you've brought him *The Dancing Barber* instead of Voloshin...' He laughed, 'I doubt he'll help install you as Tsar if you are incapable of completing even the simplest of assignments...'

'But that won't happen,' insisted Stanislaw, 'because I will bring him Voloshin. And when I am Tsar, he will do exactly as I say or I will send him to the Gulag!'

Taras looked puzzled. He said, 'but you're a Colonel, and Borodov is a General... so surely he should become Tsar?'

'No,' said the Colonel. 'Borodov is just a pawn... he is not part of my organisation. Once he has helped me dispose of Khrushchev, my organisation will dispose of him!'

'How big is your organisation?' asked Taras.

'Big enough,' replied the Colonel. 'Enough with the chit-chat... come on Voloshin, it's time we were going...'

'Before you go,' said a constipated Zena, 'we should celebrate the success, yes?' She waited for Stanislaw to blink, before she winked discretely at Klem. She said, 'we have *always* known Taras is Voloshin...' Her gaze drifted between Halyna and Lenka, 'is this the truth?'

The women nodded their agreement; Halyna adding, 'err, yes... there's no point in lying any more... I am married to Voloshin.' She looked at a stunned Taras and discretely shrugged, 'sorry Voloshin, the truth's got to come out sometime... and *now* is the time.'

Taras swallowed; what was his wife playing at?

Stanislaw smiled, then laughed raucously, causing the sludgy "stew" to slop all over the pan. He sang, 'I *knew* I was right... I am *always* right!' He shook his free fist in the air, 'and they said I was mad...'

Zena smiled at the Colonel, 'of course you are,' she said, 'err, right, I mean... And you are surely the densest of all. So if you untie me, I will go and get the samahon – there is the plenty of it upstairs – and then the success, it can be the celebrated, yes?'

Taras cringed: even Stanislaw wasn't stupid enough to fall for such an obvious trick.

Stanislaw shuffled in his seat, 'samahon is the drink of a

peasant... *Vodka* is the drink of a Tsar... Don't you have any vodka?'

Taras tried to hide the bottle he'd taken from the Club, but Stanislaw's eye was locked onto it. Taras frowned; begrudgingly, he held it up, 'would this do?'

'Unscrew the cap and give it to me,' instructed Stanislaw, 'and no funny business!' He stretched out his hand, beckoning Taras to approach. 'No sudden movements or I smash the egg!'

'As you wish,' Taras said, standing up. As he approached the table, he noticed Mister Pushkin hunkered by the Colonel's feet, looking extremely fed up. If only the cat could lay claim to the crackpot's ankles; or better still, jump onto the table and lay claim to his face...

Impatiently, Stanislaw grabbed the bottle. Holding the label close to his eye, he read, 'Russian Vodka... Voloshin you certainly have taste...'

Taras cringed as the man's fleshy lips wrapped themselves around the clear glass neck of the bottle, and cringed even more when as much vodka spilled down the man's purple cassock as had glugged into his mouth.

'This is good stuff,' declared Stanislaw, wiping his mouth on the back of his hand before taking another enormous swig. Again, he spilled vodka down his cassock, which dripped from the hem and bounced off Mister Pushkin's head.

The cat shook itself dry and plodded directly out to the yard... that was the final straw.

Taras considered how best to incapacitate Stanislaw... He thought about offering him a Benton and Wedges cigarette, hopeful that the cyanide and arsenic might do him in... But the fumes would probably do everybody in... Besides, someone like Stanislaw would be immune. Although offering to light his cigarette would provide an opportunity to drop a lighted Swan Vesta onto the man's vodka-soaked cassock... But did he want to risk the whole house going up in flames? Alternatively, he could offer him a "Mint Imperial"... hopeful that he might choke... but Stanislaw's breath was so appalling that the flavour of mothballs would likely go undetected... he'd probably crunch through an entire bagful without noticing...

Then he observed how twitchy Stanislaw's fungal growth of a

The Dancing Barber

nose was becoming... something in the kitchen was seriously irritating him... One of Halyna's plants on the windowsill was emitting pollen... Discretely, he looked around, realising it was the Pussy Willows Halyna had brought from church on Palm Sunday... they'd rooted, and had also produced the finest yellow pollen that – being placed by an open window – was slowly circulating around the kitchen... All Taras had to do was wait for Stanislaw to sneeze, then he could snatch away the egg and take control of the situation... but that might take too long. He looked at the wilting daffodils in his hand, and a wry smile flickered across his face...

Without asking permission, Taras strode over to the sink, filled a blue vase with water and proceeded to arrange his pilfered daffodils, humming the Ukrainian National Anthem.

Discretely, he slipped Halyna's sickle-like knife up his sleeve, fixing the wooden handle under the worn leather strap of his wristwatch. He knew the very sight of its long, curved blade would strike fear into Stanislaw, inducing him to remember what Zena did with a similar implement three decades ago...

Taras carried the vase to the table and placed it directly in front of Halyna. 'Doesn't that look nice?'

'Very,' said Halyna, shakily.

'I'm pleased,' said Taras, 'I *picked* them especially for you...'

Halyna noted he said "picked" instead of "bought"; in any case, they looked pretty. 'They smell nice too...' she said, sniffing the delicate aroma.

Stanislaw slammed the empty bottle of vodka onto the table, and commanded, 'Voloshin! Hand me the telephone!' He clicked his fingers, 'quickly!'

Halyna held her breath, expecting Taras to lose his temper... but he didn't. What was the matter with him? How was he managing to stay so calm?

With gritted teeth, Taras strode across the kitchen and picked up the telephone, hopeful the wire wouldn't reach, so as to coax the crackpot from his chair. Unfortunately it was longer than a skipping rope.

He clattered the telephone onto the table in front of Stanislaw and watched the stout finger repeatedly dial an endlessly long number that seemed to be perpetually engaged.

'Oh Tsar Stanislaw?' said Zena, 'as the vodka, it has gone, would you like the samahon now? I know you think it is the drink of the peasants... but our samahon, it is...' she smacked her lips together, '...wonderful!'

'It is the delicious,' added Lenka, 'the best we have ever made and it has the plenty of the *Slyna*...'

Frustrated by the endless monotony of the engaged tone, Stanislaw slammed down the receiver and stared at the twins. '*Slyna*... that is like sugar, isn't it? So it will be sweet...' He clicked his fingers, 'let me have it.'

Despite being tightly bound with washing line, the twins prepared to stand up. The wooden chairs on which they sat creaking with relief, as indeed did they when their trapped wind was released.

'Where do you think you are going?' snapped Stanislaw, 'sit down on your fat backsides!' He looked at the plastic pendulum clock on the wall and then directly at Taras, 'I want Voloshin to go and get it! Bring as much as you can carry, but if you're not back here in *one* minute, the egg will be no more! And remember, it's worth at least ten thousand of your English pounds.' When Taras didn't move he clicked his fingers harshly and shouted: '<u>Go</u>!'

Taras took the deepest breath he could, 'very well, I will *get* your samahon.' He looked at Zena, 'could someone please tell me where it is?'

Zena said, 'the bottles of samahon, they are in my cupboard in the attic.'

Taras nodded his thanks to his future sister-in-law, deciding not to correct her: it was *his* cupboard, not hers. He turned to Stanislaw and said, 'but before I go, I *must* insist you apologise to Zena and Lenka...'

'What for?' said the red-eyed Colonel.

'They do not have fat backsides,' said Taras, pushing the daffodils closer to the Colonel's twitchy nose.

'Of course they do,' insisted the Colonel, expelling so much air from his lungs that the room was enveloped by fumes of over-boiled cabbage and alcohol.

Klem grinned at the Colonel. He realised what Taras was doing, and thought it was deviously cunning... Although he knew he shouldn't, he said, 'their backsides aren't as fat as yours...'

The Dancing Barber

'And how do you know?' said the Colonel. 'No-one has ever seen my other end!'

'I have,' said Klem, 'just before I shot it from under the stage...'

'That was <u>you</u>?' Stanislaw shouted, the pain in his buttocks suddenly becoming more noticeable.

'It wasn't my fault,' Klem said rather pompously. 'It was an unfortunate accident... Like you being born...'

Stanislaw's head swelled with anger; he flared his nostrils, clenched his free fist and hammered the table so hard that the vase of daffodils almost toppled over. He shouted, 'I will kill you for what you've done to me!'

Taras moved around the table and stood next to the Tsar. He said, 'you should learn to stay calm... getting annoyed is terribly bad for the heart. Klem said it wasn't his fault... it really was an unfortunate accident.' He gestured to the vase of daffodils, 'calm down and sniff the flowers... their fragrance is wonderful.'

Klem said, 'I am *truly* sorry for shooting you and for everything else.' He glanced at Zena and Lenka, 'and the twins are sorry for how they treated you...'

'We are?' the twins said in unison, resuming their constipated looks.

Upon seeing Klem's taut expression, Zena said, 'oh yes, we are the *very* sorry.' She gave her sister a nudge.

Begrudgingly, Lenka added, 'we are *so* apologetic...'

Don't over-do it, thought Klem, watching Taras edge ever closer to the Tsar.

'Those flowers *do* look nice,' said Taras, 'and they *smell* even nicer...' He slid the vase under the Tsar's increasingly twitchy nose, 'you can have them if you'd like; they'll be a nice present for your General Borodov...'

Stanislaw unclenched his fist and grumbled something mildly obscene. Eventually, he said, 'you're right. I shouldn't get so worked-up... but I just can't help it...' He admired the daffodils, 'flowers do calm me... and it's been a long time since I've taken the time to sniff them...'

Much to Taras' and Klem's delight, Stanislaw positioned his fungal growth of a nose directly above the bright yellow daffodils and inhaled a deep lungful of the honeyed fragrance.

Klem's eyes met with Taras'. They counted down, 'three, two, one...'

Right on cue, Stanislaw embarked on a sneezing frenzy that Taras hoped would last at least five minutes. The Colonel must have been a real crackpot to have forgotten he suffered so badly from hay fever... but The Asylum was in a part of Siberia where summer lasted barely half a day... and even then, the air was thick with a fog of biting midges.

The man's streaming nose took on the appearance of an enormous aubergine... he repeatedly sneezed and blew it on his purple cassock. He had no choice but to drop the pan of stinking stew. Thankfully, Taras had snatched away the precious Fabergé Egg, placing it safely in his pocket.

Taras then fulfilled a desire he'd had ever since first meeting this Stanislaw. Holding his breath, he heaved up the heavy pan in both hands and upturned it on the Colonel's head, screwing it down for good measure.

With the incessant sound of sneezing echoing from within the pan, Taras said, 'no-one clicks his fingers at me...'

The Dancing Barber

Chapter 102

---✂---

'Who let the cat in?' complained Natalka, 'there's barely enough room for us in this bleeding coal-shed...' She watched the cat turn its back on her, and hoist its tail into the air, 'don't you dare!'

Sofia said, 'shut up Natalka, I'm trying to listen.'

Oksana sniffed, 'don't you think he smells nice today?'

'No, I bleeding don't,' said Natalka, 'he smells like a distillery.'

'Shut up you two,' said Sofia. Using her zippy boot, she shifted Mister Pushkin out of the way, 'not now Pushkin... and keep away from the chinchillas.'

The cat growled, but continued encircling Sofia's ankles, head-butting her and purring like a tractor.

'Shhh,' said Sofia. She nudged Natalka, whose head was still wedged next to Oksana's windy quarter. 'Can you hear that?'

'Sorry,' said Oksana, holding her stomach. 'Maybe I shouldn't have eaten so much for lunch.'

'<u>No</u>, not you,' said Sofia. 'Listen... can you hear that noise coming from the kitchen?'

Oksana and Natalka listened intently. After a while, they said, 'what noise? We don't hear anything...'

'Precisely,' said Sofia.

Natalka stretched out her arms, grateful for being able to stand up for the first time in half an hour. She said, 'Oksana, you go first!'

'I will not,' replied an out-of-breath Oksana, who'd only just managed to reverse her way out of the coal-shed, her ample body coated with brick dust and cobwebs. 'Any way, I think Sofia should go first: it is <u>her</u> house.'

'Why should Sofia go first?' asked Natalka, shaking the pins and needles from her fingers. 'You are the "Golden Girl"... Mr Taras wouldn't shout at you if you go in uninvited...'

'He will,' insisted Oksana, 'he always shouts at me.'

'Oh for Heaven's sake,' said Sofia, brushing the dust off her Tato's blue blazer, 'that's enough arguing.' She gently placed the chinchillas into the folds of Oksana's woolly jumper, 'you look after these two... And try not to sit on them... And keep them away from the cat!' She then turned and marched up the stone steps to the kitchen.

'But chinchillas hate me,' Oksana said, watching Sofia scamper away.

Natalka smirked, 'they're good judges of character.'

Oksana looked at the chinchillas that stared up at her from the comfortable folds of her woolly jumper. She gently stroked one of them on the head, inducing it to plunge its chisel-sharp incisors into the soft flesh of her index finger... The other chinchilla immediately did the same, both rodents gnawing down to the bone. If it wasn't for Natalka's hand over her mouth, Oksana's cries would have been heard in Manchester.

'Damn it, Oksana,' whispered Sofia, 'keep your mouth shut, or you'll go back in the coal-shed!'

Oksana whimpered, but said nothing. She watched the two rodents chewing her fingers, and for the first time realised what it must have been like for Mr Taras, after what she'd done with Brenda... How could she have been so cruel?

Sofia nudged the cat with her zippy boot, 'I said *not now* Mister Pushkin.' She put her ear to the kitchen door and listened, but all she could hear was deathly silence.

She peeked through the keyhole, but couldn't see anyone. 'Where have they all gone?' She attempted to look in through the window, but couldn't quite reach over the tall railings. She plucked up the courage to place her hand on the cold door handle. As she slowly turned it, she could hear her Tato screaming at her to get out... but it was only her imagination. The door creaked open and she gingerly crept inside... She relaxed... there was no-one there, apart from her and Mister Pushkin. The cat persistently encircled her ankles in a figure of eight, meowing, purring and head-butting her zippy boots, as if deliberately trying to trip her up. 'Leave me alone,' she said, nudging it away.

And it seemed every bluebottle in the neighbourhood was dive-bombing the splattered gungy remains of what looked like "the stew of the meat". The carpet was now completely ruined, but her Mama wouldn't be bothered... a new one was being delivered tomorrow.

The Dancing Barber

With the cat keeping step, Sofia followed a cool draught from the direction of the shop, the connecting door having been left slightly ajar. And in the distance, she was sure she could hear voices... But then her concentration was broken...

Oksana tried to tiptoe silently across the kitchen floor, yet managed to step on every creaky floorboard. Sofia put a finger angrily to her lips, glaring at Natalka to keep the heifer quiet.

Natalka shrugged... *I'm trying my best*...

Sofia peered through the gap in the door, the stench of rotten "stew" now intermingling with the rancid stench of over-boiled cabbage and alcohol. She looked to her feet and noticed the cat pawing at a torn fragment of purple cloth. She picked it up and sniffed it... it smelled just as boozy as the cat... And this shade of purple was very distinctive... it could only have originated from one source...

Distracted by a loud clatter, she turned to watch Oksana fumbling around with an aluminium pan, banging on the lid as deafeningly as possible. 'Shhh,' she said, 'why can't you be quiet? Is it too much to ask...?'

With relief, Oksana mouthed, 'sorry...' standing as still as she could. 'I'll be as silent as a church mouse... promise.' After Sofia turned around, Oksana weighed down the lid of the pan with a loaf of stale bread, her bleeding fingers staining the mouldy crust. She could hear the four pairs of paws scrambling up the walls of the pan containing the remnants of "stew", the chinchillas only managing to climb so far before inevitably sliding back down, plopping into the festering swamp of cooked hamster and dog food.

With her hands now free, Oksana tore noisily into a packet of cheese and onion crisps, filling her mouth until her cheeks bulged.

Sofia gestured for Natalka to take the noisy heifer back outside, a task that made shifting a disobedient elephant seem easy.

Scrunching an unopened packet of Golden Wonder with one hand, Natalka beckoned the greedy heifer out to the yard, whispering, 'there's *plenty* more out here...'

Oksana couldn't move fast enough.

With Oksana gone, Sofia turned her attention to what was occurring in the shop...

Through the gap in the door, Sofia saw what looked like a

bulbous roll of carpet laying on the red linoleum floor. She thought: *That was quick... unusual for new carpet to be delivered so quickly, and so late in the day...*

But then Sofia noticed Zena and Lenka were sat on each end, while her Mama kicked it repeatedly. Eventually her Tato calmed her down, but she couldn't resist giving it another powerful kick just before a pair of men wearing black leather coats and wide-brimmed black hats heaved it up and manoeuvred it outside. Through the distant shop window, Sofia glimpsed the carpet being shuffled into the back of a waiting estate car and driven away.

'What was all that about?' she muttered. 'And why does everyone look so angry?'

Mister Pushkin was equally curious, so he head-butted the door and weaved his way into the shop.

As the door creaked open, her Tato turned around and shooed the cat away, 'get away from me, Cooking Fat!'

Sofia froze, hoping he hadn't seen her. When he looked away, she sprinted to the back yard as fast as she could. Never before had she seen him look so angry...

'What was that?' asked an exhausted Halyna, roughly pinning her hair back into position, finally able to catch her breath.

'Only the Cooking Fat,' said Taras, calming his nerves with a cigarette, the smoke hissing from between his teeth; his nose singed after accidentally trying to light it with a Swan Vesta.

'Oh,' she said, not really caring. When she regained her composure, she asked, 'what do you think they'll do with him?'

'I don't know,' said Taras. 'But whatever it is, it can't be as bad as what Zena had planned for him...'

'Don't be so sure,' said Klem, straightening the ribbon on the collar of his crumpled shirt. 'You've heard of The Asylum, yes? Well, Stanislaw is going somewhere that makes that place seem like Sunday School...'

'As long as justice is done,' said Halyna, wiping her eyes with an old tissue.

'Rest assured,' said Klem, 'it will be. Remember, there's a particularly hot corner of Hell reserved for Stanislaw and all

The Dancing Barber

people like him.'

Taras looked as though he was chewing a bee. He said, 'it seems Sofia heard correctly after all... I just knew you were fobbing me off about this Stanislaw...' He tried to put his hands in his pockets, but in his attempt to mend the holes, he'd inadvertently sown them up completely. 'I knew all that talk about bungalows was a load of – !'

'Taras,' pleaded Halyna, 'how many more times?'

Taras held up his hand apologetically. He said, 'if only you'd told me about Stanislaw straight away, then none of this nastiness would have happened, understand?'

Halyna snorted, 'and what would *you* have done, hmmm?'

Taras folded his arms, 'that is not the point...'

'That is *precisely* the point,' said Halyna. 'With your temper, you'd have made things *much* worse!'

'Not necessarily,' said Taras, secretly knowing his wife was right. 'In any case, it was very dangerous to restrain him yourselves.' He looked at Zena, 'and for you to have imprisoned him in my loft for a whole week... I just don't know how you managed to get him up there, let alone keep him so quiet...?'

Zena shrugged, 'it was the nothing... he may be the crackpot, but he is the weakling compared to the wild boar.'

'Yes,' said Lenka, 'once you grab hold of the right parts, controlling the beast, it is easy!'

Taras smirked, 'but how did this particular beast manage to escape the loft and tie everyone up with washing line? I remember nailing the hatch shut... I used *a lot* of nails!'

Klem shook his head, 'you *don't* want to know...' He had yet to tell him about the enormous hole in the roof; and he doubted that Zena and Lenka would admit to being outsmarted by a man wielding nothing more than a rusty knitting needle. Stanislaw had taken Zena completely by surprise... there was nothing anyone could do but cooperate... in Stanislaw's hands, a knitting needle was just as lethal as a Kalashnikov...

'In the end,' said Lenka, 'everything, it worked out the well, yes?'

'Of course,' said Zena, massaging the bruised knuckles of each hand in turn. 'I like the good fight!'

'Yes,' said Lenka, 'he made the perfect punch bag...'

Zena wafted her unbuttoned cardigan, 'but it was the very hot work, yes? I am sweating like the herd of the pigs!'

Klem held his nose, and thought: *You smell like "the" herd of "the" pigs too.*

'Time for tea,' said Klem, retreating to the kitchen to switch on the kettle. 'After all the excitement, I think I'll make Earl Grey for everyone... it'll help us all relax...' When no-one acknowledged him, he shrugged and decided to use the PG Tips... they wouldn't know the difference...

'Taras?' said a puzzled Lenka, 'why did Stanislaw call you Voloshin? It makes not much of the sense?'

Taras shrugged, 'what do you expect from a man who's escaped The Asylum? I have a theory that he was the notorious "Siberian Strangler"... the nuttiest nutcase in the Soviet Union... *and that's saying something!* So he's bound to talk himno.' Taras screwed his cigarette into the ashtray, 'and from now on, I do not want to hear any more about it, understand? The subject is never again to be mentioned, understand?'

Returning from the kitchen, Klem twisted his moustache back into position, and said, 'someone like *Taras* could never be Voloshin... It's ridiculous...' He glanced at Taras, 'isn't it?'

Taras lit another cigarette and looked away.

'Now that the Kremlin has announced Voloshin's *second* assassination,' said Klem, 'I doubt anyone will ever know what the man looks like.'

'So you think it's true?' asked Halyna. 'You think he's *really* dead?'

Klem smiled, 'when he's reincarnated again... you can ask him...'

'But what does that mean?' asked Halyna.

'It is Klem who talks the himno,' said Zena. 'I do not think this Voloshin was reincarnated at all...' She looked at Klem, 'I think Voloshin was a figment of the imagination!'

'Whatever you say,' said Klem. He picked up his Fabergé Egg. 'At least we have some good news... it looks as though old Stanislaw won't get to add *this* to his collection after all...' He laughed, 'the new "Tsar" of the Soviet Union... you couldn't make it up...'

Taras admired the egg. He said, 'I still can't believe it... After

The Dancing Barber

all this time, I had no idea that thing was *real*.'

Unscrewing the two halves of the egg, Klem said, 'a-ha, without question, this is the missing *Imperial Easter Egg 2½*! In its current state, it's worth around ten thousand pounds at the right auction, minus commission. But...' he placed his finger into the recess flanked by emeralds, 'when the missing element is added, it'll be worth ten times as much.'

'What goes in there?' asked Taras, 'a big diamond or something?'

Klem shook his head, 'actually, my research suggests that it's for an ornate timepiece manufactured by *Vacheron Constantin*...' He fished the gold watch from his pocket, and pressed the discrete button on the rim of the half-hunter case. 'Take a look,' he said, holding up the pure white enamel dial for Taras to observe.

'*Vacheron Constantin*,' Taras read, 'so that...'

'Precisely,' said Klem. 'Like all watches, the movement can be removed from the case for servicing...' He flipped the watch over in his palm and opened the back to reveal the intricate movement, dancing and spinning.

Taras was mesmerised, 'it's a work of art. Isn't it amazing that something so small has been made by human hands...?'

'A-ha, that's why such watches are so expensive,' said Klem. 'There are more components in this tiny movement than there are bones in the human body.' He carefully extracted the movement and held it next to the egg's recess. 'Unfortunately... this watch is too large for the space, and it doesn't have a screw thread... See...'

'What a shame,' said Taras. He scratched his grey hair, 'you could glue it on? I've got some Super-Glue in the shop...?' Upon seeing Klem's look of disbelief, he said, 'it was just a thought...'

Klem sighed, 'if only I knew what was missing... Just think of what Katya could do with one hundred thousand pounds!'

'But ten thousand's not to be sniffed at,' said Taras. 'When you go back to Chaplinka, you can live like a Lord.'

Klem watched Zena ferret around beneath her skirt. He said, 'if I'm a Lord, she'll *never* be a Lady...' He looked away, 'but the money is not for me... Remember, funding election campaigns is an expensive business...'

Sofia stumbled down the stone steps to the yard.

'What's happened?' enquired Natalka, 'was it something awful?'

Sofia was still out of breath. 'I don't know whether it was or whether it wasn't?' She scratched her curly hair, 'who would deliver a carpet at this time of day, only to take it away again? It doesn't make any sense?'

'Carpet?' said Oksana, screwing up an empty packet of crisps, 'are you sure?'

'I know what a carpet looks like,' Sofia said, watching Oksana rip open yet another packet... the heifer seemed to have a never-ending supply. 'I thought you'd given them up? What happened to your diet?'

'I decided dieting wasn't for me,' Oksana said, spraying fragments of crisp from her full mouth.

Sofia shook her head, 'how do you know? You never even tried...'

'Never mind her,' interrupted Natalka, 'you were saying something about a carpet?'

'Carpet?' said Sofia, 'oh yes, there was a great big one on the shop floor... and it had a bulge right in the middle of it...'

Oksana cleared her mouth, 'maybe they delivered the wrong colour?'

'Maybe?' said Sofia, 'and that could explain why Mama was kicking it... She must have *really* hated it!'

'A bulge?' said Natalka, 'you said something about a bulge... Carpets only bulge when they're wrapped around something...'

'Such as...' asked Oksana, refilling her mouth.

Natalka narrowed her eyes, 'a dead body...'

Sofia cringed, 'please Natalka, don't be so ghoulish...'

'But it might be,' said Natalka. 'Maybe it's this "Stanislaw" you've been going on about...? Or this mythical "Bishop" that visited Klem's attic, but never left...? Or it could be Santa Claus or the Easter Bunny!'

Oksana almost choked on her crisps. 'Natalka, you don't half talk some twaddle.'

'Get stuffed,' said Natalka, 'if I want your bleeding opinion, I'll ask for it!'

'Hang on,' said Sofia, pulling the torn fragment of purple cloth from her pocket. 'Take a look at this...' She placed it in Natalka's hand, 'and smell it...'

'So what...' said Natalka, instantly detecting the smell of alcohol. 'It probably belongs to one of your aunties; you know how much they like their samahon.'

'No,' said Sofia, 'I recognise Bishop's purple when I see it... This is going to sound *seriously* odd, but what if... what if... Stanislaw and the Bishop are the *same* person?' Seeing Natalka and Oksana shake their heads in disbelief, she said, 'remember, I told you about all that noise I heard up in the attic, noise that even Mama denied hearing? It sounded like someone being beaten up... And then all that talk about Stanislaw... And no one ever saw the Bishop leave!' She gripped Natalka's arm, 'you don't suppose they've done him in?'

'Of course not,' said Natalka, 'I think you need to lie down...'

'I'm serious,' said Sofia, 'Tato was sure he could hear movement up in Klem's loft... Klem blamed it on the cat, but he never believed him... I bet he's kept this Bishop Stanislaw prisoner up there! I bet he tried to escape, so he did him in!'

'Have you heard yourself?' said Natalka, 'Klem couldn't hurt a fly...'

Oksana swallowed, 'but my Mama could... There's no messing where she's concerned...'

Natalka cringed, *no messing, but plenty of mess...* She looked at Sofia, 'and your Tato is hardly a pacifist...'

'And my Mama,' said Sofia, 'she can be mean with a rolling pin... and even meaner with a Hoover! And if Stanislaw is the one Klem's written about, then no-one would blame her...'

'That's true,' said Natalka. 'Come to think of it, every member of your family has an aggressive streak.'

'Shhh,' said Oksana, 'I can hear the kettle whistling in the kitchen. Do you think it's safe to go back inside yet?' She put a hand to her rumbling stomach, 'I'm hungry...'

'She's hungry...' said Natalka, shaking her head...

'No-one move,' insisted Sofia, 'we wait until Tato invites us in... He's in an awful mood. The look on his face really frightened me... much more than usual.'

'But its dark,' moaned Oksana, 'and I don't like being outside when it's dark...'

'Shut up,' said Natalka. 'Here,' she tore open another packet of crisps and thrust it into Oksana's chubby hand, 'have some more.'

'None of you believe me,' said Sofia, 'but I just know something *terrible* has happened... and when the truth finally comes out, I'll be proved right!'

Natalka said, 'you've been watching too many Hitchcock films... and you're hungry and tired... it's the ideal combination for having strange thoughts.'

'I am a little hungry,' said Sofia. She glanced at the gluttonous Oksana, 'but I'll never be as hungry as her...'

After emptying half the packet, Oksana screamed, 'yuck, Salt and Vinegar...'

The Dancing Barber
Chapter 103

Klem sat by the kitchen fire and put up his feet. He sipped his PG Tips, and for the first time, realised just how tired he was. With his Fabergé Egg nestled in his lap, he instantaneously fell asleep.

Halyna yawned so broadly that her dentures could have fallen out. She looked at the empty pans on the hob, then at the cheap Chinese pendulum clock above the mantelpiece and then yawned again. She never did like that clock... it wasn't because it was unattractive, or tacky, or loud... but because of where it came from... or rather *who* it came from... Nevertheless, it kept pretty good time and the pendulum glistened as though it was made of solid gold... but was probably just brass.

She watched Taras unfasten his cuff button and pull up the sleeve of his billowing blue shirt. She was horrified to see her sickle-like kitchen knife fastened, by the leather strap of his wristwatch, to his muscular forearm. She said, 'oh my goodness!'

'Just in case,' Taras said, clattering the knife back in the drawer. 'But I must admit... I'm glad it wasn't needed...'

Halyna couldn't agree more. She sighed, 'the strain of the past few hours has probably shortened my life by about a week...' Hearing Taras' stomach rumble, she said, 'what had you planned to make for dinner?'

Taras groaned, 'I can't be bothered now... not after everything that's happened.' He thought carefully before suggesting, 'err... can't we have fish and chips? For the last time, I promise... I'll cook something proper tomorrow, but today I think it should be plain fish and chips.' He yawned, 'I'm just too tired.'

Halyna smiled, 'fish and chips sounds goodski to me... with mushy peas, salt and vinegar!'

Taras sighed with relief, then searched for his money, which – much to Halyna's dismay – was kept somewhere in the depths of his bulge.

A confused Lenka said, 'but I thought it was the *stew* that you wanted?'

The sound of a meat cleaver guillotining down onto the wooden chopping board silenced the entire kitchen.

'Nobody mentioned stew,' said Zena, 'even I cannot stand the thought of it anymore.'

'What the – !' shouted Taras, a sentiment echoed by Halyna, who rather than reprimanding him on his bad language, chose to add a few words from her own repertoire.

'But they were in the pan,' Lenka stuttered, 'I thought...'

'That is the trouble,' shouted Taras, 'you <u>never</u> think! You stupid, <u>stupid</u> woman!'

All the noise awakened Klem from his short, yet wonderfully restful catnap. Shielding his ears, he said, 'why are you shouting at each other?' But he didn't have to wait for a response, because Mister Pushkin was having a wonderful time batting two objects at the skirting boards that were definitely not marbles... 'Good grief!' said Klem. 'We mustn't let the girls see this!' He stared at the cat, '*please* Pushkin... stop it! It's *not* nice!'

As expected, the cat did as it pleased, ignoring its former owner.

Taras rushed out to the yard, where the girls were seated on the stone steps, waiting patiently. He said, 'Sofia, here's some money... All three of you go to the Chippy and get our dinner... And don't come back for half an hour...'

Sofia looked up at her frantic father and shrugged... She'd hoped he'd cook something nutritious tonight... She sighed, 'does everyone want the usual?'

'Yes,' said Taras, 'but your Mama also wants mushy peas, and salt and vinegar...' He closed the door behind him, so the girls didn't see Klem trying to separate Mister Pushkin from his two new toys.

Oksana chirped up, 'can I not have *two* fish? I'm *starving* and one won't be enough...'

'Certainly,' said Taras, '<u>NOT</u>! Have you forgotten that you are supposed to be on a diet?'

'But Mr Taras,' pleaded Oksana, straightening her well fingerprinted milk bottle glasses, 'I seem to remember that *Swan Lake* received such good reviews because of me... if I lose weight, I won't be able to dance in the same way, and so future reviews might not be as good...'

Sofia dragged Oksana away before her Tato erupted. 'Don't worry,' she said, 'you can have my fish... All I want is a few

The Dancing Barber

chips.'

'Why do we have to stay away for half an hour?' asked Natalka. 'The Chippy's only five minutes down the road!'

Sofia shrugged, 'who knows... who cares... They've probably got a lot of cleaning up to do after what they've done to Stanislaw... Come on, we'll go the scenic route.'

'You're still going on about this Stanislaw, aren't you...' said Natalka. 'Even if you're right... why are you bothered? He's only a stinking Soviet?'

Sofia couldn't believe Natalka's attitude. She said, 'Soviet or not, he is – or was – a human being.'

'That's me told,' said Natalka, deciding not to start an argument she could never win.

With the glowing neon sign of the Chippy fast approaching, Natalka turned to Sofia and asked, 'how are you getting on with your new little friend?'

'Whatever do you mean?' snapped Sofia, fidgeting inside her Tato's blue blazer... she never did have opportunity to get changed.

'Mister Pushkin, of course,' said Natalka, bemused by her friend's reaction. 'Who did you think I meant?'

'No-one,' said Sofia, 'sorry, I'm just tired... Yes, it seems Mister Pushkin has chosen me as his new owner... I don't think Klem will be happy about it? But the cat seems pleased that I got rid of that silly leash.'

'Good,' said Natalka, 'it never did look right... you can't walk a cat like you walk a dog...'

One corner of Oksana's mouth curled ever so slightly upwards; somehow she didn't think Mr Taras would be pleased with the identity of Sofia's *other* little friend... But for once, she had no inclination to "stir it".

'Good evening,' said Sofia, unfastening the blue blazer as she stepped into the aromatic warmth of the Chippy.

'Hello So-fear,' said the Urchin, who despite only just being able to see over the stainless steel counter, was momentarily speechless at the sight of Sofia's stockinged legs and mini-skirt. 'You come for some, err for some... err... fish 'n' chips?'

'No,' interrupted Natalka, raising an eyebrow, 'we've come for some steak and ale pie...'

'Have you?' said the Urchin, ''fraid we don't 'ave any stale pie. But we got plenty o' fish – of the battered variety – chips, peas – of the mushy sort – and err, not forgettin' the salt and the vinegar... Oh, and we got plenty of these little wooden forks with which to eat it all with...'

Natalka rolled her eyes to the ceiling, 'give me strength, how can he not understand sarcasm?'

'It's the lowest form of wit,' said the Urchin smugly.

Natalka looked down her nose, 'it also happens to be the highest form of intelligence.'

'Modest as ever,' said the Urchin. 'Just like your father: the doctor who pretends he's an 'ospital porter... or is it t'other way round? I can never remember?'

Sofia giggled, despite Natalka's pursed expression. She turned to the Urchin, 'we'll have our usual order, please...' She counted on her fingers, 'eight times. And put a dollop of mushy peas on one portion... that's for my mother.'

'And scraps,' demanded Oksana, 'give me a bag of scraps!'

'So that's fish 'n' chips eight times, one with peas, and a bag of scraps,' said the Urchin. 'Does anyone else want peas? We got plenty of 'em...'

'Go on then... but not too many,' said Sofia. 'And forget the scraps, Oksana is on a diet.' She glared at the heifer, 'and she's going to stick to it!'

'What about a pickled egg?' Oksana asked. But her shoulders slumped when her request was met with shaking heads all round.

Sofia rested an elbow on the stainless steel counter, her eyes scanning the Urchin's face. She said, 'you look different today...'

'Got new clothes, 'aven't I,' said the Urchin, gently submerging eight freshly battered haddock into the molten lard, being careful not to get splattered. 'Not that you can see 'em under this smock... And I 'ave to 'ave a bath once a week, every Friday, like.'

'How come?' asked Sofia.

The Urchin sighed, 'yesterday, the filth came round to our 'ouse and nicked me Pap and me Mam; they said they were pilferers or somethin'...'

Natalka raised both eyebrows.

'How awful,' said Sofia, ignoring her friend.

'It ain't so bad,' said the Urchin, examining the chips nestled

The Dancing Barber

within the stainless steel basket, deciding they weren't quite brown enough. 'You see, me Mam, quite frankly, she were a bit of a keff, and me Pap, well 'e were always drunk and didn't like me going t'ballet. 'e said it's for pansy poofters, but it ain't I said, but 'e wouldn't believe me... Your father dances the ballet, and 'e ain't a pansy poofter, is he?'

'True,' said Sofia. 'But when his face is daubed with make-up and he's wearing one of his flamboyant costumes, some people do begin to wonder...'

'Are those chips ready yet?' demanded Natalka, tapping her foot impatiently on the floor, which crunched with grains of spilled salt.

'Another minute should do it, Miss,' said the Urchin, 'but 'addock'll be another couple o' minutes; or maybe a little longer...'

'Bleeding hell,' said Natalka, 'can't you hurry it up? Because if Oksana salivates any more, we'll all drown!'

'Be patient,' said Sofia, 'good cooking can't be rushed...'

Oksana muttered, 'trust you to take *his* side.'

'Don't you let the customers rush you,' shouted the Chippy's owner from the back room. He was sat, as usual, with his feet up, watching *Danger Man*. 'Brown and crispy is the way they should be... Brown and crispy...'

'Yes Sir,' said the Urchin. He muttered, 'after three months, you'd think 'e'd trust me without interferin' all the time.'

Sofia peeked behind the counter, 'where's that old bed sheet of yours?' She knew how inseparable he was from it, and was surprised to see it missing.

The Urchin looked glum, 'before she got nicked, me Mam, she burned it... said it were dirty. But it were cleaner than 'er!'

Sofia sympathised; her Mama made her watch her own comfort blanket burn in the fire. It seemed silly, but it was like a pet to her... She screamed the house down so much that the neighbours thought someone was being killed... and they were right: it may have been an inanimate object, but it was her comfort blanket!

The Urchin admired Sofia's blue blazer, and said, 'why you dressed as a fella?'

'It's my father's,' said Sofia, 'he made me wear it.'

'I think it suits him better,' said the Urchin.

Sofia giggled. 'I think you're right.'

The Urchin decided not to comment on how filthy the blazer looked... He doubted Mister Tar-Arse would be happy to see it damp with rain and covered in dust. He'd told him at least twice that it'd cost fifty shillings...

Sofia counted out eight wooden forks from the cardboard dispenser, lining them up neatly in her hand, all the prongs pointing upwards. Watching the Urchin expertly examine the brownness of the chips, she asked, 'you know, none of us know your name... And my father can't keep calling you "Urchin" all the time, it's not nice...'

The Urchin blushed, 'a lass 'as never asked me what me name is before...' He brushed his fringe from his eyes, 'if I tell you, you promise not to laugh?'

'I promise,' said Sofia, 'cross my heart.'

'But I might,' muttered Natalka. She looked at Oksana, 'and she certainly will...'

'Well, in that case, I'm not tellin',' said the Urchin, arranging the salt and vinegar bottles so angrily that the contents scattered and slopped across the stainless steel counter.

Sofia gave Natalka a nudge, 'don't be mean...' She glared at the salivating Oksana, 'and you can forget all about me donating my fish to you, if you dare to emit so much as a titter, understand?'

Both girls nodded their understanding. For a moment, they thought Sofia sounded just like Mr Taras... Perish the thought...

'Well, alright,' said the Urchin, 'come closer and I'll whisper it in y'r ear.'

After a brief hesitation, Sofia leaned over, keeping her elbow out of the spilled vinegar and cupping her ear in her palm.

With a mischievous twinkle in his eye, the Urchin whispered something so quietly, that despite their best efforts, neither Natalka nor Oksana could make out anything. It didn't help that an old Morris van clattered to a halt outside the Chippy and Mrs Wiggins' husband disembarked, marched across the pavement and barged straight in, almost knocking the rusty doorbell from its fixings.

'What's wrong with that?' asked Sofia, 'I think it's a nice name... It's certainly unique...'

'Thanks,' said the Urchin, blushing even more. 'Glad you like it, but,' he put a finger to his cherryade-stained lips, 'don't tell

The Dancing Barber

anyone...'

'Watch them chips don't burn,' hollered the Chippy's owner, 'I smell charcoal in the air!'

'Yes Sir,' the Urchin shouted, filtering the brown and crispy chips from the molten lard and shovelling them onto yesterday's newspaper. He waved at Mrs Wiggins' husband, who was leaning against the counter and tapping his wristwatch. The Urchin shouted into the back room, 'this is me last serving! Me Step-Pap is here to collect me!'

The Chippy's owner grumbled, 'you can have an extra shilling if you stay until *Danger Man* finishes... I've got right into it...'

The Urchin looked at Mrs Wiggins' husband and said, 'that alright, Stan?'

'Aye, I suppose so... a shilling is a shilling,' said Stan. He whispered, 'slip me a bag of chips while I'm waiting, there's a good lad.'

'And make sure your "Step-Pap" pays for them chips this time,' shouted the Chippy's owner. 'We don't give away freebies in this shop!'

'He don't,' said the Urchin. He looked at Stan and whispered, 'he's a right skinflint, he is...'

'I heard that,' said the Chippy's owner, smiling, because he was supremely proud of his miserly status.

A few minutes later, the Urchin placed the eighth newspaper parcel of fish and chips onto the counter, and handed Sofia her change. 'There you are,' he said, 'bon appetite.'

'Thank you,' said Sofia. 'See you at practice... and...' She pretended to zip her lips, 'your secret is safe with me.'

The Urchin winked, then went into the back room for his wages, looking forward to receiving that extra shilling.

Sofia warmed her hands on a small parcel of chips. The Urchin had wrapped them beautifully in yesterday's *Times*, even lining up the text so that it could be easily read. She noticed an article, and the accompanying photograph of a smart-suited Voloshin, taken thirty years ago... She gasped when she discovered who could have been hiding beneath that Cossack's moustache... 'No, it *can't* be...'

'Hands off,' said Natalka, slapping Oksana's chubby arm. 'You can wait until we get these back to Mr Taras' house!'

Oksana sulked, 'I might die of starvation by then...'

'Don't be so melodramatic,' said Natalka, carefully stacking the newspaper parcels in an old Fresh Fair carrier bag. 'Right then, fatso... I'll race you back...' she said, dashing out of the Chippy, then sprinting up Great Horton Road. 'The last one back's a pile of manure!'

'Wait!' shouted Oksana, half-heartedly trying to chase after Natalka.

Sofia was left standing in the shop, transfixed by the grainy photograph of Voloshin, which slowly absorbed the chip fat, glistening under the light-bulbs.

'You alright?' asked the Urchin. 'You look like you seen a ghost...'

'Come on fatso!' shouted Natalka. 'Run faster! Your chips are getting cold!'

'You're cruel,' said an out-of-breath Oksana, barely able to keep pace with Natalka as she raced up the steep incline of Great Horton Road, the aromas of freshly fried fish and chips providing the ideal carrots of encouragement.

'Dieting is more than just watching what you eat,' said Natalka.

'But I *always* watch what I eat,' said Oksana, 'just before I shove it in my mouth!'

Natalka sighed, 'you know perfectly well what I mean! Doing plenty of exercise is important too... So we'll sprint the rest of the way!' Accelerating up the steepest part of the hill, she shouted, 'Move it!'

Oksana's body crunched into second gear, her chubby feet pounding the pavement, almost cracking the flagstones, the resultant vibration causing her bouncing belly to rupture her corsetry and nearly give her a pair of black eyes.

'Come on!' shouted Natalka. 'Faster!'

'I'm going as fast as I can,' wheezed Oksana, regressing back to first gear.

'There's no hope for you,' said Natalka. 'No hope at all.'

Oksana stopped to catch her breath. She looked into the distance, only just making out the glowing neon sign of the Chippy at the foot of Great Horton Road. She thought: *Sofia couldn't still*

The Dancing Barber

be talking to that common boy. He may no longer drag his comfort blanket around with him, but he was still an Urchin... and Mr Taras would not want his daughter associating with the likes of him, especially when wearing a mini-skirt, even if it was disguised beneath a blue blazer. And I bet Mrs Wiggins regretted putting her name down on the foster parent register... surely there were nicer children in Bradford? Me, for instance...

'Come on, Oksana!' shouted Natalka, annoyed at having to run back down the hill to give the heifer a slap of encouragement. For the first time, she noticed Sofia wasn't with them... She thought: *Is Sofia still talking to Stan and his grubby little Urchin? And I bet I know what they're talking about...*

Natalka hoped Sofia's obsession with this Stanislaw wasn't going to get out of hand... She could only hope that Sofia kept her theories to herself... if the Police ever found out, her entire family would be arrested. She'd speak to her about it later.

Right now, she had to coax Oksana up the final few hundred yards to Mr Taras' house... 'Will you come on!' she shouted. 'Or I'll give your fish and chips to Zena and Lenka!'

But Oksana couldn't move another inch. 'Give it to them,' she said, panting with exhaustion. 'I don't care anymore!'

The old Morris van clattered to a halt by the kerb just in time for Oksana to keel over onto its bonnet, denting the metalwork.

'Hello,' said Sofia, who was sat on the bench seat between Stan and the Urchin. 'Fancy a lift?'

The Urchin got out and ran around the back, immediately swinging open the double doors, the handles of which had been tied together with frayed rope. 'There should be enough room,' he said, observing the gap between Stan's tools. He looked at the circumference of Oksana, 'but only just...'

'What about me?' said Natalka, 'after all, it's me who's just lugged our bleeding dinner up this bleeding hill...' But the van had already driven off... 'Thanks a bunch...' she said, dropping the bag of fish and chips to the ground. 'I *won't* forget this!'

AC Michael

Chapter 104

When Taras ambled back into the kitchen, he almost tumbled over Halyna's crouching body. He asked, 'what are you doing down there? I could have broken my neck!'

'What does it look like?' snapped Halyna, who continued wiping down the skirting boards with an old cloth, displaying as much enthusiasm for the task as the cat would have to the prospect of a vet taking its temperature.

She glared at the Cooking Fat that was still sat depressingly in front of the fire, disappointed that its fun had been thwarted; its stomach groaning and moaning...

Dreading the answer, Taras asked, 'what have you done with them?'

'One's in the bin,' said Halyna, 'but I think Pushkin ate the other one...'

After listening to Taras' tirade, Zena asked, 'what is this "uck" that Taras, he always says?'

Halyna resisted the urge to fling the blood-soaked cloth at her husband. She said, 'how many more times... I don't want them learning any more of your bad language...'

Taras shrugged, 'I never used to swear until your sisters appeared... It's all their fault!'

Zena turned to Lenka, 'do you know what this "uck" means?'

But Lenka was too busy. After skinning the decapitated chinchillas, and skewering them with Stanislaw's rusty knitting needle, she barbecued them on the hob, enjoying listening to the hiss and sizzle of charred rodent flesh. 'Ah,' she said, 'the music to the ears...'

With the smell of singed rodent filling the kitchen, Klem opened the window before striding across the room to stare inquisitively at the television set. After verifying the time on his pocket watch, he impatiently slapped the side of the television, 'how do I get the BBC on this thing?'

'What for?' asked Taras, 'I thought you said television rots the mind?'

The Dancing Barber

'Maybe I was wrong,' said Klem, 'Lenka has never seen a television in her entire life, and look at the state of her...' He shook his head, 'in all seriousness, I must watch the BBC News... I'd have gone up to the attic to listen to the World Service on my radio, but Stanislaw smashed it.'

'There's my radio in the shop?' Taras asked, 'that might get the World Service?'

'No, err... thank you' said Klem, picking up the television aerial, and re-enacting the dance Halyna performed in the attic. 'I can't breathe in there with all your stale tobacco...'

'Suit yourself?' shrugged Taras. He watched Klem pirouette and stretch his arms in all directions, but the television screen remained resolutely black. Taras coughed, swinging the plug as if it were a miniature lasso, 'perhaps this may help?'

Klem shook his head, 'electrics... I haven't got a clue...'

Taras nodded over to the kettle, 'if Lenka's finished barbecuing her chinchilla kebabs, switch on the kettle again... The girls won't be long... then we'll all have some Darjeeling with our fish and chips... I must admit, I much prefer it to PG Tips...'

'Kettles, I understand,' said a blushing Klem, 'televisual sets, I do not...' He was pleased he'd finally converted Taras into appreciating the quality of Darjeeling... he'd make a connoisseur of him yet... No-one else noticed the last pot was only PG Tips...

Klem gazed down at an increasingly sickly-looking cat, 'if you're going to spew, go outside and do it... Silly cat... That'll teach you for eating such deplorable things...'

The cat's stomach groaned and moaned even more. It tried to settle in front of the fire, hoping the warmth of the gas flames would aid digestion... but it soon felt even worse...

Klem sat down and waited for the hissing snowstorm to clear... Five minutes later, he was still waiting.

Straining to hold the aerial at arm's length, three feet above the television, Taras said, 'at last... if no-one moves, the picture shouldn't be affected...' He glanced down at the tatty copy of The Radio Times with Patrick McGoohan on the cover, annoyed that he'd missed *Danger Man* again. But at least they were in time for the BBC News...

'You're kidding,' said Klem, almost spilling his freshly-decanted Darjeeling. 'Katya is just a plain fishing boat... Why the hell would the Soviets sink her?'

He turned up the volume and listened to the upper-crust voice of the newsreader:

"A statement released by the Kremlin states that the capsized fishing boat, Katya, may have inadvertently strayed into military waters and thus triggered an automatic defence system. There were no reported fatalities, and all the survivors were taken for what the Kremlin terms 'debriefing'. In a related story, it has been reported on many of the news-wires that Voloshin, the so-called Peaceful Partisan, was involved in a fatal accident with an umbrella. As a result, there is a great deal of unrest on the streets of Kyiv, with demonstrators surrounding every government office, demanding to know the truth."

Taras was fed up of holding the aerial as if he were the Statue of Liberty... his arm was shaking and he couldn't hold his position much longer. He said, 'sinking Katya is one thing, but how can the Kremlin lie so blatantly about Voloshin?'

Klem sipped his cooling Darjeeling. He said, 'remember, Khrushchev's biggest weapon is his propaganda... Soviets and Ukrainians alike will believe anything they're told...'

'That used to be true... but all those demonstrators in Kyiv don't seem to believe it...' Taras' arm ached, 'please, can I put this down now... the News has finished?' He didn't wait for Klem's reply... the television snowed and hissed once more, while he massaged his sore muscles. He looked at Klem's depressed expression, 'what will you do?'

Klem shook his head, 'it's up to Katya now... I'm retired...'

'But the boat was sunk,' said Taras, 'and if everyone's been arrested, then there is no Katya...?'

Klem took out his pocket watch and wound it the usual seven times, the clicking of the ratchet focussing his thoughts. 'Importantly,' he said, 'I still have faith...' He reached into the pocket of his pinstriped jacket and extracted his miniature copy of the Holy Bible.

Peering through his half-moon spectacles, he found Mark 11:24, as marked with a length of green ribbon. He read: *"Therefore I tell you, whatever you ask for in prayer, believe that you have received it, and it will be yours."*

The Dancing Barber

He closed the book and placed it on the table in front of him, his fingers resting on the worn leather cover. Standing up, he said, 'and that is what I shall do... If you need me, I'll be up in the attic.'

Klem looked at the nauseous cat, still hunched up by the fire, 'you coming, Mister Pushkin?' When the cat didn't emit so much as a growl, he said, 'I have some nice sir-a-loin for you... fresh from the butcher's today...'

Taras shook his head, 'I don't think he's interested...' He looked at the cheap plastic pendulum clock on the wall, and wondered what was taking the girls so long...

'The chips, they are here,' announced a ravenous Lenka, upon hearing the yard gate creak open... the chinchilla kebabs in no way filling her rumbling stomach.

'About the time,' said Zena. 'I could eat the horse...'

Taras sighed, *that's about all you haven't eaten since you've been here!*

After setting the table by throwing the earthenware plates as if they were discus, Lenka immediately took her place between Zena and Halyna, and waited, fork in hand, for Natalka to lug the heavy bag through the door.

Natalka muttered, 'bleeding making me carry this bleeding bag up that bleeding hill, and they couldn't be bleeding bothered to bleeding offer me a bleeding lift!' She lobbed the newspaper parcels onto the plates and made a start on her own dinner, stabbing her chips with a two-pronged wooden fork.

Sofia skipped into the kitchen, washed her hands and sat next to her Mama. 'Sorry we're late,' she said, 'but it was all Oksana's fault... we were lucky the Fire Brigade weren't needed to cut Oksana from Mr Wiggins' van...'

The heifer took her place at the table, the wooden chair creaking under the strain.

Sofia turned to Oksana and said, 'maybe now you'll start to take your diet a little more seriously? You've completely crushed Mr Wiggins' suspension!'

Oksana may have sulked, but it didn't stop her arranging her chips between her two battered haddock, thus creating a curious sandwich. With an over-filled mouth, she said, 'Mrs Halyna, will you tell Sofia to tell everyone what the Urchin's name is?'

Sofia turned to her Mama and said, 'ignore her… I promised to keep it a secret. And a promise is a promise. Besides, Oksana will only laugh…'

Halyna looked sternly at Oksana, 'you are to leave that boy alone; he has been through enough trauma lately…'

'What trauma is this?' asked Taras, picking several flakes of greasy haddock from his lap that had fallen from his two-pronged wooden fork. 'It can't be as traumatic as me having to teach him ballet?'

'Excuse me,' said Halyna, watching everyone wolf down their dinner. 'But just because Klem isn't here, it doesn't mean we shouldn't pray before we eat!' She waited for everyone to put down their forks, and for Oksana to put down what remained of her curious sandwich. Holding her hands together, Halyna said, 'thank you Lord, for the assistance you have given us today, and thank you also for providing this delicious meal, for which we are supremely grateful. Amen.'

'Amen,' came the unanimous reply.

Halyna crossed herself in the Orthodox fashion, then allowed everyone to resume eating.

'Apparently,' said Sofia, 'the Urchin's Pap and Mam were nicked, err… arrested…' She whispered, 'because they were caught pilfering…'

'Pilfering?' said Taras, 'that's terrible…'

'It's worse than terrible,' said Halyna, munching a soggy chip. 'I think Mrs Wiggins has a heart of the purest gold to take that Urchin in… You see, his Pap and Mam – old Pot-Belly and Fag-Ash-Lil – were caught burgling *her* house… Stan caught Pot-Belly emptying the mattress of Mrs Wiggins' Bingo winnings, while Mrs Wiggins caught Fag-Ash filling a pillowcase with Stan's collection of Sovereigns. Can you believe it? Mind you,' she said, mopping up a puddle of vinegar with another soggy chip, 'I'm surprised they hadn't been burgled sooner… Mrs Wiggins has been telling *everyone* how much money she had stashed away… she may as well have put an advertisement in the Telegraph & Argus… But to have taken that Urchin in,' she shook her head with admiration, 'she must have a heart of *pure* gold.'

'I wouldn't have bothered,' said Taras, 'that Urchin's more

trouble than he's worth... And he's worth – in his own words – "nowt"!'

'Don't be so nasty,' said Halyna, 'the Urchin can't help the way he is... especially with Pot-Belly and Fag-Ash-Lil as role-models...' She looked at Oksana, 'just look at how different Oksana is now she's with Klem and Zena instead of Ivan and The Gossipmonger...'

'Mmm,' said Taras, watching Oksana scratch herself in all the same places as Zena. 'Like mother like daughter...'

Sniffing her fingers, Oksana said, 'so Sofia, are you going to tell us what the Urchin's name is? Hand on heart, I promise not to laugh. Honest.'

Sofia closed her eyes, 'a promise is a promise. I shall say no more.'

Oksana tore off another chunk of haddock and swallowed it without chewing.

'Halya, go see who that is,' said Taras, upon hearing a stout knock on the kitchen door. 'I don't like being interrupted during dinner, understand?'

'And I do?' said Halyna, 'answer the door yourself!'

Wiping his greasy mouth on an unwashed hankie, Taras begrudgingly strode over to the door, swinging it open so forcefully that it nearly flew off its hinges. 'We've just been talking about the three of you,' he said, feigning politeness, 'come in... but I know you're too busy to stay for more than a couple of minutes...'

'We're never too busy,' said Stan, taking in a deep breath. 'Ahhh... Don't your fish and chips smell lovely...?'

Mrs Wiggins agreed. She said, 'mmm... they smell divine...'

The Urchin didn't concur... working in the Chippy completely put him off them. He combed his hair into place, then nervously went to stand next to Sofia, waiting to be spoken to.

Taras said, 'we're in the middle of dinner... whatever you want, make it quick...' There was barely enough fish and chips to go round without having to apportion some to the Wiggins' and their wretched Urchin.

'Taras!' said Halyna, 'our friends don't need an excuse to visit... Please, why don't you join us? Here,' she said, unwrapping

AC Michael

Klem's fish and chips, 'we have a spare portion... Help yourselves...' She knew that Klem, being in one of his praying moods, wouldn't eat for the rest of the day.

'That's very kind of you,' said Mrs Wiggins, helping herself to a handful of chips.

'Very kind indeed,' said Stan, devouring the haddock that complemented the free chips his step-son had slipped him earlier in the evening.

Mrs Wiggins slid a brown envelope across the table to Taras. 'I have a present for you,' she said, with a full mouth, 'a present you'll really appreciate!'

'What is it?' asked Taras, picking up the bulky envelope.

'One *thousand* pounds,' said Mrs Wiggins, much to her husband's dismay. 'It ain't safe at home, and it ain't safe in the bank... So rather than spending it, I want to *invest* it...'

'You want to invest it?' said Taras. 'But where?'

Mrs Wiggins smiled, 'I want to invest it in your Ballet Studio... I know you want to expand, and I'm sure a *thousand* pounds will go a long way...' She muttered, 'it'll pay for the piano to be tuned for a start...'

'But,' interrupted Stan, 'it's all to be above board, a *proper* investment with a *proper* contract. Every year, she is to get a share of the profits... That's the only way I will allow my wife to waste, err... to *invest* her money in your Ballet Studio.' He held out his coarse workman's hand, 'is it a deal?'

'Well... shake the man's hand,' said Halyna, completely unaware that Taras' expansion plans involved building on her back yard...

'Very well,' said Taras, firmly shaking Stan's hand, 'a *proper* investment and a *proper* contract... I'll get my solicitor to draw something up first thing tomorrow...' He then shook Mrs Wiggins' hand, careful to avoid being clawed by her three-inch false nails. 'This will be the perfect partnership... with *my talent* and *your money*, we can only succeed!'

Mrs Wiggins smiled. She knew she'd only truly be happy with a more active role in the Ballet Studio, and reckoned she'd suit the title of "Musical Director" rather well... But she wouldn't tell Taras, not yet any way...

Zena grinned, 'this calls for the celebration, yes?'

The Dancing Barber

Lenka rubbed her hands together, 'I will go fetch the samahon!'

'Hello So-fear,' said the Urchin, fed up of being ignored.

'Oh hello,' said Sofia, 'I didn't see you there. How long have you been stood behind me? Why didn't you say hello sooner?'

The Urchin shrugged, and tried not to blush. He said, 'I've got a present for you...' He put his hand up his jumper and rummaged around.

Taras stared at the Urchin. He'd seen this joke before... it was neither funny, nor appropriate.

The Urchin said, 'daisies, they don't grow at the moment... But dandelions, they do... So I made you a chain o' dandelions instead... It's up 'ere somewhere... Here it is.' He attempted to drape the chain around Sofia's neck, 'oops, it seems I misjudged the circumference... oh well, it makes a nice hat-sort-o-thing...'

'It's lovely,' said Sofia, admiring her reflection in the mirror. 'Thank you Eustace.'

'Eustace,' snorted Oksana, 'I knew it'd be a silly name... and it is!'

Natalka smiled, 'more like Useless...'

'Stop it,' said Sofia, 'Eustace is my friend...' She smiled at him, 'aren't you Eustace?'

Taras cringed, especially when Eustace's eyes glazed over... 'Give me strength... Sofia, after dinner, you and I need to have a *serious* talk, understand?'

Chapter 105

After tearing out the photograph, Sofia scrunched up the greasy newspaper, and threw it into the bin. She didn't particularly enjoy her chips, and knew they'd be repeating on her until morning... At least there wasn't any washing up.

And she couldn't wait to have her "serious talk" with her Tato... She could predict precisely what he'd say... "Sofia! I forbid you to associate with such working class urchins!" She could also predict that he'd soon change his mind, when he discovered how talented Eustace really was...

Sofia yawned... it was very late and she wanted to do nothing more than curl up in bed. She watched her Mama yawn so widely that she could see her pink tonsils... it was obvious that she too had similar plans... Unfortunately, there was too much commotion in the house for either of them to contemplate going to bed any time soon...

'What's up with Oksana?' asked Sofia, 'it's not like her to be helpful...?'

'I don't know,' said Halyna, 'but I hope it continues... it's about time those sisters of mine had a proper bath... A goodski scrub will do them the world of goodski!'

Sofia smiled, 'it'll probably be the first proper bath they've ever had.' Watching Oksana pour a whole bottle of strawberry-scented Avon Bubble-Bath into the tin bath in the centre of the kitchen floor, she said, 'at least they're using soap this time... but I doubt anyone will want to get in after them...'

'Halyna cringed, 'I don't think anyone could... the water will be thick with mud!'

'Oh my God!' cried Sofia, covering her eyes. Seeing her Mama's appalled expression, she said, 'sorry for blaspheming... but that is going to give me nightmares! I can't bear to look!'

'Look at what?' said Halyna. But when she saw Zena and Lenka waddle into the kitchen with nothing but a towel draped around their necks, she too said, 'oh my God!'

'It's obscene,' said Sofia, keeping her eyes tightly shut.

The Dancing Barber

Halyna said, 'thank Heavens those two got all the hairy genes...' She whispered, 'imagine having so much hair on your back that you have to comb it...'

Sofia cringed, 'on your back and everywhere else!'

'The privacy!' demanded Zena. 'Me and Lenka, we do not want the audience when we are having the bath! Please go away!'

Halyna and Sofia were glad to escape to the pitch-black yard. Sofia turned on the porch-light and they both planned to sit on the cold sandstone step and wait.

The tin bath became a Jacuzzi the instant Zena submerged herself in it... and the water turned from clear to grey and from grey to luminous green in less than a second, an oily scum floating on the surface, an inch of grime clinging to the sides.

The last thing Halyna heard before closing the door was Oksana rasping the last of the strawberry-scented Avon Bubble-Bath all over the twins, rubbing it in thoroughly, making the sound of sandpaper on wood...

Out in the fresh air of the yard, Sofia showed her Mama the article she'd torn from *The Times*, holding it up to the dim light. Pointing at a photograph of a moustachioed man, taken circa 1933, she said, 'who does that remind you of?'

'Goodski Heavens,' declared Halyna, peering through her plastic-framed glasses, 'it could be a very young Taras...' She admired the image, which – despite being marred by congealed chip fat – was of exceptionally good quality. 'This is just how your Tato looked like... *many* years ago...'

'I thought it might have been,' said Sofia. 'Don't you want to know who this actually is?'

Halyna shrugged, 'it's probably some boring politician...?'

Sofia revealed the headline, displaying it for her Mama to see:

```
IS THIS VOLOSHIN, THE PEACEFUL PARTISAN?
COULD UKRAINE'S SAVIOUR REALLY BE CALLED PETRO?
```

'Petro...?' said Halyna. She gasped, then whispered, 'but Petro is Taras' real name...'

'Is it?' said Sofia. She knew her Tato's life prior to marrying her Mama was a bit of a mystery. Some people called him an

Enigma, whereas Zena and Lenka called him an Enema...

'Yes...' said Halyna. 'You see, during the Second World War, we were both Ostarbeiters, slave labourers, taken to Germany via Cracow in Poland. Apparently, the Soviets wanted to arrest your Tato very badly, and made a deal with the Nazis... so he had to change his name for "security reasons"... And all his credentials were forged... I never asked why...'

Sofia was fascinated...

Halyna adjusted her plastic-framed glasses. 'Petro, the Ballet Dancer was replaced by Taras, the Gentleman's Barber... only a few of the Germans knew the truth... When the war ended and we were sent to Market Drayton in Shropshire, before being transported to Bradford, it was agreed that your Tato should continue to be called Taras.'

'Why do you think the Soviets wanted to arrest Tato?'

Halyna shrugged, 'he never said. I knew so little about his past... I still don't know everything... but never did I think... No...' She laughed, '...the idea is ridiculous!'

Sofia wasn't so sure...

And the more she thought about it, neither was Halyna...

'Ahhh!' screamed Zena. 'Look at the state of me!'

'Ahhh!' yelped Lenka. 'What has the happened?'

Halyna and Sofia ran into the kitchen, dreading what they were about to see...

A giggling Oksana fled upstairs, her belly bouncing in all directions – Sofia had never seen her move so quickly – leaving Zena and Lenka stood alone on the soaking wet carpet.

It looked as though the Michelin Man's twin sisters had come to visit... every inch of Zena and Lenka's bulbous bodies was white, smooth and utterly devoid of all hair!

Halyna picked up the empty bottle of Avon Bubble-Bath and sniffed the contents. Peeling away the label, she burst into uncontrollable laughter.

Sofia took hold of the bottle and read out, 'Imaac!' She laughed so loudly that it hurt...

The Dancing Barber
Chapter 106

---------------------------------✂---------------------------------

Even after praying solidly for three hours, Klem still didn't know what to do. He undid the green ribbon and unfastened the collar of his embroidered shirt. The attic was too noisy, and far too hot and stuffy, so he ambled down to the cooler kitchen, which was – for once – blissfully quiet since everyone had gone to bed.

Klem despaired... 'Why is *everything* going wrong?' He tried to calm his mind by watching the swinging pendulum of the cheap Chinese clock above the kitchen mantelpiece, but it had little effect. Even his soothing Darjeeling made no difference... and without the cat to talk to, he talked to himself... He had so many woes that he didn't know where to start...

'What am I supposed to do about Katya? The ten thousand pounds I'll get for the Fabergé Egg can't even begin to replace what's been lost...' He shook his head, 'and until I know what became of all those poor souls aboard her, I can't actually do anything...'

His thoughts then turned to the Imaac'ed snoring machine he'd left in the attic. He could still hear her two floors down... 'Zena is going to become the Wife from Hell... and there's *nothing* I can do about it.' A shiver ran down his spine at the thought of her ear-wax candles, her cushions stuffed to bursting with short and curly hairs, her roasted rodents and her endless singing of "Tar-Ra-Ra-<u>Bum</u>-Di-Yey". Not to mention the horrendous pongs she so frequently emitted from every orifice... And the aggression she'd shown towards Stanislaw completely terrified him...

'The woman has no decorum, no manners, no idea about personal hygiene and absolutely no respect for anyone or anything... And now – thanks to Oksana – she has no hair at all!' He dreaded Taras discovering what she'd done to his beloved Eames chair... the thing wasn't designed to support twenty-five stones of woman...

Earlier that day, he'd taken Zena back to Manningham Park... he knew the Warden was off duty, and he wanted to give her a second chance... But she insisted on playing "The" Bowls, lobbing bowling balls as if they were coconuts at a fairground coconut shy, denting the pristine green so badly that by the time she'd finished, it looked more like the surface of the moon. And when the elderly green-keeper insisted she moved her bowls, no-one knew where to look when she proceeded to squat in one of the craters...

He muttered, 'marrying such a creature, it's... it's unthinkable. More than unthinkable, it's insanity!' He cursed that drunken night twelve years ago.

He sipped his cooling Darjeeling... Katya and Zena were not his only woes...

'Why has Mister Pushkin disowned me? It could only be Zena's fault... Pushkin's nose is so much more sensitive than mine... But *I* certainly haven't done anything to offend the cat...?' He shook his head, '...Sofia can't possibly provide him with as much sir-a-loin as I can...'

He clasped his hands together and prayed for a few more minutes, all to no avail.

Allowing himself to be mesmerised by the clock's swinging pendulum – its golden shape morphing into a hypnotist's pocket watch – the stresses finally began to melt away, his mind becoming calmer and clearer.

His priority had to be getting Katya functioning once again... dealing with Zena and that ungrateful cat would have to wait. He continued to watch the pendulum swing to and fro, just like the Priest's incense-filled Cadyllo at the All-Night Easter Service that seemed such a long time ago.

This cheap Chinese clock was the most accurate timepiece in the entire house... He'd often thought it was strange that Gunter would buy him such an expensive Vacheron Constantin pocket watch, yet only give Halyna such a low-cost clock to hang on the wall. But his pocket watch would frequently gain three minutes per day, whereas that cheap plastic clock hadn't gained so much as a second in months...

When the clock chimed two o'clock in the morning, Klem fished out his pocket watch and reset it. And Halyna was right... the clock's pendulum did look as though it was made of gold...

Out of curiosity, he stood up and peered at it closely through his half-moon reading glasses, following it swing to and fro. Its surface appeared to have been machined into closely-placed concentric circles that swirled from the centre... The more he thought about it, the more he realised how incongruous this shiny pendulum was to the rest of this inexpensive timepiece.

After swigging the remnants of his Darjeeling, he carefully caught the pendulum in his steady hand and unhooked it from the mechanism... Immediately, the clock began ticking three times faster... it didn't matter, he'd reset it later.

Klem held the heavy pendulum in the palm of his hand, and imagined there must have been a disk of lead beneath the gold paint. But then he turned it over, and was so surprised by what he saw, that he had to sit down...

'Gunter... you crafty *so-n-so*... How you like to make life difficult for Klem...'

Holding the reverse of the pendulum close to his eye, Klem examined the finely decorated bezel that looked sufficiently grey in colouration to have been made of platinum, inlaid with marquise cut sapphires. And in the centre, was nestled an enormous round brilliant cut yellow diamond, obviously designed by Karl Fabergé himself, displaying the fifty-eight perfect facets. The colour of the diamond was evenly yellow and it was completely flawless...

The diamond was big enough to examine without a loupe... The table and diameter were perfectly proportioned, the crown height and angle ideal, and the pavilion angle and depth couldn't be improved... It twinkled majestically in the dim kitchen light... he imagined how much better it would twinkle in daylight...

The diamond alone was worth millions... He couldn't even begin to imagine how much that Fabergé Egg would be worth, now the *surprise* was in its rightful place...

Klem clasped his hands together, cast his eyes to the charred ceiling, crossed himself in the Ukrainian Orthodox fashion and said, 'Thank You... You never let me down!'

Chapter 107

Stanislaw's bruised body smashed onto the cold metal floor, the heavy steel door slamming shut behind him. He groaned... his plan wasn't supposed to turn out like this... by now, he should have been occupying the Presidential Office in the Kremlin, sipping the strongest vodka, eating the finest caviar and deciding how best to dispose of Khrushchev...

He groaned even louder when he sat up, the hard floor doing no favours for his most horrific injury. He hadn't eaten in over a week... he could feel the loosened skin draped over his protruding cheekbones, his receding gums and the contours of his ribs. He wrapped the rags of his cassock around his shivering body and examined the dim confines of his cell...

Amongst the gloom, there was a small rectangle of bright light. Stanislaw sat up and looked closely... A pair of beady eyes stared at him through the small feeding hatch in the reinforced door. 'Let me out!' Stanislaw demanded, the fog of his breath dissipating into the icy air. Standing up, he shouted, 'you have no right to imprison me!'

Beneath the beady eyes, the embers of an expensive cigar glowed in the dimness of the dungeon. 'I have *every* right to imprison *scum* like you! The world will be a better place without you in it!' Clouds of smoke blew into the windowless cell, inducing Stanislaw to cough and splutter.

'When I escape,' screamed Stanislaw, catching his breath, 'I will strangle you with my bare hands!'

'But you'll never escape,' came the reply. The feeding hatch creaked shut and was bolted, plunging the dank cell into complete darkness.

'Oh yes I will,' shouted Stanislaw, hammering the door with both fists. He immediately set to work, looking for any weaknesses in the cell walls... The walls were made of stone, and he was sure they sloped slightly towards him, as though they'd eventually meet a dozen yards above his head in the form of an isosceles church spire. They felt very smooth and impossible to

The Dancing Barber

climb... And beneath his bare feet, the circular floor was entirely made of perforated steel, the holes equally spaced.

After he'd followed the walls full circle, he tripped over something big and soft... 'What the hell's this?' he said, prodding and kicking it.

'C-C-Colonel?' said a voice from the darkness, 'is that y-y-you?'

Stanislaw demanded, 'who's there? Speak up! Identify yourself!'

'W-w-what...' said the voice. 'D-d-don't you recognise m-m-me...?'

'Of course he doesn't!' snapped a second voice. It was much deeper, and possibly female. Then followed the sounds of hawking and spitting.

'Oh no,' said Stanislaw, detecting the stench of mothballs. 'Please, tell me it's not...'

'Y-y-yes it is,' said the first voice. 'It's m-m-me, Ivan, and m-m-my m-m-mother!'

'Hello Stani,' said The Gossipmonger, poking him with her clubbed hand. 'Long time, no see...'

Stanislaw punched the steel door, not even denting it slightly. He couldn't believe what was happening to him... After a few seconds of deliberation, he said, 'so if I've been sent where you've been sent... then that means I'm...'

'In The Convent,' said Ivan, his teeth chattering, for he still only wore what remained of the itchy hessian sack. 'It's n-n-not as b-b-bad as you th-th-think...'

'No,' said The Gossipmonger, spitting to the floor. 'It's far worse!'

Stanislaw muttered, 'I can't possibly be in Kyiv? Can I?'

The man with the beady eyes and expensive cigar had been listening at the door. He unstuck his ear and said, 'isn't that nice... It looks like "Stani's" making friends...'

'When do we turn it on?' asked the Mother Superior standing by his side, her gleaming white habit helping to illuminate the eerie, gas-lit corridor, and her aroma of incense masking the whiff of cigar smoke. 'The Nuns and I have been waiting a *long* time for this moment...'

'Patience...' said the man, dropping the spent cigar and

screwing it into the damp floor with his muddy boot. 'Don't forget... it's a virtue...'

'It is nearly time for Vespers,' said the Mother Superior, 'and you shall have to get changed...'

The man looked at his grubby dungarees. 'You're right... I'll get one of the Nuns to fetch my formal clothes from the Jeep...'

'I'll fetch them myself, it will be my pleasure...' said the Mother Superior. She listened to the bells ringing high above the nearby Saint Sofia Cathedral and thought how wonderful they sounded today. 'And will you need the Jeep refuelling?'

'Thank you, you are very kind,' said the man, 'it was a long drive from Askanya Nova...'

The Mother Superior floated down the gas-lit corridor, grateful for the compliment. She shouted, 'General Borodov... Won't you consider turning it on... only for a short while...?'

General Borodov smiled, 'why not... It won't do any harm...' Peering through the tiny hatch, he could see the three prisoners were sat on the floor. 'Perfect,' he said, his hand on the gas tap. 'Let the *re-education* commence...'

The Mother Superior whizzed back along the corridor to have a sneaky peek... She salivated with anticipation...

And never before had three candidates been more in need of *re-education*... especially the former Colonel Stanislaw... She chuckled at the thought of how a durak like Stanislaw planned to overthrow the mighty Khrushchev... poisoned caviar was *so* 1950's... And his lifelong obsession with apprehending this mythical Voloshin had to stop... It was doing terrible damage to Ukraine-Soviet relations... Stanislaw was beyond psycho analysis... not least, because he'd strangled the Soviet Union's preeminent expert, prior to escaping from The Asylum... But before he'd escaped, he'd admitted that his every action was the result of following the orders of the "Spirit of Stalin".

The Mother Superior had never heard such rubbish. Stalin was so heinous that he'd have gone directly to Hell, and had probably ousted Satan and installed himself in his place.

This small cell was one of the Mother Superior's own personal inventions... The entire floor was dotted with powerful Bunsen-Burners that ignited and extinguished randomly, delivering ferocious heat where and when the prisoners least expected it, thus

The Dancing Barber

ensuring they could never rest... And the more tired they became, the more randomly, frequently and ferociously did the flames ignite...

General Borodov hadn't been so excited since – being a high-ranking General of the Soviet Union – he'd helped launch Sputnik in 1957... It was a happy time, five years before he was coerced into heading-up the Secret Police... but at least he was allowed to conduct his operations lethargically from the quietest backwater in Ukraine.

General Borodov counted down, 'three, two, one...' He trembled with anticipation... the first Bunsen-Burners to ignite were positioned directly beneath the seated prisoners.

Both he and the Mother Superior looked forward to witnessing plenty of weeping and gnashing of teeth...

Chapter 108

It may have been three o'clock in the morning, but when Klem had an idea, he had to act on it immediately.

Taras was so sleepy that he didn't know what was happening. In five minutes, he was shaved, shampooed, dressed in his best suit and now sat in the attic with his hair neatly combed, and dyed jet black. Gradually, his brain switched on and he realised what was about to happen. He got up and made a dash for the door…

'Just *one* photograph will be enough,' insisted Klem, loading his Leica M3 with a fresh roll of colour film. 'Then everyone will know Voloshin really is alive.'

'No chance,' said Taras. 'I'm not doing it!' He clenched a fist, 'I don't know what I have to do to make you understand – once and for all – that I'm not doing it!'

Klem closed the camera's hinged back and screwed on the chromium base plate. He said, 'if you wear one of your prosthetic moustaches, no-one will ever know it's you…' He handed him a luxuriant Cossack's moustache, 'go on… put it on…'

'Forget it,' Taras said, turning the door handle, only to realise the door was locked. He put his hands on his hips, 'look, I happen to like my life the way it is. I am Taras Panas, The Dancing Barber. I have no intention of resuming my Partisan activities… Forget it! And my decision is final!'

'But all I want is *one* photograph,' said Klem, clicking a 90mm lens onto the Leica's bayonet mount, his favourite focal length for portraiture. 'When, all those years ago, I agreed to pretend to be Voloshin, I promised to keep you out of it. And I *never* break a promise.' He wound on the film, then adjusted the focus on the calibrated dial. 'What the Ukrainian people need most of all is proof… proof that Voloshin… that you… are still around… Voloshin must be more than a silhouette with a voice. Ukrainians must see Voloshin in the flesh!'

Taras folded his arms, 'why don't you dress up like Voloshin… You can wear that ridiculous prosthetic moustache and take a photograph of yourself!'

The Dancing Barber

Klem laughed, 'how can I?' He examined his reflection in the mirror, 'I look nothing like the Voloshin people remember!'

Taras shook his head. He said, 'you can't imprison me in my own attic!' He flung the prosthetic moustache onto Klem's desk, where it lay like a lifeless bat.

Klem raised the camera to his eye and looked through the viewfinder, fine tuning the focus until the two images of a pompous Taras merged into one. 'Just one photograph... that's all I want... Just one...'

'Oh Tato, you must do it...' pleaded Sofia, 'you simply *must*!'

'Where did you spring from? And why aren't you in bed?' Taras asked, upon Sofia appearing like a Jack-in-the-Box from behind the remains of his Eames chair. 'And what I *do* or *do not* do is entirely *my* business!'

'Not today, it isn't,' stated Halyna, emerging from the twins' side of the attic, having satisfactorily chastised and thanked Oksana for bathing and defoliating Zena and Lenka. 'I think you have to do precisely what Klem says!'

Klem's idea had made him so excited that he simply had to wake up the entire household... And since Sofia had guessed the truth, and convinced Halyna, then there was no longer any point in lying... But he preferred to leave the Imaac'ed twins in bed, where they frantically scratched themselves as they slept.

Sofia hugged her Tato tightly. 'I am so proud of you, but I... we all... will be even more proud of you if you help Klem with his plans! It's time someone stood up to those nasty Soviets... who better than you?'

'You don't understand what you're saying...' Taras put his hands on his hips and faced the wall. 'You're asking me to play a very dangerous game.'

'There isn't any danger... not now,' said Klem, 'Stanislaw was the worst thing that could have happened... Lightening doesn't strike in the same place twice...'

Halyna picked up the dead bat of a prosthetic moustache. She looked at Taras and smiled, 'it always did suit you...'

Taras put his hands in his pockets. 'No way... I am not letting any of you talk me into it... No... Not a chance...'

Halyna smiled. When it really mattered, she could convince her husband to do anything.

'Mmm... I'll think about it,' said Taras. 'But on one condition...'

Halyna looked at him above the rims of her plastic-framed glasses. She said, 'and what would that be?'

Taras displayed the holes in his pockets. He said, 'I think it's time you ended your silly strike... Don't you think?'

The Dancing Barber

Encore

A few days later...

> 'Therefore each of you must put off falsehood and speak truthfully...'
>
> Ephesians 4:25

The City of Bradford, West Yorkshire, Northern England

'Hello officer,' Taras said to the grumpy Policeman standing patiently at the shop door. He shielded his ears from the incessant buzzing of the faulty doorbell, 'I must remember to get this fixed.' He swiftly took off the frilly apron he wore while doing the housework and hid it behind his back. 'Are you here for a haircut?'

The officer removed his helmet to reveal a head of closely-cropped greying hair. He said, 'that won't be necessary sir, I'm here on *official* business.'

'What kind of *official* business?' Taras asked, hoping the "Benton and Wedges" cigarettes he'd sold a few weeks ago hadn't killed anyone. He also hoped he hadn't been seen helping himself to those daffodils. Maybe Zena and Lenka had been reported for their samahon distillery? I'd be their own fault... they were hardly discrete about it... Their apparatus exploded several times a day, and – despite being told not to – they insisted on selling bottles of the stuff to the tramps in the alley... One thing he knew... this official business wouldn't concern a certain crackpot Colonel... the Mafia never made a mistake when "re-education" was concerned.

The grumpy officer unfastened the silver button of his breast pocket and extracted a black notebook. Flicking off the elastic fastener and leafing to the required page, he said, 'I understand you have a couple of women staying with you who go by the names of, err let me see,' he examined the paper closely, 'Zena and Lenka?'

'Yes, sadly these women are staying with me,' Taras sighed. He lowered his voice, 'why? What have they done?'

'Several days ago, there was a spate of shoplifting, sir. And these women are the prime suspects. You see, several retail establishments in Bradford have reported them for taking many expensive goods without paying.' He once again examined the paper closely, 'and it comes to quite a substantial sum.'

'There must be a misunderstanding,' said Taras, 'because they told me the shopkeepers agreed that I would go and pay for the goods myself... unfortunately, I haven't got around to it just yet... but I will! And I have all the receipts if you want to see them?'

'That's not what the shopkeepers have told me,' said the officer sternly. 'Perhaps I could speak with the women concerned?'

'Zena! Lenka!' Taras turned and shouted, 'come in here now!' He said to the Policeman, 'they are my sisters-in-law... and most people find them rather "odd"...'

'I'm used to "odd" in this job,' said the Policeman. 'I reckon that over the years, I've pretty much seen it all.'

Taras cringed, but said nothing.

The Policeman confidently flicked to the next page in his notebook to reveal a long list, neatly written out in block capitals, using the sharpest of pencils. He said, 'your sisters-in-law have also been reported for beating up several members of The Alhambra backstage staff, indecent exposure in a public convenience, defecating in a rosebush, vandalising a fairground, butchering and cooking wild animals, assaulting the Park Warden and his Assistant and also driving a pink Mini motorcar into the boating lake of Manningham Park!' With one hand, he closed the

The Dancing Barber

notebook. Despondently, he said, 'this really isn't on, you know... Oh, I almost forgot... the one called Zena has allegedly damaged a bowling green before using it as a,' he coughed, 'toilet... Appalling behaviour, truly appalling!'

'Zena! Lenka!' Taras screamed, 'come in here <u>this instant</u>!' He listened as the twins' stomping feet made the floor shake and the picture frames rattle on the walls. 'They're coming...' he said to the increasingly impatient Policeman.

When the Policeman saw the twins, he promptly put on his helmet and tightened the chinstrap. He said, 'oh no, not you two again!' He backed away, 'you stay away from me! I've only just got rid of the fleas you gave me the last time we had the misfortune to meet! No wonder you shaved your heads... all that hair was infested with fleas and Lord knows what else!' He turned to Taras and said, 'see that you pay for the goods they took <u>first thing</u> tomorrow and nothing more will be said of it. I'm sure I can trust the word of the famous "Dancing Barber"!'

Taras said, 'but what about all that other stuff?'

The Policeman was already halfway down the road. He shouted, 'forget it! Just make sure none of it happens again! And the sooner they leave the country, the better!'

Taras couldn't agree more.

The twins shrugged their shoulders and sloped back to the kitchen.

Taras looked at his calendar, which was affixed to the wall with a drawing pin. 'This time next week,' he said, rubbing his hands together with glee, 'they'll all be gone! And I'll get some peace and quiet at last!'

Zena, Klem and Oksana had decided to go to Chaplinka... Klem thought it would be for a week or two, but Zena clearly had other ideas... Lenka was going back for good and had invited Halyna and Sofia to go and visit in May, coinciding with the Spring Bank holiday...

So this time next week – with the exception of his housekeeping duties – things would be back to normal. It would just be the three of them, and importantly, he'd get his attic back! He'd have to get Stan Wiggins to redecorate it... the place looked an utter bomb site. And then there was all that carpet to replace, and his beloved Eames chair to repair...

He'd heard mutterings that Natalka's house was still in utter chaos... Her aunties Lyudmila and Valentina weren't allowed to board the aeroplane to Kyiv, because of "hygiene reasons". So they'd returned to Natalka's parents' house, where they promptly annoyed Gunter – who'd only popped in to deliver new rent books – by wiping their filthy hands on his black leather coat after using his wide-brimmed black hat in the same way Zena and Lenka use yellow buckets. Taras sighed... at least none of this was his problem...

Taras looked up at the bright blue sky; the sun was warm and because he'd confiscated the yellow buckets, all danger of a turd landing on his head had passed, so he hoisted up his trouser legs and sat on the warm sandstone of the doorstep. Rolling up his sleeves, unfastening the collar of his nylon shirt, and angling his face to the glorious sun was one of his few pleasures in life. And the warming rays helped alleviate the residual headache caused by a Hoover and a rolling pin... not to mention all that *other* stress...

Gently massaging his temples, he still couldn't believe Halyna's attitude towards him... How could she not appreciate his anniversary gift of two tickets to see *Taras Bulba* again at *The Gaumont*...?

He'd never understand how her mind worked. Manipulative wasn't the word... only she could make him wear a frilly apron for the housework... That was no way to treat the famous Dancing Barber...

Something sharp jabbed him in the chest. He reached into his shirt pocket and removed a copy of the photograph Klem had been most insistent to take... something else Halyna had manipulated him into doing.

Despite the Cossack's moustache, it was obviously him underneath. He took comfort in the fact that when reproduced in tomorrow's newspapers, it'd be in black and white, so he'd be barely recognisable.

Taras recalled another one of Klem's Biblical quotations: Matthew 6:27, *"Who of you by worrying can add a single hour to his life?"* He lit a cigarette and decided to forget all his troubles... at least for the next few minutes.

And where worries were concerned, Klem had plenty of his own. What on earth possessed him to agree to marry Zena? At

The Dancing Barber

least he didn't waste any money on her wedding ring... but even a plumber's olive was too good for the likes of her.

But in the wake of what happened to Katya, somehow he thought Klem's retirement wouldn't last much longer... especially with Oksana to look after...

He watched Oksana run around randomly in the street, narrowly avoiding being knocked down by several cars. He shook his head at Sofia's latest idea to encourage Oksana to exercise... the heifer had a fishing rod strapped to her back, which arched over her head, at the end of which dangled an opened packet of cheese and onion crisps... No matter how fast she ran, it was always two feet out of reach...

A taxi braked harshly and bumped up onto the kerb, startling Taras so much that he dropped his cigarette, the embers almost igniting his crotch...

The grubby driver wound down the squeaky window and waved at him, simultaneously turning off his "For Hire" light.

Taras shook his head and said, 'but I didn't order a taxi!'

The taxi driver consulted his notepad and said, 'err, a Missus Zena ordered it, sir. She used a lot of bad language, so I came as fast as I could, sir.'

'Just a minute,' Taras said, 'I will go and investigate.' He knew that Zena couldn't afford to pay taxi fares, and after the money she and Lenka had already cost him, he certainly wasn't going to fund their excursions. But then a thought entered his mind: *what if she and Lenka were planning to leave even sooner... now for instance...? In that case, I'd happily pay for a limousine to take them to the airport...*

'Zena?' Taras said, skipping into the kitchen, noticing the hairless twins were wearing their great-coats and carrying their suitcases. 'Have you ordered a taxi?' he asked hopefully, 'to the airport, by any chance?'

'Do not be the silly,' said Zena, examining the third finger of her right hand, wondering why it and her golden wedding ring had turned green. She picked up her suitcases and said, 'we thought it was about the time we all went to stay at your beautiful The Bolling Hall!'

Sofia said nothing. She was too busy sulking, especially after discovering Mister Pushkin had thrown up a chinchilla's head all over her freshly-ironed mini-skirt.

Halyna immediately looked at Zena and said, 'I think *Taras* has got something to tell you…'

'Really?' said Zena as she and Lenka turned to look at him, 'and what would that be?'

Thud! Taras collapsed and lay spread-eagled on the floor… If it was good enough for his wife, it was good enough for him!

There was a timid knock on the kitchen door. 'Just a minute,' said Halyna, knowing perfectly well that her husband was play-acting. 'I'll see who it it…'

'Hello,' said Natalka, looking deeply embarrassed.

Halyna smiled, 'hello… What's the matter?'

Natalka said, 'I assume you've heard about what my aunties did in Mr Gunter's hat…?'

'I'm afraid so,' said Halyna. 'Was he angry?'

'No, he wasn't angry,' said Natalka. 'I was bleeding furious! So furious that he kicked us all out onto the street!'

'Oh dear,' said Halyna. 'I'm truly sorry to hear that… Is there anything I can do to help?'

Taras' eyes opened. He muttered, 'Halya… don't you dare…'

When Halyna insisted that Natalka, her parents and her abominable aunties, along with all their luggage, could stay for as long as they needed in the attic, Taras fainted for real! Neither he, nor the attic floor could take the strain…

About AC Michael

AC Michael was born in Yorkshire, England and enjoyed writing stories and drawing cartoons from a young age.

When not writing, his diverse interests range from hill-walking to gardening, and from watercolour painting to quantum physics.

His favourite authors are Roald Dahl, Leslie Charteris and Ian Fleming.

AC Michael has also written and illustrated the "Curious Characters" series of children's picture books.

www.acmichaelbooks.co.uk

Made in the USA
Charleston, SC
21 January 2016